THE GIRL'S EYES WERE OPEN . . .

But she looked dazed and only half awake. And there was a set of ugly bruises on her neck.

"Roger, snap out of it. We have to get her home."

"No, we have to call the police," Roger countered.

"We can call them from the apartment. We have to get her out of the cold before she catches pneumonia."

"The police have to be called," Roger insisted. "This is a crime scene. They'll want to look for clues."

"We can tell them where we found her," Caroline shot back. "They can look for clues with us back home just as easily as they can with us standing here."

Roger ground his teeth. But she was probably right. And given the unlikelihood of a quick police response to a non-emergency situation, the girl could well freeze to death before they even got a car here.

"Fine," he growled. "Come on—uh—Caroline, what's her name?"

"She doesn't seem to be able to talk. It looks like someone tried to strangle her."

"Yeah, I noticed." Roger turned around, his skin tingling with the odd impression that someone was watching them. But there was no one in sight.

He just hoped that whoever had tried to do this to the girl wouldn't get to them first.

BOOKS BY TIMOTHY ZAHN

*Denotes a Tom Doherty Associates book

The
GREEN
and
the
GRAY

TIMOTHY ZAHN

TOR®

A TOM DOHERTY ASSOCIATES BOOK
NEW YORK

This is a work of fiction. All the characters and events portrayed in this book are either products of the author's imagination or are used fictitiously.

THE GREEN AND THE GRAY

Edited by James Frenkel

A Tor Book
Published by Tom Doherty Associates, LLC
175 Fifth Avenue
New York, NY 10010

www.tor.com

Tor® is a registered trademark of Tom Doherty Associates, LLC.

ISBN 0-765-34645-1
EAN 978-0-765-34645-2

First edition: September 2004
First mass market edition: October 2005

Printed in the United States of America

0 9 8 7 6 5 4 3 2 1

*To my agent, editors, former
editors, and publishers in New York*

*With thanks for all the advice,
local information, and free lunches*

PROLOGUE

The sun had long since set behind the trees of Riverside Park, on the western edge of Manhattan Island, and the lights of the New Jersey coastline were glittering on the Hudson River. Melantha Green found herself gazing at the lights, and the dark sky beyond them, as she and the two Warriors on either side of her walked along the cool grass of the upper promenade toward the stone steps leading down to the main part of the park. It had been the last sunset she would ever see, she knew, and she felt a deep sadness that it hadn't been more spectacular. But it hadn't been, and it was over. The sky was dark, and the marginal warmth of the daylight had given way to the chill of a New York October evening. A steady northerly breeze ruffled through the last remaining leaves, and through the fear and anguish pounding in her heart she could imagine that the trees themselves were saying their farewells. Even as they settled into their yearly winter's rest, she, too, was about to settle into the quiet nothingness of death.

Except that their death would end a few months from now with the warm sunlight and the glorious renewal of spring. Her death would be forever.

The others were waiting at the top of the steps by the John Carrere Memorial as she and her escort arrived, the two small clusters of Greens and Grays standing a little apart from each other. An uneasy truce there might be right now, and genuine peace there might someday be, but that didn't mean either group particularly trusted the other. Some of the faces she could recognize in the glow from the Riverside Drive streetlights: Cyril and Aleksander, the leaders of the Greens, who had talked long and earnestly with her before this decision had been made. Her parents were there, too, trying valiantly to be stoic and loving and supportive even through the agony that was tearing their hearts apart. A couple of the Grays were familiar, too, their wide faces staring silently and emotionlessly at her from atop their squat bodies. The hope of both their peoples, they had called her, the one whose sacrifice would mean peace.

She hoped they were right. It would be a terrible thing to die for nothing.

Her escort led her to a spot midway between the two small knots of people. Cyril had a few words of greeting and encouragement, but it was clear that no one really felt like conversation, and thankfully it was soon over. With the sun down and the night growing cold, even Melantha couldn't see any point in postponing the inevitable any longer.

The preliminaries finished, Cyril and an elderly Gray with a long scar on his left cheek—Halfdan, she vaguely remembered his name—led the way down the steps into the lower part of the park, Melantha and her escort behind them, the rest of the observers joining in behind her. They walked past the small flower garden which she had been told would be her final resting spot, and she found herself wondering whether the flowers would come up extra beautiful in the spring because of it. The grass seemed springier beneath her feet than usual, though that might have been the strange shoes she'd been given to wear along with the ancient ceremonial clothing. Pinned high on her left shoulder, the unaccustomed weight of a *trassk* tugged uncomfortably at her dress.

They continued past the garden to the chosen spot between a pair of majestic oaks. A few more Greens were waiting there, eyeing and being eyed in turn by three more Grays silently hanging onto the side of the fifteen-foot stone wall that separated the lower part of the park from the upper promenade they'd just come from. The Gray leader beside Cyril gave a quiet order, and the Grays reluctantly came down from their perches, joining with the rest of their group. The lights of Riverside Drive blazed cheerily down from beyond the wall, and Melantha wondered briefly what would happen if some passerby stumbled upon the drama about to unfold. But most of the Humans who lived in the area were already nestled into their apartments for the night, and the wall and height differential effectively shielded them from anyone who might still be out.

She looked around her, trying to get a last taste of the world before she left it forever. The bare branches seemed to be calling to her as the wind brushed them together, and she found herself almost overwhelmed by the delicate scents of the grass and the earth and the trees themselves. Here and there above her, she could see stars peeking through the haze of the city, and even the traffic noise seemed muted tonight. It was, a small part of her mind whispered, a fitting place, and a fitting way, for a Green to die.

Even one who was only twelve years old.

The groups had shuffled into their positions for the ceremony, forming a loose circle with Melantha, her escort, and Cyril and the Gray leader in the center. "Melantha Green," Cyril said, his voice dark and solemn, "we have gathered here tonight to do that which must be done for the survival of our two peoples. Understand that what we do, we do for the best. We ask your forgiveness, and that of your family, and promise to dedicate ourselves to assuring that your sacrifice will not be in vain."

"I understand," Melantha said. As last words, she thought distantly, they were pretty pathetic. But the sadness and dread had seized her again, and how her death was remembered by others didn't seem very important. Her parents were out of her line of sight, and she thought about turning around and making sure they were still there.

But she resisted the urge. This was going to be hard enough on them without leaving a last, lingering look to ache forever in their memories.

"Thank you, Melantha," Cyril said. He took a step back, and nodded to her escort.

One of the Warriors stepped from her side and turned to

face her. With his eyes carefully avoiding hers, he reached
his hands up and got an almost gentle grip around her
throat.

And began to squeeze.

Reflexively, she tried to twist out of his grip, her hands
darting up of their own accord to grab at his wrists. But he'd
been prepared for the reaction, and his adult Warrior's
strength was far beyond that of a twelve-year-old girl. The
blood roared in her ears, drowning out all other sounds, but
in her mind she could feel the anguished calls coming from
the Greens over what had to be done, even from those like
Cyril who had persuaded them that it was the only way.
Lancing through it all like lightning through storm clouds
was the last call from her parents, a vibration of fear and
pain and hopelessness.

She could feel her strength ebbing away now, her arms
falling loosely to her sides, her knees starting to buckle.
Vaguely, she sensed the second Warrior gripping her under
her arms, supporting her so that the first could finish the job.
White spots were dancing in front of her eyes, and the distant streetlight reflected on his face seemed to be fading
away. Did that mean the end was near? Feeling like a dying
flower wilting in his grip, she closed her eyes.

Even through the closed lids she saw the brilliant burst of
light. The grip on her throat abruptly eased, and she had a
vague sense of the anguish swirling around her suddenly replaced with surprise and consternation. There was a distant-
sounding shout—the word *Betrayal!*—

The clutching hands were suddenly torn away from her
throat, and she heard a gasp as something threw the Warrior
to the ground. Even as she fought to suck air into her lungs,
the hands that had been supporting her let go, and she felt
herself collapsing toward the grass. Another arm reached
out from somewhere, grabbing her around the waist. For a
moment her rescuer seemed to totter; and then they were on
the move, Melantha's jaw and neck bouncing painfully as
he ran with her across the grass. The spots of her near-
suffocation were fading away, but to her surprise she found

she still couldn't see anything. The streetlights that had been blazing earlier from Riverside Drive had gone completely dark.

"She's gone!" a deep Gray voice boomed from behind her.

There was a flurry of movement from that direction, footsteps and shouts and voices calling to her mind. Her forward motion was abruptly halted, and she felt herself being clutched closer to her rescuer's body as he began to climb the wall the Grays had been hanging onto a few minutes earlier.

She tensed as he climbed, waiting for the inevitable shouts of discovery and the sounds of pursuit. But all the activity seemed to be moving away from her, either deeper into the darkness of the park or back toward the garden and the stone steps. A moment later she and her rescuer reached the top of the wall and the upper promenade, and once again she found her chin bouncing painfully against his shoulder as he ran silently along the ground.

"You okay?" a gruff voice murmured in her ear. "Melantha?"

It took two tries to get any words out through her half-paralyzed throat. "I'm okay," she wheezed. Her voice was the voice of a stranger. "Who—?"

"It's Jonah," he said; and this time, she recognized the voice. "Don't try to talk."

Melantha stiffened. That last word had been more grunted than spoken, and for the first time she noticed how labored his breathing sounded. Lifting her left hand from the arm still wrapped around her waist, she carefully touched his chest with her fingertips.

And jerked away as she touched wetness. "Jonah!"

"Don't try to talk," he said again, his breathing sounding even more ragged. "It's okay."

He slowed to a walk, his head turning back and forth as if taking his bearings. A moment later he came to a complete stop, letting her slip a bit so that her feet were touching the ground. She stretched her legs, trying to take some of her own weight away from him. But her knees were too weak to give any support, and a terrible fatigue was beginning to wash over her. In the distance behind them she could feel the calls of chaos and consternation and growing anger. "This . . . isn't right," she managed to whisper. "I need . . . to go back."

He leaned down and lifted her again off her feet, stifling her protest. "It'll be okay," he murmured as they headed off again.

The last thing she remembered before drifting into a nightmare-filled sleep was the sensation of her head bouncing rhythmically against his shoulder as he ran through the night.

1

The play at the Miller Theater had been one of those modern psychological dramas, exactly the sort of thing Roger Whittier would expect from a Columbia University student production: dark and pretentious, relying heavily on deep sociological quirks, without any pretense of rationality in its plot. From the polite applause bouncing off the lowering curtain, he guessed that most of the audience had found it as mediocre as he had.

Which was practically a guarantee that Caroline would love it.

Suppressing a sigh, he continued to slap his hands together, trying not to be embarrassed by the fact that his wife was one of the half-dozen people who had jumped to their feet in standing ovation. In four years of marriage he had yet to figure out whether Caroline's enthusiasm in these situations was genuine, driven by sympathy for the underdog, or just stubborn defiance of popular opinion.

The applause went down, the house lights came up, and the rest of the audience got to their feet and began unscrunching their coats from the backs of their seats. Roger joined the general chaos, mindful of his elbows as he pulled on his topcoat and buttoned it. He'd endured the play; and now came the verbal diplomacy as he tried not to tell Caroline exactly what he'd thought of it. The more enthusiastic her response, in general, the stonier the wall of silence that went up if he tried to point out how much the thing had actually stunk.

A flying elbow jabbed him in his right shoulder blade. "Sorry," he said automatically, half turning.

The offender, a small wizened man with an expensive

topcoat and bad comb-over, grunted something and turned away. Roger turned away, too, muttering under his breath as he struggled to get his right arm into a sleeve that had pretzeled itself into a knot. *What in hell's name was I apologizing for?* he growled to himself. He finished with his coat and turned to see if Caroline was ready.

Caroline wasn't ready. Caroline, in fact, had vanished.

He looked down, a fresh wave of annoyance rolling over the pool of resentment already sloshing through his stomach. She was on her knees on the floor, her back twisted into half an S-curve as she scrabbled around in the shadows. "Which one is it this time?" he demanded.

"My opal ring," Caroline's voice came back, muffled by distance and the dark hair draped along both sides of her face.

Roger looked away, not bothering to reply. It was always the same lately. If she wasn't running late because the water heater had drained too far for another shower, then she was misplacing her watch or losing her ring or suddenly remembering that the plants needed watering.

Why couldn't she ever get herself organized? She was a real estate agent, for heaven's sake—she certainly had to have her ducks in a row at work. Why couldn't she do it at home, too?

She was still bobbing around, searching for the missing ring. For a moment he considered getting down and seeing if he could help this along a little. But no. She knew better than he did where it had slipped off, and he would just be in the way.

Taking a deep breath, trying to calm himself, he watched the other people streaming out the doors. If she didn't hurry, he told himself darkly, they weren't going to get a cab.

• •

The last stragglers were strolling toward the exits by the time Caroline finally spotted her ring, hiding behind the front leg of the chair in front of hers. "Found it," she announced, retrieving the wayward jewelry.

Roger didn't reply. *He's angry,* she realized, an all-too-familiar sinking feeling settling into her stomach. Angry, or annoyed, or frustrated. Like he always seemed to be lately. Especially with her.

She felt her eyes filling with tears as she carefully climbed back to her feet, tears of frustration and some annoyance of her own. *I didn't drop it on purpose,* she thought angrily in his direction. *I didn't see you offering to help, either.*

But it was no use. He hadn't liked the play, and he was probably steaming over that man who'd bumped into him a minute ago. But no matter what happened, or whose fault it was, in the end it all got focused on her. On her slowness, on her lack of organization, on whatever else she did that irritated him.

He was already moving toward the aisle by the time she had collected her coat and purse, his back rippling with impatience. Roger never yelled at her—that wasn't his style—but he could do a brooding silence that hurt more than her father's quicksilver temper ever had.

In some ways she wished he *would* yell. At least then he would be talking honestly instead of pretending everything was all right when it wasn't.

But that would require him to be assertive. No chance of that happening.

No chance of getting a cab now, either. That would irritate him all the more, especially given the near-argument they'd had on the subject as they were getting ready to leave this evening.

With a sigh, she headed off behind his impatient back, her vision blurring again with tears. Why couldn't she ever do anything right?

●●

Sure enough, by the time they stepped out into the cool October air, the line of cabs that would have gathered at the curb for the post-performance crowd had vanished. "Blast,"

Roger muttered under his breath, looking up and down Broadway.

But the Great White Way was quiet tonight, or at least this stretch of it was. The university had a significant chunk of the street blocked off with a construction project up around 120th, and the city's own orange-cone mania had similarly struck down at 103rd, sealing off most of the street there. The cabbies, who had enough trouble just battling regular Manhattan traffic, had taken to avoiding these particular twenty blocks entirely.

Of course, they could always walk over to Amsterdam and flag down something there. But Amsterdam turned one-way-north at 110th, which would force the cabby to head farther east to Columbus, which was currently handling much of the Broadway traffic in addition to its own. It probably wouldn't get them home any sooner than just walking the twenty blocks, not to mention the expense involved. There was always the subway, of course, but Caroline had an absolute phobia about riding it after dark.

But to walk would mean giving in.

"I suppose we could walk," Caroline offered timidly from beside him, her voice sounding like someone easing her way onto thin ice.

"I suppose we could," Roger echoed, hearing the hardness in his own voice. That had been their pre-theater argument: a brief staking out of turf on Caroline's current favorite subject of exercise, and how both of them needed more of it.

And once she got an idea or crusade into her head, there was no getting it out of her. Three cheers for the underdog, four cheers for the noble cause, damn the torpedoes, and full speed ahead.

He frowned sideways at her in sudden suspicion. Could she have lost her ring back there on purpose, staging the whole thing to force them to walk home like she wanted?

For a long second he considered calling her bluff, either walking them over to Amsterdam or using his cell phone to summon a cab right here and insisting they wait until it arrived. But the wind was starting to pick up, and standing around freezing would definitely qualify as a Pyrrhic victory. Better to get home as quickly as possible, even if it meant giving in.

Besides, she was probably right. They probably *could* both use more exercise.

"Sure, why not?" he said, turning south along Broadway. "Unless you think you'll be too cold."

"No, I'm fine," she assured him. His sudden capitulation must have caught her by surprise, because she had to take a couple of quick steps to catch up. "It's a nice night for a walk."

"I suppose," he said.

Caroline fell silent, without even a passing mention of exercise. At least she was being a gracious winner.

Broadway's vehicular traffic, as he'd already noted, was running sparse tonight. What he hadn't anticipated was that pedestrian traffic would be similarly low-key. Once they'd made it out of the immediate Columbia area, they found themselves with the sidewalk virtually to themselves. Construction blockages wouldn't explain that; there must be a football game or something on. Or maybe it was still baseball season. He was a little vague on such things.

Though it could also be the weather that was keeping everyone inside. The wind had picked up since their arrival at the theater, and had become a steady blast of Canadian air pressing against their backs and carrying the promise of an extra-cold winter ahead.

Caroline was evidently thinking along the same lines. "We're going to need to bring the trees in soon, before it gets too cold," she commented as they hurried across 104th Street in anticipation of an imminent red light. "We let it go too long last year, and they did poorly when spring came."

"What constitutes too cold?" Roger asked, glad to have something to talk about that didn't involve either exercise or the play.

"Certainly before we get a hard freeze," she said.

"Okay," Roger said, though he had only a vague memory

of tree problems last spring. The two semidwarf orange trees, like the rest of their indoor jungle, were Caroline's responsibility. "You want to put them in the bedroom again?"

"I'd like to," Caroline said. "I know you don't like them blocking the balcony door there; but the alternative is to block the living room door, and we certainly look out that one more often—"

"Shh," Roger cut her off, looking around. "Did you hear that?"

"Hear what?" Caroline asked.

"It was like a cough," Roger told her, frowning. Aside from two more couples a block up the street, there wasn't a single human being in sight. "A very wet cough, like you get when you've got fluid in your lungs."

"I hate that sound," Caroline said, shivering.

"Yeah, but where did it come from?" Roger persisted, still looking around. All the shops in the immediate area were closed, there were no alleys, and the nearby doorways were too well illuminated by the streetlights for anyone to be hiding there. He couldn't see any open windows above them, either.

"I don't see anyone," Caroline said. "Maybe you imagined it."

I didn't imagine anything, Roger groused silently to himself. But he couldn't argue against the fact that there was no one in sight. "Maybe," he said, taking her arm and starting forward again, the back of his neck starting to creep in a way that had nothing to do with the wind. "Come on, let's go."

They continued south, past the torn-up pavement and flashing yellow lights at 103rd, heading for 102nd. Ahead on their left, he could see the theater he and Caroline sometimes went to, its marquee and windows dark. Had they started closing early on Wednesday nights?

"Roger, what's wrong with the lights?" Caroline asked quietly.

He frowned. Focusing on the theater, he hadn't even noticed that the light around them had gone curiously dim. The street lamps had turned into children's nightlights, putting out hardly any glow at all and looking like they were having to strain to manage even that much. The headlights of the passing cars seemed unnaturally bright, the doorways now resting in deep puddles of shadow. Ahead, as far down Broadway as he could see, all the streetlights had gone equally dim.

He looked back over his shoulder. The lights had dimmed just behind them, too, but only for a single block. North of 103rd, they were blazing away normally.

It was probably something to do with the road construction, of course. Something to do with torn-up streets and damaged power lines.

But then why hadn't he noticed it as they approached? Why had the lights only now gone so oddly dim?

And why had they dimmed just as he and Caroline had entered this particular stretch of sidewalk?

Caroline had gone silent, gripping his arm a little tighter. Setting his teeth, Roger kept them moving, staying as far away from the shadowy doorways as he could. Just six blocks to go, he reminded himself firmly. It would be no worse than a nighttime walk in the woods, with the added bonus that there were no tree branches to trip over. "So what did you think of the play?" he asked.

It took Caroline a second to shift mental gears. "I liked it a lot," she replied, her mind clearly miles away from the safe and artificial world of university experimental theater. "How about you?"

"The acting was pretty decent," he said. "Though the Latin lover's accent was a little thick for my taste."

"You mean Cesar?" Caroline said, frowning. "He wasn't Latin, he was French."

"I know," Roger said. "I was using Latin lover in the generic sense."

"I didn't know there *was* a generic sense for Latin lover," Caroline said. "Are you meaning a 'when in Rome' sort of thing?"

"No, it's more a general melodramatic expression," he said. They were halfway down the block now, well into the darkened area. Five and a half blocks to go. "The smooth-talking romantic guy women swoon over. Usually he either seduces them or else entices them unknowingly to their doom."

"Ah," Caroline said. "Though in this case it was hardly unknowing. LuAnn knew exactly what was going on."

"Then why did she let Cesar manipulate her that way?" Roger countered, knowing full well that getting started on the play's logic would only get him into trouble. "Especially when good old solid Albert was standing there waiting for her to come to her senses?"

"I don't know," Caroline murmured. "I still don't think it was Cesar's fault."

"Maybe not," Roger said, forcing himself to let it drop. "I liked the set design, too," he added, hoping the production's technical aspects would be safer ground. "And the music was pretty good. Chopin, I think."

They had reached 101st street, and he was searching for something else positive he could say, when the dim street-lights went completely dark.

Caroline jerked to a halt with a short, involuntary gasp. "Easy," Roger said, looking around as his stomach tight-ened into a hard knot. The streetlights were gone, but at the same time the various apartment windows above them were still lit, giving off a cheerful glow.

Which was, to Roger's mind, the eeriest part of all. He'd never seen a power outage yet that didn't take out everything in a six-block area, streetlights and buildings alike. What the *hell* was going on? "Just keep walking," he murmured.

"No," a deep voice said from their left.

Roger jumped, spinning around to face the vague shape standing on the sidewalk just around the corner from them. "What do you want?" he demanded, cursing the quaver in his voice.

"You have trees?" the man asked.

Roger blinked, the sheer unexpectedness of the question freezing his brain. "Trees?" he repeated stupidly.

"Trees!" the man snarled. "You said—" He broke off,

coughing hard. It was the same cough, Roger realized with a shiver, that he'd heard back at the corner.

Except that this man hadn't been there. No one had been there.

Beside him, he felt Caroline loosen her grip on his arm. "Yes," she said, raising her voice to be heard over the man's hacking. "We have two semidwarf orange trees."

With an effort, the man brought his lungs under control. "How big?" he rasped.

Now, too late, it occurred to Roger that they might have escaped while the other was incapacitated. But maybe they would have another chance. Bracing himself, he got ready to grab Caroline's hand and run the instant another fit took him.

"About six feet tall and four across," Caroline said. "They're in pots on our balcony."

The man took another step forward. The light from the apartment windows wasn't good enough for Roger to make out his features, but there was enough to show that he was short and broad, with the build of a compact boxer.

It was also quite adequate to illuminate the shiny pistol clutched in his left hand.

"Small," the man muttered. "But they'll do." He gestured back along 101st Street behind him. The streetlights there were also dark. "Come."

Roger could feel Caroline trembling against his side as he silently steered them past the mugger and down the sidewalk, trying desperately to come up with a plan. The man was obviously weak and sick. If he jumped him and wrestled away the gun . . .

No. If he jumped him, he would get himself shot. The mugger was a head shorter than he was, but judging by the width of his shoulders he probably outweighed Roger by a good twenty pounds. Probably outmuscled him by a hell of a lot more, too.

"Here," the mugger said suddenly from behind him. "In here."

Roger swallowed hard, focusing on the iron fence set across an alley between two buildings to their left, its gate

standing wide open. The dark concrete beyond the fence
sloped downward to a flat area, beyond which he could see a
set of concrete steps leading to a higher platform, beyond
which was a flat, featureless wall. On the right, between the
entrance and the back steps, was a shorter wall leading into
a little courtyard-like area; just past that was a fire escape attached to one of the buildings. Inside the fence to the left
was a stack of garbage bags.

"In here," the mugger said again.

"Do as he says, Roger," Caroline murmured.

With his heart thudding in his ears, Roger stepped
through the gate and started down the slope, Caroline still
clutching his arm. They had gone perhaps three steps into
the alley when, behind them, the dead streetlights abruptly
came back on.

"Stop," the mugger ordered. "There."

Roger frowned. The man, now in silhouette against the
light, was pointing at a long bundle of rags lying at the far
end of the line of trash bags. "There what?" he asked.

"Oh, my God," Caroline breathed, letting go of Roger's
arm and stepping over to kneel beside the bundle.

And then Roger got it. The bundle wasn't rags, but a
young girl, fourteen or fifteen years old, dressed in some
odd patchwork outfit made of green and gray material. She
was curled into a fetal position against the cold night air, her
eyes closed.

"Take her," the mugger's voice said in Roger's ear.

Something swung toward Roger's face; reflexively, he
flinched back. But the something didn't connect, merely
stopping in midair in front of him.

It was the mugger's hand. In it was the mugger's gun.

Its grip pointed toward Roger. "What?" Roger asked
cautiously.

"Take her," the other repeated, thrusting the gun insis-
tently toward him. "Protect her."

Carefully, Roger reached up and touched the weapon.
Was this some sort of trick? Was the other going to suddenly reverse the gun and shoot him? His fingers closed on

the gun, and the weapon's gentle weight came into his hand as the mugger let go. "Protect her," the other said again softly. Brushing past Roger, he headed silently down the slope farther into the alley.

"Roger, give me your coat," Caroline ordered. "She's freezing."

"Sure," Roger said mechanically, watching the man's broad back retreating. Was he staggering a little? Roger couldn't be sure, but it looked like it. A mugger who'd lingered too long after happy hour might explain why Roger was now the one holding the gun.

But the man hadn't sounded drunk. And there certainly hadn't been any alcohol on his breath when he'd handed over the weapon.

And that cough . . .

"Roger!"

"Right." Still watching the man's unsteady progress, he stripped off his coat and handed it over. He glanced down long enough to see Caroline sit the girl up and get the coat around her shoulders, then looked back down the alley.

The mugger was gone.

He frowned, peering into the semidarkness. The man was gone, all right. But gone where? Cautiously, he crossed to the low wall and peered over it.

The man wasn't there. He wasn't on the fire escape, either, or on the stone steps, or the platform across the end, or huddled around the corner against the cul-de-sac around the back. There were no doorways Roger could see, nothing a person could hide behind, and all the first-floor windows were barred. And he certainly hadn't gotten past Roger and escaped out the alley mouth.

He'd simply vanished.

Roger looked down at the pistol in his hand. He'd never held a real handgun before, but he'd always had the impression the things were heavy. This one didn't seem to weigh much more than the toys he'd played with as a boy. Could it be one of those fancy plastic guns the newspapers were always going on about?

But it didn't look plastic. It was definitely metal, and it sure as hell *looked* like one of those army pistols from World War II movies. He turned it over in his hand, angling it toward the streetlight for a better look.

And for the first time noticed that there was something marring the shiny metal on the right side of the barrel. A streak of something dark that came off as he rubbed his finger across it.

Blood?

"Roger, stop daydreaming and give me a hand," Caroline called.

Taking one last look around, he walked back up the sloping concrete. Caroline had the girl wrapped in his coat and on her feet, propping her up like a rag doll. The girl's eyes were open, but she looked dazed and only half awake.

And there were a set of ugly bruises on her neck.

"Roger, snap *out* of it," Caroline ordered into his thoughts. "We have to get her home."

"No, we have to call the police," Roger countered as he dug into his pocket for his phone, feeling his face flush with annoyance. Did she really think he'd just been standing there with his brain in idle?

"We can call them from the apartment," Caroline said. "We have to get her out of this air before she catches pneumonia."

"The police have to be called," Roger insisted. "This is a crime scene. They'll want to look for clues."

"We can tell them where we found her," Caroline shot back. "They can look for clues with us back home just as easily as they can with us standing here."

Roger ground his teeth. But she was probably right. And given the unlikelihood of a quick police response to a non-emergency situation, the girl could well freeze to death before they even got a car here.

Or rather *he* could freeze to death. It was *his* coat she was wearing, after all.

"Fine," he growled. "Come on—uh—Caroline, what's her name?"

"She doesn't seem to be able to talk," Caroline said, her

voice low and dark. "It looks like someone tried to strangle her."

"Yeah, I noticed." Roger turned around, his skin tingling with the odd impression that someone was watching them. But there was no one in sight.

But then, there hadn't been anyone in sight when he'd heard that first cough, either.

Shoving the gun into his pocket, he stepped to the girl's side and put his arm around her slim waist. A fair percentage of her weight came onto his arm; she really *was* in bad shape. He just hoped he wouldn't end up carrying her the rest of the way to the apartment.

He hoped even more that whoever had tried to do this to her wouldn't get to them first.

2

He did not, in fact, end up carrying the girl, but it was a near thing. By the time they reached their building, she was staggering like a drunken tourist, with the two of them supporting nearly her entire weight. The night doorman was nowhere to be seen, and it was all Roger could do to keep her from collapsing as Caroline fished out her keys and let them in.

The elevator was deserted, as was the hallway leading to their sixth-floor apartment. With Caroline again handling the door, Roger maneuvered the girl inside.

"No—the bedroom," Caroline panted as Roger started toward the living room. "She'll be more comfortable there."

"Okay," Roger grunted, changing direction.

They made it to the bedroom and got the girl up onto the bed. She was already asleep as Caroline folded the end of the comforter up to cover her legs. Roger straightened the lapels of his coat across her shoulders, and as he did so his fingers brushed across her shoulder. The material of her tunic felt odd, like some cross between silk and satin.

"She looks so young," Caroline murmured.

"How old do you think she is?" Roger asked. "I was guessing about fifteen."

"Oh, no—no more than twelve," Caroline said. "Maybe even eleven."

"Oh," Roger said, focusing on the girl's face. He could never tell about these things.

But however old she was, she certainly had an exotic look about her. Her hair was pure black, her skin olive-dark in a Mediterranean sort of way, and there was an odd slant about her eyes and mouth he couldn't place. He hadn't had a chance to see her eyes before she fell asleep, but he would bet money they were as dark as her hair.

"Better leave the closet light on," Caroline said. "She might be frightened if she wakes up in the dark and doesn't know where she is."

Roger nodded and flipped the switch, and together they tiptoed out, closing the door behind them.

"What do you think?" Caroline asked as she pulled off her coat and hung it on the coat tree by the door.

"I think we should call the cops and let *them* sort it out," Roger said, plucking his shirt distastefully away from his chest as he headed for the kitchen phone. Coming suddenly from the cold night air into the warmth of the building had popped sweat all over his body, and his shirt was sticking unpleasantly to his skin. "Deadbolt the door, will you, and put the chain on? And then check the balcony doors."

The 911 operator came on with gratifying speed. He explained the situation, gave her the address, and was assured that a patrol car would be there as soon as possible.

Caroline was pacing around the living room when he returned. "Everything locked up?" he asked.

"I didn't check the door off the bedroom," she said. "I

didn't want to wake her up. But I remember seeing the broomstick in the rail this morning."

"So did I," Roger confirmed. Crossing to the couch, he moved one of the throw pillows aside and sat down. "You might as well get comfortable. This might take awhile."

"I suppose," she said, crossing to one of the two chairs in front of him. She sat down, but immediately bounced up again. "No, I can't."

"Sit," Roger ordered, searching for some way to get her mind off her nervousness. "I want you to look at something."

He pulled out the gun the mugger had given him as she reluctantly sat down again. "You and your dad used to go shooting together, right? Tell me if this feels too light to you."

Her eyebrows lifted as she took it. "*Way* too light," she said, frowning as she hefted it. "Is it a toy?"

"Don't ask me," he said. "Could it be some kind of high-tech plastic gun?"

"I don't know," Caroline said. "It looks like a standard 1911 Colt .45." She turned it over, and her searching eyes widened slightly as she saw the blood smear. "Is that—?"

"I doubt it's tomato juice," Roger said. "Anything else you can say about the gun itself? I *really* don't want to have to tell the cops I got mugged by an F.A.O. Schwartz Special."

"Well, the slide works," Caroline said, pulling the upper part of the gun back and then letting it go, the way Roger had seen them do in the movies. "Toy guns usually don't do that."

She fiddled with the bottom of the grip. "But the clip seems to be glued in place," she added.

"So that means no bullets?" Roger asked, trying to decide if that made him feel relieved or just more ridiculous.

"I don't know," Caroline said, pulling the slide back again and peering inside. "There's *something* in there that looks like a cartridge. But—"

She let the slide go, pulled it back again. "But if it was real, it should eject when I do this. Either the round is jammed, or else it's a fake."

"Any way to tell for sure?"

"You want me to try pulling the trigger?"

Roger snorted. "No, thanks. So what exactly have we got here?"

"I don't know," Caroline said again, handing the gun back. "The slide works, but the slide release doesn't. The safety catch works, but not the clip release. There seems to be a round chambered, only I can't get it to eject. It's like it was designed to look like a real gun, but only up to a point."

"You mean like a movie prop?"

"Maybe, but why go to the trouble of making a prop that only works halfway?" she pointed out. "Why not just use a real gun filled with blanks? It doesn't make sense."

"Yeah." Roger fingered the gun. "Speaking of making sense, what did you think of her outfit?"

"A little out of style for New York," Caroline said. "Reminds me of the costumes they wear at madrigal concerts."

"I meant the material," Roger said. "What is it?"

"I didn't really pay attention," Caroline said. "It shimmered like silk, though."

"But it doesn't feel like silk," he told her. "It's too smooth."

"I don't know, then," Caroline said. "Maybe something new."

Across the room, the doorbell chimed. "Here they are," Roger said, standing up. "They made better time than I expected."

"Wait," Caroline said suddenly, jumping to her feet and grabbing his arm. "Are we sure that *is* the police?"

Roger stopped short, a fresh chill running across his skin. "Stay here," he said, dropping the gun into his pocket and moving past the front door into the kitchen. The bell rang again as he pulled a carving knife from Caroline's knife rack and returned to the door.

The two men he could see through the peephole certainly *looked* like cops. "Who is it?" he called.

"Police," a muffled voice said. "You called in a foundling report?"

Roger got a good grip on his knife. "I'm going to open the door," he said, making sure the chain was secure. "I want to see your identification."

He opened the door a crack, fully expecting the heavy wood to come crashing back at him as the two men tried to break it down. Instead, a hand eased gingerly through the gap holding a police badge and ID card for his inspection.

Roger gazed at the card a moment, uncomfortably aware that he didn't have the slightest idea what a real police ID looked like. But he *had* called them, and there wasn't much he could do now but hope they were genuine. "Thanks," he said. "Hang on, and I'll unchain it."

The hand withdrew, and he closed the door. Caroline's knickknack shelf was a step to the right; hurriedly sliding the knife out of sight behind one of the enameled plates, he unchained the door and opened it.

The two cops looked like they'd walked off the set of a TV show: one of them burly and Caucasian, with the look of long experience etched into his face, the other young and Hispanic and barely out of rookiehood. "I'm Officer Kern," the older cop identified himself, his eyes resting on Caroline a moment and then taking a quick sweep of the living room behind her. "This is Officer Hernandez. You said you'd found a missing girl?"

"That's right," Roger said. "At least, we assume she's missing. There was this mugger in an alley on 101st Street—"

"Only he wasn't actually a mugger," Caroline interjected. "He wanted us to take her and—"

"Quiet!" Roger cut her off as a soft *thud* came from somewhere behind him. "What was that?"

"What was what?" Caroline asked tautly.

"I didn't hear anything," Kern said.

"Something went clunk," Roger said grimly, heading for the bedroom. "Like someone getting hit on the head."

He thought he was hurrying; but even so, both cops got to the bedroom door ahead of him. "Stay here," Kern ordered, his gun ready in his hand. Turning the knob, he shoved it violently open.

Hernandez was ready, diving through and ducking to the left. Kern was right behind him, breaking to the right. The closet light was still on, and from the doorway Roger could clearly see the bed and his coat lying open and rumpled.

The girl was gone.

"The balcony!" Caroline said in a shaking voice, pointing over Roger's shoulder at the sliding door. "The broomstick's been moved."

"And the latch is open," Roger said grimly. "They've got her out there!"

Kern grunted something as both cops made for the sliding door. Hernandez got there first, shoving the door open and disappearing onto the balcony, the older cop right on his heels. Clenching his teeth, Roger followed, the cold air cutting across his damp shirt like a late-June breaker at Coney Island. He ducked through the opening—

And nearly ran full into Kern's back.

"What is it?" he demanded, skidding to a halt. Both cops were just standing there, looking around.

At the empty balcony.

Roger looked again. Aside from himself, the two cops, and the two heavy ceramic pots with Caroline's orange trees sticking out of them, the balcony was completely empty.

The outside lights suddenly came on, making him jump, and the living room door slid open. "Where is she?" Caroline asked anxiously, poking her head through.

"Good question," Kern said, his voice suddenly darkly suspicious. "You got a good answer to go with it?"

"But she can't be gone," Caroline objected, looking around. "She was right there in the bedroom. Where else could she be?"

"Not here, anyway," Kern said, holstering his gun as he looked along the sheer wall. "And it's too far to jump to the next balcony."

"Couldn't have gone down, either," Hernandez added, leaning over the solid balcony wall and gazing down. He twisted his head and looked up along the wall of the balcony above theirs. "Or up, either. Railings you could climb, but not solid walls like these."

"But she *was* here," Caroline insisted. "She has to still *be* here."

"Okay, fine," Kern rumbled. "Come on, Hernandez. By the book."

They spent the next fifteen minutes going systematically through the apartment, looking everywhere anything bigger than a Chihuahua could be hiding. In the end, they found nothing.

"Well, it's been fun, folks," Kern said as they headed for the front door. "Next time you feel like pulling someone's chain, leave the NYPD out of it, okay?"

"Sure," Roger growled. "Thanks for your time."

He let them out, deadbolting and chaining the door after them. Caroline had gone back to the balcony, looking around as if she still expected to see the girl hiding in a corner. With a tired sigh, he crossed the room and went out to join her.

"I don't understand," she said as he stepped to her side. "She *was* here, wasn't she? We didn't just dream it."

"If we did, we dreamed this, too," Roger told her, pulling the gun from his pocket.

"The gun!" Caroline gasped, all but pouncing on it. "Quick—call them back. This proves it!"

"This proves what?" Roger countered disgustedly. "A toy gun? It doesn't prove a thing."

"But—" Caroline seemed to sink back into herself again. "You're right," she said, her voice quiet again. "But then where did she go?"

"I don't know," Roger admitted, looking around the balcony. "I just hope . . . never mind."

"That whoever tried to strangle her didn't come back and finish the job?" Caroline said, her voice almost lost in the whistling of the wind.

"Yeah." Roger took a deep breath of the cold northern air. Winter was indeed coming early this year. "Come on," he said, not knowing what else to say. "Let's go to bed."

3

They slept poorly that night. At least, Caroline slept poorly, and she assumed from the strained and mostly monosyllabic conversation between them the next morning that Roger hadn't done very well, either.

But at least they'd never gotten around to arguing about the play. That was something, anyway.

October was usually a quiet month in the real estate business, and this October had been no exception. Summer vacation rentals were only memories and bills, families with small children were firmly settled into the school year, and the Christmas bonuses that drew young couples' thoughts toward a nice co-op with a view were still two months away.

Which left Caroline plenty of time to think about the events of the previous evening. To think and to try to pick at the knots of the mystery in hopes of untangling them a little.

But all her efforts yielded nothing. She searched the local papers and Internet news sources for stories of urban violence that might connect with the bruises they'd seen on the girl's neck, but found nothing that matched both the crime and the girl's description. The man who'd left a streak of his blood on the strange gun also seemed to have slipped back into the shadows without any notice. She spent what seemed like hours on hold at the Missing Person's Bureau, only to come up empty on both the girl and the man.

She didn't talk to Roger at all that day. Sometimes he called her at lunch, but today she was so busy with the Internet that she never even noticed it was one-thirty until the twelve-thirty lunch shift swept back into the office. For an hour after that she worried about whether she should have called him, even if he hadn't called her, and spent the rest of the day sitting vaguely on pins and needles as she wondered if interrupting his afternoon would make things better or worse.

It was with considerable relief that she returned home that evening to find Roger not only not angry with her but already working on dinner.

"Hi, hon," he greeted her, giving her a distracted sort of kiss. "How was your day?"

"Slow," she said, hanging up her coat and returning to the kitchen. "Yours?"

"The same," he said, opening a can of tomatoes. "Judge Vasco is down with the flu, so the contract-dispute argument I was putting together for Bill is on hold for at least a week. And Sam and Carleton are out in the wilds of corporate Delaware on some big rainmaking expedition."

"At least they're not running you off your feet like they usually do," she commented.

"Which was handy, given how much time I spent on hold with Missing Persons," he said a little sourly. "Turns out they don't have anyone on their books who matches the girl's description."

"I know," Caroline said, peering at the open recipe book and pulling a block of cheddar out of the fridge. "They don't have anything on the man, either."

He glanced at her, a flicker of surprise and perhaps even respect flashing across his face. "You called them too?"

She nodded. "I also checked the news sources to see if I could come up with any events that might link to the bruises on her throat. But there was nothing."

He grunted. "I took the subway up to 103rd at lunchtime and walked back along last night's route," he told her. "I couldn't get into the alley—the gate was locked—but I couldn't see an single thing that looked out of the ordinary."

Caroline selected a knife and started cutting slices of cheese. "It's like it never happened."

"Pretty much," Roger agreed. "I did hear one interesting

tidbit, though. Seems there was a massive power outage up in Morningside Heights last night. The west part, over by Riverside Park."

Caroline frowned. "How far up?"

"Kelly said everything around his place on West 115th was completely dark." He paused. "Or at least it was after the big flash."

"Flash?"

"Yeah," Roger said. "Like all the streetlights blew at once, he said."

"Did ConEd have any explanation?"

"Just the usual bafflegab," Roger said. "Overloads, cable stress, squirrels in the wiring, or maybe the Broadway construction."

"You think that might have had something to do with our streetlight problem?" Caroline asked.

"I'd like to," Roger said. "But there are three problems. One, it doesn't sound anything like what we ran into, so I don't know how they could be related. Two, the Morningside outage happened nearly an hour before our lights did their magic trick. And three, there's still the problem of why the streetlights went out and not the power in the buildings themselves."

Caroline grimaced. "So we're back where we started," she said. "We've got a wild story without a single bit of proof. Except the gun," she corrected herself. "What did you do with it?"

"I put it in the junk drawer last night," he said. "Underneath your latch-hook stuff."

The latch-hook stuff she hadn't done anything with in years, she recalled, a brief flush of warmth rising into her cheeks. She should either pick up the hobby again or get rid of the trappings. "It's like one of those old ghost stories we used to tell around the campfire," she said. "You ever do that?"

"Nope," Roger said. "And if she was a ghost, she was a damn heavy one."

"Oh, they can be substantial enough," Caroline assured

him. "I remember one story about a high-school guy who picked up a girl at a dance and lent her his sweater on the way home."

"Caroline—"

"Anyway," she said, ignoring the interruption, "the next day when he went to the house he'd dropped her off at—"

"Caroline!"

She broke off, startled at the harshness in his voice, shrinking automatically into herself. What had she done now?

Roger was staring into space, the muscles in his throat gone suddenly rigid. "Listen," he said softly.

She frowned, holding her breath and straining her ears.

And there it was. A quiet tapping sound coming from the direction of the living room.

The kind of sound made by knuckles rapping on glass.

"I think," Roger said, his voice sounding unnaturally casual, "we've got company."

He headed for the living room. Caroline looked for a moment at the knife in her hand, then set it down beside the block of cheese and followed.

She found Roger standing just inside the living room, gazing across at the balcony door. There, standing outside looking in at them, her slim figure framed by the darkening sky and the lights of the cityscape behind her, was the girl from last night, still wearing the same patchwork tunic and tights.

Taking a deep breath and letting it out in a whoosh, Roger crossed the room, popped the broomstick out of the rail, and slid back the door.

The girl ducked her head toward him in a sort of abbreviated bow. "May I come in?" she asked. Her voice was deep and throaty, with a slight accent Caroline couldn't place.

"Sure," Roger said, stepping to the side. "Unless you want to stay outside with the trees all night."

It seemed to Caroline that she gave Roger a sharp look at that. But with only that one moment of hesitation, she stepped inside. "Thank you," she said. "And thank you for helping me last night."

"It seemed the right thing to do," Caroline said, ungluing herself from the floor and moving forward as Roger closed the door and latched it. "I don't believe we've properly met," she added. "I'm Caroline Whittier. This is my husband, Roger."

"Hello," the girl said, ducking her head again. "I'm Melantha Gre—" She broke off abruptly.

Gre? "Green?" Caroline hazarded, glancing at the green-and-gray color scheme of her tunic.

The girl's lips compressed briefly. "Yes," she conceded.

"Melantha Green," Caroline repeated. It was, she decided, an attractive combination of the exotic and the down-to-earth. "That's a nice name. How old are you?"

"Twelve," Melantha said. "I'll be thirteen next May."

"I'll bet you're looking forward to becoming a teenager," Caroline commented. "Do you have any family?"

The girl sent a furtive glance back over her shoulder at Roger. "I'm really hungry," she said. "Do you have anything I could eat?"

So family wasn't a topic she wanted to talk about. Interesting. "Certainly," Caroline said, taking her hand and leading her back toward the kitchen. Her skin was cool, but not nearly as cold as it should have been if she'd been sitting out on the balcony all day. "The casserole's not ready, but I can get you something to tide you over. Do you like cheese?"

"Goat's cheese?" Melantha asked hopefully as they stepped into the kitchen.

"Sorry," Roger said from behind them. "Just plain old cow-brand cheddar."

"That's okay," Melantha said, eying the cheese hungrily as Caroline pulled out one of the two chairs at the small breakfast table and settled her into it.

"You can start with this," Caroline said, piling the slices she'd already cut onto a plate and setting it in front of her. "Would you like some milk or juice? We have orange and apple."

The girl had one of the slices in hand before the plate even hit the table. "Some apple, please?"

"Certainly," Caroline said, getting a glass out of the cabinet and turning toward the fridge. She had to make a quick sidestep around Roger, who was suddenly and inexplicably moving past her toward the table. "Tell me, why did you leave us last night?" she asked as she pulled out the bottle of juice.

"Do you have any bread?" Melantha asked.

"Sure," Roger said. He had settled in at the spot where Caroline had been cutting the cheese earlier, his back to the counter as he faced the girl. Keeping his eyes on her, he pulled open the bread drawer and snagged a bag of dinner rolls. "Why *did* you leave?" he asked as he handed them over.

For a half second Melantha looked up at him. Roger gave her a smile—a forced smile, Caroline could tell, but a smile nonetheless. "I was afraid," she said, dropping her gaze back to the table and undoing the twist tie on the rolls. "I heard voices."

"That was just the police," Roger told her. "They were here to help."

"Someone attacked you," Caroline said, carrying the glass of juice to the table. "Do you remember that? Someone tried to . . ."

She trailed off, staring at Melantha's throat. The dark bruises that had been there the night before were now barely visible. "Someone tried to strangle you," she continued slowly, touching the girl's throat gently with her fingertips.

Melantha twitched away from her touch. "I know," she said.

"Who did it?" Roger asked. "The man with the gun?"

"No," she said firmly. "He was . . . trying to help."

"Then who?" Roger demanded.

Melantha flinched. "I don't know."

Roger looked at Caroline. *Liar,* his expression said. "What about your family?" Caroline asked, deciding to try that approach again. "Is there someone we should contact, to tell them you're all right?"

A shiver ran through the girl. "No," she said, biting hungrily into one of the dinner rolls and following it with a mouthful of cheese.

Caroline looked at Roger. He shrugged microscopically; reluctantly, Caroline nodded agreement. Whatever the girl knew, she wasn't ready to talk about it.

They watched in silence as Melantha finished off the rest of the sliced cheese and two more rolls. "That was good," she said, draining her glass. "Thank you."

"You're welcome," Caroline said. "Do you understand that we want to help you?"

Melantha stared down at her empty plate. "Yes," she said.

"Then tell us what happened," Caroline urged. "You can trust us."

Melantha's eyes were still on the empty plate, but Caroline could see her lips making uncertain little movements. As if she was trying to think, or about to cry. "Melantha?" she prompted.

"Because if you don't," Roger added, "we'll just have to call the police again."

It was probably the worst thing he could have said. Melantha's thin shoulders abruptly tightened, her wavering emotional barriers suddenly slamming up full strength again. "I'm real tired," she said, all the emotion abruptly gone from her voice. The barriers there had gone back up, too. "Is there someplace I could lie down for awhile?"

"Certainly," Caroline said, throwing a frustrated glare at Roger and getting a puzzled look in return. Clearly, he didn't even realize what he'd done. "Would you prefer the couch or the bed?"

"The couch is fine," Melantha said, staggering slightly as she stood up. "No, that's okay—I can get there by myself," she added as Caroline took a step toward her. "Thank you."

She left the kitchen. A moment later, Caroline heard the faint but unmistakable sound of couch springs settling under a load. "Well, that was brilliant," she muttered to Roger, keeping her voice low. "Did it ever occur to you that it might have *been* the police she's afraid of?"

"So?" Roger countered, pitching his voice equally low.

"You want to sugarcoat it, or you want to give her reality? If she doesn't let us help her, then she *has* to go to the police. Unless you want to throw her back out into the street."

"She's scared, Roger," Caroline said with exaggerated patience. "And you towering over her like that doesn't help any."

"Maybe not," Roger said, half turning and picking up the knife Caroline had been using to cut the cheese. "But it didn't seem smart to give her a clear shot at grabbing this."

"That's ridiculous," Caroline insisted. Still, she felt an unpleasant shiver run down her back as she eyed the knife. "*She's* the one who's in danger."

"Desperate people sometimes do desperate things," Roger reminded her, setting the knife back onto the counter. "Look, I know how gaga you get when there's an underdog involved—"

"That's not fair."

"—but the fact is that we don't know the first thing about this girl," Roger plowed on over her protest. "And even if she isn't a threat to us herself, she could still be putting us in danger just by being here."

He gestured toward the living room. "Like if whoever started that job decides to come by and finish it."

Caroline shook her head. "I think it has to do with her family," she said. "Domestic violence, probably from a father or stepfather."

Roger frowned. "How do you figure that?"

"That look she gave you in the living room, for one thing, when I first asked about her family," Caroline said. "She's nervous in your presence."

"Interesting theory," Roger murmured. "Problem is, she wasn't looking at me."

It was Caroline's turn to frown. "Are you sure?"

"Positive," he said. "Because at first I thought the same thing you did. What she was doing was making sure I'd locked the door, then doing a quick scan of the balcony itself."

"Of the *balcony*?"

Roger shrugged. "*She* came in that way," he pointed out.

"If she can, why can't someone else? And don't forget our husky friend with the handy Broadway dimmer switch. If this is a case of family violence, we're talking one very weird family."

"You're right," Caroline sighed, conceding the point. "So what do we do?"

"Good question," Roger said, tracing a finger along the edge of the knife handle. "We can't call anyone; cops *or* Children and Family Services. She'd just disappear again. And we can't throw her out, either, not in the middle of the night."

"So she stays here?" Caroline asked.

"At least for tonight," he said, not sounding very happy about it. "Maybe tomorrow she'll be more willing to talk."

"And if she isn't?"

Roger exhaled noisily. "Let's just hope she is."

• •

Dinner that evening was a quiet and rather strained affair, at least on Roger's part. He was fine when talking to Caroline about the details of her day, or discussing the latest political scandal from upstate. But all his conversational gambits with Melantha fell as flat as last year's campaign promises. Maybe Caroline was right; maybe the girl *was* afraid of him.

Caroline did a little better. She was able to get Melantha talking about her hobbies, her favorite foods, and her taste in music. The first centered around painting and gardening; the second included Greek and Moroccan cuisine and any kind of seafood; the third ran to current preteen heart throbs, most of whom Roger had never heard of.

But all attempts to draw her out on what had happened the previous evening brought either silence or a quick change of topic.

Still, the girl was polite enough, and had the table manners of someone who'd been properly brought up. She was also quick to praise the simple macaroni-cheese-tomato casserole he and Caroline had thrown together.

Neither of which meant she might not murder them in their sleep, of course. As they loaded the plates into the dishwasher, he made a mental note to move the sharp knives into their bedroom before they turned in for the night.

Once the table was clear and they moved into the living room, things picked up a little. Caroline produced a deck of cards, and Melantha quickly joined into the games with an eagerness that for the first time made her seem like a genuine twelve-year-old.

But her strangeness continued to peek through. She used odd terms for some of the card combinations, and occasionally would make an exclamation in a foreign language Roger couldn't identify. Even more telling, after they had run through Caroline's repertoire of hearts, Crazy Eights, Go Fish, and Kings-in-the-Corner, Melantha taught them a new game, one neither he nor Caroline had ever heard of before.

Exuberant card player or not, though, she was clearly still running at half speed. At nine o'clock, as they watched her eyelids drooping, Caroline called a halt.

"Time for bed, Melantha," she said, collecting the cards and putting them back into their box. "We have to get up early for work, and you look like you could use a good night's sleep, too."

"Yes." Melantha hesitated. "I—maybe I'd better—I should probably go now."

"You'll do no such thing," Caroline said firmly, standing up and collecting the throw pillows from the couch. "Let me go get a sheet, some blankets, and a pillow and we'll set you up right here."

"Unless you'd rather we take you someplace," Roger suggested. "Do you have any family you could go to?"

Melantha lowered her eyes; and suddenly the relaxed, card-playing twelve-year-old was gone. "No," she said. "Not . . . no."

"Then it's settled," Caroline said cheerfully, as if she hadn't even noticed the awkward transition. "Let me get that bedding and find you a toothbrush."

Fifteen minutes later, they had her settled in on the couch. Roger confirmed that the balcony door was locked and that the broomstick was in its groove and drew the curtains. "All safe and sound," he announced as Caroline turned out the lights. "Sleep well."

"'Night," Melantha said, her voice already fading.

Caroline headed to the bedroom. Roger double-checked the locks on the front door, then followed. "What do you think?" he asked as he closed the bedroom door behind them.

"She's scared, and she's on the run," Caroline said, pulling her nightshirt from beneath her pillow. "And I still think it has something to do with her family."

"I think you're right," Roger agreed as he unbuttoned his shirt. "I'm not sure I buy the abuse angle, though. Aside from those bruises on her throat, she seems healthy and well cared-for."

"I suppose," Caroline said, sitting down on the edge of the bed and starting to pull off her shoes. She was tired, Roger could tell, far more tired than she should have been for nine-thirty on a Thursday night. This business with Melantha must really be getting to her. "Speaking of bruises," she added, "did you notice they're almost gone?"

"Yeah, I did," Roger said. "Fast healer?"

"I don't know," Caroline sighed, pulling on her nightshirt. "So what do we do now?"

"You got me," he admitted. "All I can suggest is that we try the police again in the morning."

"She didn't want to see them last night," Caroline pointed out, making a face as she climbed under the comforter and blankets and hit the chilly sheets. "I doubt she'll want to see them tomorrow, either."

"Then she has to tell us what's going on," Roger said firmly. "She tells us, or she tells the cops."

"Or she does her disappearing act again."

"Maybe by morning she'll trust us a little more," Roger said, climbing into bed beside her. "Pleasant dreams."

"You, too," she said, rolling half over to give him a kiss.

He turned off the bedside light and nestled down under

the comforter, shivering against the cold sheets. At least Caroline seemed to have forgiven him for whatever it was he'd done wrong earlier in the evening.

It had been a long twenty-four hours, and he was deathly tired. But perversely, sleep refused to come. He lay quietly beside Caroline, listening to her slow breathing, staring at the edges of the sliding door where the glow of the city seeped in around the light-blocking drapes. Over and over again he played back the incident in the alley, trying to remember every word the man had said, every nuance of his tone or body language, every unusual thing or event that had happened before or after he'd shoved that gun into Roger's hand. But the mystery remained as tangled as ever.

And it was way beyond people like him and Caroline. In the morning, he decided firmly, they would give Melantha one last chance to come clean; and after that it was the cops, whether she liked it or not. And as for her disappearing act, this time he would sit on the girl to make sure she stayed put. Literally, if it came to that.

And then, from somewhere on the outside wall, he heard a soft thump.

He froze, straining his ears. Had he imagined the sound? Or could it have just been Melantha tossing in her sleep?

The sound came again. Definitely from the outside wall, and definitely near the bedroom door.

Someone was on their balcony.

4

He slid his legs out from under the comforter, a sudden fury burning inside him. So Melantha wasn't even going to wait until morning before pulling her vanishing trick again.

Like hell.

It took only a few seconds to retrieve his workout sweats from the laundry hamper and pull them on. Easing the bedroom door open, he slipped out.

His bare feet seemed to shrink as they hit the cold hardwood of the hallway. But he didn't care. She was not, repeat *not,* going to get away with this two nights running. He rounded the corner into the living room—

And came to a sudden stop. The curtains here weren't the same heavy-duty ones as in the bedroom, and enough light was pressing its way through to clearly show Melantha still wrapped in her blankets on the couch.

There was more than enough to show the silhouette of someone on the balcony.

Call 911! was his first reflexive impulse. But an instant later he realized that would be a useless gesture. By the time the cops arrived, the intruder would be long gone. Or would have broken in and murdered all three of them.

And Roger had nothing to defend them with except a few carving knives and a stupid little toy gun.

A toy gun which nevertheless looked very real.

The shadow shifted as the intruder moved stealthily across the balcony. Easing his way back into the kitchen, Roger went to the junk drawer and dug beneath Caroline's latch-hook stuff.

The gun was gone.

For a long moment his fingers scrabbled frantically among the collected odds and ends. It couldn't be gone. He'd put it right here only yesterday.

In the living room, Melantha stirred beneath her blankets, and he grimaced. Of course—the girl had taken it. She'd searched through the drawers after he and Caroline had gone to bed and retrieved it.

He stepped back out of the kitchen. The shadow had disappeared, but he could hear a faint scratching sound. Was the intruder trying to find a way through the doors?

Most of the kitchen knives were down the hall in the bedroom, where he'd taken them while Caroline was hunting

up a spare toothbrush. But the one he'd left on the knickknack shelf last night when the cops arrived was still there.
Sliding it out from behind the plate, he wrapped it in a firm
grip and started across the living room.

The twenty-foot walk seemed to take forever. Reaching
the curtains, he crouched down and silently rolled the
broomstick up out of the track onto the carpet. Then,
straightening up again, he stepped to the other end of the
door and slid his hand around the edge of the curtain. Taking a deep breath, he popped the latch, shoved the door to
the side, and leaped out onto the balcony, knife at the ready.

There was no one there.

He looked back and forth twice. There was nobody
skulking in a corner; no ropes hanging down from above; no
grappling hooks on the balcony wall leading up from below.
Nothing but Caroline's stupid dwarf orange trees.

But someone *had* been there. He hadn't dreamed the
sound or the moving shadow. He shifted his attention to his
left, wondering if someone could have leaped across from
the next balcony.

And there, sixty feet away at the far corner of the building, was the silhouetted figure of a man.

Hanging onto the outside wall like a human fly.

Roger stared, a creeping sensation twisting through his
stomach. The man wasn't standing on a ladder, his eyes and
brain noted mechanically: he was on a section of the wall
between balconies, with no place for a ladder to be braced.
He wasn't hanging from a rope or trapeze: the roof overhang would have left him dangling a couple of feet out from
the wall, and he was instead snugged right up against the
stone facing.

And then, as Roger watched, he began to climb. Not like
people climbed walls in movies, where there was always
just that little bit of something wrong in balance or flow or
movement that betrayed the presence of the hidden wires.
The man's hands reached up one at a time, pressing against
the wall and pulling as the alternate foot lifted and pushed.
He moved as casually as if he were walking down the street;

but at the same time, Roger could sense the genuine exertion of muscles working at their task. It looked real.

It *was* real.

The figure angled across the wall between two floors and disappeared around the corner to the other side of the building. Roger stared after him, part of him hoping the man would come back, most of him fervently hoping he wouldn't.

"Roger?" Caroline whispered.

He jumped, the sound of her voice jarring him back to reality. She was standing in the balcony doorway, her robe clutched tightly around her. "What is it?" she hissed.

Roger threw a last glance at the corner and took a deep breath. . . .

And then, behind Caroline, he saw Melantha sitting up on the couch, her eyes wide, her face taut.

"Nothing," he told Caroline, trying to keep his voice casual. "I thought I heard something, that's all. Must have been dreaming."

"Oh," Caroline said, and he wished he had enough light to read her expression. "Well, you'd better come in before you freeze to death."

"Yeah," he said, shivering as he followed her inside.

He made sure he locked the balcony door solidly behind him.

● ●

He waited until they were back in bed, with the lights off and the door closed between them and Melantha, and then told her the whole story. "You're sure you *weren't* dreaming?" she asked when he had finished.

"I don't end up on the balcony in bare feet when I dream," Roger pointed out, annoyed in spite of himself. *Yes,* it sounded impossible. But she was his wife, damn it. She was supposed to believe him when he told her something.

"I'm not saying you were," Caroline hastened to assure him. "I'm just trying to cover all the possibilities."

"I've already covered them," Roger muttered, his annoyance fading into guilt at his outburst. "Sorry. I'm just . . ."

She squeezed his hand under the blankets. "I know," she said quietly. "I was just thinking out loud."

"Well, don't stop now," he said. "I'm at a dead end myself."

"All right," she said hesitantly. "Well. He wasn't on a ladder—you'd have seen that—and he wasn't on a rope, because of the roof overhang. Suction cups?"

Roger shook his head. "He seemed short, but reasonably bulky. Any suction cups strong enough to hold him up ought to have been visible."

"Short but bulky," Caroline repeated thoughtfully. "Like the man who gave Melantha to us last night?"

"I wondered that, too," Roger said. "But this one seemed smaller, and not nearly so bulky."

"And the gun's gone."

"The gun's gone," Roger confirmed. "I assume Melantha took it."

"Why?"

"How should I know?" he growled. "Maybe it's a real gun that just needs a special trick to work."

"I don't think it's a real gun," Caroline said slowly. "You saw how she was sitting up on the couch, wide awake, scared to death. If she'd had a weapon, I think she'd have had it ready."

"So where did it go?" Roger objected. "It didn't just evaporate."

"I don't know," Caroline said. "Do you want to go look for it now?"

Roger sighed. "No, we can do it in the morning. Let's try to get some sleep."

"All right," Caroline said, squeezing his hand again. "Good night."

"Again," Roger reminded her dryly. "Let's hope it takes this time."

"Yes." She paused. "That was very brave of you, you know. Going out there all alone."

"That was very stupid of me, you mean," Roger corrected. "Still, my life insurance is paid up."

He felt her stiffen beside him. Wrong thing to say, apparently. "Sleep well," she murmured.

"You too," he said. Rolling onto his side, he punched his pillow into shape and tried to settle in.

But before he did so, he reached to the floor and made sure the kitchen knives were within easy reach. Just in case.

• •

Caroline lay quietly in the darkness, listening as Roger's breathing settled down into the slow, even rhythm of sleep. Usually, she was the one who could drop off at a moment's notice; but tonight, the pattern seemed to have been reversed. Now she was the one lying fully awake, staring at the light seeping around the edges of the curtains, ears straining for the slightest unusual sound. But their mysterious visitor had apparently moved on.

Roger's flippant comment about his life insurance hadn't helped, either.

She spent half an hour listening to the soft noises of the traffic below before finally giving up. Sliding carefully out of bed, she snagged her robe and slipped out of the bedroom.

Melantha was still on the couch, a half-twisted figure wrapped in her blankets. For a moment Caroline wondered if she might be more willing to talk if Roger wasn't present. But the girl needed her sleep, too. Turning back to the kitchen, she flipped on the microwave's nightlight setting and opened the junk drawer.

Roger had told her he'd put the gun under her latch-hook equipment. Lifting up that last half-finished project, she pulled it out and set it aside.

The gun was gone, all right. She probed with her fingers, wondering if it could have worked its way underneath something else. Roger could call this junk if he wanted to;

but to her, everything in here had a history, something that reminded her of a time or event in their life together. There was the black Phillips-head screw that had gotten lost from the old bentwood rocking chair they'd given to Caroline's sister when her baby was born. There were the two partially used rolls of plastic tape left over from last Christmas, Roger having started the second when he missed seeing there was one already in use. In the months since then, they hadn't managed to work either of them down to where it could be thrown away.

Her searching fingers paused. There in the center of the drawer, beside the box of rubber bands and twist-ties, was a large brooch.

She picked it up and angled it toward the light. It was a beautiful thing, a dozen silver leaves woven into two concentric circles, with a violet stone in the center, all tied together by a delicate silver filigree mesh. It was about three inches across and heavier than it looked, with the kind of weight that could easily tear a blouse if it wasn't fastened properly.

She'd never seen it before in her life.

She hefted it in her hand. Too heavy to be silver, she decided. White gold or platinum? She peered at the back, but aside from a rather elaborate and antique-looking pin arrangement there was nothing there.

But at the same time, there was something about it that tweaked at her memory. Something that seemed oddly familiar.

The connection didn't come. Giving up, she set it aside on the counter and slid the junk drawer back in. Then, from the drawer under the telephone, she pulled out the Manhattan phone book and carried it to the table.

Gre, Melantha had started to say the previous night when asked her last name. *Green,* Caroline had guessed, and Melantha had reluctantly confirmed it. She didn't want to send the girl back to whatever it was she'd run away from, and in fact had more or less promised herself that she wouldn't.

But it was becoming increasingly clear that there would be no way of resolving this without talking to someone on the other end of the situation.

Of course, even if she found Melantha's family, what then? Take their word for what was going on? Insist on counseling, or that Family Services be brought in before she and Roger would return Melantha?

Roger wouldn't want to do that, of course. Roger hated confrontations, and would go to incredible lengths to avoid them. That was one of the things that had first attracted her to him, in fact. He'd been a welcome relief from the overgrown teenagers and macho types who went around with permanent chips stapled to their shoulders.

But there was a world of difference between being meek and gentle and simply playing doormat for rude and uncaring idiots. Sometimes she wondered if Roger really understood that difference.

With a sigh, she put that particular group of frustrations out of her mind and opened to the G's. There were more Greens than she'd expected, covering three full pages and half of a fourth. Snagging a notepad and pen, she started making a list of all those living within walking distance of the alley where they'd found her.

She was finished with the first page when she noticed something strange. She was midway down the third when the second oddity struck her. By the time she made it to the end, she was almost ready to wake up Roger and show him.

But sleep was finally starting to tug at her eyelids. Anyway, there was nothing they could do about it in the middle of the night. Tucking her notes into the phone book, she replaced it in its drawer and turned off the light.

Roger had taken over the middle of the bed in her absence. Easing her way in beside him, she pressed gently against his side until he grunted in his sleep and rolled over.

Three minutes later, with the sounds of passing cars beating softly against her ears, she fell asleep.

5

The rest of Roger's night passed restlessly, crowded with strange dreams and punctuated by long intervals of lying awake listening to the wind outside their window. At one point he had the impression that Caroline was gone, but the next time he awoke she was back where she was supposed to be.

It made for a hazy sort of grogginess the next morning that even a hot shower couldn't completely eradicate. He could smell the coffee as he shaved, and hoped Caroline was making it strong.

Not only was she making coffee, he discovered as he emerged from the bedroom into the kitchen, but she'd pulled out all the stops on breakfast as well. Along with coffee and orange juice, the table was loaded with bacon, bagels, grapes, slices of cheese, and a nearly depleted plate of scrambled eggs. Caroline was at the stove, busily scrambling another batch.

It was a far cry from the bagels and granola bars that were their normal breakfast, but the reason for the feast wasn't hard to guess. Melantha was already at the table, digging in with an energy only a preteen hitting a growth spurt could manage.

"Morning, Roger," Caroline greeted him, giving him a tentative sort of smile. "You sleep well?"

"Pretty good," he fibbed, sitting down across from Melantha. "Good morning, Melantha."

The girl's mouth was full, but she gave him a smile in return. The smile, he noted, didn't reach all the way to her eyes.

"Had a little excitement last night, didn't we?" he commented casually as Caroline left her egg-scrambling long enough to pour him a cup of coffee. Such restaurant-style service, too, was out of the ordinary. "I hope you weren't scared."

"No," Melantha said, not looking at him as she cut a triangle of cheese with her fork and shoveled the last bite of her eggs on top of it.

"You got back to sleep all right afterward?"

"Uh-huh," she said. "Caroline, can I have some more eggs?"

"Of course," Caroline said. "Help yourself. If you don't mind waiting, Roger?"

"No, go ahead and finish them off," Roger said.

"Thank you," Melantha said, and scraped the rest of the eggs onto her plate.

Roger watched her out of the corner of his eye as he poured himself some juice. Once again, he noted, she'd evaded his questions.

But this time, at least, he hadn't come away completely empty-handed. The most obvious question she should have asked was what he'd been doing on the balcony in the first place. The fact that she hadn't asked it implied she already knew.

Perhaps she sensed his eyes on her. "On second thought," the girl said suddenly, "I think I'd rather have a shower instead. May I?"

"Certainly," Caroline said. "There are towels in the cabinet beside the tub."

"Thank you." Scooping a quick double forkful of eggs into her mouth, she got up from the table and disappeared down the hallway toward the bathroom.

"So much for questioning her," Roger said pointedly as Caroline piled the fresh batch of eggs onto the serving plate.

"She wouldn't have told us anything," Caroline said, picking up her own coffee cup and sitting down on the chair Melantha had just vacated. "Besides, this gives us a chance to talk." She glanced the direction Melantha had gone, then reached into her robe pocket and pulled out a piece of jewelry. "Take a look."

Roger took it, frowning. It was a large pin of some sort, made of silver leaves and threads with a purple stone in the middle. It didn't look like anything he could remember Caroline ever wearing. "I take it it's not yours?"

"I'd never seen it before last night," Caroline confirmed. "The point is that I found it in the junk drawer, right where you said you'd put the gun."

Roger looked up under his eyebrows at her. "Are you suggesting," he said slowly, "that this *is* the gun?"

"It's about the right weight and color," Caroline said. Her voice was dogged, but Roger could sense her backpedaling from her position. If he thought it was ridiculous, and said so . . .

With an effort, he looked back at the pin in his hand. Yes, it was ridiculous. But no more ridiculous than anything else that had happened since they'd gone to that stupid play. "Let's assume it is," he said. "First and most obvious question: *How?*"

Caroline shrugged helplessly. "How does a man climb up the side of a building?"

"Touché," Roger admitted.

"I don't like it, either," Caroline said. "You ready for the next one?"

"Hang on." He took a long swallow of his coffee. She had, indeed, made it strong this morning. "Okay, hit me."

"I went through the phone book last night," she said, getting up and pulling the directory from its drawer. "I thought we might be able to locate Melantha's family."

"With just the name 'Green' to go on?"

"I couldn't sleep anyway." Opening the directory, she pulled out a piece of notepaper and handed it to him. "Anyway, I found two very interesting addresses: one on Riverside Drive near 104th, the other on West 70th just off Central Park. Each of them lists over thirty Greens living there."

Roger frowned down at the paper. His first thought was

that she must have double-counted some of the listings. But she'd have to have been *really* foggy to have double-counted *that* badly. "You have any reason to assume Melantha's from either building?"

"Not really," Caroline said. "I just thought it was strange enough to be worth mentioning."

"It's definitely that," he agreed. "The Riverside Drive address is closer to where we found her. Maybe we should go check it out."

"We could," Caroline said, staring into her coffee cup. "But I keep thinking about the bruises on her throat. If her family didn't do that, why is she so reluctant to go back home? Or to even talk about them?"

"Good point," Roger conceded. He glanced at his watch and shoveled a last forkful of eggs into his mouth. "And speaking of going places, we need to get to work."

Caroline seemed to brace herself. "Actually, I thought I'd stay home today. Keep an eye on Melantha."

Roger blinked in surprise. Skipping work was a very un-Caroline thing to suggest. But under the circumstances—"Good idea," he said. "Maybe I should stay, too."

"No, that's all right," Caroline said. "We'll be fine."

"What if our midnight visitor comes back?"

"In broad daylight?" Caroline pointed out. "Besides, she might be more willing to talk just to me."

Roger felt his lip twitch. But she was right. "Fine," he grunted. "See what you can get out of her." Picking up the pin, he dropped it into his pocket.

"You're taking the brooch with you?"

"I thought I might look in on one of those Green-intensive buildings at lunchtime," he told her. "If this *does* have something to do with Melantha, it might help prove we have her."

"Ah," Caroline said, her tone suddenly odd. "You think it would be better if we both went later?"

In other words, you don't think I can handle it? "I'll be fine," he said instead. "You concentrate on Melantha; I'll take the outside world."

"All right," she said in that same odd tone. "Just be careful, will you? This whole thing is very strange."

He snorted as he stood up. "That, sweetheart, is the understatement of the month."

She managed a faint smile at that one. "You'll call later?"

"At lunchtime," Roger promised, circling the table to give her a quick kiss. "And you call *me* if anything happens here."

"Don't worry," she said. "We'll be fine."

• •

He brooded about it all the way to the office, barely noticing the overcast sky or the as-usual crammed subway. This thing with Melantha was bad enough; but what was worse, he couldn't seem to figure out Caroline these days, either. One minute she would be fine, and the next she would be looking like a bug that had been stepped on.

Was this some kind of woman thing? Or was it just Melantha?

The sun was starting to peek more cheerfully through the clouds by the time he reached his office. But his own dark mood persisted; and after an hour and a half of blankly pushing papers around he finally gave up. Nothing was going to get done, he realized glumly, until the Melantha problem was cleared up.

Five minutes later, he was back on the street. Of the two addresses Caroline had ferreted out, the one near Central Park was the closer. He might as well start there.

The building turned out to be a modest little four-story place on a tree-lined street within view of the park, with a stone stairway that led up a half dozen steps from the sidewalk to a landing and then made a right-angle turn and continued another half dozen steps to the entrance foyer itself. An interesting anomaly struck him as he approached the building: unlike most of those he could see on the street, this one didn't have bars on its ground-floor windows.

There was a young man sitting on the top step, idly rubbing his fingers together and gazing down the street. "Can I help you?" he called as Roger started up the steps.

"Possibly," Roger said. The man looked to be in his early thirties, not exactly the sort Roger would expect to see hanging around doing nothing in the middle of a workday. He was slender with black hair and smooth, darkish skin that reminded him of Melantha's own Mediterranean complexion. He also had something of her exotic eyes, too. "I'm looking for someone named Green."

"Really," the other said. His voice was casual enough, but Roger had the distinct feeling that he was being scrutinized, as if visiting strangers were uncommon.

Still, this was New York, where people were naturally aloof. "Yes, really," he said, stopping at the midway landing. "I understand there are some Greens living at this address."

"Actually, all four apartments are owned by Greens," the man said. "Which one are you looking for?"

Roger frowned up at the building. "*Four* apartments?" he repeated. "That's all?"

"Isn't that enough for a building this size?" the other countered. His tone was faintly jocular, but there was no humor in his eyes.

"Must be really big families," Roger said. "I was given to understand there are over thirty Greens living here."

"Ah," the other said, nodding. "Actually, it's just a matter of thirty phone lines coming in. Two of the families run specialized solicitation services for one of the banks—Chase Manhattan, I think."

"Interesting," Roger said. That story might satisfy the casual passerby, but he knew better. "So this building is zoned for business?"

The other's eyes narrowed slightly. "I don't know anything about legal stuff."

"Maybe not," Roger said. "But I do."

"You a cop?"

Roger shook his head. "Just a concerned citizen."

"Concerned about zoning?" the man countered. "Or something else?"

It was as good an opening, Roger decided, as he was likely to get. "Actually, I'm looking for one particular family," he said, throwing a casual glance back at the sidewalk behind him to make sure there was no one within eavesdropping distance. "A family who might have misplaced a young girl Wednesday night," he continued, turning back to the man.

"He knows," a voice said darkly from behind him.

Roger spun around. Standing at the base of the steps beside one of the trees lining the sidewalk was another young, dark-haired man.

Gripped in his hand was a gun.

6

For that first stretched-out second Roger just stood there, frozen with the impossibility of it. The man hadn't been on the sidewalk—he'd checked everything in sight not more than three seconds earlier. He hadn't come up from the walk-down apartment below the steps, either—Roger would have seen any movement from that direction. And there was literally nowhere anyone could have come from.

Yet there he was.

"I see we've got something more serious here than just a zoning violation," he said, managing somehow to keep his voice steady.

"Porfirio, are you nuts?" the first man hissed.

"Shut up, Stavros," the gunman said, his eyes smoldering as he walked up the steps to the landing and came to a halt facing Roger. "You heard him. He knows where—"

Abruptly, he broke off, and for a long second he and Stavros stared silently at each other. Roger held his breath; and then Porfirio's lip twitched, and with clear reluctance, he lowered his gun. "My apologies," he said, the words coming out like they had to be forcibly extracted. "My concern for—"

Again, he stopped in mid-sentence. "You were about to tell us your business here," Stavros suggested into the silence.

"Yes," Roger said, watching Porfirio and mentally crossing his fingers. "I'm looking for the parents of Melantha Green."

Porfirio muttered something under his breath. "I told you he knew," he said.

"What's your interest in the girl?" Stavros asked, ignoring the comment.

"We want to return her safely to where she belongs," Roger assured him. "That's all."

"That's great," Stavros said, a hint of cautious enthusiasm in his voice. "Just bring her here. We'll take care of her."

"Her parents live here, then?" Roger asked. "Good. I'd like to speak to them."

Stavros glanced at Porfirio. "Unfortunately, her parents aren't available at the moment," he said. "Would someone else do?"

"Who do you suggest?" Roger asked cautiously.

There was another of the short staring contests between the two men. "The one you need to see is Aleksander," Stavros said. "I could have him back here in half an hour."

"Sorry, but I have other business," Roger improvised. The longer he hung out with these people, the creepier he felt. "I'll come back another time," he added, trying to maneuver around Porfirio.

The other took a quick step to block him. "Uh-uh," he said, lifting his gun a couple of inches for emphasis. "If we say you wait for Aleksander, you wait."

"Porfirio, put that away," Stavros ordered. "Look, Mr.— What's your name, anyway?"

"Roger Wh—" Roger broke off, catching himself in time. "Just Roger."

"All right," Stavros said. "I understand that you can't wait for Aleksander. But won't you at least talk to *someone?*"

"Again, who do you suggest?" Roger asked.

"There's a woman here named Sylvia," Stavros said. "Would you be willing to give her a few minutes?"

The sweat gathering on Roger's neck was starting to turn to ice as the breeze hit it. The last thing he wanted to do was stay here a second longer than he had to.

But Porfirio was still holding the gun. And after all, he *was* here to talk to someone about Melantha.

"You'll be free to leave at any time, of course," Stavros assured him. "But it would be in your best interests, *and* Melantha's, if you talk to Sylvia."

"What exactly is her relationship with Melantha?" Roger asked, feeling a trickle of hope. Apparently, Stavros had misinterpreted his hesitation, seeing careful and judicious thought instead of weakness and indecision. Maybe he could get away with pretending to be the strong, reserved type.

"She's family," Stavros said. "It'll be all right. Really."

Roger pursed his lips, as if weighing the options, then nodded. "All right," he said, trying to pitch his voice like he was doing them a favor. "Where is she?"

"I'll take you in," Porfirio volunteered, tucking his gun out of sight in a side pocket.

"No, I'll do it," Stavros said. "This way, Roger."

There was a four-button intercom set in the wall beside the inner door. Stavros didn't bother pushing any of the buttons, but simply turned the knob and pushed the door open. The foyer had a feeling of age, the sense of a place that had somehow managed to avoid the advances of time. Stavros gestured to the polished wooden stairway and they started up.

"You said Sylvia was family," Roger said as they walked. "Melantha's family?"

"We're all Melantha's family," Stavros said over his shoulder.

"Really," Roger said, frowning. Stavros's eyes and skin tone were right, but aside from that there wasn't any particular resemblance. Part of Melantha's extended family? Or did he simply mean they were both members of the same ethnic group?

They got off at the third-floor landing. An odd mixture of aromas swirled through the air, and Roger felt his nose crinkling as he tried to sort out the various components. It was definitely cooking, but not of any ethnic category he could identify. "In here," Stavros said, stepping to the door and opening it.

A stronger wave of the exotic aromas rolled out into the hall. Bracing himself, Roger stepped inside.

He found himself in a room that seemed at first glance to be a copy of a nineteenth-century parlor, complete with flower-patterned wallpaper, a simple dark rug, and furniture of a style his grandmother would have felt right at home with. His second glance picked up the more modern touches: the abstract pictures on the wall, the desk phone, the late-model computer tucked into a rolltop desk in the back corner.

Standing in the center of the room was a thirtyish woman, dark-haired and with the same Mediterranean features he'd noted in both Melantha and the two men downstairs.

And pinned high up on her blouse was a brooch made of delicate silver fibers. A brooch that looked a lot like the one he had in his side pocket.

"Come in, Roger," the woman invited as Roger hesitated by the doorway. "My name's Cassia. I'm a colleague of Sylvia's."

"Thank you," Roger said. "Just a colleague? Not family?"

"We're all family," Cassia said. "In here, please."

She stepped back into an archway leading from the back of the parlor and gestured through it. Roger walked past her, taking the opportunity to look at her brooch more closely. It wasn't a duplicate of the one in his pocket, but it was definitely of the same style. Offhand, he couldn't decide whether that was a good sign or a bad one.

The dining room had been assembled from the same hodgepodge of modern and antique furnishings that he'd already noted in the parlor. Dominating the center was a long wooden table with enough straight-backed chairs to accommodate fifteen or sixteen adults. A half-dozen children were currently seated around it, ranging in age from preschool to perhaps eleven years old. At the near end of the table was a middle-aged woman who seemed to be the one in charge. At the far end, across from her, sat a much older woman with white hair and deep age lines in her face. The children were in high spirits, laughing and chattering away in an unfamiliar language as they dug eagerly into their dinner.

He frowned. Their *dinner*?

It was dinner, all right. The serving platters were heavy with slices of steaming meat—lamb, he tentatively identified it—plus rice, three different kinds of vegetables, dark bread that looked homemade, butter, and milk. Definitely dinner.

At eleven o'clock in the morning.

"You must be Roger."

Roger lifted his gaze from the table to the older woman's face. For all the erosion of the years, he could still see echoes of what must once have been a striking beauty. Her eyes were bright and aware, sparkling with intelligence. Like Melantha and Cassia, her skin had that olive Mediterranean look.

And like Cassia, she was wearing a delicately styled silver brooch, this one with a green stone in the center.

"Yes," he acknowledged. "You must be Sylvia."

"Indeed," she said. "I appreciate your willingness to see me."

"No problem," Roger said. "But I don't want to interrupt your party."

"Six children hardly constitutes a party," Sylvia said with a smile.

"They must be voracious eaters," Roger said, nodding toward the table. "That, or you're expecting more company."

The children and the middle-aged woman had stopped their conversation and were looking curiously at their visitor. "Perhaps we should step out to the front room," Sylvia said, pushing her chair back and standing up. A few words in that same strange language, and the children returned to their meal. "They're all home-schooled," she explained as she circled the table toward Roger.

"And the meal?" he asked. "Dinner, at eleven in the morning?"

"Their fathers work the night shifts," she said. "They're running late today, so we let the children start without them."

"I see," Roger said through suddenly stiff lips. So a whole crowd of these people was about to descend on him? Terrific.

Cassia was standing beside a high-backed sofa when he and Sylvia returned to the parlor. "Sit down," Sylvia invited, gesturing Roger toward a wing-back chair as she lowered herself onto the sofa beside the younger woman. "I understand you've brought word of Melantha. You have her?"

Roger eyed the old woman. She was leaning slightly forward, her eyes bright with anticipation. "I know where she is," he said cautiously. "May I ask your relationship to her?"

"We're family," Sylvia said briefly. "What exactly has she told you?"

Roger felt his throat tighten. *What has she told you?* No questions about Melantha's health; no inquiry about her safety or well-being. Sylvia's first question had been about Melantha's location; her second had been whether the girl had talked.

Someone had tried to strangle Melantha. Someone, perhaps, who was worried about what she might say to strangers?

"I know someone tried to kill her," he said evenly, watching the lined face carefully. But there was no surprise there he could detect. "I know she's terrified for her life."

"Anything else?"

Roger hesitated. This could be risky, but it might be interesting to see her reaction. "I know there are others interested in her," he said.

Again, Sylvia's face didn't even twitch. But Cassia

wasn't in such good command of her face. The sudden compression of lips and throat were all he needed to know he'd hit a nerve.

So they knew about the mugger in the alley. Did they know about the nighttime human fly, too?

"Really," Sylvia said. Her voice, like her face, was perfectly calm. "And who might they be?"

"I thought you might like to tell me," Roger invited.

"I'd prefer to talk about Melantha," Sylvia said.

"That's fine with me," Roger said. "You could start by telling me why you don't seem to care about her well-being."

"That's not true," Cassia protested. "We're more interested—"

She broke off abruptly. "Cassia speaks out of place," Sylvia said. "But she's right. We're more interested in Melantha's well-being than you could possibly understand. Far more than you yourself are, for that matter."

"An interesting assumption," Roger said, feeling warmth flowing into his face. "Especially since I haven't heard either of you even ask about her health."

Sylvia shrugged. "We know she's alive, and the fact that you're here means she must be at least reasonably well. Otherwise, how would you have known where to come?"

"Of course," Roger said. So very logical. The kind of argument he himself might have made, in fact.

"But the danger to her has certainly not ended," Sylvia continued, her voice turning a shade darker. "That's why we need you to bring her here."

Roger shook his head. "I can't hand her over to anyone except her parents."

The lines in Sylvia's forehead deepened. "You can't protect her, Roger. Only we can do that."

"Perhaps," Roger said. "Who exactly are we protecting her from?"

Sylvia's face hardened, her eyes boring into Roger's. "Listen to me closely," she said, her voice low and strangely resonant. "Melantha isn't the only one in danger. This entire city stands on the edge of chaos and destruction. If you don't want to be responsible for the deaths of thousands of people, you will tell me where she is."

Abruptly, she rose to her feet. "And you will tell me *now*."

7

For a moment the room seemed frozen in time. Sylvia seemed to tower over the room, her face burning like that of an ancient Greek goddess, the fire in her eyes demanding instant and total obedience. Roger hunched back in his chair, flinching back before that gaze, too paralyzed to even make a break for the door.

And then, unexpectedly, two other images flickered into view, superimposed on Sylvia's. One was that of Melantha, her face twisted with fear, the way she'd looked the night he'd seen the man climbing the outside of their building. Beside it was Caroline's face, the way she always looked when he'd backed down from a confrontation.

He thought about that face, and how it would look if he had to tell her he'd given in and handed Melantha over to these people.

And suddenly he knew which confrontation he more urgently preferred to avoid. "I'm sorry," he said, forcing himself to stand. "I'll be in touch."

For that first second he thought Sylvia was going to physically try to stop him. Her eyes glinted even more brightly, the wrinkles around her mouth deepening. Roger stood motionless in front of his chair, trying to work up the nerve to move past her to the door. If she decided to get in his way— or worse, if she called down to Porfirio and Stavros—

And then, to his relief, the wrinkles smoothed out and the

fire faded from the old woman's eyes. "Very well," she said, her voice calm again. "I can't force you to stay. But give Melantha a message from us. Tell her that if she comes to us, Aleksander stands ready to protect her."

"I'll tell her," Roger promised, a fresh shiver running up his back. Ungluing his feet from the floor, he walked across the room, heart still thudding with anticipation and dread. But the two women merely watched him in silence.

Until he reached the door. "As for you," Sylvia added as he took hold of the knob, "I warn you that city is no longer a safe place for those who stand beside Melantha."

Roger swallowed. "Is that a threat?"

"Merely a statement of fact," she said. "Good-bye, Roger."

He half expected to find the whole night-shift crew Sylvia had mentioned gathered out on the landing, ready to jump him. But there was no one in sight. Making his way down the stairs, he went outside to discover that Porfirio and Stavros had likewise vanished. He headed back down the street, trying not to look like he was hurrying, an eerie feeling between his shoulder blades. He reached the bustling activity of Central Park West—

And suddenly, it was as if he was in New York again.

He walked six blocks before the tingling began to fade away into the familiar noises and smells of the city. Not until he'd emerged into the sunlight had he realized just how much of a spell the old building had spun around him.

He'd gone there hoping they could help clear up some of Melantha's mystery. All they'd done was make it worse.

He kept walking, trying to figure out what to do next. Going home was definitely out, or at least going home by anything resembling a straight line. He couldn't tell if he was being followed, but he had no doubt that he was. Sylvia's people wanted Melantha, and this was too obvious an opportunity for them to pass up.

He was halfway to his office when it suddenly occurred to him that it wouldn't be safe to go there, either. Even given that his firm was only one of a hundred in the building, he still couldn't take the chance that they might track him down and learn his name and address.

Maybe it was too late already. Even though he hadn't given them his full name, there couldn't be all that many Roger Wh-somethings listed in the phone book.

On his left was a little restaurant busy with early lunchtime patrons. Ducking into the doorway, shaking his head at the offer of a menu, he pulled out his cell phone.

Caroline answered on the third ring. "Hello?"

"It's me," Roger said. "Any problems?"

"No, not at all," Caroline assured him. "We're having a fine time. I'm teaching Melantha how to latch-hook—"

"Calls?" Roger cut her off. "Visitors?"

There was a brief pause. "Neither," Caroline said, her voice suddenly subdued. "What's happened?"

Roger hesitated, wondering if he was jumping at shadows. Out here in the sunshine and brisk New York breezes, it all seemed so silly.

But he hadn't imagined Sylvia's veiled threats. He hadn't imagined the bruises on Melantha's neck.

He certainly hadn't imagined Porfirio and his gun.

"Maybe nothing," he told Caroline. "I was at your Central Park West building a few minutes ago. I found some people who claim to know Melantha's parents, but they wouldn't let me talk to them."

"That seems strange."

"You don't know the half of it," he assured her. "Maybe I'm overreacting, but I want you and Melantha to get out of there."

The pause this time was longer. "Right now?" Caroline asked, her voice not giving any clues as to what she was thinking.

"Yeah, I think so," Roger said, trying to think. "You'll need a hotel. A decent one, hopefully not too expensive."

"How about Paul and Janet's place?" Caroline suggested. "They're not due back from Oregon for another week, and I know they wouldn't mind."

Roger pursed his lips. The Young family lived way over in Yorkville, on the east side of Manhattan, beside a little patch of trees and playground equipment called John Jay Park. If Porfirio and his buddies started their search near the Whittiers' apartment, they'd be hunting a long time before they got to that neighborhood. "Do we have a key?"

"We don't need one," she said. "Remember? They've got electronic locks on their building and apartment now."

"Oh, right," he said, remembering the conversation they'd had about the co-op's latest innovation the last time he and Caroline had been over there for an evening of pinochle. "I don't suppose you happen to remember the combinations."

"Of course," she said. "Got a pen and paper?"

"Hang on." The pen was easy, clipped as always inside his shirt pocket. The paper turned out to be easy, too: the program from Wednesday night's play was still folded lengthwise in his coat pocket. "Shoot."

"Four-oh-five-one is the outside door," she said. "Their apartment is six-one-five-nine-three."

He shook his head in quiet amazement as he wrote down the numbers. How *did* she retain stuff like that, anyway? "Got it," he said as he stuffed the program back into his pocket. "Pack up whatever you need for a few days and get over there."

"Should I take the car?"

Roger thought about it a second. Their old Buick Century had been a gift from Caroline's grandmother, and they seldom used it except for occasional weekend trips and their twice-yearly visits to Caroline's family in Vermont. But getting over to the parking garage and pulling it out would take time, and his skin was starting to feel tingly again. "No, just go," he told her. "And take a cab—it'll be more private than the subway."

"Shall I pack for you, too?"

"Yeah, you'd better," he said. "It would be kind of counterproductive to shake off their tail and then just let them pick me up again at home."

He heard Caroline's sharp intake of breath. "They're *following* you?"

"I don't know," he said. "But *I* would if *I* wanted Melantha this badly."

"We'll be out of here as soon as we can," Caroline said, her voice shaking a little.

"Good," Roger said. "But don't worry too much. Whoever these people are, they seem to prefer playing their games at night or behind closed doors. You should be okay in daylight in a crowded city."

Caroline gave a forced laugh. "You make it sound like we're dealing with vampires."

"Don't laugh," Roger warned. "At this point I'm not ready to toss out *any* possibilities. You just get the two of you out of there."

"I will," she said. "Be careful."

"Sure," he promised. "You too."

• •

The Columbus Circle subway platform was bustling with midday traffic as Roger ran his Metrocard through the reader, passed through the turnstile, and headed down. The train, when it finally came, was just as crowded. Roger managed to find a couple of square feet of standing room at one end and settled in for the trip.

And as he held onto the overhead bar and rode the bumps and sways, he found himself studying the rest of his fellow passengers.

So far all the Greens he'd met had had Melantha's same black hair and olive skin. But it would be silly to think they wouldn't have more variation than that, even among the immediate family. It would be even sillier to assume they didn't have any friends they could press into service.

Which meant the tail could be pretty much anyone. That

squat man over in the corner, say, the one pressing the ear-
bud of his CD player firmly into his ear with his middle finger, his head nodding gently to the beat as his lips moved
along with whatever song he was listening to. He was about
the same build as the man who'd accosted them in the alley
two nights ago. For that matter, there were also resem-
blances between him and the figure who'd been wandering
around their balcony last night.

Were they all working with Sylvia? Or could the alley
guy have been working against her while the human fly was
working for her?

Or it could be the black girl about Melantha's age seated
midway down the car with her nose buried in an algebra
textbook. There was a recent-immigrant look about her
clothing, and Melantha's accent wasn't anything European
that Roger was familiar with. Could it be Caribbean or
North African? Melantha would probably fit either ethnic
group.

Or it could even be that German-looking couple poring
over a subway map. Offhand, he couldn't come up with
even a tenuous connection between them and Melantha,
which might make them exactly the kind of spies Sylvia
would go for.

Unless, of course, they all wore that same style of brooch
as Sylvia and Cassia. In that case, picking out the tail would
be a piece of cake.

The brooch . . .

Shifting his grip on the bar, he dug into his pocket for the
one Caroline had found in the junk drawer. It seemed overly
heavy for a piece of jewelry, just as the gun had seemed
overly light for a firearm. But whether the weights corre-
sponded he couldn't tell. And in the artificial lighting of the
subway car, he wouldn't trust his eyes with *any* color, let
alone one as odd as this one.

He dropped it back into his pocket. Once he was out in
the sunlight again he'd give it another look.

The subway bounced its way south, discharging passengers and picking up new ones at each stop. Roger stayed in his corner, even when an occasional seat opened up which he could have taken. He was more interested in watching his fellow passengers than he was in comfort, and he could see the whole car better standing up. For awhile he tried to keep track of which people got on or off at which stop, but after awhile he gave up the effort as pointless.

Still, with a little luck, maybe he could throw Sylvia's tail a surprise.

He got off at Sheridan Square, on the western edge of Greenwich Village, and climbed back to street level. A few blocks' walk southeast would take him to the West 4th Street station, where several different lines intersected. That meant several possible trains, with lots of people taking each of them. If he could get just a little bit ahead of the tail, he stood a good chance of losing him completely.

He was striding briskly down the sidewalk, working out his plans, when a hand closed on his left upper arm.

"Hey!" he snapped, twitching instinctively against the grip as he turned his head to look.

But it wasn't a dark Mediterranean face that he found himself gazing into, the sort of face he'd expected to see. This one was wide and craggy, edged with a sparse framing of brown hair, and sat on shoulders a good two inches lower than Roger's own. The body the face was attached to was equally wide. From the casual strength of the grip around his arm, Roger guessed that most of the bulk was muscle.

"Relax," the man said, smiling encouragingly as he gazed up at Roger with bright blue eyes. "All we want to do is talk."

"Talk?" Roger asked cautiously, trying again to pull away. But the grip wasn't going anywhere, and neither was his arm. "About what?"

"Not *what*," the man corrected. "*Who*. Your young friend, of course."

"What young friend?"

"Who do you think?" the man said. "Melantha Green."

8

Roger had been heading southeast toward the West 4ᵗʰ Street station near Washington Square. Now, with his new friend in charge, they angled off in a more easterly direction. "Where are we going?" Roger asked.

"MacDougal Alley," the squat man said, guiding him around a knot of chattering schoolkids. "And we really *do* just want to talk."

"Yeah," Roger muttered. "Do I get to know who 'we' is?"

"Who 'we' *are*," the man corrected. "For starters, I'm Wolfe."

"Nice to meet you," Roger said. "I'm Roger."

They continued on in silence to Sixth Avenue. A block to the south was the subway station Roger had been making for, and for a brief moment he considered trying to make a break for it. With his longer legs, he ought to be able to outrun Wolfe in a flat-out sprint.

But Wolfe was apparently thinking along the same lines. Even as they stepped to the curb his grip tightened on Roger's arm, not enough to hurt but more than enough to make his point.

MacDougal Alley was a half block of two- to four-story walk-ups, with an iron gate at one end and a cul-de-sac at the other. Another of the squat men was loitering by the gate, fiddling restlessly with a small pocketknife. He opened the gate as they approached, falling in behind them as they passed through. Wolfe took them to a building midway down the short block and led the way up the stairs to a door on the top floor. He knocked, and a moment later the door was opened by a middle-aged woman built along the same lines as his escorts, though not nearly as wide. "This is him?" she asked, looking Roger up and down.

"This is him," Wolfe confirmed. "His name's Roger."

"Hello, Roger," the woman said. "I'm Kirsten. Please come in."

They filed inside. To Roger's mild surprise, the place wasn't a standard apartment, but rather a single large room laid out as an artist's studio. A few paintings, framed and unframed, rested at various places against the walls, with an easel holding a work in progress. Across by one of the windows, two children sat at a long table working with various colors of modeling clay. An old man wearing a stained smock leaned over them, watching their progress and occasionally making a comment in a low voice.

"Father?" Kirsten called. "Wolfe and Roger are here."

The older man straightened up. He was, to Roger's complete lack of surprise, short and rather wide. "You're sure it's him?" he called back.

"Very sure," Wolfe said. "Derek saw him leave Aleksander's place. *And,*" he added, his voice deepening significantly, "he has Melantha's *trassk* with him."

"Has he, now," the old man said. Patting one of the children on the shoulder, he started across the room, limping noticeably as he walked. "Roger, was it?" he asked, stopping a couple of paces in front of him.

"Yes," Roger confirmed.

"My name's Torvald." He held out his hand. "May I see the *trassk*?"

"I'm sorry," Roger said, frowning as he looked down at the broad palm lifted toward him. The loose sleeve of the smock had fallen away with the movement, and he could see that Torvald was wearing a wide bracelet around his right wrist, snug-fitting and made of tooled metal. Some sort of artsy watchband, perhaps? "But I really don't know what you're talking about."

"You want me to search him?" the man with the pocketknife asked darkly.

"Patience, Garth," Torvald said, his blue eyes steady on

Roger. "I'm sure Roger isn't being difficult on purpose." His eyebrows lifted. "Are you?"

"Not at all," Roger assured him, trying to keep his voice from trembling. Torvald didn't have Sylvia's grace or half-buried beauty, but in his own massive way he was just as intimidating. "I don't know anything about a—what did you call it?"

"A *trassk*," Torvald repeated, frowning slightly. "Did Derek see it up close, Wolfe?"

"No, from across the subway car," Wolfe said. "But it was definitely silver with a purple stone, just like the one—"

"Wait a second," Roger interrupted. *Silver with a purple stone* . . . "Are you talking about *this*?" Digging into his pocket, he pulled out the brooch Caroline had found in the junk drawer.

"There," Wolfe said, jabbing a finger at it. The motion pulled the sleeve away from his wrist, and Roger saw that he, too, was wearing a metal wristband like Torvald's.

"That's the one," Garth seconded. Shifting his pocketknife to his other hand, he plucked the brooch out of Roger's hand and held it out to Torvald.

"Yes, I see," Torvald said. He made no move to take it, but merely gazed thoughtfully at it. "What exactly is your role in this, Roger?"

Roger shook his head. "I'm just an innocent bystander."

"Yet you carry Melantha's *trassk*," Torvald pointed out. "That implies a rather closer relationship."

"Only peripherally," Roger said. "I'm just trying to look out for Melantha's interests."

"Melantha has no interests anymore," Wolfe insisted. "The bargain's been made."

"Of course, not everyone agreed with it," Garth said, fingering the brooch restlessly. "And he *did* come out of Aleksander's just now."

"It wasn't Aleksander," Torvald told him. "I was specifically watching him, and he was still there after all the commotion settled down."

"But he could have gotten her out of the circle and passed

her to someone who'd been primed for the occasion," Garth argued. He gestured at Roger. "Someone like him, maybe."

"Pretty risky," Wolfe said doubtfully. "Especially with Cyril standing right there."

"Unless Cyril was cooperating with him," Kirsten offered. "Maybe he had second thoughts about the agreement."

"Or never intended to go through with it in the first place," Torvald said, studying Roger's face. "How about it, Roger?"

Roger shook his head. "I'm just trying to help Melantha," he said, fighting to keep his voice steady. "I don't know anything about the rest of it."

"Maybe we need to ask him a little harder," Wolfe suggested ominously, his eyes steady on Roger.

"Don't be crude," Torvald admonished him. "Roger is our guest."

"Or he's a Green agent," Wolfe countered. "What do we do with him?"

Torvald pursed his lips. Roger held his breath. . . . "We let him go," the old man said.

"You sure that's wise?" Wolfe asked.

Torvald didn't say anything, but merely lifted his eyebrows. "Fine," Wolfe said with a sigh. "What about the *trassk*?"

Torvald looked at Garth and inclined his head toward Roger. "Give it back to him."

Wordlessly, Garth stepped back to Roger and dropped the brooch into his hand. "But tell this to your Green friends," Torvald continued, his voice suddenly ominous. "Matters cannot and will not remain as they are. They have five days, until Wednesday night, to decide what they're going to do. After that . . . well, there will be consequences."

The room suddenly felt very cold. "I'll tell them," Roger promised. "Assuming I ever see any of them again."

"I'm sure you will," Torvald said, digging into a pocket of his smock and pulling out a business card. "If you should want to discuss this further, give me a call," he added, sliding the card into Roger's breast pocket. "Or feel free to drop by any time."

"Thank you," Roger managed.

Torvald nodded gravely. "Good-bye, Roger."

● ●

Two minutes later, Roger found himself back on the street, walking again amid the sunshine and the determinedly oblivious New York pedestrians.

His whole body shaking like a leaf.

It was ridiculous, he told himself over and over as he retraced his steps back toward the West 4th Street subway station. They hadn't pulled a gun on him, the way Porfirio had at the Greens' building. They hadn't twisted his arm, or threatened him, or even talked especially roughly to him.

And yet, even more than when he'd left the Central Park West building, entering the sunlight here felt like escaping from something dark and oppressive.

But why? Torvald's loft had been well lit, soaked in the same sunshine pouring down on him right now. And there certainly hadn't been anything mysterious or eerie about the furnishings or décor. The matching jewelry? Hardly. In an island as steeped in artsy ethnic stuff as Manhattan, Torvald's wristband wouldn't even rate a raised eyebrow.

No, it had to be the people themselves. But what? Their common physique, the fact that all of them seemed built like wrestlers? Unlikely.

So it wasn't the place, the conversation, or the people. Which meant there was no logical reason for Roger to feel the way he did.

But the feeling remained.

He'd made it a block from Torvald's loft when his phone rang. He jumped at the sound, dropping Melantha's brooch into his coat pocket as he pulled out the phone and punched the button. "Hello?"

"Roger?" Caroline's voice came tentatively.

He felt his muscles relax a bit. "Yeah, it's me. Why, didn't I sound like me?"

"No, you didn't," she said, her own voice a little odd. "Are you all right?"

"Oh, I'm fine," he growled. "I just got strong-armed into a guided tour of another of New York's finest mystery houses, that's all."

"You *what?*"

Roger shook his head irritably at himself. There was no reason to dump his frustrations on Caroline. "Sorry," he apologized. "Let's just say I was encouraged to meet another player in this crazy game we seem to have gotten ourselves into." He dug the card out of his pocket. "A gentleman named Torvald Gray. You settled in yet?"

"Actually, we're at Lee's," she said, naming the little market on 96th Street kitty-corner from their apartment building. "Don't worry, no one can hear us—I'm using the phone in the back room. Melantha's lost something, apparently at the apartment, and won't leave without it. We compromised by coming here until we could talk to you."

"Whatever it is, you're not going back for it," Roger insisted. "The whole idea of this exercise was to get out before anyone came looking for you."

"I understand that," Caroline said, a little shortly. "But she's very upset, and I promised her we'd try to work something out."

Roger glowered at the skyline. Terrific. "What exactly is she missing?"

"I'm not really sure," Caroline said. "She called it a *task,* or something like that."

"Not *task; trassk,*" Roger corrected, feeling his lip twist. "Tell her to relax—I've got it."

"You do? What is it?"

"It's that brooch you found in the junk drawer," Roger said. "Torvald and his friends were kind enough to tell me its name."

There was a moment of silence from the other end. "You're talking about the brooch that might have once been a gun, right?" Caroline asked. "And this Torvald knows about it?"

"He knows more than we do," Roger said. "But never mind that now. Get going, okay? And call me right away if there are any more problems."

"I'll try," Caroline said. "Good-b—"

"Wait a second," Roger cut her off. "What do you mean, you'll *try*? You *call,* period."

"I can only call if you've got the phone on," Caroline said patiently.

"It *is* on," Roger said, pulling the phone from his ear for a quick check of the battery indicator. "Has been, ever since I left the office this morning."

"Then you must have been under a pile of metal," Caroline said. "I tried calling you fifteen minutes ago and got the 'out of range' message each time."

"That's crazy," Roger protested. "Fifteen minutes ago I was—"

He broke off. "I was in Torvald's," he went on slowly. "A small, old building without any metal structure to it. No reason a cell shouldn't have worked perfectly."

"Like there was no reason for a group of streetlights to go dim the way they did two nights ago?" Caroline asked quietly.

Roger winced. "Yeah," he agreed. "You be careful, okay? No telling how many other players there are in this game."

"I'll bet Melantha knows," Caroline said. "Maybe I can get her to talk."

"*After* you get to Paul and Janet's," Roger warned.

"Yes, of course," Caroline said with a half-audible sigh. "We'll see you later."

Roger clicked off the phone, glancing around as he put it away. Sylvia probably still had someone following him, hoping he would lead them to Melantha. Now, more than likely, Torvald had added a tail of his own. Two very different groups of people, both of them desperate to get hold of Melantha.

And he still didn't have the faintest idea why.

But Caroline was right: Melantha knew. He could see it in her eyes, in her evasiveness, in her fear. She knew.

And tonight, one way or another, he was going to get some answers out of her.

9

With a frustrated grunt, Caroline dropped the phone back onto its hook. *After you get to Paul and Janet's.* Right—like she was going to stand here in front of all New York and get into some long involved conversation with Melantha. Didn't he think she could figure that out for herself?

Didn't he think she could *think* for herself?

"What did he say?"

Caroline turned to the anxious face looking at her from just inside the office door. "It's all right," she assured the girl, carefully filtering the annoyance out of her voice. There was no point in dumping any of this on Melantha, after all. "Roger's got your *trassk.* He'll bring it to the new place with him."

"Oh," Melantha said, sounding a little uncertain. "He'll be careful with it, won't he?"

"I'm sure he will," Caroline said, studying her face. Some of the tension had eased at the news that her brooch was safe. But only some of it. "So off we go," she continued, trying to force some cheerfulness into her voice. "As long as we're here anyway, is there anything you need? A snack, maybe, to keep you going until we can get a real meal?"

Slowly, Melantha turned around to peer into the main part of the store, that same uncertain look still on her face. "Yes," she murmured. Turning her head to the side, she started slowly toward the front.

Caroline watched her go, frowning. For the past fifteen minutes all the girl had been able to think or talk about had been her *trassk*. Now, like a light switch flicking on in her brain, her top priority had apparently shifted to checking out the snack section.

"You get through?"

She turned as the store manager eased past her from the storeroom, three boxes of cigarettes balanced across his forearms. "Yes, Lee, thanks," she said. "And thanks for letting me use your phone."

"No problem," he said. "First rule of business is to treat your customers right."

"I appreciate it," Caroline said. "One of these days we really need to get a second cell phone."

"Yeah, but then you start depending on the things," Lee warned. "Then the cells get overloaded, or the system crashes, and then where are you? Give me good solid wires any day."

"You may be right," Caroline said diplomatically.

"So who's the young lady?" Lee asked, nodding toward the front of the store. "Relative?"

"No, just a friend," Caroline said, turning her head to follow his gaze. "She's been visiting for awhile and—"

The rest of the carefully prepared story caught abruptly in her throat. Melantha had not, as she'd expected, stopped by the snack food display. She was still walking in that same slow, deliberate pace.

Heading straight for the door.

"Excuse me," Caroline said, dropping her suitcase inside the office and hurrying after her. No mistake; the girl was heading outside. For a second Caroline considered calling to her, realized in time that shouting the name *Melantha* might attract the wrong kind of attention. Picking up her pace, she concentrated instead on getting to the door first.

Strangely enough, even with Melantha's head start it didn't look like it would be much of a contest. Even as Caroline dodged around and past the other browsing customers, leaving consternation and the occasional New York expletive in her wake, the girl continued on in that same measured pace. It was almost as if she didn't really want to get away at all, Caroline thought, but was simply going through the motions.

She caught up with the girl a few steps short of the door. "Hey, there," she said, taking hold of her wrist. "Where do you think you're going?"

Melantha looked up at her . . . and Caroline caught her breath. The girl's face was blank, her eyelids drooping as if she was half asleep. Behind the eyelids the pupils were so dilated that the black nearly filled the irises. "I have to go back," she said, her voice low and husky. "It has to be done. I have to go back."

She started to pull away. "Oh, no you don't," Caroline insisted, tightening her grip. "You're not going anywhere without—"

Bring her to me.

Caroline jerked. The voice that had spoken had been like nothing she'd ever heard before. It had felt distant, yet at the same time strangely close, a voice that was completely unfamiliar yet carried the sense that she'd known the speaker all her life.

And it hadn't spoken in her ears, but in her mind.

Bring her to me, the voice continued. *Open the door and bring the Peace Child to me.*

Caroline frowned. Open the door? But the shop's door was already open. "Who are you?" she whispered. *"Where are you?"*

You must understand that what I do, I do for the best, the voice said. *Unlock the door and bring her to me.*

The store seemed to waver in front of Caroline's eyes, like pavement on a hot July day. The voice was so persuasive, so insistent, so confident. How could she not obey it? How could she not take Melantha to him?

Melantha. The girl who'd looked up at her with hopeless eyes as she huddled in the cold of a darkened alley. The girl who'd found enough comfort and safety in their living room that for awhile she'd seemed like a normal child before the weight of the world had settled on her shoulders again.

The girl with bruises on her throat where someone had tried to murder her.

"No," she muttered aloud to the voice. "Go away and leave us alone." She shook her head hard; and like a camera coming back into focus, her vision suddenly cleared and everything seemed to snap back into place.

And then, from somewhere nearby came the soft chime of a doorway electric eye, and she realized that Melantha's arm had somehow escaped from her grip. Spinning around, she saw that the girl had made it two steps outside the store. "Come back here," she snapped, taking a pair of quick steps and grabbing the girl's arm again. "You're not going anywhere."

Bring her to me. The voice was still there, still as insistent as before. But there was no power in it anymore.

At least, not for Caroline. But apparently Melantha wasn't as free from its influence. She was straining at Caroline's grip like a dog on a leash, trying to pull them both back toward the corner. "Come on, Melantha," Caroline said soothingly, digging her feet into the pavement as best she could, trying not to make a scene of this. The last thing she needed was for someone to call the cops with a child-abuse complaint. She sent a quick glance around the sidewalk, but no one seemed particularly interested in the two of them.

And then, for no particular reason, she lifted her eyes to their building half a block away.

Someone was on their balcony. Two men, standing beside her orange trees.

Caroline felt her arms starting to tremble. "Come on," she told Melantha, trying to pull the girl back out of sight. It was like tugging on a bag of cement. "We have to get out of here."

"No," Melantha said, her voice as blank as her face. "I have to go back."

"Melantha, snap out of it," Caroline ordered, managing to pull her at least into the partial protection of the store's

small awning. Swiveling her around, she got a grip on both
of the girl's upper arms. "You hear me? You don't have to
go back. *Look* at me, Melantha."

Melantha blinked . . . and then, slowly, her face seemed
to sag. "Caroline?" she whispered.

"Yes," Caroline said firmly. "You don't have to listen to
him, Melantha."

"But they'll all die if I don't go back," Melantha said, her
voice pleading. Her eyelids were still half-closed, but at
least the pupils were back to normal again. "They'll *die*."

"Who will die?" Caroline asked, an eerie feeling seeping
through her.

"He said I shouldn't have run away," Melantha said. "But
I didn't. Not really."

"I know that, sweetheart," Caroline assured her. "Who's
going to die if you don't go back?"

"The Greens," Melantha said, tears welling up in her
eyes. "The Grays." She squeezed her eyes shut, sending the
tears trickling out onto her cheeks. "Everyone."

Caroline felt a shiver run up her back. *Gray.* Wasn't that
the name Roger had mentioned? "You mean Torvald and his
family?" she asked.

"All of them," Melantha repeated. "And it'll be my fault."

Caroline took a deep breath. "No, it won't," she said as
firmly as she could. "Because Roger and I won't let it happen."

"But—"

"No buts," Caroline cut off her protest, trying to ignore
the voice still prodding at the edge of her mind. "It won't
happen. Understand?"

Melantha swallowed hard. "But if it's the only way?"

"We'll find another way," Caroline promised, squeezing
her arms reassuringly. "But right now, we have to get out of
here."

"Mrs. Whittier?"

She turned around, tensing. But it was only Lee, holding
her suitcase. "Here, you forgot this," he said.

"Thank you," Caroline said, not sure she dared let Melantha out of her two-handed grip yet. "Just set it down, would you?"

Lee's forehead wrinkled. "You okay?" he asked, setting the suitcase beside the door.

Caroline hesitated. What could she say? "We're just having a little discussion," she said.

"Oh?" Lee peered at Melantha. "You okay, miss? You don't look so good."

Melantha looked questioningly at Caroline, then back at Lee. "I'm all right," she said, her voice quavering only a little.

"You sure?" he asked, clearly not convinced. "Anything I can do?"

"Actually, yes, there is," Caroline said suddenly. "You could call 911 and tell them someone's burgling our apartment."

Lee's eyes widened. "How do you know?"

"They're on our balcony," Caroline said. Carefully, she eased her head out from under the awning to look.

The balcony was empty. "Well, they *were*," she amended, moving back under cover again. "They must have gone inside. Please?"

Lee pursed his lips, but nodded. "Okay. What's the address?" She gave it to him, and he nodded again. "Okay. Wait here." Turning, he hurried back into the store.

Caroline sneaked another peek out from under the awning. The balcony was still clear; but if the men up there had seen her, they would already be on their way down. "We've got to go, Melantha," she murmured to the girl, letting go with one hand and snagging the suitcase.

"No, wait," Melantha said suddenly, grabbing at her arm. "They're still there."

Caroline frowned up at the empty balcony. "Where?"

"On the wall to the left of the balcony," Melantha said, pointing. "Two Grays."

Caroline frowned a little harder. *On the wall to the left . . . ?*

Abruptly, she caught her breath. On the side of their building, right where Melantha had said, she saw something. Not people, but a pair of what looked like ripples or perhaps giant drops of water.

Only they were moving *up* the side of the building, not down. "What *is* that?" she breathed.

"They're Grays," Melantha hissed. "They're coming for me."

"Grays?" Caroline echoed, Roger's nighttime story racing through her mind.

But his human fly had been just that: human. This was something else entirely. "Are they wearing camouflage?" she asked, knowing full well that couldn't possibly be it.

"They're masked," Melantha said, her breath starting to come in ragged gasps. "We have to get out of here." The ripples stopped moving, and even knowing where to look Caroline couldn't see anything.

And then something caught her eye, and she felt her throat tighten. There was indeed nothing to be seen of the two figures themselves . . . but just beneath where the two ripples had stopped moving she could see small dark crescents against the lighter color of the wall.

The two men had vanished. But their shadows were still there.

"We have to *go*," Melantha said again.

"I know, honey," Caroline said, looking back into the store. Invisible men climbing walls, someone calling into her mind . . .

Her eye caught a small rack of scarves beside the checkout counter. "Here," she said, pulling Melantha back into the store. "Tuck your hair into the back of your collar," she ordered, pulling the most conservatively patterned scarf free and digging into her purse. She found a ten-dollar bill and dropped it onto the counter, then turned back to Melantha and flipped the scarf over her head, tying it under her chin the way she'd seen elderly women wearing them. "How does that feel?"

"Like I'm an old woman," Melantha said distastefully, her fear receding momentarily into the background as preteen fashion dignity asserted itself.

"Let's hope everyone else sees you that way, too," Caroline said. "Walk a little stooped over, and we'll pretend I'm taking my mother for a walk."

Melantha's face screwed up, but she nodded. "I'll try."

"Okay." Putting the girl's hand on her crooked elbow the way she'd seen other women walking, Caroline reached down and picked up the suitcase. "Let's go."

They left the store and headed east, away from the apartment. Caroline could feel Melantha's hand trembling, and found herself fighting against the impulse to abandon their mother-daughter act and take off running. Setting her teeth, she split her attention between walking slowly and keeping an eye over her shoulder for an available cab.

They were halfway down the block before Melantha spoke again. "Are we still going to your friends' apartment?" she asked.

"Of course," Caroline said. "Why? Do you want to go somewhere else?"

"No," Melantha murmured, reaching up to push a lock of hair back up behind the scarf.

It wasn't until they had found a cab and were heading south that Caroline understood what the girl had been really asking.

Heading east on 96th, the direction they'd taken from the store, would ultimately have taken them to Central Park, and the apartment Roger had visited that morning.

The place where all the Greens lived.

10

It had been a long day, the paperwork at the 24th Precinct had been worse than usual, and the last thing Detective Sergeant Tom Fierenzo wanted to do was look at yet another crime scene.

"I hope this isn't going to take very long," his partner, Detective Jon Powell, commented as they showed their badges to the doorman and crossed to the elevator. "Sandy was hoping we could have the whole weekend to ourselves for a change."

"We'll be out in an hour, tops," Fierenzo promised, hoping it was true. Powell, fourteen years his junior, was still able to actually relax on his days off, and he'd been looking forward to the weekend since Wednesday morning. More to the point, so had his wife, and Fierenzo didn't particularly want to disappoint either of them with last-minute paperwork. "Nice simple robbery," he reminded the other as he punched for the sixth floor. "No homicide, no hostage situation. Easy as pie."

"Maybe," Powell grunted. "But you know Smith. If there are any complications, he'll find them."

"Point," Fierenzo conceded. Officer Jeff Smith had the detective bug as badly as Fierenzo had ever seen, and everyone from Lieutenant Cerreta on down knew it. Even routine crime scenes got the full treatment when Smith and Hill were the cops of record. "On the other hand, maybe he's got a big weekend coming up, too."

Powell snorted. "Right. Rereading the NYPD Detectives' Manual."

Fierenzo shrugged. "*Somebody* has to know what's in it."

Smith was standing by an open door halfway down the hall when they arrived, talking with a middle-aged man wearing a khaki shirt and slacks. The older man seemed to have come down with a case of the nervous twitches, not an uncommon occurrence under circumstances like these.

What *was* uncommon was that Smith wasn't wearing his calm, the-policeman-is-your-friend expression. In fact, behind a rather stiff guardian-of-the-people face, he had the look of a cat with a cornered lizard in his sights.

He looked up as Fierenzo and Powell joined them, and something in his stance clued Fierenzo to play this one formally. "Officer Smith," he greeted the other. "What've we got?"

"This is Mr. Umberto," Smith said, his voice equally formal. "He's the building super."

"Mr. Umberto," Fierenzo said, nodding.

"And this is the scene of the crime," Smith continued. "The apartment of a Roger and Caroline Whittier."

"Doesn't look like forced entry," Powell commented, peering at the door.

"It wasn't," Smith confirmed. "Perps were three males, Caucasian but dark in a Mediterranean sort of way, all of medium height and slender build. One was sixty to seventy years old; the other two in their mid-twenties."

"And how exactly do we know this?" Fierenzo asked.

Smith looked sideways at Umberto. "Because Mr. Umberto is the one who let them in."

"Really," Fierenzo said. That explained the severity of the man's twitches, anyway. It was an all-too-familiar story: some smooth-talking con man would show up, spin an impressive wall mural of smoke and mirrors, and get someone to let him past a set of deadbolts. "May I ask why, Mr. Umberto?"

Umberto winced. "I guess . . . because he told me to."

Fierenzo frowned. This was usually where the defensiveness and excuses started. "What do you mean? What exactly did he say?"

The hapless super winced again. "He just . . . said to open the door. And I . . . did."

"Did he have a work order?" Fierenzo asked, moved by a desire to give the man every benefit of the doubt. "A weapon? Did he threaten you?"

"No," Umberto said, sounding more puzzled than embarrassed, as if even he wasn't sure what exactly had happened. "He just said to open the door. And I did."

"How did they get in far enough to find you?" Powell put in. "Isn't the doorman supposed to screen out people like that?"

Umberto shrugged helplessly. "He must have just let them in, too."

"What a pleasantly accommodating staff," Fierenzo said, turning to Smith. "Have the tenants been notified?"

"We tried their offices," Smith said. "Mr. Whittier, a paralegal, clocked out about ten-thirty this morning and didn't come back. Mrs. Whittier, real estate agent, never made it to work at all."

"Cell phones?"

"One," Smith said, holding out his notebook. "Mr. Umberto just gave me the number. I thought you might want to make the call yourself."

"Thanks," Fierenzo said, copying the number into his own notebook. "Let's look at the apartment first."

"Good idea," Smith said. "That part's a little strange, too."

"Oh?" Fierenzo lifted his eyebrows. "Show us. Mr. Umberto, please wait here."

Hill was waiting for them in the middle of the living room, her hands on her hips. "Detectives," she greeted them. "Interesting robbery scene, wouldn't you say?"

"Very nontraditional," Fierenzo agreed as he looked around. Not a single lamp, picture, or throw pillow seemed to be out of place. If the room had been tossed, they were talking some obsessively neat tossers. "Bedroom?"

"Same as here," Hill said. "There's a jewelry case on the dresser; doesn't look touched."

"Who called it in?" Powell asked.

"Manager of a convenience store on 96th," Smith said. "He said Mrs. Whittier told him she could see people on her balcony and to call 911. She took off right after that."

"Right after an altercation she had with her young friend," Hill added. "A young girl, ten to twelve years old."

"What kind of altercation?" Fierenzo asked, stepping over to the sliding glass door and giving the balcony a quick look. Nothing out there but a pair of potted trees.

"He was too far away to hear what they were saying," Smith said. "He did see Mrs. Whittier grab the girl by the arms, though. *And* after she told him to call 911 she grabbed a scarf off a rack and the two of them hit the sidewalk with it tied babushka-style around the girl's head."

"Interesting," Powell said thoughtfully. "Who wears scarves that way these days?"

"Women over eighty, and people trying to disguise themselves," Fierenzo said, slipping on a pair of latex gloves and crouching down beside the sliding door. There was an odd circular area of hairline cracks in the glass just beside the lock.

"Creditors, you think?" Powell asked. "Or stalkers?"

"Or are we talking about a kidnapping?" Smith added darkly.

"Women usually snatch babies, not ten-year-olds," Fierenzo said, running a fingertip across the crack pattern. The glass on this side was smooth. "Jon, take a look."

He moved out of the way as Powell came over and crouched down. "Looks like it was hit with a hammer or something," the younger detective suggested.

"Only the pattern doesn't seem concentrated enough to be a hammer," Fierenzo pointed out. "Not enough of a central bashed section."

"You're right," Powell agreed. "So it was hit with something softer than your basic ball-peen."

"*And* it was hit from the outside," Fierenzo said. Carefully, trying not to smudge any prints that might be there, he rolled the broomstick out of the track and snapped open the lock. "Hill, go back to the door and make sure Umberto stays put."

The other three stepped out onto the balcony. "I wonder what someone might want out here," Powell commented, looking around. "Besides a nice tan in the summer."

"There's another door," Smith said, nodding toward the far end of the balcony. "Someone trying to eavesdrop on the bedroom?"

"Be a good trick to hear anything over the traffic," Powell grunted, stepping around the trees and crossing to the other door.

Fierenzo crouched down for a closer look at the living room door. "This is definitely the side that got the hammer treatment," he said, running his gloved finger over the cracked glass by the lock.

"Hold everything," Powell said suddenly, dropping onto one knee beside one of the potted trees. "Did you say a *hammer*? Or an *axe*?"

"What?" Fierenzo asked, frowning.

Powell gestured at the base of the tree. "Take a look."

Fierenzo stepped to his side. There was a shallow gash about an inch long just above where the tree trunk disappeared into the pot. "Well, now, that *is* interesting," he said, crouching down for a closer look. The gash had barely broken the bark and, like the crack pattern on the door, seemed oddly soft-edged. "Looks like they were using a pretty dull axe."

"There's one over there, too," Powell said, pointing to the other tree.

"I see it," Fierenzo said, nodding. "Smith, go ask Umberto if his visitors had any tools."

"Right." Smith disappeared through the door into the apartment.

"You ask me, this sounds like some kind of strange joke," Powell commented.

"On who?" Fierenzo asked. "The Whittiers?"

"Or us," Powell said sourly. "There are plenty of nuts out there who love attention. Especially police attention."

"Strange, but true," Fierenzo agreed. "Have Hill call in and see if Umberto has a record."

"Done and done." Standing up and brushing off his knees, Powell went back inside.

Fierenzo eyed the gash in the tree another moment, then heaved himself to his feet and looked down at the street below. Just past the corner he could see the convenience store where the 911 call had allegedly come from.

So it *was* possible to see the balcony from there. For whatever that was worth.

He went inside, sliding the door shut behind him. Smith and Powell were talking together in low tones at the far side of the living room, while Hill stood off to the side, talking quietly into her radio. "Umberto says no axes or hammers," Smith reported as Fierenzo crossed the room and joined them. "Also no bags or backpacks."

"Though Umberto himself probably has a well-equipped workshop," Powell pointed out.

"Did you want to call the Whittiers' cell phone yet?" Smith asked.

Fierenzo hesitated. Unfortunately, intriguing aspects notwithstanding, a simple home invasion wasn't the sort of thing a detective team should be spending their limited time on. "No, you two might as well run with it," he told Smith. "I'd be interested in seeing your final report, though."

Hill popped her mike back onto its shoulder patch. "Preliminary search shows nothing on Mr. Umberto," she reported.

"Fine," Fierenzo said. "Then I guess we'll leave this in your capable—"

He broke off. Across the apartment, from the direction of the kitchen, came the familiar trilling of a phone.

"Should we get that?" Powell murmured.

"No," Fierenzo said, heading toward the sound. "Anybody notice if they had an answering machine?"

"Yes, built into the phone," Smith said.

"Probably the dry cleaner telling them their sweaters are ready," Powell muttered as they all trooped into the kitchen.

The machine picked up with a click and they listened in silence as a man's voice ran through a quick and perfunctory response: Hi, Roger and Caroline, not available, leave message. A stereotypical Manhattan couple, Fierenzo tentatively tagged them: solid and hard-working, but not overly endowed with either imagination or humor. The message ended, there was the usual beep, and he made a last-minute private bet with himself that the caller would turn out to be a telemarketer.

"Hello, Roger, my name is Cyril," a smooth voice said, with a hint of an accent Fierenzo couldn't place. "I understand you spoke to Sylvia at Aleksander's this morning. I also understand you know where Melantha is."

Fierenzo frowned. Melantha. The girl who'd been seen with Mrs. Whittier?

"I imagine Sylvia tried to persuade you to bring her there," the voice went on. "But I warn you, that would be a terrible mistake. Taking her to anyone but me will spill the blood of thousands of New Yorkers squarely onto your hands."

Fierenzo's chest tightened. *The blood of thousands of New Yorkers?*

"And as Sylvia may have mentioned, time is short," the voice said. "You have just five days to bring the girl to us at Riverside Park before chaos descends upon the city. We'll do whatever you want, pay whatever you ask, in order to get her back. I hope you'll do the right thing, and that we'll see you and Melantha here soon."

There was another click, and the phone disconnected.

Fierenzo looked over at Powell. "If this is a joke," he said, "it's just gone way over the line."

"Okay, I'm lost," Powell admitted, his forehead wrinkled. "Did we just jump from a home invasion to a kidnapping to a terrorist threat?"

"We went from something to something," Fierenzo agreed. "I'm just not sure where exactly we ended up. Smith, go ask Umberto if he's seen the Whittiers with a ten- to twelve-year-old girl lately. Hill, find out if either of the Whittiers have a sheet."

Smith nodded and headed toward the door as Hill unhooked her radio mike. "You come with me," Fierenzo added to Powell. "I want a look at that bedroom."

They headed down the hall to the bedroom. "What exactly are we looking for?" Powell asked.

"Evidence of an extra person living here," Fierenzo said, glancing around. "Check the closet; I'm going to look in the hamper."

They worked in silence for a minute. "Nothing," Powell reported. "All the women's stuff seems to be the same size."

"Make sure there's no double-hanging," Fierenzo reminded him as he pulled a slightly wrinkled bed sheet from the hamper and laid it out on the bed.

"One outfit per hanger," Powell confirmed. "You got something?"

"A bed sheet, one," Fierenzo said, gesturing to the linens on the bed. "A pillowcase, also one. A normal change of bedding ought to yield two of each."

Powell nodded. "Someone's been sleeping on the couch."

"My thought exactly," Fierenzo agreed.

He looked over as Hill appeared at the bedroom door. "No records on either Whittier," she reported. "*But*, two nights ago, Whittier called 911 reporting that he and his wife had picked up a foundling girl in an alley off Broadway."

"Bingo," Powell said.

"Maybe not," Hill warned. "When the cops arrived, there was no girl here. The Whittiers claimed she'd gone out on the balcony and disappeared. The cops searched, found nothing, and left."

"Looks like wherever she went, she came back," Fierenzo said. "Let's see if Umberto can shed any more light on the subject."

They retraced their steps down the hallway and out the front door. "He says he's only seen the Whittiers with kids when they've got friends visiting," Smith reported. "Not even any of that in the past month."

Fierenzo nodded. "Mr. Umberto, we'll need the name and address of the doorman on duty Wednesday night about—" he lifted his eyebrows at Hill.

"The call came in at ten-forty-three," she supplied.

"From nine-thirty to eleven-thirty." Fierenzo looked back at Smith. "Then you call the guy and see what he remembers about the Whittiers that night. When they went out, when they came in, who was with them—you know the drill."

Smith nodded and turned to Umberto. Fierenzo caught Powell's eye and nodded his head to the side, and together they went back into the apartment. "Time to call the store manager?" Powell asked.

"Let's try a little cage-rattling first," Fierenzo said,

pulling out his phone and consulting his notebook. Punching in Whittier's cell number, he gestured Powell over where they could both hear.

The phone was answered on the second ring. "Hello?" a tight voice answered.

"Mr. Whittier?" Fierenzo asked.

There was a slight pause; and when the voice came back it was subtly different. "Yes?"

"This is Sergeant Thomas Fierenzo of the NYPD," Fierenzo identified himself. "We're investigating a break-in at your apartment this afternoon."

"A break-in?"

"That's right," Fierenzo said. "I thought you might be able to help us."

Another brief pause. "Yes, of course," Whittier said. "What can I do?"

"First of all, is your wife there with you?"

"No, she's—not here."

"What about your friend Melantha?"

The pause this time was noticeably longer. Fierenzo strained his ears, listening to the rumbling he could hear in the background. A subway car, he tentatively identified it. "I don't understand," Whittier said at last.

"I just want to know whether Melantha's with you or with your wife, that's all," Fierenzo said, keeping his own voice casual.

"Sorry. I don't know anyone by that name."

"I see," Fierenzo said, cocking an eyebrow at Powell. His partner nodded, a knowing look on his face. It was the correct response from an innocent man, only it was about five seconds too late. "Where exactly are you, Mr. Whittier?"

"Why?" Whittier countered, his voice suddenly suspicious.

"We'll need a statement as part of the investigation," Fierenzo said.

"Oh," Whittier said. "I . . . where do I need to go?"

"We're out of the 24th Precinct," Fierenzo said. "One-fifty-one West 100th. When can you come by?"

"I'm kind of tied up right now," Whittier said evasively. "How about tomorrow morning?"

"Tonight would be better," Fierenzo said, mentally flipping a coin and deciding not to push. He didn't want the man rabbiting before he'd even figured out what the hell was going on here. "I'll be here until nine o'clock."

"I'm sorry, but tomorrow is the soonest I can make it."

"I guess I'll see you tomorrow, then," Fierenzo said, trying to sound as if it didn't much matter to him either way. "Good-bye."

He shut off his phone. "He doesn't want to talk to us, that's for sure," Powell commented. "And he never once asked if anything had been taken."

"Because he knew they weren't after any of his worldly goods." Turning, Fierenzo gazed across the living room at the city lights twinkling beyond the balcony, an icy tightness settling into his gut. If there was one thing guaranteed to capture his full attention, it was the thought of innocent blood flowing in his streets, whether from serial killers, gang warfare, or terrorism. "Let's go talk to the store manager and find out just how much of a hurry Mrs. Whittier was in," he decided. "If someone's after the girl, she wouldn't have risked waiting for a bus or subway."

"Which means a cab," Powell said, nodding. "So we call the cab companies and see who picked up a woman and girl on that block at that time."

"Right," Fierenzo said. "We also have Smith and Hill take Umberto down to the station house and put him together with Carstairs. Maybe we can get a decent sketch of these intruders of his."

"We might also want to play the answering machine back for him," Powell suggested. "See if he recognizes Cyril's voice."

Umberto was still waiting when they returned to the hall, shifting nervously from foot to foot. "These officers are going to have you listen to an answering machine message and see if you recognize the voice," Fierenzo told him. "After that, we'd like you to go to the station with them and describe these intruders for a police artist."

The other swallowed. "Yes, sir. Anything I can do to help."

"One last question," Fierenzo said. "How long had these people been gone before Officers Smith and Hill showed up?"

Umberto frowned in concentration. "Half an hour. Maybe a little more."

"And in all that time it didn't occur to you to call the police?"

"Sure it did," Umberto said, sounding a little indignant. "After a break-in? Of course I thought of it."

"Then why didn't you?"

Umberto opened his mouth . . . closed it again. "I don't know," he said at last. "I guess because he told me not to."

Fierenzo felt his lip twist. "I see," he said. "Well, at least you had a good reason."

Jerking his head at Powell, he headed down the hall toward the elevators.

11

It had been a long time since Roger had ventured into Queens, and as he stepped off the train he remembered why that was. After the towering buildings of Manhattan, something about the borough always felt a little quaint to him.

But it was modern enough to have a compact mall within walking distance of this particular station. Tonight, that was all he cared about.

He went through the mall at a fast walk, zigzagging between stores and levels, trying to spot the tails he still suspected his new acquaintances had put on him. But he couldn't see anyone, and began to hope that his tangled journey through the New York City subway system over the past couple of hours had thrown them off the scent.

Nevertheless, he kept up his pace for another ten minutes before slipping into one of the mall's department stores. Ten minutes later, wearing a new hat and reversible jacket and trying to navigate through the blurring of a set of horn-rimmed reading glasses, he left the mall and headed back to the subway station.

His timing was perfect. Thirty seconds after he arrived, the next train to Manhattan pulled out, with him aboard.

He found a stray newspaper and spent the trip with it held in front of him, pretending to read as he peered over the top at the people moving into and out of his car. It wasn't quite as sparse a group as he had expected for a train running against the general rush-hour flow, and it finally occurred to him that on a Friday night more people than usual would be heading in to sample the city's night life.

He hunched down in his seat as the train rattled along. He was tired, he had a headache from the reading glasses, and he was growing increasingly resentful of the situation Melantha had pushed them into. The minute the girl had reappeared on their balcony, he knew, he should have grabbed her by the scruff of her neck and hauled her down to the police station. If he had, he and Caroline would be sitting comfortably in their kitchen eating dinner right now.

But of course, Caroline and her weakness for underdogs would never have let that happen. She would have insisted Melantha stay, and he wouldn't have had the backbone to stand up to her. And nothing about the situation would have changed.

He got off at Grand Central, wondering if he should take a few more trips around Manhattan. But he was too tired to bother. Besides, if they'd been able to follow him through everything else he'd done, it would probably be a waste of time. Catching a northbound train, he headed for Yorkville.

It was another chilly October evening, and again the streets were largely empty as he left his final subway station of the day and trudged the five blocks to the Youngs' apartment. There were still a few people out and about, but most of the neighborhood's residents seemed to be already home from the day's activities. He spotted a couple of shadowy figures in the park across the street as he climbed the steps of the apartment building, but they were too far away to worry about. Pulling out the play program, he stepped into the entryway alcove and punched the number Caroline had given him into the shiny new electronic lock.

It clicked open with a gratifying lack of fuss, and he continued on into the welcome warmth of the hallway and the aroma of a rosemary pork roast from somewhere in the building. Climbing the steps to the third floor, he punched the second number into the keypad on the Youngs' door and went inside.

There was a single dim light burning in the far corner of the living room. Aside from that, the apartment seemed to be completely dark.

And completely deserted.

He went through the place room by room, his heart beating faster with each empty space that confronted him. It had been hours since he'd spoken to Caroline—she and Melantha should have been here long ago.

And indeed they had, he discovered as he reached the last of the three bedrooms. One of his suitcases was sitting against the far wall, with a couple of Caroline's shirts and slacks stacked neatly on one of the two twin beds.

So where had they gone?

He went back down the hallway and pushed open the swinging door that led into the kitchen. A bag's worth of groceries was there, stacked neatly on one of the sideboards beneath a row of shiny copper pans.

He stepped over for a closer look, the acid taste of fear seeping into his mouth. So they weren't out shopping, at least not for food. Shopping for clothing for Melantha? But it seemed unlikely that Caroline would take such a chance, especially with evening upon them. They hadn't gone to a restaurant, either, not with everything they needed for a simple dinner right here.

Had they been abducted? But there weren't any signs of a struggle, and he couldn't imagine Caroline letting anyone take Melantha away without one.

Unless it had happened under the soothing aura of official authority. Roger had already gotten a call from someone purporting to be a cop trying to lure him back to his neighborhood. If that same someone had traced Caroline here, he might have tried the same trick on her.

Would Caroline have given Melantha up to a stranger with a uniform and the right credentials? Probably.

But if all they wanted was Melantha, why was Caroline gone, too?

He glared at the pile of groceries. Where *was* there for two footloose women to wander off to after dark? A movie? A doctor? The park?

The park.

He frowned, a stray bit of conversation suddenly popping back into his mind. The mysterious mugger with the mysterious gun, asking what kind of trees they had on their balcony.

The balcony Melantha had disappeared from when the cops arrived. The balcony she'd been standing on when she'd reappeared nineteen hours later.

And then, suddenly, a current of cool air flowed across his feet. Had someone just opened the door? But the air in the hallway hadn't been nearly this cool.

Someone had opened a window.

In the center of the counter, nestled between the cutting board and the bread box, was a wooden block holding an assortment of knives. Silently, his heart pounding, Roger crossed to it and pulled out the biggest one he could find. He returned to the kitchen door and gently pushed it open.

There were two of them: youngish middle-aged men, squat and wide. The first, his massive shoulders straining against a blue pea coat, was already inside, standing at the far end of the living room. His only slightly smaller companion, wearing gray slacks and a gray jacket with fleece collar, was just finishing the task of pulling himself in through the open window.

The first man spotted Roger at the same time he spotted them. "Where is she?" he demanded in a gravelly voice, stretching his right hand toward Roger as if offering to shake hands.

"Get out," Roger ordered, his voice shaking. "You hear me?"

He stepped forward, lifting his knife in what he hoped was a threatening manner. The men didn't move, but the second now lifted his hand toward Roger in the same hand-shaking gesture as the first. As he did so, his sleeve fell back a little, and Roger saw that he was wearing the same style of wide metal wristband that he'd seen earlier on Torvald and his friends.

That clinched it. "I said get *out*," he repeated. "Tell Torvald he can't have her." He took another step forward, hoping desperately that they wouldn't call his bluff, and wondering what he would do if they did.

"You're right, he can't," the blue-coated man agreed. He twitched his hand—

Roger stopped short as something silvery flashed into view across the man's right palm, thin metallic-looking tendrils that flowed up along his fingers like the burst from a tiny fireworks explosion. Even as he caught his breath, the filaments twisted back again, wrapping against and around each other in a pattern too fast and complex for him to follow. The wrapped tendrils settled into place against the man's palm, flattening and darkening and reforming themselves into a boxy sort of T-shape—

And a second later Roger found himself looking down the barrel of a small gray handgun.

He felt his mouth drop open, staring at the weapon in disbelief. The man's hand had been empty, his sleeve open, no sign of a holster or any other place the gun could have come from. Another flicker of silver caught his eye, and he looked at the second man to see another set of metallic tendrils twist in his hand and settle themselves into a second gun.

And impossible or not, there were now two guns pointed straight at his chest.

"Now, then," the second man said, his voice tinged with scorn. "You want to do this the easy way, or the hard way?"

Roger took a deep breath. It was, by his count, the third time in as many days that someone had pointed a gun his direction.

And deep inside him, something snapped.

"Figure it out," he snarled, lifting his knife and starting forward again. So they were calling his bluff, were they? Fine. It was time to see how far they were willing to go to get to Melantha.

The first man's face settled into hard lines as Roger started toward him. The expression didn't even twitch as he squeezed the trigger.

There was no thunderclap of a bullet going off, or even the softer snap the movies always used when the gun was equipped with a silencer. This weapon merely gave a quiet but sharp rising-pitch *tzing,* like a tight electric guitar string being plucked while the guitarist slid his finger down the fingerboard. A thin line of white shot out from the muzzle toward him—

And he was rocked backward on his heels as something slammed hard against his chest.

He gasped, staggering back as he grabbed for his breastbone. The impact had felt like someone had lobbed a bowling ball at him. He looked down, cringing at the thought of the blood that he knew must be streaming out of the gaping hole that had surely been blown in his chest.

There wasn't any blood. There wasn't any hole, gaping or otherwise. The brand-new jacket was completely unmarked.

Were they shooting blanks?

He looked back up, frowning. The men were gazing steadily back at him, as if waiting to see what he would do next.

Under the circumstances, Roger decided, there wasn't

much he could do. Taking a deep breath against the throbbing ache in his chest, he lifted his knife and again started forward.

Both men fired this time, a matched set of guitar twangs and arrow-straight white lines. This time it was a pair of bowling balls that hammered into his torso, shoving him even more solidly backward. Before he could even catch his balance they fired again, and this time the twin impacts threw him flat onto his back.

He shook his head to clear it, his entire torso now a throbbing mass of pain. At some point along the way he'd dropped the knife, and he rolled half over on his side to try to snag it. There was another *tzing*, and the knife skipped up off the floor and bounced away into the corner. Roger turned back to the two men, still gazing unemotionally at him, and started to get to his feet.

And then, through the open window, he heard a scream.

Not an ordinary scream, though. This was something thin and wailing, yet somehow with a weight and strength behind it that rattled his legs straight out from under him and sent him sprawling again onto the carpet.

The two men staggered as well; and suddenly Roger and his knife were apparently forgotten. Turning back to the open window, they scrambled one at a time through it. Something tugged at Roger's ears as the second one disappeared, not a scream this time but something more felt than heard, like an ultrasonic dog whistle. The apartment floor seemed to tilt beneath him—

And as the half-heard cry trailed off into the night he heard something that froze his blood. It was a woman's voice, twisted with pain, shouting the name *Melantha*.

Caroline's voice.

● ●

Caroline had the taxi let them out two buildings over from the Youngs' apartment, in case someone questioned him about it later, walking the rest of the way after the vehicle disappeared around the corner. Her memory of the lock combinations proved to be correct, and a few minutes later they were in the apartment. Dropping the suitcase in one of the bedrooms, they made a quick run to a nearby grocery store for dinner supplies.

Through it all, Melantha said little, except in reply to direct questions. For her part, Caroline didn't feel much like talking, either.

It was after four by the time they returned. Melantha set her half of the groceries on the kitchen counter, then silently disappeared to somewhere else in the apartment. Caroline unloaded the bags, then began cutting slices from the turkey breast and leg of lamb she'd bought, her stomach growling as she worked. With everything that had happened that day, she and Melantha had missed lunch, and she was ravenous. Piling the slices onto a plate, she set it in the microwave to heat while she arranged the rest of the sandwich makings on the kitchen table with its wraparound bench seat. When the meat was hot, she added it to the array and went in search of Melantha.

She found the girl sitting by the living room window, gazing out at the park across the street. "I've got sandwiches ready," Caroline announced.

"I'm not hungry," Melantha said, still staring out the window.

"You ought to eat something," Caroline advised. "You're a growing girl, you know."

Melantha reached up and touched her throat. "Not for much longer," she murmured.

"It'll be all right, Melantha," Caroline said, stepping up behind her and resting her hand on the girl's shoulder. "We're not going to let them hurt you."

Melantha made as if to say something, but merely shook her head. "Come on," Caroline said, giving her shoulder an encouraging squeeze. "*I'm* hungry, and I hate to eat alone."

Melantha heaved a sigh, but got to her feet. She gave the park one final look, then followed Caroline through the swinging door into the kitchen.

"I got the lamb especially for you," Caroline commented as she slid behind the table on the bench seat and gestured Melantha to join her. "Do you want some cheese with it?"

Melantha hesitated, but the aroma of the food was apparently too tempting even for her dark mood. "Okay," she said, taking a seat on the bench across from Caroline and peeling two slices of bread from the end of the loaf.

"I didn't see any goat's cheese there," Caroline commented as she carved off a slice of cheddar. "Where does your family buy it?"

"There's a place on West 204th," Melantha said, loading her bread with slices of the lamb. "A lot of our people live up there."

"Ah," Caroline said, trying to keep her voice casual. *Our people.* "Where exactly do you live?"

"Inwood Hill Park," the girl said, adding two slices of cheese to the stack. Her fingers paused. "I mean," she corrected herself carefully, "in Inwood, *near* Inwood Hill Park."

"Any brothers or sisters?" Caroline asked, taking a bite of her sandwich.

Melantha shook her head. "No."

"What about your parents?" Caroline asked. "What does your father do?"

"He's a Laborer," Melantha said. "My mother's a—" She broke off, giving Caroline a haunted look. "I shouldn't be talking about this."

"It's all right," Caroline assured her. "Do you mostly get along with your family?"

Melantha's throat tightened again as she closed her eyes, and Caroline could see tears gathering beneath the eyelids. "I love them," she said, almost too quietly for Caroline to hear. "I can't let them die."

"You mean, along with the rest of the Greens and the Grays?"

Melantha's eyes snapped open. "What do you know about that?" she demanded.

"Just what you told me," Caroline said, startled by the reaction. "In Lee's, remember? What happened back there, anyway?"

Melantha hunched her shoulders. "It was Cyril," she said, her voice shaking. "He was calling to me."

"It was more than just calling, though, wasn't it?" Caroline asked. "He was trying to make you come to him."

She frowned. "How do you know?"

"Because he had a go at me, too," Caroline told her. "Though I think he assumed we were still in the apartment."

"He *talked* to you?" Melantha asked, surprise momentarily displacing the gloom in her face. "I didn't know he could do that."

"Well, *someone* was talking in my head," Caroline said. "Who is Cyril, anyway?"

Melantha's lip twitched. "He's one of our leaders," she said. "Not a real Leader, just a Persuader. We don't have any real Leaders right now."

"I see," Caroline said, keeping an encouraging expression on her face as she tried to sort all this out. A Laborer she could understand, even with the capital letter she could somehow hear in the way Melantha said the word. But what kind of job was Persuader? "Why did he call you the Peace Child?"

Melantha lowered her eyes. "They say I can stop the fighting," she said softly. "Cyril and Halfdan say that if I . . ." She trailed off, a shiver running up through her.

"Is Halfdan another Persuader?"

Melantha shook her head. "He's a Gray. They don't have Persuaders."

"And how do he and Cyril think you can stop the fighting?"

There was no answer. "Melantha, what happened Wednesday night?" Caroline asked gently.

The girl closed her eyes again, her body suddenly heaving with silent sobs. "Did someone try to kill you?" Caroline persisted. "Someone who doesn't want the fighting to stop?"

Melantha shook her head, her silent shaking intensifying. "You don't understand," she managed between gasps. "It's all of them. All the Greens. All the Grays.

"They *all* want me dead."

• •

They spent the next hour sitting together on the bench seat, Caroline holding Melantha tightly to her side, whispering soothing words as the girl cried with a depth of grief and agony that Caroline had never before seen in someone so young. Even when the tears finally ran out she continued to hold onto Caroline as if clinging to a life preserver, her face buried in her shoulder as she groaned and whimpered half-heard words in a language Caroline couldn't understand.

The eastern sky outside the kitchen window had grown dark by the time she finally fell silent. Caroline gazed at the remains of their meal as they continued to hold onto each other, the barely nibbled sandwiches long since cooled, her own gnawing appetite long since evaporated.

Finally, Melantha pulled away. "I'm sorry," she said, sniffing against the aftermath of the tears.

"You don't need to apologize," Caroline assured her, snagging another napkin from the holder and handing it to her. "Anyway, it's better to get that kind of emotion out of your system."

Melantha blew her nose and added the napkin to the pile of tear-soaked ones that had already accumulated on the table. "Cyril's going to be mad at me."

"Cyril can go jump in the East River," Caroline said flatly. "You still hungry?"

Melantha looked at her sandwich. "Not really."

"Me, neither," Caroline said. "Let's put the food away and go unpack."

Melantha's eyes drifted to the window. "Could we go to the park instead?" she asked.

"I don't know," Caroline said, peering into the gathering dusk. The clusters of mothers and children who'd been in the playground earlier had disappeared, though the tall gate was still open. "If you want air, I could open a window."

"It's not the air," Melantha said, a little hesitantly. "It's the trees."

"What about them?" Caroline asked, frowning.

"I just want to see them," Melantha said. "Please?"

"We shouldn't be outside more than we have to," Caroline said, thinking about Roger's warning to stick to crowds and daylight.

"But it might be the last time—I mean—" she broke off, tears welling in her eyes again, and she fought to blink them back. "No one should be there yet," she said at last. "And I'll be careful."

Caroline peered into her face. No half-closed eyelids, no pupil dilation. "All right, but just for a few minutes," she said, giving in. "And not until we put the meat and cheese in the refrigerator and unpack the suitcase."

There was still some pink sky visible between the buildings to the west as they walked down the steps, but the evening's darkness had already settled firmly over their part of the city. The air was even colder than Caroline had expected, and she zipped up her coat tightly as they reached the street.

Melantha didn't seem to notice the temperature. Barely even pausing to check for traffic, she hurried across and through the gate into the park, her own coat flapping wide open as she ran. Caroline followed more slowly, her eyes probing the growing shadows for anyone who might be lurking around.

Melantha didn't seem concerned about that, either. Settling down to a walk, she moved along the rows of trees, her outstretched hand brushing across each as she passed. Occasionally, she lingered by one of them, fingering the rough bark with both hands as if trying to memorize the pattern. When she reached the end of the row she crossed to the next group of trees and started the procedure all over again. Caroline picked out a spot midway from the gate and waited, trying to be patient.

Eventually, the girl ran out of trees. "Finished?" Caroline asked as she came slowly back to her.

"I suppose," the girl murmured, turning and giving the trees a last lingering look.

"Time to go in, then," Caroline said, reaching for the girl's hand.

Melantha's gaze shifted to a point past Caroline's shoulder. "Could I just go look at those first?"

Caroline turned. Beyond the park's gate was an open-ended courtyard sort of place sandwiched between the fence and the building to the west. There were several tall trees there, rising from openings in the patterned brickwork covering the ground. The trees alongside the building itself had clumps of bushes all around their bases, this more delicate greenery protected by a foot-high wire fence. "I don't know, Melantha," she said doubtfully. "We shouldn't be outside more than we have to."

"Please?" Melantha said. "It's on the way."

Caroline sighed. "You've got two minutes."

"Thank you." With a renewed burst of energy, she trotted ahead through the park and out the gate. Caroline picked up her own pace, unwilling to let her get too far ahead this time. Melantha ran her fingers along the tree just outside the park, then headed across the brickwork toward the ones inside the low enclosure. Hopping the wire fence, she began wading through the bushes toward the biggest of the trees.

Caroline was looking at the tree, idly wondering what kind it was, when a ripple seemed to run through the lower part of the trunk. The ripple became a long bulge; and, suddenly, a human figure pushed its way outward, melting effortlessly through the bark.

And before Caroline could do more than gasp, there was an old woman standing knee-deep in the bushes in front of the tree.

Melantha jerked to a halt, twitching as if she'd stepped on a downed power line. But in her stunned disbelief Caroline hardly even noticed. The tree was far too narrow for the woman to have been hiding behind it, and she certainly hadn't risen up from the bushes around her.

But yet there she was, snarling at Melantha in a strange language as the girl backed away, shaking. She reached the fence, nearly tripping over it before she cleared it and stepped again onto the brickwork. The woman spat one final comment, then started walking through the bushes toward her.

And with that, Caroline's stunned paralysis finally snapped. "Leave her alone," she ordered, rushing up behind Melantha and clapping her hands protectively on the girl's shoulders.

"Go home, meddler," the woman said scornfully. "Leave the Peace Child to her own people."

"No," Caroline said, stepping around Melantha and putting herself between them. Distantly, it occurred to her that Roger wouldn't understand what she was doing, that he would never forgive her if she got herself killed out here tonight. But she had no choice. Melantha needed her, and she was here, and that was all there was to it. "*You* go away," she insisted. "Or I'll call the police."

The woman stopped, her expression in the glow of the streetlights going cold and hard. She drew herself up, filled her lungs with air, opened her mouth—

And screamed.

Caroline staggered back as the sound washed over her, feeling like she'd been slapped hard across the face. There was an underlying power beneath the wordless cry, a twisting of rage and control and command within the wailing, a hammering of ancient dread and weakness vibrating across her ears and through her head.

Suddenly, without any memory of even losing her balance, she found herself sprawled on the bricks. She looked up, fighting against the dizziness that was spinning the world around her, trying desperately to locate Melantha.

She found the girl standing over her, apparently unshaken by whatever had sent Caroline herself spinning. And yet, somehow, she was no longer the same little girl Caroline and Roger had knelt over two days ago, huddling alone and miserable in an alley. Melantha's lips were pressed together, her eyes blazing with a wild and dangerous fire as she looked down at Caroline. She lifted her gaze to the other woman and inhaled deeply, and Caroline braced herself for another scream.

But the cry Melantha sent through the nighttime air was something entirely different. It was almost completely silent, rattling Caroline's skull and stomach directly without passing first through her ears, bucking her up into the air and then slamming her back down onto the bricks. The ground seemed to heave again, this time throwing her sideways and rolling her onto her stomach. "Melantha!" she heard herself shout, the words hurting her throat. "Melantha, stop!"

Another of the old woman's terrible screams slashed through the night air, and again Caroline tensed as the world seemed to spin around her.

And then, in the echoing aftermath of the scream, she heard a gasp. "Caroline!" Melantha cried out.

Caroline rolled over, blinking away her blurred vision. The old woman had a grip on Melantha's wrists and had pulled her back to the low fence, their arms swinging wildly to the sides as Melantha struggled. Clenching her teeth, Caroline forced herself up onto her knees.

She was trying to get to her feet when something unseen shot past her and the struggling couple and blew a hole in the brickwork.

She twisted around. The shot, or whatever it was, had come from behind her, from the direction of the Youngs' apartment. But there was no one in sight beneath the streetlights.

And then, from midway up the side of the building she caught a flicker of movement, and a slender line of white zipped outward over her head. There was a thundering *crack* from behind her, and she twisted around again to see one of the lower limbs of the tree behind Melantha and the old woman shatter at the trunk and crash to the ground.

The old woman snarled, shoving Melantha away from her onto the bricks. Straightening up defiantly, she once again sucked in a deep breath.

But if she was preparing another scream, she never made it. Even as she opened her mouth, another of the white lines arrowed through the air squarely into her chest, and she was thrown backward as if she'd been hit by a speeding car. She slammed into the tree behind her with crushing force, bounced off, and collapsed onto the bushes.

Caroline looked at her, an icy chill adding to the pain in her head. There was something about the way the woman lay draped across the greenery that told Caroline she was dead. "Melantha?" she called tentatively. "Melantha!"

"I'm here," the girl's voice came shakily from somewhere off to her side. Fighting against her lingering dizziness, Caroline once again pushed herself up onto her knees.

And suddenly the night sky lit up with a brilliant strobing of red lights. There was the roar of a car engine; and with a screech of brakes a police car skidded to a halt by the end of the courtyard. "Police!" someone yelled, shoving open the door. "Stay where you are! You—stop!" There was a sound of rapid footsteps—

And then Roger was there, dropping onto his knees beside her, his arms wrapping tightly around her. "Caroline!" he gasped, breathing hard.

"I'm all right," she assured him, clutching at his arms. The flashing red lights had been joined by the white beam of a floodlight, and in its stabbing glare she looked around for Melantha.

The coat she'd given the girl was a few feet away, lying crumpled on the ground. Melantha herself was gone.

So was the dead woman.

12

The Crime Scene Unit's floodlights threw multiple shadows in front of him as Fierenzo walked across the courtyard and stopped by the freshly gouged hole in the bricks. "Here?" he asked.

"No, here," the cop walking beside him corrected, pointing to a spot three feet closer to the low wire fence. "I saw her lying right here."

Fierenzo looked at the mangled bushes alongside the building. A squirrel might be able to hide in there, but not a teenaged girl. "And then she got up and went where?"

"I don't know," the cop said, carefully filtering most of his frustration out of his voice. "And she only got *halfway* up before I got the spotlight on the scene."

"What about the older woman?"

"She was over there," the cop said, pointing at a group of squashed bushes just in front of the tree with the broken limb. "I saw *her,* too, before we got the spot going."

Fierenzo looked around. Two women vanished into thin air, one of whom had allegedly been shot and killed.

Only there was no body, no blood, and no bullet. She and the girl had both disappeared, as had the two men Whittier had been babbling about when he and Powell arrived. There was, in fact, nothing to prove this whole thing was anything other than a hallucination or a hoax.

Except, of course, for the shattered bricks and the broken tree limb.

He stepped over to the limb. This wasn't some delicate little branch a careless ten-year-old might break if he put his weight on it. It was long and healthy and two inches in diameter, the kind of limb you would normally take off with a chain saw.

But this one hadn't been chainsawed. The cut was rough and compressed, like someone with immense upper-body strength had taken a slightly dull axe to it.

In fact, it rather reminded him of the much smaller gashes he'd seen on the trees at the Whittiers' place.

He crouched down beside the downed limb, glowering with frustration. It had taken them over an hour to track down the cabby who'd brought Caroline Whittier and the girl here, and as a result they had arrived only minutes before the incident. If the cabby had given him the right address in the first place, he and Powell might have been in position to witness the incident themselves instead of being two buildings up the street looking at mailbox names.

But they only had what they had. Glancing around, he started to stand up.

And paused. From this angle, and this elevation, he could see something he hadn't noticed before. Etched across several groups of the bricks were long, narrow cracks. Stress lines, apparently, only they weren't centered on the hole that had been blasted in the brickwork. Instead, they were radiating outward from a spot near the low wire fence. "Where did you say the woman was lying when you came around the corner?" he asked the cop.

"Right about there," the other said, pointing to a spot a foot away from the center of the crack system.

"Thanks," Fierenzo said, straightening to his feet. Retracing his steps across the courtyard, he crossed the street, making his way through the line of neighborhood gawkers gathered on the far side. The cop standing guard on the building door let him in, and he trudged his way up the stairs to the third floor.

Powell answered his knock. "Anything?" Fierenzo asked.

The other shrugged. "They've given a statement," he said. "Doesn't make any more sense than what they'd already told us downstairs."

The Whittiers were sitting side by side on the couch, Caroline nursing a cup of tea as another cop stood watch against the opposite wall. "Mr. and Mrs. Whittier," Fierenzo said as he crossed the living room and sat down in a chair facing them. "I'm Sergeant Thomas Fierenzo. You and I talked earlier this afternoon, Mr. Whittier."

Whittier's lips compressed briefly. "Yes."

"Let's start with Melantha," Fierenzo said. "I want her full name, and where exactly she is."

The Whittiers glanced at each other, and the husband give a microscopic shrug. "We think her name's Melantha Green," Mrs. Whittier said, her voice tight. "And we don't know where she is. When I looked for her after the police arrived, she was gone."

"What about you?" Fierenzo asked, shifting his gaze to Whittier. "Did *you* see where she went?"

Whittier shook his head. "I noticed her a few feet away from Caroline as I was running up," he said. "But I was concentrating on my wife."

"Did you see her get up or start to crawl away?" Fierenzo persisted. "Do you remember which direction she was facing? Anything?"

"All I remember is seeing Caroline's coat on the ground."

"Where was she hiding when the two officers came to your apartment Wednesday night?"

"I don't know that, either."

Fierenzo looked at Powell. The other detective nodded fractionally and started for the door, gesturing to the cop standing by the wall. "Officer?"

The cop followed him out into the hall, Powell closing the door behind him. "All right," Fierenzo said, leaning back in his chair and eyeing the Whittiers. "It's just you and me now; and if you'd like, all of this can be off the record. Just tell me what happened."

"What do you mean?" Whittier asked cautiously.

"I mean all the strange things you've been afraid to tell anyone," Fierenzo said, studying their faces and trying to judge whether or not he was hitting anywhere near the target. "Melantha's habit of disappearing whenever cops show up, for instance. Or tell me about the people on your balcony this afternoon trying to break into your apartment."

That one got definite twitches from both of them. "Breaking in from the *balcony?*" Whittier demanded, frowning.

"They tried to hammer their way through the glass," Fierenzo said. "My guess is that they were scared away by the second group, the ones who came in through the front door."

"Wait a second," Whittier said, sounding thoroughly confused now. "Are you saying we had *two* different sets of intruders?"

"Three in through the front, two in from the balcony." Fierenzo lifted his eyebrows at the wife. "It *was* two people you saw up there, wasn't it, Mrs. Whittier?"

Whittier looked at his wife. "You saw someone on our balcony?"

"Yes, from Lee's," she said, an odd note of dread in her voice. "And yes, there were two of them."

"Who also apparently tried to chop down your potted trees," Fierenzo went on.

The reaction this time was pure surprise, with no guilt or hidden knowledge mixed in. "The *trees?*" Whittier asked. "Why?"

"No idea," Fierenzo said. "Who's Cyril?"

The sudden change of subject caught both of them by surprise, and in the half second before they could cover it up, Fierenzo spotted the twin flashes of recognition.

Whittier tried the dumb approach anyway. "Cyril?"

"He called your apartment while we were there," Fierenzo told him. "He said that if you didn't return Melantha to him thousands of New Yorkers were going to die." He let his gaze harden. "I trust I don't need to tell you how we react to threats like that these days."

Whittier winced. "No, sir."

"Then tell me what's going on."

Whittier sighed. "Before God, I have no idea," he said. "Like we told the other detective, Melantha was handed over to us at gunpoint. We've been bouncing around like Ping-Pong balls in a hurricane ever since."

Fierenzo suppressed a grimace. Unsatisfying though the answer might be, Whittier's voice and body language were finally carrying the ring of truth. "And Cyril?"

"Melantha told me he was one of her people," Mrs. Whittier said, lifting her hands helplessly. "That's all I know."

"I get the impression he was involved with some agreement, too," Whittier offered. "But what agreement, and between whom, I don't know."

"Possibly with someone named Halfdan," Mrs. Whittier offered. "Melantha mentioned that name, too."

"What about the thousands of dead New Yorkers?" Fierenzo asked. "Any idea what he was talking about?"

The Whittiers looked at each other again. "Melantha told

me the Greens and the Grays would all die if she didn't go back," she said hesitantly. "But I didn't think there were that many of them."

"The Greens, as in Melantha Green?" Fierenzo asked.

"Yes, though that might just be a coincidence," Mrs. Whittier said. "But then she said they all wanted *her* dead."

"Did Cyril say anything else?" Whittier asked.

"Nothing that made sense," Fierenzo said, deciding not to mention the references to Sylvia and Aleksander just yet. "We let the machine take the message. You can listen to the whole thing later if you want."

"So what happens now?" Whittier asked cautiously.

For a moment Fierenzo gave him what Lieutenant Cerreta referred to as the Official NYPD Stare. "If you mean are you under arrest, the answer is no," he said. "But this is *not* the end of this. If the girl shows up, or if you learn anything else, you *will* call me immediately. Understand?"

Whittier swiped the tip of his tongue across his upper lip. "Yes, sir."

Standing up, Fierenzo pulled out his wallet and slid out a card. "Here are my office and cell phone numbers," he said, handing it to Whittier. "Call me any time."

"Yes, sir," Whittier said again, handling the card carefully.

"Then I'll say good-night," Fierenzo said, nodding to each of them. "I suggest you lock the door behind me."

Powell was waiting for him in the hallway. "You get any of that?" Fierenzo asked.

The other shook his head. "Not really. That door's pretty thick."

"To summarize: they don't know Cyril, they don't know where the girl went, and they don't know anything else."

"Did you tell them Umberto had matched Cyril's voice with the ringleader of his polite break-ins?"

"No, I thought we'd keep that to ourselves for the moment," Fierenzo said. "Because for all their wide-eyed surprise at the news that someone had tried to get into their apartment from their balcony, neither of them remembered to ask how someone could have gotten up there in broad daylight in the first place."

"So how *does* someone do that?"

"Damned if I know," Fierenzo conceded, heading toward the stairs. "But I'm pretty sure *they* do."

"You want to haul them in for obstruction?"

Fierenzo shook his head. "I'd rather put them on a leash and let them run."

"I doubt Cerreta will spring for the extra manpower," Powell warned.

"I wasn't planning to ask him," Fierenzo said as they headed downstairs. "I figured we could cover this ourselves."

Powell turned a dark look on him. "As in, there goes my weekend?"

"The blood of thousands of New Yorkers, Jon," Fierenzo reminded him.

"Easy for *you* to say," Powell grumbled. "With Claire and the girls gone, you can keep whatever crazy hours you want."

"Sandy will understand," Fierenzo assured him.

"Sandy's getting tired of understanding," Powell countered. "What the hell. We're starting right away, I suppose?"

"They're not going anywhere tonight," Fierenzo said. "If they really *don't* know where the girl went, they're bound to stick around at least until morning in case she comes back."

"And if she does?"

"She won't," Fierenzo said grimly. "Wherever she went, I get the feeling she didn't go voluntarily."

They crossed the entryway alcove past the duty cop and stepped out into the chilly night air. The CSU investigators were closing down shop, their lights switched off and being broken down. A pickup truck with the Department of Parks and Recreation logo on the side was parked at the curb, and a pair of figures were dragging the broken tree limb toward it. "I still don't think we should let them out of our sight," Powell said.

"We won't," Fierenzo assured him. "I think I can find

someone who'll baby-sit the building until we get back in the morning."

Even without looking, he could feel Powell's eyes on him. "You wouldn't," the other said. "Smith?"

"Why not?" Fierenzo countered, pulling out his cell phone. "He wants to be a detective. It's only fair that we show him what the job entails."

"I suppose you even have his number memorized?"

"Don't be silly," Fierenzo admonished him. "I've got it on speed-dial."

• •

Roger locked the door behind the detective, fastening both the deadbolt and chain. Then he went through the apartment, making sure every window was locked.

Caroline was still on the couch, gazing into her teacup, when he returned. "How are you doing?" he asked.

She gave a little shrug. "Okay."

"How's your side?" he asked, his own chest throbbing a little harder in sympathy.

Another shrug. "It's okay."

With a sigh, he sat down beside her. "It's not your fault, Caroline," he told her quietly. "It really isn't."

"I'm the one who let her go into the courtyard," she said, her lower lip trembling visibly as she fought back the tears. "I could have said no, but I didn't. How can it *not* be my fault?" She shook her head. "That woman came straight out of the tree," she murmured with a sudden shiver. "I know you don't believe that part, but she did."

"Where she came from doesn't really matter," Roger said, ducking the implied question. Caroline had only been able to give him a quick summary before the cops marched them back to the apartment, and the mysterious woman and her baffling appearance had been one of the many things he hadn't understood. "My point is that if you *had* stayed inside, Melantha would have been here when *my* two gorillas showed up. There was going to be trouble no matter what you did or didn't do."

Caroline sniffed back some tears. "They must have followed the cab."

"We don't know that," he said, determined to snap her out of this quagmire of self-recrimination. "Maybe they followed *me*."

"No, it was me," she insisted. "We saw them climbing our building, just as we were leaving Lee's."

"They were *climbing?*" Roger asked, frowning. "You mean the outside?"

She nodded. "And Melantha called them *Grays*."

"Grays," Roger murmured. The Greens, and the Grays. This was starting to make an unpleasant sort of sense. "What did they look like?"

"I don't know," Caroline said. "They seemed short and squat. Sort of like the way you described our visitor last night."

Roger nodded. "*And* like the two who shot at me just now."

Caroline looked up sharply. "They *shot* at you?"

"With a gun that appears from nowhere and fires invisible bowling balls," he said, gingerly rubbing his sore chest. "Knocked me straight across the room."

"Let me see," Caroline said, hurriedly setting down her cup and unzipping his jacket. "You didn't tell me you were hurt."

"It's nothing," Roger assured her as she got through the jacket and started on his shirt buttons. "Like I said, it was like getting hit with a bowling ball."

"Well, there's no blood, anyway," Caroline said, peering through the gap she'd opened. "There's going to be some bruising, though."

"That I can live with," he said, buttoning up the shirt again. "I'm just glad the things weren't on whatever setting blows off tree branches."

Caroline caught her breath. "Is *that* what happened?"

"What else?" he said. "I wasn't outside in time to see the branch go, but I *did* see the woman get slammed into the tree. It was exactly what happened to me, only worse."

"Maybe that's what happened to Melantha, too," Caroline said. "Oh, Roger, what are we going to do? She trusted us, and we've let her down."

"I don't know," Roger said, taking her hand as he fought back his own gnawing sense of guilt. Maybe if he hadn't been so intimidating—maybe if Melantha had felt free to tell them the whole truth—this could have been avoided. But it was too late. Now, most likely, the story was lost to them forever.

Unless . . .

Letting go of Caroline's hand, he got to his feet. "Where are you going?" she asked as he headed across the living room.

"Fierenzo said we had a message on our machine," he reminded her, picking up the handset and punching in their number.

Caroline came up beside him as the answering machine picked up. Roger punched in the retrieval code, then switched to speakerphone so they could both hear. "Hello, Roger, my name is Cyril," an unfamiliar voice said. "I understand you spoke to Sylvia at Aleksander's this morning . . ."

They let the message run to the end. Caroline gave a little shiver, Roger noticed, when he came to the part about the blood of thousands of New Yorkers.

". . . I hope you'll do the right thing, and that we'll see you and Melantha here soon," the voice concluded.

There was the click of a disconnect. "Lovely," Roger growled. "Nothing like a little veiled threat to—"

"Hello, Roger, my name is Aleksander," a new voice unexpectedly came on. "I wanted to apologize for not being here when you came by this morning. Sylvia told me about your conversation, and I sense her zeal may have skewed your perception of us. I'd like to make that up to you, as well as give you the complete story before you make any decision on what to do with Melantha. You'd be more than welcome to come back here; alternatively, there is one of your own who's familiar with the situation."

Roger felt his throat tighten. *One of your own?*

"His name is Otto Velovsky, and he lives in the apartment building across from Jackson Square," Aleksander went on. "Please go and listen to him. I don't exaggerate when I say that the fate of the entire city may hang in the balance."

The disconnect click came again, and this time it was followed by silence. Roger waited a moment to make sure there weren't any more messages, then clicked off his end of the connection. "Where's Jackson Square?" Caroline asked.

"No idea," Roger said. "Do you know if the Youngs have a good city map?"

"Should be here," Caroline said, pulling open the telephone stand drawer.

The map was indeed there, tucked beneath a small stack of notepads and pencils. They took it back to the couch, and for a minute searched through it in silence. "There," Caroline said suddenly, pointing to a spot in the West Village near 14th Street and Eighth Avenue. "One of those little neighborhood pocket parks."

"Right," Roger said, nodding as he studied the area. It wasn't too far from a little Italian place he'd taken Caroline to a couple of times before they were married. "Did he give an address? I don't remember hearing one."

"We can look him up in the phone book," Caroline said. "I wonder who he is, and how he fits into this."

"I'm more worried about that 'one of your own' comment," Roger said. "It sounded really strange."

"And the woman by the tree told me to leave Melantha to her own people," Caroline said slowly. "Roger . . . these aren't just two ethnic groups, are they?"

He shook his head. "No ethnic group *I've* ever heard of can climb walls or pop out of trees."

"Trees!" Caroline clutched suddenly at his arm. "Roger—if that woman could come *out* of the tree, maybe Melantha went *into* it."

"Oh, *damn*," Roger muttered as a cluster of mismatched puzzle pieces suddenly fell into place. "*That's* how she disappeared Wednesday night. She just popped into one of the orange trees." He snorted under his breath. "I can't believe I'm saying this."

"Never mind that," Caroline said, jumping up and starting across the living room. "Come on."

"Whoa," Roger said. "Where are we going?"

"To the courtyard, of course," Caroline said, scooping up her coat from the chair where she'd draped it. "We have to see if Melantha's in that tree."

"With the cops still out there?"

Caroline froze with one arm halfway into its sleeve. "Oh. No, I guess not."

"Definitely not," Roger agreed, trying to think it through. "And even after they leave, it might not be a good idea. If the woman's still out there, and if she *didn't* see where Melantha went, that might give her away."

"I don't know," Caroline said, her eyes going strangely distant. "She looked awfully dead to me."

"Then where did the body go?" Roger countered. "Besides, even if *she's* not there, there may be more of her people around."

"Or the men who shot you," Caroline agreed with another shiver. "Did I tell you they can turn invisible?"

Roger felt something catch in his throat. "No, you did not," he said, trying hard not to yell. Of all the things to forget to tell him— "How do you know?"

"The Grays on the building today did that," Caroline said. "You could see them moving against the wall, but only because they were moving. Once they stopped, it was like they weren't even there."

"Terrific," Roger said, looking surreptitiously around the room.

"But they weren't completely invisible," Caroline added. "You could still see their shadows."

"Really," Roger said, a spark of an idea finally coming to him. "Wait here."

He found the hefty four-cell flashlight the Youngs kept on hand for power outages and went through the apartment again, sweeping the light across walls and ceilings and looking for unexplained man-sized shadows. To his relief, there weren't any. "Looks clear," he reported as he returned to the living room.

"I hope so," Caroline said. "What now?"

Roger looked out the window. The extra lights that had been set up around the park had been taken apart and were being loaded into their van. "There's nothing we can do until morning," he said. "We don't know who's going to be watching, and even if we find Melantha we haven't got any place to run but back here. We've already seen how vulnerable this place is."

"But we can't let her stay out there all night."

"We're assuming she was inside one of your orange trees all night and most of the next day," he reminded her. "She ought to be able to hold out until morning."

"I suppose," Caroline said reluctantly. "What then?"

"We'll call a cab," Roger said. "Once it's standing here with the engine running, you'll go over to the tree and see if you can get her to come out. If she's there, and if she answers, we can hopefully all be on the FDR before anyone can stop us."

He looked out the window again. "If so, then you two can hole up in a hotel somewhere while I go talk to this Velovsky character and see how much of this mess he can clear up."

Caroline sighed. "I just wish there was more we could do."

"Me, too," Roger said. "But I don't know what else to suggest."

"I know," Caroline said reluctantly. "Could we at least . . . ? No, never mind."

"What?" he asked. "Come on, tell me."

"Could we at least use the hide-a-bed here instead of one of the bedrooms?" she asked hesitantly. "I know she was watching when I did the code downstairs. That way, if she gets into the building but can't remember the apartment code, we'd hear her knocking."

"Sure," Roger said, suppressing a grimace. He never slept well on hide-a-beds, and Caroline knew it. But aside from that, it was a good idea. "Go get our stuff and I'll get the bed set up."

"Okay." To his mild surprise, she leaned over and gave him a quick kiss. "Thank you."

"No problem," he assured her.

And besides, he thought as he stacked the couch cushions against the wall, no matter where they settled down for the night, he wasn't going to sleep well.

13

The sun was just coming up over Queens, and Fierenzo and Powell had been sitting in the stakeout car for half an hour, when the Whittiers finally made their move. "There they are," Fierenzo announced, nudging his partner as he peered back over his shoulder.

"Where?" Powell asked, turning around.

"Cab," Fierenzo said succinctly, pointing to the vehicle that had pulled up in front of the apartment building behind them. A moment later the Whittiers appeared, the husband going straight to the cab's back door and opening it. To Fierenzo's mild surprise, though, the wife headed instead across the street.

"Where the hell is she going?" Powell muttered.

"Looks like she's revisiting the crime scene," Fierenzo

said, frowning as she stepped over the low fence and waded her way through the bushes to the tree with the broken-off limb. Crouching over, she leaned her face right up to the bark. "Looking for something, maybe?" he added.

"If she is, she's talking to herself while she's doing it," Powell told him.

"You're right," Fierenzo agreed, frowning harder as he watched the woman's lips. Movement, then a pause; then movement, then another pause. As if she was saying something and then waiting for an answer.

An answer that apparently wasn't coming. Thirty seconds later she gave up and turned back toward her husband and the cab. "Here they come," he said, swiveling back to face forward and turning the key. The engine sputtered for a moment and then caught, blowing cold air through the vents at them. In the mirror he watched as the Whittiers climbed into the cab and the driver pulled away from the curb. It passed Fierenzo and Powell and headed for the next street, its left turn signal flashing. "Here we go," Fierenzo muttered, pulling out onto the street as the cab slowed for the turn. "Five bucks says they're going for the FDR—"

"Hold it," Powell interrupted, pointing to their right. Beyond the tall fence that encircled the park, a dark-haired man was running toward them, waving both arms frantically. "What's he doing in there with the gate still locked?" Powell muttered.

"See what he wants," Fierenzo said, glancing toward the cab as it disappeared around the corner. "Maybe we can call it in and keep going."

Powell cranked down the window, letting in a fresh flood of cold air. "What's the matter?" he called.

The man skidded to a halt, opened his mouth, and screamed.

Fierenzo jerked as the sound hammered through his head, the car leaping beneath him like a bucking horse. The wheel twisted in his hands, the street and park and whole damn city tilting sideways as up and down suddenly lost their meaning. Dimly over the sound he heard Powell yelling something—

And then the world straightened out; and with a rush of adrenaline he saw he was headed straight for the curb.

He twisted the wheel, but it was too late. With a spine-jolting bounce the car careened up over the curb and rolled itself up against a lamppost.

"You okay?" Fierenzo asked, shaking his head to clear it.

"Yeah," Powell grunted, sounding as dazed as Fierenzo felt. "Hell—there he goes."

The man had reversed direction and was running back across the park toward the fence at the far side. "Oh, no, he doesn't," Fierenzo growled, popping his seat belt and shoving open his door. Scrambling awkwardly out against the upward tilt, he hit the ground and charged across the street. He'd heard echoes of that same scream last night, and he had no intention of letting this one get away.

He was across the street and making for the gate when his quarry spun around in mid-run and let loose with another scream.

He was at least twice as far away from Fierenzo as he'd been the first time, but the extra distance didn't seem to make a bit of difference. Once again the ground tilted violently; and this time, with no car wrapped protectively around him, he fell face first toward the iron fence. More by luck than anything else, he managed to grab one of the bars, halting his forward momentum and giving him something to hang onto as the world took itself on another spin. A moment later, without any memory of having fallen the rest of the way, he found himself lying on the ground. Blinking away the last few sparkling stars, he lifted his head and looked around.

The man had disappeared.

There was the sound of hurrying footsteps, and he swiveled around on his hip as Powell dropped to a crouch beside him, gun in hand as he stared through the fence into the park. "Where'd he go?" he demanded.

"What are you asking *me* for?" Fierenzo grunted, using the fence for balance as he pulled himself back to his feet. "Weren't you watching?"

"Of course I was," Powell said disgustedly, giving Fierenzo an assist with his free hand. "Right to the point where he ran behind one of the trees, and that was the last I saw of him. You okay?"

"I think so," Fierenzo said, rubbing his palms against his pant legs to dry them as he peered through the fence. The man had vanished, all right, just like Melantha and the old woman from last night. This was starting to get very annoying. "That song of his sound familiar?"

"Like the one we heard last night," Powell confirmed. "Reminds me of those nonlethal sonic weapons the military's been playing around with."

"Only this guy was doing it without assistance," Fierenzo said.

"Unless he had something hidden under his coat."

"Maybe," Fierenzo said, looking down the street. "Regardless, he's given the Whittiers a nice little head start on the day."

"So they've been lying the whole time," Powell said sourly. "Damn. I'd been hoping they really *were* just innocent bystanders."

"Don't give up on them just yet," Fierenzo cautioned. "People smart enough to successfully lie to experienced cops like us should also be smart enough not to make their getaway in a cab with big numbers plastered all over it."

"Good point," Powell said, frowning. "It's almost like they didn't even know we were here."

Fierenzo nodded. "Which suggests our friend with the noisemaker may have been running interference without their knowledge."

"Cyril?"

"Or Aleksander, or Sylvia, or someone whose name we haven't heard yet," Fierenzo said. "Take your pick."

Powell grimaced. "Who the hell *are* these people, anyway?"

"I don't know, but we're going to find out," Fierenzo promised, trudging around the car and climbing into the driver's seat. "Come on, let's see if we can get this thing unstuck."

• •

"Nothing, I take it?" Roger asked as the cab pulled away from the curb.

Caroline shook her head, trying hard not to berate herself for not trying to find Melantha last night. She tried equally hard not to blame Roger for talking her out of doing so. "If she *was* there, she isn't anymore."

"I'm sorry," he said quietly. "I guess we should have gone looking for her last night."

Caroline didn't answer.

It was still early in the morning, with traffic sparse by New York standards, and the cabby got them down to 14th Street in probably close to record time. After that, it was a straight shot west to Jackson Square.

They didn't ride the entire way, though. Remembering yesterday's traceable cab ride, Caroline insisted they get off at Fifth Avenue and walk a couple of blocks north before turning west and making for their true destination. It was too early to go knocking on apartment doors, so again at her suggestion they found a deli and went inside for breakfast.

The meal was a quiet one. Somehow, everything Caroline saw around her—from the cheeses to the thin-sliced meats to the serving girl's dark hair—reminded her of Melantha. Roger was equally quiet as he plowed through his bagel and coffee, but whether he was thinking along the same lines she didn't know.

They emerged from the deli a little after eight to find that the early-morning sunshine had disappeared behind a ceiling of dark clouds and a light rain was falling. "Perfect," Roger muttered, glancing around and heading for a street vendor with a rack of compact umbrellas prominently displayed beside his magazines and packaged snack foods.

"You don't need to buy that for me," Caroline told him as he picked out a black one and dug into his pocket for some cash.

"It's not just for you, sweetheart," Roger assured her, taking her arm with his free hand and popping open the umbrella with the other. "See?" he said, lifting it over their heads and pulling her close beside him. "Instant anonymity."

"Ah," she said, finally understanding. "Good idea."

"Thank you," Roger said. "Let's just hope the rain keeps up."

Velovsky's building turned out to be an old brick structure right across the street from the Jackson Square park. They found the proper intercom button, and with only a slight hesitation Roger pushed it.

The reply came with surprising promptness. "Yes?"

"We're looking for Otto Velovsky," Roger said into the grille.

"You've found him," the voice said briskly. A middle-aged voice, Caroline guessed, belonging to a man probably in his mid-fifties. "Who are you?"

"Roger and Caroline Whittier," Roger said. "We were told—"

"Apartment four-twelve," the other cut him off.

The door buzzed, and Roger pushed it open. The staircase was off to the side, and they climbed to the fourth floor. One of the doors opened as they approached, and a man stepped into the doorway.

He wasn't the fifty-something man Caroline had expected. He was in fact at least thirty years older than that, with a lined face, a slender build, and a fringe of pure white hair.

"Come in," he said, beckoning with bony fingers, and Caroline revised her estimate upward even further. Lower nineties at the youngest, possibly even pushing ninety-five, but apparently still quite spry. With Roger's hand gripping her arm nervously, they stepped past him and went inside.

"We appreciate you seeing us on such short notice, Mr. Velovsky," Caroline said, glancing around the living room as the old man closed the door behind them. The décor was quite homey, with antique-style furniture, a dark carpet, and tasteful wallpaper patterned with small abstract figures.

There were a couple of framed prints on the wall, and a computer hummed away in a rolltop desk in the far corner. Beside the computer was a mug of gently steaming coffee. "I hope we're not intruding."

"Not at all," Velovsky assured her, waving them toward a couch with lace-fringed throw pillows scattered around it. "Can I get you some coffee?"

"No, thanks," Roger put in, his voice sounding a little strained as he glanced around. "You and Aleksander must use the same decorator."

"Like minds run in like ways," Velovsky said, retrieving his mug from the computer desk and settling into a wing-backed chair across a low coffee table from the couch. "Please; sit down."

"What exactly did Aleksander tell you about us?" Roger asked as they sat down together on the couch.

"Nothing at all," Velovsky said. "He simply told me I was to tell you everything." His bright eyes shone as he looked back and forth between them. "I trust you recognize the honor implicit in that request. Aside from me, you'll be the first humans to hear the whole story."

Caroline felt a shiver run through her. She and Roger had speculated about who the Greens and Grays might be, and had more or less concluded they weren't human. But she hadn't really accepted that conclusion, at least not on a gut level.

Until now.

"We're listening," Roger prompted.

"I'm sure you are." Velovsky took a sip from his mug and set it down on the table. "The year was 1928," he said, his eyes taking on a faraway look as he leaned back in his chair. "Shiploads of Europeans were pouring weekly into the immigration office on Ellis Island, where I was a very junior forms processing clerk. At about ten-thirty in the morning on a rather warm July twenty-seventh, I was sent downstairs to one of the storerooms for a fresh box of medical release forms. I was heading down the hallway when I saw the door to one of the other storerooms standing wide open and a line of dark-haired people coming out of it."

"Not fellow employees, I presume?" Roger hazarded.

"Worse than that," Velovsky said. "That particular room wasn't much bigger than a broom closet. Clown cars might have been all the rage at Ringling Brothers; but ten people had already come out, and I *knew* you couldn't get that many people in there.

"Well, they saw me the same time I saw them, and they weren't any happier about it than I was. The first two in line—big, slender fellows, but with plenty of muscle—came toward me like a pair of lions sizing up the gazelle du jour. They did something with their hands, and suddenly each was sporting a long-bladed and very nasty-looking knife. That was when I realized I was in serious trouble."

"And they killed you, of course," Roger murmured under his breath.

"Shh!" Caroline murmured back. "Let him tell it his own way."

"Yes, Roger, do be patient," Velovsky said. "I've been rehearsing this tale for over seventy-five years, and this is the first time I've been allowed to tell it. Let me savor it a little."

Roger waved a hand. "Sorry."

"Thank you," Velovsky said. "At any rate, an older man in the group said something in a foreign language and beckoned me over to where he and a young boy—his twelve-year-old son, I found out later—were standing. With all those knives around me, I decided I'd better do what he wanted. As I came up, he reached out a hand to my forehead and . . . touched me."

Velovsky stopped, his eyes drifting to the cityscape outside the window. "I've been trying ever since then to put words to what happened," he said, his voice as distant as his gaze. "But I still haven't found the proper way to do it. It was like I was inside his mind, and he was inside mine, and we were speaking together in the basic underlying core language of the human soul. I could remember his memories;

image and sound, smell, touch, and taste. I was looking over his shoulder as he thought, watching his logic and his multiple trains of thought. It was exhilarating and terrifying, alien beyond imagination, twisted and confusing and yet as comfortable as an old sweater."

Reluctantly, Caroline thought, he brought his eyes back to focus. "They called themselves the Greens. There were sixty of them, refugees from another world."

"Which one?" Caroline asked.

"They don't know," Velovsky said. "The stars here are nearly identical to those they could see from their home, though there are a number of subtle differences."

"An astrophysicist might be able to pin it down," Roger suggested. "They could draw up some star maps for comparison."

"They could also announce their presence on the eleven o'clock news," Velovsky said tartly. "They're trying to keep a low profile, if you hadn't already guessed."

"But if they don't know where they are, how did they get here?" Caroline asked. "Did they lose their charts afterward?"

"They didn't have any charts," Velovsky said. "Or navigators, either, at least not the way we use the term. Back on their world their remaining Farseers had been able to pull up images of Earth, and their Leaders decided this was where they would go. The Farseers and remaining Groundshakers were able to throw the transport through space to Earth, bringing it out in the Atlantic somewhere off Long Island."

"How long did the trip take?" Roger asked.

Velovsky shrugged. "Apparently instantaneous. The transport was capable of underwater travel, so they brought it to the base of Ellis Island, buried it partway in the silt, and dug a tunnel up to the storage room."

"Have you seen this transport yourself?" Caroline asked.

Velovsky nodded. "I was feeling woozy after that contact—so was the Leader, for that matter—so they took us back to the transport to rest while the Lifesingers did some quick healing. I've been down several times since then, just visiting. They use it as a sort of hydroponics farm to grow some of their native herbs and spices."

"What's it like?" Roger asked.

"Relatively small, but nicely laid out," Velovsky said. "The fact that it matched with the mental images I'd just been given helped convince me that everything else he'd shown me was genuine, too."

He smiled. "My boss chewed me out royally when I finally got back upstairs," he added. "He was particularly mad that he couldn't figure out where I'd disappeared to. If he'd only known."

"Sounds like a lot of unnecessary risk, sneaking into Ellis that way," Roger pointed out. "Why not just come in along the coast of Maine or something?"

"I don't know how the decision was made," Velovsky said. "I do know they chose the United States deliberately, and I can only assume they'd decided that if they were going to live here they should be official about it. The Greens always look at the long-term aspects."

"Is Aleksander the Leader you met?" Roger asked.

"Aleksander's a Persuader, not a Leader," Velovsky said.

"Can't he be both?"

"Actually, no, he can't," Velovsky said. "Or rather, a Leader *is* a Persuader, but the Persuader Gift has to be combined with the Gift of Visionary. They don't have any true Leaders or Visionaries at the moment, and Persuaders are next in line. It's not ideal, but it's the best they have right now."

"But the one you met *was* a true Leader?" Caroline asked.

Velovsky nodded. "Leader Elymas, who unfortunately died within a week of reaching New York. I've often wondered if the strain of sharing his mind with me was part of what killed him." His lip twitched. "Or maybe I absorbed a share of his strength and stamina along with those thoughts. I've certainly aged more gracefully than most of my contemporaries."

"So if Aleksander is their acting leader, what's the story with Cyril?" Roger asked.

Velovsky grimaced. "Unfortunately, the lack of a true Leader has allowed two factions to form among the Greens," he said. "Aleksander and Cyril each lead one of them."

"And what's Cyril's job?" Roger continued. "Is he a Persuader, too?"

"They're *Gifts,* not *positions,*" Velovsky corrected. "Special talents Greens are born with that define what they're going to be as adults. And yes, Cyril is also a Persuader."

"What did you mean by the *remaining* Farseers and Groundshakers?" Caroline asked. "Was there some sort of catastrophe on their world?"

"There was indeed," Velovsky said, the corners of his mouth tightening. "Their entire civilization was nearly wiped out in a devastating war."

"Let me guess," Roger said, his voice graveyard dark. "They were at war with a people who called themselves the Grays."

"Very good," Velovsky said bitterly. "The same Grays, in fact, who now threaten to destroy everything the Greens have spent the last seventy-five years building. They want to begin the war all over again, to finish what they started on their home world.

"And to perhaps destroy *this* world in the process."

14

For a long minute the only sound in the room was the quiet popping of the radiator beneath the window. "But why now?" Caroline asked. "Why, after all these years?"

Velovsky sighed. "That's one of the genuine ironies of this whole situation," he said. "I helped get the Greens get through immigration, figuring they would do best in northern New England or Colorado. But they apparently liked the idea of living in a city for a change, so at Leader Elymas's insistence I set them up in Manhattan. There were certainly enough trees in Central Park for a colony that small."

"Yes—the trees," Roger pounced. "What's that all about?"

"The Greens' bodies aren't like anything found on Earth," Velovsky said. "Their cells are much smaller, their whole physical structure far more mutable. They also have a strange—well, let's be honest; a rather parasitic relationship with trees. They can melt their way through the bark and settle into the core of the tree, wrapping themselves into a much smaller volume than you'd expect. While inside, they're able to draw nourishment and strength from the tree's own biological processes."

"Doesn't sound very efficient," Roger said, sounding doubtful.

"Efficiency isn't the only consideration," Velovsky pointed out. "A few milligrams of Vitamin C make a world of difference for a man with scurvy, after all. If you need something, no matter how small or seemingly insignificant, you still need it. In the Greens' case, they need periodic contact with trees."

"Can they also be healed that way?" Caroline asked, thinking back to Melantha's bruises.

"To a certain extent," Velovsky said. "Spending time inside trees also nurtures growth, particularly in the children."

"A block east of Jackson Square," Roger said suddenly.

"What?" Velovsky asked.

"I was just remembering how Aleksander described your location," Roger said. "Not Greenwich at Eighth, or the West Village, but across from Jackson Square."

"Typical Green directions," Velovsky agreed. "They always think in terms of parks and trees."

Caroline nodded. "And Melantha told me she lived *in* Inwood Hill Park—"

"Melantha?" Velovsky cut her off, his eyes widening, his voice suddenly intense. "You know where Melantha is?"

"Yes, let's talk about Melantha," Roger jumped in before Caroline could answer. "Why does everyone want to kill her?"

Velovsky hesitated, his eyes shifting back and forth between them. "If you know where Melantha is, it's absolutely vital you tell Aleksander."

"So we've heard," Roger said. "You were telling us about Ellis Island?"

Velovsky eyed him a moment longer, then lowered his gaze. "I got some jobs lined up and found them a nice little building off Central Park for their—well, call it their headquarters. A couple of apartments was all they needed, since they really only used them for official residence purposes. Mostly of their off-work time was spent in the park itself."

"Is that the building on 70th near Central Park West?" Caroline asked. "I saw a lot of Greens listed at that address."

"Yes," Velovsky confirmed. "They've also spread out over the years."

"How many of them are there now?" Caroline asked.

"About eight hundred and fifty," Velovsky said. "Anyway, they settled in, and I'll admit I was feeling pretty proud of myself. Savior of a whole race, and all."

His lips compressed into a thin line. "I got to feel that way for exactly one week. Seven days after they all moved to Manhattan, forty Grays arrived at Ellis."

"Through a different storage room, I presume?" Roger asked.

"Actually, they came in much less dramatically," Velovsky said. "They'd simply parked their transport and waited until a likely refugee ship sailed past. They climbed up the side, mingled with the rest of the passengers, and walked down the gangway half an hour later."

"They can climb ships, too?" Caroline asked.

"Ships, buildings, mountains—you name it," Velovsky said. "Anything with enough metal traces in it. They were originally cliff-dwellers back on the Greens' world, you know. Well, no, you probably didn't. Anyway, I recognized them immediately from the images I'd gotten from Leader Elymas's mind, and made sure to deal personally with their case."

"Sounds like *they're* the ones who should have gone to Colorado," Caroline suggested.

"And I tried," Velovsky told her, shaking his head. "Believe me, I tried. But they were as stubborn as the Greens, and they also insisted on New York. It was partly the tall buildings, but I also got the impression they thought they could hide better in the city's ethnic mosaic than someplace where the population was more homogenous. Maybe that's why the Greens wanted New York, too, now that I think about it."

"Why do the Grays care about blending in when they can turn invisible?" Roger asked.

"It's not true invisibility," Velovsky said. "What they can do is freeze in place on the side of a cliff or building, something with a nice simple background, and camouflage themselves to blend in. The technical term is *masking*."

"Handy," Roger commented.

"Handy, but very limited," Velovsky said. "It wouldn't work while walking down a street, or even sitting in a room with as much variation as this one. Even on the side of a building you can see them if you're close enough. Still, it's useful enough when they want to hang onto the side of the Flatiron Building and spy on the Greens in Madison Square."

"Is that where you sent them?" Roger asked. "Lower Manhattan?"

Velovsky snorted. "Give me a little more credit than *that*. It took some fancy footwork, but I finally managed to talk them into moving to Brooklyn and Queens."

"Queens," Roger muttered. "Of course."

"What?"

"I tried to lose a Gray tail by going to Queens." Roger waved a hand. "Never mind. So: Brooklyn and Queens?"

Velovsky nodded. "I assumed they'd take some time to adjust to the new culture and then move to the mountains where they belonged. I thought that if I could keep the two groups separated and unaware of each other for a year or two, I'd be in the clear." He grimaced. "Unfortunately, I failed to take into account the stubbornness of both groups. Once they'd put down roots in their communities, they were in for the long haul."

"How did they discover each other again?" Caroline asked.

"I don't know," Velovsky said heavily. "It could have been the aftermath of the 9/11 attacks—maybe Greens and Grays were both involved in the rescue or cleanup operations. It could have been as simple as a group of Green teenagers taking a day trip to Brooklyn and spotting people their Pastsingers had told them had died three-quarters of a century and a dozen light-years away."

"And you think they're going to start their old war again?" Roger asked.

Velovsky snorted. "My dear boy, it's already started. Or did you think that comment about Grays spying on Madison Square was just a figure of speech?"

Caroline looked at Roger. "But then why haven't we heard about it?" she asked.

"Don't be naïve," Velovsky said with another snort. "World War II didn't start the day Hitler marched into Poland, either. The two sides are still in their opening maneuvers: staking out positions, locating the other's strongholds, planning their strategy."

He waved a hand toward the window. "Unfortunately, most of the maneuvering seems to be happening here in the city, with the Grays pushing against Green areas instead of being forced to defend their own homes. Torvald, for instance, one of the chief Grays, moved rather brazenly into MacDougal Alley near Washington Square a couple of months ago, chasing all the Greens away from the park. Thanks to moves like that, they've penetrated a considerable ways into lower Manhattan."

"Maybe even farther north than that," Caroline murmured.

"I wouldn't be surprised," Velovsky said grimly. "They've

got their hammerguns, their tels, their instant-rappelling tension lines, and who knows what else. About all Nikolos has to fight back with is a few Warriors and the Shriek."

"Who's Nikolos?" Caroline asked.

"Elymas's son, and the Greens' only Command-Tactician," Velovsky said. "He'll be commanding their forces when the actual fighting breaks out." He grimaced. "What there is of them, anyway. Between the Group Commanders and the Warriors themselves, I don't think there are more than sixty who can fight."

"Can't they train more?" Roger asked. "You said there were eight hundred and fifty of them."

"It doesn't work that way," Velovsky said. "Like I said before, each Green is born with a particular set of skills, and those skills are what defines him or her. If you're born a Lifesinger or a Laborer or a Warrior, then that's what you are and always will be."

"Sounds like a caste system," Caroline said.

"That's exactly what it is," Velovsky agreed. "But it's imposed by genetics, not society. Don't try to judge the Greens by human standards. They're not like us."

"What *are* they like?" she countered.

His gaze drifted to the window again. "I've known these people for seven decades, Caroline," he said, his voice quiet and earnest. "I've seen what they do, how they work, the subtle but very real benefits they bring to this city. Go look at police reports and see how many purse-snatchers and muggers fleeing through parks suddenly seem to trip and fall all over themselves. Chances are, a Green Warrior was nearby. Or go to a rehab center and find out how many of their success stories used to sleep on the benches in Central Park. A lot of Lifesingers live there, and their songs of healing can help humans in remarkable ways."

"I'm glad for them," Caroline said shortly. "Now tell us why all these fine and noble people want Melantha dead."

Velovsky hesitated. "All I know is that they need her back," he said. "Aleksander's the one you should talk to. He lives in Central Park, near the Seventh Regiment Memorial by the bowling greens. If you go there and wait, someone from his group will contact you."

"We'll think about it," Roger said, taking Caroline's arm and getting to his feet. "Thanks for the history lesson."

"Gray aggression cost the Greens their first home, Roger," Velovsky said, not moving from his chair. "Don't give them the chance to do the same to their second."

"We understand," Roger said. "By the way, where does Cyril hang out?"

Velovsky shook his head. "Cyril's approach won't work," he said. "All that kind of appeasement ever accomplishes is to buy a few months or years of peace. Aleksander is the only one who can finally end this."

"Yes," Roger said. "Cyril's home?"

Velovsky pursed his lips. "Riverside Park, near the Carrere Memorial."

"Thank you," Roger said. "We'll be in touch."

The drizzle had intensified while they'd been inside, though it was still short of what Caroline would have characterized as a full rain. Hoisting their new umbrella, Roger led them back toward 14th Street, threading them deftly through the streams of other pedestrians. He kept a firm grip on Caroline's arm as they walked, almost as if he thought she was a child who might suddenly dart out into traffic.

Or perhaps he just needed the comfort of her touch right now. As much as she needed his.

She waited for him to open the conversation. A block later, he finally did. "What do you think?" he asked.

"For one thing, he's lying about Melantha," she said. "He knows perfectly well what they want her for."

He eyed her oddly. "You sure?"

"Absolutely," she said. "I could see it in his face."

"Oh," he said, sounding a bit taken aback. "Actually, I was asking more about what you thought we should do about Melantha if we find her again."

Caroline gave him a sideways look. "Roger, they want to *kill* her."

"I'm not sure I believe that anymore," he said. "How can killing a twelve-year-old girl prevent a war?"

"Maybe we should try to find out before we throw her to the wolves," Caroline shot back.

"They're not all wolves, Caroline," he said. "No matter what Melantha told you, they can't *all* want her dead."

"What makes you so sure?"

"Weren't you listening?" he said. "Velovsky as good as admitted there was a power struggle going on between Aleksander and Cyril. They both want Melantha, only for different reasons."

"Or maybe they just disagree about the best way to kill her," Caroline muttered.

"No," Roger said, shaking his head. "Remember that crack about appeasement. Cyril apparently has a plan to somehow buy off the Grays."

"With Melantha's death?"

"Possibly, though I still don't see how that would work," Roger said. "Aleksander, on the other hand, seems to be going for final victory."

Caroline shivered. "So we basically have a choice between letting Melantha die or letting the Grays get slaughtered."

Roger snorted. "*We* have no choice of anything," he reminded her sourly. "With Melantha gone, we're out of the game."

"No, we're not," Caroline said firmly. "Number one: they still think we know where she is. That gives us some leverage."

"Leverage in what? Caroline, this isn't any of our business."

"With our city about to become a battleground?" Caroline countered. "Of *course* it's our business. And number two: if Melantha's free, she *is* going to come back to us. I know she is."

Roger sighed, and she braced herself for more argument. To her relief, though, he just shook his head. "Well, if it comes down to Melantha or the Grays, I don't think there's much of a choice," he said. "After all, it was the Grays who destroyed the Greens' world."

"Or so Velovsky says," Caroline said. "But don't forget that his attitude toward them started with a brain-meld or whatever with the Green Leader, not to mention seventy-five years of cozying up to them. Of *course* he's going to take their side."

"Well . . . maybe."

"And there's one other point," she added. "It wasn't a Green—from *either* side—who gave Melantha to us in the first place. It was a Gray."

"It was, wasn't it?" Roger said thoughtfully. "Both the body type and disappearing act show that."

"So at least some of the Grays want her alive, too," Caroline concluded.

Roger snorted. "Unfortunately, the only Gray contact we have is Torvald, who's doing his best to push the Greens out of Manhattan."

"According to Velovsky."

"Velovsky wasn't the one using me for target practice last night."

"We still need to hear their side of the story," Caroline insisted.

Roger sighed, shifting their direction toward an artist's supply shop just ahead. "Fine. Torvald likes art. He'd probably appreciate it if we called from an art store."

They ducked into the store, Roger closing the umbrella and shaking it on the doorstep before bringing it inside. Finding a quiet corner, he pulled out his cell phone. "I don't suppose you'd like to talk to him?"

"You're the one he knows."

"I didn't think so." Digging a business card out of his wallet, he glanced at the number and punched it in.

Caroline touched him on the arm and pantomimed putting a phone to her ear. He nodded and leaned his head close to hers, angling the phone so they could both hear.

There was a click. "Hello?" a woman answered.

"I'd like to speak to Torvald," Roger said.

"Who's calling, please?"

"This is Roger," Roger said. "We met yesterday over a *trassk*."

There was a slight pause. "Just a minute."

The phone went dead. Caroline counted off ten seconds; and then there was another click. "Hello, Roger," a much deeper voice said. "What can I do for you?"

"Hello, Torvald," Roger said. "I called to see if you could clear up a couple of points I'm confused about."

"Certainly," Torvald said. "What would you like to know?"

"Why do you and the Greens both want Melantha dead?"

There was another pause. "You certainly are a direct one," Torvald said. "I'd be happy to discuss the matter. But in person, not over the phone."

Out of the corner of her eye, Caroline saw Roger smile tightly. "Fine," he said. "How about the bar at the Ritz-Carlton? Central Park South at Sixth Avenue."

There was a soft chuckle. "Across the street from Aleksander's private estate?" Torvald asked dryly. "No, thank you. How about the benches in Police Plaza instead?"

Roger gave a soft snort. "Fine. When?"

"Will an hour from now give you enough time to get there?"

"Sure," Roger said. "See you then."

He broke the connection. "Cute," he said, tucking the phone back into his pocket. "I knew he wouldn't want to go anywhere near Central Park, but I expected him to compromise with someplace as far north as he felt comfortable."

"Which might have told us how far the Grays have penetrated onto Manhattan," Caroline said, nodding her understanding.

"Right," Roger said. "But this doesn't tell us anything at all. With all the cops roaming around Police Plaza, he could probably walk into a Green town meeting and still be safe."

"So are we going to meet him?"

Roger turned and stared out the window. "We could," he said slowly. "Or *we* could try being cute."

"What do you mean?" Caroline asked suspiciously.

"We assume Torvald will soon be on his way to Police Plaza," Roger said, clearly still working it through. "While he's gone, maybe I should drop by his studio and see what I can dig up."

"You can't be serious," Caroline said, her heart tightening in her chest. "What if they catch you?"

"What if they do?" he countered. "Don't forget, as far as Torvald knows we're still holding the trump card. If he wants Melantha, there's not much he can do, no matter what he catches me doing."

Caroline shook her head. This was undoubtedly the craziest idea Roger had ever come up with. Still, she had to admit that it felt good to see her husband taking a more proactive stance for a change. "All right," she said. "But I'm going with you."

"Caroline—"

"You'll need someone to keep watch," she interrupted him. "And if Torvald can't do anything to you, he can't do anything to me, either."

"I suppose," Roger said, a note of resignation in his voice. "Fine. Let's go."

15

They left the art shop and headed back toward Greenwich Avenue. The rain had faded to barely a drizzle, but Roger nevertheless kept the umbrella snugged low over their heads. "You said Torvald's apartment was north of Washington Square?" Caroline asked as they reached Greenwich Avenue and turned southeast.

"Right," Roger confirmed. "We'll go a couple more

blocks, then swing south of the park. That way we'll be able to see if Torvald actually leaves."

A broad-shouldered man in a blue pea coat, his collar turned up against the rain, suddenly stepped out of a doorway in front of them. Roger flinched to his side, nearly throwing Caroline off balance as he broke step. But before he could say or do anything else, the man had taken a pair of quick strides and wrapped a large hand around his upper arm.

Caroline inhaled sharply as a second man, this one wearing a gray jacket with a fleece collar, came up alongside her and closed a hand on her arm as well. Both men, she noticed with a sinking feeling, were short and squat. "Well, well," Roger said grimly. "Caroline, meet my shooting buddies from last night."

Caroline turned as far as she could with her arm pinioned to her side to look at her captor's face. It was wide and almost cheerful looking, but with a strange coolness in his eyes. "You shot at my husband?" she asked him.

"Yeah—sorry about that," he apologized. "But don't forget, he was coming at us with a knife." He looked questioningly at Roger. "You *did* tell her that part, too, didn't you?"

"Save it for later, Ingvar," the man holding Roger's arm said. "Let's just get them out of here."

"Sure," Ingvar said, giving Caroline's arm a gentle nudge toward a narrow side street angling off to their right. "This way."

"Where are you taking us?" Caroline asked, her voice trembling as she took a step that direction.

"They're not taking us anywhere," Roger said, tightening his grip on her other arm. "Stand still, Caroline."

Caroline looked at him in surprise. Resistance from Roger, especially under such circumstances, was the last thing she would have expected.

It was apparently the last thing their captors expected, too. "What do you think you're doing?" Ingvar demanded, sounding more startled than angry.

"We're not leaving this spot," Roger told him flatly. "You

want to say something to us, you say it right here. You want to *do* something to us, let's see how you like doing it in front of fifty witnesses."

The man holding Roger's arm snorted. "Listen, friend—"

"Easy, Bergan," Ingvar soothed him. "Look, Roger, there's no need for dramatics. All Father wants is a little chat."

"Father?" Roger asked, frowning.

"Our father, Halfdan Gray," Ingvar said. "Torvald may have mentioned him."

"No, he didn't," Roger said grimly. "But Melantha did."

"So you *do* still have her," Bergan said. "Good. He'll *definitely* want to talk to you."

"Fine," Roger said. "Bring him here, and we'll talk."

Bergan gave a deep sigh. "I'd have thought you'd have learned your lesson last night," he said, shifting hands where he gripped Roger's arm. He twitched his right wrist—

Caroline stiffened as five lines of silvery liquid shot out from under the sleeve of his blue coat onto his palm, twisting together and settling into a dark gray mallet-like object nestled in his hand. "You remember what getting pounded with a hammergun feels like, right?" Bergan went on, pressing the weapon against Roger's ribs. "You don't want your wife to have to feel it, too, do you?"

"We don't want to hurt you," Ingvar added as something hard pressed against Caroline's side as well. "But as I said, Father wants to talk."

"Okay," Roger said, his voice tight. "Let my wife go, and I'll come with you."

"Sorry, but it's a package deal," Bergan said.

"Come on, let's not make a production of this," Ingvar said reprovingly. "Let's just walk down this street to where we parked our car, then take a nice little ride. Nothing to it."

Roger looked sideways at Caroline. "I don't think we have much choice," she said.

"Yeah, listen to your wife," Bergan said. "Come on, come on—we haven't got all day."

Roger's shoulders sagged slightly in defeat, and with the two Grays still holding their arms they turned onto the side street, their feet kicking up a spray of water. It was a one-way street, Caroline noted, very residential, with the lines of parked cars on both sides leaving only a narrow lane open for traffic. A short block away they reached another small street, this one angling off to the left. "You might as well wait here," Bergan said, letting go of Roger's arm and continuing up their original street. "I have to come back this way anyway."

"Make it fast," Ingvar told him, glancing around.

"Right." Lengthening his stride, Bergan marched off down the sidewalk.

Caroline looked around. There was a café on the corner, but it appeared to be closed. The only moving cars were the ones she could see zipping past back on Greenwich Avenue a block away, and all the apartment windows below the level of their umbrella were blank. Bergan and Ingvar had certainly picked a nice quiet spot for their kidnapping.

"Where exactly did you park?" Roger growled as Bergan disappeared over a slight rise. "New Jersey?"

"We got as close as we could," Ingvar said, nudging Caroline toward the connecting side street. "Let's walk down here a little, shall we?"

This street was also one-way, in the direction they were currently walking, and narrow enough to allow for only one curb's worth of parked cars. Two blocks ahead, Caroline could see the steady traffic of a major street angling across it. "Sorry for the extra exercise," Ingvar apologized. "There was someone sitting in a window back there watching the rain."

"And you'd like there not to be any witnesses," Caroline murmured.

"What we'd *like* is not to be noticed at all," Ingvar countered. "So far, that's not working too well."

"What do you expect?" Roger countered. "You didn't have to kill that old woman, you know."

"That was an accident," Ingvar said, stretching his arm

out and opening his hand. Like a reversed movie, the weapon came apart into silver tendrils and flowed back down his palm to disappear up the sleeve of his gray jacket. "Bergan was just trying to get her to back off. But she'd Shrieked us, and his aim was a little too scrambled."

"So she *is* dead?" Caroline asked, her stomach tight.

"Afraid so," Ingvar conceded. "For whatever it's worth, Father was as mad about it as you probably are."

They had reached the cross-street midway down the two-block length now, and Ingvar brought them to a halt. To their left, Caroline could again see the traffic on Greenwich Avenue, and for a moment she wondered what would happen if she and Roger made a break for it. Would Ingvar chase them, or simply bring out his gun again and shoot them down in cold blood?

"So how does Melantha fit into all this?" Roger asked, turning to face the other.

Ingvar frowned at him. "Velovsky didn't tell you? Figures. I assume that's one of the things Father wants to discu—"

And right in the middle of a word, Roger dropped the umbrella and drove his fist hard into Ingvar's stomach.

Ingvar didn't fall. He didn't even grunt. For all the effect Caroline could see, Roger might as well have hit a three-hundred-pound hanging bag.

She looked at Ingvar's face, fearing the worst. But there was no anger there, only a faintly mocking look of amusement. "Come on, Roger," he admonished. "You can do better than *that*."

Roger was staring at him, his breath coming fast and ragged, his fist opening and closing as if he was gauging his chances of getting the punch to work the next time. "But let's not even try," the Gray added before Roger could make up his mind.

From the corner behind them came the sound of an engine, and a dark blue sedan turned carefully around the parked cars onto their side street. "Where are you taking us?" Caroline asked.

"Brooklyn," Ingvar told her, giving Roger a last appraising look and then turning toward the approaching vehicle. "About half an hour's—"

He broke off as the car suddenly leaped forward, accelerating straight toward them. As Caroline watched, an arm and shoulder came through the driver's side window and leveled another of the gray guns at them.

"Shee!" Ingvar bit out, shoving Roger out of his way toward the line of parked cars. Jumping toward the sidewalk on the opposite side of the street, he twisted his wrist and snapped his own gun back into his hand.

But he was too late. Even as he brought the weapon to bear, a white line shot out from the driver's hand and landed squarely in the center of his chest.

Roger's desperate punch hadn't even rocked Ingvar back on his heels. The white line hurled him three feet backward to sprawl onto the pavement. He rolled up onto his side, twisting his wrist over again—

"Come on!" Roger's voice snapped in Caroline's ear. Before she could even turn around, he had grabbed her wrist and was dragging her between the parked cars and down the cross-street toward Greenwich Avenue. It took two staggering steps for her to catch up to his stride; and then they were sprinting together down the sidewalk. Caroline heard the sudden change in engine noise as the car behind them shot past their cross-street and kept going.

No one stopped them or shot at them. A taut half minute later, they emerged onto the avenue.

"Wait," Caroline gasped as Roger turned them to the right and slowed to a fast walk. "What about Ingvar?"

"What about him?"

"Did whoever was in that car run him down?" Caroline clarified. "We can't just leave him back there."

"He'd probably have left *us* there."

"You don't know that."

Roger hissed an annoyed sigh. "We'll go over to St. Vincent," he said, pointing to the hospital across the street. "There are bound to be some cops there. They can go check it out."

"I suppose that'll—" Caroline broke off, jumping as a vehicle suddenly squealed to a halt at the curb beside them.

She spun toward it, expecting to see the blue car with Bergan glaring at her through the windshield. To her relief, it was only a taxi. "Cab?" the driver shouted out the window at them.

"No, thanks," Roger said.

"Actually," a soft voice said from behind Caroline, "you should."

Carefully, Caroline turned. But again it wasn't Bergan. Instead, it was a pair of slender young men with black hair and eyes and dark, Mediterranean features.

And long, slender knives held inside their open coats.

"Oh, no," she murmured.

"Get in," the Green ordered. His voice was still quiet, still civilized, almost pleasant.

Caroline looked at Roger. He nodded, his posture drained of all its earlier energy. Too many shocks, she realized, coming too quickly on each other's heels.

Silently, she slid into the backseat. The driver, she saw now to her complete lack of surprise, also had black hair and olive skin.

Roger climbed in after her, one of the Greens getting in beside him as the other Green took the front passenger seat. "Just sit back and relax," the driver said over his shoulder as he pulled away from the curb. "It's a nice day for a drive."

16

"So," Fierenzo murmured aloud, parking his fists on his hips as he stood by the iron fence at the mouth of the alley. "This is the place."

There was no answer. Not that he'd expected one, of

course. Aside from the usual assortment of trash, the alley where the Whittiers claimed to have been accosted was pretty much empty.

For a minute he gazed over the fence, taking it all in. Alleys were alleys, as far as he was concerned, but this one at least had the virtue of an interesting layout. Three different buildings faced into it, with a six-foot concrete wall along the right cutting off a small courtyard that didn't seem to serve any purpose he could see. A door led from the courtyard into the building on that side, a door the Whittiers' mugger might have found useful if he'd been able to get over the wall.

Of course, if he'd gotten up on the wall, he could just as easily have gone up the fire escape at the back end. Alternatively, he might have made it up the concrete steps beyond the fire escape, gone across the platform that filled the back quarter of the alley, and climbed over the chain-link fence at the far end. Whittier claimed he'd only turned his back for a second, but Fierenzo knew how unreliable witnesses were at judging times and distances.

One thing that *was* certain was that this whole thing was becoming as frustrating as hell. On the one hand, he had the Whittiers and their wild story, which sounded almost plausible until you started poking at its various corners. On the other hand, he had a collection of equally improbable stories from such diverse sources as the Whittiers' building manager and the cops who broke up whatever the hell was happening in Yorkville last night. On the third hand, he had his own observations, ranging from the strange marks on the Whittiers' trees to whatever had made him drive his car up the side of a lamppost this morning.

And on the fourth hand, he had not a single shred of tangible evidence to tie any of it together.

He shifted his attention to the fence in front of him. The lock on the gate was good and solid, and looked new. A key type, too, which meant it could be picked by someone who knew what he was doing.

"Can I help you?" a deep but courteous voice called.

Fierenzo looked up. A smallish woman was standing on the landing just outside the building to the right, half hidden behind a large black man with the word "Security" embroidered on his shirt. "Yes," Fierenzo told him, digging his badge wallet out of his pocket and holding it up for the other's inspection. "You have the key to this gate?"

"Yes, sir," the security guard said.

"I'd like to take a look inside," Fierenzo told him. "Tell me, how new is this lock?"

"I put it on Thursday morning," the guard said, pulling a key ring out of his pocket as he came down the steps.

The morning after the Whittiers had allegedly found the gate standing wide open. "What happened to the old one?"

"Someone broke it," the guard said. "Looked like they took a sledge hammer or something to it."

"Did you keep it?"

The other shook his head. "May I ask what you're looking for?"

"Evidence of a possible crime," Fierenzo told him. "Do you mind if I go inside?"

The guard's lips puckered. He'd undoubtedly been carefully drilled in the laws regarding building searches and when and where warrants were and weren't needed. But he'd probably never had anyone ask to inspect his alley before. "You can come in with me if you want," Fierenzo added, trying to smooth over his uncertainty.

"No, I need to get back," the other said, reaching down and unlocking the gate. "Can I trust you not to try opening any of the windows or doors?"

"Scout's honor," Fierenzo assured him. "If there's anything at all, it'll be out here."

"All right," the guard said, pulling open the gate. "I'll be inside if you need me."

"Thanks," Fierenzo said. "By the way, anything unusual happen Wednesday night besides the broken lock?"

The guard shrugged. "I wasn't on duty then, but the night man didn't say anything the next morning. I can get you his name if you want."

"Not just yet, thanks," Fierenzo said. "I'll let you know if I need him."

"Okay," the other said. "Lock up when you're done, please." Turning, he lumbered up the steps, and he and the woman went back inside.

Fierenzo spent the first minute in a low crouch, examining the area around the lock. The lad with the sledge hammer, he decided, had been remarkably accurate. There was a fresh-looking indentation where the previous lock might have been shoved into the metal behind it, but aside from that there didn't seem to be any damage to the gate itself. Straightening up, he went inside, his eyes fixed on the sloping pavement beneath his feet, and walked back to the stone steps.

Nothing.

He walked the route again, eyes tracking slowly back and forth, covering every inch of the ground. But if there had ever been anything there, the morning's drizzle had apparently obliterated it. He finished back at the gate, then retraced his path one more time down to the bottom of the slope and the black metal fire escape zigzagging its way upward.

He stopped beneath it, shading his eyes against the mist still drifting out of the sky and trying to recall everything the Whittiers had said. They had been accosted on Broadway by a short, wide man with a hacking cough who had stuck a .45 Colt in their faces. He'd brought them here, shown them a girl named Melantha, and told them to take care of her. He'd then handed Whittier the gun and staggered away toward the rear of the alley, disappearing the moment Whittier's back was turned.

And sometime along in there, the dimmed-out streetlights had come back on.

Fierenzo frowned, his thoughts flicking back to when he'd left Broadway and started down 101st Street fifteen minutes ago. He'd been preoccupied at the time with locating the alley; but he vaguely remembered seeing that half a block north . . .

He left the alley and walked back to Broadway. There it was: a ConEd cherry picker with someone in the basket working on one of the streetlights.

The crew foreman standing beside the truck turned a New York glare his direction as Fierenzo walked up. "You want something?" he asked in a pronounced Brooklyn accent and a tone that made the question a challenge.

"Just a little information," Fierenzo said, holding up his badge. "What's wrong with the lights?"

"Now? Nothing," the foreman said, the glare softening a little. "But we got a bunch of complaints Wednesday night from here down to 86th that something was screwy with them."

"What time was this?"

The foreman shrugged. "Ten, eleven o'clock. Something like that."

Roughly the same time the Whittiers claimed they'd seen the streetlights go dim, then come back on. "And you're just getting on this now?"

"Hey, like I said, there's nothing wrong with 'em," the other protested, the attitude starting to come back. "Anyway, it took us the last two days to clean up the mess over on Riverside Drive."

"Yes—the big power outage," Fierenzo said, nodding. "That was Wednesday night, too, wasn't it?"

"Yeah." The foreman shook his head. "Hell of a thing. The people up there said the lights went dim, then a couple seconds later blew up like a six-block fireworks show."

"And what do *you* say?"

"What do you mean, what do I say?" the other retorted. "They blew up, all right. Dim, I don't know about."

"What caused it?"

"Damned if I know that, either," the foreman said. "It was like something overloaded 'em, only there wasn't any sign of something that coulda done that. Mostly, we just checked the cables and brought in a spitload of new bulbs."

"'Spitload'?"

The foreman shrugged. "The wife wants me to cut back on the language. The kids are starting to pick it up."

"Mm," Fierenzo said. "Thanks."

He turned and went back to 101st. So there was some marginal confirmation to at least part of the Whittiers' story. Unfortunately, it was once again purely anecdotal. If the Whittiers had been up on Riverside Drive, at least they'd have some blown-out bulbs they could point to. Here on Broadway, there wasn't even that much.

He reached the alley and once again headed down the slope. All right. Whittier had said he'd seen what looked like blood on the gun when the mugger handed it over. An injury might explain the staggering he'd also reported; and if the wound was in the man's chest, it could also explain the wet-sounding cough.

But if he was bleeding on the gun, maybe he'd bled on the ground, too. Bending low, his eyes panning back and forth across the dirty pavement, Fierenzo went slowly down the alley one more time, wishing he'd thought to bring a Luminol kit with him.

He reached the stone steps without spotting anything. The man's clothing had probably absorbed most of the leaking blood, at least long enough for him to get out of the alley.

He straightened up, wincing at a sudden kink in his back. Time to cut his losses and get back to the more promising thread of the investigation. By now Powell should have tracked down the cab the Whittiers had blown out of Yorkville in this morning and gotten their destination. Turning around, he glanced one last time up at the building beside him.

And froze. There, on the wall, was a faint patch of darkness on the brick, like the mark left by a man with a blood-saturated shirt who had pressed tightly to the wall trying not to be seen.

Only the spot was eight feet up.

Fierenzo stepped back from the wall, shading his eyes against the drizzle. There were more of the stains, smaller than the first and more smeared out, as if the bleeder had been moving up and sideways along the wall.

He swore gently under his breath. Finally, some tangible evidence. Unfortunately, it made no sense. If the mugger had had a block and tackle setup on the rooftop for a quick getaway, why bother going sideways along the wall? Why bother hugging the wall at all, for that matter? And Whittier's own testimony said the streetlights had been back on by then. How could he possibly have missed seeing someone pressed against a wall twenty feet away?

But logical or not, the evidence trail itself was clear. Assuming the dark stains were indeed blood that had managed to survive the rain, the man had definitely been moving up and sideways along the wall.

Heading straight for the fire escape.

The wall blocking off the tiny courtyard was a good six feet high, and it had been years since his academy days when Fierenzo had routinely had to climb such things. But he wasn't as out of shape as he'd feared, and he made it to the top with a minimum of sweating and hardly any cursing at all. From there it was a simple matter of hauling himself up onto the fire escape.

There were no bloodstains on the bottom two landings. But then, he hadn't expected there to be. The pattern on the wall had been angling upward, toward the third or possibly the fourth of the seven landings.

He found the expected stain on the third-floor railing: a small one, wrapped halfway around the bar as if the bleeder had barely had the strength to pull himself up and roll over onto the landing. For a moment Fierenzo studied the mark, then crouched down to examine the grating that made up the landing's floor.

He was still searching for bloodstains when he heard a faint noise from above him.

He looked up. There was nothing on the next landing, and the interference between the grating meshes made it impossible to see anything higher than that. But he had definitely heard something. Moving as quietly as he could on the metal steps, he continued up.

He had passed the fourth landing and was halfway to the fifth when the noise came again. This time it was loud enough for him to identify as a suppressed cough.

For a few seconds he stood still, thoughts of desperate men and shoot-outs flashing through his mind, wondering if it was time to call for backup. But then the cough came again: and this time, he could hear an edge of pain or fatigue to it.

And if he couldn't handle a lone, injured man who'd been out in the cold for three nights, he had no business being a cop in this city. Checking to make sure his Glock 9mm was riding loose in its shoulder holster, he continued up.

There was no one on the fifth landing, or the sixth. He was on his way to the seventh and final landing when he heard the cough again.

Only this time it had come from *below* him.

He looked down. The fire escape was bars and metal mesh, without a single shred of cover anywhere on it. And yet, unless the mugger was also a ventriloquist, Fierenzo had somehow walked right past him.

He was back on the fifth landing, looking for something—anything—out of the ordinary, when something like a movement at the building side of the landing caught the corner of his eye.

He looked quickly in that direction, but there was nothing there but more mesh and wall. He was staring at the spot when the movement came again, a subtle rippling in the pattern of the building's brickwork. His eyes seemed to refocus themselves. . . .

And there, tucked into the angle between the mesh and the wall was a vague, half-curled-up outline of a human being.

He had no memory later of having drawn his gun, but suddenly it was in his hand. "Freeze!" he snapped at the outline, wondering fleetingly if this was what it was like to go insane. "Police. Let me see your hands."

For a handful of seconds nothing happened, the pause giving Fierenzo time to notice both the irony and the absurdity of his standard cop's command. *Show me your hands, he said to the invisible man.* . . . The outline quivered with another cough; and then, like a window curtain being pulled back, the image hardened and solidified.

And there on the landing lay a short, stocky young man, curled around himself against the cold, gazing at Fierenzo with half-hooded blue eyes. His shirt beneath a thin jacket was stained dark with dried blood. "Who are you?" he asked hoarsely.

It took Fierenzo two tries to find his voice. "Detective Sergeant Thomas Fierenzo, NYPD," he said, squatting down beside the man. "Who are *you*?"

The man's eyes dropped to the gun in Fierenzo's hand, and he smiled weakly. "You won't need that," he said.

"Probably not," Fierenzo agreed, slipping the weapon back into its holster. Judging from the man's drawn face and half-closed eyes it was clear he wasn't in any shape for a fight. More importantly, both his hands were in sight and empty. "What's your name?"

The man took a careful breath, as if still uncertain of the state of his lungs. "Jonah," he said. "Who are you working for?"

"I already told you," Fierenzo said. "The police."

"I mean who are you *really* working for?" Jonah asked, his face hardening. "Cyril, or Aleksander?"

"My boss is Lieutenant Cerreta, 24th Precinct," Fierenzo said stiffly. "If you're implying—wait a second," he interrupted himself as his numbed brain began to catch the rails again. "Cyril? As in . . . *Cyril?*"

For a moment Jonah stared at him with an expression that made Fierenzo wonder if he ought to rethink the man's threat potential. Then the look faded, and the eyelids half-lowered again. "You're not with them," he said, breathing hard as if the simple act of giving Fierenzo a hard stare had worn him out. "But you *do* know them?"

"By reputation only." Fierenzo cocked an eyebrow. "I haven't met Melantha yet, either."

He'd hoped dropping the girl's name would spark a reaction. He hadn't been prepared for quite the reaction he got. Jonah's eyes snapped fully open, his throat suddenly tight. "Where is she?" he demanded, his right hand groping to a grip on the lapel of Fierenzo's coat.

"None of that," Fierenzo warned, grabbing the other's hand and starting to pry the fingers away. Jonah's left hand lifted—

And to his astonishment, Fierenzo found himself looking down the muzzle of the strangest-looking gun he'd ever seen.

"Take it easy," he said quickly, abandoning his efforts to pry Jonah's hand away from his coat. "I already said I haven't met her. I don't know where she is, either."

For a moment Jonah didn't move. His weapon, Fierenzo noted distantly, looked more like an elaborately carved judge's gavel with flattened sides and a shortened grip than a real handgun. But there was no mistaking the purpose of the small hole pointing at the detective's face.

And then, to his relief, Jonah's right fingers loosened their grip on his coat, the hand falling limply onto the landing. "She has to be all right," he murmured. His gun-hand wavered away from the detective's face, opening as he let go of his gun.

Fierenzo was ready, darting his hand down to catch the weapon before it fell onto the landing. But his hand caught nothing but empty air. "I'm sure she is," he said absently, his eyes searching vainly for the gun. Still, with appearing and disappearing men, what was the big deal about appearing and disappearing guns? "Right now, we have to get you to a hospital."

"No!" Jonah insisted, grabbing weakly at Fierenzo's hand as he reached for his cell phone. "No hospital. If you take me there, they'll find me."

"We can put you under police protection," Fierenzo assured him. "You'll be perfectly safe."

"Aleksander will walk right past them," Jonah said wearily. "He'll ask nicely, and just walk on past."

Fierenzo opened his mouth . . . closed it again. Cyril had walked past the doorman and super in the Whittiers' building simply by asking. Did Jonah think cops would behave the same way if Aleksander showed up and also asked nicely? Apparently, he did.

And he might be right. "You still need medical attention," he said.

Jonah shook his head. "All I need is food and rest."

"What, from *that*?" Fierenzo countered, gesturing to the blood-encrusted shirt.

"It happened Wednesday night," Jonah said. "If it was that bad, I should already be dead."

He had a point, Fierenzo had to admit. "I'll make you a deal," he said. "If you can get down the fire escape without bleeding, blacking out, or coughing up blood, I'll take you somewhere besides a hospital. Otherwise, it's straight to St. Luke's. Agreed?"

Jonah gazed at the detective a moment, as if weighing the other's trustworthiness, then nodded. "Agreed."

"Good," Fierenzo said, straightening up and extending a hand. "Let's get you out of the cold."

Jonah was built like a wrestler, and felt like he weighed as much as two of them. Fortunately, once Fierenzo got him on his feet he was mostly able to navigate on his own. They made it down the fire escape, and Fierenzo left him in the alley while he retrieved his car.

"Where are we going?" Jonah asked when they were finally on their way.

"My apartment near Lincoln Center," Fierenzo told him. "My family's visiting relatives in Illinois, so it'll just be the two of us."

"Sounds good," Jonah said. Already his breathing sounded better, Fierenzo decided. At the same time, he seemed considerably sleepier than he had on the fire escape.

And in fact, before they even hit the next street, he was snoring away.

Fierenzo grimaced. Lieutenant Cerreta, he suspected, would have a world-class fit when he found out about this. But if it finally gave Fierenzo a handle on the case, it would be worth it.

In the meantime, he still had the Whittiers to deal with. With a little luck, maybe he would have their set of puzzle pieces in hand by the time Jonah was ready to give up his.

And with a little *more* luck, maybe the two sets would actually fit together.

Fishing out his cell phone, he popped it open. Time to check Powell's progress with the Whittiers' cab.

17

Even before the cab made it to the eastern edge of Manhattan, the drizzle began to taper off. By the time they reached the FDR and turned northward, Roger could see a little blue sky starting to peek through the clouds in the west. Just as the Green had predicted, it was turning into a nice day for a drive.

Not that either of their passengers was in the mood to appreciate it. Caroline hadn't said a word since they'd driven off, and every time Roger looked her direction he found her face turned slightly away from him as she gazed out the window. She *was* holding his hand, nestled there in her lap. But the fingers were stiff and cold, and he knew that only part of that was from fear and uncertainty.

The rest was undoubtedly anger . . . and it wasn't hard to guess where the slow burn was coming from. *Wimp* was certainly one of the words bouncing around her skull. *Coward* was probably in there, too.

He couldn't really blame her.

His first thought as they got on the FDR was that they

were being taken back to the Youngs' apartment and the site of Melantha's latest disappearance. But the cab passed the turnoff without even slowing down. His next guess was that they were being taken to Central Park West. But they passed the likely turnoffs for that, too.

He had just started to wonder if they were being taken off the island entirely when the driver turned off onto 116th and headed west across East Harlem. They passed through that neighborhood, through Harlem itself, and finally came to a stop at Morningside Park.

"End of the line," the Green beside Roger announced as he opened the door and climbed out. "Come on, come on."

Silently, Roger obeyed, offering Caroline a hand as she slid across the seat to the door. The Green in the passenger seat had gotten out, too, and gestured into the park. "This way," he said.

"Where are we going?" Roger asked, looking around.

"There," the Green said, pointing up the slope to the tall stone wall towering above them. "Columbia University."

"Why don't we just drive around to the other side?" Roger asked, a shiver running through him as he looked up. Columbia University, home to the Miller Theater, where he and Caroline had been just before they'd met Melantha. Coincidence?

"Because it's more anonymous this way," the Green said. "Besides, you look like you can use the exercise. Let's go."

It was a long way up from the park to the university, and even with the various sections of more or less level ground interspersed with the stairs Roger's leg muscles were starting to complain by the time they reached the top. The two Greens took them a short way down the street, through an open gate into a small brick-and-pavement courtyard, then down another short walkway to a building identifying itself as the Faculty House. Another Green was waiting, and opened the door as they walked up. "President's Room," he told their escort as they filed through. "Second floor."

They arrived at the President's Room to find a single occupant waiting at one of the round tables by the windows, an older man with a lined face and patches of silver twisting through his otherwise black hair. "Roger and Caroline Whittier," he greeted them, rising from his chair as they approached. He was dressed in a white turtleneck, black slacks, and a green blazer with a tapering filigree of muted copper pinned to the left lapel. "Please; sit down."

Roger took the chair across from him, giving the other a quick study. Despite the wrinkles and patches of silver hair, he had the same sort of grace and dignity that Roger had noticed earlier in Sylvia.

"I'm glad you could come here today," he commented as Caroline sat down at Roger's left. "My name is Nikolos Green."

"Ah," Roger said, nodding. "The Command-Tactician."

"And Leader Elymas's son," Caroline added quietly. "You're a well-preserved octogenarian."

"Thank you," Nikolos said, smiling wryly as he reseated himself. "Though to be fair, Greens don't age quite the same way as Humans do."

He looked over at the other two Greens. "You're dismissed," he said.

"Yes, Commander," one of them acknowledged. Together they crossed the dining room and left.

"Nice quiet place you have here," Roger commented. "According to the sign downstairs, it's only open on weekdays."

Nikolos shrugged. "I have certain privileges."

"Do those privileges include kidnapping and assault with a deadly weapon?" Roger countered.

Nikolos lifted his eyebrows. "Kidnapping? Come now. You were invited to visit me, and you accepted."

"And the knives those invitations were engraved on?"

"Knives?" Nikolos asked, looking politely puzzled. "No, no. I'm sure all you saw was a *trassk*." He reached up and unfastened the pin from his lapel. "Like this one."

"It was nothing like that," Roger growled, starting to feel annoyed at this childish game.

"Perhaps it was the lighting." Nikolos turned the pin over in his left hand, the copper filaments catching the light from the windows, and for a moment he stroked it meditatively with the fingertips of his right. Then he closed his right hand over the pin, squeezed it and slid his hand away toward Roger—

Roger caught his breath. The pin had vanished. In its place, stretched across Nikolos's open left palm, was a long, slender knife. "You can see what sort of tricks lighting can play on your eyes," Nikolos said. He closed his right hand over the knife again, pushing the point of the blade back toward the hilt as if collapsing a telescope. "It can make you think you've seen something that can't possibly be there."

He squeezed his right hand a few times as if kneading bread dough; and when he lifted it away again the knife had been replaced by a small, copper-colored replica of the Statue of Liberty. "Very nice," Roger commented. "May I?"

"Of course." Leaning forward, Nikolos handed the statue across the table.

Roger looked closely at it. The statue seemed perfectly solid, perfectly ordinary, the sort of trinket sold by the thousands in Times Square souvenir shops. It was about the same weight as the gun the mugger had given him Wednesday night, he decided, and approximately the same weight as the *trassk* he was still carrying in his pocket. "Impressive," he said, handing the statue to Caroline.

Nikolos shrugged. "A parlor trick," he said, his voice sounding oddly sad. "Useful enough, but little more than a memory of happier times."

"How do you work it?" Caroline asked, turning the statue over in her hand. "Is this one of the Gifts?"

"No, any Green can manipulate a *trassk*," Nikolos said. "And *only* Greens, of course. We can make it into anything we can visualize, consistent with its mass. Still, the metal is very strong, and like gold can be stretched almost infinitely thin."

He held out his hand, and she returned the statue to him. Again he kneaded it, then pulled it outward into a disk the size of a dinner plate. "As you see, it looks much bigger than should be possible, considering its original size," he said, holding it up. "What you don't see is how thin the metal has become in order to stretch this far."

He banged the disk gently on the table. "Yet even now it's strong enough to easily maintain its shape. It can also be made flexible or even completely elastic." He manipulated it again, turning it into a giant rubber band. "Like so," he said, stretching it nearly to arms' length before letting it collapse again.

"How long will it stay that way?" Caroline asked.

"Left on its own, it reverts in anywhere from a few minutes to a few hours, depending on how solidly its owner fixed it," Nikolos told her. "Obviously, a Green can alter it before then if he or she chooses."

"The multitool every well-dressed Green is wearing this season," Roger murmured.

"Once, that was literally true," Nikolos said. "But not anymore. We collected all the *trassks* we could before we fled our homeland, but our numbers have long since outstripped our meager supply. Nowadays, there are only enough for our Warriors and a few of our top people."

"Melantha had one," Caroline pointed out.

"A special dispensation for a special occasion," Nikolos said. "That particular *trassk* had once been my mother's." His lips compressed briefly. "She was killed in the war, before we came here."

"I'm sorry," Caroline murmured.

"Why don't you make more of them?" Roger asked. "Did you forget how?"

"You can't forget what you never knew," Nikolos said ruefully. "The truth is, the *trassks* were made and given to us a long time ago . . . by the Grays."

Roger blinked. "The *Grays?*"

"Back when we lived together in peace and harmony." Nikolos placed his hands on opposite sides of the coppery rubber band and squeezed, and the *trassk* returned to its original shape. "As I said, memories of happier times."

"What happened?" Caroline asked.

"We met largely by accident," Nikolos said, his eyes taking on a faraway look as he refastened the brooch onto his lapel. "Both of our peoples were fleeing from conflicts with the Others, the ones who dominated our world. The Greens had been migrating northward, the Grays coming south, and we met in a place we always referred to simply as the Great Valley."

He shook his head. "You never saw such a place," he said quietly. "A swift-flowing river cut through the ground at the base of a line of bluffs rising from the riverbed. Hundreds of Gray families moved in there. On the other side of the river, a vast forest stretched across the rolling ground, eventually rising to a line of craggy mountains where the Grays set up a second colony. The forest itself went on for miles, filling the area between the ranges, with enough room for generations of Greens to come. The approaches were difficult to traverse, and lay a considerable distance from the Others' trade routes. We had every expectation that we could live there for a long time in peace."

He stroked his *trassk*. "The Grays made little toys like this for us—they were cunning toolmakers, skilled beyond the capabilities of even our best Creators and Manipulators. In return, we used our Gifts to work with nature in ways their metalsmithing skills couldn't match. Our Manipulators and Laborers created gardens and specialized tree forms for them, while our Farseers located game and hidden fish schools for them to hunt. In many cases, our Lifesingers could also heal them of illnesses or injuries."

"I'm still unclear as to how these Gifts work," Roger said.

"There are only a few basic ones, which can mix together in different ways," Nikolos said. "The Higher Gifts, also called Mind Worker Gifts, are those of Visionary, Persuader, Pastsinger, Lifesinger, Command-Tactician, and Groundshaker. There are distinctions according to strength: a Farseer is a less focused Visionary, while a Farspeaker is a less powerful Persuader. A Leader, on the other hand, is the rare person who combines both the Visionary and Persuader Gifts. Overall, about one in eight of our people are Mind Workers."

"And the rest?" Roger asked.

"They're called Arm Workers," Nikolos said. "Creators have a smaller degree of the Visionary Gift than that possessed by Visionaries or Farseers, while Manipulators are less powerful Groundshakers. Most of the rest possess the Gifts of strength and stamina and dexterity that permit them to work as Laborers. Overall, they make up between half and two-thirds of our population."

"And the Warriors?" Caroline asked.

"They have the same Gifts of stamina and strength as the Laborers, but with extra measures of speed and agility," Nikolos said. "They also have considerably more power and control of the Shriek."

"And you know in advance which of these categories each child is going to fit into?" Caroline asked.

Nikolos eyed her. "You disapprove?"

"I find it hard to believe a Green has so little control over his or her life," Caroline said, taking his gaze without flinching.

"I'm sure you do," Nikolos agreed calmly. "But we're not like you, Caroline. The Gifts aren't like Human talents for art or spelling or mechanics, something that can be used or ignored as the owner chooses. They're something we're born with, like the color of our eyes and the texture of our skin. At the age of twelve, each child sits down with Leader or Visionary and is put through the series of tests that formally identifies his or her Gift. That gives the child three years to learn the responsibilities and potentials of that Gift before assuming the full mantle of adulthood."

Caroline's lip twitched. "It doesn't seem fair."

"In some ways, it isn't," Nikolos conceded. "And I admit there have been times I've envied you Humans your ability to choose your own destiny, despite the handicap of having to spend weary years learning a skill which to us comes naturally." He shrugged. "But we are what we are, whether Human or Green. All we can do is accept it and move on."

"Perhaps," Caroline said, her voice carefully neutral. "How long did you live in the Great Valley?"

"I don't know the exact number of years," Nikolos said. "I do know that my father's grandfather told him of the journey northward, and of their first contact with the Grays."

"So about three generations," Roger said, relieved to be back to a less contentious topic. "Did you see this Great Valley yourself?"

"Of course," Caroline said before Nikolos could answer. "Velovsky said Elymas and his son were both there when they arrived at Ellis Island, remember?"

"That's correct," Nikolos said. "I saw the Great Valley at the very end of the good times, and at the very beginning of the bad."

"How did the war start?" Caroline asked.

"With a simple disagreement," Nikolos said, shaking his head. "Don't most things start that way? The Grays were running low on some of their metals and wanted to expand their mining operations downriver. Our Leaders pointed out that the Others had gradually been settling closer to that end of the Great Valley and that the noise of mining might lead them to us. We suggested instead that the Grays send an expedition into the outside world and purchase the metals from the Others."

"What didn't the Grays like about that?" Roger asked.

"They said the Others thought we were all dead, and that appearing in the open would bring them down on us even faster than the sounds of mining would." Nikolos snorted under his breath. "I don't know what they did to the Others they lived among before they fled from their original homes, but knowing their rough behavior and lack of discipline I can think of several reasons they might be concerned about being found. At any rate, they made it clear they would oppose any attempt by anyone, Green *or* Gray, to reestablish contact with the Others."

"Who exactly were these Others?" Roger asked.

Nikolos shrugged. "I never actually met one, of course, but the Pastsinger memories record a people very similar in appearance to you or I. Some Greens even speculated they were an actual, physical cross between Greens and Grays, since they built with stone and metal like the Grays but also cultivated the soil and used wood from trees as we ourselves did." He waved a hand. "A completely ridiculous theory, of course, given the vast differences between Green and Gray physiology. But culturally and artistically, at least, it's fair to say the Others stood midway between our peoples."

"So which way did the decision go about the metals?" Roger asked.

"We never made it that far," Nikolos said grimly. "One night, when all were asleep, some of the Grays from the Eastcliffs slipped across the river and set fire to our end of the forest."

Caroline inhaled sharply. "No," she breathed.

"Yes," Nikolos said. His eyes were closed now, his forehead pinched. "You can't imagine what it was like," he said in a low voice. "Panicked children in their trees, their parents struggling to get them out as the fire burned all around them. Other adults and children running frantically across a carpet of burning leaves, trying to reach the safety of the river."

His eyes opened, a black fire burning suddenly within them. "And all the while, the whistle of Gray hammerguns as they fired volley after volley into the forest at us."

"What about your Warriors?" Roger asked. "Didn't they fight back?"

Nikolos smiled bitterly. "Of course they did. But sitting across the river midway up their cliffs, the Grays were too far away to be affected by the Shriek. The archers could find no target in the darkness, and the Warriors couldn't climb up to engage them hand to hand. In desperation, our Leaders summoned the Groundshakers and ordered them to bring down the cliffs."

"What do you mean, bring down the cliffs?" Roger asked carefully.

"Exactly what I said," Nikolos told him. "As the Grays had used our dependence on trees against us, so we now used the stone and rock they loved against them."

The skin on the back of Roger's neck began to tingle. "Are you saying they created an *earthquake?*"

"The Greens are a people of great strength," Nikolos said, the anger in his voice momentarily eclipsed by pride. "As moral authority lies with the Leaders and Visionaries, so physical power rests with the Groundshakers."

"But you said there were Gray families on those cliffs," Caroline protested. "Women and children."

"Did they care about *our* women and children when they set fire to our forest?" Nikolos snapped. He broke off, passing a hand in front of his eyes. "I'm sorry," he said, his voice more subdued. "Of course we regretted the deaths of innocents. But we had no choice. The Grays were still firing, shattering our trees all around us, and we had to protect our own. The only way to stop them was to bring down their cliffs."

He closed his eyes again. "The Grays continued to fire as the rock began to splinter around them, now specifically targeting the Groundshakers. But they were too late. The Eastcliffs broke and fell, and their attack was finally ended."

"Yes," Roger murmured. "But there was still the Gray colony on the other side of the Great Valley."

"A much larger colony, too," Nikolos agreed quietly. "By the time the morning light began to struggle through the smoke rising from our ruined trees, the war had begun in earnest. In the space of a few days it had spread to the entire Great Valley."

He shook his head sadly. "And within a handful of months, it was clear there was no hope. The Great Valley we'd loved had become a killing ground: thousands of us dead, thousands of our trees burned or shattered into splinters. Many thousands of our enemies were dead too, of course. But if we continued as we were, the only end could be the mutual destruction of both our peoples."

"Which is where Velovsky's story picks up," Roger said as understanding struck him. "Your Leaders decided to leave."

"They decided to save a remnant," Nikolos corrected. "Sixty of us were selected, representing most of the Gifts, with my father chosen to lead them. The Farseers had located a new home, and a vehicle was constructed to take us there. The remaining Groundshakers and Manipulators joined their strength together beneath the guidance of the Visionaries; and in the beat of a hummingbird's wing we were here."

His eyes drifted to the tall windows. "It was a strange world, noisy and dirty, full of people whose speech we couldn't understand," he said in a low voice. "But all we could see was the fact that the terrible war with the Grays was over, and that at last we were safe."

Roger snorted gently. "And so, of course, eleven years later Adolf Hitler would touch off the worst war *our* world had ever known."

Nikolos smiled. "The universe does have a sense of irony."

"Did your people fight in that war?" Caroline asked.

"Not in that one, or in any since," Nikolos told her. "I'm sure you realize that allowing military doctors to examine us would be a disaster. No, our Persuaders kept us out of the army, while we found other ways to serve our adopted country."

"In war factories?" Roger asked.

"Many of our Arm Workers did so, yes," Nikolos said, nodding. "Others found more creative ways. Have you ever heard about the German sabotage team who slipped ashore from a U-boat on Long Island in June of 1942?"

Caroline shook her head. "No."

"Actually, I think I have," Roger said, frowning as he searched his memory. "Didn't they run straight into a soldier patrolling the beach?"

"A Coast Guardsman, actually," Nikolos corrected. "A young man, only twenty-one, alone and in heavy fog. But instead of killing him and moving on, the saboteurs tried to bribe him, then simply let him go. Historians generally put it down to their reluctance to kill someone so young in cold blood."

"But you have a different theory?" Roger suggested.

"We know the truth," Nikolos said. "Our Warriors were

patrolling the New York coastal areas, including Long Island, watching for precisely this sort of thing. The one who detected this particular group was close enough to a Persuader to call her in. She manipulated them into letting the young man go."

His lips twitched a smile. "She also persuaded one of the saboteurs to give himself up a week later, after the efforts by the Coast Guard, Naval Intelligence, and the FBI had come up empty."

A stray memory popped into Roger's mind: Stavros, at the Green apartment building near Central Park, opening doors without bothering to knock, as if he already had permission to enter. "I presume the Warrior didn't need a radio to call in the Persuader?"

"We can communicate with each other over short distances, yes," Nikolos confirmed. "For most of us, the range is no more than the length of a city block. Those with the particular Gift of Farspeaking are stronger, able to send and receive thoughts over much greater distances."

He smiled faintly. "We can't read Human minds, either, in case you were wondering."

"But you can talk *to* our minds," Caroline spoke up. "The Greens who came to our apartment yesterday afternoon were calling to me."

Nikolos made a face. "That would have been Cyril," he said. "Only a Persuader or Farspeaker would have the strength to send a message to a Human."

"Or to talk our super into unlocking our apartment," Roger put in. "How did he find us, anyway?"

"We'd seen a Gray searching that area the previous night, and guessed that they knew something we didn't," Nikolos said. "When Cyril got your name from Sylvia, he took it upon himself to check out all the Roger Wh-somethings in the area."

He looked at Caroline. "Once he learned *your* name, Caroline, he apparently decided to try to contact you."

"And to see if he could get Melantha back directly?" Caroline asked.

Nikolos hesitated. "Like all the rest of us, Cyril uses his Gift only for what he thinks best for our people."

"And how exactly does killing Melantha fit in with that noble goal?" Roger asked, folding his arms across his chest. "So far everyone we've met has done a tap dance around that question."

"I'm far too old to dance," Nikolos said tiredly. "The fact is that she was an unexpected surprise, a Gift that shouldn't have appeared until our population was at least twice the size it is now."

He sighed. "Melantha, you see," he said, "is a Ground-shaker."

18

Something hard and cold settled into the pit of Caroline's stomach. That couldn't be right. Not the fragile young girl with bruises on her throat whom she'd helped carry to their apartment. Not the girl she'd played cards with, and fed eggs and cheese to, and dressed in her own clothes. Not the girl who'd sobbed on her shoulder in misery and grief and loneliness.

But even as the reflexive denial rose in her throat, another, darker image flashed through her mind. Melantha, no longer young or fragile, standing tall and strong in the courtyard last night, unflinching as the old woman's scream washed over her and sending back a terrible, defiant scream of her own.

A scream that had sent the ground heaving beneath Caroline like a stung horse.

"That's crazy," Roger insisted. *"Melantha?"*

"Believe it," Nikolos said darkly. "The test was run by the Farseers and confirmed by the Manipulators. It *is* accurate."

"It is, Roger," Caroline told him. "She did it last night, before you got there. She shook the whole courtyard."

"And that was only a fraction of the power she'll have when she reaches adulthood." Nikolos turned to look out the window. "The skyscrapers of New York are earthquake-proof, or so their designers claim," he said quietly. "But they have no idea how much focused power a Groundshaker can unleash. She will literally be able to bring down any building she chooses."

"Like 9/11," Caroline murmured. "Only a hundred times worse."

"Exactly," Nikolos said, nodding. "You see now why it's vital that we get her back."

"I'm sorry, but I still don't understand," Roger said. "I can see why the Grays would want to get rid of her. But she told Caroline *everyone* wanted her dead. Grays *and* Greens."

"Well, *I* don't want her dead," Nikolos said. "Neither do Aleksander and his supporters. But Cyril's managed to persuade more of us that her sacrifice would be in our best long-term interests. Now that the decision's been made, there's nothing the rest of us can do about it."

Caroline frowned. But if that was the case, why had Sylvia tried so hard to get Roger to bring Melantha to her and Aleksander? "So it's like a democracy?" she asked. "You vote on what to do, then assume everyone will fall into line behind the decision?"

"It's not quite that chaotic," Nikolos said hesitantly. "It's difficult to explain to people who don't share our ability for mind-to-mind contact. Basically, Cyril and Aleksander used their persuasion Gifts to state their positions to the other Greens."

"In the strongest terms possible, I suppose," Caroline murmured.

"Why do you say that?" Nikolos asked.

"You *do* call them Persuaders," Caroline reminded him. "I presume their particular Gift is to make people do what they want, like Cyril tried to do to Melantha and me."

"You make it sound more manipulative than it really is," Nikolos said. "As I said, it's hard to explain to Humans."

"Velovsky seemed to understand," Caroline said.

"Velovsky's a special case," Nikolos said, a little tartly.

"Okay, so they try to persuade the others," Roger cut in. "What happens then? You vote?"

"Not in so many words," Nikolos said. "Those who agreed with Cyril added their mental strength in his support, as did those who agreed with Aleksander. When the two Persuaders then faced off against each other, the one with the stronger position was empowered to make the decision. In this case, that was Cyril."

Roger snorted gently. "Town meeting meets prize fight."

Caroline fought back a grimace. To her, it sounded more like the worst of Madison Avenue meeting the worst of manipulative pressure politics. "But how could he possibly persuade them to kill Melantha?" she asked. "Isn't she your best weapon?"

"Not yet she isn't," Nikolos said. "All she has is potential; and that's the point, really. At the moment, we and the Grays are fairly evenly matched, with neither side holding enough advantage to feel confident in launching an attack. But by the time Melantha reaches fifteen, that will change."

He lifted his eyebrows. "Which means that, from the Gray point of view, if they intend to try to destroy us, they need to move now."

"Only they can't, because you're at parity," Roger said, his voice carrying sudden understanding. "So you made a *deal* with them?"

"It's called a truce," Nikolos said stiffly. "Is that so hard to understand?"

"But they *attacked* you," Roger objected. "They burned your forest."

"And I personally will never forget that," Nikolos said quietly, and Caroline shivered at the edge in his voice. "Neither will any of my generation, most of whom would gladly risk everything by throwing my sixty Warriors into a final battle against our enemies."

"And where do *you* stand?" Caroline asked.

Nikolos took a deep breath. "I'm a Command-Tactician," he said. "I lead Warriors, not the Greens as a whole. Whatever our leaders decide, I have no choice but to support that decision."

"So in exchange for peace," Caroline said darkly, "Cyril agreed to murder a twelve-year-old girl."

"Easy, hon," Roger said. But his voice sounded strained, too. "It's the kind of decision nations have to make all the time."

"And it certainly wasn't made as casually as you imply," Nikolos insisted. "We explored every other possibility first, from sending Melantha and her family into exile to seeing if it was possible to surgically remove her ability to use her Gift. It was only with the greatest reluctance that we finally concluded that this was the only way."

"So what went wrong?" Roger asked.

"We still don't know," Nikolos said, making a face. "A delegation of Greens and Grays met in Riverside Park that night, assembling by the Carrere Memorial."

"Wouldn't the other side of the Parkway, by the river, have suited you better?" Caroline muttered.

"The river?"

"She's talking about how you'd dispose of the body afterward," Roger explained, sounding more than a little uncomfortable.

"No need," Nikolos said, his eyes still on Caroline. "A Green body in contact with vegetation or soil is quickly absorbed, vanishing without any trace Humans can see."

"Like the woman who vanished last night in the courtyard," Caroline said, finally understanding that particular mystery.

"The first casualty of our new war," Nikolos said, his eyes boring into Caroline's. "*Unless* that war can be quickly ended."

Caroline forced herself to hold his gaze. "You were telling us what happened at the park," she reminded him.

The Green's lip twitched. "We'd taken Melantha to a secluded spot and . . . begun . . . when the lights on Riverside Drive suddenly dimmed," he said. "Naturally, like idiots, we all turned to look; and as we did, the lights suddenly exploded with such devastating brilliance that we were temporarily blinded."

He reached up and fingered his *trassk*. "At least, most of us were. But someone in the delegation was obviously in on the plan. The moment the rest of us were blinded, he struck down the Warriors holding Melantha and made his escape."

"What makes you think it was someone from the group?" Roger asked.

"Anyone slipping in from outside the circle would have brushed against at least one of us as he passed," Nikolos said. "But no one did."

"How about from above?" Roger asked. "Velovsky said something about a Gray rappelling gadget."

"Tension lines," Nikolos said, nodding. "Like invisible wires they use to travel between buildings. But in this case, there was no place to set one up except on one of the buildings across Riverside Drive. In order to pass cleanly over the trees, a Gray would have had to start so high, and to slide in at so steep an angle, that the impact of his landing would have been clearly felt."

He shook his head. "No, it had to be someone in the group, someone who grabbed Melantha and then shoved his way out. Before we could react, they were gone."

"But not before someone got in a parting shot," Roger said, remembering back. "He was bleeding."

Nikolos looked sharply at him. "You *saw* him? What did he look like?"

"He was just there for a minute," Roger fumbled, clearly startled by the other's reaction. "All we saw—"

"All we saw was a shadowy figure," Caroline cut him off,

touching his hand warningly. "The lights on Broadway were acting funny that night, too."

"What about his body type?" Nikolos persisted. "He *was* a Gray, wasn't he?"

"Why didn't you just take a head-count afterwards?" Caroline countered. "If it was someone from the group, he obviously would have been missing."

"Obviously," Nikolos said sourly. "Unfortunately, the group didn't stay together the way it should have. Someone panicked and shouted that the Grays had betrayed the truce, and most of the non-Warriors instantly scattered. The Grays did the same, retreating to their strongholds in south Manhattan and Queens. They never got a head-count for their delegation, either." He grimaced. "Or so they say."

"But why would any of the Grays have wanted to keep her alive?" Roger asked.

Nikolos hissed between his teeth. "Because with a truce in place and Melantha dead, the faction who wants war would have no way to draw the rest of the Grays onto their side. They by themselves certainly don't have the strength to defeat us. But if they could kidnap Melantha and claim we had reneged on the agreement, they might be able to rekindle the old rage and envy."

"What about the Greens?" Caroline asked. "Could any of *them* have decided to go against Cyril's pronouncement?"

"Greens do not 'decide' to go against a Leader's pronouncements," Nikolos said stiffly. "Not even Melantha's parents would have dared do something like that."

"I see," Caroline said, letting that pass for the moment. "At any rate, there's nothing more we can tell you about Melantha's rescuer. As I said, the lights had gone strange."

She looked at Roger, noting the frown creasing his forehead. But to her relief, he'd gotten the message. "That's right," he seconded. "Sorry."

Nikolos pursed his lips, his eyes flicking back and forth between them. "I suppose it doesn't really matter," he said. "Once we have Melantha back, we can simply ask her."

"What will happen then?" Roger asked. "I know you plan to—" he glanced at Caroline "—to pick up where you left off. But after that, what? Are you just going to trust the Grays to stick to their part of the bargain?"

"I don't know what Cyril will decide," Nikolos said. "Personally, I think Manhattan's grown far too crowded of late anyway. My advice would be to sacrifice Melantha to prove our good faith, then pull back to upstate New York where we'll have all the trees we could ever want." He shook his head. "But that will be a decision for all the Greens to make," he added. "At any rate, you understand now how important it is that Melantha be returned to us. When and where can we pick her up?"

Caroline sensed Roger bracing himself. "We appreciate your time, Mr. Green," he said, his tone suddenly formal. "If you'll give me your phone number, we'll be in touch."

Nikolos's face had gone stony. "We don't have time for games, Roger," he said, a layer of ice coating his tone. "We need her back; and we need her back *now*."

"No, you don't," Roger said, his voice almost calm. "You need her back by Wednesday. That leaves us plenty of time to decide what to do."

He touched Caroline's arm and pushed back his chair. Caroline followed suit, and they stood up together. "You're making a mistake," Nikolos warned, not moving from his own seat. "We cannot allow you to jeopardize our lives. We *will* have Melantha back."

"If she's willing to return, we'll deliver her personally," Roger promised. "If not, I guess we'll have more talking to do. Your phone number?"

"Just come back to the park," Nikolos gritted out. "Someone will contact you."

The two Greens who had ridden in the cab with them were waiting outside the door as they emerged from the dining room. Caroline gripped Roger's arm tightly as she walked beneath their silent glares, but they made no move to interfere. "What now?" she asked as they emerged from the building into the chilly afternoon air.

"Subway," he said shortly, turning them to the west and picking up his pace.

He lapsed into silence as they headed across the university. Probably angry with her again, Caroline realized with a sinking feeling.

Even on a Saturday, the campus was comfortably crowded with students and faculty wending their way between the various buildings. Roger led them past Dodge Hall, and Caroline found herself wincing as she looked at the doors leading into the Miller Theater. If she hadn't insisted on walking home from that performance Wednesday night—if she'd just put a leash on her phobias for once and had been willing to ride the subway a few short blocks—they never would have been marched at gunpoint into that alley and gotten themselves into this mess.

Of course, in that case, Melantha would probably be dead. Maybe she was anyway.

The subway car was rumbling its way south before Caroline plucked up the courage to speak. "Are you mad at me, Roger?" she asked tentatively.

To her relief, he merely frowned at her. "No, of course not," he said, sounding puzzled. "Why would I be?"

"I don't know," she said. "I thought maybe I talked too much in there. You've been so quiet since we left."

"I was just trying to sort it all out," he said, reaching over to take her hand. "What do *you* make of it?"

"Mostly, it seems inconsistent," Caroline said. "Nikolos makes the Greens sound all noble and civilized, but admits they're willing to murder a twelve-year-old girl in cold blood."

"For the good of the rest of the Greens," Roger reminded her.

"I don't care if it's for the good of the known universe," Caroline countered. "It's still wrong. I also can't believe the Grays are so callous that they'd demand it."

"They were the ones shooting into the trees during the war," Roger reminded her. "Or are you going to tell me there's another side to *that* story, too?"

"There's another side to every story," Caroline said, trying to keep her voice even. Arguing with him wasn't going to get her anywhere. "And we need to hear theirs before we make any kind of judgment."

Roger grunted and lapsed back into silence. The 96th Street stop—the one by their building—came and went, apparently without him noticing. Caroline thought about pointing it out, decided it would be safer to pretend she hadn't noticed it, either.

"All right," he said as the train pulled into the 86th Street station. "Compromise. Let's go back to the Youngs' and look around. If Melantha's lying low, she has to expect we'll come back for her."

"If she's there, why didn't she answer when I called to her this morning?"

"Maybe she was afraid to," he said. "Maybe there were still Greens or Grays hanging around."

"You think they'll be gone by now?"

"No idea," Roger admitted. "But right now, it's all I've got."

"Okay," she said. "That sounds fine."

"Yeah." He exhaled, just loudly enough for her to hear. "Sorry," he added. "I'm just—I'm not very good at this."

"You did just fine," Caroline assured him, a bit surprised by the vehemence of his confession. Usually when he felt this strongly about his weaknesses, she got the brunt of his self-anger. "In fact, you did better than fine," she added. "You kept control of the conversation, and probably got a lot more out of him than he planned to give us."

"I doubt that," Roger muttered. "But thanks anyway. I'm just sorry I didn't do better when they forced us into that cab."

"I'm not sorry," Caroline told him, frowning. Why was he apologizing about *that*? "We wouldn't have learned any of this if they hadn't taken us to Nikolos."

"As it turns out, yes," he said. "But you sure weren't happy about it at the time."

"I wasn't upset," Caroline protested. "Really."

"You were awfully quiet."

She frowned. Was *that* what had put him in this mood? "I was listening," she said. "Trying to make out what they were saying."

It was Roger's turn to frown. "What are you talking about? They didn't say a single word the whole trip."

"Not out loud," Caroline agreed. "But it was like—" She paused, trying to find the right words to describe it. "You know how sometimes when you're by a stream that's running over a lot of rocks you can hear a kind of murmuring? When I was young I used to pretend the stream was talking to the woods. It was kind of like that."

"Really," Roger said, clearly intrigued. "Could you get any words, even ones you couldn't understand?"

She shook her head. "I could tell they were talking to each other, but that was it."

"What about with Nikolos? Could you tell if he ever talked to anyone?"

"Not really," she said. "Of course, he was farther away from me than the Greens in the cab."

"Which probably means your range is pretty short," Roger concluded. "Too bad."

"Sorry," Caroline said automatically.

To her surprise, he grinned at her, possibly the first genuine smile she'd gotten from him since this whole thing began. "Don't apologize, hon," he assured her. "It's not exactly your fault. I wonder why you could hear it and I couldn't."

"Maybe I was sensitized when Cyril tried to get me to bring Melantha to him," Caroline suggested.

"Maybe," Roger said. "It's as good an explanation as any." He nodded out the window at the subway tunnel wall flashing past. "Times Square coming up. We need to change trains."

Caroline braced herself. "Roger . . . what happens if we *do* find Melantha? Do we just hand her over to Nikolos?"

Roger shook his head. "I don't know," he said. "Let's worry about it then."

19

Jonah was plowing his way through his fourth sandwich when Fierenzo's cell phone finally rang. Scooping it off the table, he popped it open. "Fierenzo."

"It's Jon," Powell's voice came back. "I've got good news, bad news, and weird news. Which do you want first?"

"I believe it's traditional to start at the bottom," Fierenzo said, getting up and crossing to the kitchen door. Preoccupied with his meal, Jonah didn't even look up as Fierenzo let the door swing shut behind him. "Let's hear the bad news."

"The Whittiers have learned not to take cabs to their actual destination," Powell said. "Smith and I canvassed the whole area around 14th and Fifth, and none of the shopkeepers remember seeing them."

"Not a huge surprise," Fierenzo said, walking to the far end of the living room where he could look out the windows. The city always seemed so clean and cheerful and crime-free from up here.

"I suppose not," Powell conceded. "The good news is that Smith then picked up a report of an incident that happened an hour ago down at Waverly Place and West 11th Street. On a hunch I showed the Whittiers' photos around the area, and we got lucky: a coffee shop manager at the corner of Greenwich and Bank Street remembered them walking around his corner between a pair of short, wide guys."

Fierenzo frowned. Short wide guys. Like the man sitting in his kitchen eating up all his bread and lunchmeat? "Turning the corner which direction?"

"From Greenwich onto Bank," Powell said. "Quiet neighborhood back that way, especially on a Saturday."

"He's sure it was them?"

"*I'm* sure it was them," Powell said. "Because a few minutes later an ambulance driver waiting at St. Vincent Hospital saw them come tearing out again onto Greenwich, this time minus their escort."

"Really," Fierenzo said, frowning as he tried to visualize the street layout down there. "So they left Greenwich, went down Bank, turned again at either Waverly Place or West 4th, then came back up to Greenwich again?"

"It was Waverly," Powell told him. "According to the driver, they met up with two other guys and all got into a cab together."

"Not their original escort?"

"The driver described this pair as tall and thin," Powell said. "Unfortunately, he didn't get the medallion number."

"It's still a start," Fierenzo told him. "The cab companies are going to love us today."

"That's okay—I'm used to being loved," Powell assured him. "You ready for the weird news now?"

Fierenzo frowned. "I assumed that *was* the weird news."

"Not even close," Powell assured him. "The reason we came down here in the first place was that there was some kind of altercation on Waverly Place—which is how we know that's where the Whittiers turned—involving a man and a car that was apparently trying to run him down. A witness crossing the street a block away said he saw the man shooting at the car, and that the car was bouncing around as the bullets or whatever slammed into it."

"'Or whatever'?"

"Patience, partner," Powell said. "Let me give it to you in order. Just before the car reached the pedestrian, he managed to jump out of the way. The car kept going; the intended vic then turned around and *he* commenced shooting at the back end of the car."

"What did the vic look like?"

"Shortish and built like a wrestler," Powell said with a note of satisfaction. "I'd bet money that he was one of the two men the coffee guy saw hustling the Whittiers around the corner. No idea what happened to the other one."

"How do we know he wasn't the driver?" Fierenzo asked.

There was a faint snort from the phone. "Because the driver was a kid."

"A *kid*?"

"Yep," Powell said. "Like I said, the car kept going down Waverly after it passed the intended vic. Our witness saw it coming toward him and ducked around the nearest building so he wouldn't get creamed when it ran into the cross-traffic at Seventh. He heard the car brake to a halt, and a few seconds later a kid ten to fifteen years old went charging around the corner. He reached Greenwich Avenue, and that was the last the witness saw of him."

"I don't suppose he got a good look at the kid's face."

"Better than that," Powell said. "He saw both the kid's *and* the intended vic's faces. He's also an amateur photographer with an eye for features, and would be happy to describe both of them to a police artist. I've already sent him back to the precinct."

"We should have more citizens like this," Fierenzo said.

"Sign me up for a dozen," Powell agreed. "Anyway, after the kid disappeared our good citizen looked down Waverly again and saw the vic running back toward Bank Street. This weird enough for you yet?"

"Why?" Fierenzo asked suspiciously. "Is there more?"

"There is indeed," Powell said. "Because now we get to the 'whatever' part you asked about a minute ago. Like I said, the car had been battered pretty good; but it hadn't been shot, like the witness assumed. It was more like it had been worked over by a bunch of guys with sledgehammers. Lots of dents, not a single bullet hole."

Fierenzo frowned. "Like the hammer marks we saw on the Whittiers' balcony door?"

"That was the first thing I thought of, too," Powell agreed. "They seem to be the same kind of impact marks, only more so."

"Maybe you'd better tow it in and have CSU look at it."

"Already in the works," Powell said. "The owner's listed as a Halfdan Gray from Queens. That ring any bells?"

"The Whittiers mentioned someone named Halfdan," Fierenzo said, frowning. "Does he have a son with a penchant for joyriding?"

"I don't know—we haven't been able to contact him yet," Powell said. "Of course, it could also be that the kid was no relation and simply boosted a convenient car. One more thing. Our witness claimed he didn't hear any shots; but when I pressed him, he *did* remember hearing something like a bass guitar string being plucked. Does *that* one ring any bells?"

Fierenzo rubbed his cheek thoughtfully. "The cops at last night's Yorkville fiasco."

"Bingo," Powell said. "A violin or rubber-band sound, one of them said, just before they heard the tree limb come down. I'm starting to see some very interesting connections here."

"Does look that way, doesn't it?" Fierenzo agreed, keeping his voice neutral. Powell was right: it meshed very nicely with everything else they knew.

So why were his cop's instincts screaming like a Met soprano going for a high C? "You say you've sent the witness to the station?"

"Yeah, about ten minutes ago. Why?"

"Do me a favor," Fierenzo said slowly. "As soon as CSU gets there to deal with the car, you get yourself back to the office and keep him there."

"Sure," Powell said. "For how long?"

"Until I can talk to him," Fierenzo said. "There are a couple things I have to do first."

"Not a problem," Powell assured him. "I've gotten people lost in there without even trying. Just try to make it today, okay?"

"I will," Fierenzo said. "And get Smith tracking the Whittiers' latest cab."

"Right," Powell said. "Don't you want to know the witness's name?"

Fierenzo frowned. "Do I?"

"I think so," Powell said, sounding grimly amused. "He's a Mr. Oreste Green."

"Oreste *Green*?"

"That's right," Powell said. "Granted, Green's a common enough name. But it's still an interesting coincidence, don't you think?"

"If it's a coincidence, I'm a frog," Fierenzo growled. "I hope you didn't mention that his name sounded familiar."

"Don't worry, I played it cool," Powell assured him. "So I'll hang onto him until you get here?"

"Right," Fierenzo said. "And hang onto whatever sketches Carstairs comes up with, too."

"Got it," Powell said. "See you later."

Fierenzo keyed off the phone and slid it back into his pocket. Leaning his shoulder against the wall beside the window, he scowled out at the city below.

Green. Caroline Whittier had talked about Greens and Grays last night, suggesting they might be at least some of the thousands of New Yorkers Cyril had been threatening in his phone message. Up to now he'd been tentatively assuming that the Green reference was to the left-wing environmentalist political party, with Melantha's last name being just a coincidence, and the Grays being some kind of slang reference he wasn't familiar with.

But now an Oreste Green had popped up into the case, along with a Halfdan Gray. Could the references be to names, after all?

He looked over at the kitchen door. Jonah had never given him a last name, he realized suddenly. Jonah Gray, perhaps?

Whether it was or not, it was definitely time to ask the man some questions. Detaching himself from the wall, he retraced his steps across the living room to the kitchen.

He was just reaching out a hand to push open the door when he heard a quiet voice coming from beyond it.

He froze in place, listening hard. Just one voice, which implied Jonah was talking on the phone. Hooking his fingertips into the louvers, Fierenzo carefully pulled the door open an inch.

"—course not," Jonah was saying, his tone managing to sounding indignant and hurt at the same time. "I'm just wondering what in blazes I'm doing here."

There was a brief pause. "Because it's a waste of time, that's why," he went on. "No one's going to bring Melantha *here*."

Fierenzo felt a tingle on the back of his neck. *Melantha.* He was talking about the missing girl.

But who was he talking *to*?

"Because it would be stupid," Jonah said. "If they want her under Warrior protection, they put her in Central. If they just want her hidden, they pick any one of the five gazillion trees lining the streets."

Carefully, using the sound of Jonah's voice as cover, Fierenzo eased the door open a few more inches.

To find himself faced with an extraordinary sight. Jonah was still at the table, his back to Fierenzo, half a sandwich temporarily abandoned on his plate. But he wasn't talking on the kitchen phone, as Fierenzo had assumed. Instead, he was sitting with both hands up along the sides of his head, palms pressing against his cheeks and middle fingers poking into his ears in a classic hear-no-evil posture.

"If I *had* seen any, don't you think I would have reported it?" Jonah asked patiently. "What do you—? Fine. You want a traffic report? I'll give you a traffic report."

He exhaled an annoyed sigh. "Okay. Vehicular traffic's pretty much the same as it has been all day, maybe picking up a little on Canal in the past hour. Not many pedestrians, what with the rain and all. . . . No, Bergan, I'm not being insubordinate. Trust me; if I was, I'd be doing a *lot* better job. . . . Because I'm being wasted here, that's why. I already explained they're not going to put her in some little pocket park. They're *certainly* not going to put her in a pocket park down here, with Torvald's crowd between them and Central. You want me to be of some actual use, send me to Riverside or Washington. Even Gramercy's a better bet than this place."

He paused again. Fierenzo peered closely at his hands, trying to figure out which of them held a radio or phone. But he couldn't see anything in either one.

"Yes, and I'm sorry," Jonah said. "But I have to sleep *sometime*. . . . Yeah. Don't worry—I'll call you the *minute* they show up. . . . Sure."

He lowered his right hand away from his head—his *empty* right hand, Fierenzo saw now—leaving the left still pressed against his cheek. The right hand's little finger twitched once—

"Okay, he's off," Jonah went on, his voice suddenly ominous. "You want to tell me where you were about ten this morning? . . . Come on, Jordan—this is *me* you're talking to. . . . Oh, terrific. Let me tell you something kiddo: that was Bergan himself at the third corner of this little conversation, and he's spitting granite right now. . . . Look, forget the Greens for a minute and concentrate on what Bergan and Ingvar are going to do if they ever find out that was you. And consider yourself lucky that some cop didn't see you climbing into that car."

A second tingle ran up Fierenzo's back *Climbing into that car. . . ?*

"Yes, I understand," Jonah went on, his tone marginally more sympathetic. "But I really don't think there's anything to worry about. Even if Halfdan *had* gotten hold of them, there really isn't anything useful they can tell him. Same goes for the Greens. . . . Yes, even the Persuaders. Just quit with the impromptu heroics before someone catches you, okay? . . . No, I should be fine for awhile—I'm getting some food, and that's mostly what I needed. You just stay put and keep feeding me updates. And *start* with the traffic report next time, okay? Especially the pedestrians. That's what Halfdan's looking for, and it's a hard topic to vamp on. . . . Good. And *stay* there this time."

He sighed. "I know," he said. "Don't worry, we'll find her. Look, I have to go. Watch yourself."

Carefully, Fierenzo eased the door shut. He ran a ten count, then stepped on the loose floorboard by the wall and gave it a nice loud squeak. Pushing open the door, he strode nonchalantly into the kitchen. "Sorry about that," he apologized, circling the table. "Business. How you holding up?"

Jonah was munching away at his sandwich again as if nothing had happened. "Finally starting to get filled up, I think," he said. "A nap's starting to sound better and better, though."

"Well, you should have plenty of time for one," Fierenzo said, watching the other's face closely. "I have to get back to the Two-Four. Someone nearly got run over near Washington Square a couple of hours ago, and I need to check it out."

"Really," Jonah said. He was trying hard to keep his voice casual, but Fierenzo could hear the sudden underlying tension. "Anyone hurt?"

"I don't think so, but the details are kind of confused," Fierenzo said. "That's why I want to talk to the witness personally."

Jonah's face had gone very still. "Witness?"

"Somebody named Green," Fierenzo said offhandedly, getting up from his chair. "My partner is taking him in to describe the driver for a police artist."

"That should be useful," Jonah murmured.

"It can make or break a case," Fierenzo agreed, pulling on his coat. "Don't open the door or answer the phone—the machine can take any calls. If you get hungry again, help yourself to anything in the fridge. I'll be back soon." He smiled encouragingly as he pushed open the door and stepped into the living room. He was still smiling as he let the door swing shut.

The smile evaporated, and for a moment he glowered at the closed door. Jonah knew about the incident, all right—his voice and posture had shown that as clearly as if he'd held up a poster. And Fierenzo would bet money that his friend Jordan had been the kid behind the wheel.

How Jonah knew what Jordan had done still begged for an explanation. But even if the details were still foggy, one thing was crystal clear. A case that had started as a simple apartment break-in had escalated to kidnapping, assault, and possibly attempted murder. It was a trend Fierenzo didn't care for at all.

Still, the incident had allowed him to dangle some interesting bait in front of his mysterious houseguest. If Jonah was obliging enough to take it, the 24th Precinct might soon be getting some interesting visitors.

He shook his head as he headed for the elevators. This was turning out to be one hell of a day off.

* *

Roger had planned to take them on the same kind of convoluted route he'd used the previous evening after leaving Torvald's studio. But with the sun now well past the meridian, and Caroline's reminder that both the Greens and the Grays seemed to know pretty much everything about their movements anyway, he decided it wasn't worth the effort. They changed trains only twice, at Times Square and Grand Central, reached their final stop, and set off on the five-block walk to the Youngs' apartment. The drizzle, which had stopped while they were talking to Nikolos, began again a block into the walk, and Roger bought another umbrella to replace the one they'd lost during the escape from Ingvar and his lunatic driver buddy.

They checked the apartment itself first in case Melantha had managed to find her way back. But she hadn't. Caroline insisted on leaving a short note with Roger's cell phone number, and then they headed back outside.

The park gate stood open, but the intermittent drizzle had apparently kept everyone away except for a couple of kids who seemed to be enjoying not having to share the playground equipment for once. "So what's the plan?" Roger asked as they crossed to the courtyard and stopped by the damaged tree. "I don't think getting up on one of the benches and shouting 'Melantha!' is going to cut it."

"I was actually thinking of . . . well, of listening to each of the trees," Caroline said, a bit hesitantly. "If I can hear Greens talking to each other when they're outside their trees, maybe I can hear them doing it from inside, too."

"Worth a try," Roger agreed. "And if there's nothing in the courtyard, we can try the park. She might have switched trees after . . . uh-oh."

"What?" Caroline asked, looking around.

"There," Roger said, pointing down the street at the pickup truck rolling toward them, RCS Landscaping plastered prominently across the hood. "Looks like someone's here to deal with the tree."

"Is that a problem?" Caroline asked.

"Only if they see you talking to their patient," Roger said. "Better go start at the other end while I keep them occupied."

Caroline nodded and headed off across the bricks. Roger stepped to the curb as the pickup rolled to a stop. "That was fast," he commented as a man and woman got out and headed around toward the back of the truck. "It usually takes forever to get someone here when a tree gets damaged."

"The owner put a rush order on this one," the man said as they hauled a stepladder out of the truck. "What happened, anyway?"

"You got me," Roger said, glancing at the other end of the courtyard. Caroline was leaning close to one of the trees, gazing intently at the bark. As he watched, she straightened up, glanced around, and moved off toward the next one in line. "There were a couple of screams, something that sounded like a gunshot, and then cops as far as the eye could see."

"Must have been some gunshot," the woman said, eyeing the tree as she collected a saw and spray can from the truck's toolbox. "What happened to the branch?"

Roger frowned. "You didn't already take it?"

"Of course not," the man said. "You think we'd have hauled away the branch and then made a second trip just to seal the gash?"

"Someone from the city probably took it," the woman added.

"Probably," Roger said, a bad taste in his mouth as he backed away. Too late, of course, he finally had it.

He intercepted Caroline on her way to her fourth tree. "Forget it," he said, taking her arm and steering her back toward the street. "She's gone."

"You know where she is?"

"I know where she *was*," he corrected grimly. "She was hiding in the broken tree branch."

Caroline inhaled sharply, her eyes darting back over his shoulder. "Oh, Roger," she breathed. "It's already gone!"

"Yeah, and it wasn't the landscapers who took it, either," he told her. "They thought it might have been the Parks Department, but you know as well as I do no one down there would have moved anywhere near this fast."

"They found her," Caroline said softly, her voice edged with despair. "Oh, Roger."

"Don't panic just yet," Roger cautioned. "It may not be as simple as it looks."

"What do you mean?"

"I've been trying to remember what the courtyard looked like this morning," he said. "I'm pretty sure the branch was already gone."

"Yes, I think you're right," she agreed slowly.

"So it was taken last night," he concluded. "Probably during all the confusion with the cops and CSU people running around."

"She's probably already dead," Caroline murmured.

"No, I don't think so," Roger said firmly. "Remember, there were Greens and Grays all around the park last night. If whoever it was just wanted to kill her, he could have waited until the cops left and had the ceremony right then and there."

Caroline shivered. "Unless he wanted to kill her later, in private."

"I can't see any reason for either side to do that," Roger said. Actually, there *were* a couple of possible reasons, but there was no point worrying Caroline any more than she already was. "So let's assume she's alive, and get busy and find her."

He felt his wife straighten up. "You're right," she said. "Any ideas?"

They had reached the northern edge of the park, and Roger turned them west. "We're assuming they took the branch out under the cops' noses," he said, working it out as he went. "They couldn't have just dragged it away—that would have been way too suspicious. So they must have had a truck."

"And it had to be something official," Caroline said, picking up the thread of his logic. "Either a Parks truck or some landscaper's."

"Right," Roger agreed. "And unless they had the unbelievable luck to already have access to such a vehicle, they would have had to steal something."

"*And* they couldn't risk taking the branch very far," Caroline mused. "The first red light, and Melantha would have been out of the branch and gone. So the truck and branch may still be nearby."

"That's my guess," Roger said. "*I* sure wouldn't have driven a stolen truck any farther than I had to. They'd have stopped as soon as they could, gotten Melantha out and transferred to another vehicle, and taken off. *And* they wouldn't have done it near any other parks, since that's where the Greens are."

"The Grays, too," Caroline said. "Velovsky said they're mostly keeping an eye on the Greens."

"Right," Roger said. That last part hadn't yet occurred to him. "So they would have ditched the truck somewhere away from parks."

"That still leaves a lot of ground to cover," Caroline said, her enthusiasm fading a bit.

"I know, but right now it's all we've got," Roger said.

"There's still a chance she managed to escape before they could get her out, and if so she may be in hiding near wherever we find the truck."

Caroline walked in silence for a minute. "Who do you think it was? A Green, or a Gray?"

Roger shook his head. "The Greens would probably be better at figuring out she was in the branch," he said. "The Grays seem more mechanically minded, which probably means they'd be better at hot-wiring a truck."

"We also know it was a Gray who gave her to us," Caroline pointed out. "And only a Green could have turned her *trassk* into that gun he threatened us with," she added, her voice suddenly odd.

"You have something?"

"I was just thinking," she said. "The Gray who gave her to us couldn't have created that gun. Obviously, it had to have been Melantha."

"Obviously," Roger agreed, wondering where she was going with this. "All that proves is that, down deep, she doesn't really want to die."

"Except that Greens don't just casually violate the decisions of their leaders like that," Caroline reminded him. "Especially when you've been told that your death is the only way for your people to survive." She shivered in the shifting breeze. "I hate this, Roger. All these people getting ready to restart a war that should have ended three-quarters of a century ago. And all of them trying to find a way to use Melantha to their advantage. We have to stop it."

"I'd love to," he said. "It is interesting, though, what Nikolos said about the universe's sense of irony. Just look at who got picked to be dropped into the middle of this: me, who hates conflicts; and you, who automatically stands up for the underdog. Between us . . ."

He paused, an odd thought suddenly occurring to him. "Between us . . . ?" Caroline prompted hesitantly.

"I never thought of it this way before," Roger said slowly. "But between us, we make a pretty good team."

"I've always thought so," Caroline said, slipping her hand into his. The hand was cold, but he could hear a new whisper of hope in her tone. "You think they're watching us?"

"What if they are?" Roger countered, trying to keep his voice light. "They probably know our life histories by now."

"I suppose," she said. "I just feel creepy with the thought of them looking over our shoulders."

"Yeah." Roger took a deep breath. "One other thing. If they *did* sneak off with Melantha when we think they did, then you and I going out to look for her after the cops left wouldn't have made any difference. There's no sense kicking yourself about that."

"I know," she said quietly. "I still can't help thinking we failed her."

"Caroline—"

"So we'll just have to make up for it," she said, her voice tight but brisk. "Let's start by finding that truck."

●　●

Still talking together, the Whittiers turned the corner and disappeared from sight. Setting his folded newspaper onto the seat beside him, NYPD Officer Jeff Smith turned the key in the ignition. He'd known that coming back this afternoon and staking out the neighborhood had been a long shot, especially after so many hours had passed. But he hadn't had anything particularly interesting planned for the day anyway, and sometimes long shots paid off.

This one just had.

Checking his mirrors, he pulled the car slowly away from the curb, steering with one hand as he punched the buttons of his cell phone with the other. "Powell," Powell's voice answered on the third ring.

"It's Smith, Detective," Smith said, smiling tightly as he turned in the direction the Whittiers had gone. "I've got them."

20

Powell was in the squad room, his phone pressed to his ear, when Fierenzo arrived. "About time," he said, waving Fierenzo to his own chair across their paper-strewn desk. "Smith is on four. You want to talk to him?"

"Absolutely," Fierenzo said, dropping into his chair and punching the extension as he scooped up the phone. "Fierenzo. You still on the Whittiers?"

"For what it's worth," Smith's voice came. "They've spent the last hour and a half walking around the Upper East Side, checking out every cross-street and driveway."

Searching for Melantha? "Are you on foot?" Fierenzo asked.

"Not yet," Smith said. "I've been trying to stay with my car in case they suddenly decide to grab a taxi."

"Is there any particular pattern to their search?" Powell asked.

"Just that they're focusing entirely on the streets," Smith said. "No apartments or shops, just the streets."

"Looking for something parked," Fierenzo murmured. "Did they go into their friends' place before they started their walking tour?"

"Yes, but they didn't stay long," Smith said. "Right after they came out they went back to the courtyard. The wife went to the south end and looked at several of the trees, while the husband went and talked for a minute to the landscapers who'd come by to fix the gash on that tree."

Fierenzo looked sharply across the desk at Powell. "There was a Parks truck there last night picking up the branch."

Powell nodded. "That was my thought, too," he said. "I've checked, and they say no one was out last night."

"So someone borrowed one of their trucks?"

"One of their trucks *is* missing," Powell confirmed. "I've got an alert out to watch for it."

Fierenzo scowled. "So in other words, someone just waltzed out from under our noses with something they didn't want us to find."

"Yeah, but what?" Powell objected. "CSU had already been all over that area. They wouldn't have let anyone take the branch otherwise."

"Unless the men in the truck asked them nicely," Fierenzo said. "Like the super at the Whittiers' building."

"Right," Powell said slowly. "But Umberto freely admitted what he'd done when Smith and Hill questioned him. As far as I know, no one in CSU has come forward to announce they let someone walk off with evidence."

"Has anyone asked them?"

Powell's forehead wrinkled. "Well . . . no, probably not."

"Maybe somebody should," Fierenzo said. "Smith, you didn't happen to bring a camera with you, did you?"

"Actually, I did," Smith said. "I've got a telephoto lens, too."

"Good," Fierenzo said. "If they talk to anyone, get a picture of it. And call me right away if anything changes."

"Yes, sir," Smith said.

"Talk to you later," Fierenzo said, and hung up. "What's happening with our Mr. Green?" he asked Powell.

"He and Carstairs finished a while ago," Powell said, picking up a file folder and sliding it across the desk. "Here's what they came up with."

Fierenzo opened the folder and spread the papers in front of him. There were four drawings, each giving a front or a side view of one of the suspects, all of them far more detailed and refined than the vague sketches Carstairs was usually forced to turn out. Green apparently had an excellent memory for detail. "Like pre–Matthew Brady mug shots," he commented.

"Pre-who?"

"Civil War photographer," Fierenzo explained. "Very famous."

Powell made a face. "Let me guess. American history unit?"

"Very good," Fierenzo complimented him. "Nineteenth-century, to be specific."

"Yeah, whatever," Powell said. "Just try to go easy on that stuff around the others this time, will you? They were starting to call *me* Professor during that English lit unit last year."

Fierenzo shrugged. "Wait till *you* have a kid or two asking for help with their homework," he warned. "That stuff just sinks straight into your brain, whether you want it to or not. Anyway, that was Greek classics and mythology, not English lit. The English lit unit doesn't come until spring."

"I can hardly wait," Powell murmured.

"Me, too," Fierenzo said, picking up the two front-view drawings for a closer look. One of the subjects was definitely a young, probably preteen boy. The other was a man in probably his mid-fifties, with a wide face and weight and height estimates consistent with a short, wide body type. The boy's face was thinner, but Fierenzo could see the same squat build starting to appear in his own numbers.

And there was something else about him, too. Something Fierenzo couldn't quite put his finger on. "Where is Green now?" he asked, looking up again.

"In the lounge," Powell said, gesturing back over his shoulder.

"Not alone, I hope."

Powell shook his head. "I've got Wong and Abramson tag-teaming him."

"Good," Fierenzo said. "Has anyone tried to get in to see him?"

Powell frowned. "Not that I know of. Who are we expecting?"

"Anyone who doesn't want these getting out," Fierenzo told him, collecting the drawings back into the folder and standing up. "I have to drop something off at the lab, then I'll go talk to him."

"You want me there?"

"No need," Fierenzo said casually. In actual fact, he definitely did *not* want his partner sitting in on this one. "I'd rather you tackle CSU about the branch, and then see if you can chase down that missing Parks truck."

He smiled tightly. "Call it pride, but I'd rather we find it before the Whittiers do."

• •

They'd covered probably twenty blocks when something deep inside Caroline finally gave up. "This isn't going to work," she said with a sigh, gazing at the miles of traffic swirling through the streets like a swarm of determined bees. "The truck isn't here. And if it isn't here, neither is Melantha."

"I wish I could disagree with you," Roger admitted. "I guess I was wrong about them dropping the truck nearby."

"But how could they keep her in the branch?" Caroline objected.

"They didn't have to," Roger said, sounding disgusted with himself. "All they needed to do was drive a couple of blocks, get Melantha out of the branch and into the cab, and then go anywhere they wanted. Stolen or not, who's going to stop and question a Parks truck?"

"But how would they get her out?"

"I don't know," he said. "But remember what Fierenzo said about the Grays on our balcony trying to cut down our trees with their—what did Velovsky call them? Hammerguns? Maybe they thought Melantha was in there and were trying to draw her out."

"Yes," Caroline said, shivering at the thought. Would shooting at the tree feel like someone hitting her body? "And of course, if it was Greens who took her, they could probably just reach in and pull her out."

"Which means we need a new strategy," Roger said, looking at his watch. "And personally, I don't think well on an empty stomach."

Caroline suddenly realized how vacant her own stomach felt. Preoccupied with her hopes and fears, she hadn't even noticed. "We missed lunch again, didn't we?"

"Yep," he said. "Let's find a restaurant and discuss it over dinner."

"You don't need a restaurant," a man's voice said from behind them.

Caroline spun around, nearly twisting her ankle in the process. A young couple was standing there, both of them dark-haired and olive-skinned. "I'm sorry," the man apologized quickly, lifting his hands with his palms outward. "I didn't mean to startle you."

"How long have you been following us?" Roger demanded.

"Only a block or two," the man assured them. "And we weren't following you so much as we were trying to catch up."

"Well, now you have," Roger said warily. "What do you want?"

"To invite you to our homestead for dinner," the man said. "My name is Vasilis; this is my wife, Iolanthe."

"Greens, I presume?" Roger asked.

"Of course," Vasilis said, as if it should have been obvious. "We live over in Carl Shurz Park, just a couple of blocks from here."

"Convenient," Roger growled. "And what comes after dinner?"

Vasilis's forehead wrinkled. "I don't understand."

"Thumbscrews?" Roger suggested. "Hypnosis? Because we're still not going to tell you where Melantha is."

"Oh, no, nothing like that," Vasilis protested. "Just dinner and conversation, and you can leave whenever you want."

"We're told you haven't been shown a very good side of our people," Iolanthe added, sounding a little embarrassed. "That's why we were asked to invite you. We were hoping to remedy that."

Roger leaned his head over to Caroline's. "What do you think?" he asked quietly.

For a moment she studied the couple, trying to get a feel for them. "At least this time we're being asked," she said. "I don't see why not."

"Wonderful," Vasilis said briskly, gesturing behind him. "Then this way, please."

They turned around and headed back east. "So what are you two?" Roger asked, looking them up and down. "Pastsingers? Warriors?"

"I'm a Laborer at one of our restaurants," Vasilis told him. "Iolanthe's a Manipulator, though right now she mostly stays home to help with our group's child-rearing."

"You have your own restaurants?" Roger asked. "I sort of assumed you'd keep more to yourselves."

"We have to earn a living like anyone else," Vasilis said. "Apartments and food cost money, even when you spread the costs out the way we do. Fortunately, Green cooking is close enough to Greek for us to safely bill ourselves as Mediterranean or southern European."

"Do you have children of your own?" Caroline asked.

"Yes, we have three," Iolanthe said, a note of pride in her voice. "Xylia, thirteen; Phyllida, eleven; and Yannis, seven. Xylia's visiting one of her friends in Central Park tonight, but you'll get to meet the others."

"You'll meet a few of the others in our homestead, too," Vasilis said. "Most of them are working or otherwise out tonight, though."

"How many of you are there?" Roger asked.

"In our homestead, six families," Vasilis said. "Mostly couples with young children, like us."

"We came here five months ago from Washington Square," Iolanthe added quietly. "The Grays were moving into the neighborhood, and we were worried about our safety."

"But we can't retreat forever," Vasilis said, his voice dark. "Somewhere, we're going to have to draw a line in the dirt and make our stand."

They arrived at a modest apartment house on the edge of Shurz Park, and Vasilis led the way inside and up the stairs to one of the corner apartments. A young boy was standing at the door with an air of expectation. "This is our youngest, Yannis," Iolanthe said, and once again Caroline could sense the almost-words as the two adults communicated silently with their son. "He'll be performing the ancient pass-warder ritual tonight."

There was another almost-word, and the boy straightened up. "Who comes to this homestead?" he asked, his voice proud and strong.

"The master of the homestead and his wife," Vasilis answered.

"And who comes alongside you?"

"Honored guests of the Greens," Vasilis said, holding his right hand out, palm upward, toward Caroline.

"Take it with your right hand," Iolanthe murmured in her ear. Hesitantly, shooting a glance at Roger, she complied.

"And does the mistress of the homestead concur?" Yannis asked, looking at his mother.

"I do," Iolanthe said, taking Roger's right hand in hers.

"Then you may enter," Yannis intoned. Bowing from the waist, he stepped to the side, turning the doorknob and pushing open the door. The aroma of cooking food wafted out as he did so, an aroma rich in lamb and vegetables that made Caroline's empty stomach growl. Still holding her hand, Vasilis stepped past the boy into the apartment, Iolanthe and Roger following.

"I guess we should have warned you about that," Vasilis said, letting go of Caroline's hand. "The holding of knife-hands is supposed to guarantee that no one is readying a weapon as they pass. I hope you weren't offended."

"Not at all," Roger assured him. "It's not much different from our own custom of shaking hands."

"Normally, it would be a Warrior who would challenge guests that way," Iolanthe said. "Since our group doesn't include any Warriors, Yannis asked if he could do it."

"I thought your roles were rigidly enforced," Caroline said.

"They are," Iolanthe agreed. "But Yannis isn't old enough

for the testing, so we don't yet know what his Gift is. Until we do, it's permissible for him to play at any role he wishes."

"The loopholes of a modern society," Vasilis said, grinning at Roger. "As a paralegal, I'm sure you can appreciate that."

"All too well," Roger conceded. "It's certainly a lot friendlier than the reception I got at Aleksander's place yesterday."

"You weren't an invited guest then," Iolanthe reminded him.

"Speaking of whom," Vasilis added, his eyes flicking over Caroline's shoulder, "here's our other guest for the evening."

Caroline turned to see a tall Green with an age-lined face and short-cropped salt-and-pepper hair step into the living room through an open doorway. "Roger and Caroline," Vasilis said, gesturing toward him, "may I present one of the leaders of our people. This is Persuader Aleksander."

"Good evening," Aleksander said, his voice calm and cultured and resonant, his eyes glittering as he looked back and forth between them. "I'm so very pleased you could join us."

● ●

"Did you get any pictures of this couple?" Fierenzo asked into his phone.

"About half a dozen," Smith said. "You want me to stay with them?"

"Definitely," Fierenzo said. "I want to know how long they stay in there, and whether they come out alone, with this first couple, or with someone else."

"Got it," Smith said. "Talk to you later."

Punching off his phone, Fierenzo pushed open the door beside him and stepped back into the lab. "Secret conference all done?" the short redhead in the lab coat asked blandly, straightening up from her microscope.

"Just trying to give you a little room to work," Fierenzo

told her in the same tone as he returned the phone to his pocket. "Anything?"

"Well, it's definitely blood," she said. "Whether it's human or not—" She shrugged. "I don't know."

"Why not?" Fierenzo asked. "Can't you do a DNA or something?"

"Sure," she said. "I can also do glucose levels, tox screens, and about a hundred different tests for various genetic diseases. But you asked for something fast and cheap. Are we changing our instructions?"

Fierenzo made a face; but there was no way he was going to get the lieutenant to pop for a whole battery of expensive tests and the personnel to run them. "No," he conceded. "So what *can* you tell me?"

"Like I said, it's blood," she said. "The sample you gave me was pretty minuscule, but there were definitely red cells in it. Where did you get it, anyway?"

"Off the wall of an alley near 101st and Broadway," Fierenzo told her. "What makes you think it's not human?"

"Mainly, because I can't get it to type," she said.

"Could it be something rare?" Fierenzo suggested. "AB negative or something?"

She shook her head. "The test should work with anything, and I can usually do it with even less than I've got here. A few days' exposure to the elements shouldn't have messed it up, either."

"Any guesses?"

She shrugged. "Could be animal blood," she said. "I can't tell without further tests; and I'm out of time for any more freebies. You get me an official request, and I'll put it in the stack with all the rest."

"Pass," Fierenzo said, heading for the door. "By the time you got to it, it'd probably be too late to do me any good anyway."

"So get me more personnel," she suggested.

He snorted. "You must be kidding. We get more people in the department and *I'm* taking them. Thanks, Kath."

He left the lab and headed for the lounge, a creepy feeling

shivering along the surface of his skin. So Jonah's blood wasn't human. It was a thought that had been trying to force its way into his mind ever since he'd found the injured man at the end of that vertical blood trail. But up to now he'd been reasonably successful at tap-dancing his way around it.

Now, the dance had come to an end.

So who were they? A lost Neanderthal colony? A vampire nest? An alien invasion?

Of more immediate concern, what should *his* response be to the situation? Alert the mayor? Call out the S.W.A.T. team?

He grimaced as he strode down the hallway. No. So far, no one seemed to be doing anything dangerous to the city or its inhabitants. True, a girl was missing, but he still had no proof that any crime had been committed.

So he would sit on this, and wait until such time as he could determine that such a threat did exist.

Sergeant Abramson was chatting with a young, dark-haired man when Fierenzo reached the lounge. "You must be Oreste Green," Fierenzo said, nodding to him. "I'm Detective Fierenzo. We appreciate you giving up part of your Saturday to come here today."

"More of it than I'd expected," Green said pointedly as he stood up.

"I know, and I apologize," Fierenzo said, glancing at the other cops sitting around the lounge. "Let's go someplace where we can have more privacy," he suggested, backing toward the door.

"Why?" Green asked, making no move to follow. "I gave my statement, and I gave the descriptions to your artist. What more do you want?"

"I'd like to go over all of it with you," Fierenzo said.

"I did that with the other detective," Green said. "Don't you talk to each other?"

"Come on, fella, give me a break," Fierenzo said, lowering his voice. "His handwriting's lousy. I'll get a migraine if I have to get this from his report."

Green hissed between his teeth. "Fine," he said. "But make it fast."

The interrogation room was just down the hall. "Can I get you some coffee?" he asked as he ushered Green inside.

"No, thanks," the other said, his pace faltering as he looked at the bare walls and simple table and chairs. "The other place was cozier."

"But not as private," Fierenzo said, sitting down at the table and gesturing to the chair across from him. "Have a seat."

"Ten minutes," Green warned, reluctantly sitting down.

"Ten minutes," Fierenzo agreed, pulling out the sketches and spreading them out across the table. "Tell me what happened."

Green sighed. "I saw a car racing down Waverly Place toward a man—"

"This man?" Fierenzo interrupted, tapping the sketches of the adult.

"Right," Green said. "He was pointing some kind of gun at the car, but I never heard any shots. The driver had his hand out the window, and I think he was pointing something back."

"No gunshots from him, either?"

"Nothing that I heard," Green said. "The car missed the guy and kept going—"

"Missed him how?"

"What do you mean?"

"I mean how exactly did the man avoid the car?"

"He jumped between two of the parked cars along the curb," Green said. "The car kept going, coming toward where I was standing. I ducked around the side of the building, heard the car stop, then saw a kid come running out."

"This kid?" Fierenzo asked, indicating the other set of sketches.

"That's the one," Green said. "He ran to Greenwich Avenue and disappeared around the corner; and when I looked back down Waverly I saw the car sitting there with the other man running the other direction."

"I see," Fierenzo said, collecting the papers together again. "And why exactly did you help our artist make these sketches?"

Green frowned. "I was just trying to be a good citizen."

"No, I don't think so," Fierenzo said, leaning back in his seat. "Good citizens in your situation generally make more of an effort to tell the truth."

"What are you talking about?" the other demanded cautiously. "I told you exactly what I saw."

Fierenzo shook his head. "Neither the man nor the boy would have just run away," he said mildly. "At least, not at street level."

Green's face had suddenly gone very still. "What do you mean?" he asked.

"I mean I know all about these folks," Fierenzo said, watching him closely. "They don't run alongside buildings. They climb them."

He had expected some kind of guilty reaction. To his mild surprise, Green merely settled back into his chair and leveled a hard stare at the detective. "So you're working for them."

"I'm working for New York City," Fierenzo corrected. "Why do all you people assume I'm working for the other side?"

"Because there *are* only two sides," Green bit out. "If you're not with us, you're against us."

"Whatever." Fierenzo tapped the stack of sketches. "You want to tell me now why you wanted these?"

"You're the clever one," Green countered. "You tell me."

"Okay," Fierenzo said agreeably. "These two are part of the group your people are gearing up to fight. You saw them playing Waverly Place Chicken, possibly over who was going to get first crack at the Whittiers. You *do* know who the Whittiers are, don't you?"

Green didn't answer, but the question had been rhetorical anyway. Fierenzo had already caught the reaction in the other's eyes at his mention of the Whittiers' name. "At any rate, you saw them, but didn't recognize them," he went on. you could have gone back to your group and tried to describe them, but verbal descriptions to untrained people are always a little dicey. So when Detective Powell showed up, you decided to avail yourself of a police artist's services to get some actual pictures made. How am I doing?"

Green pursed his lips. "You can't keep me here, you know."

"I know," Fierenzo agreed. "Fortunately for you, I have no interest in doing so." He stood up and stepped to the door. "Thank you for your assistance; you're free to go. Have a nice day."

Green's forehead creased uncertainly. "If you're not going to hold me, why did you keep me here all afternoon?"

"Mostly, to make sure we were both on the same page," Fierenzo told him. "And also to make sure *you* knew where *I* stood on this; namely, for life, liberty, and peaceful streets. I hope your people won't get in my way on that."

Green snorted. "You'd better hope instead that *you* don't get in *our* way."

Fierenzo lifted his eyebrows. "Is that a threat?"

"Merely a statement of fact." Almost leisurely, the other unfolded himself from his chair and got to his feet. "What about my pictures?"

"I'll hold onto them for now," Fierenzo said. "If your friends want to see them, they're welcome to come down here and discuss it."

"I'll tell them that," Green said, circling the table. "I can find my own way out."

"I'm sure you can," Fierenzo said, stepping out of his way. "The officer down the hall will make sure you don't get lost. Good-bye, Mr. Green."

Silently, Green pulled the door open and left the room, leaving it ajar behind him. Fierenzo watched long enough to make sure the duty cop down the hall was escorting him to the exit, then returned to his chair and sat down. Swiveling the sketches around to face him, he spread them out again.

There had been something about the boy's picture that had been nagging at him earlier. Now, having given his subconscious time to mull it over, it practically leaped off the paper at him.

The boy was a younger version of his new houseguest Jonah. Brothers, most likely, or at least close cousins.

He leaned back in his chair, scowling. Yet another puzzle piece that didn't seem to connect with any of the others in his collection. This kid was almost certainly the Jordan that Jonah had been talking to back in his kitchen, the Jordan who was apparently sitting somewhere near Canal Street collecting traffic reports.

Only from the way the rest of the conversation had gone, he had the feeling that it was actually Jonah, not Jordan, who was supposed to be on spotter duty out there.

But what it was all ultimately about, he still didn't have a clue.

With a sigh, he gathered the sketches back into a pile. He might not know what was going on, but he would bet dollars to donuts that Jonah did. Actually, from the way the other had been behaving earlier, he'd rather expected him to have shown up here already. Apparently, he'd decided catching up on his sleep was a higher priority.

Which was fine with Fierenzo. He was going to have to spend the next couple of hours here anyway, trying to come up with something plausible to write about this case.

Once the paperwork was done, though, there was definitely going to be an earnest little conversation back at the apartment. Folding the sketches lengthwise, he slid them into his inside coat pocket and headed back to his desk.

21

"Before we continue," Aleksander said when they were all seated in the living room, "I'd like to apologize to you, Roger, for Sylvia's behavior yesterday morning. I'm afraid she was a bit overzealous in her desire to obtain your cooperation. Please understand that what we do, we do for the best."

"I'm not sure 'overzealous' even begins to cover it," Roger countered, his heart pounding painfully in his ears. Aleksander, the Persuader. Was that how they intended to get Melantha back? "She was trying to use the Persuader's Gift on me, wasn't she?"

"'Trying' being the operative word," Aleksander said, smiling faintly. "At best, it was pure intimidation. At worst, it was probably fairly ludicrous. Sylvia has no more ability to persuade than a three-year-old finger-painter could reproduce a Renoir masterpiece."

"Unlike you?" Caroline asked, her voice tight.

Aleksander shook his head. "I'm not going to try to persuade you," he said. "For one thing, I'm not even sure it would work. Particularly on you, Caroline, now that you've successfully resisted one attempt. Besides—" the lines in his face deepened "—you don't know where Melantha is anymore, do you?"

Roger felt Caroline's hand tighten in his. "Of course we do," he insisted.

"There's no need to lie," Aleksander said. "People like you would never have simply deserted her in the park last night or this morning."

Roger sighed. "You win," he said, ignoring Caroline's sudden stiffness. "So what happens now?"

"We have dinner, of course," Aleksander said, sounding surprised. "That *is* why you were invited."

"I thought you just wanted Melantha," Caroline said.

"Melantha is the key to our survival," Aleksander said. "But that doesn't mean we can't pause to thank those who have been our friends."

"Are you sure we're your friends?" Roger asked bluntly.

"You took in a helpless child and protected her as best you could," Aleksander said. "Those are the actions of a friend, whether you understood that or not."

"And if we'd rather leave?" Caroline asked.

Aleksander shrugged. "You'd miss a good dinner. But no one will try to stop you, if that's what you mean."

Roger looked sideways at Caroline. But her face held no

cues. "Personally, I'm too hungry to go hunting for a different restaurant," he decided. "Besides, I'd kind of like to see how this tree thing of yours works."

"Then you shall," Aleksander promised, standing up. "But first things first. Dinner is ready."

• •

"Thanks," Powell said, dropping the phone back into its cradle and scribbling a final note. "Bingo, Tommy. They found the Parks truck."

Fierenzo looked up from his report. "Where?"

"Way the hell down in Chelsea, near Pier 59," Powell said. "The branch was still in back, too, which pretty well proves picking it up was just a pretext to get something else. You want to get down there before they take it back to the garage?"

Fierenzo hesitated. But at this point, finishing his report and having that talk with Jonah were higher priorities. "No, I'd better stay here. You can go check it out if you want."

"What's the trouble?" Powell asked, craning his neck to see what Fierenzo was doing.

"Oh, it's this report," Fierenzo said, waving at the papers in front of him. "It wasn't until I started writing it down that I realized how insane the whole thing sounds. I need to find a way to phrase it so it'll be taken seriously."

"Good luck," Powell said, standing up and snagging his coat from the back of his chair. "I guess I'll go take a look at that truck."

"Thanks," Fierenzo said, looking at his watch. "And after that, you might as well go home. It's already past five, and you weren't even supposed to be working today. Say hi to Sandy for me, and have yourselves a nice quiet evening."

"If it's all the same to you, I think I'll leave your name out of it," Powell said dryly. "Just make sure *you* get some sleep, too." Threading his way between the desks, he left the squad room.

"Yeah," Fierenzo muttered after him. "Right." Taking a

sip of room-temperature coffee, wishing he'd paid more attention during his lone creative writing course in college, he turned back to his report.

• •

"The first few years were the hardest," Aleksander said, taking a sip of dark red wine from the delicately sculpted glass beside his plate. "Velovsky had helped us through the Ellis Island experience, but once we were on our own there was little he could do."

"I can imagine," Roger said. "Buildings were something brand new to you, weren't they?"

"They were certainly new to our generation," Aleksander said. "The Others had lived in buildings, though, and our Pastsingers had preserved those memories. Of course, our own short time in the transport had also given us a taste of what it was like to live with a roof over our heads."

"And of course, those of us who grew up here are quite comfortable with it," Iolanthe added. "There are times, especially in the winter, when our children would rather stay indoors than go out to their trees."

"Though I suspect the existence of video games has something to do with that," Vasilis murmured.

"Is that why you don't want to leave Manhattan?" Roger asked. "Because you've become accustomed to this way of living?"

"We don't want to leave Manhattan because it's our home," Aleksander said, a little tartly. "We fought for a place here; fought to learn the language and the culture; fought for jobs and livelihood and a safe place to raise our children. Why should we let ourselves be pushed out?"

"Yes, of course," Roger said. "I'm sorry."

"We don't ask for your sympathy," Aleksander said. "Just your understanding. And, if you choose, your presence at our side in this struggle."

"We'll do what we can," Roger said, wincing as a flurry

of ear-piercing giggles erupted from the other end of the table. "Practicing the Shriek, are they?"

"It's more a lack of control over their vocal range," Iolanthe said, leaning forward to look that direction. "Yvonne, can you keep it down a little?"

"Sorry," the woman at the far end of the table apologized. She snapped her fingers twice. "Children: silent manners. Eat."

Instantly, the six children subsided, their chatter and quiet laughter replaced by the industrious staccato clicks of fork on plate as they returned their attention to their food.

"As you can see, they're not that different from Human children," Aleksander commented with a smile.

"You've definitely acclimated to life in middle America," Roger agreed, looking at the children. "This setup reminds me of Christmas dinner with Caroline's family in Vermont."

"We're used to it, of course," Iolanthe said. "Do you have a large family, Caroline?"

"There are about twenty of us," Caroline said shortly, her voice studiously neutral.

Roger frowned at her. Her profile had a tightness about it, as if masking some emotion she wasn't interested in letting out. "You all right?" he murmured.

"Yes, you seem uncomfortable," Aleksander seconded. "Is something wrong?"

Caroline hesitated, then set her fork down and looked him squarely in the eye. "Yes, there's something wrong," she said. "We're all in here eating while Melantha's out there, alone and cold and hungry."

"I see," Aleksander said calmly. "And what makes you think no one's out in that cold looking for her?"

Caroline's expression cracked slightly. "Are you saying there *are*?"

"There are over eighty Greens right now walking the streets of Manhattan and calling to her," Iolanthe said gently. "Nearly everyone from Central and Morningside Parks, in fact. Does that ease your mind?"

Caroline's cheek twitched. "A little."

"Only a little?" Aleksander asked with a smile. "Please; speak on. What else can we do to quiet your concerns?"

Caroline took a careful breath. "Nikolos said you're leading the faction that wants to fight the Grays. Is that true?"

"Absolutely," Aleksander said calmly. "Like Nikolos, I was there. I saw what the Grays did, and I don't believe there can be peace between us."

"But not all the Greens agree with you," Caroline said. "And if you're going to fight, you need all of them on your side. True?"

"Actually, I only need a majority," Aleksander corrected. "Once I have that, the rest will follow."

"The point is that you need a way to rally the other Greens to your side," Caroline said. "I was just thinking that supposed treachery by the Grays might do the trick."

"'Supposed?'" Vasilis asked.

"I'm wondering if you might have snatched Melantha and are trying to blame it on the Grays," Caroline said.

Roger felt his stomach tighten. But to his relief, Aleksander didn't seem offended. "I see," the old Green said calmly. "And then?"

"And then what?" Caroline asked.

"How were we supposed to maintain the illusion of Gray treachery after Melantha had been brought back?" he asked. "Do you think Cyril and the others would ever follow me again after she'd told her story?"

Caroline swallowed visibly. "I suppose you'd have to kill her."

"Absolutely," Aleksander said, nodding. "And therein lies the flaw in your argument. Melantha is our key to victory in this battle, our ultimate weapon against the Grays. The last thing we would ever want is for harm to come to her." He shook his head. "No, Caroline. If I had Melantha, I wouldn't be pretending it was the Grays who had taken her. I would be reopening my argument and demanding another face-off with Cyril."

"We understand," Roger said quickly. "And I apologize for even suggesting you might do such a thing."

"That's all right," Aleksander said, his eyes still on Caroline. "Caroline?"

Her lip twitched, but she nodded. "I understand, too," she said.

"Good," Aleksander said, his voice almost cheerful again. "Then let's return to our meal, and hope that the searchers will find our lost child."

● ●

The sun was long gone by the time Fierenzo finally trudged out of the station house. The good news was that the report was finished: truthful enough to be legal, yet vague enough in the right places not to get him hauled in front of the departmental shrink.

The bad news was that the whole thing was little more than thin air tied together with fishing line. And Cerreta was bound to notice.

He scowled as he strode down the sidewalk toward where he'd parked his car a block away. The really annoying part was that he had witnesses who *could* put substance to the whole thing if they wanted to. But Oreste Green wasn't talking, the Whittiers weren't talking, and Jonah wasn't talking. Until one of them did, he wasn't going to be able to get much official traction on this.

He zipped his jacket a little tighter, hearing the faint crackle of the folded papers in his inside pocket as he did so. Now, though, maybe he had something to get at least one of those witnesses off the blocks.

He reached Amsterdam and turned north, looking through the tall chain-link fence beside him into the playground as he went around the corner. The place was undergoing some renovation, with a stack of long round timbers that looked like a Paul Bunyan version of Lincoln Logs piled near the fence. They were eventually going to be assembled into a new climbing structure, but up to now the only progress Fierenzo had seen had been the creation of a shallow pit entirely surrounded by orange mesh fences.

He was pondering the odd pace of construction in his city when two figures suddenly appeared in the middle of the sidewalk ten yards ahead of him.

Fierenzo slowed his pace, feeling his heart rate pick up, wondering where in hell the two men had come from. The chain-link fence didn't allow for any cover, there were no cars parked along the street, and the trees lining the sidewalk by the fence wouldn't conceal anyone over the age of two.

And yet, there they were. Friends of Jonah's, maybe?

They made no move as he continued toward them. They were both young, probably in their mid-twenties, and wiry looking. The taller had short dark hair and a narrow face with a long aquiline nose, while his companion was half a head shorter and had an abundance of curly black hair.

"Evening," Fierenzo called. "Chilly night, isn't it?"

"Yes, indeed," Aquiline Nose called back. "Are you Detective Sergeant Fierenzo?"

So they weren't just random if gutsy muggers, working in the shadow of the 24th Precinct House, but had been waiting for him specifically. "Yes," he confirmed, coming to a halt a double arm's length away from them. "What can I do for you?"

"We need the sketches," Nose said.

"All of them," Curly added.

"Sketches?" Fierenzo asked, deciding to try the dumb approach first. That tended to make people angry, and angry people often talked too much.

"The sketches Oreste Green made for you," Nose said calmly. "The ones of the two Grays on Waverly Place this morning."

"You mean Halfdan Gray and his son?" Fierenzo suggested.

"Halfdan?" Curly asked, frowning. "Oreste didn't say it was—"

"We'd love to have a nice chat about this," Nose cut him off. "But right now, all we want are the sketches."

Fierenzo shook his head. "Sorry, but they're back on my desk."

"Fine," Nose said agreeably. "Let's go get them."

"Okay," Fierenzo said. He turned around, making a quick visual sweep of the area as he did so; but instead of ending his turn pointed back down the sidewalk, he made a complete three-sixty, coming around again to face the two men, his Glock ready in his hand. "On second thought," he said as he wrapped his finger around the trigger, "you two can walk in front."

In the harsh glare of the streetlights, he saw Nose's lips curve into a patronizing smile. Opening his mouth wide, he screamed.

Fierenzo jerked as if he'd been kicked in the stomach. It was the same scream he'd heard outside the park that morning, the scream that had first driven him up a lamppost and then dropped him flat on the sidewalk.

But it was the same in quality only, in the eerie, unearthly tone and reverberation. For sheer force of impact, this blast was incredibly more powerful. Fierenzo found himself staggering backward as the sound slammed across his face and torso like hurricane-driven sand, battering his ears and eyes and face, turning his muscles to quivering rubber, twisting through his stomach and leaving a trail of agonized cramping in its wake.

Something slapped against the back of his head, and with a start he realized he'd blundered sideways into the chain-link fence. His gun was still clenched in his right hand; groping blindly over his shoulder with his left, he managed to get a grip on the cold metal rings. For a long moment he just hung there, struggling to keep his balance against the vertigo that was spinning the city around him like a carnival fun ride. Opening his eyes—he hadn't even realized until then that he'd shut them—he saw the two men walking confidently toward him. "Now, then," Nose said casually. "You were saying?"

Clamping his teeth against the nausea trying to turn his stomach inside out, Fierenzo lifted the dead weight of his gun from his side. "Police," he managed.

Nose didn't even break stride. Even as Fierenzo tried to

sort out which muscles controlled his trigger finger, the other stepped up and deftly twisted the gun out of his hand. From six inches away, he gave another short, bark-like scream, sending Fierenzo's head slamming backward into the fence. The fingers of his left hand spasmed, losing their grip, and he collapsed into a shivering heap on the sidewalk. Blinking tears from his eyes, he saw the two pairs of shoes in front of his face shift position as the men squatted down beside him. "That was very foolish," Nose said. "Now you're going to hurt for hours, and we're still going to have the sketches. Where are they?"

It would be so easy to give in, a corner of Fierenzo's mind whispered through the pain. All he had to do was point to his jacket pocket, and they would take the papers and leave him alone.

Even more importantly, he wouldn't have to suffer the shame of being walked through the station house like a staggering drunk or drooling Alzheimer's patient. He might still hurt for hours, but at least he'd be able to hang onto some shred of dignity.

He twisted his head around to look up into Nose's eyes. "I told you already," he croaked. "They're on my desk."

"Fine," Nose said, taking one of Fierenzo's arms. Curly took the other, and they hauled him to his feet. "Let's go take out a police station."

22

"—*Siv thuysen mecidu-noens fyl errea!*" eleven-year-old Phyllida called, standing tall and proud in a posture that reminded Roger of Melantha after she'd won her first game of Crazy Eights. The girl lifted her arms toward the ceiling, gave a flourish of hands and fingers that was too complicated for him to follow, then let her arms drop to her sides again.

"—and in peace they lived there all," her younger brother Yannis said with equal drama. "The Song of Tros-partia," the two children said in unison, and bowed low toward the five adults seated on the chairs and couches in front of them.

"Very nice," Caroline said approvingly, her tone finally carrying some genuine warmth. But of course, Caroline had always been a sucker for a good performance, especially one involving earnest amateurs. The children's impromptu recital had been just the thing to bring her around.

"Definitely," Roger seconded, wondering if he should point out that it had been far more interesting than that psychological drivel they'd suffered through three nights ago at the Miller Theater. Probably not. "Did they do the translation themselves?"

"Oh, no," Iolanthe said. "The Song of Tros-partia is a landmark saga of our earliest recorded history. We wouldn't trust it to any but the most Gifted of our Pastsingers."

"That was actually the third English translation of the Song," Aleksander added. "As we've grown more knowledgeable about your language's nuances over the years, the Pastsingers have tried to render it ever more accurately while still maintaining the classic form and sentence structure. This version was completed only two years ago."

"The children did a wonderful job," Caroline said. "Do you suppose one of them might grow up to be a Pastsinger?"

"We've wondered that ourselves," Vasilis acknowledged. "But then, every parent wants his or her child to be blessed with one of the Higher Gifts. We'll just have to wait and see."

"How exactly do these Gifts work?" Roger asked. "Is it genetic, or something else?"

"It's basically genetic," Vasilis said. "A pair of Laborers will tend to have Laborer children, a pair of Farseers will tend to have more Farseers, and so on."

"The whole dominant/recessive thing is more complicated than with Humans, though," Aleksander added. "Take Vasilis and Iolanthe, for example. As a Manipulator, Iolanthe has a small bit of the Groundshaker Gift, so if there was to be a true Groundshaker born among us, you might reasonably guess he or she would come out of this homestead. But their eldest daughter, Xylia, has already tested out as a Laborer, and there's no particular reason to assume Phyllida and Yannis will have any of the Mind Gifts."

"How about Melantha's parents?" Roger asked.

"Another good example," Aleksander said, nodding. "Zenas and Laurel are both Laborers, who by all rights should only have Laborer children. It just shows you can never predict where the lightning will strike."

"At any rate, we very much appreciate you sharing that with us," Roger said, looking back at the children.

"Children?" Iolanthe prompted.

"You're welcome," the two children said, again in unison.

"And now it's time for bed," Vasilis said. "Go get your night things on."

Yannis made a face, but apparently knew better than to argue. Nodding acknowledgment of their instructions, they left the living room.

"They do a very effective dramatic reading," Roger commented. "Though that unison thing is a little unnerving. Do they practice that, or does it come naturally?"

"It's mostly a side effect of our close-range empathic communication," Vasilis said. "And siblings often have clearer communication among themselves than usual."

"But I think they *do* practice, as well," Iolanthe added. "They've always been fascinated by coordinated movement, whether in dance routines or Olympic synchronized swimming."

"Any word yet from the searchers?" Caroline asked.

"Only that Melantha hasn't answered any of their calls," Aleksander said. If he was startled by the sudden change in subject, he didn't show it. "Trust me: the minute she does, you'll be among the first to know."

"Can't you just sense her presence or something?" Roger asked.

"Unfortunately, it's not that easy," Aleksander said. "If it was, we'd have found her at your apartment that very first night. No, if Melantha chooses not to answer a call, the searchers could walk right past her without knowing it."

"What about you?" Caroline asked. "Couldn't you order her to respond?"

"I think you're under the impression that Persuaders have considerably more power than we actually do," Aleksander said. "We don't *order* people to do anything. It really *is* just persuasion: the pushing of our particular point of view while still allowing the other person to make up his or her own mind."

"And thanks to you, Melantha has had a chance to rethink her earlier decision to allow this insane sacrifice," Vasilis added. "As long as that hasn't happened, there's still a chance for Aleksander to persuade enough of the Greens to our side."

"What happens if you do?" Roger asked. "Nikolos said Melantha isn't at her full strength yet."

"No, but merely the threat she poses might be enough," Aleksander said. "If we can convince the Grays that we would be willing to create a wholesale slaughter—which, of course, we aren't—perhaps we can make them leave New York of their own accord."

"Why don't *you* just leave?" Caroline asked. "There's a huge country out there just waiting for you."

"Because this is our home," Iolanthe said. "How do you just pick up and leave your home?"

"You did it once before," Caroline reminded her.

"It's not that simple."

"Why not?" Caroline persisted, starting to sound a little cross. "I'm still waiting to hear a good reason."

"No offense, Caroline, but it's really none of your business," Vasilis said, sounding a little cross himself. "If we choose to stay here—"

"It's all right, Vasilis," Aleksander interrupted him quietly. "We've told them this much. We might as well tell them the rest."

He looked back at Roger. "It has to do with our transport, the one buried under Ellis Island," he said. "We still use it to grow some of the herbs and spices we knew back on our own world."

"Yes, Velovsky mentioned that," Roger said. "Is there a problem with it?"

Aleksander sighed. "Just the rather awkward fact that we can't move it."

"Its propulsion systems don't work anymore?"

"They work just fine," Aleksander said dryly. "Unfortunately, so does Human sonar."

Roger grimaced, suddenly understanding. "Oh."

"'Oh,' indeed," Aleksander agreed heavily. "It was probably risky enough bringing it into New York harbor through all the traffic back in 1928. Now, with modern underwater detection, we couldn't move it a hundred yards without triggering an early-warning system somewhere."

"Especially after 9/11," Roger said.

"Indeed," Aleksander said. "So now you know the truth. We can't move the transport, and we also can't abandon it to the risk of being found by the Humans or, worse, by the Grays."

"Which leaves us only one choice," Iolanthe said. "We have to stand and fight."

"And the only way to do that is with Melantha," Aleksander concluded. "I'm convinced that if I can talk to her, I *can* bring her onto our side—" He broke off. "Ah—I see we're ready for bed."

Roger turned. Vasilis and Iolanthe's son and daughter had returned, along with the four other children who had been at dinner that evening. All were clothed in leotard-like outfits of various shades of green, with dark brown half-boots of a soft-looking material on their feet. "Nice pajamas," he commented.

"Has everyone cleaned their teeth?" Iolanthe asked, standing up. Six heads nodded silently. She nodded back, then turned to Roger and Caroline. "Would you like to come, too?" she invited. "You, especially, Roger, said you wanted to know more about the tree thing."

"Definitely," Roger said, getting to his feet. "Come on, Caroline. This should be interesting."

● ●

At first, Fierenzo's legs wouldn't work at all. He sagged in the middle of the sidewalk, muscles trembling uncontrollably as his attackers held him up by his arms like a puppet with broken strings. "You can do it," Nose said encouragingly. "You want to be here all night?"

"Go to hell," Fierenzo gritted out, fighting to get his feet under him. This time his knees held as he cautiously put a little of his weight on them. He tried taking a step, and collapsed again into his captors' grip as he let the joints buckle again.

Curly swore in an unfamiliar language. "Come on, Fierenzo—we didn't hit you *that* hard."

"Maybe you've never hit a diabetic before," Fierenzo snarled back. "Give me a chance, will you?"

"We're wasting time," Curly growled. "I say we go in and get them ourselves."

"Patience is a virtue," Nose said. "He can have one more minute."

Fierenzo smiled tightly to himself. In actual fact, despite the lingering pain, his muscles were recovering quite nicely. Already, he judged, he ought to be able to at least hobble if he had to.

But his captors didn't know that, and the throwaway fib about diabetes should have muddied the waters that much more. If his helpless act could buy him a little more time, he should be able to run or fight if and when a suitable opportunity presented itself.

He spent Nose's extra minute in a great show of agony and unsteadiness. All too soon, though, it was over. "That's long enough," Curly declared, balling his hand into a fist and giving Fierenzo's kidney a none-too-gentle prod. "Move, or we leave you here."

"You'll never get in there alone," Fierenzo ground out, the warning buying him another couple of seconds. He was definitely coming out of this now, and should be back to a reasonable level of strength by the time they reached the station house. Remembering to keep his movements shaky, letting the two men take as much of his weight as they were willing to, he started walking.

They had taken five steps, and were passing beneath one of the streetlights, when a section of sidewalk two yards in front of them exploded.

Fierenzo twitched reflexively as a thundercrack and a cloud of concrete dust washed over him. An instant later he lost his balance completely as his captors yanked him backward and twisted him around the other direction, hustling him back the way they'd come. They hadn't taken more than two steps when a second sledgehammer blow shattered another section of sidewalk, again a couple of yards ahead of them.

The two men got the message. They brought Fierenzo to a halt; and then, even as Nose hauled the detective out of his sag, Curly let go entirely and took off at a dead run down the sidewalk, zigzagging like a soldier crossing an enemy field of fire. Nose swiveled Fierenzo around again, this time to face the street, and shifted to a one-armed hold beneath his rib cage. His other hand snaked around to join it, and for a moment he seemed to be fiddling with something just beneath Fierenzo's sternum. His hands separated; and Fierenzo winced as a gleaming, short-bladed knife flashed into view, clutched in Nose's right hand. It waved in front of his eyes a moment, a silent warning to behave himself, then came to rest against his throat. "Show yourself or the cop dies!" he shouted past Fierenzo's ear.

The only answer was another crack of exploding sidewalk, this one a yard to their right, followed by another the same distance to their left. Fierenzo strained his eyes against the glare of the streetlight and the headlights of the oblivious drivers zooming past, trying to spot the shooter.

But there were no figures moving around in the shadows of the buildings across the street, and no obvious silhouettes in any of the windows. Another chunk of pavement disintegrated to their right without even a hint of a muzzle flash that he could see.

Nose apparently couldn't find the shooter, either. He snarled something under his breath and again shifted grip, this time grabbing a handful of Fierenzo's hair and yanking his head up and back to expose his throat more conveniently to the knife. "Last chance!" he shouted. He hauled Fierenzo backward, and there was a metallic rustle as he brushed up against the playground fence. "Show yourself!"

Fierenzo stiffened. With his face pointed upward at this new angle he couldn't see what, if anything, was going on with the shooter across the street.

But he was in perfect position to see the shadowy figure that glided silently across the night sky above the glare of the streetlights to his right, dropping toward the playground behind him.

He barely had time to wonder whether he had imagined it when a voice came suddenly from across the street. "All right!" it called. "I'm here! Don't hurt him!"

"There you are," Nose muttered. Taking a deep breath, he screamed.

The earlier screams, aimed at Fierenzo from six feet away, had been bad enough. This one, bellowed practically in his ear, was a hundred times worse. His whole body stiffened and then turned to jelly, sagging him toward the ground in spite of the grip on his hair. Whereas before the world had seemed to twist around him, now it was as if he no longer had any direction at all. His chest and gut were a whirlpool of agony as his internal organs seemed to grate violently against each other. He wanted desperately to be sick but his stomach muscles couldn't even organize themselves enough to vomit.

The scream cut off into a fainter echo. At first he thought it was just a trick of his ears or mind as they vibrated with an afterimage of the sound. But then the fainter scream came again, and he realized that it was coming from Curly, somewhere down the street. He hadn't run off in panic, as Fierenzo had thought, but had merely moved away to deprive their attacker of the advantages of a bunched target.

Curly screamed again, too far away for Fierenzo to feel any fresh effects from the noise; and as some of the other agony began to subside he became aware of a duller secondary pain coming from the top of his head. Nose was still holding him mostly upright by his hair, the knife still resting against his neck, using him as a human shield against the silent gun across the street.

And as Curly's screams continued and Fierenzo's brain started sluggishly working again, he realized that the attacker's gun had indeed gone completely silent. Twisting his neck, he got one eye turned far enough to look toward the street.

There, on one of the twenty-story buildings on the far side of the pavement, was a sight that a week ago would have made his jaw drop all the way to the ground. Halfway up the side, midway between two of the darkened windows, a human figure was pressed against the sheer wall, arms and legs spread-eagled as if he'd been shot out of a cannon and slammed bodily into the brickwork. There was no sign of ropes or a platform, no indication even of any climbing hooks.

The scream came again; and as the sound echoed off the building, he saw the figure's right foot twitch loose from the wall as if his magic glue had suddenly evaporated. He scrabbled frantically for a grip, sliding a couple of feet down the side before he could catch himself again. Clearly, the screams were having the same debilitating effect on him that they'd had on Fierenzo.

Just as clearly, he was hanging on for dear life. Curly gave another scream, a short one this time, and the human fly slid another foot downward.

Fierenzo felt his jaw tighten as he finally caught on to the strategy. By moderating the length of their scream attacks, his captors were trying to bring the attacker down in a controlled fashion; not hard enough to drop him ten stories to his death, but also not giving him a chance to fight back.

Only they didn't know about the other man, the one who had glided over their heads during the noisy attack on the sidewalk an eternity of pain ago. The man who might at this very moment be moving stealthily up behind him and his captor.

The only problem was, the way things stood right now there was precious little he or anyone else could do from back there without putting Fierenzo's life at risk. The chain-link fence effectively blocked any way of getting to Nose's knife hand, and Nose himself showed no sign of letting down his guard any time soon.

Of course, for all he knew the stalker might be focused exclusively on rescuing the figure being forced down the building across the street. He might not care at all whether or not a police detective ended the evening with his throat still intact.

It was Fierenzo's job to make sure he had that option.

"Let me go," he gasped, putting all the agony and fear into his voice that he could. It didn't take much effort. "Please. You've got him—he can't do anything to you anymore. Please—my stomach—I'm going to be sick—"

"Oh, for—" Lifting the knife away from Fierenzo's throat, Nose let go of his hair and disgustedly shoved him away to sprawl onto the sidewalk. Fierenzo tried to catch himself, but his disobedient muscles weren't up to the task, and a chorus line of stars flashed across his vision as the side of his head slammed into the cold concrete. Stifling a groan, he flopped over onto his back to look up at Nose. The other looked back for a moment, his face expressionless, then shifted his attention back to the building across the street. From down the sidewalk, Curly gave another of his short screams, rattling Fierenzo's ears still further.

And as the two of them concentrated on bringing down their opponent, they completely missed the giant Lincoln Log that came swinging up out of the darkness of the school ground to land across the top of the chain-link fence.

The figure who ran up the makeshift ramp was nearly to the top when the rattle of the metal rings finally woke Nose to his danger. He spun around, searching for the source of the noise, his knife arcing up into guard position. But he was too late. Even as he spotted the log and looked up, the new-comer had reached the top and taken off upward in a high, arching leap. Nose spun around to follow his motion, knife held high, his mouth opening for another scream.

He never got it out. As the newcomer reached the top of his arc there was a sound like a guitar string being plucked, and something gripped in his left hand sent a slender line of white shooting into Nose's chest.

The shot staggered him backward, the intended scream coming out as an agonized cough instead. The gunman got off a second shot, this time bouncing Nose off the fence, be-fore he landed on the edge of the street. His knees bent to absorb his momentum; and as he crouched in place for a second, Fierenzo finally got a clear look at him in the street-light. Short and squat, he was dressed in dark clothing with a ski cap pulled down to his eyes and a patterned scarf cov-ering his nose and mouth.

A scarf that looked suspiciously familiar.

A long, ululating scream erupted from down the block. Clenching his teeth against the renewed surge of pain, Fierenzo twisted his head around to look. Curly, of course; but to Fierenzo's surprise, the other wasn't running for cover, but was instead charging full-tilt toward the crouch-ing gunman.

For a heart-stopping pair of seconds Fierenzo thought that the tactic was going to succeed as the gunman stag-gered under the sonic assault. But then he regained his bal-ance and leveled his weapon at his attacker. Bracing his left hand with his right in a traditional marksman's stance, he fired.

Curly didn't just stagger the way Nose had. The white line that ran into his chest not only stopped him dead in his tracks, but delivered enough impact to throw him backward off his feet. He hit the sidewalk with a sickening thud and lay still.

Beside Fierenzo, Nose was trying to get to his feet. Shifting aim, the gunman fired again into his chest. Nose went down again, and this time stayed there. For a moment the gunman peered at him, as if trying to decide whether he needed an insurance shot, apparently decided against it, and turned to Fierenzo. "You okay?" he grunted.

"Oh, just dandy," Fierenzo wheezed back. The scarf was familiar, all right. So was the voice coming from behind it. "You have a good nap?"

Jonah shook his head. "You came *that* close, Detective," he said darkly. "You play games with these people, you're going to be burned."

"Tell me about it," Fierenzo said, wincing as he rolled onto his back and tried to work his trembling hand into his coat pocket. "Your fingers working any better than mine right now?"

"What do you need?" Jonah asked, squatting a little unsteadily beside him.

"My phone," Fierenzo said, his fingers finally closing on the device. "I have to call an ambulance."

"You'll be all right," Jonah assured him. "There's nothing a hospital could do for you anyway."

"It's not for me," Fierenzo said, easing out the phone. "And while I appreciate you coming to my assistance, I'm going to have to ask you to surrender your weapon."

"What, you mean the ambulance is for *them*?" Jonah asked scornfully. Reaching down, he plucked the phone from Fierenzo's fingers. "Sorry."

"*Damn* it," Fierenzo snarled, making a useless attempt to grab it away. "Give that back."

"They don't need *or* want an ambulance," Jonah said, turning the phone off and dropping it into his own pocket. "Trust me. Anyway, what are you feeling so charitable for? They attacked you, remember?"

"Doesn't matter," Fierenzo bit back. "I still can't just leave them bleeding on the sidewalk."

"This isn't like the guns you're used to," Jonah said patiently, hefting the flattened mallet Fierenzo had seen him holding earlier that afternoon on the alley fire escape. "Though I'll admit the one down the block will probably hurt a lot longer than you will. Anyway, you're the only one who's bleeding."

Frowning, Fierenzo reached up and touched his cheek. There was blood there, all right, a thin trail rolling down into his collar from the bottom of his ear. "I still need that weapon," he said, wondering what kind of permanent hearing damage he'd managed to sustain tonight.

"Sure," Jonah said, holding the gun out in front of him. "Now you see it—"

He opened his hand; and right in front of Fierenzo's eyes, the gun seemed to come apart into a set of slender, silvery snakes. For an instant they stretched out along the insides of Jonah's fingers and then vanished up his sleeve.

"—now you don't," Jonah finished, and Fierenzo could imagine a grin behind the concealing scarf. "It's all in the wrist."

"Look—"

"Later," Jonah cut him off, taking his upper arm and starting to pull him upright. "We've got to get out of here before their friends arrive."

"You mean there are more—aaah," Fierenzo interrupted himself as his whole body seemed to explode in new pain. "Easy—*easy!*"

"Sorry, but we can't wait," Jonah said, continuing to pull. "The only reason they're not on top of us already is that they're scattered all over Manhattan looking for Melantha."

"For Melantha?" Fierenzo asked. "What do they—aaah!"

"Yeah, I know," Jonah said sympathetically. "Try not to groan too loudly, will you? It attracts attention."

He worked Fierenzo to his feet, then ducked over and grabbed his leg. A second later, Fierenzo found himself hanging over the other's shoulder in a fireman's carry. Be-

fore he could protest, they were heading down the sidewalk
at a fast trot, each step adding an extra jolt to his pain.

He was clenching his teeth against the agony, staring at
the swaying sidewalk flowing beneath Jonah's feet, when
the blackness finally took him.

23

The group didn't go out the front door, as Caroline had
expected, but instead slipped out the back. "There's
someone in a car watching the building," Vasilis explained
as he led the way around a group of bushes and across the
street toward the park. "Probably one of Detective
Fierenzo's associates. It wouldn't do to let him see this."

"You're sure he can't?" Roger asked.

"Our trees aren't in his line of sight," Vasilis assured him.

Aleksander seemed to stir. "And we're watching him, in
case he decides to leave his car," he added.

Caroline eyed him, frowning. He'd done it again, just as
he had a few minutes ago. For a moment he'd seemed to drift
away into his own private world of thought or meditation.

Or communication? Casually, she angled her path to
come alongside him.

There it was: the same almost-words flowing around the
corners of her mind that she'd heard in the cab that morning. And if she was judging the texture of the thoughts correctly, there was a definite urgency to the communication.

Had someone found Melantha?

"What do you do about these fences?" Roger asked as
they came up to the gate. "A lot of Manhattan's parks are
locked up at dusk."

"We have ways," Vasilis said, stepping up to the gate and

getting a grip on the hinge side. He glanced around; and then, to Caroline's surprise, he pulled the gate open from that end, swiveling it around the latch and lock. "All the gated parks we use are gimmicked," he explained, as the others filed through the opening. "Usually it's a trick gate, but some of them have a section of the fence itself we can open up."

Once inside, the Greens split into two groups, Vasilis and Iolanthe and their children turning south while the other two adults herded the rest of the children to the east. Aleksander gestured toward the first group, and he and the Whittiers fell in behind them. Caroline found herself looking at the trees with new eyes as her feet crinkled through the dead leaves. Were there Greens hiding in all of them, she wondered, nestled in comfortably for the night? Or was Shurz Park something of a new frontier, with room still available for expansion?

"Here we are," Iolanthe announced as they reached a small clump of trees. "Okay, children. Hugs."

In turn, Phyllida and Yannis gave her and Vasilis a hug and kiss. "Now say good-night to our visitors, and it's off to sleep."

"Good-night, Persuader Aleksander," the children said gravely in unison, bowing to the old Green. "Good-night Roger. Good-night Caroline."

"Very nice," Vasilis said approvingly. "Yannis, do you want a boost?"

"Nuh-uh," the boy said. Stepping to the tree, he wrapped his arms around the trunk. Pressing himself against it, he melted into the bark and vanished.

Roger let out a huff of air. "Whoa," he murmured. "That's . . . really weird."

"I suppose," Aleksander said with a shrug. "We're used to it ourselves, of course."

"Yes," Roger said. "Vasilis, what did you mean about a boost?"

"That's his branch up there," Vasilis said, pointing to a

large limb veering off from the main trunk about eight feet from the ground. "I'll be lifting Phyllida up to hers in a minute, but Yannis prefers to climb up for himself."

"From *inside* the tree?" Caroline asked.

"It's tricky for a seven-year-old," Vasilis said. "But he's always been a little chipmunk, and he enjoys the challenge." He turned to his daughter. "Your turn, Phyllida."

He gave her one last hug, turning the embrace into a lift as he caught her under her rib cage and hoisted her up to a branch coming off the opposite side of the trunk from Yannis's and a couple of feet lower. He spun her halfway around to face the branch, and she wrapped her arms and legs around it. For a moment she stared solemnly at her father, and Caroline again felt the sense of communication as they apparently shared some private joke together. Then, crinkling her nose at him, the girl melted into and through the branch the way her brother had.

"Clothes and all," Roger murmured. "Special material?"

"Special material, special preparation, special weave," Iolanthe told him. "We used to have to do everything by hand, but now we own a small manufacturing plant where one of the lines makes clothing for all of us."

"That whole line handled by Green Laborers and Manipulators, of course," Vasilis added. "Do you want to stay, Iolanthe, or would you rather go back to the apartment and our conversation?"

"Actually, we need to be going," Caroline put in before Iolanthe could answer. "Thank you for the wonderful dinner."

"Yes, thank you," Roger added, frowning a little at Caroline. "We enjoyed spending time with your family and learning more about your culture."

"It was our privilege," Vasilis said. "Would you like me to escort you home?"

"No, that's all right," Roger said. "We'll be fine."

"As you wish," Vasilis said. "Let's go back to the homestead—I believe you left your purse there, Caroline—and we'll say good-night."

"I'll say good-night now," Iolanthe said. She reached out

and took Caroline's hand, squeezing it gently rather than shaking it, then did the same with Roger. "I'll see you soon, Vasilis," she added, giving her husband a kiss. Stepping to the tree, she wrapped her arms around the trunk and melted inside.

They passed again through the trick gate, and after another roundabout path they were back at the apartment. "Again, we're glad you came," Vasilis said as he ushered them into the living room. "Please feel free to drop by anytime you're in the neighborhood."

"We will," Roger promised. "I'd like to try one of your restaurants sometime, too. Do you have a list of their names and addresses?"

"I have one," Aleksander said, reaching into an inside pocket and pulling out what looked like a business card. "In fact—just a moment." Turning the card over, he pulled out a pen and wrote briefly on the back. "Here you go," he said, handing it to Roger.

Caroline peered over his shoulder. Beneath two lines of cryptic symbols were two more lines written in English: *The bearer is entitled to two meals.* It was signed *Aleksander.*

"That's great," Roger said. "Thank you."

"What's this other writing?" Caroline asked.

"It's *Kailisti,* the language we spoke back on our own world," Aleksander identified it. "Not much use here, of course, but we still teach it to our children."

"In some homesteads, the adults insist they speak it at home for a few years to make sure they don't forget it," Vasilis added.

"Did Melantha's homestead do it that way?" Caroline asked, thinking back to Melantha's accent.

"Probably," Aleksander said, smiling. "Melantha's maternal grandmother was a Pastsinger who felt very strongly about maintaining our ties to our heritage. I doubt she let Melantha and her brother even learn English until they were three or four years old." He shook his head. "She's gone now. Two years ago."

"I'm sorry," Caroline said automatically.

Aleksander shrugged. "In general, we live longer than Humans," he said. "But in the end, death comes to us all. At any rate, thank you for coming tonight. Now that you truly understand the stakes involved, I hope you'll do the right thing if Melantha comes back to you."

"I hope she will," Caroline said. "Good-night."

Roger didn't say anything as they stepped out into the darkened street, but Caroline could sense the familiar tension in his stance and walk. They'd made it a quarter of the way down the block, and Caroline was trying to figure out how to break the ever-thickening wall of silence when he finally spoke. "There he is," he said quietly, nodding back over his shoulder. "That car pulling out—see it?"

She pretended to look at something on the ground and caught a glimpse of a car easing away from the curb. "Yes," she said. "I hope you're not too mad at me."

"I'm not mad at you at all," he said, his voice puzzled but definitely not angry. "Why would I be mad?"

"You were obviously having a good time in there, and I pulled us out," she said, feeling a sense of relief as the imaginary wall melted away. "And you were so quiet on the way out."

He shook his head. "You know, Caroline, I'm not angry with you nearly as often as you seem to think. I wasn't talking as we left because I wasn't sure who might be listening. I didn't want anyone eavesdropping while you told me what was bothering *you*." He looked sideways at her. "Or was *I* wrong about that?"

"No, I wanted to get out of there," she confirmed. "There's something wrong about all this, Roger."

He was silent for another three paces. "Can you give me a hint?" he asked. "Sorry—I didn't mean it that way. What I meant was, can you narrow it down?"

Caroline chewed at her lip, trying to put her uneasiness into words. "Maybe it's the stiffness of the whole culture," she said slowly. "The children seem almost *too* well behaved, the adults a little *too* upright and noble. And it seemed like Aleksander and the others were bending over backwards not to talk about Melantha except when we brought her up."

"Well, of course they were putting their best foot forward tonight," Roger said. "They want us to like them."

"Yes, but why?"

"Well, for starters, Velovsky's not going to live forever," Roger pointed out. "Maybe they want to establish another friendly contact in the human world for after he's gone."

"Or maybe they're just trying to manipulate us onto their side so we'll give Melantha to them if she comes back," Caroline countered. "Because they're still hiding things, Roger. That business about Persuaders not being able to order people around, for starters. I was there; I *know* Melantha was under Cyril's control until I snapped her out of it. And I know he was trying it with me, too."

Roger was silent a moment. "If that's true, a Persuader ought to be able to order her to reveal herself, too," he pointed out. "In which case, why wasn't Aleksander out helping with the search?"

Caroline shivered. "Maybe because he already knows where she is."

"In which case, you can say good-bye to any peace treaty," Roger said. "Hell."

"There's something else about Aleksander," Caroline went on. "There at the end he was talking to someone with that telepathic or empathic thing they do. It seemed to be something very serious or urgent."

"Something about Melantha?"

"That's what I'm wondering," Caroline said.

"In that case, I wonder if the whole evening might have been staged," he said slowly. "Something to keep us occupied while they did something with her."

Caroline thought back. "I don't think so," she said. "The family stuff seemed genuine, anyway. I'm sure the Greens have a great love for each other, both their immediate families and their people as a whole. But that doesn't mean

Aleksander wouldn't lie to get what he wants. In fact, it might make it more likely that he would."

Roger was silent another five steps. "Let's assume you're right, and that they're trying to manipulate us," he said at last. "Let's further assume that they have Melantha, having either snatched her last night or found her just now. Then the first question is whether they would hide her in the city or—"

He broke off as a car suddenly roared up from behind them and squealed to a halt. Before Caroline could do more than grab Roger's arm, the door swung open and the driver hopped out, turning to glare over the car roof at them. "Police!" he called, holding out a badge. "Roger Whittier?"

"Yes," Roger said nervously. "Is there a prob—?"

"Get in," the cop cut him off, gesturing emphatically toward the back door.

"Wait a second," Roger protested. "What are you charging us with?"

"You're not being charged—yet," the other said. "You're wanted as material witnesses."

"Witnesses to what?" Caroline asked, her heart suddenly pounding in her throat. *Melantha? No—please not Melantha.*

"Detective Fierenzo has disappeared," the cop bit out. "He may have been murdered."

24

"According to witnesses, the screaming started about an hour ago," Detective Powell said, swiveling one of the interrogation room's plain wooden chairs around and sitting down straddling it, his forearms resting on the back. "It was accompanied by the sounds of someone hammering their way through several sections of sidewalk. The whole thing lasted maybe ten minutes before someone called it in and we got out there. By then, Detective Fierenzo was gone."

"And no one in the station heard any of it?" Roger asked.

Powell shook his head disgustedly. "They definitely didn't hear the screams. If they heard the hammering, they took it for something else and ignored it." His eyes bored into Roger's. "But from the descriptions, it sounds a lot like the stuff that went down by your friends' apartment in Yorkville yesterday evening."

"It does, doesn't it?" Roger agreed heavily, a cold chill running through him. So that was it. The battle lines had been drawn, and the war had begun. With or without Melantha, it had begun. Was that in fact the urgent communication that Caroline had detected from Aleksander? That the fragile peace had finally been shattered?

Or worse, did it mean Aleksander himself had coldbloodedly ordered the war to begin? "You said the screaming started *before* the shots?" he asked.

"That's what two of the witnesses said," Powell said, eyeing him closely. "The others weren't sure. Is it important?"

"I don't know," Roger said. "It might be."

Powell hitched his chair a couple of inches closer. "Try me."

"I don't have anything solid," Roger hedged, throwing a quick glance at Caroline's pale face across the table. "This may be part of a—well, sort of a gang war."

"Between the Greens and the Grays?"

"Possibly," Roger conceded. "Like I said, I don't know anything for sure."

"What about Fierenzo?" Powell persisted. "What happened to him?"

"Are you sure something *did* happen to him?" Caroline asked.

"His gun was found at the scene," Powell told her. "His car's still parked nearby, and there's no answer at either his apartment or cell phones."

He shifted his glare back to Roger. "*And* we found traces of blood at the scene that match his type. Why is it important whether the screams or cracked concrete came first?"

"It might tell us who started the fight," he said. "But if the witnesses aren't sure, it doesn't help."

Powell grunted. "Who were you visiting this evening?"

"A couple named Vasilis and Iolanthe," Roger told him. There was no point in waffling on that one; a simple canvass of the building would pinpoint the Greens' apartment quickly enough.

"Friends?"

"New acquaintances," Roger said. "They invited us to dinner."

"Anybody at this party make any phone calls?"

In spite of the seriousness of the situation, Roger had to suppress a smile at that one. Checking out the phones was a time-honored police method for ferreting out links between suspects. Unfortunately for them, the technique was useless against Greens. "I didn't see anyone use a phone while I was there," he said truthfully.

For a moment Powell eyed him in silence. "You know, Roger, we've been assuming you and your wife were more or less innocent bystanders who got dropped into this situation," he said at last. "But that assumption could change at any time."

"We haven't lied to you," Caroline said.

"You haven't told the whole truth, either," Powell countered. "And you might want to bear in mind that complicity in a police officer's murder carries the death penalty in New York."

Roger felt his skin prickle. "We were all the way across the city when Detective Fierenzo disappeared," he said, fighting to keep his voice calm. "That other cop—Smith—was watching the building the whole time."

Powell shrugged. "You're the legal expert," he said. "But if I were you, I might take another look at the laws concerning conspiracy and obstruction."

With an effort, Roger met his gaze. "Are you charging us?" he asked. "If not, we're leaving."

Again, Powell let the silence hang in the air a few seconds. Then his lips puckered slightly. "Have a good evening," he said, gesturing toward the door.

They had to pass by the site of the attack on their way home. It was like a replay of the previous night, Roger thought morosely as he gazed at the bright lights and the purposeful men and women looking for clues.

Experienced investigators with nothing to investigate. However the Grays' hammerguns worked, Roger's experience with them had already shown they left no bullets or other evidence behind. The Greens' Shriek was by its very nature impossible to analyze after the fact. And once again there was no body left at the scene.

Only this time it wasn't a Green body that had melted quietly into the bushes. This was the body of a human police officer.

"You think Fierenzo accidentally walked into the middle of a skirmish?" he asked Caroline quietly.

"Doesn't seem likely," she said. "Both sides have gone to a lot of effort to keep their existence a secret. I would think they'd cut and run if someone showed up, especially a police officer."

"Unless that's why they made off with him afterward, either alive or dead," Roger pointed out. "In fact, that could be what Aleksander was so hot and bothered about back at the park. Maybe what you were picking up was him trying to figure out how to cover over the mess."

"Maybe," Caroline murmured. "But if they decided Fierenzo knew too much, what does that say about *us*?"

Roger felt a shiver run up his back. "They *did* let us go," he pointed out.

"Because Smith was watching the building," she said. "I wonder if we should stay away from our apartment."

"Or should get out of Dodge completely," Roger said grimly. "Unfortunately, both sides seem perfectly capable of finding us anytime they want."

"Yes," Caroline agreed, her voice suddenly sounding odd.

He glanced at her. She was staring straight ahead, an intense look on her face. "What is it?" he asked.

"Aleksander wants Melantha to destroy the Grays so that the Greens can stay in Manhattan," she said slowly. "Right?"

"Right," Roger said, wondering where she was going with this.

"Cyril wants to sacrifice Melantha so that the Greens and Grays can both stay in Manhattan," she continued. "Either way, they all want to stay in Manhattan."

"And Aleksander told us why," Roger said, feeling a touch of impatience. He didn't need a recap of the obvious. "They need to stay with their transport."

"Right," Caroline said. "So why did Nikolos suggest sacrificing Melantha and then leaving?"

Roger frowned into the darkness, his impatience evaporating. "He *did* say that, didn't he?" he agreed. "He said they should sacrifice Melantha and then pull back to upstate New York."

"I could understand that coming from one of the younger Greens," Caroline went on. "They might not have the same hatred as their parents, or might not be so attached to the place they'd escaped a war to reach. But Nikolos is one of the original settlers."

"Yes," Roger said, rubbing his cheek. "I don't know much about warfare, but it seems to me a good tactician wouldn't run *away* from something as much as he would run *to* something. I wonder if there's a way to find out if he has any interests upstate."

"If you mean real estate interests, sure," Caroline said. "I can pull up the database from my office."

"Upstate records, too?" Roger asked, lifting his eyebrows. "I thought you were limited to the city."

"No, I can get everything in New York state," she said. "Of course, if it's not in his name we're never going to find it."

"These are people who insist on hanging onto the Green name even when they're jammed thirty to an apartment,"

Roger reminded her. "I think we can assume it won't be listed under John Doe."

"Probably," Caroline agreed. "When should we start? Tomorrow morning?"

Roger looked around. He didn't see anyone nearby; but with Greens and Grays that didn't mean much. "Let's do it now," he decided abruptly. "Let's get the car out of the garage and do it right now."

"The *car*?" she echoed, sounding startled. "I thought you hated driving in Manhattan on Saturday night."

"I hate getting murdered in my bed even worse," he told her grimly. "Besides, if we find something, we'll want to get right on it. I just hope I remembered to fill the tank before we put it away."

• •

It took Caroline two hours to compile a list of all the Greens with large land holdings within two hundred miles of the city. After that came two more hours of battling the organized chaos of Saturday night traffic before they finally made it out of the worst of the metropolitan traffic. They found a modest motel near Tarrytown, begged two sets of toiletries from the desk clerk, and settled in to study Caroline's list.

Half an hour later, they'd found it.

"That's the place," Roger declared, tapping the listing for a hundred-acre estate tucked away in the hills between Shandaken and Bushnellsville. "E. and N. Green Associates. 'E' for Elymas; 'N' for Nikolos."

"Certainly looks like it," Caroline agreed. "Though I still don't know what we're expecting to find."

"Me, neither," Roger confessed. "Maybe it's nothing but an emergency refugee area Nikolos set up when they first got here. I still want to know what he's up to." He glanced at his watch. "We'd better turn in, too. We'll have another couple of hours' drive in the morning, and we'll want to get as early a start as we can."

"Yes," Caroline murmured, her voice suddenly dark. "Roger . . . you don't suppose Fierenzo could have been so scared by the Shrieks and hammerguns that he just ran away, do you?"

"It's possible," Roger said encouragingly, squeezing her hand. He didn't believe it for a minute, of course. But then, neither did she. "But whatever happened, there's nothing we can do about it tonight," he added. "Come on, let's get to bed."

25

The first thing Fierenzo noticed as he dragged himself back toward consciousness was that he seemed to be surrounded by a diffuse glow of light. The second was that the familiar city noises reaching his ears were distant, yet too distinct to be filtered through the walls of his apartment.

The third thing he noticed was that he was freezing.

Cautiously, he opened his eyes. The glow was just as diffuse with his eyes open as it had been with them closed, a sort of light cream-colored glow that seemed to fill the sky above him. Blinking to try to clear his vision, he reached a hand tentatively upward.

His fingertips twitched back as they unexpectedly ran into something soft and springy. He blinked again; and suddenly his eyes found the proper focus. He was lying under a length of fabric angling downward over him like the side of a tent.

He turned his head. Not a tent, actually, but a simple lean-to attached at its upper edge to a rough concrete wall about three feet to his right. Wincing as a stab of pain shot through his neck, he followed the concrete wall down to where it ended at a flat expanse of what looked like roofing material on which he was lying.

"Welcome back," a familiar voice said from somewhere in the direction of his feet. "How do you feel?"

Fierenzo lifted his head to look that direction, noting as he did so that he was covered from feet to armpits in a thin blanket the same color as the tent material. Jonah was sitting at the far end of the lean-to, his back braced against the concrete wall. "I've been better," Fierenzo said. "Is it me, or is it cold in here?"

"It's mostly you," Jonah said. "One of the more delightful side effects of getting hit by a Green Shriek is that your body's not quite sure what to do with all the pain that's been dumped on it. Three times out of five it decides you must be sick, and kicks up a fever for a few hours. I can get you another blanket if you want."

"No, that's all right," Fierenzo said, turning halfway up onto his right side and resting his head on his right palm. Now that he was awake and moving, he could feel the chill starting to recede. Lifting his wrist, he peered at his watch: just after two o'clock on Sunday afternoon. He'd slept nearly eighteen hours. "Where am I?"

"On a rooftop in Chinatown," Jonah said. "This is my assigned station for keeping an eye on the Greens in the Sara D. Roosevelt Park and watching for Melantha to make an appearance."

"Really," Fierenzo said. Chinatown was in the southern end of Manhattan, miles from where he'd been attacked. "How did I get here?"

Jonah shrugged. "We have ways of getting around town quickly."

"Ah," Fierenzo said. Surreptitiously, he touched his chest and heard the reassuring crackle of paper from his inner pocket. At least the sketches were still safe. "Who assigned you here?"

"Halfdan and his sons are in charge of the surveillance and sentry arrangements," Jonah said, giving him an indulgent smile. "Does that actually tell you anything?"

"Enough," Fierenzo assured him, only lying a little. "As a matter of fact, I know all about the Greens and the Grays of

New York." He lifted his eyebrows significantly. "Jonah *Gray*."

Jonah's smile didn't even flicker. "Not bad," he said. "Actually, my name isn't Gray. We're not as fastidious as the Greens about wearing our affiliation on our sleeves for the world to see. In fact, we've been branching out for several decades now, name-wise."

"But you *are* a Gray?"

"I am," Jonah said. "Though I doubt you understand what that means."

"Let me take a crack at it," Fierenzo offered. "You can climb buildings, you can turn invisible, you have disappearing guns, you can fly, and you aren't human. Did I miss anything?"

Jonah's lips puckered. "You've been paying better attention than I thought," he acknowledged reluctantly. "That puts me in kind of an awkward position."

"Sorry to hear that," Fierenzo said, gently rubbing his left elbow along his rib cage where his shoulder holster was nestled. From the feel of it, he could tell that the gun itself was gone. "It seems a waste of effort, though, to save my life, then turn around and kill me yourself."

"Oh, those Greens wouldn't have killed you," Jonah said. "A cop? They wouldn't have dared."

"They tried to kill *you*," Fierenzo pointed out.

Jonah waved a hand in dismissal. "Different situation. And don't worry, I'm not going to kill you, either. It's just that your dropping in like this is going to make everything more complicated than it already was."

"Complication seems to be the order of the day," Fierenzo said. "Can you at least tell me why you're here?"

"I already did," Jonah said. "I'm watching for Melantha."

"I meant your people," Fierenzo said. "What do you want here on Earth?"

Jonah shrugged. "The same thing everyone else wants," he said, an odd note of sadness in his voice. "To live and work and raise our families in peace. 'Give me your tired, your poor, your huddled masses yearning to breathe free.' That's us."

"Very nice," Fierenzo complimented him. "I see you've been here long enough to take the tour of Liberty Island."

"Actually, I've never been out there," Jonah admitted. "But then, most of us natives never have."

Natives. Fierenzo's heartbeat picked up a little. Now they were getting somewhere. "Natives of what?" he asked carefully. "From where?"

"Natives of New York, of course," Jonah said, sounding puzzled. "I was born and raised in Queens."

Fierenzo blinked, the whole Space Invaders scenario threatening to unravel in front of his eyes. "What?"

There must have been something in his expression, because Jonah chuckled. "No, really," he said. "And *I'm* third-generation. Our people have been living here since 1928."

"Really," Fierenzo said, not sure whether to be relieved or not. Was a Space Invasion less of a threat if it waited three-quarters of a century to get moving? "Doing what?"

"What I just said," Jonah told him. "Living and working and raising our families." His lips compressed. "Of course, that was before we found out the Greens were here, too."

"I take it you have a problem with them?"

"Aside from the fact that they want to destroy us?" Jonah countered, his voice turning grim. "If you knew what—excuse me," he interrupted himself, lifting his left hand to his cheek the way Fierenzo had seen him do back at the apartment. "Yes?" he said.

Only this time, Fierenzo was able to see that the hand was empty. Another of his now-you-see-it, now-you-don't gadgets?

"On my way," Jonah said, lowering his hand and twitching his little finger. "I'll be right back," he added to Fierenzo, hopping up into a crouch and opening the cloth flap that closed off the end of the lean-to. A momentary burst of cold air rolled over Fierenzo, and he caught a glimpse of a section of rooftop and gray sky beyond it as the other stepped through, closing the flap behind him.

Fierenzo shivered. So he'd been right. Jonah and his fellow Grays were indeed not of this world. And apparently they'd brought not only a load of high-tech gadgets with them, but also a full-fledged war. Wincing at the muscle twinges, he slowly turned his head and began a systematic inspection of his current living quarters.

There wasn't much to see. Aside from the blanket covering him and another one folded beneath him as a pad, there were only a pair of small mechanic's toolboxes against the wall near where Jonah had been sitting. Throwing off the blanket, he got up on slightly unsteady hands and knees and headed over to investigate.

He had just reached the closer box when the flap opened and Jonah reentered the tent. "Sorry about that," he apologized as he sealed it again behind him. "Jordan spotted some commotion down in the park and I wanted to check it out."

"Melantha?" Fierenzo asked, momentarily forgetting he'd just been caught red-handed sitting where he probably wasn't supposed to be.

Jonah shook his head. "Just a couple of gangs having an argument."

"What kind of argument?" Fierenzo asked, reaching for his cell phone. To his annoyance, it was missing, too.

"Don't worry, there was a patrol car just pulling up to take a look," Jonah assured him. "And Jordan's still watching." He gestured toward the toolbox Fierenzo was kneeling over. "You hungry?"

He was, in fact, starving, Fierenzo suddenly discovered. "I could use a snack," he said. "Just back the butcher truck up to the table."

Jonah grinned. "No butcher trucks, but you're welcome to what we've got. Help yourself."

"Thanks," Fierenzo said, popping the catches and lifting the lid. Inside, instead of tools, was a selection of granola-bar-sized packets in an impressive array of wrapper colors.

Aside from the colors, there were no other distinguishing features he could see. "Do I at least get a hint?"

"Sure," Jonah said. "Sorry. The blue ones are basically different shades of beef and pork; the red ones—"

"'Shades' of beef?"

"Varieties might be a better way to put it," Jonah said. "The light blue ones taste like roast beef, with the darker ones more toward the steak end of the scale, while the turquoise drift off toward roast pork. Red are types of poultry, yellow are fish, green are fruits or vegetable mixes."

"The ultimate salad bar," Fierenzo said, picking up one of the green bars and peering doubtfully at it.

"Amazingly enough, you're not the first person to make that joke," Jonah said. "That one's a kind of multi-vegetable sort of thing. It goes well with any of the beef bars."

Peeling back the wrapper, Fierenzo took a cautious bite. To his mild surprise, the bar was as flavorful as freshly picked vegetables would have been. "Not bad," he said as he chewed. The texture was also more interesting than he'd expected, with subtle variations that kept his teeth and tongue guessing from one bite to the next. "Goes well with beef, you say?"

"This one especially," Jonah said, picking out a robin's-egg-blue packet. "I find it works best to alternate bites."

The blue bar was equally tasty, reminding Fierenzo of a particularly good beef Wellington he and Claire had once had in SoHo. "Is this standard Gray cuisine?" he asked.

"No, at home we cook up real food just like you do," Jonah assured him. "I'm partial to Italian and Chinese myself. These are watchmeals, designed for Grays who are traveling or on sentry duty."

"Beats the hell out of army MREs," Fierenzo said, shifting around and settling his back against the wall. The cold concrete sent another chill through him, but he ignored it. "You have anything to drink?"

"I've got some water," Jonah offered, pulling open the second toolbox to reveal a neat row of plastic bottles.

"Sounds good," Fierenzo said. "So how deep *is* the trouble you're in?"

"Deep enough," Jonah admitted as he handed over one of the bottles. "We could wind up with everyone in this whole thing mad at us."

"Sounds like you need a friend," Fierenzo commented, twisting off the bottle cap and taking a long swallow.

"You, for instance?" Jonah shook his head. "Sorry, but like I said, you know too much already." He lifted a finger. "Oh, and just for the record, we don't fly."

"You sure did a good imitation of it back at the playground."

"I was sliding down a tension line," Jonah explained. "Nothing to it."

"Ah," Fierenzo said. "And a tension line is what?"

Jonah snorted. "You *are* the persistent one, aren't you? Look, I'll protect you until you're recovered—I owe you that much for getting me off that fire escape. But after that we're going to have to call it even and go our separate ways."

"No, I don't think so," Fierenzo said, draining the rest of the water and taking another bottle out of the box. "You see, I happen to know that your rescue of me last night was just a side effect of you pulling your own bacon out of the frying pan."

Jonah's eyes took on a wary look. "What are you talking about?"

"I'm talking about the fact that you and your brother Jordan are mixed up with the Whittiers and Melantha Green," Fierenzo said calmly. "So far you've managed to keep your involvement a secret, mainly by creating the illusion that you've been here in Chinatown watching the park, while in fact you've been in the Upper West Side trying to stop bleeding. You've done that by having Jordan sit here feeding you reports, which you then pass on to your pal Halfdan and his surveillance coordinators."

He took a swallow of water. "Unfortunately for you, one of the Greens got a good look at Jordan yesterday during that stunt he pulled near Washington Square, and he conned us into making up some nice sketches. You knew that if the

Greens got hold of them, they'd eventually find someone who recognized Jordan, at which point they would give you both the kind of long, hard look you can't really afford."

He gestured at Jonah's hands. "Oh, and whatever that radio or cell phone is you have built into your hand, you actually have *two* of them," he added. "One per hand, which I gather is not standard issue. Private and party lines?"

Jonah's face had taken on a slightly sandbagged look. "Something like that," he managed. "Damn. You *are* good at this."

"Come down to the station sometime and explain that to my boss," Fierenzo said. "I've been telling him for years that I deserve a raise. Jordan *is* your brother, then? All I could tell from the sketch was that he was a close relative."

"Half-brother, actually," Jonah said, sounding a little more on balance. "Same father, different mothers. His last name isn't Gray, either, if you're still keeping score." His face puckered. "I presume that politely asking you to fade back into the woodwork is out of the question?"

"Not until and unless I get the whole story," Fierenzo told him. "And I mean the *whole* story."

"But—"

"But nothing," Fierenzo cut him off sharply, letting him have the NYPD Stare with both barrels. "A Green named Cyril said the blood of thousands of New Yorkers was going to flow in the streets. That is *not* acceptable in my town. You'll tell me what's going on, or so help me I'll bring so many local, state, and federal agencies down on you that Manhattan will have to open a branch island."

For a half-dozen heartbeats Jonah didn't reply. Fierenzo held his gaze, hoping he hadn't pushed too hard and wondering what he would do if he had. If Jonah decided he needed to be shut up, the obvious solution lay no more than half a rooftop away. Even if no one ever figured out how a NYPD detective had come to fall off the top of a building in the middle of Chinatown, it would certainly close his mouth in an unpleasantly permanent way.

And then, to his quiet relief, some of the starch seemed to

melt from Jonah's body language. "I am going to be in trouble forever," he muttered. "Okay, you win. It all started a long time ago, on a world not all that different from this one. . . ."

• •

The early-morning sunshine had been replaced by low, gray clouds by the time Roger left the Thruway toll booth and turned the car onto Route 28, heading westward toward the Catskills. He'd never liked driving in unfamiliar areas, and as the road meandered back and forth through the hills he had to bite his lip to keep from asking every two miles if Caroline was still monitoring their progress on their maps.

It was after noon by the time they reached the turnoff onto 42 and turned north again. "It shouldn't be more than a couple of miles," Caroline said, peering at the maps spread out over her lap. "This side of Bushnellsville, past Damme Road, off to the west."

"Got it," Roger said. "With any luck, there'll be a sign."

"Yes." She paused. "Have you thought about what you're going to say when we get there?"

"Not really," he admitted, his stomach tightening as it always did when he knew there was a confrontation ahead. "I mostly thought I'd drop Nikolos's name and play the rest by ear."

Caroline shifted in her seat. Probably didn't think much of the plan, he guessed. But then, he wasn't exactly wild about it, either. "I've been trying to think what he might be up to," she said. "It's occurred to me that Cyril's the one who's come off looking the worst in this whole thing."

"How do you figure?"

"Well, from what you told me about your conversation with Torvald, it sounds like Cyril was closely connected with this whole Peace Child thing," she pointed out. "Having it blow up in his face makes him look foolish or naïve, which automatically elevates Aleksander and his pro-war faction."

"True," Roger agreed. "Problem is, we know it was a Gray who took her. How could Nikolos have gotten one of them to do his dirty work?"

"Maybe he conned one of their factions into—there it is," Caroline interrupted herself, pointing a finger ahead. "E. and N. Green."

"I see it," Roger confirmed as he spotted the modest sign beside the equally modest gravel drive heading up into the woods. He flipped on his signal; and just as he started into his turn, he spotted a young man dressed in dark green standing beside one of the trees near the driveway entrance. "Uh-oh," he said. "We've got company."

"Should we stop?" Caroline suggested hesitantly.

But the Green made no move, merely watching silently as they drove past. "I guess not," Roger said. "Probably just a watchman, like the one I ran into at Aleksander's building."

"Roger," Caroline said slowly. "Was that man wearing a *trassk*?"

Roger glanced at the mirror, but the Green was already out of sight. "I didn't notice."

"I think he was," she said, her voice suddenly tight. "In fact, I'm sure of it. Didn't Nikolos say they only had enough *trassks* for the top leaders and the Warriors?"

"Yes, but so what?" Roger asked. "It makes sense for them to have a Warrior standing guard."

"With the main battle setting up to happen in Manhattan?"

"Point," he said slowly. "Unless he's expecting the Grays to attack here."

"Or else is *planning* for them to attack here," Caroline murmured.

"How do you *plan* for your enemies to attack you?" Roger objected. "Besides, an area like this would be tailor-made for Greens to fight in. The Grays would have to be nuts to walk into it without a good reason."

"Maybe Nikolos *has* a good reason," Caroline said. "Like Melantha."

Roger felt something twist in his stomach. "In which case, they would definitely have Warriors on duty."

"There's another one," Caroline said, pointing to Roger's left. "No—three of them."

Roger looked. All three Greens were young and tall, striding purposefully toward the road they were driving on.

All three were definitely wearing *trassks*.

"I'm thinking we should find a place to turn around and get out of here," Caroline said, her voice starting to tremble.

Roger looked in his mirror. Five more Greens had appeared on the road behind them. "Too late," he said.

"There's another," Caroline said.

He shifted his attention forward. Fifty yards ahead, a small road angled off to the right from the main drive. Standing unsmiling in the intersection was a Green, his hand held palm outward in the universal gesture to halt, the *trassk* on his jacket gleaming dully in the diffuse light seeping through the clouds. Roger let the car coast to a halt, rolling down the window as the Green stepped around to his side. "Hello," he greeted the other, trying to keep his voice cheerful and unconcerned.

"Hello," the Green replied, his voice as neutral as his face. "Are you expected?"

"Not really," Roger admitted. "But I'm sure he'll see us."

The Green lifted his eyebrows. "'He'?"

Roger felt his throat tighten. He'd banked on there being somebody obviously in charge here, and that his casually vague comment would make him sound like he knew what he was talking about. Now, instead—

"Your Group Commander," Caroline spoke up from beside him. "We need to see him as soon as possible."

The Green's forehead wrinkled slightly, and with a shiver Roger noticed his eyes unfocus for a moment. Communicating with his companions, no doubt. "Very well," he said suddenly, pointing down the side road. "There's a cabin that direction. You can wait there."

"Isn't he up there?" Roger asked, pointing ahead along the main drive.

"You'll be directed," the Green said in a voice that made it clear it was an order.

Roger grimaced. "Fine." Shifting the car into reverse, he backed up a few feet and turned into the side road.

"I don't like this," Caroline murmured.

"Understatement of the day," Roger said grimly, digging his cell phone out of his pocket and handing it to her. "Here—see if you can get a signal."

"Who are we calling?" Caroline asked, sliding it out of its case and turning it on.

"I don't know," he told her. "I just want to see if we *can* call anyone."

"Doesn't look like it," she said, peering at the indicator. "I'll try our apartment."

She punched buttons and held the phone to her ear. "Nothing," she said with a sigh, turning it off and handing it back to him. "We must be in a dead spot."

"Yeah," Roger said. "Probably on purpose."

They passed two more intersections, each of which had a Green waiting to point them the correct way. Finally, perhaps a half mile from the main drive, they reached the end of the road and a small, rather run-down cabin. Two more Greens were standing by the door, flanking it like guards. "They look like Yannis from last night," Caroline murmured.

"Somehow, I doubt we'll be getting a friendly pass-warder ritual," Roger said as he rolled to a halt in front of the building. Putting the gearshift in park, he shut off the engine and pocketed the keys. "Come on."

"This way, please," one of the Greens called, reaching over and opening the cabin door as they got out of the car.

"Thank you," Roger said, determined to at least maintain the illusion that they were all friends here. Beyond the door-way was a living room full of drifting dust and an almost chokingly musty smell. Clearly, the place hadn't been used in years.

And yet, this was where the Group Commander had decided to put them. That wasn't a good sign.

"Interesting," he commented, trying to sound unconcerned as he looked around. The furnishings consisted of an old couch and a pair of wicker chairs that were starting to fall apart, threadbare rugs, drab curtains, a beam-ribbed ceiling, and a stone fireplace with a wooden mantel above it. "Looks like a Learning Channel frontier life special."

"It's not that old," Caroline told him, her nervousness momentarily submerged beneath professional interest. "The construction dates to just after the war. The rug's probably from the late fifties, the furniture late fifties or early sixties."

"Any idea how long since anyone's lived here?" he asked.

She shivered. "Twenty years. Maybe longer."

There was a sound behind them, and Roger turned as a third Green stepped into the cabin, a load of firewood stacked across his arms. "I apologize for the accommodations," he said, crossing to the fireplace and setting down his load. "I was told to bring wood so that you could start a fire."

"I'm sorry, but this is unacceptable," Roger said firmly, putting every bit of righteous indignation into his voice that he could muster. "Is this your Group Commander's idea of hospitality?"

"Again, I apologize," the Green said as he stacked the wood beside the fireplace. "I'll be back with more wood and some kindling."

He went out the door, closing it behind him. Roger took a deep breath, nearly gagging on the floating dust in the process. "I'm sorry, Caroline," he said quietly. "This isn't turning out the way I'd hoped."

"It's not your fault." Caroline took a shuddering breath of her own. "So what do we do?"

Roger looked back toward the door, half minded to try opening it and seeing what happened. But the two Warriors playing pass-warder were almost certainly still outside, and he'd seen how fast a Green could convert a *trassk* into a knife. "I guess we wait," he decided reluctantly, turning back toward the fireplace. "You're the one who grew up in the country—you build the fire. I'll see if I can pry some of these windows open and get us some air."

26

"That is one hell of a story," Fierenzo said, shaking his head in wonderment. "And in all that time nobody's figured out that you're here?"

"Not as far as I know," Jonah said. "But then, why would they? We became legal citizens three-quarters of a century ago, and all we've done since then is try to live our lives quietly and peacefully."

"Until now," Fierenzo said.

"This was hardly our decision," Jonah insisted stiffly. "It was the Greens who pushed us into it."

"And then came up with a plan to murder one of their own," Fierenzo murmured, a cold anger stirring inside him. He'd always had a particularly unforgiving spot in his heart toward people who abused children, and ritual murder of any sort made his skin crawl. As far as his score sheet was concerned, the Greens were going into this with two strikes against them. "But that was seventy-five years ago. Why restart the feud now?"

Jonah snorted under his breath. "Oh, come *on*. You have ethnic feuds on Earth that have lasted for millennia."

"Sure, but those are usually fought over the same hereditary plot of dirt," Fierenzo pointed out. "Your private Götterdämmerung happened a dozen light-years away."

"Our private what?"

"Götterdämmerung," Fierenzo repeated. "The Norse version of Armageddon, with everything going up in flames like your valley. My point is that it's hard for people to forget the injustices of the past when someone can point out the exact spot where Uncle Igor got murdered by the Cossacks. But when you transplant those people onto different ground, the arguments tend to become less virulent. Especially when they all have to live among other people in a new society."

"You don't understand the Greens," Jonah said with a sigh. "They're—well, call it centralized thinking. Their whole lives, from their jobs to the way they think, are locked into this rigid genetic caste structure of theirs, which is guided by the people they've decided are genetically entitled to be their leaders. If those leaders decide to lock themselves into the patterns and prejudices of the past, the rest of the people haven't got much choice but to let themselves be dragged in along with them."

"And the Grays are different?" Fierenzo asked.

"Compared to the Greens, we're the poster boys of anarchy," Jonah said. "We have people who mediate disputes, lay down guidelines for our behavior toward each other and Human society, and sit in judgment when somebody crosses the line. But that's about it."

"Every Gray for himself?"

"Basically, though it's not as bad as it sounds," Jonah said. "A Gray's behavior is also moderated by his or her network of friends. Since we all have our own networks, and since all those networks intertwine, we end up being more or less accountable to the entire group."

"Government by village peer pressure?" Fierenzo suggested.

"Why not?" Jonah said with a shrug. "In effect, that's exactly what we are: a small town spread invisibly throughout New York City."

"So why can't you just pull up stakes and leave?"

Jonah's face hardened. "You can't back down in front of bullies, Detective. A cop should know that better than anyone. If the Greens succeed in pushing us out of New York, we'll never be free of their threats. The only way to end this—the *only* way—is to convince them that there's no reason we can't live here together in peace. We don't have to be best friends—in fact, they're welcome to ignore us completely if they want. But we have as much right to live here as they do, and we're not going away."

"Mm," Fierenzo said, taking another sip of his water. "Let me see that gun again, will you?"

Jonah's forehead wrinkled, but he set his own water bottle aside and held out his left hand. "Here's what it looks like sheathed," he said, pushing up his jacket sleeve to reveal an elaborately decorated metal wristband. "I twist my wrist so to throw it—"

He turned the wrist sharply over, and Fierenzo watched in fascination as silvery tendrils shot out of the wristband's underside, flowing up along the insides of Jonah's fingers and thumb and then bending and curving around each other like a mutant pretzel before melting together into the now familiar flattened cylinder shape. "And there it is."

"Yes," Fierenzo said, nodding. Now that he had a clear look, he saw something he hadn't noticed before: where the wide wristband had been only a slender loop of wire remained, encircling Jonah's wrist and attached to the grip of the hammergun by an equally thin metal wire. "Is that loop supposed to keep you from dropping it?"

"It does that, too, but it's mostly there to give the hammergun a path to flow back along when you sheathe it," Jonah told him. "Like so."

He opened his hand and the hammergun went into reverse, untwisting itself and flowing back along the fingers to re-create the original wristband. "That is truly amazing," Fierenzo said, shaking his head. "How exactly does it work? It doesn't fire slugs, does it?"

"In a way it does," Jonah said, flipping his wrist and bringing the weapon out into his hand again. "It fires small force bubbles that accelerate away—"

"Wait a second," Fierenzo interrupted. "It fires *what?*"

"Force bubbles," Jonah repeated. "Little spheres or disks of non-solid force. A bubble accelerates away from the muzzle, growing bigger and gaining speed along the way, until it runs into a solid object. At that point it dissipates, transferring its energy and momentum to the target."

"How many settings are there?"

"Just the two: ball or disk," Jonah said. "The ball is spherical and delivers its energy like a hammer, while the disk has an edge to it and is more suitable for cutting."

"So the ball is what you hit the Greens with yesterday night by the station house," Fierenzo said slowly, trying to sort this out. "While the disk is what that other Gray cut off the tree branch with over in Yorkville?"

"Yes to the first; I don't know to the second," Jonah said. "Depending how far away the tree was, either setting could probably have taken off a branch."

"Wait a minute," Fierenzo said, pressing his fingertips to his forehead. "I thought you said you hadn't killed the two last night."

Jonah sighed. "Watch," he said. Sticking his free hand directly in front of the hammergun muzzle, he squeezed the trigger.

There was a faint *pop,* but as far as Fierenzo could see nothing else happened. "Like I said, the shot picks up energy and momentum as it travels," Jonah said. "Right up close—" he fired into his palm again "—nothing much happens. A little farther away—"

Taking his hand away, he fired at one of the empty water bottles a foot away from him. The shot sent it skittering across the concrete. "—and you can start to feel it," he said. "Farther away yet—" he lifted the weapon to aim at an imaginary horizon "—and you could theoretically crack off a piece of a mountain."

Fierenzo shook his head. "Sounds pretty damn dangerous. I've never even heard of a weapon that doesn't work up close."

"That's probably because hammerguns aren't technically weapons," Jonah said. "They were designed as mining and stoneworking tools. Low-power at close range for delicate shaping; high-power farther away to give a kick to the ore vein or surface formation you're working."

"Uh-*huh,*" Fierenzo said as something suddenly occurred

to him. "Which means that when you shoved that thing in my face on the fire escape it was a hundred-percent bluff."

"Basically," Jonah admitted. "But what else could I do?"

"I suppose," Fierenzo conceded. "And that's why the second Green last night ran *toward* you instead of away. He was trying to move in to where you couldn't hit him as hard."

"That, plus the fact that the sonic nature of the Shriek means it gets stronger as you get closer to it," Jonah said.

"Tell me about it," Fierenzo said ruefully, rubbing his ear gingerly. "Was that Jordan up on the building playing target?"

Jonah nodded. "He was trying to hold their attention so I could get behind them." He grimaced. "Though if I'd realized how strong the Shriek could be even at that distance, I'd never have let him do it. I guess I've never seen a Warrior in action before."

"So the Greens will always want to fight up close, while the Grays will always want to fight at a distance," Fierenzo concluded. "That'll make for some interesting battlefield tactics. Where exactly do these force bubbles get their energy?"

"They draw heat from the air molecules along their path and convert it into kinetic energy," Jonah explained. "That's why you usually see a white line, at least if the bubble's traveled far enough. That's frost that forms where the air's suddenly had some of the energy sucked out of it and gone cold. Sometimes you can even get snowflakes drifting off the line."

"Sounds very festive," Fierenzo said. "What do you use to hang onto buildings?"

"Nothing but natural talent," Jonah said. "It has to do with van der Waals forces between our bodies and the metal in the walls, or some such thing. I'm a little vague on the details."

"Close enough," Fierenzo said. Physics had never been his strong suit, either. "Now, what about this tension line thing you mentioned earlier? How does *that* work?"

Jonah made a face. "What do you want, Fierenzo, a short course in Gray tech?"

"Humor me," Fierenzo said. "You're trying to convince me to keep my mouth shut, remember?"

"And there's no point in keeping quiet about one secret when you can have a hundred secrets to keep quiet about instead?"

"Exactly," Fierenzo said. "Come on, give."

With an exasperated sigh, Jonah reached beneath his coat to the side of his belt and pulled out a device about the size of a cigarette pack but flatter. "Fine," he said, tossing it into Fierenzo's lap. "There it is. Go ahead—figure it out."

He leaned back against the wall, folding his arms across his chest. Picking up the device, Fierenzo gave it a quick study. It looked something like a tailless manta ray, with one side flat and the other smoothly curved, and seemed to be made of the same metal as Jonah's wristband. In the front, where the manta's mouth would have been, there was a finger-sized ring connected to a slender thread that disappeared inside the metal. Set into the concave top was a small round glass-like disk with a knurled bezel around it.

And that was it. No switches, no buttons, no controls of any sort that he could see. For all he could tell, it might have been the inner workings of one of the pull-ring talking dolls his sisters had played with when he was a boy.

He looked up. Jonah was watching him like a dog trainer with a new student. "You don't really want me to just start playing with it, do you?" Fierenzo asked him.

"Why not?" Jonah asked. "You can't hurt it."

"Come on, Jonah, I'm too tired for puzzle box games," Fierenzo said. "Give."

"Okay," Jonah said agreeably. "But if I do, show-and-tell is over. Deal?"

"I don't know," Fierenzo hedged. "There's still those radios of yours, and that invisibility trick—"

"Deal?" Jonah repeated.

Fierenzo sighed. "Deal."

"All right," Jonah said, uncrossing his arms. "Put the flat side against the wall, with the ring hanging downward."

Fierenzo set the device against the wall as instructed

about a foot above the rooftop. "Now rotate the bezel around the eye a quarter-turn counterclockwise to loosen it," Jonah instructed.

Fierenzo did so, and found the glass disk now floating freely in its socket. "Aim it downward at an angle to the roof and tighten the bezel again," Jonah continued. "Now hold the projector against the wall so that your hand is away from the eye, pull the ring out an inch or so, and let go of the projector."

Carefully, Fierenzo got a two-fingered grip on the top of the device. Leaning as far back out of the way as he could without looking obvious about it, he took hold of the ring and pulled.

Nothing happened. Frowning, he let go of the projector. To his amazement, it remained firmly in place against the wall.

He looked at Jonah. The other had a faint smile on his face, the kind Fierenzo had often seen on amateur magicians. "Now what?"

Jonah gestured. "Wave your hand between the eye and the roof."

Frowning, Fierenzo eased a single finger downward—

And twitched it reflexively away as it hit something solid. "What the *hell*?"

"There's your tension line," Jonah said. "A thin line of force running between the projector eye and whatever solid object you've got it aimed at."

Carefully, Fierenzo eased his finger around the invisible line. The shape and feel were like a very tight, very slick rope. "How much weight can it handle?" he asked.

"You could hang a dozen guys from it without making the projector work very hard," Jonah said. "We use them sometimes to travel between skyscrapers."

"Very impressive," Fierenzo said, sliding a finger up and down the line. "What kind of range does it have?"

"Like a hammergun shot, the line runs outward until it hits something solid," Jonah said. "I'm told it was once considered the quick and easy way to travel between mountains."

"And then, what, you just leave the projector behind?" Fierenzo asked, the discomfiting image of a thousand invisible wires crisscrossing Manhattan flashing to mind. "Or can you climb back up it?"

"Not a chance," Jonah said. "The coefficient of friction is way too low." He pointed to the ring Fierenzo was still holding. "That's what the ring's for. You slide it on over one of your fingers before you set off, and it feeds out thread until you reach the other end. Then you just give it couple of back-and-pulls, and it shuts the line off and brings the projector back to you." He gestured. "Try it."

Sliding the ring onto his middle finger, Fierenzo pulled it out a couple of feet from the box. He paused, then backed it up and pulled it out; backed it up and pulled it out—

Without warning, the box detached itself from the wall and shot over to Fierenzo's hand, reeling itself in along the thread like a carpenter's tape measure. "And you're ready for your next trip," Jonah concluded, holding out his hand. "I'd offer you a ride, but you really need to be able to hold onto the side of your destination building for it to be a properly enjoyable experience."

"I'm more than happy to pass, thank you," Fierenzo assured him, handing back the projector. "I'd probably twitch my arm the wrong way and shut the thing off in midair."

"You can't," Jonah said. "As long as there's any significant weight on the line it won't shut off. Safety feature."

"And this is what you used to pull Melantha out of the frying pan Wednesday night?"

Jonah nodded. "The tricky part was coming up with a way to keep them from realizing it was somebody outside their group who'd snatched her," he said. "The only way to get over the trees was to set up the tension line several stories up on one of the buildings east of Riverside Park. The problem was that if I'd just slid down to the ground at that angle, I'd have been going so fast I'd have bowled over half the circle when I landed."

"So how *did* you do it?"

"I set the line nearly horizontal, running it to a building

across the Hudson in New Jersey," Jonah said. "Then instead of just hanging on as usual, I hooked an elastic rope onto it and held onto that. When I got over the circle, I bungeed down into the middle, grabbed Melantha, and ran."

"Clever," Fierenzo said. "But why didn't they find the bungee afterwards?"

"Because it wasn't there," Jonah said. "I didn't use the projector's retrieval ring myself, but left Jordan back at the jump-off building to handle that. He waited until the bungee was over the middle of the river before shutting it down. The bungee sank, and there was nothing left to tell anyone how it was done."

"And so they spent the next few days throwing suspicious glares at each other instead of looking for an outsider," Fierenzo said. "I suppose it was you who blew out all the lights on Riverside Drive, too?"

"Yeah, and I'm sorry about that," Jonah said. "But we had to make sure they couldn't see what was happening."

"So how did the Whittiers come into the picture?"

"The original plan was for me to get Melantha across Manhattan and offshore to Roosevelt Island," Jonah said. "Neither side was occupying it, so we figured it would be a safe place to hide her for awhile. But you need both arms to carry someone on a tension line, and one of the Warriors had managed to get me with a knife before I flattened him. At the same time, Melantha wasn't in any shape for a long walk."

"Why didn't you just hop a cab or the subway?"

"What, with me bleeding all over my shirt?" Jonah countered. "Besides, a fair number of Green Laborers drive cabs these days. All I could think to do was take us northeast toward Nikolos's stronghold in Morningside Park, hoping it would be the last direction anyone would expect us to go, while I tried to come up with a new plan. But Melantha wasn't even up to that, so I found an alley to hide her in and went scouting."

"Having blown the padlock off the gate with your hammergun?"

Jonah nodded. "Anyway, I'd just about decided we were going to have to risk that cab after all when I heard the Whittiers talking about the trees on their balcony. It was the perfect solution: being inside a tree would protect Melantha from prying Gray eyes, while being off the ground would keep inquisitive Greens from probing around and finding her. So I called Jordan and had him pop the lights on Broadway. Well, to try, anyway; the gadget we'd rigged up didn't work as well there as it had earlier on Riverside Drive. But it worked well enough. Melantha was awake by then, so I had her turn her *trassk* into something I could scare the Whittiers with long enough to hand her over to them."

"You were taking a pretty big chance," Fierenzo pointed out. "Picking a pair of New Yorkers at random doesn't necessarily get you the cream of the crop."

"I know," Jonah said. "But like I said, I was out of options. Anyway, I figured we could always get her back from them if we had to. We just couldn't afford to get caught with her ourselves. As long as the Greens didn't know who'd snatched her, even if they got her back, we'd be free to try again. But if we got caught, Halfdan would make sure we never got another chance."

"Halfdan being the head of your peace faction?"

"Halfdan being the one ready and willing to sacrifice Melantha to maintain the status quo," Jonah corrected bluntly. "You can call that peace if you want to. Anyway, I made the handoff, then hid on the wall until they'd taken Melantha away. I called Jordan, told him to get ready to cover for me when the you-know-what hit the fan and all adult Grays got scrambled into search or sentry duty, then climbed up to the fire escape to hide and heal. You know the rest."

"Except what exactly was going on in the Whittiers' apartment when I got dragged into this mess," Fierenzo said. "What do you know about that?"

"Not much, but I can connect the dots," Jonah said. "Jordan had wanted to follow the Whittiers home, but the search got under way faster than he'd expected and he had to get clear of the area. The next night, after most of the commotion had moved elsewhere, he went back to the neighborhood to try and find her. My guess is that some people from both sides spotted him climbing around the Whittiers' building and got curious."

"So the next day we get two separate groups converging on the place," Fierenzo concluded. "The Grays went up the outside and tried to get Melantha to come out of the trees by shooting at them. When that didn't work, they started trying to break the door glass enough to get in, only they were interrupted by a set of Greens who'd gotten the building super to open the door for them."

"You've got it," Jonah agreed. "We were just lucky that Mrs. Whittier and Melantha had already left."

Fierenzo nodded. "I think that brings me up to date," he said. "Except for two questions. One, where is Melantha now? And two—" he cocked an eyebrow at Jonah "—just whose side are *you* on in this?"

"To answer the second: I'm on Melantha's side," Jonah said.

"And which side is that?"

"Like I said: Melantha's," Jonah repeated. "As to the first—" He shook his head. "I wish I knew. Somebody's got her—that much I'm sure of. If she were free we would have heard from her by now. But as to who or where, I have no idea."

"Sounds like Number One on our things-to-do-list," Fierenzo decided, unzipping his coat and fishing inside. "You'd probably better take charge of these, too," he added, pulling out the folded sketches. "All I really wanted them for was to force the truth out of—"

He broke off in mid-word, staring at the pages in his hands. Back at the precinct house, he'd put four sheets of paper in his pocket: two pictures each of Jordan and the adult Gray.

Now, two of the sheets were missing.

He snapped open the remaining pages, tearing one of them in his haste. To his complete lack of surprise, they were both of the adult.

Jordan's pictures were gone.

"What is it?" Jonah demanded.

"We've been robbed," Fierenzo said tightly, crumpling the sheets and shoving them into his side pocket. "Somehow, while they were hauling me down the sidewalk, the Greens managed to grab Jordan's pictures."

For a split second, Jonah just stared at him. Then, abruptly, he jerked his left hand up to his cheek. "Jordan, we're blown," he snapped. "Get out of here—go to Meeting One. And call Mom and Dad and tell them to join us."

He waited for an acknowledgment and dropped his hand. "We'd better get out of here," he added to Fierenzo, closing the supply box lids and refastening them.

"You think they'll give Halfdan the sketches?" Fierenzo asked, starting to fold up the blanket and wincing as twinges of pain shot through his shoulders.

"They probably showed them around to their own people first," Jonah said, folding the pad Fierenzo had been lying on and tucking it under one arm. "If none of them recognized him, yes, they'd certainly give them to Halfdan."

"Who will probably not be very happy with you," Fierenzo said, finishing with the blanket. "What's this Meeting One?"

"It's a place where we've met before," Jonah said, picking up the food box and getting up into a crouch. "We should be safe there, at least for awhile." He opened the lean-to flap and picked up the water box.

And froze. "What is it?" Fierenzo asked.

Jonah took a deep breath. "We've got company," he said, setting down the food box and pushing the flap all the way open. Across the roof, striding purposefully toward the lean-to, were a half-dozen short, squat men.

The Grays had found them.

27

Fierenzo's hand twitched toward his shoulder holster before he remembered his gun wasn't there anymore. "Who are they?" he asked.

"Halfdan's inner circle," Jonah said. "The one in front in the blue pea coat is Bergan, his eldest son. He's the one Jordan clobbered yesterday morning for the car he used to get the Whittiers away from Halfdan's other son, Ingvar."

"Who I see is also here," Fierenzo said, recognizing the gray-jacketed man on Bergan's left from the crumpled sketches in his pocket. "You think they know you're the ones who snatched Melantha?"

"I can't think of any other reason why Jordan would have tried to drive over Ingvar," Jonah said grimly. "And Halfdan normally doesn't have any trouble putting two and two together."

"Well, he'll just have to do his arithmetic alone," Fierenzo said, coming to a decision. Pulling out his badge wallet, he brushed past Jonah and ducked through the flap onto the rooftop. "Afternoon, gentlemen," he called to the converging circle of Grays as he held the badge up high. "What's going on?"

Bergan stopped short, his mouth twitching at the sight of the badge. The other Grays took the cue and also stopped. "Who are you?" he called back.

"Detective Sergeant Thomas Fierenzo," Fierenzo told him, waving the badge around so that the entire circle could get a look before returning it to his pocket. "You up here for a party?"

Bergan's eyes flicked past Fierenzo's shoulder. "We

came to see Jonah McClung," he said. "He's a friend of ours."

"Mr. McClung hasn't got time to chat right now," Fierenzo said, making a mental note of the name. Jonah had said that it wasn't Gray, but he'd been careful not to say what it actually was. "He and his brother Jordan have to come down to the station with me."

The lines around Bergan's eyes deepened. "Why?" he asked. "What have they done?"

"They're possible witnesses to a felony," Fierenzo said, glancing around. "Jordan? Jordan! Damn—where's that kid gotten to? Jordan!"

"What felony?" Ingvar asked.

Fierenzo turned to face him, and out of the corner of his eye he saw one of the other Grays put a hand up to his cheek. Calling to have Jordan brought back before the cop got suspicious, he hoped. "Sorry?"

"What felony are Mr. McClung and Mr. Anderson witnesses to?" Ingvar amplified.

So Jordan's last name was Anderson. Halfdan's sons were just chock full of useful information. "They may have seen a kidnapping from the park over there," he told the other, gesturing toward the edge of the roof. "I need to get their statements and have them look through some mug books."

"So neither of them is being charged with anything?"

And that was the critical question here, Fierenzo knew, at least as far as Ingvar and Bergan were concerned. A formal charge would mean fingerprints and mug shots and all the rest of the attention these people had taken such pains to avoid all these years. Faced with that possibility, they might well decide desperate action was called for.

On the other hand, *not* being faced with that possibility would make the temporary loss of Jonah and Jordan seem considerably less critical in comparison. "No, of course not," he assured Ingvar. "Like I said, I just want their statements." He glanced around. "Where in hell did Jordan get to?"

"Here he is," a voice called from behind him.

Fierenzo turned to see two Grays escorting a tight-lipped

youth toward him. It was the first time he'd actually seen
Jordan in the flesh, but like Ingvar he was the spitting image
of his police sketch. "About time," he said peevishly, gesturing the boy forward. "Come on, come on—it's freezing up
here. You too, Jonah. Leave the stuff—you can come back
and get it later."

Trying to act nonchalant, he marched his prisoners
through the line of Grays to the roof stairway and pulled
open the door, ushering them inside. "The rest of you get
out of here, too," he ordered the others over his shoulder.
"There are laws against hanging out on roofs without the
owner's permission." He gave Jonah a nudge. "Let's go."

No one spoke until they'd reached ground level. "Where
are we going?" Jordan asked as Fierenzo got his bearings
and turned toward the nearest subway station.

"Back to the Two-Four to get my car," Fierenzo told him.
His muscles still twinged occasionally as he walked, but he
was definitely on the mend.

"And then?"

"You'll see." He cocked an eye at Jonah. "'McClung,'
huh?"

Jonah shrugged. "Like I said, we've been branching out."

"That wasn't what I meant," Fierenzo said. "I was thinking about your habit of clinging to walls. Cling—clung—
McClung?"

Jonah frowned. "No," he said firmly. "My grandfather
wouldn't have lowered himself to a joke that bad." He
paused. "At least, I don't think so."

They caught an uptown subway at Canal and Lafayette,
changed lines at Grand Central and Times Square, and were
soon back on 102nd Street where Fierenzo had parked his
car the previous evening. To his mild surprise, it hadn't been
towed.

"Get in," he told the others, unlocking it with the remote
and getting stiffly into the driver's seat. Jonah climbed in
beside him, Jordan taking the back. "So where *are* we going?" Jonah asked.

"We'll start by losing the tails I'm sure Bergan and Ingvar put on us," Fierenzo said, starting the car and fastening his seat belt. "Get my spare gun out of the glove box, will you?"

"What are you going to tell your lieutenant?" Jonah asked, popping the glove box door and gingerly pulling out Fierenzo's spare Glock.

"I'm working on that," Fierenzo said, looking in the mirror. "Hang on a sec," he added as Jonah started to hand him the gun. A car-sized hole had opened up in the traffic flow; twisting the wheel, he cut into it, shifted over a lane, and made the turn north at the next block on the tail end of the yellow light. "Okay," he said, holding out his hand. Jonah gave him the gun, and he slid it into his shoulder holster. The familiar weight felt reassuring, somehow. "Thanks."

"You're welcome," Jonah said. "And after we lose them?"

"We'll go to Meeting One, of course," Fierenzo told him. "I want to meet the rest of your conspiracy."

Behind him, Jordan inhaled sharply. "What conspiracy?" Jonah asked, his voice suddenly tight.

"You talked about having meetings there," Fierenzo reminded him. "That implies more than just the two of you, or even just the two of you and a set of parents. And I don't believe for a minute you and Jordan pulled this whole thing off alone. It's time I found out whose side you're actually on."

"But we can't," Jordan protested. "Jonah, tell him—"

Jonah silenced him with a gesture. "All right," he said. "But only if you can lose Halfdan's people."

"Trust me," Fierenzo assured him. "A couple of parking garages, a cab or two, maybe some new coats for you and your brother, and we'll shake them."

Jonah took a deep breath and settled back into his seat. "Okay," he said. "I just hope you know what you're doing."

Fierenzo nodded. "Yeah. Me, too."

● ●

The afternoon was starting to fade away, and Caroline had restoked the fire twice, when they finally had a visitor.

"Good afternoon," Nikolos greeted them as he stepped into the cabin between a pair of Warriors. "I wish I could say I was pleased to see you."

Caroline glanced at her husband, caught the quick twitch of his lip. Clearly, he wasn't any more surprised to see Nikolos than she was. "Likewise," Roger told the Command-Tactician. "Cozy setup you have here."

"We like it," Nikolos said, gesturing them to the couch as he eased himself into one of the two rickety cabriolet chairs. The wicker protested under his weight, but held. "Let me guess," he went on. "It was that comment I made about pulling back to upstate New York."

"Basically," Roger confirmed as he and Caroline also sat down.

Nikolos nodded heavily. "I knew it was a mistake the minute I said it, but all I could do was hope you hadn't noticed. Dare I ask how you found this place so quickly?"

"Dare we ask where Melantha is?" Roger countered.

"I wish I knew," Nikolos said ruefully. "I certainly don't have her."

"Of course not," Roger said. "And this is just your summer retreat, right?"

"No, this is precisely what I'm sure you've already surmised," Nikolos said calmly. "Our last fallback position, prepared in the event that the Grays succeed in pushing us out of the city."

"Where you can continue the fight on your own terms?"

Nikolos shook his head. "If we're pushed back here, the war will already have been lost," he said. "This will become little more than our final resting place, a land where our remaining people can fade back into the shadows of the hills and woods."

"Or a place where you can relax in comfort while Melantha destroys New York and the Grays?" Caroline suggested, her throat tight.

There was a smoldering fire in Nikolos's eyes as he turned to her. "Look, *Humans,* it's my job to protect my people from our enemies," he bit out. "If dropping a few buildings is what it takes to accomplish that, then yes, that's exactly what I'll do."

"But only if you can persuade Melantha to cooperate," Roger said.

"I don't need Melantha," Nikolos shot back, leaning forward in his emotion, his hands gripping the armrests of his chair. "Damian can—"

He broke off abruptly. "I'm afraid you're going to have to be our guests for awhile," he said, his voice suddenly stiff and formal as he stood up. "Accommodations are being prepared for you at the main house. The Group Commander will send for you in about an hour."

Turning his back on them, he headed for the door. "Just remember one thing," Roger called after him. "If you want to kill Grays, you're right, we probably can't stop you. But if you start wrecking buildings and killing *our* people, this retreat of yours won't hide you for long."

"We hid from the Others for generations," Nikolos countered, half turning to look over his shoulder at them. "And *they* at least knew who and what they were looking for. You really think we can't hide from a people who don't even know we exist?"

He strode out into the gathering dusk. The two Warriors followed, closing the door behind them. "Yeah, but there you had a whole valley to hide in," Roger muttered at the door. He took a deep breath, let it out in a ragged sigh, and turned to Caroline. "Was it my imagination, or did Nikolos actually lose control there for a minute?"

"It certainly looked that way," Caroline agreed, thinking back to that suddenly cut off sentence. "Has anyone mentioned Damian before?"

"Not to me," Roger said. "I'm still trying to figure out whether or not he has Melantha. One minute he'll say something that sounds like he does, the next minute he'll say something just the opposite."

Caroline shivered. "Roger, we've got to get out of here," she said. "Get back to the city and warn someone."

"I'm open to suggestions."

She looked around the room, trying to think. The cabin was late forties or early fifties, she'd already decided. A lot of such summer hideaways had sprung up about that time throughout the Catskills, many of them of rather hasty construction. The windows would be single-paned, the walls minimally insulated if at all, the floor—

The floor.

She looked down at the floor. Standard overlay flooring, the boards with that rough and rustic look. Getting down on her knees, she held her palm just over the floorboards. With the fire drawing air from the rest of the cabin . . . "Do you feel air coming through the floor?" she asked.

Roger got down beside her, licking a finger and holding it over one of the larger cracks between boards. "I think so," he said after a moment. "But that fire's drawing in a lot of air. It could be a leak from somewhere else."

"I don't think there's any subflooring here, Roger," she said. "Just these boards nailed to the joists, with a crawl space underneath."

"No slab?"

"Wasn't required back then for this type of building," she told him. "And I remember seeing skirting boards on the outside at ground level as we were coming in. It's a crawl space, all right."

Roger tapped the board thoughtfully. "And if we can get through, then we can get out."

For a long moment they looked at each other. "There's still the guards outside," she reminded him.

"Let's worry about that when we get there," Roger said. "How do we start?"

"Go see if there's anything we can use to pull nails," she said, straightening up again. "Don't forget to check the kitchen drawers. I'll look for a place to—"

She gave a strained chuckle. "What?" he demanded.

"I almost said I'd look for a place to dig," she said. "Like we were on Treasure Island or something."

"More like a prisoner-of-war camp," he pointed out, heading for the kitchen. "I'll see what I can find."

By the time he returned, she'd located their best bet. "The previous occupants did a good job of cleaning it out," he told her, dumping a double handful of junk onto the couch. "But this potato peeler might get a couple of the nails started before it gives out."

"Maybe even more than a couple," Caroline agreed, looking over the rest of his loot. Half a hinge, a bent drill bit, a piece of an egg beater, and a power cord like the one on her mother's old waffle iron.

"And for actually prying up the boards once the nails are out, I thought we could use that spark-blocking thingy," he added.

"It's called a fender," Caroline identified it, eyeing the low metal barrier in front of the fireplace. "Yes, that might work."

"So that's our tool kit," he concluded. "Where's our spot?"

"Right here," Caroline said, pointing to the corner she was standing in. "You see the stains on the ceiling? That's from rain or snow leakage. It's partially rotted the boards here—you can feel how soft it is compared to the rest of the floor."

He pressed a foot down onto the spot. "Looks good," he agreed. Picking up the potato peeler, he knelt down and got to work.

Caroline picked up the broken hinge, her stomach twisting inside her. They could certainly get out of the cabin—she was sure of that now. But after they did . . .

She stepped to the other end of the board he was working on. Clearly, Roger hadn't thought it all the way through yet. Better not to distract him.

Getting down on her knees, she started digging into the softened wood.

• •

"What do you mean, the car's gone?" Powell demanded into the phone. "I left orders for it to be watched."

"There was a glitch in the stakeout schedule," Smith said,

sounding as frustrated as Powell felt. "By the time I realized that, it was too late. But I found a newsstand guy who saw them get in and drive off."

"But it *was* Fierenzo?" Powell asked, some of the tension in his chest easing a little. Whatever else was going on, his partner was still alive.

"The news guy identified his photo," Smith confirmed. "The others were two males: one mid-teens, who got in back, the other mid-twenties, who got into the front passenger seat. He described them as both being dark-haired and kind of squat." He paused. "He also said that as the car pulled away, he saw the older one holding a gun."

The decreasing pressure in Powell's chest reversed itself. So instead of a murder, they now had a kidnapping. "Get your guy to the station," he ordered. "And get Carstairs and his sketch pad down there."

"Carstairs won't be happy about being pulled in on a Sunday," Smith warned. "Especially not after coming in on Saturday, too."

"Tell him I'll buy him dinner," Powell growled. "Then put out an APB on Fierenzo's car and get a canvass going to see if you can find someone in the neighborhood who can fill in more of the picture. And don't let your witness walk until I get there."

"I won't," Smith promised. "See you."

Powell hung up the handset, and for a couple of seconds he glared blackly down at it. What the *hell* was happening out there, anyway?

"Jon?"

Powell looked up to see his wife Sandy standing in the doorway. "Sorry, honey, but I've got to go back in," he said with a sigh, reaching down and retrieving his shoes.

"Tommy?"

He nodded. "At least now it sounds like he's alive. Kidnapped, but alive."

"Be careful," Sandy said quietly. "If someone doesn't want him walking around, they might not want his partner doing it, either."

"Hey, don't worry," he assured her, pulling on his coat and turning to give her a quick but serious hug. "We're not on any cases right now that anybody would kill for."

"Sure," she said, clinging to the hug a bit longer than usual. "Just be careful."

"I will," he promised, kissing her. "I'll call if I'm going to be later than midnight."

His last image as he left the apartment was of her standing in the middle of the room watching him go. A cop's wife, with all the pain and hope and determination that came with that job.

The blood of thousands of New Yorkers, the mysterious Cyril had said. Could Fierenzo have been marked to be the first of those thousands?

Was Powell himself marked to be the second?

28

The floorboards were even softer than Caroline had hoped, and it took less than fifteen minutes for them to tear the first one away from the joists beneath it. After that, with the advantage of leverage, the job went quickly. Ten more minutes, and they had a hole big enough to fit through.

"I wish I had a flashlight," Roger said, peering down into the dankness. "On second thought, maybe I'm glad I *can't* see what's down there. All sorts of creepy crawlies, probably. Any idea how tough the skirting boards will be?"

"It shouldn't be bad," Caroline told him. "They're completely exposed to the weather, and this place obviously hasn't been maintained for decades. I'm guessing a good strong push will knock them right off their nails. Especially the ones by this corner—we know this part of the roof leaks."

"Good enough," Roger said, looking around. "Anything in here we want to take with us?"

This was it. Bracing herself, Caroline took the plunge. "Take anything you think you could use," she said. "You're going alone."

He jerked as if he'd been poked with a live wire. "*What?* Caroline—"

"Roger, it's the only way," she cut him off quickly, trying to keep her voice from shaking. If she let him argue, she might weaken and give in, and then they'd both be doomed. "No matter how loose the skirting boards are, you're not going to push them off without making at least a little noise. Besides, there are those Warriors on guard. Someone has to create a diversion to get them away from the car."

"So we make a diversion and jump them and just go out the door," he countered stubbornly.

"How?" she asked. "What kind of diversion?"

"*I* don't know," he snapped. "Maybe—well, maybe we start the rest of the kindling burning in the middle of the room and yell *fire.*"

She shook her head. "It won't work. Even *I* would know better than to fall for that. They're not going to just charge in blindly and let us jump them."

"Then we yell *fire,* and when they open the door *we* charge *them,*" Roger offered. "We leave together, or we don't leave at all."

"Then you condemn the Grays to death," she said. "If Nikolos has Melantha and can make her use her Gift, they won't have a chance."

"Maybe I don't care about the Grays," Roger snarled. "Maybe they deserve whatever they get."

"And the city?"

The muscles in his jaw tightened. "Fine," he growled. "But *you* go. *I'll* stay here and make the diversion."

"It won't work," she told him gently. "If they hear me shouting *fire* and see me jumping around in a panic, they'll assume you're somewhere waiting to jump them. All their attention will be inward, toward the inside of the cabin and the trap they're expecting you to spring. That should give you the chance to get behind them to the car. It won't play with you doing the jumping around and me supposedly in hiding."

"I can't just leave you here, Caroline," he said pleadingly, his voice shaking the way she was trying so hard to keep hers from doing.

"And besides," she went on, "before you get to the road, you'll have to drive through anyone who gets in your way. I'm not sure I could do that."

"You think *I* can?"

"If you don't, it'll all be a waste of effort." She looked at her watch. "And if we don't hurry, it'll be a waste anyway. Nikolos said they'd be bringing us up to the main house in an hour, and half that time is already gone."

"Maybe it'll be easier to escape from up there."

"No," Caroline said flatly. "If there's anyplace on this property they'll have kept maintained for appearances' sake, it'll be the main house. No flimsiness, no rot, and Greens all around. If you don't escape now, from this cabin, you're not going to escape at all."

Roger closed his eyes. "Caroline . . ."

"Please," she said. "For me?"

"But what if they—?"

"They won't," Caroline told him quickly, trying to chase the same terrifying thought away from her own mind. "If you get away, they won't dare hurt me. You'll know I'm here, and they'll know you know it."

He exhaled loudly, a sigh of defeat. "How will I know when to move?"

"You'll know," she assured him, feeling limp with relief. The last thing she wanted was to have Nikolos burst in on them while they were still standing here arguing. For once, Roger's tendency to back away from confrontations was proving useful. "Actually, that fire idea of yours sounds like the best way to go. I'll try to scream loudly enough to cover the sound of you breaking the skirting boards."

"But not loud enough to bring every Green within half a

mile running to see what's wrong," he warned. Reaching over, he took her in his arms and gave her a lingering hug and kiss. "I love you, Caroline."

"I love you, too, Roger," she said, a lump forming in her throat. It had been a long time since he'd said that in a way that made her feel like he really meant it. "Be careful."

"You too." Taking another deep breath, he lowered himself into the crawl space.

Caroline crossed to the fireplace, her momentary relief that the argument was over replaced by fresh tension as she focused on the task at hand. Now she was actually going to have to go through with it.

She could only hope that she was right about them not killing her afterward.

The Warrior hadn't brought much kindling with the firewood, just a double handful of flat sticks and a half-inch stack of newspaper. But she'd used less than half of it making their original fire, and there should be enough left for what she had in mind. Separating the newspaper into individual sheets, she crumpled each one and made a loose pile of them near the fireplace. She'd heard once that perfume would burn, so she retrieved her purse and dumped the contents of her spray bottle onto one corner of the pile. Then she went to the wicker cabriolet chair Nikolos had been sitting in earlier and lugged it over to the fireplace, positioning it just over one edge of the newspaper.

Roger should have chosen his target skirting boards by now and be in position to knock them out. Crossing to the hole they'd made in the floor, she replaced the boards over it so that it wouldn't be instantly obvious as to what was going on. Her eye fell on the pile of stuff he'd collected from around the cabin and, on impulse, picked up the spare power cord and folded it up in her hand. Back at the fireplace, she lit one of the kindling sticks from the main fire and held the lighted end against the wicker seat of the chair until it started to smolder. Leaning close, she blew carefully on it until a small flame finally appeared.

The chair was as dry as twenty years of neglect could

make it, and within half a minute the fire had spread to half of the seat and the wicker was beginning to crackle with the heat stress. Lighting the newspaper beneath the chair, she stepped back and went into the cabin's kitchen area where the newly blazing fire was out of her direct sight. There she waited until the sound of her fire was clearly audible. Then, taking a deep breath, she ran across the living room, making as much noise on the wooden floor as she could. "Fire!" she shouted, putting panic in her voice as she hammered on the door with her fists. "Help! Fire!"

She was still pounding when the door was abruptly pushed open. "What?" one of the Warriors demanded, looking over her shoulder.

"It caught on fire," Caroline gasped, pointing frantically toward the burning chair. "There's no water in the kitchen—nothing to put it out with. Please—help us."

"Move away," the Warrior ordered, stepping into the doorway. He paused there, and she saw his eyes flick to both sides and then up as he searched quickly for the trap he obviously expected. "Just relax," he added, stripping off his jacket and wrapping it around his hand as he strode into the cabin. "It'll fit just fine into the fireplace."

"But it's a *chair*," Caroline objected. "We can't—I mean—"

The Green didn't bother to answer. Grabbing the back of the chair with his protected hand, he lifted it up and turned it sideways, lining it up to slide in with the rest of the fire.

Surreptitiously, Caroline glanced back at the door. The second Warrior was watching the proceedings from just outside the doorway, showing no signs of coming in. From where he stood, she realized with a sinking feeling, it wouldn't take more than a slight turn of his head to see Roger making for the car.

She would have to do something about that.

The first Warrior had the chair wedged firmly into the fireplace now, sticking out into the room but mostly over the hearth where dropped sparks and ashes wouldn't pose any danger. Easing toward him, Caroline put her hands together in front of her as if nervously wringing them. Under cover of the movement she shifted one end of the power cord to the other hand. With the threat from the chair mostly neutralized, the Warrior turned his attention now to the newspaper, methodically stamping out the bits that were still burning and grinding his shoes hard where the floor looked like it might be smoldering.

Clenching her teeth, Caroline stretched the power cord out in front of her and leaped up onto his back, looping the cord around his throat and pulling back with all her strength.

The Green was fast, all right, faster than she would have expected. Before she could even get the cord tightened around his neck he had spun ninety degrees to the side, grabbing her right wrist in an iron grip and bending violently forward with the clear intent of judo-throwing her over his shoulder.

But she'd grown up with three brothers and knew how to counter that one. She leaned sideways as he bent over, sliding off his back but keeping a grip on the cord. The maneuver ended up flipping her all the way over; and suddenly she found herself with her heels on the floor, hanging at an angle by the cord now looped around the back of the Warrior's neck, staring up into the Green's startled and increasingly angry face. "I've got him!" she shouted, realizing full well that that was a bald-faced lie. "Hurry!"

And then the other Warrior was on her, grabbing at her wrists. She tried to kick him, but he was at the wrong angle and she could only knee him weakly in the side of his leg. He got a grip on her wrists and forced them apart, tearing the cord from her grip. With her support suddenly gone, she fell backward onto the floor, grunting as her back and head slammed onto the rough wood. The first Warrior said something venomous-sounding, rubbing the back of his neck with one hand where the cord had dug into his skin. He lifted the other hand over his head, and Caroline flinched back as the open palm poised over her face.

The slap never came. Even as the Green started to swing

his hand toward her cheek, the cabin filled with the sudden roar of a car engine.

The two Warriors reacted instantly, making a mad scramble for the door. Caroline grabbed at them as they fled, but they were out of reach before she could catch hold of anything. The engine changed pitch as Roger threw the car into gear, roared briefly as he backed into a tight half-circle, then changed pitch and roared even louder as he tore back down the drive, throwing a spray of dirt and leaves and gravel against the front of the cabin. Hoisting herself up on one elbow, Caroline caught a glimpse of his taillights as they disappeared over the first rise.

She took a deep breath, her heart pounding in her ears as her fingers rubbed the back of her head. She'd done her part. The rest was up to him.

● ●

The first part was the hardest. As Caroline had guessed, the skirting boards hadn't been much of a barrier, though to Roger's hypersensitive ears snapping them off their nails had sounded like cannon being fired. He slipped through the undergrowth alongside the cabin, wincing at every leaf that crackled beneath his feet and hoping desperately he didn't trip over some hidden vine. He reached the corner of the cabin as Caroline's diversion was in full swing, only to find one of the Greens still standing in the doorway between him and the car.

He stayed pinned to the corner for what seemed like an hour, agonizing over whether he should try to sneak up on the Warrior or bypass him and head for the road on foot. But then the commotion hit a higher pitch, and the Green charged inside, and Roger sprinted with desperate recklessness for the car. For once the Buick started without protest, and he managed to get turned around and onto the drive before the Greens could stop him.

Which didn't mean they didn't try. Glancing in the mirror as he tore along the narrow drive, he shivered as he caught a glimpse of the knife sticking up out of the trunk. Whether the Warrior had been trying to hit something vital or whether he'd planned to hang onto the weapon and pull himself aboard Roger didn't know. But his muscles trembled with the realization of how close he'd come in that split second to losing everything.

And he was hardly out of the woods yet, literally as well as figuratively. He'd paid careful attention to the scenery as they drove in earlier, and he was pretty sure he knew how to get out again. But in the gathering dusk and the light and shadow thrown by his headlights he might as well have been on a different planet, and all the logic and reason in the world couldn't help the pounding of his heart.

Ahead, a road branched to the right. He hit the intersection and turned hard to the left, hoping fervently that he was going the right way. They'd always turned right on the way in, and he hadn't spotted any other side roads but the ones they'd taken, but it was always possible that he'd missed one. If he had—if he took a wrong turn anywhere in here—he would be instantly lost.

The car shot over another rise, and he winced as it hit the ground hard enough for the rear end to bottom out. He veered to miss a pothole, nearly running off the drive in the other direction, and threw another shower of gravel rattling against his rear bumper as he manhandled the car back on course. Ahead, he caught a glimpse of another intersection, and again turned to the left. One more left turn, he reminded himself, and he would be on the last leg. The intersection after that would be Route 42, and from there he was pretty sure he could find his way back to the Thruway and the relative safety of the city.

And then, abruptly, a figure appeared in the middle of the drive ahead of him, the knife in his hand glittering in the headlights. Clenching his teeth, Roger jammed the accelerator to the floor. Caroline was counting on him; and somewhere out there, so was Melantha.

And just for once, he was damned if he was going to let either of them down.

The Green barely made it out of the way in time, diving sideways to safety behind a large tree. Roger kept going, dimly aware that he was going way too fast for the terrain and visibility, but no longer caring. He nearly missed the final left turn, but managed to make it with only a glancing blow against a small sapling at the intersection. Another Green was waiting just beyond the intersection, this one standing prudently off to the right, and as Roger gunned the engine his arm whipped over his head like a baseball pitcher throwing a fastball. Something thudded into the side of the car; and then Roger was past, driving hell for leather for the highway. There was another rise, another brief surge of weightlessness as the car went momentarily airborne before slamming with a protesting squeal back onto the gravel.

There it was, dead ahead. He hunched forward, fingers tightening on the steering wheel as he braced himself. This would be their last chance to stop him. . . .

And then, suddenly, he was at the end of the drive, standing on the brake pedal as he tried to slow down enough to make the turn. He caught a glimpse of another face as he swung the wheel hard, fishtailed a little as he straightened out, then floored the accelerator and pushed the Buick for all it was worth.

He was half a mile down the road before he realized he was holding his breath, and forced himself to inhale again. He was another half mile past that when he noticed his fingers had the wheel in a death grip, and that his jaw was frozen in something halfway between a scowl and a grin.

He was another mile past that when it occurred to him that he'd roared out onto the road without ever once checking to see if there was any other traffic.

He continued south, staying as far above the speed limit as the curves would allow. Fortunately, traffic was light. He came up behind only three other cars and passed all of them before reaching Route 28 and turning east. Traffic here was somewhat heavier, with fewer opportunities for passing, and he found himself swearing softly to himself every time he wound up trapped behind a slow-moving vehicle, tensing for the attack that must inevitably be waiting beyond the next curve.

But no attack came, and by the time he reached the Thruway he began to finally believe that he had in fact gotten away.

Which meant it was time to start figuring out what he was going to do next.

The obvious answer was to call the police. But the more he thought about it, the more he wondered if that would actually get him anywhere. Surely the Greens had had some experience dodging the law over the years. Besides, what could he say that would convince anyone he was telling the truth? He'd never seen the main house on the Green property, which meant he couldn't describe the place itself or even the road leading to it. He could probably identify the various Warriors who'd been directing traffic or lugging firewood; but when those same Greens could vanish into the nearest tree without a trace, that approach would be a dead end, too. He could take them to the cabin, but with a little effort Nikolos could probably erase everything that might corroborate his story. They could replace the missing floorboards and crawl space skirting, trade out the furniture with an entirely different set, maybe even resettle the dust so that the place would look as abandoned as it had when he and Caroline first arrived.

And if he took the authorities there and they found something different than he'd described, that would be the end of his credibility. After that, no amount of pleading would do any good.

Ahead, he could see the lights of a service area. He was still uncomfortably close to Green territory, but the car needed gas and he needed coffee and something to soothe an increasingly distracting acid stomach. A big place like this, with a lot of people around, was probably as safe as he was going to get.

He pulled in to the pumps, stuck his credit card in the

slot, and filled the tank. Relocating to a parking space by the store, he went inside and bought a cup of coffee and a plastic-wrapped turkey sandwich.

He had made it back to the car when there was a call from his right. "Hey! Buddy!"

He turned, tensing. The man was big and rough-looking, wearing a baseball cap and down vest over a set of denims, and was walking toward the store entrance with the stiff gait of someone who'd spent too long a stretch behind the wheel. "What?" Roger called back cautiously.

"Better check your hood ornament," the other said, jabbing a finger toward the far side of the Buick. "Looks like it's slipped a little."

Roger frowned. *Hood ornament?* "Yeah, thanks," he said, wondering what in the world he was talking about.

The man nodded and disappeared into the store. Still frowning, Roger left his sandwich and coffee on the roof and circled around the front of the car.

There, sticking out of the fender, was another knife. So that was what that last thud had been as he tore along the drive. One final gift from the Greens.

An almost not-so-final gift, he realized with a shiver as he wiggled it free of the metal. Another foot forward, and it might well have punched a hole in the radiator reservoir. If it had, they could have simply strolled the mile or two it would have taken the car to overheat and die.

The new discovery reminded him he still had a knife sticking out of his trunk lid, as well. Walking around to the back, he pulled it free, then got the car open and tossed both knives onto the passenger seat. For all the supposed rarity of their damned *trassks,* he thought grimly, the Greens seemed more than willing to spend them trying to get him and Caroline out of their way. Retrieving his coffee and sandwich, he got in and locked the door behind him.

He sat there for a few minutes, watching the people going in and out of the store as he ate, a black anger chewing at him. They had Caroline, they might have Melantha, and the only cop who might have been willing to listen to his story had vanished. As far as Nikolos and his friends were concerned, Roger was the lone figure still standing against them. Roger, and the Grays.

The Grays.

He picked up one of the knives again, studying its texture as he turned it over in his hand. A few minutes or hours from now, and he wouldn't even have these to show any cop he tried to talk to. They would have reverted back to elaborate pieces of jewelry, and nothing Roger could do would change them back again.

But the Grays wouldn't need any convincing. They already knew all about the Greens and their *trassks*. Having two more to show them might be all the proof he needed to convince them he was telling the truth.

And if part of that truth was that Nikolos had Melantha hidden away in the Catskills, he might just be able to persuade them to go up there and rescue his wife.

To rescue his wife . . . and to trade her life for Melantha's.

He stared at the knife, feeling cold as that realization hit him for the first time. Because that was exactly what he would be doing if he brought in the Grays. If they raided Nikolos's retreat and found Melantha there, she would die.

And he would have to face Caroline and tell her what he'd done.

With a soft curse, he tossed the knife back onto the seat and turned the key in the ignition. He was too tired to untangle his way through the ethics, too tired and too scared and too numb. He hadn't asked to be dropped into the middle of their war, and it wasn't up to him to figure out how to resolve it. All he knew was that Caroline was in danger, and that he would do whatever he had to in order to get her back safely. And if it cost Melantha's life . . .

He shook his mind sharply, refusing to finish that thought even in the privacy of his own mind. Backing out of his parking space, he took the ramp back onto the Thruway. Torvald Gray, Greenwich Village artist, was about to have a visitor.

29

The Warriors sat Caroline back down on the couch, one of them standing guard over her while the other monitored the burning chair and continued to feed it deeper into the fireplace as necessary. By the time that task was finished, they had been joined by two more Warriors, all four of whom proceeded to stand silently around the cabin like a set of Macy's manikins. No one spoke, not even to answer her questions or respond to her comments, but she was able to pick up the tantalizing almost-speech that indicated they had plenty to say to each other. It was almost a relief when one of them suddenly announced that the Group Commander was ready to see her.

They set off through the woods, the four Warriors arrayed in a loose square around her. It was pitch-black outside, and her first reflexive thought was that this might be her chance to get away. But common sense quickly prevailed. The Greens would hardly let themselves be caught by surprise twice in one night, and wandering around blindly in a strange forest would be a complete waste of effort.

Besides, it was clear after the first dozen steps that her escorts had far better night vision than she did. They walked across the uneven terrain with casual confidence, while she spent much of her time hesitating and stumbling and batting branches away from her face. After a couple of near falls, one of the Warriors finally stepped close and took her arm, guiding her as he would a blind woman through the darkness.

But if she couldn't see very well, the sounds around her more than made up for it. Instead of the usual bird and insect noises, she could hear rustling bushes and grunts of exertion and voices calling to each other in an unfamiliar language.

The main house, when they finally reached it, was something of a surprise. It was larger than she'd expected, rambling outward in two angled wings and rising to three stories in places, set at the back of an expansive and well-kept lawn. Every window in the place seemed lit, and she could see half a dozen shadowy figures walking briskly toward and away from it. Without better light it was impossible to tell what kind of construction it was, but from the design and placement of the windows she guessed it was much older than the cabin, possibly even late 19th century.

Her escorts led her up the steps onto a wide porch and through a door flanked by ornate sidelights, with an equally ornate fanlight above it. Beyond the door was a large foyer, high-ceilinged, rimmed with carved pillars and sporting a hardwood floor. One of the Warriors detached himself from her side and stepped to a set of double doors leading off the foyer to the left. "In here," he said, pushing open one of the doors. "The Group Commander is waiting."

"Thank you," Caroline said, fighting to keep her voice steady. Stepping past him, she walked inside.

And stopped short. The room was a library, complete with built-in bookshelves filled with dark volumes in a variety of sizes. In the center of the room was a massive oak desk flanked by a pair of floor lamps with three antique bergère armchairs facing it.

But it wasn't the furnishings or the room itself that had startled her. It was, rather, the room's single occupant.

"Good evening, Caroline," the silver-haired woman said calmly, the soft glow from the lamps highlighting the deep age lines in her face. "I'm Group Commander Sylvia Green." She smiled slightly. "I take it I'm not exactly what you expected?"

Caroline found her voice. "I'm sorry," she said. "We've heard a lot about Green Warriors in the past couple of days. I guess I just assumed that they would all be men."

The woman shrugged. "The Gifts choose us," she said, rising to her feet and gesturing to one of the armchairs. "We do not choose them. Please; sit down."

"Thank you," Caroline said, frowning as the name suddenly clicked. "You said your name was *Sylvia*?"

"The same Sylvia your husband met at Aleksander's apartment, yes," the woman confirmed. "I presume that was your next question?"

"Yes, it was," Caroline said as she took one of the chairs. "I hope you aren't too angry about Roger's escape."

"It was embarrassing," Sylvia conceded as she resumed her seat. "But hardly fatal. There's nothing he can do to trouble us."

"Really," Caroline said politely. "Then why are your people all stirred up out there?"

"Stirred up?"

"Making noises in the night."

"Oh, that," Sylvia said. "They're just making your cabin disappear."

"They're *what*?"

"Not literally, of course," Sylvia assured her. "You may have noticed how narrow the side roads were that you drove along earlier today. The Laborers are merely brushing away the gravel at those intersections and quick-planting bushes across them. Even if Roger finds someone willing to listen to his story, he'll come back to find that none of the drives he described are there anymore."

Caroline felt her stomach tighten. "Clever," she managed.

"Deception has always been a part of warfare," Sylvia said with a shrug. "One of the many aspects of my Gift."

"An interesting Gift," Caroline murmured. "May I ask what you intend to do with me?"

"Nothing sinister, I assure you," Sylvia said. "You'll be kept here until it's all over, then allowed to return to your home."

Caroline's throat tightened. "Assuming Manhattan is still there."

The lines in Sylvia's face deepened. "What exactly would you have us do, Caroline *Human* Whittier?" she demanded. "You speak as if *we* weren't the ones the Grays tried to exterminate, setting fire to our forest and cold-bloodedly shooting as we tried to escape the flames. Should we simply lie down and die to keep from inconveniencing your people? Or should we make a stand and defend ourselves and our loved ones? What would *you* do in our place?"

"I might worry a little more about the innocents caught in the middle," Caroline told her. "Three thousand people died when the twin towers went down. How many buildings and lives are you planning to destroy in your defense?"

"Don't misunderstand me, Caroline," Sylvia said stiffly. "We're Warriors, not butchers. We will not inflict any more damage or death than necessary to protect our people. But if it comes to a choice between Green survival or a few lost Human lives . . . well, there is no choice there."

"Even if those lost humans are your own friends?" Caroline persisted.

"I have no Human friends," Sylvia said. "As a matter of fact, before I met you and Roger, I'm not sure I even knew any Humans by name."

"You're joking," Caroline said, looking at the other in surprise. "How long have you lived here?"

"I was one of the original refugees," Sylvia said. "Oh, and I knew Velovsky by name, too. But he was about the only Human I knew before you two."

"How in the world did you manage that?" Caroline asked, still not quite believing it. "I thought all of you moved into the city together."

"All except for a small group who came here," Sylvia said. "Leader Elymas wasn't entirely happy with the idea of living in a city, so he sent our group to look into the possibility of a more permanent home."

"I thought he died before you even left Ellis Island."

"He did, but he'd seen the Farseers' visions and knew what to expect," Sylvia said. "Actually, to be precise, it was his son Nikolos who relayed his instructions to us. Leader Elymas was too far gone to speak during his final hours, and Nikolos was the only one who could still communicate with him and interpret his messages."

"What do you mean, interpret?" Caroline asked. "I thought you have a direct mind-to-mind link."

"We do, but some things transfer better than others," Sylvia said. "Words and simple sentences usually work, and emotions are seldom misunderstood. But images and abstract ideas can be difficult, both to send and to receive. Sometimes only those who know each other well can manage it without distortion. Pastsingers and Farseers do much better than the average, of course, but they're a small minority."

"I see," Caroline said, nodding. "I've been wondering why you bothered with speech at all."

"If we could communicate clearly and consistently without it, we would," Sylvia said. "At any rate, I've sent for some food, and then you'll be taken to your room."

"Thank you," Caroline said. "I'm still not clear as to why you haven't had more contact with humans. Don't you like us?"

"I neither like nor dislike you," Sylvia said candidly. "It's simply that I've spent my life here in the woods, preparing this place for future generations. I just never got around to making contact with the locals."

The door opened behind her, and Caroline turned to see a Green step into the room with a box the size of a half-pound chocolate sampler in his hand. "Your meal," Sylvia identified it. "I'm afraid it's all we have to offer."

"Thank you," Caroline said, eyeing the box dubiously as the Green handed it to her. She opened the lid and found herself gazing at a double row of tubes the size of granola bars and the shape of manicotti. "What are they?"

"Warrior field rations," Sylvia told her. "Designed to keep a Green healthy and strong during long campaigns."

"I see." Closing the box, Caroline set it on the edge of the desk. "I'm sorry, but it won't do."

It was clearly not the response Sylvia had been expecting. "I'm sorry?" she asked.

"I said it won't do," Caroline repeated. "Food designed to keep Greens alive could be dangerous or even lethal to humans."

"Nonsense," Sylvia said stiffly. "Greens eat human food all the time. I ate some there myself, in fact, at Aleksander's. It's never bothered any of us."

"So Greens can eat human food," Caroline said. "That doesn't mean it necessarily works the other direction." She gestured toward the box. "For all either of us know, there may be trace chemicals or vitamin concentrations in there that would kill me." She lifted her eyebrows. "Unless, of course, Nikolos *wants* me dead."

"Don't be absurd," Sylvia said, throwing a scowl at the other Green. Without a word, he retrieved the box and left. "Unfortunately, as I said, that's all we have."

"I understand that," Caroline said, choosing her words carefully. "But there must be restaurants nearby."

Sylvia barked a laugh. "Of course."

"No, really," Caroline insisted. "Roger won't have called any of the local police—he'll have assumed you already have them in your back pocket. And he can't possibly get up here with anyone from the city until after midnight at the earliest."

Sylvia was staring at her, an odd expression on her face. "You're serious, aren't you?"

"Absolutely," Caroline said. "I'm starving, and this is the best way for me to get something safe to eat. I won't make any trouble—I promise. All I want is to go and eat." She cocked her head. "I'll even treat," she cajoled. "Unless you're afraid a Green Warrior can't ride herd on a lone human female."

Sylvia smiled cynically. "No, you don't," she said. "You can't maneuver me into doing something just because I think I'll look weak or afraid. A Group Commander never makes decisions based on emotion."

"Good," Caroline said. "Then do it because your people may retreat here someday, and you'll need as much first-hand knowledge about the area as possible."

The wrinkles in Sylvia's forehead deepened again, and Caroline held her breath. Then, so abruptly that it caught her by surprise, the older woman gave a sharp nod. "You're on," she said, standing up. "There's a vehicle out back behind the house that I think still runs. You drive."

The vehicle turned out to be a vintage Ford pickup that looked like it hadn't been driven in years. But there was gas in the tank, and with a little persuasion Caroline got it started.

They passed two groups of Greens at their bush-planting party as she drove down the narrow road. One or two of the workers glanced up as they passed, but no one seemed shocked or even particularly surprised to see their prisoner driving away with their Group Commander.

But then, Sylvia had said these were Laborers. Maybe matters involving Warriors was of no concern to them.

"Which way do I go?" she asked as they reached the end of the drive.

"Left," Sylvia said. "I'm told there's a small diner just before you reach town that might suit us."

"As long as they have decent food," Caroline said, turning onto the highway. "You're going to join me, aren't you?"

She heard Sylvia's snort even over the growling engine. "You weren't expecting me to let you go in alone, were you?"

"No, I meant were you going to eat with me," Caroline corrected. "You know: share a meal together?"

"Does this come under that same heading of firsthand knowledge?"

"It comes under the heading of hospitality," Caroline said. "I just want to try to understand you people."

"Why?"

"Because I like Melantha," Caroline told her. "I'd like to be able to appreciate the rest of her people, too."

"And it's hard to appreciate freaks of nature who can climb inside trees?"

"It's hard to appreciate people who kidnap us," Caroline said tiredly, quietly conceding defeat. If Roger did his best to avoid confrontations, Sylvia clearly went out of her way to create them.

For a few minutes the only sounds in the truck were those of the engine and road. "Did Nikolos tell you how many Warriors we have?" Sylvia asked at last.

Caroline searched her memory. "I think he said you had about sixty."

"Did he also tell you we're facing nearly seven hundred Grays?"

Caroline swallowed. "No."

"And unlike us, all of them *can* pick up hammerguns and fight if they want to," Sylvia said. "Even if we assume a Green Warrior can handle four or five untrained Grays, the odds are still badly against us. I'm not here to be liked, Caroline, by you or anyone else. My job is to do whatever is necessary to give my people their best chance to survive."

"We don't want you destroyed," Caroline said earnestly. "All we want is to find a way to keep Melantha alive."

"So do we all," Sylvia murmured. "Right now, the threat of her Gift is all that keeps the Grays from attacking."

Caroline grimaced. That wasn't what she'd meant at all, and Sylvia knew it.

The grimace turned into a frown. Or *did* she know it? Was Sylvia so fixated with her job that she was incapable of seeing Melantha or anyone else except in military terms?

She looked sideways at the older woman's profile in the dim glow of the dashboard lights. One of the original refugees, she'd said, which probably put her somewhere in her eighties or nineties. How many of those years been spent out here in the woods, with only a handful of Laborers and fellow Warriors to keep her company? Had she ever married and had a family? Did she have any genuine friends, or only colleagues?

How much of her life had she sacrificed in the name of her Gift?

She turned back to the winding road, an odd sensation prickling across the back of her neck. Ever since this whole thing had started she had felt angry at the Greens, or distrustful of them, or simply flat-out frightened of them. Now, for the first time, she was starting to feel sorry for them.

"There," Sylvia said, pointing at a small lighted sign ahead. "That's the place."

"Right," Caroline said, slowing and turning into the lot. She eyed the two other cars already there as she maneuvered the pickup into a parking space, wondering if having witnesses around would make Sylvia rethink the whole idea.

But Sylvia said nothing as Caroline turned off the engine. They climbed out of the truck, and walked across the lot and into the diner.

Inside, the place was exactly what Caroline had expected: a reasonably modern restaurant disguised as a nostalgic relic of the fifties. A sign said to seat themselves, and Caroline led the way past the other two occupied tables to one of the booths in the back. Sylvia took the far side, the seat that gave her a view of the rest of the diner, as Caroline slipped into the one facing her. The aromas made her empty stomach growl impatiently.

"I presume you read English," Caroline said, pulling a pair of menus from the clip at the end of the table and handing Sylvia one.

"Perfectly," Sylvia said, a little frostily, as she took the menu and opened it. "I've just never been in a restaurant before."

"Really?" Caroline asked. "Not even one of the Green restaurants?"

Sylvia shook her head. "I've only been to the city a few times." She gestured to the menu. "What do you recommend?"

"What did you have at Aleksander's?" Caroline asked,

glancing down the menu. "Roger said you were sitting down to eat when he got there."

"I've had lamb, fish, rice, various vegetables, and bread," Sylvia told her. "I suppose I should use this opportunity to extend myself."

"In that case, you should probably go with either a steak, cheeseburger, or fried chicken," Caroline suggested. "Steaks tend to be iffy in places like this—sometimes very good, sometimes really bad. But either of the other two should be fine."

"What are you having?"

"The cheeseburger and a side salad," Caroline said, closing her menu. "And a chocolate malt."

"Very well," Sylvia said, giving a curt and very military looking nod. "The chicken, then. Where do we go to get the food?"

"The server will bring it," Caroline said. "We just tell her what we want, and she'll go back to the kitchen and tell the cook."

"I see," Sylvia said. "Like eating at someone's homestead, except that there are choices?"

"Something like that," Caroline said. "We pay at the end, too. I'll handle that part."

"Yes," Sylvia murmured. "Will you handle the food requests, as well?"

"Certainly, if you'd like." Caroline half-turned, hoping to catch the waitress's eye.

And froze. At the far end of the diner, strolling in through the doorway, were a pair of state police officers.

Carefully, trying to keep her movements casual, she turned back around. Sylvia was watching her, her jaw tight, a warning glint in her eyes. Caroline gave her a microscopic nod of reassurance in return.

There was the sound of bustling feet behind her. "Evening, ladies," a plump woman in a white apron said cheerfully as she set glasses of water in front of them. "Getting a bit brisk out there, isn't it? Do you need another minute?"

"No, we're ready," Caroline said, opening her menu again and reading off their order as the woman scribbled onto a pad. "—and one chocolate malt," she finished. "Unless you'd like one, too, Mom?" she added, lifting her eyebrows questioningly at Sylvia.

The older woman didn't even twitch. "Yes, I think I would," she said.

Caroline nodded. "Make that two."

"You got it," the waitress said, making one final notation and finishing off with a flourish. "I'll put this in and get started on your malts." With a smile, she bustled off.

"'Mom'?" Sylvia asked dryly.

"I thought it might make things simpler," Caroline told her, replacing the menus in their clip. "A woman and her mother out for an evening together are automatically above suspicion."

"I'll take your word for it," Sylvia said. "You know your people better than—"

She broke off, her gaze slicing through the air over Caroline's shoulder. Caroline started to turn around—

"Evening, ladies," an authoritative male voice said. "You two own that red Ford pickup out there?"

Steeling herself, Caroline put on her real estate agent's poker face and finished the turn she'd started. One of the two state troopers was standing over her, one hand casually on his hip. "Yes," she confirmed. "Is there a problem?"

"I noticed kind of a smell around it on our way in," the cop said. "Are your emissions tests up to date?"

Caroline flashed a look at Sylvia— "Of course they are," the older woman said calmly. "The papers are in the glove box."

"Would you mind showing them to me?" the cop asked.

"Not at all." Sylvia looked at Caroline. "Would you get them for him, please?"

It took Caroline a second to find her voice. "Sure," she managed. Untangling her feet from the table supports, she slid out of the booth. With the cop at her side, she started down the diner toward the door, her mind suddenly spinning at top speed.

Because this might be her best chance to get away. Maybe her only chance, in fact. These troopers would have no connection to any of the local police departments that the Greens might have subtly poisoned or subverted over the years. Once she was outside with them, she could identify herself as a kidnap victim and ask for help. They'd have to take her seriously, at least enough to get her out of here while they made further inquiries. They could be gone before Sylvia and her Shriek could even make it to the door.

Sylvia.

Caroline's lip twisted, the sudden mixture of uncertainly and hope dying quietly within her. Sylvia was a Group Commander, with presumably some of the same tactical Gift Nikolos himself possessed. She would hardly have suggested Caroline go outside alone unless there was a backup plan already in place.

The cop pushed open the diner door for her, and Caroline stepped out into the cold night air. No, she and the cop weren't alone out here. Whether Sylvia had somehow set this up herself, or whether she'd just taken the opportunity when it presented itself, this was surely a test.

And with a chill in her heart, Caroline realized that if she flunked, that would be the end of it. Sylvia would probably never speak to her again, at least not on anything except official Warrior business. She would never allow Caroline off the Green estate again for a meal like this, either, and she would most certainly never join her.

And she would continue to consider humans as lesser beings not worth a second thought as she prepared for war.

They crossed the lot to the pickup, and Caroline unlocked the passenger side. "I'm not sure exactly where she keeps it," she told the cop, reaching into the glove box and pulling out a small travel folder. "Let's see . . ."

"Here," the cop offered helpfully, pulling out a flashlight and shining it on the papers.

The emissions certificate was the third one down. "Here it is," she said, sliding it out and holding it up for his inspection.

"Thanks," the cop said, nodding. "Sorry to have bothered you."

"No bother," Caroline assured him, putting everything back and closing the truck door again. "This old thing *does* get pretty pungent sometimes."

The other cop met them halfway back to the diner, holding two carryout cups of coffee. "You ready, Carl?" he asked.

"Yeah," the cop said, stopping and taking one of the cups. "Have a good evening, ma'am."

With that, they headed toward their squad car. "You, too," Caroline murmured after them. Shivering once, she glanced at the row of silent trees lining the parking lot and went back inside.

The malts had been delivered in her absence, and Sylvia was sipping thoughtfully at hers through a straw. "Did you find the certificate he needed?" she asked as Caroline rejoined her in the booth.

"Yes," Caroline assured her, unwrapping her straw. "It all seems to be in order."

"Good." Sylvia gestured to her glass. "Interesting drink, this."

"It's very popular among my people," Caroline said, taking a sip. It was rich and thick, as only a homemade malt could be. "You were taking something of a chance there, weren't you?" she added casually.

"You think so?"

"Absolutely," Caroline said. "Having one of your Warriors use the Shriek on a couple of state cops would have bought you far more attention than you would have liked. Especially since Roger will probably be raising various roofs himself sometime in the next few hours. If someone made the connection between his story and that of these cops, you could have had all sorts of unwanted visitors descending on you."

Sylvia eyed her over the malt. "Yet you said nothing."

"Are you guessing about that?" Caroline countered. "Or are you admitting you have someone on guard out there?"

The other smiled wryly. "Touché," she said. "Is that the correct term? Touché?"

"It is," Caroline assured her. "Is that a yes?"

Sylvia pursed her lips. "I misjudged you," she admitted. "You're smarter than you let on. Also more . . . sympathetic, I think."

Caroline shrugged. "We took in a girl we didn't even know and tried to protect her," she pointed out. "We're obviously suckers for people in trouble."

"Yet we're the ones who tried to kill her," Sylvia reminded her. "You might not feel so sympathetic toward us."

"You're still people in trouble," Caroline said. "And we still want to help."

Sylvia didn't reply.

The waitress appeared a minute later with their food, and they set to with a will. Sylvia's first tentative nibbles at her chicken quickly became larger bites, with the mashed potatoes and gravy getting an equally quick and enthusiastic vote of approval. Caroline attempted to probe a little into the history and organization of the Green estate as they ate, but learned nothing except that they'd owned the property since 1932. Most of the conversation ended up centered on Caroline, with Sylvia skillfully drawing out her life story in general and the events of the past week in particular.

Caroline also had to deflect three separate attempts to learn who exactly it was who had given Melantha to them that fateful Wednesday evening. "I don't know why you're so determined to protect him," Sylvia said a bit crossly after her third and least subtle probe. "We know Melantha's parents weren't involved, so it can't be out of any perceived loyalty to her family."

"I just don't want to see someone punished for saving her life," Caroline said evasively.

Sylvia shook her head. "You have it backwards. We, of all the Greens, would be the most grateful for the saving of her life. My concern is for her current safety; and knowing who took her might help us learn where she is." She shook her head. "I just hope Roger isn't foolish enough to tell the police that she's here. If he does, the Grays are bound to hear about it."

"You think they'd attack?" Caroline asked, frowning.

"Of course they would," Sylvia said in a tone of strained patience. "This place is our last hope, the refuge where any survivors would be gathered together. If they took it away from us, we would have no choice but to face them in Manhattan, where all the advantages are theirs."

"But this is hardly the last place in the country where there are forests," Caroline objected. "How could the Grays taking this particular plot of land hurt you?"

"Because this particular plot is ours," Sylvia said quietly. "Would you want to live in someone else's home the rest of your life? Or, worse, in an anonymous hotel room somewhere?"

Caroline grimaced. "Not really."

"Neither do we." Sylvia set her last chicken bone back onto the plate and began wiping her fingers. "We need to get back."

"I suppose," Caroline said. "No, no," she added as Sylvia reached for the small shoulder bag she'd brought in with her. "My treat, remember?"

"I've reconsidered," Sylvia said. "I've decided I wouldn't be a fitting host if I allowed you to do that."

"I insist," Caroline said, producing her credit card. "I invited *you* to dinner, and it wouldn't be hospitable for me to let you pay. If you'd like, you can think of it as compensation for that chair we burned."

Sylvia snorted. "That chair has been ready for the fire since 1968," she said. But she nevertheless let the shoulder bag fall back to her side. "Very well, then, I accept. Thank you."

"My pleasure," Caroline said, turning halfway around and gesturing to the waitress.

The Laborers they'd passed on their way out of the estate were nowhere to be seen as Caroline maneuvered the

pickup back up the winding drive. "Very neat," she complimented Sylvia as they passed the spot where the Warrior
had first stopped them. "I know that side road was right
there, and I still can't see a thing."

"Green Laborers are the best workers in the world,"
Sylvia said proudly. "I only wish I had more of them to
work with."

"How many do you have?"

"Only twenty," the other said. "And we have a smattering
of the other Gifts, too."

"Ah," Caroline said, her mind flashing back to that last
confrontation with Nikolos and the name he'd accidentally
dropped. "And Damian? Which is his Gift?"

There was a short pause. "Damian?" Sylvia asked, her
voice suddenly odd. "Who's that?"

"I assumed you knew," Caroline said. "Nikolos mentioned him back in the cabin."

Sylvia hissed softly between her teeth. "Did he, now.
That was . . . unfortunate."

Caroline frowned at her. "Why? Who is he?"

"No one who concerns you," Sylvia said evenly, pointing
as Caroline drove around the final curve and came within
sight of the house. "Park in back of the house. Then I'll
show you to your room."

Caroline's room turned out to be a third-floor suite at the
back of the house's central section, with a private bathroom, a multi-angled ceiling, and two expansive dormer
windows. It smelled slightly of age, but otherwise seemed
freshly cleaned and made up. "I trust you'll be comfortable
here," Sylvia said as she went around the room turning on
lights. "If you need anything, just come downstairs and find
someone."

"No guard posted at my door?" Caroline asked, trying to
make it a joke.

"I think you've proved we can trust you, at least a little."
Sylvia smiled faintly. "Besides, you know as well as I do
that you wouldn't get very far."

"And I still want to learn more about you and your people," Caroline countered. "Thank you for letting us go to dinner tonight."

"You're welcome," Sylvia said. "Perhaps we can do it again before you leave us."

"I'd like that," Caroline told her. "Good night."

"Good night." Sylvia bowed slightly and left, closing the door behind her.

It had been a long day, full of tension and fear and emotion, and the first thing Caroline did after she'd pulled the shades was to head straight to the bathroom for a good soak. The tub was an old-fashioned cast-iron job, deep and wide, set up off the floor on little molded feet. The water-heating system, fortunately, had apparently been upgraded since the tub was installed, and once the hot water finally made it up three floors there seemed to be plenty of it. A few minutes later, she was soaking gratefully in the steaming water.

And as she soothed away the lingering tightness in her muscles, she tried to sort out what exactly was going on. And, more importantly, where exactly she stood in the middle of it.

She and Roger had obviously been right about the Greens having a forest hideaway. But how many of the rest of the Greens actually knew about it was another question entirely. Aleksander had certainly never hinted that they had any recourse but to make their stand in Manhattan. Had he deliberately left out this fallback position for security reasons, or to bolster his argument for wanting Melantha back?

Or was Nikolos the one who was playing games with this place, possibly against Sylvia as well as everybody else?

And where did Damian fit into this? Nikolos had seemed chagrined that he'd let the name slip, and Sylvia had reacted even more strongly. That implied he was someone important.

But who?

She scooped up some of the hot water in her cupped hands and rubbed it across her face. It didn't matter, really, at least not to her. Whoever Damian was, there was little she could do about it here.

What she *could* do was continue the path she'd started on

tonight. If she could nurture her new relationship with Sylvia—if she could spark even a little empathy toward the humans Nikolos might soon order her and her Warriors to kill—maybe the Command-Tactician who had quietly defied Cyril's peacemaking authority might find himself facing a minor rebellion of his own.

Leaning back in the tub, she closed her eyes and willed herself to relax. She could only hope she would have enough time to teach Sylvia what it meant to be human.

30

There was no one with the distinctive Gray body type loitering by the MacDougal Alley gate as Roger drove slowly through Greenwich Village's crowded evening traffic. But as he passed, he could see lights burning in Torvald's loft apartment. Circling the block, he found a parking space and maneuvered the Buick into it.

He had already decided there was no point to trying to sneak up on them. Even if there was no one watching from street level, they undoubtedly had sentries posted on the nearby buildings. Pushing his way through the gate, he strode boldly down the alley to Torvald's building and pushed the intercom button.

There was a moment of silence. Roger stood motionless, feeling the eerie sensation of having a dozen pairs of eyes focused on his back. He reached for the button again; but before he could press it, there was a click from the lock. Taking a deep breath, he opened the door and headed up the stairs.

"Well, well," a familiar voice said dryly as he emerged from the stairway. "Look what the cat dragged in."

Roger grimaced. "Hello, Ingvar," he said, noting a couple

of fresh mud stains on the fleece collar of his gray jacket. "I'm glad to see that car didn't flatten you."

"I'm touched by your concern," Ingvar said with only a trace of sarcasm. "You been surfing the sewers?"

Roger looked down at his clothing. He had brushed away the worst of the mud at the Thruway service area, and a lot of the rest had caked up and fallen off since then. But he still did indeed look like something Caroline's mother's cat would proudly bring into the house to show off. "I've been playing with the Greens," he told the other. "Is Torvald home?"

Ingvar's forehead creased slightly. "Sure," he said, nodding toward the studio door. "Go on in."

"Thanks." Gingerly easing past the other, Roger opened the door and stepped inside.

Torvald was home, all right. But he wasn't alone. There were at least two dozen other Grays packed into the studio, some gathered into small conversation groups in various corners, the rest standing around one of the flat tables that had been set up in the center of the room. Torvald was presiding, gesturing with a pointer at a large-scale map of Manhattan spread out across the table, his middle-aged daughter Kirsten beside him.

Everyone looked up as Roger came in. Fighting against the impulse to turn and run, he gave Torvald a nod. "Hello, Torvald," he said. "Sorry to barge in on you this way."

"Have you found Melantha?" another older Gray with a long scar on his left cheek spoke up from Torvald's side.

Roger focused on him. "And you are . . . ?"

"Halfdan Gray," the other identified himself. He quirked a small smile. "Father of the two gentlemen who stopped you on the street yesterday."

"Right," Roger said. "Sorry about that."

Halfdan waved the apology away. "*Do* you know where Melantha is?"

"I might." Roger looked back at Torvald. "First, we need to discuss my price."

"By all means," Torvald said, not sounding offended. "Can we offer you anything? Coffee? Tea?"

"Dry cleaner?" Halfdan added, gesturing toward Roger's clothing.

"Nothing, thank you," Roger said, glancing around at the rest of the group. "Just a little privacy."

One of the Grays in the corner stirred. "I'm not sure I like that," he said.

"I'm not sure you have to," Halfdan told him. "Everyone out."

Slowly, and with some quiet muttering, the Grays made their separate ways to the door, a few of them giving Roger suspicious or unfriendly looks as they passed. Roger stood still, wincing as the river of bodies flowed around and past him, until only he, Torvald, Halfdan, and Kirsten remained. "There's your privacy," Halfdan said shortly. "Where is she?"

"My price first," Roger said, walking the rest of the way across the loft to stand on the far side of the table from the other three. "I want a guarantee that Melantha won't be killed."

Halfdan snorted. "Don't be ridiculous. The whole point of this exercise is to eliminate her."

"No, the point is to eliminate her as a threat," Roger corrected. "That doesn't necessarily mean she has to die."

"If she doesn't die, she can't be anything *but* a threat," Halfdan countered. "We can't take the chance that a Leader might rise up someday who decides to use her to get rid of us."

Roger shook his head. "I don't think they're nearly that blindly obedient to their Leaders anymore." He looked down at his dirt-stained clothing. "I have some recent experience in the matter."

"So do we," Torvald said. "But you assume the current tug-of-war between Cyril and Aleksander is the natural state of Green society. It's not. Give them a true Leader, and the dissent would evaporate."

"Fine," Roger said, conceding the point. "But why would a future Leader suddenly decide he wanted to wipe you out? Assuming you hadn't done anything to them, of course."

"We didn't do anything back in the Valley, either," Halfdan bit out. "That didn't stop some Leader from ordering the Warriors to attack us."

"Or to order their Groundshakers to bring down an entire cliff," Torvald added darkly. "Hundreds of families died in that—"

"Wait a second," Roger cut him off. "They told me *you* started the war. That you set fire to their forest because you weren't getting your way in the talks."

"That's a lie," Halfdan said flatly. "We didn't set that fire, and they knew it. It was probably dry lightning—we'd been warning them for years to do something about the brush around their trees."

"They also told me you were shooting at them from the cliffs," Roger said.

"Of course we were shooting," Torvald said. "But not at them. We were shooting at the trees in front of the fire, trees they'd already vacated."

Roger frowned. "The ones they'd vacated?"

Torvald sighed. "A firebreak, Roger," he explained patiently. "We were trying to create a firebreak."

"Hoping to save the rest of the valley," Halfdan growled. "But they didn't care. They saw we were distracted, figured it was as good a time as any to teach us a lesson, and started knocking down our cliffs."

"I see," Roger murmured, a hard knot forming in his stomach. Even with all his questions and suspicions about the Greens, he'd nevertheless still assumed that what they'd said about their history had been accurate. In fact, he'd rather cavalierly dismissed Caroline's suggestion that they needed to get the Grays' side of the story.

"But that's ancient history," Torvald continued. "You're here to discuss current events."

"Yes," Roger said, forcing his mind back to the subject at

hand. "And I'm still waiting to hear what you're willing to do about Melantha."

"I already told you that," Halfdan said. "We can't let her walk away from this alive."

"What kind of guarantee could you give *us*?" Kirsten put in suddenly.

Roger focused on her. "What?"

"You want Melantha to live," Kirsten said. "We want to live, too. What guarantee could you give us that her Gift wouldn't be used against us, now or in the future?"

"Kirsten—" Halfdan began warningly.

"No, let her talk," Torvald interrupted him. "Roger?"

Roger suppressed a grimace. A completely predictable question, and yet it hadn't once occurred to him to come up with an answer for it. "I assume you won't simply accept her promise that she'll leave you alone?"

Halfdan snorted. "Hardly."

"Let's try a slightly different approach," Torvald offered. "If you tell us where she is, I'll you my word we'll do everything we can to take her alive. *And* that we'll keep her that way until either you or the Greens come up with the guarantee Kirsten asked for, or else we all concede such a guarantee isn't possible. Fair enough?"

"Why should I believe you'll keep such a promise?" Roger countered. "You're the ones who have the most to gain from her death."

"You have to trust someone," Torvald said, his eyes steady on Roger. "And I have a feeling you have more need of us right now than you're letting on. Tell me, where's your wife?"

Roger felt a cold lump settle into his stomach. "The Greens have her," he said.

"In the same place where they have Melantha?" Halfdan asked.

"I actually don't know for sure," Roger admitted. "There were hints that Melantha might be there, too, but I never actually saw her."

"So that's what this is really about," Halfdan said cynically. "You don't really care about Melantha. All you want is for us to rescue your wife for you."

"Of course I want that," Roger told him. "But I also want Melantha to be safe."

"It sounds to me like the makings of a package deal," Torvald said, lifting his eyebrows. "All right. We'll still promise safety for Melantha, at least temporarily, plus we'll get your wife out as well. Fair enough?"

"Depending on what you tell us, of course," Halfdan put in.

Roger hesitated. But under the circumstances it was probably the best he was going to get. "I got these mud stains a few hours ago in a little hideaway the Greens have up in the Catskills," he said. "Caroline and I went to look the place over and were essentially kidnapped."

"What makes you think Melantha is there?" Torvald asked.

"We were accosted by several Warriors on our way in," Roger said. "I can't think of any reason why they'd pull Warriors away from defensive positions here in the city unless there was something important up there for them to guard."

"And . . . ?" Torvald prompted.

Roger shrugged. "That, plus the fact they clearly didn't want us getting out and telling anyone about the place."

Halfdan shook his head. "Not enough," he said firmly. "I wouldn't even bother to look the place over on that kind of evidence, let alone set up a raid against it."

"Not even to rescue Caroline?" Kirsten asked.

"They got into this mess on their own," Halfdan reminded her. "Anyway, there's nothing we can do without risking our own people."

Roger felt his hands clenching into fists. "There was another name Nikolos mentioned that might mean something," he said, grasping at straws. "A person named Damian. I don't know who—"

He broke off. There was a look on Torvald's face like a

man walking though a graveyard at midnight. "Damian?" the old Gray asked carefully.

"He's lying," Halfdan said before Roger could reply, his own expression suddenly hard and cold.

"Who's Damian?" Kirsten asked.

"One of the most notorious Greens from the Great Valley," Torvald said, his voice tight. "He was known as the Butcher of Southcliff."

Kirsten inhaled sharply. "I thought he was dead."

"That's what the histories say," Torvald agreed. "But histories have been known to be wrong."

"Greens have been known to lie through their teeth, too," Halfdan said, looking at Roger with sudden suspicion in his eyes. "How hard exactly was it for you to escape?"

"Hard enough," Roger told him, a shiver running up his back at the memory. "Why?"

"No reason," Halfdan murmured. "Except that I'm sure a Command-Tactician as good as Nikolos would make it seem very convincing."

Roger stared at him, suddenly understanding where he was going. "No," he insisted. "That's impossible. Caroline and I busted a gut to get me out."

"Maybe," Halfdan said, studying his face closely. "But in a contest between a Human and a Green Warrior, I know where I'd put *my* money."

"But why would they take me prisoner and then let me escape?" Roger objected.

"Perhaps so you'd do exactly what you've just done," Torvald said. "Come and tell us about their secret hideaway, with Damian's name thrown in as extra bait, and try to persuade us to raid it."

"Thereby stripping *our* positions of able-bodied fighters," Halfdan added.

Roger shook his head. "No," he said firmly. "I was there. No one let me escape."

"Believe what you want," Torvald said. "But I, for one, am not going to go charging into a heavily wooded area on the strength of your word. Certainly not on the strength of *Nikolos's* word."

"Neither will I," Halfdan said. "We've given them until Wednesday to produce her. The ball's in their court now."

Roger braced himself. "What about Caroline?"

"Their war isn't against Humans," Torvald said. "I don't think they'll harm her."

"You don't *think*?"

"I'm sorry," Torvald said, his voice and expression firm. "There's nothing more we can do."

It was a long, lonely walk back to the car. Roger listened to the rhythm of his own footsteps, oblivious to the sounds and lights of the city around him. Torvald was right, of course: Nikolos had no reason to hurt her. The two sides would have their war, and when it was over they would give his wife back to him. Their part in this strange story would be over, and they would get on with their lives.

But what if Torvald was wrong?

For a few minutes he just sat in the driver's seat, wishing he and Caroline had never gone to that play Wednesday night, and trying to make sense out of this latest chapter in the mess they'd gotten themselves into. He still didn't believe that Nikolos had deliberately let him escape, the way Torvald and Halfdan thought. But if not, why hadn't Nikolos contacted him, either to try to lure him back or else to warn him to keep quiet about what he'd seen? All the other would have to do was pick up a phone. . . .

A phone.

With a muttered curse he dug his cell phone out of his pocket. Of course Nikolos hadn't called. He remembered now hearing the beep from the phone as Caroline turned it off, right after they discovered it wouldn't work on the Green estate.

And with the cell off, there was only one other approach Nikolos might have tried. With trembling fingers, he punched in their apartment phone number.

The machine picked up on the first ring. Squeezing the steering wheel hard with one hand as he pressed the phone to his ear with the other, he waited impatiently for the message to play itself out. It did so, there was the familiar beep, and he punched in the retrieval code.

There was a single message. But it wasn't from Nikolos. "This is Fierenzo," the detective's voice said. "Call me."

Roger blinked at the faint click of the disconnected phone. *Fierenzo?* But Powell had said he'd disappeared. Had he been found again? Or was this some kind of Green trick?

There was only one way to find out. Pulling out the card Fierenzo had given him, tilting it to catch the light from the restaurant window beside him, he punched in the detective's cell number.

It picked up on the first ring. "Fierenzo."

"Roger Whittier," Roger said. "You called my home—"

"About time," Fierenzo cut him off. "You know the Marriott Marquis in Times Square?"

"Uh . . . sure," Roger said, a bit taken aback.

"There's a theatre ticket waiting for you at the box office," Fierenzo said. "If you hurry, you should be able to catch the second act." There was a click, and he was gone.

"What the *hell*?" Roger muttered aloud, thumbing off the connection from his end. Still, he had nowhere better to be right now. Returning the phone to his pocket, he started the car and pulled back onto the street.

He found a parking garage near the Marriott and headed on foot through the bustling streets of Times Square. The theatre's ticket office was just off the street, and he found himself wincing at the pointed once-over the man at the window gave his filthy clothes as he handed over an envelope. Wondering whether the ushers would be nearly so diplomatic, he found the escalator and headed up.

As Fierenzo had predicted, he had caught the play between acts, and the lobby was full of milling people. Trying not to touch any of them, he eased his way through the crowd toward the nearest door.

A hand caught his arm. He started to pull away—

"Just keep going," a voice murmured in his ear. "Elevators are that way."

Heart pounding, Roger looked sideways at his captor. The man was definitely a Gray, short and wide, with the kind of iron grip he knew would be a waste of time to struggle against. "I don't know what you think you're doing," he protested, deciding for lack of any better idea to try the innocent approach. "But I paid good money to see this show."

"No, you didn't," the man murmured back. "Relax, will you? We're all friends here."

Roger frowned. "Friends of whom?"

"Oh, come *on*," the other said reproachfully. "Don't you even recognize your favorite delivery man?"

Roger frowned a little harder . . . and then, suddenly, the voice clicked. "You're—?"

"The name's Jonah," the other said. "Come on, the others are waiting."

They caught one of the elevators and headed up into the hotel towers rising high above the theatre part of the complex. Jonah took them off at the twentieth floor, then led the way to the stairs and walked up three more flights. "Sorry about the cloak-and-dagger stuff," he apologized as they emerged from the stairway. "But we have to be careful."

"I didn't say anything about you," Roger assured him quickly. "I didn't even tell them you were a Gray."

"I appreciate that," Jonah said. "In here."

He stopped at one of the doors and tapped the wood: two quick taps, a pause, then three more. Whoever was on the other side was ready; he'd barely finished the third tap when the door swung open. Jonah hustled Roger inside, crowding in close behind him, and Roger caught a glimpse of a shorter Gray as he swung the door closed again.

"Welcome to the vast conspiracy," Jonah announced, taking Roger's arm and leading him into the main part of the room.

Roger caught his breath. There were four other people sitting in a semicircle around the room, gazing at him with expressions that ranged from anxious to suspicious to hopeful. Two were adult Grays, a man and a woman, much older than Jonah. Beside them sat another couple.

Only the second couple weren't Grays. They were Greens.

"These are my parents," Jonah said, gesturing toward the Grays. "Ron and Stephanie McClung."

He gestured to the Greens. "And these are Zenas and Laurel Green," he added quietly. "Melantha's parents."

31

"Y ou'll have to excuse me," Roger said as Jonah led him to an empty chair and sat him down in it. Distantly, he realized he was staring rudely at the Greens, but he was unable to stop. To find Greens and Grays sitting peacefully together in the same room was too far outside his range of expectations to absorb in a single gulp. "I was under the impression—I mean—"

"You thought we all hate each other," Zenas said gently into his fumbling.

Roger winced. "Yes," he confessed. "Both sides have told me flat-out that the other side tried to exterminate them. And you don't seem to have anything in common."

"Of course we have something in common," Stephanie said, smiling sadly at Laurel. "We have Melantha."

"But—" Roger looked at Jonah. "But you're *Grays*."

"And if you'll shut up for a minute or two, they'll tell you all about it," a voice suggested from the corner behind him.

Roger twisted around. Detective Fierenzo was sitting on the floor in the corner, his coat off, his shoulder holster prominently in sight. Focused on the main group, Roger hadn't even noticed him. "Are you all right?" he asked.

"I'm fine," Fierenzo assured him. "Why?"

"Doesn't matter," Roger said, feeling foolish and somewhat annoyed that he'd wasted all that worry on a man who was obviously alive and well. "So how did *you* get into this?"

"Same way you did," Fierenzo told him, flicking a look at Jonah. "Wrong place at the wrong time. You ready to listen yet?"

"Yes," Roger said, turning back to face the others. "Sorry."

"It started about six months ago," Zenas said. "Melantha had gone to the library to do some research for a school project, and was on her way home when a half-dozen toughs decided she looked like someone they could pick on. Fortunately for her—" he looked over at the young Gray who had opened the door for them earlier, now seated quietly on the floor beside Jonah "—it happened that Jordan here was passing by and took exception to their lack of manners."

"Had he also been at the library?" Roger asked.

"Nothing so respectable," Ron said dryly. "He didn't feel like studying that day and had cut school and gone into Manhattan."

"For the third time that month, I believe," Stephanie added, sending a slightly threatening look at her son.

"He's always getting in trouble," Jonah murmured to Roger.

"Like his brother before him," Ron added pointedly. "At any rate, he had his hammergun with him, so he masked and got up on a wall and proceeded to beat the toughs silly. Eventually even they figured out that something weird was happening and headed for higher ground."

"Melantha, of course, realized instantly who it must have been who'd just rescued her," Zenas said. "She'd learned about Grays and hammerguns from the Pastsingers, and she took off as soon as she had a clear path and headed for home. She was pretty shaken, she told us later."

"But by the time she got home, she'd had time to cool off and think about it," Laurel picked up the story. "She'd been taught the Grays had hated us, but she also recognized that Jordan's actions on her behalf didn't fit that pattern."

"Maybe he just hadn't realized she was a Green," Roger suggested.

"I hadn't," Jordan confessed. "There are a lot of people in the city who look kind of like Greens."

"And we don't teach Green recognition nearly as well as the Greens teach their children what Grays look like," Ron said.

"Comes from our differing teaching methods," Zenas explained. "Pastsingers can transfer fairly clear images directly to their students, which naturally include images of Grays from the Great Valley time. We wouldn't want you to think we deliberately prime our children to be on the lookout for Grays."

"And in fact, Melantha *did* conclude that he hadn't recognized her," Laurel added.

"Which was a big relief to her," Zenas said. "But at the same time, she found herself intrigued. It's not every day you see a real, live fossil walking the streets of New York. She decided not to tell anyone, but see if she could track him down herself."

"Sounds risky," Roger said, frowning. "Not to mention kind of needle-in-haystackish."

"Melantha's always enjoyed challenges," Laurel said, blinking back tears. "If she'd just left things alone—" She broke off, daubing at her eyes.

"She decided to start where he'd first appeared," Zenas said, taking his wife's hand. "As Ron said, he'd been masked while he was shooting, but she remembered seeing a boy with a red-and-blue backpack running for a nearby doorway as the gang moved in on her and guessed that had been him. On the assumption that he lived nearby, she started haunting the area waiting for him to show up again. Eventually, he did."

"She came over and thanked me," Jordan said in a quiet voice. "At first I didn't know what she was talking about— I'd mostly forgotten about it. But then I remembered . . . and then I realized who she really was."

"Were you frightened, too?" Roger asked.

There was a play of emotion across his face, which settled quickly into the groove Roger would have expected from a twelve-year-old boy. "'Course not," he said with a touch of bravado. "She was only one Green, you know."

He looked over at Melantha's parents, and the bravado faded. "Mostly, I was kind of flattered she'd gone to all that effort to find me," he admitted. "I figured—well, she offered to buy me a soda, and I said yes."

Roger shook his head. "Sounds right out of Shakespeare," he commented.

"It's not like that," Jordan insisted. "We're just friends." He lowered his gaze. "Really good friends. I don't want to lose her."

"I'm sorry—I didn't mean it that way," Roger apologized, looking back at the two couples. "How did the rest of you get involved?"

"The kids had been meeting secretly for a couple of months before Melantha finally told us," Zenas said. "We found out later they'd decided they couldn't keep sneaking around and had made a pact to tell both sets of parents on that same night. Needless to say, we were pretty shocked." He looked a bit guiltily at his wife. "We may actually have yelled at her a little, in fact."

"It was the kind of yelling you'd do if you'd just learned your child had been spending her afternoons swimming with alligators," Laurel added, a bit defensively.

"Speaking as the mother of Jonah *and* Jordan, I know that yell quite well," Stephanie said dryly, throwing a fond look at each of her sons in turn. "And we didn't react any better when Jordan broke the news at our house."

"You didn't yell at me, though," Jordan pointed out helpfully.

"Trust me, son, we were yelling on the inside," Ron assured him. "And then, of course, when we finally started to calm down, what did this audacious little nugget do but casually invite us to go out to dinner with Melantha and her family."

"We got the same invitation," Zenas said. "I think we may have yelled a little more at that point."

"But you obviously went," Roger said.

"Not that time we didn't," Zenas said. "Or the second or third times she asked us, either. We finally gave up on— what was it?"

"The eighth time," Laurel said. "And that was only because we decided it was the only thing that would shut her up."

"That's about the conclusion we came to, as well," Ron said. "Which isn't to say we didn't still have serious reservations about the whole thing."

"Serious enough, in fact, that they detailed me to stand watch outside, just in case," Jonah volunteered. "I figured with a quick dinner and maybe dessert, it'd be over in an hour, hour and a half tops." He reached down and squeezed his brother's shoulder. "I was stuck on that stupid wall for almost three hours. I was starting to think my whole family had been conked on the head and smuggled out the back by the time they finally came out."

"We'd been wrong about the Greens," Stephanie said simply. "We'd been so very wrong."

"Us, too," Zenas said. "After that, we started getting together on a fairly regular basis, probably once a month, and talking on the phone at least once a week. Melantha and Jordan, of course, saw each other a lot more often than that."

His face turned grim. "And then, apparently, someone bumped into someone else on the street . . . and suddenly our whole world came apart."

"We still don't know which side came up with this insane Peace Child plan," Ron said contemptuously. "Knowing Halfdan, my guess is that it was him. An attempt to bring parity to the two sides, or some such learned nonsense."

"Someone at Torvald's told me it was Cyril's idea," Roger said. "Not that it matters, I suppose."

"Not really," Ron said. "It was bad enough when the warnings and alerts first started, having to bury our relationship with Zenas and Laurel even deeper than it already was, never knowing what was going to happen or when we might suddenly be called on to fight each other. We kept trying to get news about this peace conference that was rumored to be going on, hoping against hope that somebody would realize that we weren't in the Great Valley anymore and that we didn't have to reopen all the old wounds."

"Unfortunately, the people doing the negotiating *were* still in the Great Valley, at least in spirit," Roger murmured. "They all had personal memories of the other side's supposed treachery and their own losses. And nobody was interested in forgiveness and a new start."

"I think you're right," Stephanie said. "Even while we were hoping for peace, everything we heard seemed to be pushing things the opposite direction. People on both sides began to stake out territory. There were occasional incidents—nothing involving Shrieks or hammerguns, but there were some stare downs and even a couple of shoving matches. I thought for sure the whole thing would blow up before the discussions even ended."

"And then they *did* finish, and announced their agreement," Ron said darkly. "And when we heard what they'd decided—well, we just couldn't believe it. We contacted Zenas and Laurel right away to see what we could do to help."

He looked over at them. "And they told us there was nothing that could be done. The Greens had made their decision, it was over, and they had no choice but to accept it and see it through."

"They didn't understand," Zenas said, the words coming out with difficulty, his gaze on the floor in front of Roger's feet. "I'm not sure they understand even now. It's our way, something that's deeply and unchangeably a part of us. There was literally nothing we could do to try to save our daughter."

"I suppose we really *don't* understand," Stephanie conceded. "Our minds just don't work that same way. Not better or worse, really, just different."

She reached over and touched Laurel's shoulder. "But we knew them well enough to know how horribly they were being torn up inside at the thought of watching Melantha die. We knew that if they physically *could* do anything to save her, they would."

"And since they couldn't," Ron said, "we, as their friends, decided to do it for them."

Roger shook his head in wonderment. "That was one hell of a risk," he pointed out. "Halfdan doesn't strike me as a good person to cross. And going up against Green Warriors doesn't sound like much fun, either."

"You don't know the half of it," Jonah said ruefully, pressing a hand gently against his side. "Mostly, though, it worked."

"We knew what was happening the instant the streetlights flashed and went out," Laurel said quietly. "And in the midst of ache and sorrow came sudden new hope. I don't think we'll ever be able to find the words to properly express our gratitude for the risks Jonah and Jordan took to rescue our daughter." She gave Roger a tentative smile. "And you, too, Roger, for the part you and your wife played. That's why we asked Detective Fierenzo to bring you here tonight. So that we could finally thank you."

"You're welcome," Roger managed around the lump that had grown in his throat. Earlier that evening, he'd wished that he and Caroline had never gotten tangled up in any part of this mess. Now, as he looked into Laurel's face, he realized that he wouldn't have missed it for the world. "I'm glad we were able to help," he added, feeling suddenly very awkward. "But you'd better hold on to your gratitude until it's over."

"I'm afraid it may be over now," Zenas said, his voice dark and grim. "We haven't heard anything from Melantha since Friday night. We fear the worst."

"The worst may indeed have happened," Roger conceded. "But maybe not. Let me tell you about *my* afternoon. . . ."

• •

"This is just how you found it?" Powell asked, gazing at the car in the parking garage. "You didn't move anything?"

"I didn't even touch it," the young cop assured him. "I recognized the tag from the APB and called it in."

Powell nodded grimly. Fierenzo's car: neatly parked, conscientiously locked, as if someone fully intended to return to it. One of his companions had been holding a gun on him; the other, if the witness and Carstairs's sketch were to be believed, might possibly have been the same kid who'd been playing chicken with a borrowed car the previous morning.

Someone had allegedly kidnapped a young girl. Someone had been involved in a shooting incident in Yorkville, where a couple of bodies were still unaccounted for. Someone had tried to run someone else over with a car. And now someone had kidnapped the police detective who'd been working on the case.

And over all of it hovered Cyril's threat: return the girl, or watch the blood of thousands of New Yorkers flow in the streets.

"Detective?"

Powell shook away the thoughts. "What?"

"I was just going to point out that the keys aren't in the ignition," the cop said hesitantly. "A lot of times if someone's been kidnapped they're hustled out of the car so fast they forget to take them."

"I know," Powell said. "Go back to your patrol. I'll wait for CSU."

"Okay." The cop hesitated, seemed to be about to say something else, then nodded and headed back to his squad car.

Powell watched him go, feeling a quiet fire burning behind his eyes. Yes, the missing keys might argue that Fierenzo had gone with the men voluntarily. It could also mean that his kidnappers were conscientious types who liked to tidy up a crime scene after them.

He still didn't know what exactly was going on. But Whittier had suggested it, and all the other indicators were falling into place. Somewhere in his city, a gang war was brewing.

He pulled out his phone as the squad car pulled away. While he waited for the wizards at CSU to get here, he would give the Gang Task Force a call and see if they were hearing anything from the street.

And after that, he decided grimly, he'd better give Sandy a call. This could prove to be a longer night than he'd thought.

32

"I don't believe it," Jonah growled when Roger finished. "Why, that rotten, conniving, little—"

"Save it," Ron cut him off, his eyes steady on Roger's face. "But you didn't actually *see* Melantha up there?"

Roger shook his head. "I'm sorry. I wish I could be more helpful."

"What about Damian?" Stephanie asked, looking at the Greens. "*Could* he still be alive?"

"I don't see how," Laurel said. "He certainly wasn't aboard the transport. The Pastsingers could hardly have missed *that*."

"Wait a minute, though," Zenas said, frowning. "I was aboard the transport a couple of years ago, picking up a supply of herbs, and I remember spotting what looked like a door at the very back end behind the engine room. It didn't look like it had been opened in years."

"Extra cargo space?" Ron suggested.

"That's not what the Pastsingers say," Laurel said, frowning now as well. "They describe the transport as having three passenger compartments with attached supply rooms, a power room, an engine room, a control compartment, an exit hatchway area, and several connecting hallways that doubled as the air-purifying system. Nothing about anything behind the engine room."

"That's what I remember, too," Zenas agreed hesitantly. "Of course, what I thought was a door *could* have just been some sort of trim or decoration."

"I don't know," Ron rumbled, scratching at his cheek. "It's starting to sound an awful lot like someone had a private room back there."

"But how could the Pastsingers hide something like that?" Stephanie put in. "I thought they were usually very accurate."

"Yes, but only about things they've actually experienced or have learned from other Pastsingers," Zenas pointed out. "If none of them ever used the door, it might not show up in their descriptions."

"What we need is a contemporary witness," Fierenzo said. "Someone from the original 1928 arrival. If there *is* a room back there, that's the group that would have used it."

"I don't know," Laurel said doubtfully. "Most of that group are solidly on Aleksander's side."

"Does it have to be a Green?" Roger asked as an idea suddenly occurred to him.

Zenas snapped his fingers. "Of course. Velovsky!"

"Who?" Fierenzo asked.

"He was a clerk who bumped into them on Ellis Island when they first arrived," Roger told him. "He helped them get settled and has been sort of an honorary Green ever since. *And* he told us he's been aboard the transport several times."

"You think he'll talk to us?" Fierenzo asked.

"He talked to Caroline and me once," Roger said, pulling out his phone. "I think I can get him to do it again."

"Wait a minute—don't call yet," Ron said quickly. "Torvald might have his line tapped."

"Torvald knows about Velovsky?" Fierenzo asked.

"Everyone knows about Velovsky," Stephanie assured him. "He helped us a little, too, when we first arrived."

"And his place is where Halfdan's men picked you up Saturday morning, Roger," Ron said. "They had the apartment staked out on the chance Aleksander or Cyril would send you to talk to him."

"I was listening to the whole thing on the tel net while they were figuring out how and where to grab you," Jonah added. He looked pointedly down at his brother. "So was Jordan, obviously," he added, nudging the other with his foot. "He was the one who chased Ingvar off you with Bergan's car."

"Really," Roger said, focusing on the boy. "Were you that worried about what Halfdan might do to us?"

"I was more afraid that if Halfdan had you he'd take you to Cyril," Jordan muttered, looking halfway between embarrassed and defiant. "I thought Cyril might be able to make you tell him where Melantha was." He threw Roger a furtive look, then dropped his eyes. "I didn't know you'd already lost her."

There was a moment of awkward silence. "The part that worries me most is that Torvald and Halfdan are cooperating again," Stephanie spoke up. "The question of what to do with Melantha caused a huge split between them, with Halfdan pulling a lot of people to his side with the claim that he and Cyril could work out a peace plan. If he's now thrown in with Torvald, that may mean he's given up on peace."

"I don't think he's given up completely," Roger said. "But he *is* close."

"How bad exactly would that be?" Fierenzo asked. "If all the Grays decided to go to war, *could* they take the Greens?"

"With only sixty Warriors on our side standing against them?" Zenas said grimly. "Cyril says it would be close, but personally I don't think we'd have a chance."

"Which brings us back to Damian," Fierenzo said thoughtfully. "You say your Pastsingers remember everything they personally saw. Any chance of finding one who remembers seeing him dead before you came here?"

Zenas and Laurel looked at each other. "We could ask around," Zenas said. "But mentioning his name would tip off Aleksander that we've been talking to Roger. Is it worth that kind of risk?"

"It might be," Fierenzo said. "Because I don't buy this Damian story for a minute."

"Why not?" Ron asked, frowning.

"Same reason I don't believe they've got Melantha stashed up there," Fierenzo said. "It's too far from the probable battle zone."

"But if Damian *isn't* there, why mention him in the first place?" Jordan asked.

"It could be that Aleksander's trying to goad you into attacking them," Fierenzo told him "Either because he figures his Warriors will have better odds in a forest setting, or because he wants to pull Gray resources out of the city in preparation for an attack here. Or Damian could be his idea of a Quaker cannon."

"A what?" Jordan asked.

"Something that seems to be a weapon but isn't," Stephanie told him. "Like painting telephone poles to look like artillery and setting them up where the enemy can see them."

"Well, if he hoping for a major attack, he's out of luck," Roger said. "It didn't sound like Halfdan or Torvald was going for it, either."

"Don't be so sure," Ron warned. "Halfdan usually argues against any idea that isn't his, but often changes his mind once he's had a chance to think it over."

"And Torvald would probably pretend to dismiss it whether he believed you or not," Jonah added. "Odds are, the minute you left he starting running numbers on how many men he'd need to hit the place."

Jordan frowned up at his brother. "But if it's a trap . . . ?"

"Then they could be in trouble," Jonah conceded. He looked at his father. "Or rather, *we* could be in trouble. There's a good chance Halfdan would pull a lot of us off sentry duty for any raid. That's you and me, among others."

"How fast could they organize a force if they decide to go that way?" Fierenzo asked.

"Well, they'd have to start by redoing the picket line," Ron told him, his forehead creased in thought. "That should give us at least a few hours' warning."

Fierenzo nodded and turned to Roger. "You said Nikolos

talked about taking you to the main house. Did you ever actually see this house, either up close or at a distance?"

Roger shook his head. "No."

"But you *could* find the drive again, right?"

"Yes, assuming they don't pull out the sign," Roger said. "If they do, I'm not sure. There were a lot of similar ones leading off that road."

"Any idea where Nikolos lives when he's in the city?"

Roger snorted. "A tree in Morningside Park. What his official street address is, I don't know."

"I think he's unlisted," Jordan said. "I tried looking him up in the phone book once, just to see where he was."

"Yeah." Fierenzo rubbed at his nose. "See, here's the problem. Once you file an unlawful restraint charge against Nikolos, I can make some calls and get the sheriff or state police to go in and take a look. But if the Greens can hide Caroline somewhere on the grounds, and you can't prove you were even there, they're not going to be very enthusiastic about any searches."

Roger grimaced. "In other words, Caroline's there until they decide to let her go."

"I didn't say that," Fierenzo said thoughtfully. "I said we couldn't get the state cops interested. I didn't say we couldn't go up there and take a look ourselves."

"Are you crazy?" Jordan blurted. "They'll grab you!"

"Not necessarily," Fierenzo said. "If they think I'm just the unlucky Joe Cop who got stuck with a delusional citizen and his ridiculous story, they may try to bluff their way through it. Especially if they think that'll be the end of it."

"But they already know you're involved in the case," Roger pointed out.

"Which is why I'm the one you'd come to with your story," Fierenzo said.

"They'll also know you've had a run-in with a pair of Greens," Jonah added.

"Not necessarily," Fierenzo said. "If they're as isolated as Roger thinks, they may not get regular news from the city.

And even if this particular rumor's made it up there, there's no way for them to know you've spilled the whole story. Trust me, I can make it work."

"Sounds risky," Jonah said doubtfully.

"Well, if you don't like that part, you're going to hate this one," Fierenzo warned, turning to the Greens. "How close would you have to get to Melantha to tell if she's there?"

"It's not like that," Laurel said, shaking her head. "If she doesn't talk to us, we wouldn't know she was even there."

"Really," Fierenzo said, suddenly thoughtful. "And it works that way with all of you?"

"Yes," Zenas said, frowning. "Why?"

"Because aside from checking up on Caroline, it would be awfully nice if we could find out for sure whether or not Melantha's there." Fierenzo lifted his eyebrows at Zenas and Laurel. "Either of you feel like taking a drive upstate tomorrow?"

"You can't take them with you," Jordan objected. "What if someone recognizes them?"

"As generations of kidnappers and mob enforcers have learned, it's hard to recognize someone when they're hidden in your trunk," Fierenzo said dryly. "Neither of you is claustrophobic, I trust?"

"No," Zenas said hesitantly. "But there could be a problem if Aleksander or Cyril happens to be visiting. If either of them suspected I was hiding nearby, he could call me by name and possibly force me to reveal myself."

"Really?" Roger asked, frowning. "That's not what Aleksander said."

"You saw *Aleksander?*" Jordan cut in.

"Don't worry, it was last night, when there wasn't anything we could tell him," Roger said. "But he told us a Persuader couldn't actually order people to do anything."

"Interesting," Zenas murmured. "What exactly did he say?"

Roger closed his eyes for a moment, trying to visualize the scene. "He said a Persuader doesn't *order* people to do anything," he said, opening his eyes again. "That all he does is try to talk the other person into his point of view. He said the other person still has the power to make up his own mind."

"Is that wrong?" Fierenzo asked.

"Not entirely," Zenas said, slowly. "But it's not quite as benign as he makes it sound. A Persuader *does* have a certain degree of power, particularly if he can call to a person by name."

"Could he force Melantha to come to him?" Jordan asked anxiously.

"They seem able to do it with humans," Fierenzo muttered. "The super in Roger's building opened up their apartment without any fuss at all."

"Different situation," Zenas said. "Normally, humans have no idea what they're up against, and therefore don't have any chance to resist. Melantha, on the other hand, would know exactly what he was trying." He looked at Roger. "Especially if, as you say, she'd already resisted a Persuader's order once. She knows now what to listen for, and how to fight it."

"She's always had a mind of her own," Laurel said, smiling at Jordan. "Otherwise she wouldn't have set off to track down a Gray in the first place."

"It's still interesting that Aleksander spent Friday evening with Roger and Caroline," Fierenzo mused. "You'd think it would have been more worthwhile to at least try to smoke Melantha out."

"Are you suggesting *Aleksander* has her, not Nikolos?" Stephanie asked.

"Or he and Nikolos might be in collusion," Fierenzo told her. "Or Damian really *is* alive and well in the Catskills and Aleksander had a leisurely dinner because he doesn't really care whether they find Melantha or not." He shrugged. "Or it could be I'm misreading the clues entirely. But no matter which way you slice it, we still need to check out that hideaway."

"I agree," Zenas said. "Which of us do you want, Detective Fierenzo?"

"Whichever one's less likely to be missed," Fierenzo said. "I doubt even Nikolos would have the chutzpah to search a cop's car, but that might change if he gets a tip that one of Melantha's family is suddenly and suspiciously AWOL."

"That would be me, then," Laurel said in a voice that allowed for no argument. "Zenas has his job to do, but I make a couple of shopping trips each month that take me out of range of anyone else. Tomorrow can be one of them."

"Will they believe you'd go shopping with your daughter still missing?" Roger asked.

Laurel smiled wanly. "My husband and I still have to eat."

"Don't worry, she can pull it off," Zenas said, clearly not thrilled with the idea but just as clearly recognizing that it had to be done. "You two just take care of her. I mean *good* care of her."

"We will," Fierenzo promised.

"Is there anything we can do to help?" Jonah asked.

"Nothing I can think of," Fierenzo said. "On second thought, yes, there is. You can lend Roger one of those hand phone things in case we get in trouble and need to let someone know what's going on. How far will they reach?"

"Several miles," Jonah said. "Though without a booster setup in place, the Catskills may be a little of a stretch. We call them *tels,* by the way, not phone things." He looked down at his brother. "Come on, Jordan. On your feet, and let's see your hand."

Jordan made a face, but obediently stood up and held his left hand out to his brother. "You *did* want the private family line, as opposed to the general-purpose tel, right?" Jonah added, picking at the heel of Jordan's hand with thumb and forefinger.

"Unless you think Torvald would come charging to our rescue if we called," Fierenzo said dryly. "How come you have a spare, anyway?"

"Blame it on another of my old school-cutting buddies," Jonah said. "He wanted us to be able to chat while we were skylarking around Queens without the rest of the community listening in. He was a whiz at tech stuff, and he figured out a way to build a tel that worked on a different frequency couple from the rest of them."

"It's not on any of the radio bands we already use, is it?" Roger asked, staring in fascination as Jonah got a grip on what looked like a sheer film on Jordan's hand and began pulling it carefully off.

"It doesn't work the way your radios do," Jonah assured him. "We basically take a pair of normal radio frequencies, but instead of modulating them, we run a harmonic coupling between them. There are only a half-dozen frequency pairs that are convenient to use, and he picked the one as far away from the usual band as possible so that there wouldn't be any chance of interference between them."

"What happened to the one your friend had?" Fierenzo asked. "He doesn't still have it, does he?"

Jonah shook his head. "He gave it to me when he thought his parents were closing in on us and told me to get rid of them."

"We assume he didn't want to get caught with the evidence," Ron added.

"Right," Jonah said, grinning tightly. "For all his private defiance against authority, he tended to panic over the possibility of getting into real trouble."

"Why didn't you toss them like he told you?" Fierenzo asked.

Jonah shrugged. "I liked having them, so I took a chance and hid them away instead. No one ever came down on me, so I guess the whole thing was a false alarm. Anyway, when we started getting to know Melantha's family, I dug them out of storage and gave one to Jordan so I could keep in touch with him while he was in Green territory."

"Too bad you didn't give one to Melantha," Roger murmured.

"Actually, we did discuss that possibility at one point," Zenas said. "We decided it would be better for Jonah and Jordan to be able to keep in touch. Jordan and Melantha were already pretty adept at keeping their time together private, and we didn't want Melantha getting caught with a Gray tel." His lips compressed briefly. "Though I wish now we'd done it that way."

"We also didn't know whether you could take a tel inside a tree without damaging it," Jonah pointed out. He had the film nearly pulled away from his brother's hand now, with only the fingertips still attached.

"That really looks weird," Roger commented. "Like a snake shedding his skin."

"Or Peter Pan trying to get his shadow back on," Fierenzo said. "How hard is it to work?"

"Not very," Jonah assured him. "I can run him through the manual in five minutes." With one final tug, he pulled the last fingertip free. Holding the tel dangling in front of him, he turned and squatted down beside Roger's chair. "Let's have your left hand."

Gingerly, Roger held it out. Jonah draped the tel into position on top of it, smoothing and prodding at it to get the various sections lined up along the fingers. "Just relax," he advised. "It won't hurt."

He began pressing the tel onto the skin of Roger's palm. "One other thing that might or might not mean anything," Roger said. "The day after Cyril tried his Persuasion trick on Caroline, she found out she could sense Green communications. It was only at close range, and she couldn't understand what was being said, but she could definitely tell when one Green was talking to another."

"Interesting," Zenas said. "I've never heard of anything like that before."

"Not even with Velovsky?" Fierenzo asked.

"If it happened, I've never heard anything about it," Zenas said.

"Me, neither," Laurel seconded.

"Maybe it seemed so natural he never thought to comment on it," Roger suggested as Jonah finished with his palm and started massaging the tel into his fingers. "He told us he'd had a telepathic crash course in all things Green from Leader Elymas. Maybe sensing your communication was part of the same package."

"I remember the Pastsingers talking about that contact," Laurel said. "I don't think anything like it had ever been tried before, not even with the Others back on our old world. I sometimes wonder if the strain of that was what killed Elymas so young."

"*I* sometimes wonder how things might have been different if he'd lived," Zenas added. "We wouldn't have this power struggle between Cyril and Aleksander, for one thing."

"On the other hand, he might already have ordered Melantha to wipe us out," Jonah said grimly.

"Melantha wouldn't have done that," Jordan insisted. "No matter who told her to."

"Well, it's a moot point now," Jonah said, giving Roger's forefinger one final smoothing. "How does that feel?"

"Weird," Roger said, wiggling his fingers experimentally. The tel didn't exactly impede his movements, but it was impossible to forget the thing was plastered to his skin. "It's like wearing half a glove."

"You'll get used to it." Jonah looked over at Fierenzo. "So what are we supposed to do while you, Roger, and Laurel head north and look for Melantha?"

"Basically, you get on with your lives," Fierenzo told him. "You act as natural as you can and wait for us to come back."

"Even Jonah and me?" Jordan asked. "Halfdan's still looking for us, you know. There've been calls about us at least once an hour since you took us off that roof."

"And they've been getting testier, too," Jonah added. "I don't think we want to be found just yet."

Fierenzo made a face. "You may be right," he conceded. "How suspicious is he going to be that you're not answering the calls?"

"Not very," Jonah said. "I've gone silent before when people were mad at me, though not so much since I left school." He lifted his eyebrows. "Still, as long as Jordan and

I are hiding out anyway, why don't we go to the Catskills with you?"

Fierenzo snorted. "What do you think I'm running, a bus service?"

"And they're hardly going to let a couple of Grays into their compound," Roger added.

"I didn't mean we'd go all the way in," Jonah said. "You could drop us off on a hill someplace where we could be ready as backup if you needed us."

"If anyone spots you and Laurel together, it'll be all over," Zenas warned.

"We shouldn't need backup anyway," Fierenzo seconded. "This is a soft probe, not a frontal assault."

"Though a little extra precaution might not hurt," Ron said. "And it would certainly keep them from running into Bergan."

"I suppose," Fierenzo said. "Well . . . okay."

"But Zenas's right about the risks," Ron continued, looking at Zenas. "Which means the boys *don't* go unless he and Laurel agree they should."

For a moment Zenas and Laurel gazed at each other in silence. Then, with a sigh, Zenas nodded. "All right," he said heavily. "They can go."

"Fine," Fierenzo said. "But I'm not driving through Manhattan with all of you sitting there for the whole world to see. Can you two take the Hudson Line train to Peekskill early tomorrow morning?"

"Why can't we just go tonight?" Jordan offered.

"Sure, that'll work," his older brother agreed. "We'll take the next train and park on one of the buildings until morning. Roger can call me on the tel when you get close and arrange for a pickup."

"Fine," Fierenzo said, levering himself to his feet. "Then I guess all that's left is to get Laurel set up with a convincing cover. Come on, you two; let's huddle."

He crossed the room to Zenas and Laurel and knelt down in front of them, talking in a low voice. Roger found himself gazing at them, and at the two Grays sitting listening beside them, marveling at this unlikely alliance that Melantha and Jordan had somehow managed to create.

"Roger?"

He turned away from his musings. Jordan was standing beside him, his face solemn. "Yes?"

"I just wanted to thank you for taking care of Melantha," the boy said, the words coming out with difficulty.

"You're welcome," Roger said, feeling a surge of sympathy for the boy. Caught in a war and a decades-old hatred he didn't understand and couldn't fight . . .

He felt his jaw tighten. Yes, they *could* fight it. And they would. "We'll get her back, Jordan," he told the boy quietly. "Don't worry. We'll get her back."

"Jordan?" Jonah called from across the room.

Jordan's lips pressed together briefly as he held Roger's gaze. Then, with a silent nod, he turned and joined his brother. For a moment they spoke quietly with their parents, and then the two youths headed out.

Roger closed his eyes as the door closed with a thump behind them, a terrible ache stabbing suddenly at his heart. The Greens and the Grays—families both, wrapped together with all the love and unity and mutual appreciation that that implied.

And on the other side of the room sat Roger Whittier, alone, his wife imprisoned away from him somewhere in the woods. A wife who, over the past few months, he'd somehow forgotten how to appreciate. A wife he'd perhaps even forgotten how to love.

If this ended badly, he might never get the chance to fix that mistake.

There was a footstep at his side, a breath of moving air drifting across his cheek. He opened his eyes to find Fierenzo standing over him, gazing down with a mixture of concern and hard, cold assessment. "We're set," the detective told him. "We'll pick Laurel up tomorrow morning at a mall in Yonkers."

Roger looked over at the door in time to see the two Greens disappear out into the hall. The Grays, he noted with mild surprise, had already gone. "Where are we staying?" he asked.

"Here," Fierenzo said. "Ron and Stephanie rented this room, but under the circumstances they decided they'll just go home and let us have it."

"Okay," Roger said, suddenly too tired to argue or even discuss. "I never found out from Jonah how to use this tel."

"He gave me a quick rundown," Fierenzo assured him. "You looked like you needed a minute alone. Don't worry— it's easier than setting a VCR. Where are you parked?"

"A garage on 44th near Broadway," Roger told him. "It's a twenty-four-hour place."

"Good," Fierenzo said. "I'll call down to the desk and see if I can get us a couple sets of toiletries, and after that we'd better hit the sack. Tomorrow's going to be a busy day."

33

The room was bathed in the soft twilight of a half-moon peeking in through the threadbare curtains, the dimness occasionally brightening as drafts sneaking around the ancient window panes rustled the curtains. Curled beneath her stack of blankets, Caroline stared at the shifting patterns of light across the ceiling as she listened to the wordless voices swirling around her. She couldn't tell what was going on, but one thing was clear.

The Greens were very busy tonight.

She let the almost-sound wash across her mind, straining as she tried to pick out a nuance here or a flicker of recognizable emotion there. There was a pattern to it—that much she was sure of—and she had the nagging feeling that if she could just get a handle on that pattern she might be able to understand what was being said. But try as she might, she couldn't break the code.

Though maybe that was because she had more important things on her mind.

Had Roger made it off the estate? Sylvia had implied that he had, but that could have been a ruse to keep her from trying anything herself in the false hope that he would be returning to rescue her. Had the Warriors caught him, either by forcing the car into a tree or ditch or by using their *trassks* directly against him? Had he been injured, or even—

Firmly, she shook the thought away. She wouldn't even think about that. Not now.

And if he *had* reached the highway, had he made it back to the city? Or had there been Green sentries waiting along the road where they could ambush him as he drove? Had they called back to the rest of the Warriors in New York and set up an attack for him there? Had they been waiting at the apartment, on the chance he'd be too weary to think of the potential for danger there?

And even if he'd survived all of that, what then? Would he go to Detective Powell, who was half convinced he and Caroline had been involved in Detective Fierenzo's disappearance?

Or would he go to Torvald and the Grays?

She shivered at the thought. Velovsky had said the war was still in its pre-combat stage; but if Torvald decided this was his opportunity to score a major coup by attacking and wiping out a small group of caretaker Greens, there might be no going back. Once a spark was lit between these two peoples there seemed to be no stopping it.

Which led to the *really* difficult question: what should she herself be doing at this point? Should she be trying to escape, or at least trying to get word to the outside world? Or should she just continue on the path she'd begun at dinner tonight, cultivating a relationship with Sylvia and trying to convince her of the value of human lives?

Because the Wednesday deadline Nikolos had warned

them about was fast approaching. Whatever Caroline decided, there wasn't a lot of time left for her to work with.

She frowned suddenly at the ceiling as the humming in her mind interrupted the flow of her thoughts. There was a *lot* of Green talking going on out there. Even with her limited experience, it seemed more than could be explained by twenty Laborers and a handful of Warriors.

What exactly was going on?

Steeling herself, she pushed back the blankets and swung her legs out of the bed, wincing as her bare feet touched the cold wooden floor. Carefully avoiding the handful of creaking boards she'd discovered during her bedtime preparations, she crossed to one of the dormer windows and pulled back a corner of the curtain.

Outside, the moonlight played softly across the expanse of forest stretching over the hills behind the house. No one was visible, but with Greens and trees that didn't mean much. The window latch clearly hadn't been moved in years, but with a little effort she pried it free and pulled the window open.

The cold air flowed in full force, and she shivered again. There was still nothing to see; but now that the window was open, she could hear faint sounds of movement and scuffling wafting over the roof with the breeze. Whatever was happening, it was happening on the other side of the house.

She got a grip on the side of the window and leaned out, peering around the side of the dormer at the peak of the roof a couple of feet above her head. The shingles on the dormer itself looked a little treacherous, but the rest of the roof seemed in reasonable shape and not too steep to climb. If she was careful, and if she could find enough handholds on the dormer, she ought to be able to walk her way the rest of the way up the roof and see what was going on over there.

First, though, she needed to make sure she didn't freeze to death out there. And, just as importantly, make sure she wasn't seen.

Her brown coat and navy slacks, she judged, would be dark enough to adequately hide her against the moonlight.

Her shoes were dark, too, but the soles weren't designed for climbing. She would have to go with bare feet and hope there was no one on this side of the house who might spot a couple of pale spots pressed against the shingles.

Her face, though, was a different matter. She took two turns around the room, looking for something to use to cover it, before inspiration finally struck. Untucking the blankets from beneath the mattress, she got her small fold-up scissors out of her purse and cut a four-inch strip from the end of the darkest one. Tucking everything back into place, she folded her new scarf back across her forehead as if putting on a headband, then crossed the two ends behind her head and brought them forward again around her nose and mouth. Crossing the ends one more time, she tied them together behind her head, leaving only a narrow strip around her eyes uncovered. Returning to the window, she pulled it open, took a deep breath, and climbed out onto the roof.

The shingles seemed even colder than the floor, and she had a fleeting longing for the jogging shoes tucked in the back of her closet in Manhattan. She got a grip on the peak of the dormer and carefully made her way up the slope to the top.

And found herself faced with an extraordinary sight. All across the wide lawn in front of the house shadowy figures were on the move: running or ducking, crouching beside the trees at the edge of the lawn, apparently even dancing with each other. Some of them had dark objects in their hands, and she could hear faint and sporadic chuffing sounds. She caught a flicker of slightly brighter light from one of the figures, and spotted the knife in his hand.

And with that, she suddenly understood. The chuffing objects were paintball guns; the flickering knives were converted *trassks;* the dancing figures were in fact Greens wrestling in close hand-to-hand combat.

These weren't late-night exercises. These were war games.

She lifted her head a little higher. There were more

Greens inside the edges of the forest, she could see now, slipping in and out of trees as they ambushed those carrying paintball guns or dodged their shots. To her right, on one of the wings angling off from the main part of the house, she could see several Greens firing from the rooftop and through some of the upper windows. Using the house to simulate Gray attacks from the buildings of New York, she realized, her stomach tightening at the thought. Another look at the forest revealed more Greens at the tops of some of the taller trees, also shooting paintballs at their comrades below.

And standing where the main section of the house angled into the right-hand wing, like a rock at the edge of a swiftly flowing river, was Sylvia.

She stood with her hands on her hips, silently observing the activities, just far enough to the side to be out of the way. Occasionally she would give a hand signal, and twice she summoned a group of Greens to her for a brief conversation before waving them back to their positions. But mostly, she just watched.

For several minutes Caroline did the same, a mixture of fascination and horror swirling within her. There was a strange beauty to the Warriors' movements, a ballet-like grace to the way they fought their mock battles. Green Laborers, Sylvia had said, were the best in the world. Clearly, Green Warriors were in that same class.

But all the grace and skill in the world couldn't mask the ultimate purpose of their game. They were training and practicing to kill. Soon, perhaps within days, they would be in downtown Manhattan using those knives against the Grays.

She squeezed the shingles hard. There was still a chance to stop this. There had to be.

Off to her left, a flicker of orange light caught the corner of her eye. A car had emerged from the woods and was approaching the house, wending its way cautiously through the melee with only its parking lights showing.

Caroline froze in place, her eyes just above the peak of

the roof, as the car rolled to a stop and a tall Green got out. He paused beside the car for a moment, scanning the battleground. Then, making sure to stay out of the way, he crossed the lawn to Sylvia.

Caroline frowned, squinting down at them. She couldn't see very clearly in the darkness, but there was something about the altered texture of the voices whispering through her mind that told her the newcomer was Nikolos himself. For a minute he and Sylvia talked together, Sylvia gesturing at different parts of the grounds as she apparently reported on the war games' progress. Occasionally Nikolos made a comment or gesture, but for the most part it was definitely Sylvia's show.

And then, Sylvia pointed toward the house.

Caroline stiffened with sudden premonition. Not waiting to see any more, she eased her head back down and started moving as quickly as she dared along the roof. She reached the dormer opening and stepped through into her room, closing and latching the window behind her. Whipping off her coat and slacks, she laid them across one of the chairs, then shoved her scarf/mask out of sight between the mattress and box spring. With her heart pounding in her ears, she slipped back under the blankets.

She had barely gotten settled when there was a quiet tap on her door.

She froze, her throat tightening, her mind spinning with possibilities. Had Sylvia or someone spotted her up there on the roof and come to check? Surely not—they wouldn't be bothering to knock if they had. She should answer the knock, then, feigning innocence and making it sound like she'd been sound asleep.

But no. A knock that soft wouldn't have woken her up at home, so she probably *shouldn't* react to it. She should wait for a louder knock, or possibly someone to call her name.

She was still trying to figure out her best move when, with a sudden squeak, the door swung open.

She twitched violently in reaction, the bed creaking in protest. "What?" she gasped.

"It's me, Nestor," one of her guards' voices came. "You have a visitor downstairs."

With an effort, Caroline got her breathing under control, feeling a tiny flicker of relief. Her reaction at being startled that way had probably been more appropriate to a suddenly awakened sleeper than anything she could have devised on her own. "Now? Who is it?"

"Command-Tactician Nikolos," Nestor told her. "He told me to send his apologies for the lateness of the hour, and promised it would only take a few minutes."

Caroline took a deep breath. "All right. Let me get dressed, and I'll be right down."

A few minutes later she came down the stairs, blinking against the handful of lights that had been turned on. Nestor and a female Warrior were waiting at the foot of the steps, showing no signs of the strenuous exercise they'd just been participating in outside. Silently, they led her to the library where she and Sylvia had first met.

Nikolos was waiting there alone, standing with his back to her as he gazed out the window into the night. "Ah—Caroline," he said, turning as Nestor ushered her inside and closed the door behind her. "My apologies for waking you at this hour."

"That's all right," Caroline said, taking one of the chairs in front of the desk. "My dreams weren't very pleasant, anyway."

"I'm not surprised," he said, swiveling one of the other chairs around to face her and sitting down in it. "I've been having rather unpleasant dreams myself lately. Dreams involving the destruction of my people."

"I'm worried about my people, too," Caroline said evenly. "What can I do for you?"

He seemed to brace himself. "We need to find out, once and for all, who it was who gave Melantha to you last Wednesday night."

"We've been through that," Caroline reminded him, feeling a stirring of annoyance. "With, I think, just about everyone involved in this, on both sides. We don't know who it was."

"I'll settle for a description," Nikolos persisted. "Starting with whether he was a Green or a Gray."

"That's an odd question," she said. "I thought all the Grays wanted her dead. Why would any of them stick his neck out to rescue her?"

For a moment Nikolos stared hard into her eyes. Then, reluctantly, he lowered his gaze. "Let me lay my cards on the table," he said, rubbing at his cheek. Clean-shaven at two in the morning, Caroline noted absently. Either that, or else Greens simply didn't have much facial hair in the first place. "It's been learned that a Gray named Jonah McClung, who was assigned to sentry duty at Sara D. Roosevelt Park, has been shirking his duty while his younger brother Jordan covered for him."

"And this information comes from where?"

Nikolos lifted his eyebrows. "So you recognize the names?"

"I've never heard either of them," Caroline said. "I just wanted to know the source before I put any effort into thinking about it."

"It was Halfdan Gray's people who discovered there was something odd going on with Jonah," Nikolos said. "When they began to suspect it might have something to do with Melantha's disappearance, Halfdan informed Cyril, who then informed me."

"And you trust this Halfdan?"

"As far as I trust any Gray," Nikolos said. "Halfdan and Cyril are the ones who worked out the original peace agreement between our peoples."

"The one that involved Melantha's murder."

Nikolos's lip twitched. "Yes. What I need from you is anything that would either confirm Jonah was the one involved or else clear him so that we can stop wasting time looking for him."

"What do you mean, looking for him?" Caroline asked, frowning. "Don't you keep track of the Grays?"

"Not as well as we thought, obviously," Nikolos said sourly. "Both Jonah and his brother seem to have gone to ground somewhere. Halfdan has repeatedly tried to contact them, but they're refusing to answer."

"Maybe they can't," Caroline suggested. "Maybe Aleksander got to them, the same way someone got to Melantha."

"Or maybe it's Jonah and Jordan themselves who have Melantha," Nikolos countered. "Tell me what happened Wednesday."

"Why?" Caroline asked. "So you can find Melantha and use her to destroy our city?"

Nikolos took a deep breath. "Listen to me, Caroline," he said, lowering his voice. "Things are not the way you think. I give you my word that if we get Melantha back she won't have to do anything to anyone. Not to the Grays; not to your city."

"I thought she was the keystone of your defense."

"Nonetheless, I give you my word," Nikolos repeated. "Melantha won't have to do anything in this war."

Caroline stared at him, her skin prickling as the pieces suddenly fell together. "Oh, my God," she murmured. "Damian is another Groundshaker."

"Who told you that?" Nikolos asked sharply.

"You did," Caroline told him. "You said you didn't need Melantha because you had Damian."

For a long moment Nikolos gazed at her. "Sylvia was right," he murmured at last. "You're more perceptive than I thought."

"So it was a fraud from the very beginning, wasn't it?" Caroline said, feeling cold all over. "You never intended to use Melantha against the Grays at all."

"Of course we intended to use her," Nikolos said. "But not as a weapon. She's still too weak and unpredictable in her Gift."

"But not too weak to be used as a decoy," Caroline said. "Someone to distract the Grays and keep their eyes away from this place and Damian."

"You make it sound so harsh," Nikolos reproved her. "Aleksander and I knew from the beginning that the Grays would never let us live in peace, that the minute they found an opportunity they would move to exploit it. But we also knew Cyril would never believe that until it was demonstrated."

"So you figured you'd lull the Grays by letting him kill Melantha," Caroline said acidly. "Never mind that it would cost the life of an innocent young girl."

Nikolos shook his head. "You must understand that what we do, we do for the best," he said, his voice strangely earnest. "Yes, it would cost Melantha her life; but once she'd been sacrificed and the Grays moved to attack, Cyril would finally recognize his error and rejoin us. At that point, we could bring Damian in and gain a swift victory over our enemies. With her life, Melantha would have purchased a lasting peace for her people."

"Such a noble plan," Caroline bit out. "Too bad someone had to go and ruin it."

Nikolos drew himself up in his chair. "I've been patient with you up to now, Caroline," he said, his voice tight. "I've assumed you've been so fixated on Melantha that you couldn't see the big picture. But now you know what's at stake, and what must happen if our people are to survive. I've assured you that Melantha will live; I've assured you that we'll do everything possible to win a quick victory over the Grays and thereby cause as little collateral damage as possible. But I *will* know who delivered Melantha to you."

Caroline shook her head. "No."

"I could remind you that Melantha herself agreed with the decision."

"I could remind *you* that twelve-year-olds usually do what adults tell them," Caroline countered, getting to her feet. "Sorry you wasted the drive up here. Good night, Commander Nikolos."

His lip twitched. "Good night, Caroline."

She turned her back on him, passed through the doorway and between the silent Warriors, and returned to her room. Two minutes later, she was back under the blankets, staring at the play of light across the ceiling and wondering dully if the war games had resumed on the other side of the house.

So it had been for nothing. All of it. Whether Melantha lived or died; whether she or Roger or Fierenzo lived or died or succeeded or failed—none of it mattered. From the very beginning Nikolos had had his plan in place for the Grays' destruction.

And there was nothing she could do to stop him. He was a Command-Tactician; and as Green Laborers and Warriors were the best in their fields, he was surely the best in his. He would have thought of every move that could possibly be made against him, and would already have a contingency in place to counter it.

She took a deep breath, fighting back the despair threatening to drown her. *No*, she told herself firmly. It *hadn't* been for nothing. They'd helped keep Melantha alive, at least for a few days, and they'd unearthed this vital bit of information about Damian and gotten Roger back to the outside world with it. That had to be at least moderately disruptive to Nikolos's neat plans. Maybe Roger was talking to the police or the Grays at this very moment, in fact, proposing or cajoling or arguing them into taking some kind of action.

Or maybe he wasn't, she realized with a sinking feeling. Roger, argue someone into action? Hardly. That would require him to deliberately walk into a confrontation, and he avoided confrontations like the plague itself.

Or did he?

She frowned at the ceiling, the events of the past few days playing across her memory. Roger standing up to Ingvar and Bergan until the two Grays literally forced them off Greenwich Avenue at gunpoint. Roger driving past, around, possibly even through Green Warriors to get out of here and go for help. For that matter, Roger refusing to tell Sylvia or Torvald or Nikolos anything about Melantha in the first place.

Maybe it wasn't that he avoided conflicts because he wasn't man enough to stand up for himself. Maybe it was simply that he avoided the petty and unnecessary ones, saving his focus for those that *were* important. Maybe she just hadn't seen him before in a situation where he had to take this kind of aggressive moral stand.

If true, it was something she'd never known about him. But then, perhaps he hadn't realized it about himself. The quiet routine of their normal lives didn't lend itself to heroics, after all. Maybe he'd never before had anything this important to measure himself against.

Throwing off the blankets, she got out of bed and crossed to the chair where she'd put her purse. A little probing, and she came up with her pen and the pack of chewing gum she kept for the people in her office who seemed perennially in the throes of cigarette withdrawal. The bedroom curtains weren't thick enough to keep out curious eyes, but the bathroom window was made of frosted glass. Taking the pen and gum in there, she closed the door and turned on the light.

There wasn't a lot of writing space on the silvery paper that came wrapped around a single stick of gum. But years of filling out real estate forms had given her plenty of practice in microscopic writing.

Roger: Damian Groundshaker, ready move on NYC—time unknown. Melantha not here. Sylvia Group Com in charge. Don't bring Grays. I love you, C.

She added their home phone number and laid her pen aside, gazing down at the note. There was so much more she wanted to say to him. So much more she needed to say. But there was no room for inessentials like love and hope and trust. Carefully, she refolded the paper around the gum and slid it back inside its outer wrapper. She would just have to hope that they would both make it through to the other end of this alive, and she could say it in person.

Turning off the light, she left the bathroom and returned the gum and pen to her purse. Then, one final time, she climbed wearily into bed. It was time to get some rest, and to prepare herself for the crucial day ahead.

34

"Well?" Fierenzo asked as the five of them stood beside a tall granite boulder on the edge of the steep hill. "Does it work, or doesn't it?"

"It works, I suppose," Jonah said, sounding a little doubtful as he peered between the trees with a compact set of binoculars. "I can see a corner of the main house, if that's really the Green estate we're looking at down there. If I can see it, we can theoretically get there."

"Pretty bumpy landing from this high up, though," Jordan added, sounding even more doubtful than his older brother. "I'd vote for someplace closer."

"Get too close and you're likely to run into a picket line," Fierenzo warned. "Anyway, there's not going to be any sliding, bumpy or otherwise. You're here to watch and listen and, if necessary, make it sound like we brought a small army with us."

Beside Roger, Laurel shivered. "But that's an absolute last resort," Fierenzo added, glancing at her. "And *only* on Roger's direct order."

"Understood," Jonah said. "Be careful."

"Trust me," Fierenzo said wryly. "Okay, Laurel. Your turn."

A few minutes later Laurel was curled in a sort of fetal position inside the Buick's trunk, completely covered by the old emergency blanket Caroline kept back there, the outline of her body camouflaged by the various department store bags Fierenzo had scattered strategically around her. "You okay?" he asked, repositioning the bags one final time.

"I'm fine," her muffled voice came.

"Okay," Fierenzo said. "Remember, now, you're only supposed to *listen* for Melantha's voice. No calling out on your own. We don't want them spotting you, and we definitely don't want them identifying you."

"I know," she said. "Let's get this over with."

"Right." Closing the lid, Fierenzo headed for the passenger door. "And you two watch yourselves," he added to Jonah and Jordan. "I don't want some Green Warrior sneaking up and sticking a knife in one of you. Let's go, Roger."

Roger got behind the wheel and turned the car back down the winding road toward the main highway below. "You've been pretty quiet the last twenty miles," Fierenzo commented as he drove.

"I've been thinking about some of the things I've said to Caroline in the past few weeks," Roger admitted. "Some of the things I've *thought* even when I was smart enough not to say anything."

"What sorts of things?"

Roger shook his head. "Oh, I don't know. Sometimes she just doesn't seem to think, I guess. Or we're getting ready to go somewhere and she suddenly heads off to do something at the last minute that she could have done anytime that afternoon."

"Mm," Fierenzo said. "How long have you been married?"

"Four years," Roger told him. "Seems longer sometimes."

Fierenzo chuckled. "Trust me, you're hardly even started. She's a real estate agent, right? You need a certain amount of brainpower to handle a job like that, wouldn't you say?"

"Of course," Roger said. "I didn't mean—"

"She gets along well with people, too?" Fierenzo went on. "Mixes well at parties, puts strangers at their ease—that sort of thing?"

"Yes, that too," Roger agreed.

"Remembers anniversaries and birthdays and when each of her nieces lost their first tooth?"

"Uh . . . yeah, I think so."

"And she's better at all this than you are?"

Roger grimaced. "Probably."

"Well, see, there's your problem," Fierenzo said. "You just don't understand how your wife thinks."

Roger snorted. "Careful," he said, only half jokingly. "You get tossed into sensitivity training these days for saying things like that."

"I'm a detective," Fierenzo countered. "Part of my job is to understand people and learn what makes them tick." He shrugged. "Not to mention twenty-two years of marriage to that same kind of woman."

"So enlighten me," Roger said. "How *does* she think?"

"Let's start with you," Fierenzo said. "If you're like me—and I think you are—you think in terms of numbers and facts and problems and solutions. We approach life as a set of difficulties and puzzles that have to be conquered. True?"

Roger thought it over. That *did* seem to be how he looked at things. "I guess so," he said. "And Caroline doesn't?"

"Nope," Fierenzo said. "I mean, she probably *can* do that if she needs to. But most of the time she looks at the world in terms of relationships. Relationships between people; relationships between events; how individual parts combine to make the whole. You as a contract-law paralegal probably see your job in terms of statute and case law and contract details. Caroline, if she was doing it, would probably see it in terms of who was in difficulty and how they could be helped and what the consequences would be for them and their families of her doing a good job. You see the difference? You'd both ultimately accomplish the same thing, but you'd have approached it from different mental angles."

"Yes, I see," Roger murmured, thinking hard. This was something that had never occurred to him before.

"Like I said, my wife's the same way, and early on it sometimes drove me nuts," Fierenzo went on. "But I've learned how to take advantage of it. Since she sees things differently, she can often fill in the gaps and blind spots in my own mental vision. I can't even count the number of times I've been discussing some brass walnut of a case with her when she's made a comment that suddenly threw light on something I either hadn't noticed or hadn't considered the right way."

"So when Caroline waters plants at the last minute . . . ?"

"She's probably got her plants connected mentally to something that also connects to the two of you going out," Fierenzo told him. "It's a convenient relationship, and it works, so she sticks to it."

"But we're always late," Roger argued.

"Are you?" Fierenzo countered. "Or are you just not as early as you'd like?"

Roger frowned. "Well . . . mostly the latter, I guess. So how does this connect to her always losing things?"

"Probably a matter of her focusing on one thing and not paying attention to everything else," Fierenzo said. "It doesn't *all* have to connect, you know."

"I guess not," Roger said, a stray memory flitting crossing his mind: Stephanie, in the hotel room last night, pointing out that Green and Gray minds didn't work the same way, but that neither was better or worse than the other. "Just different," he murmured.

"What?"

"Nothing," Roger said. "I'm going to have to think about this some more."

"You do that," Fierenzo said. "But do it later. Right now, concentrate on your upcoming performance."

"I'm frantic, insistent, and frustrated that you won't believe me."

"Right, but don't overdo it," Fierenzo warned. "You're also tired and scared, and that saps a lot of a person's emotional strength. In this kind of show, less is more."

Ahead, Roger could see the highway cutting across the end of the mountain road they were on. "When should I start?"

"Right now," Fierenzo said, pulling out his gun and giving it a quick check before returning it to its holster. "They may have sentries or observers posted anywhere from this point on. They might as well get a glimpse of the Angry Citizen with his jutting jaw."

"Right." Roger took a deep breath. "It's show time."

• •

"Check," Sylvia said, moving her bishop three squares over to attack Caroline's king. "Wait a minute. Is it check, or checkmate?"

"Let me see," Caroline said, studying the board. It was probably the latter, considering her own level of skill at this game. She'd always been terrible at chess, and this morning's matches had certainly not raised her average any. "It's checkmate, all right. Congratulations."

"Thank you," Sylvia said, eyeing her with mock suspicion. "You're not just letting me win, are you?"

"I won the first two," Caroline reminded her, starting to reset the board for another game. "I told you that this was a Warrior's game."

"That it is," Sylvia agreed, starting to reset her pieces as well.

Caroline smiled to herself. Yes, she was doing terribly. But then, the goal here had never been for her to win. She'd discovered the board and pieces tucked away in a back corner of her closet earlier that morning, along with a badminton bird and a deck of dog-eared cards with four missing, and had suggested to Sylvia that it was a game she might find enjoyable. One of the rooks turned out to be missing, but a stack of quarters from her purse had solved that problem, and they'd settled down in the library to give it a try.

As she'd expected, Sylvia had taken to the game like a cat to canaries. She'd had the moves down cold after the first game, was starting to learn the necessary strategy by the second, and had figured out counters to most of Caroline's meager repertoire of tricks by the third. Now, with the sixth game just ended, she was showing all the enthusiasm of a kid with a new toy.

"The Human who came up with this game must have been brilliant," Sylvia commented as she finished setting her pieces and swiveled the board around.

"Some of us have definitely been brilliant through the ages," Caroline agreed. Pulling her pack of gum from her pocket, she casually pulled out a stick and unwrapped it. "Games, music, art—we've had our share of geniuses."

"What's that?" Sylvia asked, eyeing the gum. "Food? Are you hungry?"

"No, this is called chewing gum," Caroline said, holding it out for her inspection. "You chew on it and get flavor in your mouth. Want to try one?"

"I suppose," Sylvia said, a bit hesitantly. "You don't actually eat it?"

"No swallowing involved," Caroline confirmed, folding the stick into her mouth and pulling out another for Sylvia. "Though it doesn't hurt humans any if we *do* swallow it. You've never seen Green children or teens chewing gum?"

"Never," Sylvia said, folding the stick into her mouth as she'd seen Caroline do. She blinked twice. "Very intense. What exactly is this flavor?"

"It's a blend of various fruits," Caroline told her, putting the pack away. "Do you like it?"

"It's . . . different," Sylvia said diplomatically. "At any rate, it's your move."

"Right," Caroline said, moving her king's pawn two squares forward. "Maybe there's someone in midtown Manhattan right now who'll be the next human to come up with a game as brilliant and elegant as this one."

Sylvia smiled knowingly as she set her queen's pawn one square forward in response. "And therefore, we should be careful what happens to the Humans in our war?"

"I would think a good Warrior would be careful about that anyway," Caroline replied, jumping her king's knight up and over to the edge of the board.

"I wish that decision was ours to make," Sylvia said, moving her queen's bishop two squares out. "But I'm afraid it's up to the Grays. If they choose to make their stand from residential buildings, in effect hiding behind the Humans, we'll have no alternative but to bring those buildings down."

"There are always alternatives," Caroline said earnestly. "Nikolos is a Green Command-Tactician. That means he's one of the best there is."

Something like a flash of annoyance flicked across Sylvia's lined face. "You make it sound easy," she said. "It isn't."

"Maybe not for you or me," Caroline agreed. "But surely Nikolos can come up with something better than an all-out war in the middle of a city."

"Even if such a thing were possible—" Sylvia broke off, her eyes unfocusing, and once again Caroline heard the almost-words of Green telepathic communication. The older woman's eyes came back; and to Caroline's surprise, she abruptly stood up. "But right now, it's lunchtime," she said briskly. "Shall we try a different restaurant?"

"Ah—sure," Caroline managed, glancing at her watch. She'd been racking her brain all morning trying to figure out how to get Sylvia to let her take her out for another meal. "But it's only eleven-thirty."

"I'm hungry," Sylvia said, stepping away from the board. "Aren't you?"

"Oh, sure, I can always eat," Caroline assured her, scrambling to her feet.

"Then get your coat," Sylvia ordered, already halfway to the door. "I'll meet you at the truck."

● ●

"There," Roger said, pointing at the gravel drive leading off the road to the left and flicking on his turn signal. "The sign's gone, but I'm pretty sure that's it."

"Let's give it a try," Fierenzo agreed.

The drive seemed a little different beneath his wheels than on his last trip in, Roger noticed uncomfortably as he turned in. But then, that could be a result of his own re-arrangement of the gravel on that mad dash out.

No one appeared as they followed the twisting path through the trees. "You suppose they've abandoned it?" Fierenzo asked as they topped a gentle ridge and started down the other side.

"More likely I've got the wrong place," Roger said, grimacing. "The turnoff we took to the cabin should have branched off before here."

"Mm," Fierenzo said, looking at the woods around them. "Maybe we should have given Jonah's tel to Laurel. At least we could have had a running commentary as to whether there are any Greens nearby."

"I think I see a house up there," Roger said, peering ahead.

"Let's take a look," Fierenzo said. "If this *isn't* the Green place, maybe they can tell us where it is."

The house was big and old, Roger noted as he followed the drive through the expansive lawn stretched out in front of it: three stories in places, with a pair of wings rambling out to the sides. Caroline could probably tell at a glance when it had been built; all he could tell was that it looked rather haphazardly designed.

The front door opened as he rolled to a stop in front of the steps, and a young man stepped out onto the porch. "Can I help you?" he called as Roger and Fierenzo got out of the car.

Roger's heart rate picked up as he got his first close look at the other. Tall and dark, with black eyes and olive skin. They were at the Green estate, all right . . . only the Greens had somehow rearranged the drive beyond all recognition. Fierenzo had been right; he *wouldn't* have been able to prove his story to anyone else. "I'm looking for my wife," he bit out. "Where is she?"

The young man seemed taken aback. "I'm sorry?"

"Relax," Fierenzo told him, holding out his badge. "I'm Detective Sergeant Fierenzo from New York City. Mr. Whittier here claims his wife has been kidnapped and is being held around here somewhere."

"Really?" the other breathed. "That's terrible."

"Oh, stop it," Roger said disgustedly. "You're not fooling anyone."

"Take it easy, Mr. Whittier," Fierenzo warned in the weary tone of someone who's already heard it too many times. "Is this one of the people you saw?"

"Not exactly," Roger admitted. "But they were similar in appearance."

"Uh-huh," Fierenzo said. "Can I ask your name, sir?"

"I'm Nestor Green," the other said, looking uncertainly at Roger. "And there isn't anyone else here. Really."

"I'm sure there isn't," Fierenzo said soothingly. "Are you the owner, Mr. Green?"

"No, that would be my Aunt Sylvia," Nestor said. "She's out shopping."

"Good," Roger said. "That'll give us a chance to search the house."

"Be *quiet*, Mr. Whittier," Fierenzo said, throwing him a warning look. "Any idea when she'll be back?"

"Not really," Nestor said. "Listen, I can't just—look, do you have a warrant or something?"

"No, and we're not going to search the house," Fierenzo assured him, holding up a placating hand. "I wonder if we could come in and wait for a few minutes? See if your aunt returns?"

"Sure," Nestor said reluctantly. "Come on in."

He led the way through the door into a large and elaborate entryway. "Good-sized place," Fierenzo commented, glancing around as Nestor led the way to a pair of double doors to their left. "How many people live here?"

"Just my aunt and me and a few caretakers," Nestor said, pushing open one of the doors. Beyond was an impressively equipped library, with a massive desk in front of a pair of tall windows looking out onto the wooded hills beyond. "She's hoping to get some investors to restore the place and turn it into a lodge."

"You've sure got the view for it," Fierenzo commented, nodding toward the windows. "How long have you lived here?"

"About three years," Nestor said. "Can I get you something to drink?"

"We're fine, thanks," Fierenzo said, stopping in the middle of the library and giving it a casual survey. "Nice collection."

"I want to see the rest of the house," Roger spoke up truculently. "I know Caroline's here."

"We don't have a warrant, Mr. Whittier," Fierenzo said patiently. "I already told you that."

"So?" Roger countered. "This is a kidnapping. Exigent circumstances, remember?"

Fierenzo took a deep breath. "Do you recognize this house?"

Roger hesitated. "Well . . . no."

"Do you recognize Mr. Green?"

"I already told you I didn't," Roger growled.

"Do you have any proof that your wife is even in this particular *county,* let alone this particular estate?"

Roger glared at him. "Now, *look,*" he warned. "I'm telling you—"

"You've already told me," Fierenzo cut him off, turning abruptly for the door. "Thank you, Mr. Green—sorry for the inconvenience. Come on, Mr. Whittier."

"Wait a minute," Roger said again, grabbing the detective's arm as he passed. "We're *leaving*?"

"Yes, we're leaving," Fierenzo said, turning to look squarely into his eyes. "I told you before that if you couldn't give me something solid, this whole trip would be a waste of time. You haven't, and it has been. Now get in the car."

"No," Roger snapped, bracing himself. Here was where he had to push it just the right amount. . . . "I swear to you that cabin is out there somewhere. We have to find it."

"Forget it," Fierenzo said. "I'm not going to waste what's left of my day tromping through a bunch of woods."

"We have to," Roger said firmly. "You're supposed to be investigating, right? Well, *investigate,* damn it."

Fierenzo held his gaze another moment, then turned and looked back at Nestor. "Are there any other roads on the estate besides the one we came in on?"

"There's one that goes from behind the house through the back areas of the woods," Nestor said carefully. "But I've been over the estate a dozen times since we moved here. This is the only building on the grounds."

"I tell you it's there," Roger insisted.

"Does the other drive take us back to 42?" Fierenzo asked, ignoring him.

"Yes, about a quarter mile north of the one you came in on," Nestor said.

"Fine." Fierenzo turned back to Roger. "Here's what we're going to do," he said in a voice that left no room for argument. "We're going to leave now, taking the other road through the estate. I'll drive; you can look out the windows. If you spot your cabin—hell, if you spot *any* cabin—we'll stop and take a look at it. If you don't, we're getting onto 42 and heading back to the city. Take it or leave it."

Roger glared at him for another second, wanting to see how Nestor was reacting to this but not daring to look at him. The cabin would certainly be nowhere near that road— Nikolos would have seen to that when he erased all the other approaches to it. But circling the grounds pretending to look would give Laurel the maximum possible range in her search for her daughter.

"Well?" Fierenzo prompted.

Roger let his shoulders sag. "Sure," he muttered. "What do you care?"

"Thanks for your time, Mr. Green," Fierenzo said as he and Roger headed toward the library door. "We can find our own way out."

They crossed the entryway and the porch and walked down the steps to the car. Roger got into the passenger side as Fierenzo went around the front and slid in behind the wheel. "Keys?" the detective asked as he closed his door.

"Did he seem worried about us taking the long way out?" Roger asked, digging out the keys and handing them over.

"I didn't see any reaction," Fierenzo told him. "Best

guess is that they've already erased or camouflaged everything leading to the cabin."

"No kidding," Roger said sourly. "They could have taken the whole building apart for all I know. I just hope Laurel's having better luck."

The drive they were on came to an abrupt end just beyond the far wing of the house, but by the time they got there Roger could see the other road Nestor had mentioned. Fierenzo eased the car across a short stretch of grass to the patch of gravel and picked up his speed a little. "Interesting," he said, pointing ahead of them. "Tire tracks. Someone's used this road recently."

"Nestor said his aunt was out shopping," Roger reminded him.

"Sure, but I assumed he was lying," Fierenzo said. "That either Sylvia was never there to begin with, or else that she'd ducked out the back and was hiding inside a tree somewhere."

"She'd have a job hiding Caroline in there with her."

"True," Fierenzo said. "And this puts a new light on things."

Roger frowned. "What do you mean?"

"Later." Fierenzo gestured toward his window. "You're supposed to be looking for a cabin, remember?"

Roger turned back to the side window, trying to figure out which direction he was facing. Starting at the back of the house, he was thinking the road had curved west. If so, then they were now heading north. . . .

He was straining his eyes, trying to catch a glimpse of anything that wasn't tree or bush or grass, when he was abruptly slammed against his seat belt as Fierenzo stomped on the brake. "What—?" he demanded, twisting his head around to look out the windshield.

The protest died in his throat. Standing across the drive thirty feet in front of the car were four Greens, long *trassk* knives shining in their hands.

"I think," Fierenzo said quietly, "that we're in trouble."

35

"You said that was called a *Reuben*?" Sylvia asked, peering across the table at the sandwich in Caroline's hands.

"Yes," Caroline confirmed, taking a bite and savoring the tang. "A little messy, but delicious."

"And these are chicken fingers," Sylvia said, picking up one of the golden-brown sticks from her own plate. "You know, I believe I've seen chickens, and I remember them having claws instead of fingers."

"The name refers to the shape," Caroline told her. "Try one of those dipping sauces."

Tentatively, Sylvia touched the chicken to the top of the BBQ sauce bowl and nibbled at it. "Interesting," she said, nodding.

"Personally, I prefer the hot mustard," Caroline told her, indicating the other bowl. "Careful, though—it packs a punch."

"So you give me a challenge?" Sylvia said, mock-solemnly, as she plunged her chicken finger an inch into the hot mustard. Defiantly, she bit off that end—

And grabbed for her water glass, eyes bulging. "I warned you," Caroline said, unable to hide an amused smile as the other woman drained half the water in a gulp. "Roger always accuses me of having a wrought-iron tongue whenever I—"

She broke off. Without warning, Sylvia had gone rigid, her eyes locked somewhere past Caroline's shoulder. "Sylvia?"

There was no response. "Sylvia!" she repeated more

forcefully, reaching over to grip the woman's hand, her heart suddenly pounding. Had the hot mustard poisoned her?

And then, as suddenly as it had begun, Sylvia blinked, her eyes coming back to focus.

But those eyes were now hard and cold, the lines of her face settled into deep wrinkles. "Get your things," she said tightly. "We're leaving."

"Now?" Caroline asked, relieved and stunned at the same time. "Sylvia, I didn't mean that—"

"Now," the older woman ordered, sliding out of the booth.

"I have to pay the bill first," Caroline protested, fumbling for her purse. "If I did something wrong—"

"Not you," Sylvia said, standing beside the booth like a statue, her eyes focused on the distance. "The stupid fools."

"Who?" Caroline asked, staring up at her.

"Your husband is in trouble," Sylvia bit out. "Hurry."

Her mouth suddenly dry, Caroline pulled the credit card out of her wallet.

And hesitated. She'd wanted to come here today for a specific purpose. If she left without fulfilling it, she might never get another chance.

But if Roger was in danger . . .

Setting her teeth firmly together, she gathered up her purse and coat and slid out of the booth. It wasn't going to work exactly as she'd planned, but she could still do it. And it would only take a few extra seconds.

She could only hope that those few extra seconds wouldn't cost her husband his life.

• •

"What do we do?" Roger murmured, his throat tight as he watched the four Greens striding toward the car.

"You've got the tel," Fierenzo reminded him, his voice icy calm. "Call it in."

Roger had completely forgotten the gadget pasted to his

left hand. Now, twitching his little finger, he held it to his cheek. "Jonah?"

"Here," the Gray's voice said promptly. "What's happening?"

"We're in trouble," Roger said tightly. "There are four Warriors coming at us—"

"Six," Fierenzo corrected. "Two more behind us."

Roger swiveled to look. "We're surrounded by six Warriors," he told Jonah.

"Terrific," Jonah said. "What did you do to set them off?"

"Absolutely nothing," Roger protested. "I don't know why they're even here—"

"Save the analysis for later," Fierenzo cut him off. "Can he help, or not?"

"Can you help us?" Roger relayed the question.

There was a brief pause. "Yeah, I think so," Jonah said. "Give me a minute. I'll give you two call buzzes when we're ready."

Roger lowered his hand. "He says it'll take another minute," he told Fierenzo, eyeing the advancing Warriors. "We may not have that long."

"Then we'd better make sure we do," Fierenzo said, unfastening his seat belt and drawing his gun. He opened the door and climbed out, leveling the weapon at the approaching Greens. "Police officer," he called. "Open your mouths, and I'll shoot."

The Warriors stopped, their expressions impassive. "Here's the deal," Fierenzo went on. "I know about the Shriek. I also know you have to open your mouths wide to use it, and if any of you so much as looks like they're about to let one off, I'll consider that an overt act and respond accordingly. I figure I can get off at least two clear shots before you scramble my aim. So the question becomes which two of you want to die for nothing?"

"What do you mean, for nothing?" one of the Warriors asked, taking care to move his lips as little as possible.

"A lot of people know where we are right now," Fierenzo

told him. "If we don't come back, they'll know where to look."

"We can tell them you left hours earlier," the Green countered. "There will be no evidence here for them to find."

"You'd be surprised what modern forensics can dig up," Fierenzo said. "On the other hand, *we* have no evidence that you've done anything illegal. If you step aside right now and let us go, there's nothing we can do against you."

"Wait a second," Roger protested, wrenching open his door and getting out. "What about Caroline?"

"She isn't here," the Green said.

"Like hell she isn't," Roger growled. "We want her. *And* Melantha."

"Roger, shut up," Fierenzo muttered across the roof at him. "We're at the short end of three-to-one odds here."

"I don't care," Roger said stubbornly. "I want Caroline back."

"I tell you she isn't here," the Green insisted.

"Fine," Fierenzo said, throwing a warning look at Roger. "Then if you'll step aside, we'll be on our way."

A look of consternation crossed the Green's face. "I'm sorry," he said, the words coming out with an odd reluctance. "That's a decision only the Commander can make."

Roger's left hand twitched as a tingle went through it. There was a second tingle. . . . "What if you and your group were in immediate danger?" he called. "Would you still have to wait for the Commander's decision?"

The Green's eyes flicked to Fierenzo's gun. "This hardly qualifies."

"Maybe this will." Hoping fervently he wasn't just blowing smoke, Roger lifted his hand to his cheek. "Go," he said into the tel. He lowered his hand, looking surreptitiously around—

And with a thunderclap that seemed to shake the whole forest, one of the tree trunks to his left exploded.

Roger jerked violently, wincing back as a cloud of splinters and sawdust rained down on them. The tree had been shattered about halfway up its trunk, and as he stared in astonishment the upper half leaned ponderously and toppled over, tearing its way through the foliage around it. It reached the ground and settled down at a sharp angle, its branches tangled with those of its neighbors.

Roger's ears were still ringing from the first blast when they were hammered by a second thunderclap, this one to their right, as a section midway up another tree disintegrated into another spray of wooden shrapnel.

He glanced across the car at Fierenzo. The detective was staring at the newly decapitated tree, his jaw and throat muscles tight. "What about it?" he called, turning back to the Warriors. "Does *that* qualify?"

The Green was staring at the second tree, his own face tight with concentration. Then, giving a microscopic nod, he looked back at Roger. Holding his knife up, he put his other hand onto the tip and shoved, collapsing the *trassk* once again into a harmless piece of jewelry. "Go," the Green said darkly, fastening the brooch onto his jacket as he and the other three Warriors stepped out of the way. "Don't come back."

Fierenzo seemed to shake himself out of a trance. He glanced once behind them and, apparently satisfied, slipped his gun back into its holster. "Come on," he said to Roger, climbing back into the driver's seat.

"Wait a minute," Roger objected. "What about Caroline?"

"I said *get in,*" Fierenzo snarled, his voice suddenly vicious.

Swearing under his breath, Roger obeyed. He had the door only halfway closed before Fierenzo peeled out, scattering gravel in all directions. They roared past the four silent Greens, whipping down the drive as fast as Fierenzo could manage and still stay on the road. Roger held on grimly, the memory of his own frantic exit echoing through his mind, the escape where he'd run away and left his wife behind.

Which he'd now done a second time.

• •

They were halfway back to the estate when, beside Caroline, Sylvia suddenly seemed to sag. "What is it?" Caroline asked anxiously.

"It's over," Sylvia said. She rubbed her eyes vigorously a moment, then turned to Caroline. "Don't worry, he's all right. The Warriors let him go."

Caroline took a deep breath, feeling the tension draining out of her. "Thank you," she murmured.

Out of the corner of her eye, she saw Sylvia look sharply at her. She braced herself; but the older woman merely nodded. "You're welcome."

There were a hundred other questions Caroline wanted to ask, but she could sense this wasn't the time for them. "So," she said instead, trying to sound casual. "Shall we go back and finish our lunch?"

Sylvia snorted a chuckle. "I rather expect the waitress has cleared it away by now, don't you?"

"Yes, probably," Caroline admitted. "Well, there's always dinner."

"Perhaps," Sylvia said, a little grimly. "Right now, I need to have a long talk with my Warriors."

"Of course," Caroline said. Stretching still-tense shoulders, she settled in to drive.

And wondered why quiet alarm bells were suddenly going off in the back of her mind.

• •

They had gone three miles down the highway, about halfway to the side road leading to where they'd left Jonah and Jordan, when Roger finally broke his silence. "When are we going to let Laurel out of the trunk?" he asked.

"When I say so," Fierenzo said shortly, checking his mirrors. The good news was that there was no sign of pursuit.

The bad news was that with this crowd, that didn't necessarily mean anything.

"What about Jonah and Jordan?" Roger asked. "We going to pick them up when you say so, too?"

Fierenzo threw him a quick sideways glance. The other was staring straight ahead, his expression rigid. Feeling angry and frustrated and guilty, no doubt, at the fact that he'd once again had to abandon his wife.

But they'd had no choice, and he was pretty sure Roger knew it. Which was a long way from accepting it, of course. "Yeah, better give them a call," Fierenzo told him. "Tell them we'll be getting to their road in about ten minutes."

"Sure." Roger put his hand up to his cheek and began to talk.

Fierenzo checked his mirrors again, his mind racing. Something strange had happened back there, something that was setting all his detective's instincts on edge, but something which he couldn't get a handle on.

"Hold it a second," Roger cut into his thoughts, waving a hand toward the steering wheel. "Jonah says to pull over."

"What, here?" Fierenzo asked, frowning as he looked around. There was nothing around them but more forest. "There could be an ambush sitting inside any of those trees."

"Just pull over," Roger said sharply. "Jonah says they've moved, and that they can rendezvous with us right here."

"Fine," Fierenzo gritted. Ahead was a slightly wider spot just off the shoulder, and he pulled over and stopped. "Tell them to hurry," he added, leaving the engine running.

"He says to hurry," Roger said. He held the tel in place another moment, then twitched his little finger and lowered the hand. "You always this surly afterward?"

"I'm not surly," Fierenzo insisted. "I'm wondering what the hell happened back there."

"I'll tell you what the hell happened," Roger bit back. "What the hell happened was that we ran off like scared puppies and left Caroline behind."

"You'd rather have stayed and fought?" Fierenzo asked, turning his Official Police Stare on the other.

For once, the stare did no good. "What, you don't have six bullets in that gun?" Roger retorted.

"Actually, I've got seventeen," Fierenzo said icily. "But that's irrelevant. You've never been hit by a Green Shriek, have you?"

The anger in Roger's face cracked slightly. "No," he said, a fraction less truculently.

"I have," Fierenzo told him. "And I was being *very* optimistic when I said I'd get off two rounds before they introduced me to the dirt. If we'd fought, we'd have lost."

"Even with Gray backup?"

Fierenzo grimaced. "Yeah—Gray backup," he murmured. "You know, I've been attacked by the Greens twice now, and both times it's been the Grays who pulled me out of it. That's left kind of a soft spot in my heart for them . . . and up to about ten minutes ago I'd have taken their side against Cyril and Aleksander and Nikolos in a New York second." He shook his head. "But after that little display . . ."

He looked away from Roger, scanning the area around them. "We've been concentrating—at least, *I've* been concentrating—on Melantha and this Groundshaker thing as the biggest threat to the city," he said. "Now, I'm not so sure. It's one thing to hear Jonah describe how a hammergun round gets more powerful the farther it travels. It's something else to watch one blow the top off a tree."

"So now you're wondering where the real threat lies?"

"I *know* where the real threat lies," Fierenzo growled. "It's this whole damn war of theirs. And I'm *this* close to rounding up every one of them I can find—on *both* sides—and digging up, thinking up, or trumping up enough charges to hold them."

"You do that and you'll condemn them to perpetual slavery," Roger warned, his voice grim. "They'll never pass whatever medical tests they get put through in prison. You really think the Feds wouldn't snatch them the second they found out who and what they really were?"

Fierenzo sighed, some of the anger draining out of him. "Of course they would," he conceded. "Which is why I'm not going to do it unless I absolutely have to. Especially not to people who've lived in my city this long without causing any trouble."

Abruptly, he reached down and popped the trunk release. "Keep your eyes peeled," he said. "I'm going to let Laurel out."

She was still lying obediently still under her blanket as he lifted the trunk lid. "We're clear," he told her, pushing the clothing bags out of the way and pulling off the blanket. "Anyone nearby?"

"If they are, they're not talking," Laurel said, squinting a little in the sunlight.

"Yeah," Fierenzo said, letting his gaze harden. "Now. You want to tell me what you did back there?"

"What do you mean?" she asked cautiously.

"Don't play me, Laurel," Fierenzo warned. "I'm not in the mood. You weren't just listening there at the end, were you?"

Her eyes shifted guiltily away from his stare. "I'm sorry," she said in a low voice. "I know you told me not to. But I didn't hear anything from Melantha, and no one had mentioned her. So I decided to take a chance. I didn't think they would even notice my voice among all the others. I certainly didn't expect them to react so quickly. I'm sorry."

"I'm sorry, too," Fierenzo said pointedly. Still, it was hard not to feel a certain degree of sympathy for her. If it had been one of *his* daughters who'd been kidnapped, he might not have paid much attention to someone else's orders, either.

There was the sound of a car door opening, and Roger appeared around the side of the trunk. "They're coming," he reported. "You okay, Laurel?" he added, offering her his hand.

"I'm fine." She took his hand, and with his assistance

climbed out onto the ground. "I'm didn't hear Melantha, though." She looked furtively at Fierenzo. "I even gave a quick call to her, just before we were stopped. But there was no answer."

Roger nodded heavily. "Well . . . we all knew it was a long shot."

"But she did hear *something*," Fierenzo said, the pieces finally starting to come together.

"What do you mean?" Roger asked, frowning.

"They knew who we were the minute we drove in," Fierenzo said, trying to put his intuitive logic train into words. "They also had to know we were there to spy on them."

"Granted," Roger said. "So?"

"So they didn't seem all that worried when they thought we were spying for ourselves," Fierenzo continued. "Otherwise, they'd have grabbed us while we were still in the house. And it didn't even seem to bother them all that much when the hammerguns went off."

"They looked startled enough to me," Roger said.

"Startled, yes, but not bothered," Fierenzo pointed out. "There's a difference. That implies they weren't even that worried when they realized we were spying for Grays."

He looked at Laurel. "But they *did* care when Laurel made that quick call for Melantha and they suddenly realized we had a hidden Green aboard. They cared a *lot,* in fact. So the question is, what was going on back there that they wouldn't want a Green to overhear?" He lifted his eyebrows in invitation.

"I don't know what to say," Laurel said, her forehead tight with concentration. "They were monitoring our progress through the forest, and there were bits of other conversations—just the casual sorts of things people talk about all the time. There was also a Farspeaker keeping in touch with their Commander, who must have been out of normal range."

"Aunt Sylvia," Roger murmured. "I wonder if she's the same Sylvia I met at Aleksander's place."

"I don't know." Laurel looked at Fierenzo. "But you were right. The minute I gave my call, they suddenly went from very calm to very excited. I went quiet again immediately, but it was too late."

"Wait a minute," Roger said, frowning. "You say she heard something that worried them. But after a couple of minutes they went ahead and let us go. Doesn't that mean they concluded she *hadn't* heard anything?"

Fierenzo thought it over. "You may be right," he conceded reluctantly. "Damn. I thought we might be onto something."

"We might still be onto half of it," Roger offered. "Because their reaction shows there was something they thought she *might* have heard."

"Could be," Fierenzo agreed. "Any ideas, Laurel?"

Laurel shook her head. "I'm sorry," she said. "I can't think of anything—"

She broke off as the sound of something brushing through tree branches came from their left. Fierenzo looked that direction, his hand automatically going for his gun.

But it was only Jordan, flying rapidly through the air toward them as he angled downward on his invisible tension line.

Beside him, Fierenzo felt Roger twitch as he caught sight of the flying Gray. "It's all right," Fierenzo soothed him, wincing as Jordan's outstretched feet slammed hard into the tree trunk anchoring the other end of the tension line. A pair of broken ankles right now would not be good.

But the young Gray's legs merely bent with the impact, absorbing the momentum like a pair of coiled springs. A second later he had let go of the line and dropped onto the ground, clearly none the worse for wear. A second later Jonah slammed into the same spot on the tree and also dropped to the ground. Turning around, he waved his hand back and forth twice as if directing traffic and then held it steady.

Fierenzo looked back in the direction the two Grays had come from. A moment later he spotted the tiny tension line projector flying toward them like a small kite being reeled in, its manta ray/airfoil shape keeping it high above the ground and any potentially entangling branches. It shot toward Jonah, and Fierenzo wondered suddenly if the Gray was going to wind up with a set of broken knuckles when it hit.

But Jonah obviously knew the proper technique. Just before the projector reached him, he swiveled a hundred eighty degrees around to let it shoot past, burning some of its speed as it braked along its retrieval thread. The projector made a U-turn and finished its trip to his hand at a much more manageable speed. "Everyone okay?" he called as he and Jordan jogged to the car.

"Thanks to you," Roger said, shaking his head. "Velovsky mentioned tension lines, but it didn't sound nearly as impressive as it looks."

"Yeah," Jonah said distractedly, his eyes on Laurel. "Laurel?"

"I didn't find Melantha," she said tiredly. "I'm sorry."

"Then where is she?" Jordan asked anxiously, looking at Fierenzo.

"I don't know," Fierenzo told him. "But we won't find her hanging around out here. Everybody in the car."

"We going back to the city?" Roger asked as they all climbed in.

"Not yet," Fierenzo said, retrieving the mental thread he'd been working on back at the estate before the Warriors had so rudely interrupted. "Nestor told us Sylvia was out doing some shopping. Laurel corroborated that a minute ago when she said their Commander was out of range of everyone except the Farspeakers. Given that, what's the simplest thing for them to have done with Caroline?"

"Sylvia took her along?" Jordan suggested.

"Exactly," Fierenzo said. "And there's just a chance that Caroline might have been permitted to do a little shopping of her own."

He looked at Roger, who was frowning blankly at him. "And if she was clever," he added, "she might even have used a credit card."

Roger's eyes widened as the light finally dawned. "Of course," he said, fumbling out his phone and his wallet. "How do I do this?"

"Call the company—number's on the back of your card," Fierenzo instructed, glancing in the mirrors and pulling out onto the highway again. "Tell them your wife may have lost her card and ask where the last place was she used it."

They had made it back to Shandaken and the intersection with Route 28 when Roger finally turned off his phone. "Got it," he announced. "The Minute Café in Bushnellsville."

"A restaurant?" Jonah asked incredulously. "She bought *lunch*?"

"As I said, clever," Fierenzo said, taking a left into a grocery store parking lot and turning around back toward 42. "Let's go see how clever she actually was."

• •

"Afternoon, gentlemen," the waitress said cheerfully as she came up to Roger and Fierenzo. "Two for lunch?"

"No, thank you," Roger said, pulling Caroline's photo out of his shirt pocket and holding it up for her inspection. "We're looking for this woman."

The waitress's eyes went suddenly wary. "Oh, yes?" she asked, her voice neutral. "Who wants to know?"

"Her husband," Fierenzo said, nodding toward Roger. "And the NYPD," he added, holding his badge wallet up beside Caroline's photo. "Was she in here today?"

The woman's eyes flicked to the badge and then back to the photo. "Yes," she said, a little reluctantly. "She and her mother."

Roger frowned. Her *mother*?

"Where were they sitting?" Fierenzo asked.

"Back there," the waitress said, pointing at the rearmost booth. "They left in an awful hurry, too. Hardly touched their food."

"Find me her charge slip, please," Fierenzo said, starting

toward the booth. "Her name's Caroline Whittier. Come on, Roger, let's take a look."

"What exactly are we looking for?" Roger asked as they sat down on opposite sides of the booth.

"Something Caroline might have left behind," Fierenzo said, picking up the napkin dispenser and rifling through the napkins. "A note slipped into a menu, say, or dropped on the floor during lunch."

"But she couldn't have known we'd even be up here," Roger objected, leaning over and studying the floor under the booth.

"No, but she could address it to you and assume *someone* would find it," Fierenzo pointed out, pulling out the stack of menus and fanning through them.

"I don't see anything," Roger said, poking his fingers carefully along the gap between the cushion and the padded seat back. "Maybe Sylvia caught her trying to do it."

Fierenzo grunted. "Let's hope not."

The waitress appeared beside them. "Here's her bill," she said handing it to Fierenzo.

"Thank you." He glanced it over; and to Roger's surprise, a corner of his lip twitched in a lopsided smile. "Well, well," he said, handing it across the table. "You definitely underestimate your wife's brains."

Roger frowned at the slip of paper. Date, time, amount, Caroline's signature . . . and the tiny word *table* scrawled just beneath her name. "'Table'?" he asked. "What does that mean?"

"I believe it's what's known as a clue," Fierenzo said, bending over and peering beneath the table. "Ma'am, did she pause by any of the other tables on her way out?"

"I don't know," the waitress said. "I was filing away the bill and wasn't really watching."

"But you *did* say she was in a hurry," Fierenzo said, sliding out of the booth and heading toward the door.

"Yes," the woman said, clearly puzzled.

"You think she put something on one of the tables on her way out?" Roger asked, hurrying to catch up.

"I've already cleaned all those," the waitress called after him.

"That's okay," Fierenzo called back as he stopped by the last table by the door and dropped down into a crouch. "Not *on* the table," he added to Roger as he peered at the underside. "*Under* it." Reaching up, he pulled out a folded silver gum wrapper with a wad of chewed gum attached to it.

"Hey, she was pulling out some gum while I was running her card," the waitress said, jabbing a finger at the gum.

"Thank you." Fierenzo dropped into one of the chairs and motioned Roger to join him. For a moment he just examined the gum and wrapper as they were. Then, carefully, he pried the gum off and unwrapped the paper.

And as Roger watched, the detective's mouth tightened. "What's the matter?" Roger asked anxiously. "Is she all right?"

Wordlessly, Fierenzo handed it over. Turning it around to face him, Roger read the tiny note. *"Roger: Damian Groundshaker, ready move on NYC—time unknown. Melantha not here. Sylvia Group Com in charge. Don't bring Grays. I love you, C."*

He looked up at Fierenzo, a hard knot in the pit of his stomach. "So they were wrong," he said. "Damian is indeed alive and well."

"So it would seem," Fierenzo said heavily. He looked up pointedly at the waitress, who took the hint and drifted away. "That would explain what happened back at the estate, too," he went on. "Group Commander Sylvia was afraid Damian might have identified himself, or that someone might have mentioned him by name. As soon as she realized that hadn't happened, there was no reason to keep us there."

Roger reread the note. "I don't know," he said slowly. "Somehow, I'm not convinced." He looked over at the waitress, busying herself at the counter. "Ma'am, you said Caroline was in with her mother. Can you describe this other woman?"

"She was old," the other offered. "White hair, really dark eyes. Darkish skin, too—looked kind of Greek or Italian. They didn't look much alike, actually—I figured she was a stepmother or mother-in-law."

"Did you notice any jewelry?"

"She had this really nice pin on her jacket," the waitress said, gesturing to her own upper-left shoulder. "Silver filigree, big green stone in the middle. That's all I noticed."

"Thank you." Roger turned back to Fierenzo. "That sounds like my Sylvia, all right. And *my* Sylvia was absolutely insistent on getting Melantha back."

"Maybe she was lying," Fierenzo suggested. "If they're trying to keep Damian a secret, they have to pretend they still need Melantha."

"Or else she's been lying to Caroline," Roger countered. "I mean, face it—how many kidnappers have you run across who take their victims out to a public restaurant?"

"And then let them put lunch on a traceable credit card?" Fierenzo shrugged. "You have a point. But we can't afford to take the chance."

"I wasn't suggesting we should," Roger said. "I'm just trying to figure out how we find out for sure without the Grays maybe charging into a trap."

"Well, we're not going to figure it out here," Fierenzo said. "Let's get back to the city."

36

The Warrior leaned past her and pushed open the library door, and Caroline walked inside. "You wanted to see me?" she asked.

"Yes," Sylvia said, looking up from a small stack of papers and gesturing Caroline to one of the chairs in front of the desk. "I wanted to apologize for my behavior at lunch this morning, and to offer you some explanation."

"Thank you," Caroline said evenly. It was a polite enough gesture, she supposed. It would have been even more polite if Sylvia hadn't sent her straight to her room after their return and left her there for two hours to stew in fear and uncertainty over what might have happened to her husband. "I appreciate your concern," she added as she settled into the chair.

"You're angry with me," Sylvia said, studying her. "I can't say I blame you." She leaned back in her chair. "Here's what happened. Your husband and Detective Fierenzo arrived here unannounced shortly after you and I reached the restaurant."

"Unannounced but not unexpected?" Caroline suggested.

Sylvia shrugged microscopically. "We keep track of what's happening nearby," she said. "Naturally, I couldn't afford to let them find you here."

"Naturally," Caroline said. "What did you do to them?"

Sylvia lifted her eyebrows. "We did nothing. A few of my Warriors overreacted when they drove off along the back way through the woods, but I got that straightened out and they were allowed to leave."

"Is that what you were doing in the restaurant and the truck, communicating with the Warriors?" Caroline asked. "Right after you called Roger and Fierenzo fools?"

"Fools?" Sylvia frowned; and then her face cleared. "Oh. No, you misunderstand. I wasn't calling *them* fools. I was referring to my Warriors and their unauthorized action."

"Ah," Caroline said, her mouth going a little drier. Because that wasn't at all what she had thought at the time. She'd had the distinct and solid impression, in fact, that Sylvia *was* talking about Roger.

But why would she lie about it?

"I appreciate you telling me," she went on. "And you said Roger was all right?"

Sylvia nodded. "As I told you then—and then repeated a

moment ago—they left unharmed. I presume that by now they're well on their way back to the city."

"All right," Caroline said, nodding. "What happens now?"

"You mean with them?"

"I mean with everyone."

Sylvia's lips compressed briefly. "The Grays have given us until Wednesday to return Melantha or face a possible attack," she said. "Since we don't *have* Melantha, we can't meet that demand. Our only option is to make sure their threatened reprisal doesn't happen."

Caroline felt her blood freeze in her heart. "In other words, you're going to launch a preemptive strike."

"I'm sorry," Sylvia said in a low voice. "I know what the city means to you, and I give you my word that we'll restrict the battle to Gray territory as much as possible. But it has to be done."

"It doesn't have to be this way," Caroline insisted, her tongue tripping over the words. "There has to be a way to stop this. There *has* to be."

"I'm sorry," Sylvia said again; and even through her anguish Caroline could sense the other genuinely meant it. "But with the Grays pressing in on us, and with Green society fragmented and Leaderless, we have no choice but to take whatever opportunities we can."

"I'm sorry, too," Caroline said. "What will you—I mean, how will you—?"

"How will we do it?" Sylvia picked up one of the sheets from the desk in front of her. "The plan is for our attack to take place tomorrow night," she said. "Late at night, when most Humans are asleep and off the streets. We'll gather together our handful of Warriors, and with Damian protected behind them we'll begin pushing southward from the northern tip of Manhattan. We'll try to take out the Grays using only the Shriek, which can knock them off their buildings if they're below the fifteenth floor or so." She grimaced. "But if they're higher than that, we'll have no choice but to have Damian bring down those buildings."

"Even residential ones?" Caroline asked.

"We find the concept of living shields repulsive," Sylvia said darkly. "I hope the Grays will be noble enough not to hide behind sleeping Humans. But if they do . . ." She shook her head. "We'll just hope they don't."

For a minute the room was silent. Caroline found herself staring out the window at the afternoon sunlight playing through the forest. She'd always loved trees and forests, and had spent hours walking in them when she was younger.

Now, all she could see out there was hidden death.

"I was also wondering," Sylvia said, "if you'd like to finish our chess game."

"Our *chess* game?" Caroline echoed incredulously.

Sylvia's lip twitched. "No, I didn't think so," she said. "Well. You may go, then. We'll be eating at six."

"Those Warrior field ration things?"

"I'm afraid that's all we have," Sylvia said. "Unless you'd like me to send someone to town for you. If you're not in the mood for my company over a chessboard, I doubt you'd appreciate it over a dinner table."

"Actually, I would," Caroline said hesitantly. "Not your company itself, I admit, but I would like to go out."

"Hoping to escape?" Sylvia asked, lifting her eyebrows.

Caroline shook her head. "I've already promised I wouldn't try that." She paused, trying to put her feelings into words. "Roger and I went out to dinner with some friends on September tenth, 2001. It was a great evening— good conversation, wonderful food, everything just calm and cheerful and relaxed."

"And the next morning, the world fell apart," Sylvia said, nodding her understanding.

"And it's never been exactly the same since," Caroline said. "But I still have the memory of that evening to look back on."

She looked back at the window. "It's about to fall apart again," she said quietly. "I'd like to have another memory I can hold onto. Even if it's just a small-town diner surrounded by strangers."

Sylvia was silent another moment. "I suppose it can't do any harm," she said at last. "Your husband is well on his way home by now, and I hardly think anyone else up here would recognize you."

She lifted a finger warningly. "But if we do go, we'll have to wait until after sunset. That detective might have tried to set up something before he left, and if he did I want to have the advantage of darkness on our side. Can your stomach wait until, say, eight o'clock?"

Caroline's stomach was already feeling pretty empty. But she merely nodded. "Yes."

"Then I'll see you at seven-thirty," Sylvia said. "And if you change your mind about that chess game, let me know."

● ●

"A chess game," Fierenzo said flatly.

"Why not?" Roger persisted, gripping the wheel tightly as he guided the car down the highway. "You saw the way the board was set up in the library. I've seen Caroline use that same opening a dozen times."

"Her, and half the chess players on the East Coast," Fierenzo pointed out. "I'm sorry, but it's not nearly enough for a search warrant."

"Then let's skip the search and move straight to an attack," Jonah said flatly from the backseat.

"Not if you want any of New York's Finest involved," Fierenzo warned. "We can't and won't do things that way."

"I was thinking more of Grays' Finest," Jonah countered. "Caroline wouldn't have written what she did about Damian unless she'd either seen him or Sylvia had specifically mentioned him. Torvald won't need much more convincing. I'll bet even Halfdan will go along."

Roger looked in his mirror. Seated in the middle of the backseat between the two Grays, Laurel was staring expressionlessly at the back of the seat in front of her. "You're awfully quiet, Laurel," he said.

"What do you expect me to say?" Laurel asked, her voice

steady. "That I would willingly consent to my people being attacked? Possibly even destroyed?"

"We aren't going to destroy you," Jordan said earnestly.

"It would be a very surgical strike," Jonah agreed. "We'd take out Damian and that would be that."

"Maybe that's all *you* would intend," Laurel pointed out. "But you wouldn't be the ones in charge. Do you really think Torvald or even Halfdan would stop once Damian was killed?"

Roger shifted uncomfortably in his seat. "This really sounds weird to me," he said. "We're breaking our necks trying to keep Melantha from getting killed; yet here we are talking about a surgical strike on Damian."

"It's an entirely different situation," Jonah said firmly. "Melantha doesn't want to hurt anybody, Gray *or* Human. Damian, on the other hand, would probably enjoy slaughtering both groups. The Gray histories I've read concluded he was at least partially insane."

"Actually, so do our Pastsingers," Laurel confirmed reluctantly. "There was one incident in particular during the war where he deliberately targeted a cave in the Southcliff region where children and injured Grays had taken refuge, even though he knew full well there were no combatants anywhere nearby."

Roger grimaced. "Oh."

"In fact, I agree with Jonah that he has to be eliminated," Laurel went on. "I'm just worried that Torvald would take the opportunity to finish us off once and for all."

"Tell me about these Others you used to live with," Fierenzo said suddenly.

Roger frowned at him. "Why do we care right now?"

"Humor me," Fierenzo said. "You said they looked a lot like humans. What was their culture like?"

"The ones we lived near were mostly pastoral," Laurel said, sounding as confused by the sudden change in topic as Roger. "They farmed and kept flocks."

"Cities? Technology?" Fierenzo asked.

"Not much of either," Laurel told him. "They were supposed to have some cities, but we didn't live near any of them. Where we lived was mostly farm and pasture and small villages."

"What about you, Jonah?" Fierenzo asked, shifting in his seat to look back at their passengers. "Were your Others like that?"

"There was farming and herding, sure," Jonah said. "The ones who lived by the ocean also did a lot of fishing."

"How about marauding?" Fierenzo asked. "Did they like to raid other parts of the coastline?"

"I suppose," Jonah agreed slowly. "They were a rowdy, clan-driven bunch who did their fair share of fighting, both among themselves and with their neighbors. And with those long oceangoing sailing ships—sure, they must have done some plundering."

"I'll be damned," Fierenzo said, very quietly.

"What's the matter?" Roger demanded, throwing a quick look at him.

"The Greens and Grays," Fierenzo said. "They didn't come from some unknown planet a dozen light-years away. They came from right here on Earth."

"What are you talking about?" Laurel asked, sounding startled. "Our world was wooded and primitive, nothing at all like this."

"What I'm talking about is the legends of our ancestors," Fierenzo said. "Specifically, the mythology of the ancient Greeks."

"The *what*?" Roger asked.

"The mythology of the Greeks," Fierenzo said tartly. "Come on, Whittier, your high school days aren't *that* far behind you. You can't have forgotten all of it already."

"I remember it just fine," Roger said. "But what do myths have to do with—?"

And suddenly, horribly, it clicked. "You're not saying . . . *wood nymphs*?"

"You've got it," Fierenzo confirmed. "One of my daughters dragged me through her mythology unit last year, and this whole thing has been bugging me ever since Jonah told me their history. I think the Greens are the real-life basis of the wood nymph legend."

"That's crazy," Roger protested. "Anyway, Velovsky told us they *did* come from somewhere else."

"Sure they did," Fierenzo agreed. "But their world and ours weren't separated by space. They were separated by time. A jump of four or five thousand years, I'd guess, into the future. After a gap that big, they might as well have been on another planet."

"The Greek Oracles," Laurel murmured. "They could have been Visionaries or Farseers."

"Falls right into place, doesn't it?" Fierenzo agreed. "Your Warriors might have inspired some stories, too, like the stuff about Hercules or Odysseus."

"What about us?" Jordan asked.

"What *about* you?" Fierenzo countered. "What direction were you heading when you hit the Great Valley?"

"South, I think," Jordan said, looking questioningly past Laurel at his brother.

"Yes, it was south," Jonah confirmed. "They traveled pretty far, too, before they met up with the Greens."

"There's your answer," Fierenzo told him. "The Greens became part of Greek myth; you Grays got worked into Norse myth."

"*Norse* myth?" Roger echoed, struggling to dredge up the long-neglected details from that high school mythology unit. "You mean as in Odin, Asgard, and the Frost Giants?"

"And the dwarves, the smiths of the gods, who made wondrous gadgets for them," Fierenzo said. "Including their masterpiece, the weapon of the god of thunder."

Roger's throat suddenly tightened. "Oh, my God," he murmured. "Thor's *hammer*?"

"A hammer with an unusually short handle," Fierenzo said. "A hammer that could be thrown into something and then come back to his hand. A hammer that could knock the top off a mountain. Stop me when this starts to sound familiar."

"I'll be cursed," Jonah murmured.

"But we don't actually throw the hammerguns," Jordan objected.

"You call it throwing when you bring them out of the wristbands," Fierenzo pointed out. "Besides, a primitive Norseman watching from the sidelines could certainly be excused if he misread what happened. You point the thing, a rock a hundred yards away explodes into dust, and when your observer opens his eyes it's back in your hand. What other conclusion could he come to?"

"Wait a minute, this is going too fast," Roger said. "Are you suggesting one of the Grays was the basis for the Thor legend?"

"Either that or some Norse warrior finagled himself a hammergun," Fierenzo said. "He'd have made quite a name for himself before he finally hung up his cleats." He hissed a sigh. "Which makes things just that much more awkward."

"Why, were you thinking of sending them all back home?" Roger asked.

"As a matter of fact, that's exactly what I was thinking," Fierenzo said bluntly. "That was my fallback position if all else failed: throw everyone back aboard their transports and kick them the hell off Earth. A moot point now."

"A moot point anyway," Laurel said. "We needed all our Farseers and Groundshakers to make it work the first time."

"All of them except Damian," Jonah countered ominously.

Laurel sighed. "Apparently so."

The car went silent. Roger looked over at Fierenzo, found the other staring hard out the windshield. "So what do we do now?" he asked.

Fierenzo shook his head slightly. "We'll think of something."

37

"**O**kay," Smith said, running his eyes down the printout. "LUDs show just one hit on Fierenzo's cell phone after he disappeared, a one-minute call to the Whittiers' apartment. About two hours after that we have a call from Whittier's cell to Fierenzo's cell. No other activity on either phone since."

Powell grunted. He'd tried Fierenzo's cell a hundred times in the nearly forty-six hours since the detective's abduction. If he'd tried one more time during that two-hour window, he might have been able to at least hear the voice of whoever was using his phone now. "Anything on the Whittiers' car?"

Smith shook his head. "We've checked all the garages around their apartment. I've got an APB out on it, but after that triple carjacking in the Bronx last night the uniforms have more plates to look for than usual."

"Did you make it clear this one was related to a missing cop?"

"Actually . . . at the time we didn't have a solid connection," Smith hedged.

Powell locked a glare on him. "You think maybe we've got one now?"

The other's lip twitched. "Yes, sir."

"Then upgrade the hunt."

"Yes, sir." Smith turned to go.

"Hold it," Powell said, feeling slightly ashamed of himself. Smith was doing the best he could, after all. "Sorry—I didn't mean to jump on you that way."

"That's okay," Smith assured him. "You think the Whittiers are involved in whatever happened to him?"

"I don't know what to think," Powell admitted. "Either they had nothing to do with it, or else they're the strangest pair of idiot savants I've ever run across. You can't be smart enough to convince Fierenzo you're an innocent bystander and at the same time be stupid enough to grab him and then walk around using his own cell phone."

"I suppose," Smith said. "Did the Gang Task Force have anything on these Greens and Grays?"

"They've never heard of them," Powell said. "They're guessing we've got brand-new players in town."

"And with just two days until Cyril's deadline," Smith muttered. "Unless he was just blowing smoke."

"Yeah." Reaching across his desk, Powell snagged his phone. "Keep working the phone angle," he instructed the other. "And run another check to see if anyone's been using Tommy's credit cards. I'm going to give the Gang Task Force's cage another rattle."

He grimaced. "And after that, I think I'll give the S.W.A.T. duty officer a heads-up. Just in case he *wasn't* blowing smoke."

• •

Roger punched off the phone. "He's not exactly thrilled about getting dragged out at this time of night," he told the others. "But he says he'll be right over."

"What do you mean, this time of night?" Jonah scoffed. "It's not even seven-thirty."

"I get the feeling Velovsky's day ends when the street-lights come on," Roger told him. "The fact he's willing to come out now shows how much Melantha means to him."

"How much the Greens mean to him, you mean," Ron said sourly. "I still don't think it's a good idea for us to be here when he arrives. Velovsky doesn't think very highly of Grays."

"Then it's time he broadened his horizons," Zenas said firmly.

Roger pursed his lips. Privately, he had his own doubts

about dropping all this on Velovsky at once. But Zenas had suggested it, and Laurel and Fierenzo had concurred, and so for better or worse they were going to give it a try. "Well, we're not very far from his place, so he should be here in a few minutes."

"Hopefully without a bunch of Green Warriors in tow," Jonah muttered. "I was thinking I might go up on the roof for a couple of minutes and check things out."

"Halfdan's still looking for you," Stephanie warned him.

"I'll be careful." Jonah looked at Fierenzo, lifted his eyebrows questioningly.

"I don't think it's necessary," the detective said. "But it probably won't hurt, either. If you want, go ahead."

Nodding, Jonah got to his feet and stepped to the door. "Keep an ear peeled, Roger," he added. Opening the door, he checked the hallway and slipped out.

"This isn't nearly as nice a place as the Marriott," Roger commented.

"Not nearly as expensive, either," Ron countered dryly. "It was our ancestors who mined the mountains for gems, you know, not us personally."

"I have a question," Fierenzo said. "I know Elymas led the Greens here to Manhattan. But who exactly was in charge of the Gray contingent?"

"Torvald and Halfdan's father," Ron said. "He was—"

"*Their* father?" Roger cut in. "Those two are *brothers*?"

"Yes," Ron said, frowning. "Didn't you know?"

"How could I?" Roger said, feeling a little sandbagged. "I thought they were rivals for control of the Grays."

"As much as Grays are under *anyone's* control," Zenas murmured.

"And may our freedom forever reign," Ron countered solemnly. "At any rate, their father Ulric had been a major clan leader back in the Great Valley. He was the one who organized our refugee group."

"We obviously don't have the same strict societal cohesion as the Greens," Stephanie said. "But Ulric was probably the closest thing we had to a leader everyone would listen to. That was certainly the case by the time we arrived here."

"And he did a terrific job of nursing us through the transition from old world to new," Ron said. "He got us through customs, set us up in homes and jobs, and pushed hard to make sure we all learned English as quickly as possible so we could fit into Human society and not simply withdraw into our own little ethnic knot."

"What happened to him?" Fierenzo asked.

"The same thing that happens to all of us," Ron said, his voice almost wistful. "He died a few years after we got here."

"Of course he *was* already pretty old," Stephanie added. "From what I've heard, people were surprised he held on as long as he did."

"After that we mostly went on with our individual lives," Ron said. "Basically ignoring anyone's authority except when someone stepped over the line and had to be dealt with." He looked over at Zenas and Laurel. "It was only when the Green crisis exploded onto the scene that there was any real need for us to get organized, at which point Torvald and Halfdan each made a bid for authority."

Roger's left hand tingled, and he lifted it to his cheek. "Yes?"

"Velovsky's entering the hotel," Jonah's voice came in his ear. "No sign of any Greens, either with him or hanging around in the shrubbery. I'm coming back in."

"Right." Roger lowered his hand. "Velovsky's on his way."

"Good," Fierenzo said. "So when you say 'the Grays,' you're really talking about a fairly amorphous mass of individuals."

"That's us, all right," Ron agreed.

"Actually, that's one of the reasons we're so terrified of fighting them," Laurel said. "There's so little central control anywhere that you never know what exactly they're going to do."

"And of course, no central control means no individual to

focus on whose loss would make the army fall apart," Zenas said.

"Zenas," Laurel said warningly.

Zenas looked at Ron and Stephanie. "Sorry," he said, a little shamefacedly. "I didn't mean it to sound that way."

"That's all right," Stephanie assured him. "We know you realize we're not the enemy, just as we know you aren't."

"At least, not yet," Zenas countered grimly. "But what are you going to do if war *does* break out? Are you going to be able to sit out the fighting when your friends and cousins are being killed?"

"And what about us?" Laurel added. "Zenas and I aren't Warriors, but we can certainly be ordered into support service. What are you going to do then?"

There as a knock on the door. "Let's focus on trying to make those decisions moot, shall we?" Fierenzo said, getting to his feet. Crossing to the door, he pulled it open. "Come in, Mr. Velovsky."

The lines in Velovsky's face deepened at the sight of the stranger in front of him. "Do I know you?" he asked.

"He's a friend of mine," Roger spoke up, taking a step toward him. "Please come in."

Still frowning, Velovsky eased past Fierenzo and stepped into the room. "I assumed this was going to be a private—"

He broke off, his body twitching violently as he spotted Ron and Stephanie. "What the—?"

"It's all right," Roger hastened to assure him. "They're friends, too."

"Friends of whom?" Velovsky countered harshly, taking a quick step backward. Too late; Fierenzo had already closed the door and was standing in front of it.

"Friends of ours," Laurel spoke up.

Velovsky's body twitched again as he seemed to suddenly notice the two Greens. He looked at the Grays, then back at the Greens, then over at Roger. "What in the name of hell is going on here?"

"Have a seat, Mr. Velovsky," Fierenzo invited, moving his

own chair into the circle and assisting Velovsky into it. "We have a story I think you should hear."

Velovsky sat in stony silence as they took turns recapping the events of the past few days, his arms crossed, his eyes mostly alternating between Ron, Stephanie, and Jordan. Jonah quietly rejoined them midway through, and got his own slot in Velovsky's glaring rotation.

The recitation ended, and for a long minute no one spoke. Finally, Velovsky stirred. "You actually expect me to believe this?"

"Why would we lie?" Roger asked.

"Why would *Grays* lie?" Velovsky asked pointedly. "Why would enemies of the Greens *lie*?"

"We're here, too," Laurel reminded him. "Do you think we would betray our own people?"

Velovsky's eyes darted to her, turned reluctantly away. "I don't know," he muttered. "Maybe I don't know as much about Greens as I thought."

"Look, all of us in this room want the same thing," Roger said. "We all want to find Melantha."

"Only for very different reasons," Velovsky countered. "*We* want her alive."

"So do we," Stephanie said.

"So you say." Velovsky looked at Fierenzo. "What *you* want her for I can't even guess. You planning to arrest her or something?"

"If that's what it takes, why not?" Fierenzo countered, his voice cold. "My job is to protect my city and uphold the law." He lifted his eyebrows. "If I were you, I'd start thinking that direction, too."

"Well, *I* certainly don't know where she is," Velovsky said.

"We're not asking you to play psychic," Roger said, feeling his patience starting to wear thin. Was Velovsky so blind that he couldn't see both sides of this? Couldn't he understand what Melantha and her family were going through?

Couldn't he sympathize even a little with the underdog?

The thought struck him like a slap in the cheek, warming his face with unexpected shame. Wasn't that same compassion precisely one of the characteristics he'd found so irritating in Caroline lately?

Was that how Caroline saw him, he wondered suddenly? As someone cold and unfeeling and uncaring?

"Then what *do* you want from me?" Velovsky demanded.

"A little information," Roger told him, pushing aside the self-recrimination. Now was not the time. "You told Caroline and me that you've been aboard the Green transport several times. Zenas tells us he thought he saw a door at the back of the engine compartment. We want to know whether you ever saw anyone use that door or, even better, if you ever saw what was behind it."

Velovsky's eyes drifted off to one of the room's corners, his antagonism fading slightly as he focused on the question. "I don't know," he said at last. "I remember there being three big rooms for the passengers, with one or two supply rooms attached to each, a power room, an airlock, and a command deck, plus the engine room itself. But I don't remember any— Wait a minute."

The lines in his face deepened. "Yes, I *do* remember that door," he said slowly. "In fact, I asked someone about it. She said . . . she said it was extra storage. But even when they were moving things in and out of the other compartments, I never saw anyone use it."

"You said 'she' told you it was storage," Fierenzo said. "Do you happen to remember her name?"

Velovsky closed his eyes, his lips puckering. "Sylvia," he said at last. "Yes. Her name was Sylvia."

Roger looked at Fierenzo, a fresh knot forming in his stomach. "As is Sylvia, the Group Commander?"

"Does sound that way, doesn't it?" the detective agreed grimly. "If so, I think we can assume that whoever or whatever was back there had a military purpose."

"What if it did?" Velovsky asked truculently. "Would you rather they have come here weak and defenseless?"

"At the moment, I'd rather they not have come here at all," Fierenzo said. "But it's a little late for that now. The question is, was it in fact Damian who was hiding in there?"

"I have another question," Ron said suddenly. "Zenas, Laurel—what happens if you have *two* Groundshakers operating at the same place?"

Zenas snorted. "Twice the mess, probably."

"I don't mean working together," Ron said. "I mean if one is working *against* the other."

"How would—?" Zenas broke off, a suddenly thoughtful expression on his face. "That's a good question."

"It's like they're giving out sound waves, isn't it?" Jordan asked. "I thought sound waves go right through each other."

"Actually, that depends on a couple of factors," Jonah corrected his brother. "How similar they are, whether they're going the same direction . . ."

He looked sharply at his father. "*And* whether they're in or out of phase."

"Maybe that's why Sylvia is so anxious to get Melantha back," Laurel said, her voice dark. "In fact, maybe that's why Nikolos and Cyril were so anxious to kill her in the first place. They were afraid she might not cooperate in their war, and that she might actually be able to work against Damian."

"Interesting thought, though still just a theory," Fierenzo warned. "Still, if it's true, it gives us that much more reason for us to find her." He reached out his hand to Velovsky. "Thank you for your time, Mr. Velovsky. If you care anything about Melantha, you'll keep quiet about our meeting."

"Of course I care about Melantha, Detective," Velovsky growled, ignoring the proffered hand as he stood up. "I care about *all* the Greens; and if I could see any way your little conspiracy could hurt them, I'd go to Aleksander in a minute."

He sent a glower toward Zenas and Laurel. "Fortunately for you," he added, "I can't."

"And we appreciate your forbearance," Roger told him,

trying not to let too much of his annoyance seep into his voice.

"Zenas, what exactly does your transport look like?" Stephanie asked suddenly. "I was thinking that if we knew its shape and layout, we might be able to figure out how big this extra storeroom actually is."

"Good idea," Zenas said, holding out his hands. "It's— well, let's see. It's curved like this."

"Roger, see if there's some stationery in there," Fierenzo instructed, pointing to the desk behind him.

Roger started to swivel around, stopped as an idea occurred to him. "How about we try a three-dimensional model instead?" he suggested, digging into his coat pocket and producing Melantha's *trassk*. "You all know how to work these things, right?"

"Perfect," Zenas said, smiling tightly. "Let me have it."

"Here, Velovsky, pass it over," Roger said. He shifted the brooch to his left hand to give to the old man—

And jerked violently as a raucous squeal erupted from his hand.

"What was *that*?" Velovsky demanded, twitching back as Roger reflexively dropped the *trassk*.

"No idea," Roger said, staring down at the brooch lying on the carpet, his ears ringing. "It's never done that before."

"Pick it up again," Fierenzo ordered, crossing behind Velovsky and standing beside him.

Gingerly, Roger did so, touching it only with his fingertips. Nothing happened. He let it drop into his cupped palm—

The second squeal sounded even louder than the first. Again Roger fumbled the *trassk;* but this time, before he could drop it, Fierenzo reached over and plucked it from his hand. "Jonah?" the detective called, beckoning him over with a short nod of his head as he reached over and turned Roger's hand palm upward. "You're our local expert on Gray electronics. What's the *trassk* doing to Roger's tel?"

"I'm hardly an expert," Jonah protested as he came over

and took Roger's hand, peering at the palm like a Gypsy fortune-teller. "It shouldn't be doing *anything* to it."

"Then explain this." Reaching over, Fierenzo touched the brooch to Jonah's left hand. There was another squeal, this one quickly cutting off as the detective pulled the *trassk* away. "Or *this*," he said, shifting the brooch to Jonah's right hand.

And paused. The *trassk* sat in that hand without so much as a squeak. "I thought you had a tel on both hands," Fierenzo said.

"I do," Jonah confirmed, cupping the *trassk* firmly in his right hand. Still no sound. He waved it toward his left hand, moved it back as another squeak sounded. "It's just our private-line tels," he concluded, sounding bewildered. "But that's crazy."

"You said they operate on radio frequencies, right?" Fierenzo asked, taking the *trassk* back.

"I also said it doesn't work the same way your radios do," Jonah reminded him.

"What about my cell phone?" Roger asked. "I always hold it in my left hand, where it's right against the tel. Could it have done something to it?"

Jonah shook his head. "Tels don't operate on cell frequencies, either."

"But this isn't a standard tel," Fierenzo reminded him.

"Maybe it's not a standard phone anymore, either," Roger said as another memory suddenly flashed to mind. "Right after I met with Torvald, Caroline said she'd tried to call while I was in there and couldn't get through."

"I thought Caroline was upstate when you met Torvald," Jonah said, frowning.

"I meant the first time," Roger said. "Friday afternoon, after I talked to Sylvia at Aleksander's."

"And you didn't mention it before?" Jonah demanded, stretching out his hand. "Give it to me."

"I didn't think it was important," Roger said, digging out the phone and handing it over. "He asked about Melantha, I didn't tell him anything, and then he let me go. Just like yesterday."

"Except that on Friday you still knew where Melantha was," Jonah pointed out grimly, peering closely at the phone as he turned it over in his hands. "Did Torvald or anyone else handle this?"

"No, it was in my pocket the whole time," Roger said, thinking back. "But it definitely wasn't working."

"That may not mean anything by itself," Ron said. "He probably had a suppressor going."

"General electronic damper," Jonah added. "Third cousin to the gadget Jordan and I used to knock out the streetlights Wednesday night. Torvald probably has his whole building blanked out to make sure no one can snoop on him." He shook his head. "I don't see anything here."

"I have a question," Fierenzo spoke up. He was holding the *trassk* close to his face, Roger saw, studying its back. "You said you set the frequency of these private tels as far from the general band as possible so there wouldn't be any interference between them, right?"

"I didn't do it personally, but yes, that's what Garth did," Jonah confirmed. "He was afraid that—"

"Hold it," Roger cut him off as a memory suddenly popped back. "*Garth?* Twitchy type, always fiddling with a pocket knife?"

"That's him," Jonah said, frowning. "Do you know him?"

"Only slightly," Roger said grimly. "He was waiting at the gate when Wolfe grabbed me outside the subway and hauled me in to see Torvald."

"Son of a bitch," Fierenzo said.

They all looked at him. "What?" Roger asked.

"Take a look." Reaching to the back of the *trassk,* Fierenzo peeled something small and filmy from the metal. "We've been outsmarted, friends," he went on, holding it up for everyone to see. "Looks like Garth built himself a bug and put it on Roger's *trassk.*

"Torvald's been listening to everything we say."

38

For a long moment no one spoke. Roger stared at the filmy patch hanging from Fierenzo's fingers, his stomach twisting in horror.

Velovsky was the first to break the silence. "You fool," he murmured, his eyes burning into Roger's face. "You stupid, careless fool."

"What do we do?" Laurel breathed.

"We start by not panicking," Ron said firmly, gesturing to his eldest son. "Jonah, take a look at the bug. Maybe it's just a tracer and not a complete listening device."

Gingerly, Jonah took the patch from Fierenzo, turning it over a couple of times and angling it toward the light as he looked closely at it. "You're right, it's just a tracer," he announced at last, a note of relief in his voice. "There's a carrier transmitter but no microphone. In fact—" He plucked at the film with his fingernails. "Yes," he said, holding it out for Roger and Fierenzo to see. "There are actually parts of *two* tels here, back to back but offset," he went on. "Two separate carrier transmitters."

"That must be how it can work as a tracer," Ron said. "Normally, you can't pinpoint a tel's position."

"That's a bit of good news, anyway," Fierenzo said. "Even if Torvald knows the *trassk* is here, he doesn't know who's in here with it. *Or* what's been said."

"Small comfort," Velovsky muttered. "They'll have the whole building surrounded by now."

"I don't know," Jonah said, his forehead creasing. "I didn't see anyone while I was up there."

"Let's find out," Fierenzo suggested, retrieving his coat

from the back of Velovsky's chair. "Get the tracer, Roger, and let's you and me take a little walk."

"What about us?" Laurel asked as Roger gingerly took the tracer back from Jonah and slipped it into his pocket.

"Stay here until we call you or come back." Fierenzo caught Velovsky's eye. "That goes for you, too," he said.

"It won't make any difference," Velovsky said quietly. He had slumped in his chair, his eyes locked onto the carpet in front of his feet. "In here or out there, the Grays will get us whenever they want us."

No one was lurking in the hallway as the two men walked to the elevator. Roger felt his muscles tense as the doors slid open; but there was no one in the car, either. They got in, Fierenzo punched for the lobby, and they headed down. "Relax," the detective advised as the floor numbers on the panel slipped swiftly downward. "It may not be as bad as it looks."

"Of course not," Roger said bitterly. "I've only wrecked everything, guaranteed Melantha's death, and probably destroyed Manhattan in the bargain. Not that bad at all."

"Don't go melodramatic on me," Fierenzo said reprovingly. "Number one: even if they can pin down exactly which room we were in, they don't know who was in there with us."

"They'll be able to figure out that it was Ron and Stephanie who rented it."

"So?" Fierenzo countered. "I've already been seen with Jonah and Jordan, and you've already been seen with me. The critical question is whether or not anyone's made the link between us and Melantha's parents."

"And with Velovsky," Roger reminded him.

"And with Velovsky," Fierenzo agreed. "But it's a good-sized hotel, and there are ways of getting people in and out without being spotted. We should be able to sneak all of them out if we have to."

No one with an obvious Gray build was waiting when the elevator reached the lobby. Fierenzo eased them through a waiting cluster of people and led the way into the foyer. "Where are we going?" Roger asked.

"We've taken our little walk," Fierenzo said as he pushed the door open and headed toward a line of waiting cabs. "Now it's time for a little ride. How much cash have you got on you?"

"I don't know," Roger said, frowning. "Maybe a hundred."

"Good enough," Fierenzo said, pulling out his own wallet. "Once we're on our way, give me fifty and the tracer."

He stepped to the first cab in line and opened the back door. "Columbia University," he told the driver as he gestured Roger in and then got in behind him.

"Where at Columbia do you want?" the cabby called over his shoulder as he pulled out into the traffic flow.

"It's the—where was Nikolos again?" Fierenzo asked, turning to Roger.

"The Faculty House," Roger supplied. "East campus, on Morningside Drive."

"The Faculty House," Fierenzo confirmed. Half-turning, he looked casually behind them, then held out his hand toward Roger and wiggled his fingers in silent command.

Pulling out his wallet, Roger selected two twenties and a ten and handed them over, setting the tracer on top of the stack. Fierenzo pressed the thin film onto the top bill, rubbing his thumb over it a couple of times. For a moment he peered at his handiwork; then, nodding in apparent satisfaction, he folded the bills into his hand, added a couple more from his own pocket, and turned to gaze out the side window. Roger tried to relax, wondering what exactly the detective had in mind.

Two blocks later, he found out. Leaning abruptly forward, Fierenzo tapped on the divider. "Pull over here," he called, jabbing a finger at an open area to their right. "This is ridiculous," he growled to Roger as the driver obediently pulled to the curb and stopped. "He's *your* father, not mine. You want to go all the way to Columbia just to take him home, fine. I'm going back to the party."

"Oh, come on," Roger argued back, not sure where the other was going with this but recognizing a cue when he saw one. "We promised. Anyway, he wants to see us."

"He wants a ride," Fierenzo said with exaggerated patience. "He doesn't care if you're even there. He sure doesn't care if *I'm* there."

"Fine," Roger said impatiently. "If that's the way you want it, go ahead and get out."

"Yeah, I'll do that," Fierenzo retorted, pulling on the handle and shoving the door open. He caught Roger's eye and his head twitched fractionally toward the open door beside him. "Have a nice drive. I'll keep Elaine company for you."

"Wait a second—Elaine's mine," Roger warned. "You keep your paws off her."

"And say hi to your dad for me," Fierenzo added with a leer. Half-turning, he started to get out.

Roger caught his arm. "Come on, Bill, we can't just leave him there."

"Sure we can," Fierenzo said. "In fact, I'd lay you odds he's already found himself another ride."

"Yeah, but what if he hasn't?" Roger persisted.

"Then he can—oh, *hell*." Muttering under his breath, Fierenzo pulled up the wad of bills he and Roger had put together. "Here, fella, here's what I want you to do," he said, reaching through the partition and slapping the money into the cabby's hand. "Seventy bucks. Go on up to the Faculty House and see if there's a white-haired old man hanging around waiting for a cab. If there is, take him home—he'll give you the address."

"What if he's not there?" the cabby asked, eyeing the money uncertainly.

"Then you've just made yourself a real big tip," Fierenzo said, sliding across the seat and out the door. "Come on, Ralph. And you owe me."

Roger got out after him, and together they watched the cab pull out again into the night. "You think he'll actually go up there?" he asked.

"Doesn't matter," Fierenzo said, looking around them.

"Wherever he goes, Torvald's tracer goes with him. Come on, let's get back."

No one accosted them along the way, and a few minutes later Jonah was once again dead-bolting the door behind them. "Well?" he demanded.

"The tracer's gone on a tour of greater Manhattan," Fierenzo told him. "I forgot to ask you to monitor the general Gray tel band."

"Actually, we'd already thought of that," Ron said. "There were a couple of sentry reports on Green activity, and Halfdan made a few positioning changes to counter Warrior movements in Central Park. It all sounded very routine."

"It also sounds like Halfdan's coming to a boil over our disappearance," Jonah put in. "All sentries with views of police precinct houses have been alerted to watch for us."

"Well, if they're watching for you there, that's several sets of eyes not watching any other directions," Fierenzo said philosophically. "Anything about Roger and me? Or about a cab heading for Columbia University?"

"Not that I heard," Ron said.

"Same here," Jonah said as his mother also shook her head.

"Well, it's been an interesting evening," Velovsky said, standing up and picking up his coat and hat. "Do I have your permission to leave yet, Detective?"

"Yes, of course," Fierenzo said, digging a card from his pocket. "If you think of anything else that could help us—"

"Just be thankful I'm not going to report you," Velovsky cut him off, ignoring the proffered card. With one final glare at Ron and Stephanie, he headed for the door.

"I have a question," Laurel spoke up hesitantly as Velovsky maneuvered past her. "Jonah and Jordan have their private tel system. What's to keep Torvald from having one of his own?"

"Good question," Ron said soberly, looking over at his eldest son. "Jonah?"

"*Very* good question, actually," Jonah said, grimacing.

"As long as he's got Garth working for him, there's no real reason why he can't."

"Actually," Fierenzo said, "he does."

"How do you know?" Zenas asked.

"Jonah said that tracer was a pair of carrier transmitters without a mike or anything else," Fierenzo said. "Can someone show me where that particular component would be on a tel?"

"About here," Ron said, holding up his hand and pointing to a spot just below the little finger.

"About the size of the tracer itself?" Fierenzo asked.

"About that," Ron agreed. "Why?"

"I had a close look at it," Fierenzo said. "It was roughly circular, but not exactly, and the edge was slightly ragged in at least two places."

"Which means what?" Zenas asked, sounding puzzled.

"Which means it wasn't something Garth or Torvald had prepared beforehand, ready to go in case Roger showed up," Fierenzo explained. "It was instead hastily cut out of something else. What could that have been except an actual tel?"

"Or a pair of tels," Stephanie murmured.

"Correction noted." Fierenzo looked at Jonah. "Jonah, you told us that the frequency couple your tels operate on are the safest to use as far as leakage into the main system is concerned. Yet I take it the tracer wasn't running on that exact pair?"

Jonah nodded. "It was close to our frequency couple— that's why we got feedback when they were together—but not exactly on it."

"That's what I thought," Fierenzo said, nodding. "So if yours was the safest frequency couple, why didn't Garth use it when he made up a new batch for Torvald's crowd?"

Ron snapped a pair of massive fingers. "Because he knew Jonah might still have his pair lying around," he said. "He didn't want to take the chance we might be able to listen in on Torvald's private business."

"That was my conclusion, too," Fierenzo said. "And now we come to the interesting bit. Did you and Stephanie have any trouble after you left our meeting at the Marriott yesterday? Specifically, did anyone seem to be following you, or come to your house later, or confront you with accusations about collaboration with the enemy?"

"No, of course not," Stephanie protested. "Don't you think we'd have told you if we had?"

"Of course I do," Fierenzo soothed her, a note of satisfaction in his voice. "But I had to ask. That's it, then."

"That's what?" Ron asked.

"The answer," Fierenzo told him. "I know who has Melantha."

There was a moment of stunned silence. "You *what?*" Jonah demanded. "Why didn't you say so before?"

"Because I didn't know before," Fierenzo said. "Torvald's tracer was the last piece of the puzzle."

"You've lost me," Zenas said, his hand gripping Laurel's.

"It's very simple," Fierenzo told him. "We know now that Torvald's been able to track Roger's movements since Friday afternoon. That's how he found out where Caroline and Melantha had gone that evening, in fact, after they disappeared from the Whittiers' apartment."

"But it was *Halfdan's* sons who nailed me in the Youngs' apartment," Roger said, frowning.

"Having probably picked you up during your side trip into Queens," Fierenzo said, nodding. "What we didn't realize until now was that there were actually two separate groups of Grays on hand: Halfdan's sons *and* Torvald's people."

"Probably Garth and Wolfe," Jonah murmured.

"Whoever, having that tracer let them track Roger straight into Yorkville," Fierenzo said. He looked over at Zenas and Laurel. "We also know there was at least one Green on hand, the old woman who got killed. With one of you on the scene, I gather word gets around pretty quickly."

"True," Zenas confirmed. "There were certainly other Greens already in the neighborhood. Most Manhattan parks have at least a couple of families living there, except for those in the south where Torvald's Grays have moved in."

"So what you're saying is that there could have been peo-

ple from each of the different factions in the area when
Melantha disappeared," Jonah said.

"Exactly, which is what had the water muddied for so
long." Fierenzo pointed to Roger. "But now we know that
Torvald could track Roger anywhere in Manhattan. We also
now know that he *didn't* do anything to the McClungs after
our meeting in the Marriott. Yet he could surely have made
some serious political capital out of a family of Grays col-
laborating with the enemy. If nothing else, he could have accused Aleksander of using his Persuader tricks to torpedo
the peace plan."

"So why didn't he?" Laurel asked.

"Because he didn't know about the meeting," Fierenzo
told her. "And why not? Because he wasn't paying attention
to the tracer.

"Because he didn't care anymore what Roger did."

Roger caught his breath. "Because he already had
Melantha!"

"Bingo," Fierenzo said with grim satisfaction. "So now
all we have to do is figure out where he's got her stashed."

"It can't be his studio," Roger said, trying to think it
through. "There's no room, and he has other Grays going in
and out." He looked at Ron and Stephanie. "Unless you
think Halfdan could be in on it, too."

"Not Halfdan." Ron was positive. "He was *very* intent on
making the peace plan work. If he knew where Melantha
was, he would have taken her straight back to Cyril."

"He can't be hiding her anywhere on Manhattan, either,"
Zenas added. "He couldn't take the chance that some Green
might wander close enough to hear her."

"What about Queens or Brooklyn?" Fierenzo asked.
"Those are your original strongholds, aren't they?"

"Actually, they're mostly *Halfdan's* strongholds now,"
Ron said. "Torvald and the majority of his supporters
moved into lower Manhattan as soon as they found out the
Greens were here."

"So she's *outside* the city?" Jordan demanded anxiously.
"But that could be *anywhere.*"

"It could," Fierenzo agreed. "But don't forget that the farther away he puts her, the riskier it is for him. He has to have people taking care of her, and that means traveling to and from their homes."

He gestured to Jonah and Jordan. "You saw how fast word traveled that you two had come up missing, and you know better than I do how much finagling it took to cover up Jonah's absence from his sentry post. I doubt Torvald would risk his caretakers being gone so long that they attracted that same sort of attention."

"Unless she's already—" Jonah threw a hooded look at the Greens.

"No," Fierenzo said firmly. "Torvald wouldn't risk killing her until and unless he was sure she wouldn't be more useful alive than dead."

"And now that he knows about Damian, he'll be taking even better care of her," Roger pointed out.

"Absolutely," Fierenzo agreed.

"So what's the answer?" Zenas asked. "If she's not *in* the city, and she's not very far *out* of the city, where is she?"

"Only one place I can think of that's close enough and has the necessary privacy," Fierenzo said, grimacing. "Unfortunately, I'm not sure it really limits our search that much."

"The transport!" Stephanie exclaimed suddenly, sitting upright in her chair. "It's right offshore somewhere, with easy access to the city."

"And undoubtedly out of range of any passing Greens," Ron added with a growing excitement of his own. "That has to be it."

"That's what I'm thinking," Fierenzo agreed. "The question is how we find it. Ron?"

The growing excitement faded from Ron's face. "I have no idea," he confessed. "I've never been aboard it. I don't think I know anyone who has."

"Garth has," Jonah said sourly. "Some of our fancier electronic stuff is still stored down there. You want me to ask him?"

There was the sound of a clearing throat from over by the door. Roger turned; and to his surprise he saw Velovsky standing there quietly, still in his hat and coat. "I thought you'd left," he said.

Velovsky shook his head, his eyes on Zenas and Laurel. "You don't need to call in any Grays," he said. His voice still sounded uncomfortable, but its earlier antagonism was gone. "I know where it is."

Roger stared at him. "You're kidding."

Velovsky shook his head again. "It was after the Grays had moved in and established themselves," he said, coming somewhat reluctantly back into the main part of the room. "I'd made a record of some of their addresses, and I used to go into Queens a couple times a month and just watch them for awhile. Just to see how they were doing."

He smiled tightly. "I had a terrible urge sometimes to walk up to one of them and tell him that I knew who and what he was, just to see what kind of reaction I'd get. But I knew it would tip them off that the Greens were here, too. Anyway, I would also sometimes follow one of them, just to see where Grays went and what they did.

"One day, I followed one onto the Staten Island Ferry."

Silently, Laurel stood up and held out her hands. A half smile flickered across Velovsky's face as he slipped off his coat and handed it and his hat to her. "My curiosity was aroused," he continued, "so I followed him to a place on the northeast shore that had a bunch of old beach supply sheds scattered around with No Trespassing signs plastered all over them. He went straight to one of them, unlocked the door, and went inside. I waited around, wondering what was going on. When he came out half an hour later, he was carrying a flat box under his arm."

"Do you remember what time of year that was?" Ron asked.

Velovsky squeezed his eyes shut. "I know it was spring," he said slowly. "The weather was nice that day, but it had been raining most of the previous week. Probably late April."

Ron nodded. "Tels and hammerguns for the May 5th

coming-of-age ceremony," he said. "All Grays who've passed their tenth birthday are formally inducted into the rights and responsibilities of adulthood at that time."

"You kept your extra hammerguns in the transport?" Zenas asked.

"We kept all our spare electronics down there in those days," Ron said. "We were afraid of having anything potentially incriminating in our apartments or businesses, so things were only brought up from the transport as they were needed."

"We sometimes had people working around the clock in there making new equipment," Stephanie added.

"Not any more, I hope," Fierenzo said.

Ron shook his head. "All our workshops are elsewhere in the city. The transport itself is mostly empty these days."

"Except for one very special resident, we hope." Fierenzo looked at Velovsky. "And you're sure this shed you saw is still there?"

Velovsky nodded. "I've been back a couple of times, just walking around and watching. I never spotted another Gray going in or out, but I doubt they've moved the transport."

"Actually, according to Aleksander, neither side can risk doing that," Roger said. "Too much danger of the Coast Guard spotting it."

"That's it, then," Fierenzo concluded. "Anyone fancy a late-night drive to Staten Island?"

"You mean *tonight*?" Zenas asked, frowning.

"Why not?" Fierenzo asked. "At this point delays gain us absolutely nothing."

"I'll go with you," Jordan said eagerly, holding up his head.

"Me, too," Jonah seconded.

"Count us in," Zenas confirmed.

"Might as well make it a party," Ron added. "When do we start?"

"Not for another few hours," Fierenzo told him. "We need to let the streets clear out first."

"I don't know," Velovsky said doubtfully. "That beach

shed is pretty small. A big crowd of you might wind up just getting in each other's way."

He looked at Zenas and Laurel. "At any rate, I don't think you two in particular should be there."

"But she's our *daughter*," Laurel said.

"And the transport is the ultimate Gray stronghold," Velovsky pointed out. "News of a Green intrusion there wouldn't sit very well with them."

"He's probably right," Ron said reluctantly. "Torvald doesn't need any more ammunition against us than he's already got."

"By the same token," Velovsky went on, turning to the Grays, "it wouldn't be a good idea for any of *you* to go, either. Unless you plan to kill whoever's in there, they'll surely be able to identify you afterward. That would hand Torvald the same political capital Detective Fierenzo talked about earlier."

"They're already after Jordan and me," Jonah pointed out.

"But they have no proof you were involved in Melantha's rescue," Velovsky reminded him.

"You'll still need one of us," Ron spoke up. "I don't know how the security's been set up, but it'll be something only Grays can get through."

"That's me, then," Jonah said. "Like I said, I can't get into any hotter water than I'm already in."

"Mr. Velovsky?" Fierenzo prompted.

Velovsky grimaced. "He can get us through their security," he said. "But after that, he stands aside."

Jonah grimaced in turn, but nodded. "All right."

"So who exactly is going?" Roger asked, looking at Fierenzo. "You and me?"

Fierenzo shrugged. "Torvald can't have more than a couple of caretakers on duty at any given time."

"Yeah—*Gray* caretakers," Roger reminded him. "Big guys with hammerguns and attitude."

"I've got a gun, too," Fierenzo reminded him.

"And what are you going to do with it?" Roger retorted.

"Kill them? I thought the whole idea here was to avoid bloodshed."

"I've also got a badge, and the authority to use it," Fierenzo said, starting to sound a little impatient. "But if you don't want to go, just say so. I can always call in a S.W.A.T. team."

"You know you can't do that," Roger said disgustedly. "Fine. Let's make it a twosome."

"Let's make it a threesome," Velovsky corrected. "I'm going in, too."

"You?" Roger asked disbelievingly.

"What, you think I'm old?" Velovsky demanded, lifting his eyebrows in challenge.

"I appreciate your willingness, Mr. Velovsky," Fierenzo said. "But Roger's right. You just show us to the place, and we'll call it even."

"No," Velovsky said, shaking his head. "I want to see firsthand the condition Melantha's in and how they've been treating her."

"A little political capital for the Green side?" Jonah suggested tartly.

"Let me put it another way," Velovsky said, gazing evenly at him. "Detective Fierenzo seems a little too friendly with you Grays for my taste. Mr. Whittier is an unknown quantity; but he certainly defied the will of the Greens by hiding Melantha from them. I want someone on this expedition who I can trust to genuinely look after Green interests."

"I think you're misjudging us," Fierenzo said calmly. "You're certainly misjudging *me*. But that's okay. If you want to come along, we'll be glad to have you."

"But you're not going in there unarmed," Stephanie said firmly, standing up. "Are you right-handed, Mr. Velovsky?"

Something flicked across Velovsky's face. "Yes," he said cautiously.

"Good." Pushing up her right sleeve, she did something to her wristband and snapped it open. "Here," she said, stepping over to him and holding it out. "Take my hammergun."

For a moment the room was silent. Velovsky stared at her, the lines in his face deepening as she continued to hold the wristband toward him. Then, slowly, he pushed back his right sleeve and held out his arm. She adjusted the metal around his forearm and snapped it closed. "It takes a bit of practice to learn how to throw it," she warned. "But Detective Fierenzo said you had a few hours. We can teach you."

"You gave me your weapon," Velovsky said, his voice sounding odd.

"You may need it," she said simply, sitting down again.

"She's right," Ron added, heaving his bulk to his feet, his wristband already unfastened and in his hand. "Give me your arm, Roger."

Jonah nudged his brother. "Jordan?" he prompted.

"But mine's left-handed," Jordan objected.

"That's okay," Jonah said, looking at Fierenzo. "I'm sure the detective can shoot perfectly well with either hand."

"Not really," Fierenzo said, pushing up his left sleeve. "But as Stephanie said, we've got time to practice."

"And to hear all about your plan?" Roger suggested, wincing a little as Ron wrapped the cold metal around his forearm.

"Yeah, a plan would be nice," Fierenzo agreed. "Let's see if we can come up with one."

39

The sunlight had long since faded from the woods outside Caroline's window, the darkness growing roughly in proportion with the increase in growling from her stomach. If Sylvia was still on her promised eight o'clock dinner schedule, they should be leaving in the next fifteen minutes.

Caroline hoped so. Not that the dinner itself was all that vital, though certainly she felt like she could eat a small cow at this point. But far more important than food was the new note she had carefully wrapped around one of the sticks of gum in her purse.

She lay back on the bed, staring out into the darkness, thinking back over the note. *Roger: Green Warriors moving NYC Tue night from N—sweep S w/Damian behind them—must intercept before buildings fall. I love you, C.*

Was there anything else she should say? There was a bit of room left at the bottom of the gum wrapper, and she was getting the hang of this Lilliputian writing technique. But anything else would be pure speculation, and she couldn't risk being wrong. Better to just stick with what Sylvia had told her and let Roger draw his own conclusions.

Assuming Roger got the note at all. And that was a *big* assumption, even with the credit card payment to point him to the right place. Maybe all she was doing was spinning her wheels, idling away her time until Sylvia finally let her go home.

Sylvia.

Caroline rubbed thoughtfully at her cheek. Something had happened after their aborted lunch, something that had set her mental alarm bells clanging. But in all these hours of idleness, she still hadn't figured it out.

Her stomach gave an extra-loud growl, and she winced as a brief ache wound its way through her. Maybe she would do better to wait until after dinner, and a quieter stomach, to try to figure it out. At least wait until she'd gotten a side salad and maybe some bread tucked away inside her. If the waitress was efficient enough—

And suddenly, there it was. *Waitress.* On the way back to the Green estate, Sylvia had commented that the waitress would have already cleared away the dishes.

Which was true enough . . . except that Caroline had never used the word *waitress* in Sylvia's presence. She'd always used the term *server*.

She closed her eyes, fighting upstream against her hunger, forcing her mind to think. So Sylvia knew the word *waitress*. Was that such a big deal?

Yes, it was. Because Sylvia claimed to have never been to a restaurant before. Sylvia didn't even know how to order a meal at a restaurant.

Yet she knew a female server was also called a waitress.

Caroline felt her throat tighten as the past twenty-four hours suddenly came into a new and devastating focus. Sylvia had been lying right from the very start. She'd lied about her ignorance of human society and customs. She'd lied about wanting to learn more about Caroline's people. She'd probably even lied about not knowing how to play chess.

She'd almost certainly lied about the Greens' upcoming attack on the Grays.

Rolling onto her side, Caroline sat up on the edge of the bed, the sudden movement sending a wave of light-headedness over her. If the battle plan was a lie, then she had to destroy that note immediately. The last thing she could afford was to take the chance that Roger would find it and give it to the Grays.

Or did chance have anything to do with it?

Sylvia the naïve, sheltered Green might not know how Caroline could pass a note. She would have no idea that Caroline's credit card could instantly show where they'd been.

But Sylvia the cunning liar would know all those things. Which mean that the only reason they were going out to-night was that Sylvia already knew Caroline's previous note had been found and passed on to the Grays.

This whole thing, in fact, had been a setup, she saw now; a clever and subtle manipulation of Caroline's unwilling-ness to stand by while innocent people died.

But then, the woman had said it herself, straight to Caro-line's face. *Deception has always been a part of warfare.*

Slowly, she lay back down on the bed. There was no Damian, then. The whole story of a second Groundshaker had been nothing but a red herring, something to deceive and distract the Grays.

So what then *was* the Green plan? Did they expect Melantha to topple the skyscrapers while the Grays hunted in vain for a phantom Damian? Could a Persuader like Aleksander force her to commit mass murder, the same way Cyril had tried to force her to give herself up outside Lee's market? If they hid Melantha inside that crowd of Warriors she'd seen practicing last night—

She frowned at the ceiling. There *had* been a crowd out on the lawn, hadn't there? Nikolos had nearly gotten run over twice, in fact, while trying to make his way over to Sylvia. There had been way more than the sixty Warriors Velovsky had said Nikolos could field against the Grays. In fact, if she added in the ones in the trees and those shooting from inside the house, there could have been as many as a hundred fifty of them out there.

And suddenly, an icy chill caught her by the heart as it all fell into place. Thanks to her first note, the Grays would be expecting the Greens to attack with a Groundshaker, which would probably get them spread out and away from the tallest buildings. If they also received the message now waiting in her purse, they would furthermore gather together at the north end of the city, preparing to take on Nikolos, Damian, and sixty Warriors. Instead, they would find themselves facing two or three times that many.

And they would be slaughtered.

Her hands curled into fists. So that was the true secret behind this hidden Green territory. And when she and Roger had threatened to stumble into that secret, Nikolos had calmly taken the opportunity to twist the potential leak to his own advantage.

Caroline had sent Roger on a mission of mercy to the Grays, hoping to save their lives. Instead, she had unwittingly conspired with Nikolos to destroy them.

"No," she muttered aloud. She wouldn't accept that. She couldn't. There had to be something she could do.

She could start by destroying her current note, which

would at least keep the Grays from walking into an Upper Manhattan ambush. But it was too late to retract her first note, the one identifying Damian as the chief Green threat. Even if the Grays avoided the trap, they still wouldn't know anything about the true number of enemies they were facing until it was too late.

Somehow, she had to find a way to warn them.

But how? The message Nikolos was obviously expecting her to write was a critical part of the Green plan. Would Sylvia simply take it for granted that Caroline would play her role as expected, or would she have someone check the note before allowing it to be found? Caroline herself wouldn't take such a risk. She couldn't imagine Sylvia doing so, either.

Unless . . .

She sat up again and went to the chair where her purse was sitting. So Nikolos wanted to be clever and devious? Fine. She could play that game, too.

Two minutes later, she had finished the addendum to her note and rewrapped it around the stick of gum. She had tried to think like her husband, to see things in his logical, efficient, problem-solving way, and to leave him a clue that Sylvia wouldn't recognize as such. Whether she had succeeded, only time would tell.

It was entirely possible that she herself would never know one way or the other.

There was a tap on her door. "Yes?" she called.

"It's Nestor," her guard replied through the panel. "Group Commander Sylvia requests your presence at dinner."

Caroline took a deep breath. "All right," she called back. "I'm ready."

• •

Powell gripped the kitchen phone tightly, a sense of exhilaration momentarily eclipsing the fatigue dragging at his mind. "And you're all right?" he asked carefully.

"Yeah, I'm fine," Fierenzo's voice replied, sounding a little bemused by his partner's intensity. "Why wouldn't I be?"

"Gee, let me think," Powell growled, a ripple of annoyance joining the emotional mix. This, he decided distantly, must be what it was like to have a teenager. "Maybe because you've been *missing* for forty-eight hours?"

"Yeah, sorry about that," Fierenzo said, sounding more preoccupied than actually sorry. "You up for a little drive?"

Powell glanced at the kitchen clock. It was just past nine-thirty. "How little?"

"A couple of hours upstate," Fierenzo told him. "Little town called Shandaken."

"Never heard of it."

"You take Exit 19 off the Thruway and drive thirty miles west on Route 28," Fierenzo told him. "You can't miss it."

"Okay," Powell said, grabbing a pad and scrawling notes. "What's there that we want?"

"There's a little restaurant called the Junction Inn where Caroline Whittier used her Visa about half an hour ago," Fierenzo told him. "I'm hoping she's left us a note on a gum wrapper stuck to the underside of one of the tables."

An eerie chill ran up Powell's back. "Cyril wasn't blowing smoke, was he?" he asked quietly. "There really is a war brewing."

"Hell itself is brewing," Fierenzo confirmed tightly. "And we've got forty-eight hours to stop it. Maybe less."

Powell looked at the clock again. "I don't suppose you know when this Junction Inn closes?"

"Probably before you can get there," Fierenzo said. "I was hoping you could be outside when they open in the morning."

"You think that'll be soon enough?"

"I don't know," Fierenzo conceded. "But the alternative is to blow in there tonight, wake up the owner and maybe a couple of state cops and demand they let you in. That would draw way more attention than I want to risk right now."

"Speaking of drawing attention, it might not be a good

idea for me to suddenly go missing," Powell said as his brain started working again. "I've got a meeting set up for nine o'clock with Cerreta and Commander Messerling."

"*S.W.A.T.* Commander Messerling?" Fierenzo asked.

"You know anyone else with that name?" Powell countered. "I got the ball rolling a few hours ago when I thought you'd been kidnapped by one of these gangs. You want me to cancel the alert?"

"Better not," Fierenzo said. "It might be a very good idea to have them standing ready."

"Okay," Powell said. "Anything else I should tell them? Aside from the fact you're all right?"

"Not really," Fierenzo said slowly. "In fact . . . let's go ahead and leave out the part about me being okay."

Powell frowned. "Tommy, you can't keep this quiet. The whole department's up in arms."

"Which is exactly how we want them," Fierenzo pointed out. "Having a missing cop in the mix should help them be a little more inspired if and when this thing blows up."

"Except that you'll eventually have to come clean," Powell warned. "This is not what they call a good career move."

"I can take the heat," Fierenzo assured him. "As for you, you never knew anything about it. This conversation never took place. Got that?"

"We'll discuss it later," Powell said, keeping his voice neutral. Like hell he would leave his partner to take all the blame himself. "So what do you want to do about the Junction Inn?"

"We still need to see if Caroline left us a note," Fierenzo said. "You think Smith might be interested in an early-morning drive?"

"I can ask him," Powell said. "But I think I should let him know you're all right."

"No." Fierenzo's voice left no room for argument.

"He gave up his whole weekend helping us look for you," Powell said, arguing it anyway. "He deserves a little consideration."

"He deserves not to have his career go up in flames,"

Fierenzo countered. "You tell him I'm okay and we'll be making him a party to this deception. You and I may be able to weather that kind of storm, but he's way too junior to get away with it."

Powell grimaced. "I suppose," he conceded. "Okay, I'll get him on it as soon as you hang up. By the way, I never got to tell you what I found on the branch that was in that stolen Parks truck."

"Let me guess," Fierenzo said. "Dull axe marks?"

Powell made a face at the phone. "I don't know why you even bother with a partner," he said sourly. "Yes, just like we found on the Whittiers' potted trees, only these went about halfway up from the broken end instead of all being clustered at the bottom."

"Don't sulk," Fierenzo soothed him. "It's still a useful confirmation."

"Confirmation of what?"

"Right now, I'm not at liberty to say," Fierenzo said grimly. "Just get Smith on the horn and point him upstate. And keep your cell handy. I might have to whistle you and Messerling up at a moment's notice."

"Don't worry," Powell said grimly. "We'll be ready."

40

Roger had been to Staten Island only once in his life, back when he was a child and his parents had taken him to see the Richmond Town Restoration. He didn't have much memory of that trip, but he'd come away with the vague impression of a place that was pretty quiet and very unexciting.

Now, at two o'clock in the morning, the island was even quieter.

"There," Velovsky said, pointing out the window at a collection of small shapes silhouetted against the reflected glow from the waters of the Upper Bay. "Third one from the left."

"Anyone around?" Fierenzo asked.

Jonah was sweeping the area with his binoculars. "Doesn't look like it," he said.

"Let's go, then," Fierenzo said, opening his door. "Roger, leave the keys above the visor."

Roger obeyed, the weight of the hammergun wrapped around his wrist still feeling strange. He climbed out of the car, closing the door to a crack instead of slamming it, and fell in behind Fierenzo, slogging through the loose sand as Velovsky and Jonah fanned out to either side.

They reached the shed without incident. "Locked," Fierenzo muttered, digging into a pocket. "I'll have to pick it."

"Don't bother," Jonah said, reaching over and pressing his thumb against the lock. "Gray general-use locks are keyed to pressure and body temperature. All I have to do is—there," he said as the lock snicked open.

Fierenzo pulled open the door and gave the weathered wood inside a quick sweep with his penlight. Looking over his shoulder, Roger saw that the shed was empty, with no other doors or windows. "What now?" he asked.

"This way," Jonah said, slipping past them and going to the far corner of the shed. He reached down and got a grip on something; and to Roger's amazement, a section of floor swiveled open on invisible hinges, revealing a set of narrow steps leading downward. "Again, general-use camouflage," Jonah explained as he propped the door back against the wall behind it. Twisting his wrist, he sent his hammergun flowing into his hand.

Roger did the same, though not nearly as deftly. Jonah gave a quick look around at the others, then turned to the staircase and started down, Fierenzo close behind. Roger followed, his heart thudding painfully, with Velovsky bringing up the rear.

The stairs were trickier than expected. Roger had grown up with the American standard of riser and step dimensions, which apparently was just slightly different from the typical Gray equivalents. Half a dozen times in the first thirty steps he caught his heel and nearly lost his balance. One of those times, as he grabbed for the smooth metal of the stairway to catch himself, his hammergun clattered against it, sounding as loud as a gunshot in his ears and eliciting a quiet but heartfelt curse from Velovsky. Letting go of the weapon, he let it flow back into its wristband, and from then on kept both hands brushing lightly against the walls for support.

Finally, with a murmured warning from Jonah, they reached the bottom.

Roger stepped off the last stair to find himself pressed close to Fierenzo in a cramped metal entryway no bigger than an office cubicle, facing an elaborately tooled metal wall. "I hope there's a door there somewhere," Fierenzo murmured.

"Right there," Jonah said, gesturing to a section of the wall that looked no different to Roger than any of the rest of it. "Problem is, I don't know how to open it."

"Try to figure it out," Fierenzo said tartly. "I'd really prefer not to have to knock."

"We may not have a choice," Velovsky warned. "The outer door would have locked Melantha in. This one might well be designed to lock everyone else *out*."

"I think he's right," Jonah said reluctantly, running his hand over the wall. "Okay. Everyone back up the stairway."

They reversed direction, climbing back up the steps. It was just as tricky going up, Roger discovered, as it had been going down.

"That's far enough," Fierenzo murmured after the first ten steps. "Okay, Jonah," he called softly as he turned around and drew his gun from his shoulder holster. Taking a deep breath, Roger threw his hammergun into his hand and tried to prepare himself for action.

From below came a pair of dull thuds that echoed off the stairway walls. There was a moment of silence, then two more. "Come on!" Jonah shouted. "Open up, will you?"

More silence followed. Then, abruptly, there was a faint creak of metal, and Roger felt a puff of oddly scented air flow past him. "What do you—?" a deep voice growled.

"About time," Jonah cut him off. "Hey, Garth. How's it going?"

"Wait a second—wait a second," Garth protested. "You can't come in here. Special orders from—"

"From Torvald," Jonah finished for him. "Yes, I know. Why do you think I'm here?"

"No, really, you can't come in," Garth insisted. "We've got some delicate tech work going and can't have people clumping around stirring up air currents."

Jonah's sigh was clearly audible. "Very plausible," he said. "I'll be sure to tell Torvald what a fine job you're doing. But right now, I have to get in to see the girl."

There was just the briefest pause. "Girl?" Garth cautiously.

"Melantha *Green?*" Jonah said, starting to sound a little irritated. "The one you're *guarding?* Torvald wants me to bring some proof to Halfdan that we've got her."

"He told *Halfdan* about her?" Garth said, sounding stunned.

"The situation's starting to unravel," Jonah bit out, his voice clearly impatient now. "Or didn't they tell you about Damian?"

"They told me Whittier spun a spiderweb story for them," Garth said contemptuously. "I don't believe it any more than Torvald does."

"Well, I guess Torvald's changed his mind," Jonah said.

"He must have changed more than that," Garth countered. The initial shock of finding Jonah outside his door was apparently fading, and Roger could hear suspicion starting to edge into his voice. "Since when are *you* working with him?"

"Since none of your business," Jonah said. "He doesn't tell *me* everything he's got on the burner, either. What, you think I just strolled over to Staten Island and came down here on a sudden whim?"

"Why didn't he tell me you were coming?" Garth demanded. "For that matter, why didn't you use your tel instead of pounding on the door just now?"

"Because I don't *have* one," Jonah said. "I was supposed to get one of the pair you cut up to track Whittier's *trassk* with. Come on, we're wasting time. You going to let me in, or not?"

"Not, I think," Garth decided firmly. "Not till I talk to Torvald."

And with that, Fierenzo jumped suddenly down the steps, the thud of his feet hitting the metal floor echoing up the stairway. "Police," he snapped. "Keep your hands where I can see them. Roger, get your butt down here."

Roger clattered back down the steps, Velovsky behind him, to find the situation just about the way he'd visualized it. Garth was standing in the middle of the open doorway, his mouth hanging open in shock, his ever-present pocketknife for once gripped motionlessly in his hand. In front of him stood Jonah; slightly to the side where he had a clear line of fire was Fierenzo, his gun pointed squarely at Garth's stomach. Garth's bewildered frown shifted over the detective's head— *"Whittier?"* he demanded. "Jonah, what in—?"

"Later," Fierenzo cut him off. "How many more in there?"

Garth's mouth clamped solidly shut. "Fine—we'll find out for ourselves," Fierenzo said, tossing Jonah a set of handcuffs. "Stay here and watch him, and make sure he doesn't use his tel. You two come with me."

Pushing past Garth, Fierenzo headed into the transport. Glancing furtively at the glowering Gray as he passed, Roger followed.

The transport's door led into a light-blue corridor that stretched back about ten feet to a T-junction. Fierenzo reached the intersection and paused, giving a quick look both directions. "Short branch to the left; longer one to the right," he murmured back over his shoulder. "Any suggestions?"

"Go right," Velovsky muttered back. "We must be near the bow. Most of the transport will still be aft."

"Sounds good to me," Roger seconded.

Fierenzo nodded. "Stay sharp," he warned. "Looks like there are a couple more turns back there, and I see at least two doorways. Perfect spot for an ambush." Giving another quick glance both directions, he sidled around the corner and headed to the right.

This corridor was longer than the first, stretching back at least thirty feet. Roger stayed close behind Fierenzo, his eyes on the two doorways midway down the corridor leading off to opposite sides. Melantha and another guard might be in one of those rooms—

"Behind you!" Velovsky barked suddenly.

Roger spun around to find that a big Gray had appeared at the far end of the corridor branch they hadn't taken and was striding purposefully toward them. Clenching his teeth, he snapped his hammergun up, peripherally aware that Velovsky was doing the same.

They were both too late. There was the familiar guitar-string whine, and suddenly Velovsky was thrown backward, slamming into Roger and sending his own shot splatting uselessly into the corridor wall. He tried to line up the weapon for a second try, but there was another whine and his arm flailed back over his shoulder as the Gray's shot caught him in his upper-right shoulder, spinning him halfway around and dropping him off-balance onto one knee. The Gray's third shot sent Velovsky careening backward into him again, throwing his aim that much farther off and leaving Fierenzo the only one still standing. With two of his opponents down, the Gray broke into a sprint, hammergun still spitting shots their direction. He reached the T they'd just passed, glanced toward the entryway as he ran through the intersection—

And was abruptly slammed sideways against the wall as Jonah's hammergun shot caught him dead center.

Roger suddenly noticed his left hand was tingling. Shouldering Velovsky off his arm, he twitched his finger and pressed the hand to his cheek. "Yeah, what?" he demanded.

"I've got this one," Jonah announced. "Keep going."

"Right," Roger said, getting shakily to his feet. He'd lost his grip on his hammergun in the fracas, he discovered; flicking his wrist, he threw it back into his hand. "You okay, Velovsky?"

"Don't worry about me," the old man wheezed, his chest heaving as he fought to get air back into his lungs. "Just move it."

"Quiet," Fierenzo admonished them both.

They continued on to the first door. It opened at a touch on a white plate set in the wall beside it, and Fierenzo and Roger looked cautiously inside.

The room was dark, but there was enough light spilling in from the corridor to show a dozen rows of dusty-looking padded seats, arranged airline style. "Passenger compartment," Velovsky identified it, peering past Roger's shoulder. "Those seats probably fold down for sleeping."

"Should we check it out?" Roger asked, trying to see around the chairs. "They could have Melantha on the floor behind that last row."

"You couldn't hide a Gray back there," Fierenzo pointed out, shining his flashlight into the compartment. "Not enough room."

"What about that storeroom?" Velovsky asked, pointing his hammergun toward a darker archway opening off the far side of the compartment. "Plenty of room in there for her *and* a couple of guards."

"Yeah, but all the comfortable seats are out here," Fierenzo pointed out, shining the light at the archway.

"They could have moved her when they heard us coming," Roger suggested.

Fierenzo shook his head. "Dust on the chairs; nothing floating in the air. Let's keep going."

The next door opened into a second compartment arranged in a mirror image of the first, and just as deserted. Beyond the two doorways, the corridor ended in another T-junction, this one with equal-length branches leading off to both sides. "Should we split up?" Roger offered as Fierenzo hesitated.

"Bad idea," Fierenzo said. "Let's try right."

"No," Velovsky said suddenly. "Go left."

Roger looked at him. The old man was staring into space, frowning hard in concentration. "Any particular reason?" Fierenzo asked, his voice wary.

"Just go left," Velovsky repeated sharply, gesturing with his hammergun.

A memory flashed into Roger's mind: Caroline in the cab Saturday morning, listening to the Greens as they communicated silently with each other. Could he be hearing Melantha's call? "Let's do it," he said, turning down the left-hand branch. Five paces ahead the corridor bent to the right; not bothering to look first, he charged around the corner.

He caught just a glimpse of the Gray kneeling marksman-style in the center of the corridor as the hammergun shot slammed into his chest, throwing him backward against the wall. He tumbled down onto the deck, vaguely aware of Fierenzo diving flat onto the floor around the corner in front of him as Velovsky leaned his right arm awkwardly around the corner—

"Roger. *Roger!*"

With a start, Roger came to. Fierenzo was crouched over him, slapping at his cheek. "You okay?" the detective demanded.

"Yeah, I think so," Roger told him. His head and chest ached fiercely, but not with the sharp stabbing pains he would have expected from broken bones. "You get him?"

Fierenzo nodded, getting a grip on Roger's arm. "Come on—Velovsky's gone ahead."

With the detective's support, Roger managed to stagger down the corridor. The Gray was lying on the floor a few feet back from a doorway opening off to the right, his hands cuffed securely behind his back. Roger got a grip on the edge of the doorway, and he and Fierenzo stepped through into another of the passenger compartments they'd seen farther forward.

Propped up on her elbow on one of the flattened-out seats, her eyes heavy-lidded with interrupted sleep as she gazed nervously at Velovsky, was Melantha. "Melantha?" Roger called, taking another tentative step inside.

Her dark eyes turned toward him and abruptly widened. "Roger!" she gasped. Hopping off the seat, brushing past Velovsky, she ran toward him. Roger braced himself—

And then she was in his arms, her own arms wrapped tightly around him, sobbing into his shoulder. "I knew you'd come," her muffled voice came from his jacket as she cried. "I knew you and Caroline wouldn't leave me."

"We're here, honey," Roger soothed, feeling embarrassed yet strangely comfortable as he held her close, trying not to wince as her arms squeezed his new set of bruises. "I'm sorry it took so long, but we're here."

"And we need to get moving," Fierenzo put in, touching the girl's shoulder. "Do you know how many Grays are in here with you?"

Melantha lifted her face from Roger's shoulder just far enough to look warily at the stranger. "It's all right," Roger told her quickly as she clutched him a little tighter. "He's a cop, and he's on our side. How many Grays are there?"

"Three," she said, still sounding nervous. "One was with me, and there were two more somewhere else."

"All accounted for, then," Roger said, feeling a trickle of relief.

"But this one probably had time to call it in," Fierenzo reminded him. "Come on."

Melantha held onto Roger the whole way back through the transport, letting go only long enough to fling herself at Jonah for another quick bear hug when they reached him at the entrance. "Is Jordan okay?" she asked as they started up the stairs. "They said Halfdan would do something terrible when he found out who helped me."

"He's fine," Jonah assured her. "He's mostly been worried about you."

"Did they hurt you at all?" Velovsky asked, an ominous undertone to his words.

"No, I'm all right," she said, giving him a curious look.

"They said they'd only hurt me if I tried to run or use the Shriek on them. Are you Velovsky?"

"That's right," he said. "Why?"

She clutched Roger's arm a little tighter. "I thought you were on Aleksander's side," she murmured.

Roger looked back at Velovsky, caught the brief quirk of his lip. "We can talk about it once you're safe," he assured the girl.

"If there *is* any place that's safe," Velovsky grunted as they reached the shed and climbed up through the trap door.

"Oh, I think we can come up with something," Fierenzo told him, opening the outer door and giving the area a quick scan. "Come on, and I'll show you."

The Buick was pretty crowded with the five of them jammed into it. But it didn't stay crowded for long. Barely a mile after Fierenzo directed Roger onto Richmond Terrace, he ordered him to pull over again. "Here we are," he announced. "Everybody out except Roger and Velovsky."

"You're kidding," Roger said, peering at the building straight ahead down the street and then turning to look at Fierenzo. "You *are* kidding, right?"

"Not at all," Fierenzo said, nodding across the street to their left. "It's a perfectly respectable motel. More to the point, it's got a very nice stand of trees surrounding the play area out back."

Beside him, Melantha suddenly stiffened. "Mom and Dad are here!" she breathed.

"Which is even more to the point," Fierenzo agreed quietly. "Room 22, I believe. Your family's in the adjoining room, Jonah," he added, looking at the Gray. "I figured that after all you'd been through, you all deserved a little time together."

"And if Torvald tracks them here?" Velovsky countered darkly. "We can't be more than a couple of miles from their transport."

"Torvald's going to expect us to head back to Manhattan as fast as the laws of Richmond County allow," Fierenzo said. "Which is where you and Roger are going, by the way, in case they've got spotters on the Bayonne Bridge. I'll bring the rest of the group in tomorrow when there's more traffic to hide ourselves in."

"Very clever," Velovsky growled, clearly still not convinced. "And if Torvald isn't cooperative enough to follow your little red herring? Are you and a few Grays going to protect Melantha single-handedly?"

"I don't think single-handedness is anywhere in the picture," Roger told him, pointing out the windshield at the building that had first caught his eye. "I gather you hadn't noticed where we are."

"The old 120th Precinct," Fierenzo identified it, a sort of malicious nostalgia in his voice. "I was here for two years before they transferred me to Manhattan. Still know quite a few of the guys." He cocked an eyebrow at Velovsky. "You think even Torvald's got the gall to try for a kidnapping on a police station's doorstep?"

"Can I go now?" Melantha asked anxiously. "Please?"

"We can all go," Fierenzo assured her. "Roger, you've got my cell number—call immediately if you spot trouble. Otherwise, I'll let you know when and where we'll be meeting. I'm not sure exactly when, but it won't be before noon."

Roger nodded. "I'll be ready."

"I just hope you know what you're doing," Velovsky muttered.

"I guess we'll find out, won't we?" Fierenzo said, popping open his door. "Now vamoose, you two. And don't pick up any hitchhikers."

Velovsky didn't speak again until they were on the Bayonne Bridge, heading into New Jersey. "We going back to that hotel?" he asked.

"Might as well," Roger said. "The room's paid for, and Fierenzo arranged for a late checkout, so we've got it until two. You have someplace else you'd rather go?"

"Yes—my own apartment," Velovsky retorted.

Roger shook his head. "Not a good idea. If Garth or the other Grays recognized you, your apartment's the first place Torvald will come looking."

"I suppose," Velovsky conceded reluctantly. "I just never sleep very well anywhere except my own bed."

"Personally, *I'm* not going to have any trouble sleeping," Roger said, yawning prodigiously. "It's been a really long day."

Velovsky was silent another minute. "They're not really in Room 22, are they?"

Roger shrugged. "I have no idea."

"In fact, they're probably not even in that particular motel," Velovsky persisted. "Fierenzo still doesn't trust me."

"I don't think he trusts a lot of people right now," Roger told him.

"He seems to trust the Grays."

"Only the ones Melantha trusts."

"He trusts *you*," Velovsky said pointedly.

"Maybe." Roger shot a glance at Velovsky. "And before you start in on the Grays, you might want to remember that it's your Green friends who are holding my wife hostage."

"So you say," Velovsky muttered, his veiled outrage subsiding a little. "If they are, it's for a good reason."

"Yeah," Roger said. "Sure."

"I'm sure they'll let her go unharmed," Velovsky insisted. "They're good people, Roger. They really are."

"Yeah," Roger said again. "I guess we'll find out, won't we?"

Velovsky didn't reply.

41

The summons Caroline had been expecting came at six o'clock the next morning. She took a quick bath, got dressed in the clothes she'd been living in for the past two days, and went downstairs.

As usual, Sylvia was waiting for her in the library. As was decidedly *un*usual, so was breakfast.

"Good morning, Caroline," the older woman said gravely as Caroline walked across the room, her nose wrinkling at the delicate aromas coming from the covered tray on the desk. "I'm sorry to wake you at such an early hour. But we're going to be doing some traveling today and need to get started."

"That's all right," Caroline assured her, stepping to the desk and gesturing to the tray. "Is that for me?"

"Yes," Sylvia said. "I thought you should have a good breakfast before we go."

Caroline lifted the lid. Beneath it were scrambled eggs, sausage, and a Belgian waffle covered with strawberries and whipped cream. On the desk beside the tray were a tall glass of orange juice and a small carafe of coffee with a mug beside it. "You've come a long way since I introduced you to human food," she commented.

She looked Sylvia straight in the eye. "But then, this whole thing has been an act from the very beginning, hasn't it?"

She would have expected Sylvia to indulge in at least a moment of gloating. But there wasn't even a hint of a smile on the older woman's face. "I'm sorry I had to lie to you," she said gravely. "But I had no choice. You and Roger had found us, and I had to do something quickly or our secret would have been exposed."

"Locking us away in a guarded cabin wouldn't have been enough?" Caroline countered.

"Actually, no, it wouldn't," Sylvia said. "The news of your sudden disappearance would have been dangerous all by itself if the wrong people got hold of it. I had to come up with a way to neutralize the entire threat."

I *had to do something quickly*. I *had to come up with a way*. Caroline stared at her . . . and suddenly, one final detail about that moonlight rendezvous clicked into place.

Because high-ranking Greens didn't go to see other people. They brought the other people to see *them*. Nikolos had done that, hauling her and Roger up to Columbia University from Washington Square. Aleksander had done it, too, sending Vasilis and Iolanthe to bring them to where he was waiting at their apartment. Even here, both Nikolos and Sylvia had invariably sent for her instead of coming to her room themselves.

But it was *Nikolos* who had walked across the yard to Sylvia. Which meant that it was *Sylvia,* not Nikolos, who was the higher-ranking person. Which meant— "Nikolos isn't the Command-Tactician, is he?" she said. "You are."

This time a smile did indeed touch Sylvia's lips. But it was a smile of admiration, not gloating. "Very good," she said. "As I said before, you're smarter than you let on."

"I'm also very confused," Caroline said. "How in the world did you pull that off? *Why* did you pull it off?"

Sylvia gestured to the tray. "Your food's getting cold," she said. "You'd better sit down and eat."

"If I do, will you answer my question?" Caroline asked, pulling a chair over to the tray.

Sylvia shrugged. "There's not much answer to give," she said, walking around behind the desk and sitting down. "Along with the usual death and destruction, the war in the Great Valley generated a huge degree of chaos and disorganization among our people. People and families were shuffled randomly back and forth, sometimes getting lost in the process. Lists of the Gifts were lost or garbled as Pastsingers died or found more urgent things in need of remembering. Sometimes Leaders and Visionaries were nowhere to be found and confirmations were missed completely, leaving those children to figure out their Gifts for themselves."

"And Nikolos was twelve when you came here," Caroline said around a mouthful of waffle as that age suddenly took on a new significance. "No one really knew what his Gift was."

"It was a bit trickier than that," Sylvia said. "We had to persuade the Visionaries in the Valley that he wasn't old enough to be tested, and that we would do so when we reached our destination. We then had to imply to those here that he had in fact been tested before we left. But as I say, all was chaos, and no one was paying as much attention as they should have."

"And your own Gift?"

"We couldn't hide the fact that I'd been in the fighting," Sylvia said. "But it was easy enough to conceal who I really was and pass me off as a Group Commander instead."

"But why do any of this in the first place?" Caroline asked. "You were going to have a Command-Tactician with the group anyway. Why did it matter who exactly it was?"

"They had their reasons," Sylvia said. "To be honest, I don't really know what all of them were."

"Except that deception has always been a part of warfare?"

"That's certainly part of it," Sylvia agreed.

"Can you at least tell me whether this was your idea or Nikolos's?"

"It was my superiors', actually, back in the Valley." Sylvia smiled at Caroline's reaction. "Yes, even Command-Tacticians have superiors, usually older and more experienced Command-Tacticians. Mine were unhappy with the way Leader Elymas was organizing his refugee expedition, and decided to take certain aspects of it into their own hands."

"Which ones?"

Sylvia shrugged. "Basically, it was a question of defense capabilities," she said. "In the mix of Gifts Elymas had chosen, they didn't think he was taking enough Warriors, especially given the unknown dangers posed by the Humans the Farseers had seen. There was an extra storage area behind the transport's engine room, so they contrived to select a number of Warriors and conceal them inside. That way, when the inevitable trouble erupted, I'd have a larger contingent to work with."

"I see," Caroline said, nodding. "Only the trouble never happened."

"Of course it happened," Sylvia said. "What do you think we're in right now?"

"I meant it didn't happen back then," Caroline said. "So why didn't you reveal yourselves to the others after you arrived?"

A grimace flicked briefly across Sylvia's face. "As you say, they were able to settle into the city without needing us," she said. "Elymas was already dead, and Nikolos and I didn't think his successors would appreciate our deception. Fortunately, my hidden Warriors had included both males and females, and I had learned there was a great deal of wooded territory north of the city where we could live and breed without really being noticed. So one night I brought the whole group here and began the long process of building a sanctuary and creating an army to defend it, should our people ever need us."

She gestured toward the south. "Now, they do."

"How many of you are there?" Caroline asked. "I was guessing around a hundred fifty."

"Close," Sylvia said. "The enclave numbers a hundred fifty-six, a hundred twenty of them Warriors and Group Commanders. Add those to the sixty already in the city, and I should have enough of a fighting force to quickly and decisively defeat the Grays."

Caroline shivered. Nearly two hundred Green Warriors, with the Grays prepared to face only sixty. It wouldn't be a defeat, it would be a slaughter. "I thought you could only do what your Gift allowed," she said. "How is Nikolos able to handle tactics?"

"Obviously, he can't," Sylvia said. "I've had to coach him the entire way, from the moment we boarded the transport to our last conversation just a few hours ago. Everything you've heard him say has been basically a direct parroting of what I've told him."

She snorted gently. "Except for that little throwaway line he dropped on Saturday about retreating to upstate New York, of course, the comment that put you and Roger on our trail. I was ready to strangle him for that one."

"Oh, I don't know," Caroline said evenly. "It may have started off as a mistake, but you certainly did a very good job of turning it to your advantage." She lifted her eyebrows. "You *did* turn it to your advantage, didn't you?"

Sylvia's lip twitched. "You're referring to your notes, I presume?"

"Yes," Caroline said, her heartbeat picking up its pace. Here it came; the moment of truth. "You knew all along I was going to write them, didn't you?"

"I knew you *had* written them once they were planted," Sylvia said. "But it wasn't until that first dinner, when you showed you were smart enough to pass up what looked like a clear opportunity to escape, that I realized you might also be smart enough and brave enough to find a way to contact the outside world."

"So the thing with those two state troopers was a test?"

"Actually, it was pure happenstance," Sylvia said. "Up until then my plan had simply been to allow you to waste your time and energy trying to persuade the naïve Green to defy her Command-Tactician and come over onto your side. But once you'd shown yourself to be a notch above that, I decided to offer you a more proactive role."

"As a disseminator of disinformation," Caroline said, putting some bitterness into her tone. "I feel honored. So when the Grays assemble in Upper Manhattan tonight to face you, they won't find anyone there?"

"No, there will be a few Warriors coming onto the island there," Sylvia assured her. "Enough to keep the Grays from becoming suspicious. But that isn't where the main thrust will occur. And of course, there certainly won't be any Groundshakers accompanying them."

"Damian will be elsewhere?"

Sylvia shook her head. "Damian doesn't exist," she said. "He was one of the Groundshakers left behind who sent our transport on its way."

Caroline nodded slowly. So she'd been right about that part, too. "Just one more lie?"

"One more attempt to prepare the Grays for the wrong war," Sylvia corrected. "Ever since the beginning of this, whether we were agreeing to sacrifice Melantha or else making up a Damian who didn't exist, the goal has been to deflect their thoughts and attention away from the fact that we have far more Warriors than they realize. *That's* where our hope lies."

"I see," Caroline said heavily, trying to conceal her own cautious trickle of hope. So her second note had made it through. Sylvia had missed the significance of the clue she'd planted and had let it go. "I suppose I should be relieved that you aren't planning to level New York anymore. Or will that change if you find Melantha again?"

"I never wanted to level New York or kill any of your people," Sylvia said, an odd intensity to her tone. "I still don't. I may not have any genuine affection for you, but I bear you no ill will, either."

"No, all you want is the chance to finally use your Gift," Caroline said, grimacing.

Sylvia lifted her eyebrows. "We *have* been using our Gifts," she said. "A Warrior's true Gift isn't fighting per se, but simply the protection of our people. True, sometimes that Gift involves combat, but more often it simply requires thoughtful preparation and watchful waiting."

"You've certainly done plenty of that," Caroline murmured.

Sylvia sighed. "I'm not looking forward to this war, Caroline," she said quietly. "I saw enough death back in the Great Valley to last the rest of my lifetime. But my duty is to protect my people. Whatever I have to do to achieve that end *will* be done."

"I understand," Caroline said. "Do I at least get to go to the city with you? See for myself what exactly you have to do to my people in order to protect yours?"

Sylvia smiled. "Come now, Caroline," she said, gently admonishing. "You can't manipulate me *that* easily. I thought you realized that." The smile faded. "Actually, though, I've already decided to take you with us. Whatever happens tonight, win or lose, you'll be free afterward to return to your home."

"And Roger?"

A shadow passed across Sylvia's face. "Roger's with the Grays," she said. "Whatever happens to him is in their hands now."

There was a moment of silence. Then Sylvia stirred and gestured toward the tray. "You'd better hurry if you're going to finish," she said. "The Warriors are already on the move. It'll soon be time for us to go, as well."

• •

Light was beginning to filter through the curtains across the motel room when the ringing of Fierenzo's cell phone jolted him awake. He grabbed for the arm of the chair he'd been sleeping in, pulling himself mostly upright as he fumbled the phone out of his pocket and thumbed it on. "Fierenzo," he said.

"It's Jon, Tommy," Powell's voice came. "Smith's got the note."

Fierenzo glanced across the room at the glowing numbers of the clock between the two beds—7:02 A.M.—noting peripherally that Jonah had propped himself up on an elbow and was looking a bit blearily at him. "Good," he murmured to his partner, digging out his pad and pen. "He phoned it in, I hope."

"He did indeed," Powell confirmed. "You ready?"

Fierenzo flipped the notebook open to an empty page. "Shoot."

"You were right about it being on the back of a gum wrapper," Powell said. "Smith said it's a little hard to read, but here's his best interpretation: 'Roger: Green Warriors moving NYC Tue night from N . . . sweep S w/Damian behind them . . . must intercept before buildings fall . . . I love you, C.' Any of this making sense to you?"

"All of it, unfortunately," Fierenzo said, scribbling madly. "Okay, I got it."

"Hang on, we're not done," Powell said. "There's also a P.S. It says—"

"Wait a second," Fierenzo interrupted, frowning. There

hadn't been any postscripts on Caroline's first note. "What kind of P.S.?"

"Just a P.S.," Powell said, sounding puzzled. "Your basic everyday oops-I-forgot-something P.S. Is that a problem?"

"Possibly," Fierenzo said, thinking hard. "Could Smith tell whether it was the same handwriting and pen?"

"I don't know," Powell said, suddenly thoughtful himself. "It must have been at least close or I'm sure he would have said something."

"Call him back and ask," Fierenzo said. "In the meantime, let's hear it."

"Okay," Powell said. "It just says: 'P.S. Watch out for roaming Warriors like on Wed.' Then below that are a bunch of kisses."

Fierenzo frowned. "Kisses?"

"Yeah, you know—a row of X's at the bottom like high-school kids put on their notes. Two rows, in this case: five in the first, four in the second, with three periods after the fourth X in the bottom row."

"Three *periods?*" Fierenzo echoed, thoroughly confused now.

"Yeah," Powell said. "She must really miss him."

"I guess," Fierenzo muttered, adding the three dots to his second row of X's. "That it?"

"That's it," Powell confirmed. "You really know what all this means, huh?"

"Up until the last part I did," Fierenzo admitted. "This 'roaming Warriors' part worries me. I wonder if it means we'll have to deal with a main battle group plus some independents making trouble elsewhere."

"You mean like snipers or saboteurs?"

"Something like that," Fierenzo said hesitantly. "I don't think their main target is the city itself, but we could be talking a huge amount of collateral damage."

"Any idea how many fighters we're talking about?"

"My source tells me the Greens can field up to sixty people," Fierenzo said. "Not too hard to control if they stay together. But if they drop even a few roamers, it's going to stretch our resources pretty damn thin."

"Hell on wheels," Powell muttered.

"Very possibly," Fierenzo agreed. "Look, we need to see the note itself. When you call Smith to check on the handwriting, tell him to hustle himself back down here."

"I will," Powell said. "Do you think the Tuesday in the note is *this* Tuesday? As in, today?"

Fierenzo grimaced. "That's my guess. Looks like someone's moved up Cyril's initial timetable by twenty-four hours. You said you're meeting with Messerling at nine?"

"Yeah, and I'll make sure he knows the alert's been moved up," Powell promised. "What are your plans for the day?"

"Nothing I can discuss on a cell phone," Fierenzo said. "Let me know when Smith thinks he can be back."

"Right."

There was a click, and Fierenzo punched off his phone. "Trouble?" Jonah asked quietly.

"That was my partner," Fierenzo told him, levering himself stiffly out of the chair. "We've got another note from Caroline."

"So I gathered," Jonah said. "That's not what I asked."

Fierenzo shrugged as he headed toward the bathroom. "This particular note has a P.S. that's either a secret message to Roger, a red herring Sylvia herself added on after Caroline hid it, or possibly an indication that Caroline's glue is starting to melt. We won't know until we can look at the original. Maybe not even then."

He was at the sink, splashing cold water on his face, when Powell called back. "I just talked to Smith," he said, his voice tight. "He was sitting in the restaurant parking lot waiting for my call when he saw something interesting go by: five enclosed white Dodge cargo vans in convoy, all coming south on 42 and turning east on 28."

Fierenzo felt a tingle on the back of his neck. The direction Sylvia and her people would come from if they were leaving their stronghold, and the direction they'd be going if they were headed for Manhattan. "Did he get anything on the drivers?"

"Just that they were all young and dark-haired," Powell said. "He also got the tags; I've got DMV running them."

"I don't suppose they were careless enough to put Caroline Whittier in plain sight in any of them, were they?"

"If she was there, Smith didn't spot her," Powell said. "But he was thinking that instead of hightailing it back to the city, maybe he should hang around a bit and see if there's any more traffic. Maybe follow some of it and try to figure out where they're all going."

Fierenzo rubbed the stubble on his cheek as he tried to kick-start his brain. Under normal circumstances, he would certainly want Smith to tail the convoy.

But if he did, he and Powell might not get Caroline's note for several more hours. If the Greens were on the move, they might not have those hours to spare.

"He also suggested faxing us a copy of the note," Powell said into his thoughts. "That won't tell us whether the pen is the same, but at least we could check the handwriting."

"Sounds good," Fierenzo agreed, a little annoyed that he hadn't thought of that himself. "Tell him to see if he can find a place that faxes through a computer instead of just a standard machine. Maybe they can enhance the size or contrast a little."

"He's already spotted a locksmith shop nearby that does shipping and faxes," Powell told him. "And he can even keep an eye on the traffic while he's in there."

"Perfect," Fierenzo said. "What time does it open?"

"Not until ten, but there's a number in the window to call for emergencies. I think this qualifies."

"Definitely," Fierenzo agreed. "Have him fax it to you at the station house, then call me when you've got it. I'll tell you where to meet me."

"Right. Talk to you later."

Clicking off the phone and setting it aside, Fierenzo finished washing his face. "So what's the plan?" a voice asked as he reached for a towel.

He looked over to find that Jonah had followed him to the bathroom doorway. "I'm heading back to the city," he said, rubbing the towel vigorously across his face. "We need to get this message figured out."

"Seems pretty clear to me," Jonah said. "The Greens are coming onto Manhattan tonight from the north and will be pushing their way south, with Damian behind the line to bring down the buildings from under any Grays who are too high for the Shriek to affect."

Fierenzo lowered the towel, looking at Jonah with raised eyebrows. "You left your notebook open," the other explained with a somewhat sheepish smile.

He had, too, now that he thought about it. Sloppy. "I was just amazed you were able to read my handwriting, that's all," he said, hanging the towel back on its rack. "It's mostly that P.S. we're worried about."

"You want me to get everyone up?"

"No, you all might as well get a little more sleep," Fierenzo said. "I've got a friend coming by at one o'clock with a big police van—cop named Al Chenzi; call him Creepers. He'll take you into the city to a hotel across from Police Headquarters. I've already got a room reserved in your name."

"Okay," Jonah said. "How are you getting in? Ferry?"

"No, Creepers' wife lent me her car," Fierenzo told him. "I'll be fine."

"You want me to come along?"

Fierenzo shook his head. "I'd rather all of you stay together and keep an eye on Melantha. Which reminds me."

He reached up and unfastened the hammergun still snugged against his left forearm. "Give this back to Jordan with my thanks," he said, handing it over. "Immensely handy little gadget. I wish I had one on a permanent basis."

"You're welcome," Jonah said. "Come talk to me when this is all over. Maybe we can work something out." His lip twitched. "Maybe even start a new Thor legend."

"Let's just concentrate on getting through the drama we're in the middle of right now," Fierenzo told him grimly, pulling his shirt back on. "Have everybody ready to go by twelve-thirty—the Greens, too. And make sure it's really Chenzi: fifty-five, pure white hair, tiny little mustache you can barely see, blue eyes, missing the last segment of the little finger on his right hand."

"Got it," Jonah said. "You be careful."

"I will," Fierenzo promised. "See you all later."

• •

"Okay, it's sent," the locksmith said, handing Smith the gum wrapper and the receipt. "That'll be fifty-four dollars."

Smith lifted his eyebrows. "Fifty-four *dollars?*"

"It was an off-hours emergency call," the locksmith reminded him. "That's fifty for the call, four for the fax."

"Fine," Smith said, turning around to the shop's big plate glass window as he pulled out his wallet. The traffic was starting to pick up a little, he noted, and he hoped no more of the white vans had sneaked past while he wasn't looking. An old red Ford pickup trundled along behind a more modern Chevy, one of their engines sounding badly in need of a tune-up.

Smith stiffened. The light out there wasn't particularly good, and he'd caught only a glimpse of the pickup's driver as it passed. But unless he was seriously mistaken—

"Hello?" the locksmith prompted from behind him.

Smith yanked out three twenties and slapped them on the counter. "Keep it," he said tersely. Scooping up the gum wrapper and receipt, he shoved open the door and sprinted for his car.

Thirty seconds later, he was back on the highway, roaring off in hot pursuit of the truck. Grabbing his phone, he punched Powell's number. "This is Smith," he said when the detective answered. "I think I've found Mrs. Whittier."

• •

"Absolutely not," Fierenzo said emphatically, stomping hard on the brakes of his borrowed car as he nearly rear-ended a small delivery van. "He can follow the truck, but he's to stay well back. Under *no* circumstances is he to approach it."

"But he says he can get her out," Powell argued. "There was only one other person in the truck, and he said she looked pretty old."

Fierenzo gritted his teeth. "Remember that fancy sonic blast that knocked me on my can outside the park Saturday morning?" he asked. "Sylvia, the old woman, has got the same equipment. If she thinks Smith is crowding her, he could find himself shaking bumpers with a tree."

Powell sighed audibly. "Fine. I'll warn him off, then head in and get the fax. I should be at the precinct in half an hour. How about you?"

"I'm fighting rush-hour traffic," Fierenzo growled. "It could be another hour or more before I get there."

"Do we have that much time to spare?"

Fierenzo glared at the lines of cars and trucks and vans stretching to the horizon ahead of him. No, they damn well might *not* have that much time to spare, he realized. Caroline's note had seemed to indicate the Greens' action had been moved up twenty-four hours, from Wednesday night to Tuesday night.

But the Greens were already on the move. With only a couple hours' drive between them and the city, and at least nine hours until Tuesday night really began, they were already on the move. Did that mean there were several hours' worth of preparations they needed to make once they reached Manhattan?

Or did it mean the timetable had been moved up even further than Caroline had realized? Because if Nikolos had decided to turn Damian loose on Manhattan's skyscrapers in the middle of the workday . . . "You're right," he told Powell. "Okay. There's nothing *I* can do to get in any faster, but we don't have to wait until I'm there to get Whittier started on the note. Maybe he can decipher it while I'm still on the road."

"You know where he is?"

"Room 412 at the Riverview," Fierenzo said, mentally crossing his fingers that neither side had figured out how to tap into the city's cell system. "In fact, complete change of plans," he said suddenly. "When you get to the precinct, call Whittier and tell him to meet me at the Civic Center—I can get there faster than I can to the Two-Four. Then resend Smith's fax down there. Let's see . . . send it to Merri Lang in the Municipal Building. She owes me a favor, and I can trust her to keep her mouth shut."

"Whittier and the fax to Lang; got it," Powell said. "Where do you want Whittier to meet you? You're still listed as missing, you know."

"I hadn't forgotten," Fierenzo assured him. "Lang's floor should be safe enough—no one there reads police bulletins."

"Got it," Powell said. "Anything else?"

"Just trace those vans, and don't miss your appointment with Cerreta and Messerling," Fierenzo told him.

"Right," Powell said. "I'll call if I hear anything."

The phone went dead. Fierenzo tapped the "off" button and dropped the phone on the seat beside him. Glancing at his mirrors, he cut into the next lane and sped up. It was time to show these other yahoos just what thirty-five years of New York driving experience looked like.

• •

The fax was waiting in the machine when Powell arrived at the station house. "Perfect," he muttered to himself as he looked it over. The P.S., in particular, was exactly the way Smith had dictated it.

Now all they had to do was figure out what it meant.

"Powell?" someone called from across the squad room. "DMV's on line four."

"Thanks," Powell called back. Hurrying to his desk, he scooped up the phone and punched the button. "Powell."

"Adamson here, Detective," a woman's voice said in a heavy Brooklyn accent. "I've got those tags you sent us."

"Great," Powell said, flipping his notebook to the right page. "Go."

"All five vans are registered to an E. and O. Green Associates of Bushnellsville, New York," Adamson reported. "They were purchased used two months ago."

"Mm," Powell said. So Smith's instincts had been right: the Greens were indeed on the move. "Anything else?"

"I can get you VINs and such if you really want them," Adamson offered. "I was also a little curious about that purchase date, so I took the liberty of backtracking the previous owners. You interested?"

"Absolutely," Powell said, flipping to the next page.

"Turns out all were owned by various restaurants in the city," she said. "What's really interesting is that all the restaurant owners are also named Green."

Powell frowned. "Really?"

"Really," she assured him. "Is this some sort of insurance scam or something?"

Powell smiled tightly. If she only knew. "You know I can't discuss that with you," he said in his best official-neutral voice. "You have the restaurants' names and addresses?"

He scribbled notes as she read them off. "Okay, great," he said when she had finished. "Thanks."

"Any time, Detective."

He dropped the phone back into its cradle, looking over his list with grim satisfaction. So now they had at least a few solid addresses connected with these elusive Greens. Might be worth taking a closer look at them at some point, maybe see if the businesses' finances and ownerships interlocked in any way. Might even be able to work this into a Federal RICO charge if they found they needed some extra leverage.

But that was for later. Right now, there were more urgent matters to deal with, such as what exactly Sylvia was bringing to Manhattan that required five vans to carry. More gang fighters, perhaps? But the vans Smith had described weren't usually equipped as passenger vehicles. Besides, from what

Fierenzo had said it didn't sound like there were very many people up there. Weapons, then, maybe more of those sonic gadgets? Drugs?

Explosives?

Hauling out his phone directory, he turned to the listing for hotels. He would call Whittier, as Fierenzo had instructed. But after that, he would give the State Police a quick heads-up. If there was something nasty on the highways of New York this morning, they would definitely want to know about it.

• •

"Just a second," Roger said, wedging the phone between his ear and shoulder and digging a pen and a pad of note paper from the bedside table. "Okay; ready."

"Right," Powell said. "Here goes. 'Roger: Green Warriors moving NYC Tue night . . .'"

Roger wrote down the message as the other dictated, his heart pounding with new hope even as yawns of fatigue tugged at his jaws. Caroline was still alive, or at least she had been as of last night. And not only alive, but able to write a succinct yet completely understandable warning to them.

Completely understandable, that is, until Powell got to the P.S.

"Five X's, then four, then three dots?" he asked, frowning at the notepad. "What's that supposed to mean?"

"We were hoping *you* could tell *us*," Powell said. "Could it just be the usual shorthand for sending you kisses?"

"Not a chance," Roger said firmly. "Caroline's never done that before, not in any note or letter she's ever written me."

"Then it's definitely a clue," Powell concluded. "All we have to do is figure out what it means."

Roger grimaced. Translation: now all *he* had to do was figure out what it meant. Caroline was *his* wife, after all. "Any chance of seeing the actual note?"

"It won't be here for a few hours, but we have a very good fax of it," Powell told him. "I'm sending it to a forensic accountant named Merri Lang—she's in the Municipal Building on Centre Street across from City Hall. She'll be expecting you. Detective Fierenzo will meet you there as soon as he can."

"Muni Building; got it," Roger repeated.

"One other thing," Powell said, his voice suddenly a little hesitant. "Officer Smith is currently on the trail of a pickup truck we think came from the place you and Fierenzo visited. We *think* your wife may have been driving it."

Roger squeezed the phone tightly. "Did she look all right?"

"As near as he could tell," Powell said. "Just thought you'd want to know."

"Thanks," Roger said. "Okay, I'm on my way."

"The fax will be waiting," Powell said. "Talk to you later."

Roger hung up the phone and leaned back against the headboard, gazing at the message he'd scribbled on the pad. *Watch out for roaming Warriors like on Wed. XXXXX XXXX* . . . If this was supposed to be clear to him, Caroline had missed by a mile.

But she'd taken the time to write it, and taken the risk of sending it. It had to mean *something*.

His eyes dropped to the rows of X's at the end. They were certainly not kisses; Caroline had always detested cutesy stuff like that. Had she been trying to cross something out? Did the X's mean the first nine letters of the note should be erased? Or the last nine letters? Maybe the first or last nine letters of her previous note?

"What's the word?" Velovsky murmured from the other bed.

"Sorry—didn't mean to wake you," Roger apologized. "We got a message from Caroline."

"Clear as mud, I take it?"

"Actually, mostly it's very readable," Roger said. "You're the expert on all things Green. Does a row of X's have any particular significance?"

"It's slang for smooches," Velovsky rumbled. "Like S.W.A.K., and all that. Weren't you ever a teenager?"

"My mother once said I was born forty," Roger told him. "I was asking about *Green* culture and slang."

"Nothing that I know of," Velovsky said. "Is *that* what she put in her note? A bunch of X's?"

"Among other things," Roger said, tearing off the top page of the notepad and folding it in half. "I'm going to take a quick shower, then I've got to go."

"Help yourself," Velovsky said, closing his eyes again and rolling over onto his side. "And don't slam the door on your way out. Two o'clock checkout, you said?"

"Right," Roger confirmed. "Pleasant dreams."

The other didn't answer. Grimacing, Roger got out of bed and crossed to the bathroom. Caroline, Fierenzo had suggested on the way to the Green estate, didn't think the same way Roger himself did.

He could only hope the detective had been overstating the case a little. Because if he couldn't reconstruct her thinking, the risk she'd taken would be for nothing.

He'd failed her enough times lately. He couldn't afford to fail her again.

• •

The traffic had been getting steadily heavier for the past fifteen minutes as the highway approached the Thruway and the more populous region along the Hudson River. Smith stayed on the red Ford's tail, trying to strike that magic balance between being close enough to see the subject, yet far enough back that the subject wouldn't spot *him*. He'd had some training in the technique, but all of his admittedly limited experience had been in the city, where the distance guidelines were completely different.

He frowned ahead down the highway. Coming his direction in the other lane, he could see a white van. One of the group he'd seen driving east through Shandaken an hour and a half ago? If so, what was it doing heading back west? He lifted his foot off the gas, letting the car slow down a little in hopes of catching the license plate as the van passed.

And then, without warning, it swerved into his lane, coming straight toward him.

Smith reacted instantly, leaning on the horn as he slammed on his brakes, drifting as far right as he could without going off the road. But it kept coming. He angled the car even farther right, eyes flicking back and forth between the van and the shoulder, searching desperately for someplace to escape to without going down the shallow embankment into the drainage ditch that ran alongside the road. But there was nothing; no driveways, no parking lots, nothing even remotely flat.

The van was still coming. With a curse, Smith gave up, twisting the wheel and bracing himself as the car shot off the road. He had a glimpse of the van suddenly swerving back into its own lane—

And then he was sliding down the embankment, the nose of the car dipping sharply into the ditch and then bouncing up again as he rolled up the other side.

For a moment he just sat there, his heart pounding, his body shaking with adrenaline shock. The engine idle still sounded okay, and the hood looked undamaged from where he was sitting. With luck, maybe he'd been able to slow down enough before going off the road that he hadn't done any serious damage to anything.

There was a cautious crunching of gravel from behind him. He twisted in his seat, half expecting to see the white van returning to finish the job they'd started. But it was just a late-model Lincoln with a balding, middle-aged Good Samaritan staring wide-eyed at him from behind the wheel. He was talking urgently on his cell, probably whistling up the nearest cop.

Smith took a deep breath. A cop, and a tow truck, a little bit of luck with his suspension and radiator, and he would be out of here.

But in the meantime . . .

With a sigh, he turned off the engine and fished out his cell phone. "This is Smith," he said disgustedly when Powell answered. "I've lost them."

42

"That's it," the cabby announced, pointing ahead as they turned off Broadway and drove alongside the park surrounding City Hall. "Where do you want off?"

"Anywhere along here is fine," Roger told him.

The cabby pulled over to the curb and stopped. "Thanks," Roger said, paying him and climbing out. The vehicle pulled away, and he set off down the sidewalk toward the towering Municipal Building, wondering what kind of security they had in there these days. Hopefully, this Lang person would have left word at the front desk that he was expected.

"Hello, Roger," a voice said from behind him.

Roger spun around, his heart suddenly pounding. Torvald was standing in the middle of the sidewalk a couple of paces away, his face expressionless. "Oh," Roger said, the word coming out weak and rather inane. "Hello, Torvald."

"You're late," the other said gravely.

It took Roger a second, and then he grimaced. Yes—the appointment he and Simon had arranged Saturday morning, just before Aleksander's people had swooped in on him and Caroline. The appointment, now that he thought about it, that he hadn't intended to keep in the first place. "Sorry about that," he said. "We got a little sidetracked."

"So I heard." Torvald lifted his eyebrows. "Perhaps I could have a few moments of your time now."

Roger hesitated. But here, surrounded by courts and cops, surely Torvald wouldn't be crazy enough to try anything. "I suppose I can spare a minute," he said, shifting his own voice into neutral and looking around. There didn't seem to be any benches at this end of the park. "Where?"

"Let's take a walk," Torvald suggested, stepping to his side and gesturing him ahead. "A walk around a park is always a pleasant way to pass the time."

"You do enjoy pushing the envelope, don't you?" Roger asked, eyeing the trees as they started off, slowing from his usual pace to stay with Torvald and his limp. "How did you find me, anyway?"

"Halfdan's surveillance network spotted Velovsky leaving his home last night and going to your hotel, though of course no one understood the significance of it at the time," Torvald said. "Under the assumption that you, at least, might return there for the night, I sent Garth to watch the place. He overheard you mention the Municipal Building, so I came down to await your appearance."

"I see," Roger said. "How is Garth doing, by the way?"

"Mostly fine," Torvald said, smiling faintly. "Mad enough to chew granite, though."

Roger glanced up at the buildings towering around them. Was Garth up on one of them right now pointing a hammer-gun in his direction? "I hope he realizes it wasn't personal."

Torvald nodded; agreement or simple acknowledgment, Roger couldn't tell which. "You fooled us all," the Gray said. "You and Jonah both. I take it his whole family is in on this?"

"That's not really something I can discuss."

"And that policeman, too, of course," Torvald continued. "Detective Fierenzo. Yes, you had us nicely fooled. My congratulations on an excellent job."

His eyes met Roger's. "But I need her back," he said, his voice quiet but earnest. "It's the only chance the city has. If the Greens get hold of her, we're all going to die."

"*All* of us?" Roger countered pointedly. "Or just all of you Grays?"

Torvald's lips compressed into a thin line. "So much for

the compassion of Humans," he said, an edge of bitterness in his voice. "*Yes,* it will be mostly Greens and Grays who will die. Does that make you feel better?"

"Not especially, no," Roger said, his face warming with embarrassment. It had been a stupid thing to say. "I'm sorry. I didn't mean it that way."

"How *did* you mean it?"

"I was mostly questioning your sales pitch," Roger said. "I don't especially want anyone to die, on either side. But threatening me and the city isn't the way to earn my cooperation."

Torvald shook his head. "It wasn't a threat," he said. "It was a statement of fact. Yes, the Greens are coming mainly for us; but don't think you and your fellow Humans will escape unscathed. Aleksander and Nikolos fully intend to wipe us out; and if they have to order Damian to bring down every building in Manhattan to accomplish that, they will."

Roger felt his stomach tightening. "I thought you didn't believe Damian was still alive."

"What I never believed was that a Command-Tactician like Nikolos would stand meekly by and let his ultimate weapon be destroyed," Torvald countered darkly. "I knew there was something else going on behind those earnest Green expressions, which is why I never trusted the agreement Halfdan and Cyril worked out to sacrifice Melantha. I simply didn't know what exactly the trick was that the Greens had up their sleeve. Now, we do."

Roger stared at him, the conversation with Jonah and Jordan about competing Groundshakers flashing to mind. "Is that why you snatched her from the courtyard Friday night?" he asked. "You knew about Damian and knew that Melantha was the only person who might be able to counter him?"

"No, on both counts," Torvald said. "I never had even a hint that Damian might be alive until you dropped his name Sunday night." He grimaced. "As for Melantha standing up to him, there's very little chance of that, either. She's far too young to counter an adult Groundshaker."

"Then why take her?" Roger persisted. "So you could kill her and blame it on the Greens?"

Torvald snorted. "You persist on getting things backwards, Roger. *Halfdan* is the one who worked out this Peace Child plan with Cyril. I never agreed to it."

"Because you wanted war?"

"Because I wanted us to have this out like soldiers, not politicians," Torvald bit out. "What kind of soldier demands the death of a young girl to give himself a battlefield advantage?"

"But you put a tracer on me," Roger protested, feeling his assumptions threatening to slide out from under him. Torvald, the alleged bloodthirsty warmonger, concerned about the method by which victory was obtained? "And then you snatched Melantha away from us."

"What else could I do?" Torvald demanded, his voice still charged with emotion. "Halfdan's sons were perched on the back of one of the buildings and Cyril had half a dozen Greens in trees down the street, all of them patiently waiting for the police to finish up and leave. If Garth and Wolfe hadn't gotten there first, Melantha would have been dead by morning."

"Are you trying to tell me," Roger said slowly, "that you've been holding her in protective custody?"

Torvald exhaled heavily. "What's the point?" he muttered. "She didn't believe me. Why should I expect you to be any smarter?"

Roger stared at him, feeling more adrift than ever. Could Torvald be telling the truth? Melantha had certainly been in good shape when they'd burst in on her a few hours ago; not tied or gagged, looking clean and more or less comfortable, with the remains of a good meal on a tray over on one side of the room. True, her guards had fired on them; but if Torvald was right, the most likely intruders would have been Halfdan's people, who would have taken her away to be killed. "Tell me something," he said. "Why did you move into Manhattan in the first place?"

Torvald smiled tightly. "Don't you really mean, why did I

move into Manhattan a block away from a Green homestead?"

"Consider the question rephrased," Roger said. "Why did you?"

Torvald's eyes shifted past him, to the trees rustling in the breeze in the park. "The first few weeks after the unexpected contact between our peoples were very strange," he said, his voice oddly meditative. "Like a combination of cold-war posturing and slow-motion ballet. Both sides were feeling out the other, looking for strengths and weaknesses, maneuvering politically and geographically for future advantage. It seemed to me that we were heading toward the sort of frozen trench warfare that gripped Europe in the first World War."

His eyes came back to Roger's face. "People can't live like that, Roger," he said. "It saps the energy and the will, weaving an element of distraction and fear into both sides' psyches and daily lives. Worse, it sets the stage for animosities that may never be eliminated. You've seen it happen in a hundred different places on your world. I didn't want that for my people *or* for the Greens."

He gestured toward the north. "So I decided to force the issue, one way or the other. I moved my family into MacDougal Alley, a street that was probably half owned by Greens at the time. I hoped that would either precipitate a full-fledged shooting war, which would settle things once and for all, or force us to learn to live in peace the way we had in the Great Valley. Either way, it would have been over."

"With one side possibly destroyed?"

"I was hoping we would find wisdom before that happened." Torvald grimaced. "Instead, the Greens found Melantha."

For a minute they walked together in silence. "All right," Roger said at last. "So you say you're on Melantha's side."

"I'm on the *Grays'* side," Torvald corrected him tartly. "But I also have no interest in seeing her slaughtered like a sacrificial goat." He shook his head. "But matters are out of our hands now, yours and mine both. Your upstate Greens seem to be on the move."

Roger felt his breath catch. "What do you mean?"

"There's a police alert out on five white cargo vans presumably heading this direction from the Catskills," Torvald told him. "Whatever Nikolos was building or preparing up there, he's bringing it to the city. And history suggests that Command-Tacticians never begin something until they're ready to follow through."

He gestured toward the park. "The maneuvering and posturing are over. All we can do now is brace ourselves for whatever he has planned."

Roger looked over at the gently waving trees. Powell hadn't mentioned this part. "You say you'd prefer for your peoples to live in peace," he said. "Are you willing to prove it?"

Torvald studied him through narrowed eyes. "How?" he asked.

"I don't know yet," Roger conceded. "But there may come a time in the next few hours when I'll think of something."

"You have my phone number," Torvald told him, coming to a stop and holding out his hand. "Call me any time."

"I will," Roger said, taking his hand. Torvald squeezed it briefly, then turned and started to walk away. "One more question," Roger called after him. "Is there any particular significance in Gray culture to a row of X's?"

The other turned back, frowning. "X's?"

"Specifically, a row of five with another row of four beneath them followed by three dots."

"Not that I've ever heard of." Torvald cocked his head slightly. "Does this mean you have a new message from Caroline?"

Roger hesitated. "Yes, but we haven't yet completely deciphered it. Actually, that's why I'm going to the Municipal Building."

"I see," Torvald said, eyeing him closely. "Bear in mind that both our peoples are in Nikolos's sights now. If we don't stand together, many of us will likely be dead before tomorrow morning."

"I understand," Roger said. "I'll do what I can to keep you in the loop."

"Very well," Torvald said. "In the same spirit of cooperation, it may be of use for you to know that late yesterday afternoon Nikolos was seen leaving his homestead in Morningside Park and heading south in a cab."

Roger frowned. Not north? "Where did he go?"

Torvald shook his head. "Unfortunately, Halfdan's surveillance network has become somewhat strained as of late and lost him somewhere south of Times Square." His lips compressed briefly. "Several of his people have been pulled off sentry duty to look for your friend Jonah."

"Pity," Roger said. "It might have been helpful to know where Nikolos ended up."

"I'm aware of that," Torvald said. "I've had my people out looking for him ever since I learned he'd disappeared. So far, we haven't found him."

Roger grimaced. "Keep trying."

"We will," Torvald assured him. "Call me."

"I will," Roger promised.

With a final nod, Torvald headed away down the sidewalk.

Roger watched until he had disappeared into the flow of pedestrians. Then, taking a deep breath, he turned back and headed with new urgency toward the Municipal Building and the fax waiting there for him.

● ●

"I don't know," S.W.A.T. Commander Messerling said, tapping his teeth gently with the end of his pencil as he stared at the Manhattan map on the conference room wall. "Assuming your informant is right about a sweep from the north, the Broadway or Henry Hudson Bridges are the obvious entry points, with the Washington, the George Washington, and the Cross-Bronx as secondaries."

"That's one hell of a cover zone," Lieutenant Cerreta pointed out. "Even with the tag numbers, there are a lot of white Dodge vans on the roads."

"Personally, I'm more worried about the gang members already in the city," Messerling said. "I don't suppose you have any idea where they might be centered."

"I've got five possible leads, but no actual evidence," Powell said, opening his notebook to his list of Green restaurants. "Two months ago, these businesses sold the upstate group the vans we think they're currently using."

"Way too thin for a warrant," Cerreta commented.

"We might be able to get in under one of the Homeland Security Acts," Messerling said doubtfully. "But that would mean bringing in the Feds."

"Detective Fierenzo was rather hoping we could avoid that," Powell said.

"That was *before* he disappeared," Messerling pointed out darkly. "He might be feeling differently right now."

"Assuming his disappearance and this gang war are related," Cerreta said. "Still nothing on his car?"

"It hadn't been approached during the twenty-four hours before we gave up and had it towed in," Powell said, an uncomfortable feeling churning in his gut. When Cerreta found out that Fierenzo was alive and well, there were going to be five circles of hell to pay. "So far, CSU hasn't found anything useful."

Cerreta grunted. "I don't know," he said. "Play that tape again, will you?"

Powell touched the button on his recorder, replaying the tape of Cyril's message they'd made from the Whittiers' answering machine. "A possible kidnapping, except that no one named Melantha has been reported missing," Cerreta mused. "Vague threats, but no indication of anything other than homegrown thugs. No foreign connections at all. I'm not sure we could get the Feds in on this even if we wanted them."

"So we do it ourselves," Messerling said. "Fine. When do we need to be set up?"

"That's part of the problem," Powell said. "The message indicates that the confrontation will take place tomorrow night. More recently we got information that it would be tonight instead. But those vans are already on the move, which means it could be as early as this afternoon."

"Or they may have decided it would be safer to cross the bridge when there was more traffic," Cerreta suggested. "Once they're in, it would be easy enough to go to ground and wait for nightfall." He gestured at Powell's notebook. "Possibly at one of those restaurants."

From Powell's pocket came the faint ring of his cell phone. "Excuse me," he said, digging out the phone and punching in on. "Powell."

"Jon, it's me," Fierenzo's voice came tautly. "We've got it."

• •

Roger was sitting in a small waiting area down the hallway from Merri Lang's office, staring at the fax she'd given him, when someone dropped into the chair beside him. He started; but it was just Fierenzo. "Lang told me where you went," the detective said, holding out his hand. "What do you think?"

"It's like two different people wrote this," Roger said as he handed over the fax. "The first part is obviously shorthand, but the meaning is crystal-clear. The P.S., on the other hand, is almost wordy by comparison, and about as clear as a bureaucratic form."

"But it *is* Caroline's writing on both of them?" Fierenzo asked, studying the paper.

"It all looks like her printing, yes," Roger confirmed. "I just don't understand why she would suddenly change styles that way."

"Let's assume Caroline has the first part ready to go when she suddenly learns something new," Fierenzo said, handing back the fax and leaning back in his chair. Lacing his fingers together behind his head, he stared up at the ceiling. "She wants to add it to the note; but for some reason she also wants to make sure it *won't* be understood if the wrong people find it."

"The wrong people being Sylvia?"

"That's the most obvious wrong person," Fierenzo agreed. "So now she has to write this new information in a way that only the *right* person will understand, that right person being you or one of the Grays."

Roger shook his head. "I've already run the multiple-X thing past Torvald. It didn't strike any particular chords."

Fierenzo frowned. "You talked to *Torvald*?"

"He met me on the way over here," Roger said. "We had an interesting conversation."

"You didn't tell him about the message, did you?

"I told him there was one, but that we still needed to figure it out," Roger said. "You have any thoughts?"

"Only the broad scenario I just laid out," Fierenzo murmured. "But don't forget that she doesn't necessarily think the same way you do. You may be looking at this in a literal way, whereas she might mean something symbolic."

Roger snorted. "Frankly, I was assuming the whole thing was symbolic."

"Not necessarily," Fierenzo said. "There are parts that are almost certainly literal. This 'roaming Warriors on Wed' line, for instance. The Wednesday reference seems pretty concrete."

"Well, we sure didn't see any Warriors last Wednesday," Roger told him. "At least, not that I know of. I sort of assumed the Wednesday reference meant tomorrow, not last week, and that she was trying to warn us that after whatever happens tonight there would still be Warriors around tomorrow."

"Possibly," Fierenzo said. "But I'm not ready to give up on last Wednesday just yet. Tell me everything that happened that day."

"We went to work," Roger said, frowning as he thought back. After everything that had happened in the past few days, last Wednesday seemed like an eternity ago. "We came home, ate dinner—"

"What did you have?"

"Fish," Roger said. "Then we got ready for the play, argued a little about whether to walk or take a cab and about not getting enough exercise. Then we went to the play. At the end she managed to lose a ring under the seat, so that when we left all the cabs were already gone. We started walking home, discussed the play a little . . ."

He trailed off as the whisper of something caught at the edge of his mind. *Watch out for roaming Warriors. . . .*

"What is it?" Fierenzo asked quietly.

"She liked the play a lot," Roger said slowly. "I mostly didn't. It was one of these deep, psychological things, with a typically ridiculous love triangle in the middle of it." He shook his head as it belatedly struck him. "Relational thinking," he said. "No wonder she likes things like that while I don't. *I'm* watching the plot contrivances; *she's* watching the character interactions."

"What in particular did either of you say about it?" Fierenzo asked. "Anything about Romans?"

"No," Roger said, staring at the tiny letters Caroline had printed. "No, wait a minute. I did make a comment about—" He looked sharply at Fierenzo. "About Latin *lovers,*" he said. "Roman Warriors; Latin lovers."

Fierenzo shook his head. "You've lost me."

"I called the villain in the play a Latin lover," Roger said, stumbling over the words as his tongue tried to keep up with his brain. "Caroline pointed out he was French; I said he was a Latin lover in the generic sense; she asked if that was the same sense as the 'when in Rome' cliché. You see? Latin—Roman. Roman—roaming."

Fierenzo still had a wary look on his face. "I hope there's more to this."

"Plenty more," Roger said grimly. "Because right after I dropped that reference we argued a little about whether the main female character was a victim or not. I thought the woman was dragged unknowingly to her doom. *She* argued that the character knew what was going on the whole time."

"Knew what was going on," Fierenzo murmured, half to himself. "Knew what was . . ." He broke off. "Sylvia knew she was leaving notes?"

"That's what it sounds like to me," Roger agreed. "And

that fits with Caroline suddenly having to put this into code. What I don't understand is if Sylvia found out about that first note, why didn't she just keep Caroline inside where she couldn't leave another one?"

"Obviously, because she *wanted* Caroline to leave it," Fierenzo said grimly. "Sylvia's been feeding her disinformation and deliberately letting her pass in on to us." He looked at the fax. "Which means everything above the P.S. is garbage. The Greens aren't attacking from the north at all."

"But if Caroline knew it was a lie, why send it at all?" Roger asked, frowning.

"Because by then she knew her first note was disinformation, too," Fierenzo told him. "Problem was, there was nothing she could do to call it back. Since the Greens were vetting the notes, and since Sylvia obviously wouldn't let a straight warning get through, she had to say what Sylvia wanted and then piggyback this P.S. onto it and hope they couldn't figure it out."

"And hope that we could," Roger said, thinking back to her first note and the supposed confirmation of Damian's existence. "Does this mean that there isn't any Damian?"

"I'd say there's a real good chance of that," Fierenzo agreed. "Looks like Torvald and Ron were right—the whole thing was never anything but a scam. A little bait to lure the Grays into planning for the wrong war." He tapped the fax. "And maybe being caught on the wrong part of the island to boot."

"Okay," Roger said slowly. "But if there's no Damian, then what's the trap?"

"Oh, my God," Fierenzo murmured, his face suddenly turned to stone. "What am I using for brains? Your wife's a genius, Roger. All she has is a gum wrapper; so what does she do but make her words do double duty. One clue, two different meanings."

He nodded at the fax. "'Roman Warriors' points to your Latin lover and Sylvia, all right. But it also clues us in to the X's at the bottom."

Roger caught his breath. "Are you saying . . . Roman *numerals*?"

"And at X equals ten, that's ninety Warriors," Fierenzo said. "Or more—those three dots probably mean the series continues."

He looked at Roger, his face tight. "*There's* Nikolos's dirty little secret, Roger. No wonder he didn't care if Melantha died Wednesday in Riverside Park. He's got a private army of Warriors stashed away in the Catskills."

"With the Grays only expecting the sixty they know about," Roger said, a shiver running up his back. "Nikolos is going to pull a Little Bighorn on them."

"Not if I can help it," Fierenzo said, pulling out his cell and punching the buttons. "Maybe we can intercept those vans before—Jon, it's me. We've got it."

● ●

"Okay, we're on it," Powell said, scribbling one last note. "Thanks."

He punched off the cell. "That was my informant," he told Cerreta and Messerling. "New information: those vans may be carrying soldiers. Possibly over a hundred of them."

"Soldiers?" Messerling said, frowning. "I thought we were talking about a gang war."

"So this means we *are* talking terrorists?" Cerreta added.

"No, it's still a gang war," Powell said hastily, trying to remember the precise words Fierenzo had told him to use. "But this group has been specially trained and equipped."

"So bottom line is that we're now talking between a hundred fifty and two hundred fighters on the streets?" Messerling asked.

"And that's just on one side," Powell said, nodding. "And it gets worse. There are indications the attack we've been expecting will be only a feint. That means the main thrust could come from any direction."

"Unless we can nab them before they get to choose which

bridge or tunnel they want," Cerreta said, picking up the phone and punching in a number.

"State Police?" Messerling asked.

Cerreta nodded. "That type of van normally isn't equipped for passengers," he said. "If they've got that many people crammed in there, we can get them on a traffic violation long enough to search for weapons. Yeah—this is Cerreta; NYPD. Get me Kowalsky in Operations."

"Fine, but what's our reason for stopping them in the first place?" Messerling asked.

"Smith was tracking some white vans," Cerreta said, holding his hand over the mouthpiece. "A white van deliberately forced him off the road. Since we don't know which one it was, we'll just have to stop all of them while we figure it out."

"I'll buy that," Messerling agreed, nodding. "I just hope a judge will, too."

"Let's worry about that after we get them off the road." Cerreta held up his hand. "Matt? It's Paul Cerreta. I've got a little problem for you. . . ."

43

"There!" Officer Alfonse Keely said, pointing at the row of white vans speeding toward them down the Thruway. "Ross?"

"That's them," his partner confirmed, half his face covered by the massive binoculars gripped in his hands. "Tags one . . . two . . . yeah, that's them." He lowered the binoculars, frowning. "I thought Dispatch said there were five of them."

"Yeah, I count eight, too," Keely said grimly, picking up the mike. "Dispatch; Bravo-two-seven. Got a hit on eight, repeat *eight*, white Dodge vans: tags confirmed on five of them. Heading southbound, just passing Arden."

"Dispatch, copy," a crisp female voice replied. "Pursue and observe only."

"Roger that," Keely said, setting down the mike and starting the engine. Letting the vans pass, he pulled out onto the highway behind them.

He still didn't know what exactly this alert was all about. Dispatch was being very hush-hush, and even the usual departmental grapevine hadn't been any help.

But whatever this bug was that Manhattan had up its butt, it was apparently a big and hairy one. Before they'd gone two miles a half-dozen terse positioning orders came over the radio as an unknown number of cars were zeroed in on the convoy. Over the next ten miles, Keely noticed an ever-increasing number of squad cars drifting casually into view in front of or behind the vans. The orders tapered off, and for another couple of miles Keely wondered if maybe someone had decided to forget the whole thing—

"Units four and six: close off," the radio crackled suddenly. "All units: move in to assist. Use extreme caution—driver and passengers armed and dangerous."

And with that, red lights exploded into view all around them, not just from the marked cars but from a half-dozen unmarked ones as well. "Holy Mother," Ross muttered as he flipped on their own light bar. "What the hell *is* this?"

"With this much firepower on tap?" Keely countered. "Ten to one it's terrorists."

"Terrific," Ross grunted, popping their shotgun from its rack. Chambering a round, he held it ready between his knees.

Two of the squad cars were directly in front of the vans now, with three more pacing them. The drivers took the hint, maneuvering carefully through the rest of the startled traffic flow to the right-hand lane. For another minute they kept going, as if trying to decide just how serious the cops really were. Keely gripped the wheel hard, hoping they wouldn't be stupid enough to make a run for it. He'd seen the aftermath of a high-speed gun battle once, and it hadn't been pretty.

The pacing patrol cars moved closer, solidly boxing them in. The vans held their speed another few seconds, then finally bowed to the inevitable and pulled off the road, rolling to a stop beside a cluster of tall maple trees. The cops pulled off with them, positioning themselves fore and aft to block off any chance of escape, with a couple more parking half on the road alongside them to make double sure. Keely found himself a slot five cars back, and a moment later he and Ross were hurrying forward toward the line of vans along with a dozen other cops. The ones who'd made it to the vans first were already shouting orders and pulling open doors, their weapons at the ready.

And because Keely happened to be looking at the faces of the cops at the rear van, he caught the abrupt change in their expressions. "What've we got?" he called as he jogged up beside them.

Silently, one of them gestured into the van with his shotgun. Frowning, Keely eased to the door and looked inside.

The driver was sitting motionlessly, his hands in plain sight on the steering wheel, his face composed and unconcerned as he stared straight ahead through the windshield.

The rest of the van was empty.

• •

"What do you mean, empty?" Powell demanded, staring at Messerling in disbelief. "They *can't* be empty."

"Well, they are," the other insisted, pressing the phone a little harder to his ear. "Drivers only. No passengers, no weapons, no explosives, no contraband. Not even jumper cables. Nothing."

"What about the drivers?" Cerreta asked. "How do they seem?"

Messerling relayed the question. "Pretty damn calm," he reported. "No panic; apparently not even any surprise."

"With how many cops on the scene?"

"About thirty."

Cerreta looked at Powell. "Your average Joe Citizen

would be having a stroke about now," he said. "These guys were expecting this."

"Only they were expecting it far enough in advance to offload their people before we got there," Powell agreed sourly.

"Looks that way," Cerreta agreed.

"Lieutenant, have those vehicles checked, top to bottom," Messerling ordered into the phone. "And bring in the drivers."

He waited for an acknowledgment, then hung up. "They'll be here in an hour," he reported.

"Good," Cerreta said. "Let's just hope we can get something out of them."

"Don't worry," Messerling said tightly. "We will."

* *

They had the drivers lined up beside the vans and had frisked them for weapons; and the cops were just readying their handcuffs when all eight men suddenly bolted.

It was, Keely would realize afterward, an exquisitely coordinated move. All he saw in the heat of the moment, though, was the sudden flurry of activity as each driver shrugged off the hands holding him, gut-punched anyone standing too close, and made a mad and clearly futile dash for the clump of trees beside the road.

"Hold your fire!" the lieutenant in charge shouted from the far end of the line. "Grab them!"

The cops were already on the move, surging after them like Coney Island breakers heading for the beach. Keely joined the rush, a small corner of his mind recognizing that the would-be escapees would be run to ground long before he could reach the party, but caught up nevertheless in the mass excitement.

"Where the hell do they think they're going?" Ross huffed from beside him.

"Who knows?" Keely said, wondering if the whole bunch had gone simultaneously insane. There couldn't be more than a couple dozen trees there—he could see straight through the clump to the snow fence and the rocky field behind it, for Pete's sake. Where did they think they were going to hide?

The drivers reached the first line of trees maybe five paces ahead of their pursuers, ducking and veering around the thick trunks like tight ends punching through a swarm of defenders. One of them ducked down, scooped up an armful of dead leaves, and half-turned to hurl them into the air behind him.

Reflexively, Keely winced back, his eyes flicking to the fluttering leaves just long enough to confirm there wasn't anything solid like a grenade or satchel charge flying through the air with them, then turned his attention back downward.

The drivers were gone.

He caught his breath, his feet still thudding across the loose dirt, his brain refusing to acknowledge what his eyes were telling him. In that single instant of inattention, without any fuss, bother, smoke, or mirrors, all eight men had vanished as if swallowed up by the earth itself.

The pack of cops in front of him obviously didn't believe it, either. They charged straight through into the miniature forest, guns ready, heads wagging this way and that as they searched for their quarry. Five seconds later, they ran out the other side, jogging to a confused halt. "What are you waiting for?" the lieutenant shouted, sounding as bewildered as everyone else looked. "Come on, they're there somewhere. Find them. Damn it all, *find* them!"

• •

Fierenzo held the phone to his ear, the taste of stomach acid in his mouth. "All of them?" he asked.

"*All* of them," Powell gritted, his voice as angry and troubled and just plain scared as Fierenzo had ever heard it. "Eight grown men, vanished in a clump of trees a rabbit shouldn't have been able to hide in."

"What about the vans?"

"To hell with the vans," Powell snarled. "Up to now I've been willing to play along with this without anything stronger than your personal say-so. But this has gone *way* beyond partner loyalty."

Fierenzo winced. "Should you be saying this sort of—?"

"Don't worry, I'm in the stairwell," Powell growled. "But I'm serious. You going to tell me what's going on, or do I have to bail?"

Fierenzo gripped the phone tightly, his eyes darting to where Roger sat very still across the coffee shop table. "I can't," he said, keeping his voice steady. "Not yet. I gave my word."

"Something's about to happen to this city, Tommy," Powell reminded him tightly. "If you know anything—*anything*—you have a sworn duty to report it."

"I've reported as much as I can, Jon," Fierenzo said. "I'm still working on it at my end, just as you are at yours. Trust me a little longer, will you?"

He heard Powell take a deep breath. "We are both going to burn in hell," the other said at last. "All right, a little longer. But that's all. Those soldiers of yours are on their way, and we have no idea when or where or how they're going to hit the city."

"We'll find them," Fierenzo promised, wishing he had even a shred of hope that he could actually do so.

"We'd better," Powell said. "I'll talk to you later."

Fierenzo punched off the phone. "They got away?" Roger asked.

"Of course they got away," Fierenzo bit out. "The idiots let them park their vans right beside a clump of trees."

Roger made a face. "There wasn't anything you could have done."

"Of course there was," Fierenzo snapped back. "I knew what Greens can do. I could have warned them."

"You think they would have believed you?"

"That's irrelevant."

"Hardly," Roger said scornfully. "Lot of good you'd do anyone locked in the psych ward at Bellevue."

"Lot of good I'm doing right now," Fierenzo muttered.

"Melantha's alive and free," Roger reminded him. "That's a pretty fair amount of good right there."

"I suppose," Fierenzo conceded, mentally shaking away the cobwebs. Time to stop feeling sorry for himself and attack this thing logically. "Okay. They've switched vehicles, so we can't shadow them. If they keep quiet even other Greens can't detect them, so putting Melantha's parents out as spotters won't help. What else have we got?"

"I don't know," Roger said, fiddling with a coffee stirrer. "You suppose the Grays have a way of spotting them at a distance?"

"I doubt it," Fierenzo said. "If they could, they should have nailed Melantha a lot sooner."

"It still wouldn't hurt to run it past Jonah," Roger pointed out, glancing surreptitiously around the coffee shop and lifting his left hand.

"Okay, but just ask him about Green detectors," Fierenzo warned. "Don't tell him why we need to know. *Or* what was in Caroline's message."

Roger frowned. "You're not going to tell them?"

"Not yet," Fierenzo said. "I don't want anyone else in the picture until we have a plan."

"But—"

"No argument," Fierenzo said, glaring across the table. "I'm not in the mood."

Roger glared back, but nodded. "Fine," he said. Twitching his little finger, he lifted his hand to his cheek.

● ●

This was, Smith groused silently to himself as he drove slowly through the streets of Stony Hollow, turning out to be a truly rotten day.

He'd alerted Powell and Cerreta to the existence of the

white vans, only to have the drivers of those vans somehow elude thirty cops and escape. He'd located Caroline Whittier, only to get run off the road and lose her. He'd called in the description of the red Ford pickup, including its plate number, only to be told that it hadn't been spotted since it disappeared from Smith's own sight over that hill.

On the other hand, he *hadn't* officially clocked in for work today down at the Two-Four, and even though Powell had assured him he would take care of it, he suspected his partner Hill would be claiming a big chunk of his hide when he *did* show his face at the station house again.

And now here he was, driving around in a slightly banged-up car through the modest towns scattered along the highway, looking for God only knew what. It would have been so much handier if the men in the vans had abandoned them somewhere near where they'd picked up their new rides; say, beside a car-rental agency or bus station. But they'd been smart enough not to leave behind any such obvious pointers.

But Caroline Whittier and the old woman she'd been riding with might not have been so clever. If they'd ditched their pickup somewhere around here, and if he could find it, maybe he could figure out what the whole bunch of them were now driving.

It was a faint hope, he knew. But at the moment it was the only game in town. At least it was better than going back to Manhattan and facing Officer Hill.

Ahead, an increased speed-limit sign marked the edge of this particular town. Speeding up, keeping his eyes peeled, he headed for the next.

● ●

Cerreta didn't quite slam the phone down as he hung up, but he wasn't all that far from it. "No, I take it?" Powell asked, cupping his palm over the mouthpiece of his own phone.

"Even less than no," the lieutenant confirmed with a

scowl. "He said he might just refuse my next warrant request, too, just to make up for interrupting his morning with this one."

"It didn't matter to him that a cop is missing?" Powell asked, feeling a fresh twinge of guilt over the lie.

"Sure it did," Cerreta said sourly. "He said that if we can prove Tommy's disappearance is connected with these people, he'll be happy to entertain our request for a warrant. Only we can't prove that." He lifted his eyebrows. "Or can we?" he added, his eyes suddenly very steady on Powell's face.

It took Powell two tries to get the word out. "No."

"Because I'd hate for something to happen to him if someone else could have prevented it," Cerreta went on, that half-suspicious look still on his face.

"Yes, sir," Powell said. "So would I."

Cerreta held his gaze a moment longer, then gave a microscopic nod. "Anything new with Messerling?"

Powell lifted his phone slightly. "He's activating S.W.A.T. units all over the city," he said, relieved to be on firmer ground. "I've got Hill and Grosvenor checking with DMV for any other vehicles registered to those restaurants."

"While we're at it, we'd better put someone on the restaurants themselves," Cerreta decided, picking up his phone again. "Outside *and* in. No law against a cop having a cup of coffee in the restaurant of his choice."

There was a click in Powell's ear. "I've got a preliminary deployment schedule now," Messerling's voice said. "You want to take this down?"

Powell scooped up a pen and pad. "Go ahead."

• •

"No soap," Roger said, lowering his hand. "Jonah says they don't have any way to distinguish Greens from humans, at least not at any distance. Our infrared signatures are similar, we look pretty much the same on a sonic pattern readout, and entropic metabolism detectors are no good beyond about five feet."

"What the hell's an entropic metabolism detector?" Fierenzo lifted a hand. "Never mind—it doesn't matter. What about those metal brooch things?"

"The *trassks*?" Roger shook his head. "He said they're not going to show up as anything other than ordinary metal. It's the Green psychic manipulation ability that makes them work. We could still watch for people wearing them, I suppose."

"Assuming they're stupid enough to leave them out in the open instead of in their pockets."

"There's that," Roger conceded. "What do you think they're planning?"

"Well, the basics seem obvious," Fierenzo said. "They're assuming you've relayed Caroline's disinformation to Torvald, which means they expect Grays to gather at the north end of the island to wait for the phantom Damian and his Warrior escort to show up. That gives Nikolos the choice of coming up right behind them—say, over the George or the Triborough—and slaughtering them while they're facing the wrong direction, or else coming up into Lower Manhattan to take out the women and children who've been left behind in supposed safety."

Roger shuddered. "Or head directly into Brooklyn and Queens, where the bulk of the Grays still live."

"Point," Fierenzo said, grimacing. All they needed was for Nikolos to expand this to the other four boroughs. "The question is whether Nikolos would prefer a straight-on attack against fellow fighters, man to man, or would he'd prefer the terrorist route of targeting civilians so as to throw the fighters into disarray."

"So what do we do?"

Fierenzo turned and stared out the window at the cars and people passing by. That was a damn good question. He had some ideas, but they all depended on at least partial knowledge of the Green strategy. "We go to the hotel and wait for Jonah and the others," he decided. "Maybe when we put our heads together we'll come up with something."

"Don't you think it's about time to alert Torvald and the other Grays?"

"Let's talk to Jonah first," Fierenzo said, giving his mouth a final dab with his napkin and standing up. "Whatever Nikolos has planned, I doubt he'll move until it's dark."

"You willing to bet all our lives on that?"

Fierenzo looked out the window again at the people of his city. "I don't think I've really got a choice," he said. "Come on, let's get out of here."

44

It was nearly two o'clock, and the rumbling in Smith's stomach had finally become too loud to ignore, when he arrived in downtown Kingston.

From a Manhattan perspective, of course, the term "downtown" seemed rather quaint. Still, there were a couple of small but adequate-looking restaurants in what the signs called the Historic Rondout Section of town along the riverfront. Picking one at random, he parked and headed in.

"Afternoon," a young woman greeted him as he stepped inside. "Table for one?"

"Please," Smith said, nodding. "And a red pickup if you have one."

The woman blinked. "A *what*?"

"Never mind," Smith said. He really should know better than to try to be funny on an empty stomach. "I've spent all day looking for a wayward red pickup, that's all."

"A red *Ford* pickup?" a new voice called.

Smith looked around the empty dining area, finally spotted the face peering out through the low window leading back into the kitchen. "Yes, as a matter of fact," he said. "New York tag NKR—"

"Oh, it's got plates?" the other interrupted him. "Never mind. Gail said this one didn't have any."

"Wait a second," Smith said quickly, not sure he believed this. He'd been killing himself trying to find this truck; and these people already knew where it was? "They could have taken the plates off."

"They?" the waitress echoed, frowning. "It's not yours?"

"No, but I'd really like it to be," Smith said, pulling his badge and ID from his pocket. "Officer Jeff Smith, New York Police. If that's the truck I've been looking for, it may have been involved in a kidnapping."

The woman's face settled into hard lines. "I'll call Gail right now and find out where it is."

"Gail doesn't know," the cook called to her through his window. "Call Rolf Jacoby—he's the one who actually saw it."

"Okay," the waitress called back. "I'd better get Hank on it, too. He's the police chief," she added to Smith.

"Great," Smith said, watching her hurry to the cash register podium. In certain parts of New York, he suspected, the truck could have sat abandoned for a week before anyone bothered to bring it to anyone else's attention. An hour in a small upstate town, and everyone in a five-mile radius knew all about it.

He shook his head. "God bless America," he murmured.

• •

The pickup had been left neatly parked behind one of the local lumber yards. A police car was waiting when Smith arrived, with a single uniformed cop standing beside it. "You must be Smith," the other said as Smith got out of his car and walked toward him. "I'm Hank Fishburn."

"Pleasure, Chief," Smith said cautiously. "First off, I want you to know I'm not trying to poach any of this from your jurisdiction."

Fishburn snorted. "The whole state got an alert about two hours ago on this thing," he said. "No one mentioned a red pickup, though."

"I told Manhattan about it," Smith assured him.

"Report must have gotten lost in transit," Fishburn said. "Happens way too often. Anyway, the point is that I get the feeling jurisdictional infighting is pretty much out the window. What can we do to help you?"

Smith breathed a silent sigh of relief. "For starters, I need to find out where the people from this truck went."

"The rest of my force is canvassing the area," Fishburn said. "I understand you're also looking for some people who were in white cargo vans?"

"Right," Smith confirmed. "They're long gone by now, but if we can figure out what kind of vehicles they switched to we might at least be able to find out where they've landed in the city."

"Well, there's one place in town that rents cars, plus a couple more within a ten-mile radius," Fishburn said, forehead wrinkling in thought. "Is there anything to indicate they had any business here in Kingston?"

"I think so, yes." Smith pointed at the truck. "If all they wanted was to ditch the truck, they could have had their friends pick them up someplace out in the woods. Fifty yards off the road, and we wouldn't have found it for a month."

"Yeah, that makes sense," Fishburn conceded. "Your boss Powell's supposed to be sending me a photo of this Mrs. Whittier. Once we have that, we can start a more thorough search. In the meantime—" he lifted his eyebrows "—you never did get your lunch, did you?"

Right on cue, Smith's stomach growled. "That can wait," he said.

Fishburn shook his head. "There's no point in starting before we have that photo," he pointed out reasonably. "My people are already doing everything that can be done right now. He gestured back toward his car. "Come on," he said. "My treat."

Smith gave him a tight smile. "And while I eat, you'll see if you can find out what's *really* going on?"

Fishburn smiled genially, putting a hand on Smith's shoulder and giving him a gentle but irresistible nudge toward the car. "Something like that."

"What if I can't tell you anything you don't already know?"

"Then you're buying dessert."

• •

"God of heaven and earth," Stephanie murmured, her eyes wide in a suddenly pale face as she sat on one of the beds between Jonah and her husband. "Two *hundred* Warriors?"

"We think it could be as many as that, yes," Fierenzo told her.

"And you have no idea where they are?" Ron said.

Even from across the hotel room, Roger saw Fierenzo's throat tighten. "Not yet," he acknowledged, his voice steady. "We're working on it."

"Glad to hear it," Jonah said, only a trace of sarcasm in his voice. "And when exactly were you planning to bring in the *real* experts on Greens?"

"If you mean the rest of the Grays, I don't know," Fierenzo said. "At this point I'm not even sure we should."

"You're not sure you *should*?" Jonah echoed. "Fierenzo, you're talking about a mass slaughter here. Two hundred Warriors—" He broke off, looking over at the three Greens and his brother Jordan, huddled together on the other bed. "Zenas, *you* tell him."

"The Pastsinger memories of the last war indicate that a single Green Warrior can usually handle four to seven Grays," Zenas said quietly. "And there are, what, about seven hundred of you?"

"Six hundred eighty," Ron said. "But only about four hundred of us are adults and teens who could fight." He looked over at his wife. "That includes the adult women."

"Do the math, Fierenzo," Jonah said darkly, looking back

at the detective. "With four hundred of us, the sixty Green Warriors we *thought* they had would have given us a six to one ratio, a pretty fair balance of power." He looked at Roger. "Two *hundred* Warriors is quick annihilation."

"You have to warn them, Detective," Stephanie said, her eyes pleading. "You have to."

Fierenzo sighed. "The problem is Nikolos," he said. "More specifically, what precisely he'll do if the Grays don't behave the way he expects them to."

"What are you talking about?" Jonah demanded. "You mean if we don't dance to his tune—?"

"Let him talk, son," Ron cut him off, his voice quiet but firm.

"Thank you," Fierenzo said. "Let's say we do tell Torvald exactly what we think Nikolos's plan is. Do you think he'd bother sending people to upper Manhattan to counter what we all expect to be a feint? Or would he concentrate on defending the main Gray areas?"

"Probably the latter," Ron said, nodding. "Yes, I see the problem. If we don't send a strong force to the northern end of the island, Nikolos will probably shift to another plan."

"Exactly," Fierenzo said. "Unfortunately, we don't know what this Plan B is."

"Are we sure we even know what Plan A is?" Laurel asked.

"Not entirely, no," Fierenzo admitted. "But the pieces we *do* have will be useless once he realizes Torvald and Halfdan aren't playing ball. And at that point we won't have any handle on him at all."

"Why can't we just give Torvald—I mean—just half the story?" Melantha asked hesitantly, her hands clutching Jordan's on one side of her and her mother's on the other.

"Are you suggesting we deliberately send our people into a trap?" Stephanie asked, a sudden edge to her voice.

"I'm sure she didn't mean it that way," Laurel countered, a similar edge to her voice as she came to her daughter's defense.

"I don't know what she meant," Stephanie shot back. "But what she *said* was—"

"That's enough," Fierenzo cut her off. "Everyone just calm down."

"Easy for *you* to say," Stephanie bit out, turning glowering eyes on him. "They're not out to destroy *your* people."

"Melantha's not out to destroy your people, either," Fierenzo reminded her tartly. "Or had you forgotten that?" He pointed to the Greens. "Or would you rather just give up on this pesky peace thing and start the war right here? Go on—you've all got hammerguns. Go ahead and use them."

There was an awkward silence. "Don't be silly," Stephanie said, her voice still strained but under control again. "I'm sorry, Melantha."

"That's okay," Melantha said in a small voice. "I didn't mean—"

"It's all right, sweetheart," Laurel soothed her. "We're all new to this." She looked at Fierenzo. "None of us are Warriors, Detective," she added. "We don't know the first thing about how to think and plan this way."

"I realize that," Fierenzo said. "Of all of us, I've probably had the most tactical training; and *I'm* nowhere near an expert at it. But like it or not, the nine of us in this room are the best chance we've got for heading off this thing." He looked at Roger. "The ten of us, including Caroline," he added.

For a moment he looked around the room, as if waiting for argument. But none came. "All right, then," he went on. "In actual fact, Melantha was on her way to what I was thinking of proposing myself. We obviously can't give Torvald and Halfdan just half the story and let them walk into a trap; but we *could* give them all of it and ask them to behave as if they only had the part Nikolos wanted them to hear."

He looked at Ron and Stephanie. "The question is, would they be willing to play along? Or would they instead try to turn the situation around and crush the Greens?"

"The deeper question is, isn't that exactly what we want?" Jonah put in before his parents could answer. "Not to crush the Greens themselves, but to whittle the Warriors down to a manageable size?"

"The Warriors *are* Greens, Jonah," Zenas said warningly.

"We can't let them get slaughtered any more than we can let that happen to you Grays."

"I'm sorry, but I'm not sure we have a choice in the matter," Jonah countered. "Those extra Warriors are what's causing this whole problem. They have to be neutralized somehow, or we're dead."

"But you can't just *kill* them," Laurel protested. "They're not doing anything except following the requirements of their Gift."

"*And* following Nikolos," Jonah pointed out.

"All of which is part of the Gift," Laurel said.

"I think that's Jonah's point, actually," Ron murmured. "Cyril is supposed to be your leader right now, and Cyril is proposing peace. In spite of that, Nikolos is preparing for war."

"That's only because there hasn't yet been any peace established," Laurel insisted. "Once the leaders formally make that decision, Nikolos will fall into line like the rest of us."

"But how do you *know* that?" Jonah pressed. "It's a nice theory, but you can't take it to the bank."

"You can with Greens," Zenas said firmly. "The Gifts define our thinking and our behavior. And part of the Command-Tactician's Gift is to subordinate himself to the Leader."

"Except that you haven't *got* a Leader," Jonah muttered. He waved a hand vaguely through the air. "Never mind. I don't know what to think anymore."

"Then start by thinking about the fact that we're all friends here," Ron told him quietly. "Nothing that happens between our peoples can be allowed to change that."

Jonah lowered his eyes. "I suppose," he said.

"It's ironic, isn't it?" Laurel said meditatively. "Ironic and sad both. Once *all* of us were friends, before the disaster in the Great Valley. Now, just when it looks as if we're going to lose everything, our two families have finally found that capability again."

"Thanks to Melantha," Stephanie said.

"And Jordan," Laurel added, reaching over her daughter's shoulder to ruffle Jordan's hair.

"'The wolf shall lie down with the lamb,'" Roger murmured. "'And a little child shall lead them.'"

"What?" Zenas asked, frowning.

"An old saying about better times to come," Fierenzo told him, looking at Roger. "Misquoted a bit, but the right sentiment."

"Unfortunately, sentiments aren't going to do us any good here," Jonah said.

"'And a little child shall lead them,'" Ron said thoughtfully. "Interesting that it seems to be the older Grays who are the keenest on restarting the war where it left off. The younger ones, like Jonah and Jordan, seem much more willing to accept the Greens."

"I think it's the same with the Greens," Zenas told him. "Unfortunately, it's those same elders—among both our peoples—who are in charge."

"But that's not necessarily a permanent situation," Ron pointed out. "If Melantha happened to have been born a Leader instead of a Groundshaker, she'd have automatic authority over Cyril and Aleksander, wouldn't she?"

"At her age, possibly not," Zenas said slowly. "In a couple of years, though, absolutely."

"So what we need is for a Leader to arise among the children," Stephanie said. "I don't suppose there's a chance there might be one lurking out there somewhere?"

"There's always a chance," Zenas said. "By all the usual genetic probabilities, Melantha shouldn't have been born a Groundshaker, either. There could easily be some eleven-year-old future Leader climbing trees right now in Central Park."

"Unfortunately, he's not going to do us any good unless he can grow three years in the next six hours," Fierenzo pointed out. "Let's get back to the problem at hand, shall we? Can we or can we not persuade Torvald or Halfdan to play along with the first part of Nikolos's game long enough for us to figure out the rest of it?"

Ron and Stephanie looked at each other. "I don't know either of them very well," Ron said, a little doubtfully. "But

Halfdan's the one who was pushing the hardest for peace. I vote we approach him first."

"Sounds reasonable to me," Stephanie seconded.

"Okay," Fierenzo said, looking around the room. "If there are no objections . . . ?"

Roger took a careful breath. "I have one," he spoke up. "I don't think we should trust Halfdan."

All eyes turned to him. "But he's the one who was working with Cyril toward a peace agreement," Laurel pointed out.

"At the cost of your daughter's life," Roger reminded her. "If we're going to take this to anyone, I say we go to Torvald."

"You must be joking," Zenas said with a snort. "Torvald was the one who kidnapped Melantha."

"He told me he did that for her own protection," Roger said, looking at Melantha. "He told me he tried to tell *you* that, too, Melantha."

Laurel craned her head to look into her daughter's face. "Melantha?"

"He *did* say that," the girl agreed hesitantly. "But I thought he was just lying to keep me from making trouble."

"You did look more or less comfortable when we found you," Roger pointed out. "You weren't tied up or gagged."

"You're not seriously taking Torvald's side in this, are you?" Zenas demanded. "He's the one who moved into the middle of the Green homestead in MacDougal Alley, forcing out people who'd been there for decades."

"Did he force them out?" Roger asked. "Or did they leave on their own?"

"With a Gray in the neighborhood?" Zenas countered. "None of those people were Warriors. What else could they do?"

"He also grabbed *you* off the street, remember?" Jonah added.

"So did Nikolos," Roger countered. "So did Halfdan, or at least he tried. Look, I'm not saying Torvald's not a little ham-handed in how he deals with people. But I don't think he necessarily wants to wipe out the Greens, either."

"*There's* a ringing endorsement," Jonah muttered.

"I think he's an honorable man," Roger said doggedly. "And frankly, I don't know what else to do. I just can't agree with trying to work a deal with someone who was willing to watch Melantha get murdered in cold blood."

"Then you can't trust any of the Greens, either," Laurel said.

"*I* certainly don't trust them," Fierenzo agreed. "Present company excepted, of course. For all this talk about leadership and Gifts and cooperation, there seems to be a lot of finagling beneath the surface of Green society."

"Because we don't have a Leader," Laurel said tiredly.

"Now we're just going in circles," Ron said. "What exactly—?"

"Hold it," Fierenzo said, lifting a hand for silence as he pulled out his phone and punched it on. "Yes? . . . Great." He pulled out his notebook and a pen. "Go."

For a minute the only sound was the scratching of Fierenzo's pen as he scribbled notes. Then, to Roger's amazement, a taut smile began to spread slowly across his face. "Two lanterns, huh?" he said. "How nice. Yeah, I've got it. Thanks."

He punched off and lowered the phone. "Two *lanterns*?" Roger repeated, frowning.

"That's right," Fierenzo said, continuing to write in his notebook.

"So what does it *mean*?" Roger persisted, not in the mood for word games.

"It means, my friends," Fierenzo said, an edge of grim satisfaction in his voice, "that we may just have them."

• •

When he got right down to it, Smith had to admit, he really *didn't* know very much about what was going on. Still, it was more than Chief Fishburn did. "I'll be damned," he said as Smith finished his recitation and bit into a cheeseburger just slightly smaller than his mouth. "So you think these are the guys who kidnapped Detective Fierenzo?"

"Kidnapped or killed," Smith said grimly. "The longer we go without hearing anything, the less likely he's still alive. If he was nosing too close, they wouldn't gain much by keeping him alive."

"Except you get the needle in this state for killing a cop," Fishburn said. "But then, maybe they don't give a damn."

"Maybe not," Smith said, taking another bite of his burger. Suddenly, the food didn't taste as good as it had a minute ago.

"But you *do* think they still have the Whittier woman?"

"As of the moment they drove me off the road they did," Smith told him. "I suppose they could have dumped her somewhere after that—"

"Chief?" a voice came from the radio at Fishburn's waist.

Fishburn unhooked it and lifted it to his cheek. "Yeah, Adam, what have you got?"

"Nothing on the canvass," Adam reported. "But I pulled a bunch of the charge slips from this morning, and I found a customer who remembers seeing two women leaving that truck: one old, probably sixty or better, the other much younger, probably mid-twenties."

Fishburn lifted his eyebrows at Smith. "He happen to notice which direction they went?"

"Nope," Adam said. "But from the time-stamp on the charge slip, we know it was just after nine-thirty this morning."

"Five hours ago," Fishburn commented, glancing at his watch.

"Yeah," Adam said. "Oh, and we did check the VIN against the plate Smith gave us. This is definitely the right truck."

"After all this, it sure as hell better be," Fishburn said. "You call it in?"

"As soon as we got the confirmation," Adam said. "There's a bunch of State cops on the way to give us a hand."

"Good," Fishburn said. "Try a few more of those charge slips and see if you can find someone who saw what direction they took when they left the parking lot. What's happening with the car-rental places?"

"Kate's on that," Adam said. "I haven't heard anything from her since she started."

"Check on her progress," Fishburn ordered. "And have someone run through the blotter for stolen-vehicle reports. They may have taken the plates off the pickup to use on something else."

"Got it."

Fishburn returned the radio to his belt. "Well, she was alive as of nine-thirty this morning," he commented.

"That's something, anyway," Smith agreed, taking another bite of his burger and dropping the rest back onto his plate. "But they've already got a five-hour head start," he added, wiping his hands on his napkin. "No point in letting them get any more."

For a second Fishburn seemed inclined to argue the point. But a look at Smith's face, and he simply nodded. "Okay," he said, getting to his feet. "I'll take you to the station where you can get a better idea of what we're doing and what still needs to be done." He looked around and caught the waitress's eye. "Marge, put this on my bill, will you?" he called.

"That's all right," Smith said, shaking his head as he reached for his wallet. "I can cover it."

"You're in my town, Officer," Fishburn said firmly, reaching over the table to put a restraining hand on his arm. "Your money's no good here. Come on."

They stepped back out into the afternoon sunlight. "I'm sorry you couldn't have seen our town under better circumstances," the chief commented as they headed for the car. "It really is a nice place."

"I don't doubt it," Smith assured him. "What is this Historical Rondout Section I see on all the signs, anyway?"

"It's the old riverfront area," Fishburn said. "The docks and museum and lighthouse and all. We had a pretty thriving waterway business along the Hudson a century or so ago."

Smith froze. "You have working docks?" he asked carefully.

"Yes, but you can forget what you're thinking," Fishburn said with a faint smile. "We've got a dock manager who keeps an eye on things down there. I phoned him as soon as I got the alert and told him to call me right away if anything docked here. Every cop along the Hudson will have done the same thing."

"What time exactly did this alert come in?"

"About nine," Fishburn said, frowning. "I called Tompkins as soon as I'd alerted my own force."

"About nine," Smith said, the back of his neck starting to tingle. "Has anyone seen or talked with Tompkins since then?"

Fishburn's face went rigid. "Oh, my God," he breathed as he yanked open his door. "Get in."

They reached the dock and the Port Authority building in two minutes flat. With Smith right behind him, Fishburn strode down the walk and threw open the office door.

And came to an abrupt halt as the room's lone occupant jerked in surprise. "Wha—? Oh, it's you," he said. "Hello, Chief."

"You all right, Mr. Tompkins?" Fishburn demanded, sounding both relieved and a little deflated.

Tompkins's face gave an odd sort of twitch. "Yes, I'm fine," he said quickly, his eyes behind their thick glasses flicking to Smith and then back to the police chief. "Is there a problem?"

Fishburn threw a look at Smith. "No, we were just worried about you, that's all," he said. "Carry on."

"Just a second," Smith said as the chief started to brush past him. There had been something strangely familiar about that twitch. "Are you sure you're all right, Mr. Tompkins?"

"Yes, I'm fine," the other said, his face twitching again.

Only this time, Smith remembered where he'd seen it before. "Glad to hear it," he said carefully. "Tell me: have any ships or boats docked here since nine o'clock this morning?"

For a second, Tompkins's body seemed to go rigid. He looked at Fishburn, back at Smith, turned to look out his window at the docks, then finally turned back to Smith again. "Just one," he said, sounding as if he was surprised at the sound of his voice. "A yacht, really. It docked a little after ten."

Smith looked at Fishburn in time to see his mouth drop open. "A *what*?" the chief demanded, his voice clearly on its way to a bellow. "Tompkins, what the *hell*—!"

"Easy, Chief," Smith cut him off. "I saw this same thing back in the city. Mr. Tompkins, why didn't you inform Chief Fishburn like he'd ordered you to do?"

Tompkins shrugged, a confused hunching of his shoulders. "Because . . . he told me not to."

"He told you *not* to?" Fishburn looked at Smith. "What is this, some sort of game?"

"More like some sort of hypnotic," Smith told him. "A good one, too; except that it doesn't work if you ask a direct question."

"Really," Fishburn said, reaching to one of the chairs and pulling it over to him. "Good. Because there are several *very* direct questions I want to ask."

45

"Two *lanterns*," Jordan said, clearly delighted that he was the first to catch onto Fierenzo's little joke. "I get it. 'One if by land, two if by sea.'"

"Very good," Fierenzo said, scribbling one last note on his pad. "Okay, here's the deal. A yacht named *Galen's Tenth* picked up two women from the docks at Kingston, about seventy miles up the Hudson from New York. The dock manager identified Caroline from her photo; we assume the other was Sylvia."

Roger felt his chest tighten. "Did she seem okay?" he asked.

"He never saw her up close," Fierenzo said. "But she definitely got onto the yacht under her own steam, so my guess is she's fine."

"Did he see the Warriors?" Zenas asked.

"No, but we know there was at least one other passenger aboard," Fierenzo said. "An older gentleman who came to his office as the women were getting on and instructed him not to tell anyone about the docking and pickup. And he didn't, either, until Smith asked him a direct question about it."

He looked at Roger. "Just like the super in your building," he added. "Seems to be the trademark pattern of a Green Persuader, at least one working with humans."

"Aleksander," Jonah muttered.

"Or else Cyril's joined the party, too," Ron said. "If his support for peace this whole time was really only a matter of pragmatism, the sudden revelation that Nikolos had an unbeatable force might have been all it took for him to change sides."

"I think Cyril's more sincere than that," Laurel objected.

"We'll find out soon enough," Fierenzo said. "The key point is that the yacht was moving *down*river at the time they picked up Sylvia and Caroline, so my guess is that the Warriors were already aboard. Probably taken on somewhere farther north, maybe at a private dock with less exposure to the public eye."

"It doesn't sound like Sylvia was originally intended to go on board," Zenas said thoughtfully. "Otherwise, why make the pickup in the middle of town?"

"I agree," Fierenzo said. "She probably planned to drive herself and Caroline to New York and rendezvous with the Warriors there. Once Smith spotted them and gave chase, though, she lost that option."

"So she called the yacht and had them stop at Kingston to pick them up," Zenas said, nodding. "That makes sense."

"It also means we've already disrupted Nikolos's plans," Jonah pointed out. "What makes you think he hasn't already gone to your Plan B?"

"Nothing," Fierenzo said, looking him straight back in the eye. "We just have to assume this is a minor enough glitch that he's still on track."

"Do we know where the yacht is now?" Stephanie asked.

"The State Police have people spreading out along the river to look for it. "To observe and report only," he added, looking at Roger. "They're all aware there's a hostage aboard."

"Do we know anything else about the yacht?" Laurel asked.

"It's based at the North Cove Yacht Harbor, so we assume it's eventually going to head back that way," Fierenzo said. "We don't know if the owner's aboard or not. From the ship's dimensions, I'd say it's big enough to carry a hundred people or more, though certainly not in any comfort."

"Where exactly is this harbor?" Laurel asked. "I don't think I'm familiar with it."

"It's on the southwest side of Manhattan, just north of Battery Park," Fierenzo told her. "It's surrounded on three sides by the buildings of the World Financial Center."

"Puts it just a couple of blocks from Ground Zero," Roger murmured. "How nicely symbolic."

Melantha shivered. "It's all right, Melantha," Laurel assured her quietly, letting go of the girl's hand and putting her arm around her shoulders. "No one can make you do anything like that."

"Not even a Persuader?" Ron asked pointedly.

"No," Laurel said, her eyes hard. "We won't let them."

"Question," Jonah spoke up. "We seem to be assuming they'll be coming back to harbor. What if they don't?"

"What do you mean?" Jordan asked.

"I mean what if they just sit offshore and let loose with the grandmother of all Shrieks?" Jonah said. "With a hundred Warriors aboard, they could probably knock every Gray off his building for three blocks inland."

"Is that possible?" Fierenzo asked, looking at the Greens.

"I don't know," Zenas said hesitantly. "I remember a Pastsinger once saying that a pair of Warriors can reinforce each other's Shrieks in a way that focuses direction and intensity. But I don't know if you can do it with more than two of them or whether they'd start canceling each other out."

"But if they *can* do it, it won't just affect the Grays," Laurel pointed out. "Every Human in range would be knocked off their feet, too. There would be car wrecks, people falling down stairs and onto subway tracks, maybe even out of windows."

"Probably have a rash of heart attacks and strokes, too, just from the stress of it," Zenas added. "I don't even want to think of what it might do to the mentally unstable."

"The blood of thousands of New Yorkers," Fierenzo said grimly. "Just like Cyril promised."

"We could take them, you know," Jonah said, his voice under tight control. "Before they ever had a chance to do that. A handful of Grays at the top of, say, the Empire State Building could hit the yacht hard enough to blow it into splinters."

Stephanie looked at him in astonishment. "Jonah! How can you *think* such a thing?"

"You can't slaughter that many Greens, certainly before we've even been attacked," his father agreed firmly. "We've already decided that."

"Not to mention the fact that Caroline's still on board," Stephanie added.

"I hadn't forgotten about her," Jonah said, and it seemed to Roger that the young Gray was studiously avoiding looking in his direction. "But Aleksander and Nikolos haven't exactly called us up with a declaration of war. If this kind of sneak attack is all right with them, why isn't it all right with us?"

"Because we're not going to stoop to that sort of thing, that's why," Ron said.

"And not all Greens would, either," Zenas said.

"With all due respect, Zenas, it doesn't matter what you or Laurel or even Melantha would do," Jonah said bluntly. "Nikolos is the Command-Tactician in charge; and if we let him get his Warriors to Manhattan or Queens or Brooklyn, we're dead." He looked at his father. "I don't like it, either. But I don't think we have any choice."

"We can stop them," Ron said firmly. "All of us together—" his eyes flicked to Zenas and Laurel and Melantha "—plus all the Greens who genuinely want peace. We can stop them."

"How?" Jonah countered. "Through Cyril? Even if he does still want a truce, they're not going to listen to him. Like I said, Nikolos is in charge, and all he's ever wanted to do is destroy us." Almost reluctantly, he turned to Roger. "I *am* sorry about Caroline, Roger," he said. "But it's better that one person die before their time than everything we've worked for—everything *both* of our peoples have worked for—should come to nothing."

He said other things; conciliatory things, most likely, as he tried to justify the death sentence he was proposing. But Roger wasn't really listening. Abruptly, as if Jonah's words had opened a fire hose, all the strange and confusing pieces of this terrible puzzle were flying in from dusty corners of his mind, flipping around and turning over as he saw them in a brand new light, falling together in a way he'd never anticipated.

And in the space of half a dozen heartbeats, he had it. He had it all.

"Roger?"

He blinked his attention back, to find them all staring at him. "You all right?" Fierenzo asked.

"I'm fine." Roger took a deep breath. "I've got it."

"You've got what?"

"The answer," Roger told him, looking around the room. "The answer to everything. Maybe."

"You mean how to stop the Warriors?" Stephanie asked hopefully.

"No," Roger said, smiling tightly at her. "How to stop the war."

There was a stunned silence as he stood up and crossed to the phone. "Well?" Fierenzo said at last. "Don't keep us in suspense."

"In a minute," Roger said, picking up the phone. "I have to make a couple of calls first."

"To whom?" Jonah asked, his voice dark with suspicion.

Roger smiled crookedly at him. "Trust me, Jonah," he assured the other. "You, especially, are going to love this."

• •

The last of the shadowy figures slipped off into the night, and the Greens along the side of the yacht hauled in the ramp they'd stretched out to the old Gowanus Bay dock on the west end of Brooklyn. The soft rumble of the idling engines increased in volume, and the yacht pulled away, heading toward the choppy waters of the Upper Bay and the lights of Manhattan beyond.

"That was the last stop," a voice said from behind Caroline. "The rest of us will be getting off at North Cove."

She turned to see Nikolos crossing toward her from the wheelhouse, his *trassk* glittering against the darker material of his jacket. "Where are they going?" she asked, gesturing off toward the dark landmass rapidly receding into the night as the yacht picked up speed. "To destroy the Gray women and children?"

"Actually, many of the women are standing ready to fight beside their men," Nikolos corrected, coming to her side and leaning onto the railing as he gazed off in the direction the ten Warriors had taken. "Certainly the forces I'm told are waiting for us at the various bridges are mixed groups."

He smiled at her. "Thank you for your assistance in that, by the way," he added. "Having that many Grays gathered up there out of our way will make the operation that much simpler."

Caroline turned her face away, her stomach churning

with frustration. So Roger hadn't deciphered her secret message after all. She'd been too clever, or too obscure, and he'd completely missed both of the clues she'd tried so hard to give him. All he'd gotten was the first part, which he'd obligingly passed on to the Grays.

Who now waited uselessly at the northern tip of Manhattan, preparing for a massive battle that wasn't going to happen. At least, not there. "You didn't answer my question," she said.

She sensed Nikolos shrug. "There won't be any direct attacks on the young and infirm, if that's what you're worried about," he said. "The Warriors we sent ashore will be preparing for the confused homeward rush of Grays that I expect to happen when they realize they've been duped. With their sentries in the city reporting a mass of Warriors moving across southern Manhattan, they'll assume my entire force is there and won't expect to encounter any opposition in their home bases in Queens and Brooklyn. Ten Warriors guarding each of the likely approaches should be easily able to pick them off as they charge blindly in."

Caroline's hands curled with vicious strength around the railing. "And you consider this an honorable way to make war?"

"We do what we have to," Nikolos said evenly. "They'd do the same to us if they had the chance." He paused. "I *am* sorry, though, that you had to be dragged into it. I would have preferred to leave you and your husband out of it."

"I'm sure you would," she said bitterly. "Ideally, of course, you'd also have preferred that Melantha die so that you could lull the Grays into a false sense of security."

"The Grays didn't want security, Caroline," he said darkly. "All they wanted was enough of an edge over us to guarantee victory. If Melantha had died, they'd have attacked us within days. Possibly even within hours."

"You can't know that."

He shrugged. "Perhaps not in a strictly philosophical sense. But I personally have no doubts."

"Because of what happened seventy-five years ago in another world?"

"Kindly do not presume to lecture me, Caroline," Nikolos said, his voice simmering with hatred. "I was there. You weren't."

For a long moment he stood silently. Then, he seemed to shake himself. "At any rate, it should be over by dawn," he said. "Possibly even by midnight, if the Grays are cooperative enough to act within their optimal parameters."

"Of course," Caroline said. "Sylvia's estimates, I presume?"

Nikolos snorted. "A Command-Tactician hardly needs advice and analysis from a simple Group Commander."

"I'm sure that's true," Caroline agreed, turning to look him square in the face. "But you're not the Command-Tactician. Sylvia is."

She couldn't make out the details of his face in the faint reflected light of the city around them. But the slight pause before he replied told her all she needed to know. "Really," he said at last. "Did she tell you that?"

Caroline shook her head. "I saw the two of you during your war games practice Sunday night," she said. "You crossed the yard to talk to her, instead of the other way around. With Greens, that means she's the higher rank."

"Very good," Nikolos said, a rather forced touch of amusement coloring his voice. "She was right; you *are* a clever Human. So I stand revealed as a lowly Group Commander, do I?"

Caroline smiled into the darkness. *Deception is a necessary part of warfare,* Sylvia had told her back at their first meeting. Apparently, it was an ongoing one, as well. "You're not a Group Commander, either," she said. "You're a Persuader."

The silence this time was longer. "What makes you think that?" he asked, even the forced amusement gone from his voice now.

"Many things," Caroline told him, feeling a small flicker

of satisfaction amid the tension and despair churning within her. She'd tumbled to this one too late for the information to do her any good. But caught in the middle of a situation where she had no control, it was nice to be able to surprise him, even a little. "For one thing, our Mr. Galen in the wheelhouse is being far too cooperative about having his yacht hijacked by over a hundred strangers. Only a Persuader could have kept him calm through all this."

"Aleksander could have worked with him before the yacht left the city."

"Too risky," Caroline said. "I know Sylvia well enough to know she would have insisted on having a Persuader on board in case of last-minute changes."

"So there's a Persuader aboard," Nikolos conceded. "But as you've already pointed out, we have over a hundred men and women here. Why me?"

"Because of something you said to me back in the library," Caroline said. "Do you remember? *You must understand that what I do, I do for the best.* Even then it struck me as the kind of stylized phrasing we'd heard from the children at Vasilis and Iolanthe's homestead. The kind of formal phrasing Greens really seem to like."

"And what exactly did you conclude it meant?"

"I don't know if it means anything more than what it actually says," Caroline told him. "What's important is that it's the same phrase Cyril used when he spoke into my mind outside our apartment Friday morning, when he was ordering me to bring Melantha to him."

This time the silence stretched uncomfortably out into the night. Caroline stood beside the rail, listening to the stutter of the engines and the hissing of the yacht's wake, wondering uneasily if she'd gone too far. How dangerous to him *was* this secret he'd held for the last three-quarters of a century, and what lengths would he go to to protect it? Below her, the water of the Upper Bay churned and roiled with the boat's passage. A single heave, perhaps preceded by a thrust through her ribs from his *trassk* to make doubly sure . . .

"A very clever Human indeed," he murmured at last.

"Fortunately, no one who matters would ever take your word against mine, let alone your word against mine and Sylvia's."

He straightened up. "Besides, by dawn tomorrow, it will be irrelevant," he added. "The Grays will be gone, and no one will care who or what I am. Enjoy the rest of the cruise, Caroline Human Whittier. The rising sun will shine on a brighter day for us all." Turning his back on her, he headed across the gently rolling deck.

With a trembling sigh, Caroline returned her gaze to the towering buildings of Manhattan rising from the dark water ahead of her. No, she thought distantly, the rising sun wouldn't shine on happiness. It would shine on a very dark day indeed.

Unless someone did something. Unless *she* did something.

Getting a fresh grip on the railing, she gazed across the water at the lights of her home ahead, and tried desperately to think.

● ●

"We have a confirmation on that ten-count off the boat at Gowanus Bay," the soft voice came over the S.W.A.T. van radio. "Headed south in loose formation toward Fourth Avenue. Observers moving to shadow."

"Acknowledged," Messerling said, leaning over the radio operator's shoulder toward the microphone. "Make damn sure you stay out of sight. Any luck getting a reading on the number still aboard?"

"Nothing firm," the voice said. "They weren't there long enough for an IR analysis before they were on the move again and out of range of the more sensitive gear. But what we *did* get is consistent with the eighty to a hundred that Gavin's readings gave us."

Messerling glanced back over his shoulder at Powell and Cerreta, and Powell suppressed a grimace. He'd been hoping that Fierenzo's estimate of their opponents' troop strength had been pessimistically high. Instead, if anything, it might have been a shade low. "Understood," the S.W.A.T. commander said, turning back to the mike. "What's their current heading?"

"Looks like they're making for Manhattan," the officer reported. "We got a short sound bite on the telescope mike just before they pulled away that indicated they were heading home."

"Acknowledged," Messerling said coolly. "We're ready for them."

"One other thing," the voice said. "We got a positive on Whittier on deck as they were offloading, and we've got an eighty percent confirmation that they had Galen in the wheelhouse."

Powell felt his jaw tighten. Of all the unpleasant situations he'd had to face in his career as a cop, hostage standoffs were the ones he hated the most. Especially standoffs where he actually knew one of the hostages.

"Acknowledged," Messerling said. "Stay sharp, and out of sight. And *don't* lose them."

He gestured, and the operator cut the connection. "Well, gentlemen," Messerling said, turning back again to Cerreta and Powell. "Let's go join the party."

46

"Here they come," Messerling murmured, his head lifted just high enough to put his binoculars over the low stone edging of the balcony he and the others were lying on.

Cautiously, feeling cold and awkward and more than a little scared, Powell arched his back and eased his own head up over the stone. Beyond the tree-lined esplanade to the south, he could see the lights of the *Galen's Tenth* puttering its way northward along the Hudson River, headed for the boat basin directly below them.

The boat basin. Powell lifted his head another inch, shifting his gaze downward over the balcony to look across the wide stone walkways and manicured grass and neatly trimmed trees of the World Financial Center Plaza to the dark water and gently bobbing floating docks. At any given time, he knew, there were at least a couple of yachts tied up there, as well as a tour boat or one of the city's fleet of water taxis. But at the moment the basin was empty, all other ships moved out at Messerling's orders.

The plaza itself looked just as empty. The normal daytime pedestrian traffic of financiers and clients was long gone, the evening's collection of youthful cyclists and skateboarders had retired to homework or TV, and the throngs of commuters waiting for ferries to Hoboken or Fulton or Port Imperial were already home.

But here, unlike the boat basin itself, the emptiness was an illusion. Crouching behind the hedges or lying prone behind low walls or stretched out behind balcony walls like the one he and Messerling were on were over forty armed and armored S.W.A.T. cops. Another twenty skulked around the buildings and park areas to the north and south, backup forces for a three-sided box that would theoretically trap the incoming gang soldiers against the Hudson with no way to escape.

Theoretically.

Turning his head, Powell looked to his right at the majestic glass walls and arched roof of the Winter Palace nestled between the taller but far less spectacular Buildings Two and Three of the World Financial Center. The Winter Palace was the WFC's showpiece, a glittering multilevel expanse of marble and brass and sixteen live palm trees that served as a haven of calm and stability amid the more frantic chasing after money that took place in the buildings around it all day.

It was also the site of public performances and exhibits, as well as a myriad of private functions for the city's wealthy and powerful throughout the year, and the owners had not been at all happy at the possibility of a full-bore firefight taking place on its doorstep. Messerling's insistence that this was the only way had fallen on deaf ears, as had his assurances that even rabid gang fighters were surely rational enough to surrender once they saw the firepower arrayed against them. It was only when the Police Commissioner himself had intervened that they'd finally been able to get some grudging cooperation. If any of those impressive windows got shot out, Powell mused, the gang would be the least of their worries.

"All units, stand ready," Messerling murmured into his helmet mike.

Powell shifted his attention back to the river. The yacht had reached the entrance to the harbor and was making its way inside, moving with the ease and confidence of a pilot who'd performed this maneuver dozens of times and knew exactly what he was doing. "Anyone have a view of the civilians?" he asked. "Spotters?"

"They're both in the wheelhouse," Spotter One's voice reported crisply in Powell's ear. "Along with an older male and female and . . . looks like three young males and a female."

"Copy," Messerling said. "All units, keep that in mind if we have to open fire."

Powell reached up to wrap his hand around his mike. "What do we do if they're still aboard when they spot your people?" he asked Messerling.

"We'll wait as long as we can," Messerling told him, covering his own mike. "But the primary objective here is to contain and neutralize. We do *not* want these people escaping the box and running loose in the city." He lifted his head a bit. "Damn," he muttered. "They're taking one of the north docks."

Powell hunched himself up to look. Sure enough, the yacht had turned into the open area between two of the northern docks, a spray of water roiling at its aft end as the pilot reversed the screws to brake the craft to a halt. "Is that a problem?"

"Most of my men are on the south and east sides," Messerling told him. "The only close cover we had on the north is that curved wall right beside the basin, and there was only enough room there for five guys."

"But you've got men on the other balcony over there, right?" Powell asked, nodding past the Winter Garden toward the counterpart to the balcony they themselves were on.

"Sure, but they can't do anything from there except provide backup fire," Messerling gritted. "I'd rather avoid gunfire entirely, and a massive show of force on the ground is the best way to do that. We've got the troops, but now they'll have to cross a lot of open ground to get to the debarkation area."

Two young men hopped from the yacht to the dock and began tying up the ship. Other shadowy figures had appeared from below decks, and even before the boat was completely secured they were slipping over the side onto the dock. Looking around cautiously, they moved in an orderly line toward the double set of stairs that led up in both directions from the basin to the plaza level. The reached the steps and split into two groups, one heading up each flight. Back on the yacht, other figures were appearing from the companionway, lining up on both sides of the deck as they waited their turns to disembark. "I don't see any heavy weapons anywhere," Messerling murmured. "Anyone?"

"Negative," Spotter One's voice replied.

"Negative here, too," Spotter Two confirmed. "In fact, I don't see any drawn weapons of any sort."

"Maybe we can catch them sleepwalking," Messerling said, reaching for the bullhorn at his side. "All units: stand by. One . . . two . . ."

The leading men in the line reached the top of the stairs, one group now directly beneath the curved wall where the nearest cops lay in wait—

"Go!" Messerling snapped.

And abruptly, the entire plaza area blazed with daylight brightness as a dozen small floodlights opened up from concealment on balconies and behind shrubs. At the same instant, the cops behind the curved wall popped up into view, their compact Heckler & Koch MP5 submachine guns pointed down at the line of men suddenly frozen in place along the stairways. "Police!" Messerling shouted into the bullhorn, his amplified voice echoing eerily back from the buildings around them. "You're completely surrounded. Stay where you are and put up your hands."

• •

Caroline's first terrified thought as the light burst suddenly in her eyes was that there had been an explosion in one of the dark buildings towering over the boat basin. She gasped, throwing up an arm to shield her face, her hip slamming painfully into the edge of the yacht's control panel as she jerked backward—

"Police!" an amplified voice boomed across the night. "You're completely surrounded. Stay where you are and put up your hands."

Her breath went out in a huff, her momentary panic twisting into confusion and stunned disbelief. The *police*? But how—?

And then her brain caught up with her, and the hard knot in her stomach suddenly loosened amid a surge of unexpected hope.

Her secret message had gotten through.

Squinting against the glare, she looked over at Sylvia. The Command-Tactician's face was turned away from her, impossible to read. But there was something in the way she was standing that sent a shiver up Caroline's back. If the police expected her to simply surrender, they were in for a nasty surprise. Even before the echoes had finished bouncing off the buildings she sensed a flurry of silent Green commands ripple across her mind—

And floundered off-balance as the deck of the yacht suddenly rocked beneath her and the sound of multiple splashes came from the far side of the ship.

• •

"What the *hell*?" Powell said, frowning with surprise as the entire far side of the yacht seemed to explode with whitewater spray as at least twenty of the soldiers hurled themselves into the harbor.

"They're in the water," Messerling snapped into his mike. "Units Five and Six, get down to the basin and watch for them to come up. And watch out for those sonic weapons."

There was a curt acknowledgment, and a half-dozen armored cops crouching behind the low wall fifty feet south of the harbor vaulted over their protective barrier and ran toward the harbor, MP5s held ready in front of them. "Watch it—they're at the south dock," Spotter One warned. "I can see two—make that three of them in the water, hanging onto the side."

Powell looked that direction. Sure enough, there were three heads bobbing together in the water at the section of the dock opposite the yacht's aft end. The two outside men each had a hand up on the edge of the dock to steady themselves, while the one in the middle was apparently just treading water.

"Damn fast swimmers," Messerling muttered. "Stay sharp everyone; these three may be a diversion." The six cops reached the railing by the south ramp and came to a halt, lowering their muzzles to point into the water where the three men were hanging.

And a second later jerked back in startled confusion as, with a single powerful heave, the two submerged men on the sides hurled their companion upward out of the water and over the railing to drop squarely into the center of their formation. There was a burst of stray gunfire into the air as he grabbed the two nearest cops and shoved them back into their comrades, sending the whole bunch sprawling to the pavement. Regaining his own balance, the attacker ducked

to his right and sprinted in a zigzag run toward the south esplanade and the Hudson River beyond.

"*Damn* it," Messerling snarled into his mike. "*Get* him!"

The words were barely out of his mouth when all hell
broke loose.

In the water of the harbor, a dozen of the other would-be
escapers suddenly popped into view, their heads and torsos
bobbing upward like dolphins surfacing. Each of them had
one arm cocked back behind his head like a quarterback
preparing to throw an end-zone pass, Powell saw in that
brief glance, with the other arm stretched straight forward in
front of him. He caught the glint of metal— "Watch it!" he
snapped, cringing back reflexively. The men reached the top
of their bounce and dropped back beneath the gentle
waves—

And half a dozen of the spotlights scattered around the
plaza suddenly shattered and went dark. "What the—?"

"Slingshots," Spotter Two snapped. "They're targeting
the lights—"

"There they go!" someone else cut him off.

The men lined up on the north boat basin steps, who had
been standing impassively under the glare of the lights and
guns of the cops crouched above them, were suddenly scattering in all directions. Some of them jumped back down to
the level of the dock and sprinted east, where the height differential between basin and plaza would provide cover from
the guns trained on them from across at the park. Others
leaped up over the railing and ran toward the row of trees lining the north end of the plaza and the buildings beyond,
while still others charged straight into the guns of the cops
crouched behind the curved wall. One of the cops half rose
and lifted his gun—

Abruptly, a high-pitched yelp cut through the air, sending
a violent twitch through Powell's body.

The effects on the cops below was even more dramatic.
They staggered backward, the one who'd been bringing his
gun to bear nearly falling over as the weapon's muzzle
swung drunkenly around. Before he could recover, a metal

disk came spinning at him from one of the figures sprinting toward the trees, knocking the weapon out of his hands.

At the corner of Powell's eye, another group bobbed back to the surface of the water, and he looked back just as they let fly a second slingshot volley. With a multiple tinkle of shattered glass, the rest of the spotlights went dark. By the last dying flicker of their light, Powell saw that the attackers had overrun the dazed cops on the curving wall.

"It's like a three-ring circus down there," Messerling muttered. "All right, that's it. Ground level: masks on. Flash-bangs: *fire*."

There was a stuttering chuff of grenade launchers, and Powell turned his head away, squeezing his eyes tightly shut. Two seconds later, the flash-bangs went off, bursting with a thunderclap of sound that seemed to lift him straight off the balcony and a flash of light that was dazzling even through his closed eyelids. The light faded, and he lifted his head again to look over the balcony.

Even with the spotlights gone, there was enough light filtering into the area from the city around them to see the plaza. There should certainly have been enough light for them to see the bodies laid out on the stone walkways, writhing or twitching with the aftereffects of the grenades.

Only there weren't any bodies to be seen.

The soldiers had vanished.

"Where did they go?" he demanded, looking frantically around the plaza, blinking his eyes as if that would change the reality stretched out in front of him. There wasn't anywhere down there where that many people could be hiding. There certainly wasn't any place they could have gotten to in such a short stretch of time, especially not with flash-bangs going off all around them. They *couldn't* be gone.

But they were.

"Look alive, spotters," Messerling called into his mike. "Where did they go?"

"I don't know," Spotter One said, sounding as confused as Powell felt. "They were right there. And then . . ." He trailed off in confusion.

"Flankers, move in," Messerling ordered, his voice under rigid control. "Seal the area, and I mean *seal* it. Units Seven and Two, check the buildings on the north side for open doors. Unit Nine, get aboard that yacht and retrieve the hostages."

"No," a voice said from behind them. Powell twisted around to look—

As Fierenzo and Roger Whittier dropped into a crouch beside him and Messerling.

"*Fierenzo?*" Messerling demanded disbelievingly. "I thought you'd been kidnapped."

"Forget the yacht for now," Fierenzo told him. "You have to make a perimeter—"

"Just a damn minute," Messerling cut him off, glaring up at him. "I thought this whole thing started because you'd disappeared." He shifted the glare to Powell. "*Powell* said these guys snatched you."

"Never mind that now," Fierenzo said. "Call Unit Nine back. By my count, there are another twenty-five soldiers still aboard."

"By *your* count?" Messerling demanded. "Look—"

He broke off as a sudden commotion erupted from the shrubs and trees of the park area at the plaza's south end. "We're under attack!" a voice snapped over the radio. "They just—*oof!*"

He broke off. "Gas 'em!" Messerling snapped. "Wisbaski?"

"I'm on it," a cop at the far end of their balcony snapped back. Standing up, he swiveled his multi-shot CS grenade launcher around toward the sound of the struggle below and lifted it to his shoulder.

But before he could fire, another of the strange yips swept across the balcony, sending another twitch through Powell's muscles and staggering Wisbaski backward. With a muffled curse, he stepped forward again, the muzzle of his launcher weaving noticeably as he pointed it toward the commotion below.

And as his shoulders tensed in preparation for firing, another of the metal disks shot up from the plaza, catching the underside of the launcher and knocking it back and up. The shot went wild, the gas canister arching almost straight up into the air, trailing a thin plume of tear gas behind it.

"Oh, *hell!*" Messerling snarled, grabbing the gas mask hanging from his belt. "Incoming!"

Powell fumbled for his own mask and got it free. Then, on sudden impulse, he shoved it into Fierenzo's hands. "Here," was all he had time to say. He took a deep breath and squeezed his eyes shut—

The canister hit the balcony and burst into a roiling white cloud of stinging gas. Staying as still as he could, trying to conserve his air, Powell felt his eyes begin to tingle as the gas worked its way beneath his eyelids.

For him, he knew, the battle was over.

• •

It wasn't until the hand closed on her wrist and someone began to haul her upright that Caroline realized that she had in fact been lying on the wheelhouse deck. "What happened?" she murmured through dry lips, blinking as she tried to focus on the chaos outside.

"Stun grenades," Sylvia said, her voice sounding distant through the ringing in Caroline's ears. "Sound and flash. You must have been looking at one when it went off."

Caroline blinked some more, trying to see around the purple blob floating in the center of her vision. Even with the blob in the way, she could see that the Plaza was inexplicably empty. "Where is everyone?" she asked, a sudden, horrible thought cutting through her. "Did the police—?"

"Kill them?" Sylvia snorted. "Hardly, though I do have to give them points for restraint. No, the Warriors have simply gone to ground." She pointed past the bow end of the yacht. "Many of them are in that row of trees along the north of the boat basin. Others were able to get into the trees on the south side, over by that grassy park area. Others swam out to the river and are heading farther north and south."

There was a sudden sound of commotion from somewhere. "And others worked their way to that other park over by the building," Sylvia added dryly. "Lots of nice trees there to pop in and out of. The police will never even know what hit them."

Caroline looked that direction; and as she did so, she caught a glimpse of a thin trail of white as it arched into the sky and then tumbled back down onto the balcony to explode into a flat cloud of thick white vapor. "Excellent," Sylvia murmured. "One balcony out of commission. One more to go."

Caroline looked over at the balcony on the other side of the Winter Garden, where she could vaguely see dark helmets and guns poking over the railing. "You're not going to hurt them, are you?"

"Not unless I have to," Sylvia said. "But it may come to that. They're quite good." She paused briefly. "As are you, Caroline. I see now that I missed your hidden message completely. What exactly did all those X's signify?"

It took Caroline a moment to shift gears. "I was using Roman numerals," Caroline told her. "The 'roaming Warriors' line was meant to point Roger in the right direction." She felt her lip twitch. "It was also supposed to refer back to a conversation we'd had Wednesday night that should have told him everything I'd said before had been a lie. I guess he missed that one."

"And I'd seen Roman numerals, too," Sylvia said, sounding slightly disgusted with herself. "Very clever." She shrugged, dismissing her failure. "But no real harm done. Our observers confirm that nearly all of Torvald's troops are still gathered in Upper Manhattan, awaiting our arrival there. With Halfdan's forces scattered with equal pointlessness on sentry duty, that means that once we've bypassed this little obstacle, we'll have free run of the island."

Caroline took a deep breath. "You don't have to do this, Sylvia," she said, trying one last time. "There has to be another way."

"There," Sylvia said, pointing.

Caroline followed the direction of her finger to the balcony still awash in the wayward tear gas. A pair of Warriors had emerged from the now quiet trees and low hedges of the park below, running across the ground toward a position beneath the balcony's edge. As they braked to a halt, each flung something upward toward the railing. Caroline braced herself for an explosion or another burst of tear gas; instead, the Warriors suddenly rose off the ground, pulling themselves upward hand over hand through the drifting mist on invisible lines. "Of course," she murmured. "*Trassks* as cables and grappling hooks. Tear gas doesn't bother you, then?"

"Yes, but not to the same extent as it does you Humans," Sylvia said. "In this case, these two Warriors are merely holding their breath and keeping their eyes closed."

They reached the balcony, ducking down into the drifting cloud, and Caroline caught glimpses of quick movements as they beat back whatever opposition was still left up there. One of them partially emerged from the cloud with something that looked like an oversized shotgun and pointed it past the Winter Garden at the other balcony. There was the jerk of a recoil, and another tear-gas canister flew across the open area to wrap the balcony in a white cloud of its own.

"And now we complete the neutralization," Sylvia said calmly. From one of the trees lining the walk another pair of Warriors appeared and sprinted toward the balcony with their own grappling hooks in hand.

"And they're doing all this *blind*?" Caroline asked.

"Not entirely," Sylvia said. "Their eyes are shut, true, but the Farspeaker currently floating beside one of the docks can put some of what she sees into their minds, giving them a fair idea of what's around them. The rest of the details they fill in with hearing and touch."

Caroline watched in silence as the two Warriors made it up onto the second balcony and disappeared into the tear gas cloud. A minute later, they reappeared, rappelling to the ground and then twitching their grapples to free them. There was a shout from somewhere, and Caroline winced as a burst of gunfire ricocheted off the building behind them.

The Greens didn't wait for their attackers' aim to improve, but turned and raced back across the plaza, bullets chewing up bits of the pavement at their heels as they ran. Caroline tensed, wondering if they would make it back to the trees in time and wondering how they would get back inside without any of the cops seeing them. They were nearly there when another short Shriek split the air, rocking her back on her heels and startling her eyes momentarily shut. When she opened them again, the two running Warriors had vanished.

"And now only those on the south side of the boat basin remain," Sylvia commented calmly. "They're already masked against the gas, so the Warriors are having to approach with a little more prudence. Ah."

"What?" Caroline asked, turning and peering to the south.

"No, not there," Sylvia said, pointing her back the opposite direction. "There. The police backup forces have arrived."

Caroline turned again. "Where?"

"They've just come around the sides of the buildings," Sylvia said. "Moving in very carefully." She shook her head. "Not that that's going to help, of course. Whatever information Roger gave them, he seems to have failed to mention who and what we truly are."

Caroline felt her stomach tighten. "He just wanted the police to keep you from attacking the Grays," she murmured. "He didn't want the government hauling you off somewhere to be studied like lab rats for the rest of your lives."

"More likely he didn't want to end up in a psychiatric ward," Sylvia said cynically. "At any rate, half a tale is going to buy him exactly nothing. In fact, unless they have something more impressive in reserve, we're hardly even going to be inconvenienced. Here they come."

Caroline looked again across at the buildings. Sylvia was right: she could see shadowy figures moving stealthily along the sides of the buildings. "They can search the buildings all they want," Sylvia told her. "Sooner or later, they'll come close enough to the trees."

She gave Caroline a faint smile. "Just relax," she said soothingly. "It'll soon be over, and you'll be able to go home."

"And the Grays?"

"As I said," Sylvia said softly, turning back to face the approaching cops. "It'll soon be over."

47

Across the broad balcony something popped into a cloud of white smoke; and the next thing Roger knew Fierenzo had hauled him to his feet, nearly wrenching his left shoulder out of its socket in the process, and was dragging him across the balcony toward the door they'd just come in through. "What—?"

"Close your eyes and hold your breath," the detective snapped, tightening his grip and picking up his pace.

And then it belatedly clicked, and Roger took one last quick breath and squeezed his eyes shut as he felt the coldness of the cloud wash over him. They hit the door running, Fierenzo slamming it open and pulling Roger through.

The next minute was a flurry of echoing footsteps and massive disorientation as Roger ran blindly down the empty corridor with only Fierenzo's hand on his arm to guide him. Even with his eyes closed he could feel them starting to tingle and sting. His nostrils felt the same way, and he wondered uneasily what would happen when he finally couldn't hold his breath any longer and was forced to inhale. He had no idea what kind of gas the Greens had used, but if he was incapacitated now it would all be over. The Greens and Grays would have their war, with New York City squarely in the middle of it.

They slowed slightly to turn a corner, then picked up speed again. Roger's chest was beginning to ache from the

strain of holding his breath, and he had that creepy sensation that any second now Fierenzo would accidentally slam
him full-tilt into a wall or janitor's cart. They'd surely already passed the elevator by now—

"In here," Fierenzo said suddenly, his voice sounding
oddly muffled. His hand veered Roger to the right, and there
was a hollow thud as the detective shoved a door open and
pulled him inside a room. They ran a few more paces, and
Roger noted that the echo in here seemed different.

Fierenzo jerked him to a halt. "Hold still," he ordered.

And before Roger could even guess what he had in mind,
there was the sound of a faucet being cranked on, and a
spray of cold water washed over his face, splashing across
his eyes and up his nose.

He gasped in surprise, sputtering and coughing as some
of the water got into his open mouth and tried to go down
the wrong way. "Hold still—I'm trying to clean you off,"
Fierenzo said, letting go of his arm. "Get rid of that jacket."

Roger nodded, and started stripping it off. He was midway through the procedure when the spray stopped. "Okay,
open your eyes," Fierenzo said.

Carefully, Roger eased his eyes open. Fierenzo was just
pulling a gas mask away from his own face, sniffing cautiously at the air. "You okay?" the detective asked.

Roger gave a couple of experimental blinks and took a
careful breath. There was an unpleasant tingle in the air,
but it didn't seem to be affecting him any worse than some
of the hay fever attacks he'd had as a child. "I think so," he
confirmed.

"Good," Fierenzo said, dropping the mask into the next
sink over and pulling off his own jacket. "Give your face another rinse and then shut it off."

"Right," Roger said leaning down and throwing double
handfuls of water into his face. "We don't seem to be doing
very well out there," he commented.

"We're getting our butts kicked," Fierenzo retorted.
"Time to bring in the artillery."

"Right." Roger shook the excess water from his hands,

and grabbed a paper towel from the dispenser by the sink.
Wiping them dry, he lifted his left hand to his cheek and
twitched his little finger. "Jonah?"

"Right here," Jonah's voice came promptly. "You guys
aren't doing so well down there."

"Never mind us," Roger said. "Are you in position?"

"We're ready," the other said grimly. "You're sure you
don't want us to target the Warriors?"

"You want peace, or don't you?" Roger countered. "Just
follow the plan."

There was a faint sigh. "Right. Here goes."

Roger lowered his hand. "They're on it."

"Then I guess it's show time," Fierenzo said. "Unless you
want to take a minute and tell me what exactly this grand
scheme of yours is."

Roger shook his head. "No time," he said. "I need to get
out there before Nikolos comes up with a counterattack."

"You sure that's all of it?" Fierenzo asked, his eyes boring into Roger's face.

"I *know* this will work," Roger said, keeping his voice
steady. "Just give me a chance."

Fierenzo's lip twitched, but he nodded. "You'd just better
be right," he warned, picking up the gas mask and handing it
over. "Here you go. Knock 'em dead."

• •

The first of the backup cops had reached the corners of the
buildings and were preparing to sidle around them when the
river to Caroline's left exploded in a plume of water.

She twisted around to look as the spray fell ponderously
down again, some of it drifting onto the shore. "What was
that?" she gasped. "Are they *shelling* us?"

"Hardly," Sylvia bit out, and it seemed to Caroline that
her voice had suddenly gone dark and cold. "The fools.
What in the world do they think they can accomplish?"

Another plume of water burst into the air, this one from
much closer to the yacht. "What are you talking about?"

Caroline asked, her heart pounding in her ears. "Who is it?"

"Who do you think?" Sylvia said contemptuously. "The Grays."

Caroline stared at her. "But you said they were all somewhere else."

"Most of them are," Sylvia said, stepping to the side of the wheelhouse and peering upward at the buildings. "Unless we're being attacked by children, there can't be more than three or four of them at the most." She lifted a hand. "Of course. Jonah McClung."

"Who?"

"The Gray who snatched Melantha from Riverside Park last Wednesday," Sylvia said. "Halfdan was able to backtrack him and his brother Jordan, and was kind enough to share that information with Cyril." She nodded upward. "Apparently, they're still in the rescuing business."

Another geyser burst into the air. "What are you going to do?" Caroline asked.

"What do you think?" Sylvia retorted. "I'm going to bring them down."

"And kill them?"

"I don't have time for finesse, Caroline," Sylvia said patiently. "You see those blue-gray clouds over on the balconies?"

The tear gas clouds *did* look a little different now, she saw. In fact, they seemed to be dissipating before her eyes. "Catalytic neutralizer," Sylvia identified it. "They've given up on the tear gas and are clearing it away, probably in preparation for trying something new. Unfortunately, that also means improved visibility all around, which will make it even more risky to bring our Gray snipers down in a controlled fall. We can't afford to let the cops see them hanging onto the side of a building."

"But they haven't hurt anyone," Caroline pleaded. She'd only met this Jonah briefly, but nevertheless her heart was instantly on his side. Maybe Roger was right about her and underdogs. "Those are just warning shots."

"Warning shots that are drawing far too much attention,"

Sylvia pointed out. "They might even scare the police into bringing in heavy reinforcements or doing something equally stupid." She looked out the wheelhouse window again, and Caroline could sense her giving new orders to her Warriors—

"Nikolos!" a distant voice called faintly across the plaza.

Caroline felt her breath catch in her lungs. The voice was distant and muffled, possibly by a gas mask or other protective gear. But even so, she had no doubt as to whose voice it was. "Roger," she whispered, her eyes darting back and forth as she looked frantically around for him.

She found him standing near one of the entrances to the Winter Garden, surrounded by a tight knot of half a dozen people, all of them wearing gas masks, at least one of them clearly having some kind of argument with him. "Somebody over there seems to be wasting his time," Sylvia commented beside her.

"Roger doesn't like confrontations," Caroline said, automatically coming to her husband's defense.

"I wasn't talking about Roger," Sylvia said. "He's doing just fine. I was referring to the other man."

"Which other man?" Caroline asked as the air around her head buzzed with Green communication.

"The large one, Police Lieutenant Cerreta," Sylvia said, her tone thoughtful. "He says he's not allowing any civilians into a combat zone, period. Roger is insisting right back—"

She broke off, chuckling. "What?" Caroline demanded.

"He's insisting that with the gang members vanished from the scene—which I presume he knows full well that we aren't—that there *is* no combat zone anymore. Clever."

Another figure emerged from one of the doors beside the Winter Garden and crossed to the group. "Well, well," Sylvia said. "Detective Fierenzo has joined the fray."

"On whose side?" Caroline asked, fascinated in spite of herself by Sylvia's ability to eavesdrop at this distance. Clearly, one of her Warriors must be within earshot of the conversation.

"Not surprisingly, he's on Roger's," Sylvia told her. "I don't know how effective he'll be, though. He seems to be in a certain amount of hot water himself."

"He disappeared right after the Warriors confronted him outside his precinct house and obtained the sketches," Nikolos spoke up.

Caroline looked around in mild surprise. Nikolos had been so quiet she'd almost forgotten he was there. He was crouched on the deck beside a gently snoring Mr. Galen, his hand resting on the sleeping man's shoulder. "Jonah and Jordan rescued him," Nikolos went on, "then took him into hiding while he recovered. Apparently, he never bothered to check in with his superiors afterward."

"Cerreta's displeasure is certainly colorful," Sylvia commented, frowning suddenly. "Nikolos, how are your eyes?"

"Still reasonably good," the other said, stepping to her side. "Where?"

"Inside the Winter Garden, back up on the steps," she said, pointing. "Is that Velovsky? None of my Warriors has a clear view."

Nikolos craned his neck. "It certainly looks like him," he agreed slowly. "I wonder what he's doing here."

"I'm sure Roger could tell you," Caroline said. "Why not ask for him to be sent over?"

Sylvia looked at her in surprise. "Why should I?"

"Because he's in charge of this whole thing," Caroline said. "At least, the Gray part of it."

"What makes you think that?" Nikolos asked.

Caroline gestured toward the river. "The warning shots have stopped," she pointed out. "Whoever's up there is waiting for Roger to make his move."

"Ridiculous," Nikolos growled.

"Not at all," Caroline said, her eyes on Sylvia. "And under the circumstances, I'd think a good Command-Tactician would want to hear him out."

"I've already told you that you can't manipulate me that way," Sylvia said mildly. But her voice was thoughtful as

she gazed past Caroline's shoulder at the distant confrontation. "On the other hand, you do have a point," she went on.
"Fine. Let's see what he has to say."

Caroline turned to see a Warrior emerge from one of the
trees at the south end of the plaza and stride toward the
cluster of people. He'd gotten three or four steps before
anyone noticed, and then a half dozen machine guns
abruptly snapped up to point at him. Ignoring the weapons,
he walked to within a handful of paces of the group and
stopped. "I'm still amazed at how easy it is to take you people by surprise," Sylvia said, shaking her head.

Caroline shrugged. "We're only human."

"One of your many failings," Sylvia agreed. "It's apparently easy to run you out of ideas, too. Having failed to
come up with anything else to do, they're going to let him
come talk to us."

Roger had detached himself from the group, and with the
Warrior at his side he headed across the plaza. Caroline
watched him, suddenly and rather irrationally wondering
how she looked after three days in the same clothing. He
walked down the steps and onto the dock, where the Warrior
took the lead and gestured him to the wheelhouse. Caroline
stood where she was, feeling suddenly more nervous than
she had at the height of the battle.

And then the wheelhouse door opened, and Roger
stepped inside, his eyes flicking around the cramped space
and quickly coming to rest on her. For a moment he stood
where he was, and she had the sense that he was fighting a
battle with the dignity of the situation.

Dignity lost. A second later, he had taken two quick steps
across the wheelhouse, and she found herself being
squeezed tightly in his embrace. "Are you all right?" he
whispered in her ear.

"I'm fine," she whispered back, clutching him just as
hard in return, tears of relief welling up in her eyes. "You?"

"I'm okay," he assured her. He held her another moment;
then, almost unwillingly, he slackened his grip and turned to

the others in the room. "Hello, Nikolos," he greeted the other, his voice gravely controlled. "Sylvia. I appreciate you seeing me like this."

"Actually, it was Caroline's idea," Nikolos said, straightening up from the deck and giving Roger a long, measuring look. "She seems to think you might have something useful to say to me."

"She's right," Roger agreed, stepping slightly away from Caroline but keeping a grip on her hand. "I'm here to tell you that if you keep this up, you're going to lose."

"Really," Nikolos said, a touch of amusement in his voice. "What makes you think that a handful of bumbling Humans and a couple of Grays skulking at the top of a building are even going to slow us down?"

"A couple of reasons," Roger said. If he was surprised that they knew that there were only two Grays out there, he didn't show it. "Point number one: as long as I'm in here with you and the police maintain their perimeter, you're effectively trapped."

"Nonsense," Nikolos said. "The Warriors who've taken the eastern park area can slip out around that building any time they want. We have others in the trees to the south who can probably do the same, and the ones already in the water can swim all the way to New Jersey if they have to."

"Granted," Roger said calmly. "But you need to take another look at your numbers."

Nikolos's eyes narrowed. "What do you mean?"

"You left the Catskills with a hundred thirty-five Warriors, Farspeakers, and other support personnel," Roger said, ticking off fingers. "You sent eight of them in the vans as decoys, dropped twenty-two more in northern Manhattan to provide a feint for Torvald's Grays, and landed twenty more in Queens and Brooklyn. That leaves eighty-five here within shouting distance. Subtracting the fifteen in the water, the twelve in the trees south of the harbor, and the fourteen currently in the wooded park by Building Two—all of whom you claim can get away—you still have forty-four here on the yacht or in that line of trees along the northern part of the plaza who are effectively trapped. Taking into account the sixty Warriors you already had in the city, it looks to me like nearly a quarter of your troops are pinned down." He lifted his eyebrows. "Not to mention you and Sylvia, of course. How's my math?"

Nikolos's face had gone rigid. "You can't possibly have those numbers," he insisted.

"But I do," Roger said. "Which is point number two: we have an inside track on everything that's happening here. Namely, Melantha's mother, Laurel." He looked at Sylvia. "You remember her from our visit to your little retreat."

"Certainly," Sylvia said, her voice far calmer than Nikolos's. "The one hiding . . . where was she, anyway? Your trunk?"

"That's right," Roger confirmed. "And of course I know now why your people reacted so badly when they realized she was there. At the time we thought she might have overheard Damian talking, or else someone referring to him. But there is no Damian, is there?"

Wordlessly, Sylvia shook her head. "Right," Roger said. "What you were actually afraid of was that enough of your Warriors had been chattering for her to realize how many of them you actually had. Like everyone else, she'd bought into Nikolos's story that there were only sixty of them. If she'd heard all hundred twenty talking, she'd have realized what the plan really was."

"And if she had, she should have kept it to herself like a good Green," Nikolos said darkly. "But that's behind us. What does this have to do with the situation here and now?"

"The fact that Laurel is listening in on every order you send your troops and passing the word on to Detective Fierenzo and me," Roger said. "We know where each of them is, *and* what you're planning for them."

"So that's the way of it, is it?" Nikolos murmured in a voice that sent a shiver up Caroline's back. "Laurel Green has become a traitor to her people."

"Actually, you have that backwards," Roger told him. "She may be one of the few Greens who *isn't* a traitor to their people." He lifted his eyebrows. "Want to hear more?"

For a moment Nikolos frowned at him, and Caroline could sense a quick wordless conference with Sylvia. "It won't do you any good to move your people around," Roger warned into the silence. "We'll know the minute you try anything, and can relay the information to both the police and the Grays. But I can also promise you there are no tricks here. All I want is a chance to talk."

"Fine," Nikolos said. "Talk."

Roger shook his head. "Not here." He pointed out the window at the glass and soft lights of the Winter Garden. "In there."

Nikolos smiled thinly. "Of course," he said sarcastically. "You expect us to just walk meekly into the middle of the police camp?"

"Why not?" Roger countered. "Are you in any better contact with your Warriors here than you would be there? Besides, you're actually safer in there than you are here. Right now the cops would have very little compunction about blowing this yacht into driftwood if they thought it was justified. They're going to be a lot more careful with the real estate in and around the Winter Garden."

"What exactly are you planning, Roger?" Sylvia asked.

He seemed to brace himself. "I'm planning a meeting between both sides," he told her. "I've learned a few things I think you'll both want to hear."

"Us meet with Grays?" Nikolos bit out. "I don't think so."

"There won't be more than four of them at the most," Roger promised. "Surely a Command-Tactician and Group Commander aren't afraid of four Grays."

"That's not the point," Nikolos said stiffly. "The Grays are our enemies."

"Yet you met with them at least once before," Caroline pointed out, wondering if Roger could have discovered the same secret she had about Nikolos's deceit. "Back when you decided to sacrifice Melantha."

"Cyril and Halfdan met," Nikolos countered. "I wasn't involved."

"Well, you're involved now," Roger said. "And frankly, the alternative is that the Grays go on the offensive all over New York with a quarter of your troops pinned down here."

"We can get out whenever we want to," Nikolos insisted.

"Not all of you," Roger said. "Up to now, the police have been treating you with kid gloves. After your little escapades on the balconies, they're ready to start using deadly force."

Nikolos snorted. "Overreaction," he said contemptuously. "We didn't even hurt anyone up there."

"Call it whatever you want," Roger said. "But they're primed and ready . . . and right now, this conference is the only thing standing between you and an all-out assault."

Nikolos pursed his lips, as if mulling it over. But Caroline wasn't fooled. He played the Command-Tactician role well enough, but she could sense the apprehension in his silent communication with Sylvia. She sensed Sylvia's decision—

"All right," Nikolos said, nodding slowly. "We'll come to your little party. Is that Velovsky in there?"

"Yes," Roger said. "After all, he was present at the beginning, or at least the chapter that began in New York. I thought he deserved to be in on the end of it, too."

"The end," Nikolos murmured. "I'm not sure I like the sound of that. And the other guests?"

"Torvald and Halfdan are on their way," Roger said. "They should be here by the time Cyril and Aleksander arrive."

"Cyril and Aleksander?" Caroline asked, frowning. "Are they nearby?"

"Nearby, and in the company of two Group Commanders, a Farspeaker, and forty of Manhattan's Warrior contingent," Roger said dryly. "As I said, Nikolos has no secrets from us anymore."

"Perhaps," Nikolos said, his voice silky smooth. "Perhaps not. At any rate, we'll come and see what you have to say."

"Thank you." Roger gestured to the door. "Follow me, please."

• •

"Here they come," Cerreta said, peering across the plaza at the figures filing through the wheelhouse door. He watched a moment, then shifted his gaze back to Fierenzo. "You've got until they get here to level with me."

"I already have," Fierenzo said, trying to keep his voice steady. "I went undercover to penetrate one of the sides of this gang war, and I just never had a chance to check in."

"That's a crock," Cerreta countered, matching the other's tone. "You've been manipulating this whole thing right from the start. Everything from the cop-in-distress alarm at the Two-Four, to Smith's little unauthorized jaunt upstate, to this whole damn S.W.A.T. exercise."

"Do you deny these groups pose a potential threat to the city?" Fierenzo countered, waving out at the battlefield. "And remember, you've only seen one of the two sides in action."

"That's not the point," Cerreta ground out. "The point is that your private crusade here has managed to run roughshod over just about every rule of procedure and evidence in the book. We started out thinking we had a conspiracy to commit kidnapping or murder that we could hang these people with. Now, we've got squat."

"I would think you'd be glad I *hadn't* been murdered," Fierenzo murmured.

"At the moment, it's at toss-up," Cerreta retorted. "Because anything *else* we might have been able to use will be thrown out the minute a judge sees how you handled it." He snorted. "In fact, about all we could arrest them for right now would be assault on police officers. And even *that* would be problematic, given that we don't know who did what."

"Actually, I was hoping to avoid making any arrests at all," Fierenzo said.

"Oh, right," Cerreta growled. "You and Whittier think

you can get them to talk out their differences, have a nice group hug, and become fine upstanding citizens again."

"Sarcasm aside, I think there's a good chance we can do exactly that," Fierenzo said, putting all the confidence he could into the words. A neat trick, given that he didn't have the slightest idea what Roger was even planning.

"I hope for your sake that you're right." Cerreta jerked a thumb back toward the Winter Garden. "But if you think I'm going to let you all sit around in there alone, you're badly mistaken."

Fierenzo felt his jaw tighten. Whatever Roger had in mind, the last thing they could afford would be for more people to be let in on the secret. "I don't think that would be a good idea," he said carefully.

"No?" Cerreta asked. "Well, *I* don't think letting any of these people out of my sight would be a good idea. And *my* think outranks your think."

"I understand," Fierenzo said, resisting the temptation to point out that a couple dozen of the Greens were, in fact, already out of Cerreta's sight. "But keeping us in sight doesn't mean you have to eavesdrop, does it?"

"Meaning . . . ?"

"Meaning we could go up on the steps to talk," Fierenzo suggested, pointing through the glass wall at the set of semicircular steps leading up from the center of the main floor a few yards beyond the ordered rows of palm trees. "The S.W.A.T. guys guarding us could stay down here, near the exits. We'd all be in clear view, and there'd be no way out if someone decided to try anything."

"What about the hallways into Building Two and Three?" Cerreta asked, looking doubtfully through the glass.

"Already sealed off," Fierenzo told him. "We'd be isolated, under constant guard, and still have the privacy both sides are going to insist on."

Roger and the others had climbed the steps from the boat basin and were halfway across the plaza before Cerreta spoke again. "All right," he said, his gaze seeming to bore straight through Fierenzo's retinas into his soul. "But I'll tell you this, Detective. No matter what happens here, you're going to have to answer for your behavior this past week."

Fierenzo nodded. "Understood."

Watching the Greens approach, he could only hope that it would be the only thing he would have to answer for.

48

Cyril and Aleksander were the first to arrive, passing silently through the door and between the line of stone-faced S.W.A.T. cops Cerreta had set up just inside the glass wall. They ignored Roger as he tried to greet them, brushing past him and Caroline and climbing the steps to where Nikolos and Sylvia had picked out a tier of steps to sit on just above the circular platform midway up. They did deign to glance at Fierenzo as he stood silently a few steps away, though Roger suspected that was mostly from curiosity, and nodded with some genuine civility at Velovsky where he sat a little apart from the others.

Halfdan was next, giving the rows of palm trees below a wide berth as if expecting a dozen Warriors to leap out of them as he passed. He gave Roger and Caroline a curious once-over, ignored Fierenzo completely, and nodded formally to Cyril as he chose a place on the steps at the same level as the four Greens but a quarter of the way around the circle from them. Torvald was only a minute behind him, limping past the palms without giving them a second glance and carefully climbing the steps to where Roger and Caroline waited. "I see we're mostly assembled," he commented, nodding to his brother and glancing at Velovsky and the four Greens.

"Actually, we're completely assembled," Roger said, gesturing him toward the steps. "Please have a seat."

Torvald climbed the last few steps to where Halfdan sat stolidly and lowered himself onto the marble beside him, and Caroline gave Roger's hand a quick squeeze. "You can do it," she murmured. Letting go, she crossed to Velovsky and sat down beside him.

Roger took a deep breath and stepped to the center of the circular platform. "Thank you all for coming here tonight," he said, looking at each of their faces in turn. None of them, with the exception of Caroline, looked particularly encouraging. "This is certainly a nicely symbolic place, if I do say so myself. Marble and stonework for the Grays; palm trees for the Greens. Something for everyone."

"If you have a point to make, please get to it," Aleksander said impatiently.

Roger took another deep breath, forcing himself not to be intimidated. Whether they knew it or not, whether they even cared or not, what he was about to say was going to change their lives. "But even more symbolic is the view through those windows," he continued, gesturing over their heads. "Directly behind you is Ground Zero, where three thousand innocent people died when the twin towers collapsed."

He locked eyes with Aleksander. "A fate thousands more might have suffered if certain of you had had your way in this war of yours."

"Nobody wants to kill innocent people," Aleksander insisted. "All we want is the right to survive."

"Really?" Roger said. "Who's stopping you?"

Aleksander snorted and started to get up. "This is a waste of time," he declared. "Come on, Nikolos—"

"Did you know that you all came from Earth?" Roger cut him off.

Aleksander froze halfway to his feet. "What?"

"That's right," Roger told him. "You didn't come from some alien world in some distant solar system. The only distance your transports brought you was about a quarter of the way around the planet, probably from someplace in central or eastern Europe."

"What are you talking about?" Sylvia demanded. "This is nothing like the world we left."

"That's because the transports also catapulted you four or five thousand years forward in time," Roger said. "Possibly more."

Slowly, Aleksander sat back down. "Dryads," he murmured. "The wood nymphs of Greek mythology."

"Yes," Cyril agreed, nodding as if a long-lost piece of a persistent puzzle had suddenly appeared on the table in front of him. "I wondered about that myself, years ago. But I put it down to coincidence."

"No coincidence," Roger confirmed. "You were indeed the inspiration for the dryads." He gestured behind him at the harbor. "Given your performance out there tonight, you probably inspired the myths about water nymphs, too."

He looked over at the two Grays. "And while the Greens were being worked into Greek myth, you and your manufacturing skills and Thor-inspiring hammerguns became part of the Norse tales."

"As the dwarves, I assume," Aleksander said, looking over at Halfdan and Torvald with a half-amused, half-malicious smile. "Not very flattering."

"Maybe not, but the Norse myths were more fun to read," Roger said before either Gray could respond. "But how you were perceived by the humans around you isn't important. The point is that you haven't really gone anywhere, which means that even if you wanted to leave there isn't anywhere else for you to go. This is your home; and if you can't learn to live together, you're still going to be stuck here."

"What makes you think we want to live together?" Torvald asked evenly. "What makes you think we even *can* live together?"

"You did so once," Roger pointed out. "Back in the Great Valley you lived in peace for at least three generations." He nodded at Velovsky. "Mr. Velovsky told us the whole story."

"Then I'm sure he also told you how that peace was broken by Green treachery," Halfdan bit out. "Which, as you can see, is still the way they do things." He threw the Greens a tight smile. "Fortunately, it's a game two sides can play." Still smiling, he lifted his left hand toward his ear—

"Freeze," Fierenzo said quietly.

Roger looked over at him. The detective had his gun out, tucked subtly at his side where it was out of view of the S.W.A.T. cops on the far side of the palm trees. "Lower your hand to your lap, nice and smooth," he ordered.

"And if I don't?" Halfdan countered, his hand hovering in the air halfway to his scarred cheek. "Are you going to shoot me?"

"If I have to," Fierenzo said.

The Gray shrugged. "It won't matter if you do," he said. "You didn't think I was foolish enough to come here alone, did you?"

"That's what you agreed to," Roger said, his pulse pounding suddenly in his throat. No—it couldn't come apart. Not now. Especially not like this.

"I agreed to come in *here* alone," Halfdan corrected him. "Out there in the world is a different matter entirely."

"What are you waiting for?" Aleksander demanded, looking at Fierenzo. "You can see he's betrayed us. Shoot him."

"Wait a minute," Roger said, holding out a hand toward Fierenzo. "Halfdan, you don't really want to die, do you?"

"Whether I die or not, you can't stop what's about to happen," the Gray said calmly. "My sons Bergan and Ingvar are standing ready, and they have their orders."

"What orders?" Roger asked. "What do you want?"

"To fulfill the bargain Cyril and the Greens made with us," Halfdan said, an edge of anger underlying his words. "We agreed to sacrifice Melantha with the understanding that it would return our forces to parity and thus ensure neither side could start a war with any guarantee of victory." He nodded toward the glass wall and the yacht floating in the harbor. "Now, of course, we see why Cyril was so willing to let her die. He already had a full set of aces up his sleeve."

"I knew nothing about the Catskills colony or those Warriors until tonight," Cyril protested. "That was all Nikolos." He flashed a look at Aleksander. "Or Aleksander."

"In that case, you should be on my side in this," Halfdan told him. "Regardless of whose plot it was, the fact is that there are enough Warriors in those trees and that boat to slaughter every Gray in New York. So I'm going to eliminate them, and bring us back to the parity we originally agreed to."

"You can't do this," Aleksander snarled. But there was a nervous edge beneath the bluster. "Fierenzo, you can't let him murder an entire group of Greens."

"He won't," Nikolos assured him, staring coldly at Halfdan. "Because if he does, an equal number of Gray children will die."

Halfdan's face froze. "What are you talking about?"

"I'm talking about twenty Warriors already in place in Queens and Brooklyn," Nikolos said. "Tell him, Detective—you and the other police watched them leave the yacht."

Halfdan snarled something in an alien language. "You uncivilized little—"

"Calm yourself," Nikolos cut him off. "Your children aren't their primary target. But that will change the minute the first Warrior out there dies at your hand."

For a long moment they locked eyes. Then, slowly, Halfdan lowered his hand to his lap. "Those Warriors will not leave here alive," he warned softly. "We agreed; and we *will* fulfill that agreement."

"So the truth comes out at last," Aleksander murmured. "When Grays speak about peace, what they really mean is the incremental destruction of the Greens."

"You see the problem, Roger," Torvald said. "The old hatreds and animosities run very deep."

"No, they don't," Caroline spoke up. "Or at least, they

shouldn't. You had three full generations of peace between your peoples. Doesn't that count for anything?"

"Not to those who lived through the war," Aleksander said. "Not to those who saw their homes destroyed and their families slaughtered."

"Fine," Roger said. "Hold onto your own personal hatred, if you insist. But there's no reason to saddle your children and grandchildren with it, too."

"The children will go where the adults lead," Halfdan said sourly. "Especially *Green* children."

"Maybe," Roger said. "But maybe not. Let me tell you about a couple of idealistic young kids named Jordan Anderson and Melantha Green."

He related the story of the accidental meeting between the young Green and Gray, the tentative development of their secret friendship, and the eventual expansion of that friendship to their families. Through it all, his audience listened in stony silence.

"So that's what happened," Torvald murmured when Roger had finished. "I'd wondered how Melantha's family could have persuaded a Gray like Jonah McClung to rescue her that night."

"He did it because she and Jordan were friends," Roger said. "If your own history doesn't convince you that you can live in peace, maybe that will."

He looked at Halfdan. "Not just in a state of truce, either, with both sides poised for war but knowing they can't win," he added. "I mean a real, genuine, *stable* peace."

"It's easy for *you* to talk peace," Aleksander growled. "Easy for Melantha and Jordan, too. None of you ever saw the results of Gray treachery."

"It was *Green* treachery that started the war," Halfdan countered.

"There was no treachery!" Roger snarled, suddenly sick of the whole argument. "The fire was started by dry lightning. The Grays fired into the trees trying to create a firebreak. The Greens attacked the cliffs thinking the Grays

were shooting at them. The whole thing was a massive, stupid mistake."

"How dare you talk about us this way?" Aleksander demanded, half-rising from his seat as if preparing to attack Roger bodily. "How *dare* you pass judgment on things you have no knowledge of?"

"Besides, if it was a mistake why didn't anyone back then figure it out?" Torvald added.

Roger took a careful breath, pushing away his frustration and forcing himself back into control. They'd reached the crux of the matter, and the last thing he could afford was to let his emotions obscure their chance of understanding. "That *is* the question, isn't it?" he agreed. "And that brings me to my final point . . . because the fact of the matter is, they did."

He looked at the Greens. "Tell me, Aleksander. How did you and your people get here?"

"In our transport, of course," Aleksander said. "I thought you said Velovsky told you everything."

"Yes, he did," Roger acknowledged, turning to the Grays. "And you?"

"Both our peoples had transports," Torvald said. "You should know—you and your friends had a brief tour of ours."

"They *what*?" Halfdan asked, frowning at his brother. "When?"

"Last night," Roger said before Torvald could answer. "We went there to get Melantha."

Cyril inhaled sharply. "*Torvald* had her?"

"And you have her back?" Aleksander demanded.

"We have her, and she's safe," Roger assured him. "And before you ask, Torvald treated her quite well. Better than certain others of you would have, I might add. The point is that Velovsky was with us on this little expedition, and while we were there he did something that finally put me on the right track."

He looked over at the old man. "Do you remember pausing at that last T-junction before we found Melantha? We were going to go right, but you told us to go left."

"Of course I remember," Velovsky said, a little stiffly. "And I was right."

"You were indeed," Roger said, nodding. "We found her in the aft passenger compartment." He lifted his eyebrows. "The question is, how did you know she was back there?"

Velovsky frowned. "I don't understand."

"My assumption at the time was that your close contact with Leader Elymas back on Ellis Island had sensitized you to Green telepathic communications," Roger said. "My wife has developed some of that talent, too, thanks to Cyril's attempt to use his Persuader's Gift on her."

"But that wasn't it?" Torvald asked, his voice suddenly tight.

Roger shook his head. "We arrived to find Melantha just waking up," he said. "Aleksander had already told us that Greens don't simply broadcast their presence, like sonar beacons or something. But if she was asleep, she wasn't talking, and he couldn't have heard her. And Velovsky had never been aboard the Gray transport, so he couldn't have known where that passenger compartment was." He paused. "Or could he?"

No one spoke. For a moment Roger looked around at them, noting the frowns and puzzlement on their faces. They weren't getting it, or else were refusing to get it. "Cyril, I'll be the first to agree that your people have amazing Gifts," he said, turning to the four Greens sitting stiffly in their little cluster. "But I've yet to see anything mechanical or electronic that you've built. So tell me: *who built your transport?*"

"No," Cyril whispered. "You're wrong."

"And you," Roger continued, turning to Halfdan and Torvald. "Your people could probably have designed and built that transport in your sleep. *But how did you throw it five thousand years into the future?*"

"I'll be damned," Fierenzo said, sounding stunned. "The Grays built both transports . . . and the *Greens* sent both of them here?"

"Exactly," Roger said, feeling an odd surge of relief now that it was finally out in the open. "That's how Velovsky knew his way around the Gray transport. It was identical to the Greens', which he'd been aboard any number of times."

He looked back and forth between the two groups. "Don't you get it? This whole thing was a joint mission, put together to get a remnant of both your peoples away from a war that no one wanted but that no one could stop. The Gray mechanics built both transports, and the Green Farseers and Groundshakers sent both of them on their way. That's why you both ended up *here,* outside New York City. The whole idea was that you were *supposed* to live together."

"If that was true, why didn't anyone tell us?" Sylvia spoke up. "Why didn't anyone aboard the transports even know about it?"

"Battery Park," Torvald murmured.

They all looked at him. "What?" Cyril asked.

"You remember, Halfdan," Torvald said, turning to his brother. "On the first Sunday of every month, Dad always went out alone, early in the morning, to go sit in Battery Park. He never came home until after sunset." He looked with sudden understanding at Roger. "And he always seemed somehow sad."

Roger shook his head. "I'm sorry. I don't see the connection."

"I do," Caroline said suddenly. "He was waiting for Leader Elymas, wasn't he? It was a prearranged rendezvous, a time and place for them to make contact once both of you were settled and Elymas judged his people were ready."

"I think you're right," Torvald said. "Only Elymas never came, because he was already dead."

"And of course, none of the other Greens knew anything about the plan," Roger said, nodding heavily. "So your father died thinking the Greens had decided they didn't want anything to do with you."

"It's a nice theory, Roger," Aleksander said. "But that's all it is: a theory. You have no proof of any of this."

"Actually," Roger said, "I do."

He gestured toward Velovsky. "That's the real reason I

asked Mr. Velovsky to join us here tonight. When you first arrived, Elymas gave him an instant telepathic rundown of who and what you were and what you were doing here. I gather it wasn't something a Leader had ever done before, and it affected him so badly that it may be part of what killed him."

"You aren't suggesting Velovsky can tell us what Leader Elymas was thinking, are you?" Nikolos scoffed.

"That's exactly what I'm suggesting," Roger said, looking back at Velovsky. "Mr. Velovsky? The floor's yours."

Velovsky shook his head. "No," he said.

Roger blinked. He'd been prepared for doubt on Velovsky's part over this part of the scheme, or hesitation or disbelief or even denial. But a flat-out refusal was a response he'd never even considered. "Excuse me?" he asked carefully.

"I said no," Velovsky said firmly. "It's ridiculous and stupid, and it was a long time ago. And I'm not going to do it."

Roger shot a glance at Caroline, saw his surprise and consternation mirrored in her expression. "Why not?" she asked, leaning forward a little to look the old man more fully in the eye. "All we're asking you to do is try. Won't you at least try?"

Velovsky folded his arms across his chest. "No," he said.

"Well, in that case, I'd say the festivities are over," Aleksander said, getting to his feet. "If you'll call off your dogs, Detective, we'll be on our way."

"Just cool it just a minute," Fierenzo growled. "Look, Velovsky, I don't know what game you're playing, but it ends now. Tell us what Elymas had in mind, or I'll have you up on so many charges it'll make your head unscrew at the neck."

"Leave him alone," Cyril said sharply, standing up beside Aleksander. "He's said he isn't going to talk. Creating phony charges isn't going to get you anywhere."

"Phony like hell," Fierenzo retorted, shifting his glare to the Greens. "You're about to start a war. Velovsky is preventing us from stopping that war. That's obstruction of justice, failure to cooperate with an official investigation, conspiracy to commit multiple assault and homicide—"

"All right!" Velovsky snapped, jumping to his feet, his thin hands curling into thin fists at his sides. "You want to know what Leader Elymas thought? I'll tell you what he thought. He was full of hopes and dreams: a desire for a new life for his people in this new world, a place where they could live in peace and harmony."

He turned aching eyes on Roger. "But beneath all of that," he added, his voice trembling, "there was an undercurrent of hostility and hatred at what had been done to them in the Valley."

He took a deep breath, let it out in a sigh. "Leader Elymas didn't want peace with the Grays, Roger," he said. "He wanted to kill them all."

• •

For a frozen moment in time the room was filled with a bitter-edged silence. Caroline stared at Velovsky, his words echoing through her mind like a death sentence. Death for the Greens and the Grays, for Melantha, possibly for the entire city.

"But that's impossible," she heard Roger say.

Tearing her eyes away from Velovsky, she focused on her husband. He was just standing there, frozen with the rest of the universe, his face looking like that of a lost child. He'd worked so hard on this, with all his hopes and thoughts concentrated into this single moment.

But that hope had been in vain. Here at the end, it had all come tumbling down around him like a house of cards.

And then, even as she looked at him, something stirred deep inside her. No—he wasn't wrong. He couldn't be. She might not have been able to create the same train of logic that he had, but she had certainly been able to follow it. Velovsky had to be lying.

But why? Did he genuinely want war between his old

friends and the Grays? Certainly he'd sounded aggressive enough when he'd first told them the story. He'd as much as admitted, in fact, that he was on Aleksander's side of the conflict.

But that was when it had been a question of Melantha living or dying, and how that would affect the balance of power. Surely now that he'd heard Roger's arguments—now that he'd seen in Melantha and Jordan that peace *was* possible—surely he wouldn't deliberately let a war begin. Had he been so blindly influenced by Aleksander's opinions that he couldn't think for himself anymore?

Her eyes drifted away from her husband as she suddenly understood. No, not *Aleksander's* opinions . . . "Just a minute," she spoke up as Aleksander threw a final look at Velovsky and started down the steps. "Please. Just one more minute."

"And what would you presume to add to this discussion?" Aleksander asked contemptuously over his shoulder.

"It wasn't Leader Elymas who hated the Grays and wanted them dead," she said. "It was someone else."

Aleksander turned to look at her, taking two more steps before reluctantly coming to a halt. "Velovsky just said it *was* him."

"He was wrong," Caroline said. "Yes, most of what he got *was* from Leader Elymas. But not the hatred. That leaked in from the other Persuader."

"What are you talking about?" Cyril demanded. "There weren't any other Persuaders on the transport."

"What about you two?" Roger asked.

"I was only ten," Cyril told him. "Aleksander was seven. Our Gifts hadn't even begun to show, much less been confirmed."

"Nevertheless, there *was* another Persuader present," Caroline said. "One who was never identified as such, thanks to a group of Command-Tacticians who were suspicious of Leader Elymas's motives. A Persuader who has maintained that same deception ever since."

Deliberately, she shifted her gaze to Nikolos. "A Persuader," she added quietly, "who was standing right beside Leader Elymas, in perfect position to poison his father's communication."

Velovsky inhaled sharply. *"Nikolos?"*

"Don't be ridiculous," Aleksander said with a snort. But his eyes were on Nikolos, and there were hard wrinkles creasing his cheeks.

"But that would be . . ." Cyril stopped abruptly.

"What he did, he did for the best," Caroline said. "At least, that's what he was told."

"That's why they sent all the extra Warriors along," Sylvia murmured, as if a long-standing question had just found an answer. "*And* why they insisted I keep Nikolos's true Gift a secret. They wanted a counterweight to Elymas, someone who hated the Grays as much as they did."

"These are all fascinating suppositions," Nikolos said, standing up. "But no matter how clever your logic, there's still no way for Velovsky to prove that my father wanted peace with our enemies."

"Sure he can," Roger said, flashing a quick, desperate look at Caroline. "If he can sort out the memories, he can figure out which ones came from each of you."

Nikolos shook his head. "You're arguing in circles," he said. "In order to do that, he has to begin by assuming the memories that involve hatred of the Grays came from me, which is precisely what you're trying to prove."

"Maybe he doesn't have to prove anything," Caroline said slowly. The wildest, most lunatic idea she'd ever had in her life had suddenly occurred to her. A desperate idea; but she could see no other way. "Tell me again why the Greens are split over whose decisions to follow."

"It's because we have no Leader," Cyril said. "You know that."

"Yes," Caroline agreed. "But what if you *did* have one? Would everyone obey his commands?"

"What are you suggesting?" Nikolos demanded suspiciously. "That we should all just sit and wait for the next Leader to arise?"

"I'm saying you already have one." Caroline looked at Velovsky. "Namely, the memories and thoughts and dreams of Leader Elymas that reside within Mr. Velovsky."

Nikolos threw back his head and gave a bark of laughter. "Of course," he said. "Silly me—why didn't I see it sooner? Of *course* we should let a Human lead us."

"Why not?" Roger said, jumping in to Caroline's support. "If Elymas was here, he'd be your Leader, right?"

"A Leader is by definition a Green," Cyril said tartly. "He or she must have both the Gifts of Persuader and Visionary. Velovsky has neither."

"Of course there are physiological limitations," Roger said. "But he *does* have Elymas's memories and probably a lot of his personality. He should be able to give you a good idea of what Elymas would have decided in any given situation. Certainly better than you or Nikolos or Aleksander could."

"Now you've crossed the line to insulting," Cyril said with a sniff. "This meeting is over."

"Just a minute," Caroline said.

"You keep asking for minutes," Aleksander said. "I'm sorry, but your minutes are up."

"I wasn't talking to you," Caroline said calmly. "I was talking to Sylvia."

That got their attention. "Sylvia?" Aleksander repeated, turning and frowning at her. "What does she have to do with this?"

"Everything," Caroline said, mentally crossing her fingers. "Because Sylvia is the only one of you we have to convince."

"What are you talking about?" Cyril demanded, sounding more bewildered than angry. "She's not a Persuader *or* a Leader."

"No," Caroline agreed. "But she's the Command-Tactician, in charge of your Warriors. If she agrees that Leader Elymas didn't want war, there won't be one."

"She can't decide that on her own," Nikolos insisted, all but sputtering. "The Command-Tactician is under the strict authority of the Leader."

"Exactly." Caroline looked at Sylvia. "Well, Sylvia? You once told me your job was to do whatever was necessary to give your people their best chance to survive. Was that true? Or is it war that you really want?"

Slowly, her eyes on Caroline, Sylvia rose to her feet. She walked over to where Velovsky still stood on the steps, and for a moment looked him up and down. "*Ti larocel spiroce,*" she said.

He seemed taken aback. "What?"

"If you claim to hold Leader Elymas's memories, you surely understand *Kailisti,*" she pointed out calmly. "*Ti larocel spiroce.*"

Velovsky licked his lips and threw Roger a furtive look. "Uh . . ."

"*Ti larocel spiroce,*" Sylvia repeated.

"Yes, yes, I know," Velovsky snapped peevishly. "Let me think, will you?"

"This is ridiculous," Nikolos growled, gesturing toward the door. "Sylvia, we're leaving."

Sylvia didn't move. "*Ti larocel spiroce.*"

"*Ti larocel spiroce,*" Velovsky muttered. "*Ti larocel spiroce. Ti larocel spiroce . . .*"

Abruptly, he cocked his head to the side. "Right. *Right.* Let's see: *Doub—doubul—* no; *dobulocel dinzin ehi blyi,*" he said, fighting the syllables as if he was wrestling small alligators.

Sylvia nodded slightly. "*Quis el ekt thi semutom,*" she said.

"Right," Velovsky said. "Uh . . . *dyi tu el stel eruyn-ehi curni?*"

"*Noni epethitoc dobito ampethitoc ruslir sketi,*" Sylvia said, the words starting to come faster now.

Velovsky drew himself up to his full height. "*Eoth merkidi prupin-ota,*" he said. "*Prucrest onistom slyth.*"

Caroline felt a whisper of air beside her, and turned to see

Fierenzo come up to her side. "Any idea what they're saying?" he asked quietly.

"Not a clue," she said. "But *they* seem to understand. That's what counts."

Fierenzo grunted. "Maybe." He nodded past her. "Nikolos and Aleksander don't look happy at all. That's probably a good sign."

Caroline followed his gaze. The other Greens' expressions seemed to be hovering somewhere between furious and apprehensive, with a large helping of disbelief thrown in. Cyril, in contrast, looked merely thoughtful. "Maybe," she agreed cautiously.

Abruptly, the conversation ended. For another moment, Sylvia and Velovsky stood staring at each other in silence. Then, very deliberately, Sylvia bowed her head toward him. "I hear the Leader," she said in a clear voice. "And I obey."

Aleksander took a step toward her. "Sylvia, don't be ridicu—"

She silenced him with a look. "I have heard the Leader's words from within Otto Human Velovsky," she said. "Those words order me to withdraw my Warriors from their attack positions and to return them to their homesteads." She looked over at the two Grays. "I have given that command."

"No!" Nikolos snarled, flashing a look at the Grays.

"You'd leave us open to our enemies?" Aleksander agreed tensely.

"Yet we know now what Leader Elymas wished for us," Cyril murmured.

"We know nothing of the kind," Aleksander snapped. "That Human is *not* our Leader."

"The Leader within him has spoken," Sylvia repeated, turning her back on Velovsky and walking back to face the others. "I have no choice but to obey his order."

"This is insane," Nikolos snarled. "What kind of Green *are* you?"

"She's a Green who knows there's nothing here to fight about," Roger put in. "That there never *was* anything. Most of the Grays in New York weren't even born when you escaped from the war, and the rest were only children. You can't ask them to pay for the mistakes of their parents, any more than they can demand that kind of payment from you. You can put all that behind you and start again."

"It's what both of your leaders wanted," Caroline added. "You know that's true."

"We know nothing of the sort," Aleksander bit out. "This is nothing more than a pathetic trick."

"So don't believe it," Roger said. "Why not try it anyway? What have you got to lose?"

"Our *lives,* perhaps?" Aleksander countered sarcastically.

"They can't destroy you, even if they wanted to," Roger insisted. "You've *got* the superior firepower. You can afford to back off and see if you really *can* live in peace together."

"Unless you're willing to admit that a couple of twelve-year-olds can do what you can't," Caroline added.

Aleksander shot a glance at the two Grays, his forehead wrinkling uncertainly—

"No," Nikolos ground out, taking a step forward to put himself and Sylvia face to face. "Our murdered dead *will* be avenged."

And suddenly, through the tension in the air, Caroline could feel a pressure against her mind. The same pressure she'd felt outside Lee's market, when Cyril had tried to order her to give up Melantha.

Only this time it wasn't directed at her. It was focused full-strength on Sylvia.

"What's going on?" Fierenzo demanded quietly from beside her.

It took Caroline two tries to find her voice. "Nikolos is trying to persuade her to change her mind," she said. "He's trying to make her order an attack."

She thought she'd been keeping her voice low. Apparently, not low enough. "So much for trusting the Greens," Halfdan said, his voice brittle. "Torvald, this is our chance."

"Our chance for what?" Torvald asked.

"What do you mean, for what?" his brother bit out.

"Can't you see they're completely locked up? *She can't give any new orders.*"

"You wouldn't dare," Aleksander rumbled, starting toward him.

"Come closer and I'll break your neck," Halfdan warned. "Roger was right, Torvald—they *have* overwhelming force. If we don't take those Warriors now, when they're out of position and off balance, we may never have another chance."

"Aleksander?" Nikolos muttered from between clenched teeth.

Silently, Aleksander stepped to Nikolos's side; and as he did, Caroline felt a sudden increase in the pressure on her mind. "They're double-teaming her," she breathed to Fierenzo. She took a step toward them—

"No," Fierenzo said quietly, putting a hand on her arm. "Let them work it out themselves."

"But they're ordering her to start a *war*."

"I know," the detective said, his voice grim. "But if they can really make her do something like that, I want to find it out now rather than later."

"Torvald," Halfdan said urgently. "There are too many for my men. We have to do it together."

"You can't," Roger said, his voice pleading. "Please."

"What about the guarantee my daughter asked you for?" Torvald countered.

Roger seemed to brace himself. "There are no guarantees in this life," he told the Gray. "No one can make promises for the future. But if your two peoples are at peace when the next Leader arises, what reason would he or she have to want to make war against you?"

Torvald didn't answer, his eyes seemingly focused somewhere beyond him. "Torvald!" Halfdan repeated, all but snarling the word.

And then, Torvald's gaze came back, and he turned to his brother. "You're right," he agreed. "This *is* our chance." He lifted his hand to his cheek. "This is Torvald," he announced. "All Grays, withdraw immediately and return to your homes. Repeat: all Grays withdraw to your homes. It's over." He lifted his eyebrows at his brother. "Halfdan?" he invited.

Caroline looked back at the frozen tableau of Sylvia, Aleksander, and Nikolos, locked in their silent combat. It all looked just like it had a minute earlier . . . and yet, through the pressure still flowing past her mind she suddenly sensed something was terribly wrong. Her eyes searched Nikolos's face, found no clue there, and drifted lower to his jacket.

His *trassk* was gone.

Her eyes darted lower, to his hands. There it was, the copper-colored filigree clutched almost hidden in his right hand.

And even as she caught her breath, his left hand dipped into his right palm and pulled the *trassk* into the shape of a wide, short-bladed knife. With the blade still half-concealed, she sensed him brace himself—

"No!" Caroline cried. Shaking off Fierenzo's hand, she leaped forward, reaching desperately for Nikolos's arm.

But as she had sensed his preparation, so he had apparently sensed hers. She had barely covered half the distance when he turned on his heel, swinging around to point the knife directly at her.

She gazed at the glittering weapon as she moved toward it, time seeming to slow down as the inevitability of what was about to happen flooded across her mind. It was far too late for her to break off her charge toward him now . . . and even if she could, she wasn't sure she would want to. All of her time and conversations with Sylvia flashed back to mind: the Command-Tactician's quiet pride in herself and her Warriors, her quick and supple mind as she planned her stratagems, her earnestness when speaking of the safety of her people. In spite of all the lies and deceptions, Caroline had no doubt that Sylvia's acceptance of Velovsky's word meant a genuine willingness to make peace with the Grays.

If she died on Nikolos's blade, that chance would be gone.

Distantly, she was aware of other activity beginning to erupt belatedly around her. She felt Fierenzo's hand as it grabbed at her arm and then slid uselessly off her sleeve.

From the corner of her eye she saw Torvald start to stretch out his hand toward Nikolos, but she could see that even if he could get his hammergun ready in time Sylvia's body would be blocking his shot.

And she heard Roger's gasp of fear and horror as he realized he was too far away to do anything at all to help. To do anything except watch her die.

Nikolos's knife was in motion now, still in the dreamlike slow motion created by her enhanced mental state. The pressure on her mind changed subtly as it came up toward her. . . .

And suddenly a hand appeared from nowhere, grabbing Nikolos's wrist and twisting the knife to point away from her. Another hand simultaneously slammed palm-first into her chest, bringing her mad rush to an abrupt and painful halt. Her breath went out in a huff, and for a moment she teetered on the marble floor as she struggled for balance.

Then Roger was at her side, gripping her arms tightly as he pulled her back to stability and safety. Blinking away sudden tears, she tore her eyes away from the knife and looked up at her rescuer's face.

It was Aleksander, his throat rigid, a stunned and almost terrified disbelief in his eyes as he stared at Nikolos. "What are you *doing*?" he demanded, his voice the darkness of a graveyard. "You would kill one of our *own*?"

"She's a traitor to the Greens," Nikolos snarled, his voice trembling.

"Not to the Greens," Caroline corrected, fighting to get air back into her lungs. "Only to you."

"And to a needless war," Sylvia spoke up, her voice calm and steady, with no sign of the mental battle she'd just gone through. "I have heard the Leader's words. The Warriors will stand down." Reaching over, she deftly wrenched the knife from Nikolos's hand, collapsed it back into copper filigree, and handed it to Cyril.

"Then you condemn us all to death," Nikolos accused.

"Do I?" Sylvia looked at Torvald. "One Gray leader has already shown himself willing to try the path of peace."

"Halfdan?" Torvald prompted, and ominous edge to his voice.

For a moment Halfdan stood motionless, his throat tight, his scar standing out whitely against the redness in his cheeks. Then, with a frustrated hiss, he lifted his hand. "This is Halfdan," he growled. "All Grays, go home. . . . Yes, Bergan, that means you and Ingvar, too. . . . Just *go home*." He waited for acknowledgment, then dropped his hand back to slap against his side.

Sylvia turned back to Caroline. "Thank you," she said.

Caroline licked her lips. "Thank *you*," she murmured back.

"Okay," Roger breathed, and Caroline could hear him struggling to get his mind back on track again. "Okay. Then there's just one more thing." He looked past Caroline at the S.W.A.T. cops still lined up at the far end of the Winter Garden. "Sylvia, is it possible for you to give them just enough of a Shriek to scramble their perception for a couple of seconds, but without startling them enough that they'll start shooting?"

"It's possible, yes," she said. "You want it now?"

"Please."

She nodded. "Everyone, brace yourselves." Crossing to the far end of the circular platform, she opened her mouth and gave out a sound that sounded like a prairie dog yip. Caroline jerked in spite of the warning—

The three closest palm trees seemed to bulge outward; and suddenly there were three figures walking across the marble floor toward them: a man and two women, one of the women noticeably shorter than the other. Caroline blinked, forcing her eyes back to focus; and to her surprise and delight, she saw that the shorter woman was Melantha. "Melantha!" she gasped, crossing the platform and hurrying down the steps toward the girl. Melantha gave a delighted squeak of her own and broke into a jog.

They met in the middle of the first set of stairs, and for a long moment teetered there precariously as they hugged. "I'm so glad to see you," Caroline murmured, holding the girl tightly. "Are you all right?"

"I'm fine," Melantha said, her voice muffled in Caroline's shirt.

"Thanks to you," the other woman said.

Caroline looked up to see the two adults coming up to her. "I'm sorry," she apologized, suddenly feeling awkward as she released Melantha. "You must be . . . ?"

"We're Melantha's parents," the man said. "Zenas and Laurel. And there's no apology needed."

"More like thanks," a new voice came from behind her.

Caroline turned. Two more Grays had suddenly appeared, a man and a woman, coming down the upper stairs. "I'm sorry—I didn't see you," she said.

"That's okay," the Gray man said with a smile. "We weren't exactly trying to be seen."

"These are Ron and Stephanie, Jordan's and Jonah's parents," Melantha explained, gesturing to them. "They were hiding masked up on the wall."

"Are you here to gloat?" Nikolos demanded, glaring at Melantha's family.

"Not at all," Roger assured him. "They're here to make a point. Melantha?"

Still standing beside Melantha, Caroline sensed the girl brace herself as she turned to face the other Greens. "I state here and now, Persuaders Cyril, Aleksander, and Nikolos, and Command-Tactician Sylvia," she said in a clear voice, "that I will *not* use my Groundshaker Gift to help any of you in an unprovoked attack against the Grays."

Nikolos rumbled in his throat. "So we have *two* traitors—"

"Quiet," Cyril ordered. "Let her finish."

"I also state to *you*, Torvald and Halfdan Gray," Melantha continued, turning to face them, "that I will not hesitate to use that same Gift in defense of the Greens if *they* are attacked."

"In other words, Melantha is on the side of peace," Roger said. "And she'll use or withhold her Gift however necessary to make sure that peace is maintained."

"The Peace Child," Caroline murmured, the irony of it

suddenly striking her. "Whichever of you gave her that name knew what he was talking about, after all."

Halfdan muttered something under his breath. "Is that it, then? Can we finally go?"

"That's it," Roger said, nodding. "Except for the details of how we go about integrating your peoples into the same areas. But that can wait till tomorrow."

"Why not start now?" Torvald spoke up. "There are a number of fine trees that have been going to waste in Washington Square since the Greens pulled out." He looked questioningly at Zenas and Laurel. "There are also a pair of vacant apartments across MacDougal Alley from my home. Either one would make a good homestead for any Greens who wanted to repopulate the park."

Laurel looked uncertainly at her husband. "What do you think?"

"You know, *I've* always wanted to live in Manhattan," Ron spoke up before Zenas could answer. "You said there were *two* vacant apartments?"

"You can move right in," Torvald said.

"Wait a minute," Aleksander objected. "Melantha's not going to live in the middle of Gray territory."

"That's rather up to you, isn't it?" Roger told him. "If you can get enough Greens to move back to Washington Square, it won't *be* Gray territory anymore. It'll be Gray *and* Green territory."

"I'm not sure how well our people would take to such a suggestion," Cyril said doubtfully.

"I'm sure some will be interested," Sylvia spoke up smoothly. "As a matter of fact, I was just thinking that *I'd* like to try city life for awhile."

Halfdan snorted. "Together with all your Warriors, no doubt?"

"No, just the few necessary to protect the Greens who'll be living there," Sylvia assured him. She lifted her eyebrows at Torvald. "With your permission, of course?"

For a moment, Torvald hesitated. "Are you really ready to trust the Greens with your life?" Halfdan murmured.

The uncertainty in Torvald's face smoothed away. "You don't start by trusting all of them," he told his brother. "You start by trusting just one."

He inclined his head toward Sylvia. "You and your Warriors are welcome, Command-Tactician," he told her. "As far as I'm concerned, the more the merrier. From *both* sides."

"And with that, I think that we *are* done," Fierenzo said. "I'll go talk to Cerreta, tell him everything's been cleared up, and send the S.W.A.T. team home."

"You think they'll just let us go?" Sylvia asked, frowning. "I assumed we'd have to Shriek them and disappear before they recovered."

"I'd rather not do that if we don't have to," Fierenzo told her. "Unsolved mysteries are very upsetting to the brass. Still, as I understand it, you showed no actual weapons, did no lasting damage to either personnel or property, and had Mr. Galen's permission to borrow his yacht." He lifted his eyebrows toward Nikolos. "You *did* have his permission, didn't you?"

"Don't worry," Cyril said. "I'll make sure we did."

"Then I think we're clear," Fierenzo said, offering his hand to Ron and then Zenas. "I trust I'll be invited to visit you both once you're settled into MacDougal Alley?"

"Absolutely," Zenas assured him. "As Torvald said, the more the merrier." He smiled at Caroline. "From all *three* sides."

49

"So what exactly did Cerreta want from you?" Fierenzo asked as he maneuvered the car through the late-night Manhattan traffic.

"Mostly, he just wanted to yell," Roger told him, sitting

close beside Caroline in the backseat. "In a quiet and very civilized sort of way, of course."

"Yes, he's good at that," Fierenzo acknowledged ruefully.

"But there were a few actual questions thrown in, too," Roger went on. "Mostly concerning our precise involvement in this."

"I trust you didn't tell him?"

"We pleaded ignorance and stupidity of the highest rank, which annoyed him no end," Roger assured him. "He got particularly miffed when Caroline tried to explain that it was all a mistake, that she hadn't *really* been kidnapped."

"He was a lot more than just miffed," Fierenzo told him. "He was aching to find something—*anything*—he could charge Nikolos and Sylvia with that he could make stick. But half the Greens had already vanished, and the half who were still there didn't have any contraband or weapons or anything else he could use against them. Not even those metal disks that Messerling and a dozen cops swore had been thrown at them during the fight. Apparently, no one could find anything but some bits of really nice-looking jewelry."

"Amazing," Roger agreed. "And of course, Shrieks don't leave any marks, either."

"Or even any aftereffects, at least not at the levels they were using," Fierenzo pointed out. "Cerreta was so desperate he was actually talking about putting some divers into the Hudson to see if they could find whatever had made those big splashes."

"*There's* a great use for taxpayer dollars," Roger murmured.

"Yeah, and I think Messerling realized that," Fierenzo told him. "Either that, or he decided it would be better to just let the whole thing die as quiet a death as possible."

"Getting S.W.A.T. butts kicked by a bunch of unarmed men and women will do that," Roger said, gazing out the window at the lights and the people of his city. All the accumulated tension of the past week had drained away, leaving him unutterably tired.

But they'd done it. He, Caroline, Fierenzo, and the others had actually pulled it off.

"People do tend to remember that sort of thing at appropriations time," Fierenzo agreed. "Caroline, you're being awfully quiet back there."

"I was just wondering what Cerreta's going to do to you," Caroline said as she pressed against Roger's side.

"Oh, I think by the time I walk into his office tomorrow morning he'll have cooled off," Fierenzo assured her. "For all the hoops I made the department jump through on this, we *did* stop what everyone expected to be a major gang war. And no matter how much sod Messerling tries to heap over tonight's escapade, the fact is that the Greens amply demonstrated just how bad the war *could* have been. I think he'll take that into account."

"Yes," she murmured, and Roger felt a shiver run through her. "Do you think it's going to work?"

"No way to know at this point," Fierenzo said. "But bear in mind that except for the original refugees, all the hate on both sides has been toward an *idea*, not anyone or anything real. Now that they've got actual flesh and blood to deal with, I think a lot of the clichés and stereotypes will start to fade away. And don't forget there are now leaders on both sides who genuinely want to make a go of it."

"Though there are still those who don't," Roger warned.

"Sure, but I think most of them will eventually come around," Fierenzo said. "Halfdan will probably go along with his brother—grudgingly, maybe, but he'll go along. Aleksander was so rattled by Nikolos's play tonight that he'll probably keep a low profile for quite awhile, hopefully long enough to see it all working. Cyril, of course, was all for peace in the first place."

"And Nikolos?" Caroline asked.

Fierenzo shrugged. "Probably never," he conceded. "But at least he's a known quantity now. No, I think we've made it through the hardest part."

"It did come right down to the wire, though," Roger said, wincing at the memory. "If Torvald had listened to his brother when Sylvia was fighting with Nikolos, it could still have blown up."

"Definitely," Fierenzo said. "Especially since I'm not convinced Sylvia was nearly as helpless right then as she was letting on."

Roger felt his skin prickle. "Are you saying it was a *test*?"

"Why not?" Fierenzo countered. "She'd already made her move by calling off her Warriors. As long as Nikolos was attacking her anyway, why not play possum and see how the Grays would respond?"

Roger whistled softly. "Pretty risky."

"But very Sylvia," Caroline murmured. "I just hope Torvald is as committed to peace as she is."

"He is," Roger said firmly. "Because what nobody there knew was that he was in a lot better position than he let on. Part of the deal for pretending to fall for Sylvia's feint in Upper Manhattan was for us to let him quietly siphon off some of his people to position at the Central Park and Morningside Park homesteads. He insisted on having a bargaining chip in hand in case we weren't reading the Greens' plan correctly."

"Why didn't he mention that when Nikolos was threatening the Gray children in Brooklyn and Queens?" Caroline asked, frowning.

"Because if he had, his hotheaded brother might have gone ahead and started shooting Warriors," Roger said.

"I guess your logic convinced him that was what his father really wanted," Caroline said, nestling back against his side. "He must really trust you."

"Mm," Roger said. "Almost as much as Sylvia trusts *you*."

"Whatever works," Fierenzo murmured. "Whatever works."

• •

There was, for Caroline, a vague air of unreality as she and Roger rode up the elevator and unlocked the door to their apartment. So much had happened since she'd last seen it that she half expected to find a month's worth of dust covering everything.

But then, it really *had* been only four days since she and Melantha had hurried out that cloudy Friday morning, and the apartment looked pretty much the way she remembered it. "The trees probably need watering," Roger pointed out as they hung up their coats and walked into the living room.

"I'll get them later," she told him, picking up one of the throw pillows from the couch and sitting down in its place. "They've lasted this long," she added, hugging the pillow tiredly across her chest. "I don't think another few minutes will bother them."

"You probably should knock first, too," he suggested, dropping into the chair across from her. "Who knows who might have moved in while we were gone?"

"We'll just call it our guest room for when Melantha comes to visit," Caroline said, gazing fondly across the room at him. "By the way, I want you to know how very proud of you I was tonight. For someone who doesn't like confrontations, you handled that wonderfully."

"Thank you, ma'am," he said formally, inclining his head in a little bow. "And if I may say so, your own relational way of thinking paid off pretty well, too."

"My own what?" Caroline asked, frowning.

"The way you think," Roger said. "Fierenzo explained it to me."

Caroline leaned back against the couch and closed her eyes. "Ah."

"So anyway," he went on briskly. "The night's still young. What do you want to do?"

She pried one eyelid open. "You must be joking," she said. "I was thinking bed and about ten hours of sleep."

"You sure?" he asked, his voice suddenly going all bland. "I hear there's this new play up at the Miller Theater—"

He was fast, and he was obviously expecting it. Nevertheless, she still managed to nail him dead center with the pillow.

Look for

NIGHT TRAIN to RIGEL

by

TIMOTHY ZAHN

Now Available
in Hardcover

1

He was leaning against the side of an autocab by the curb as I walked through the door and atmosphere curtain of the New Pallas Towers into the chilly Manhattan night air. He was short and thin, with no facial hair, and wore a dark brown overcoat with a lighter brown shirt and slacks beneath it. Probably no more than seventeen or eighteen years old, I estimated, the sort of person you wouldn't normally give a second look to if you passed him on the walkway.

Which was why I gave him a very careful second look as I headed down the imported Belldic marble steps toward street level. I had no doubt there were plenty of nondescript people wandering the streets of New York this December evening, but their proper place was the nondescript parts of the city, not here in the habitats of the rich and powerful. There was already one person out of his proper social position in this neighborhood—me—and it would be unreasonable to expect two such exceptions at the same place at the same time.

He watched me silently from beneath droopy eyelids, his arms folded across his chest, his hands hidden from view. A beggar or mugger should be moving toward me at this point, I knew, while an honest citizen would be politely stepping out of my way. This character was doing neither. I found myself studying those folded arms, wondering what he might have in his hands and wishing mightily that Western Alliance Intelligence hadn't revoked my carry permit when they'd cashiered me fourteen months earlier.

I was within three steps of the kid when he finally stirred, his half-lidded eyes opening, his forehead creasing in concentration. "Frank Compton," he said in a gravelly voice.

It had been a statement, not a question. "That's right," I confirmed. "Do I know you?"

A half smile touched his lips as he unfolded his arms. I tensed; but both hands were empty. His left hand dropped limply to his side; his right floundered a bit and then found its way into his overcoat's side pocket.

It was still there as he slid almost leisurely off the side of the autocab and crumpled into a heap on the sidewalk, his eyes staring unseeingly into the night sky.

And with the streetlights now shining more directly on him, I could see that his coat was wet in half a dozen places.

I dropped to a crouch beside the body and looked around. A kid with this many holes in him couldn't have traveled very far, and whoever had done this to him might be waiting to add a second trophy to the evening's hit list. But there were no loitering pedestrians or suspicious parked vehicles that I could see. Trying not to think about rooftop assassins with hypersonic rifles and electronic targeting systems, I turned my attention to the kid himself.

Three of the bloodstains were over the pinprick-sized holes of snoozer loads, the kind used by police and private security services when they want to stop someone without using deadly force. The remaining wounds were the much larger caliber of thudwumpers, the next tier of seriousness in the modern urban hunter's arsenal.

The tier beyond that would have been military-class shredders. I was just as glad the attacker hadn't made it to that level.

Carefully, I reached past his limp hand into his overcoat pocket and poked around. There was nothing there but a thin plastic folder of the sort used for carrying credit tags or cash sticks. I pulled it out, angled it toward the marquee light from the New Pallas behind me, and flipped it open.

There was a single item inside: a shimmery copper-edged ticket for a seat on Trans-Galactic Quadrail Number 339216, due to depart Terra Station at 7:55 P.M. on December 27, 2084, seven days away. The travel designation was third class, the seat listed was number twenty-two in car fifteen.

The destination was the Rigel star system and the Earth colony of Yandro.

Yandro, the fourth and final colony in the United Nations Directorate's grand scheme to turn humanity into a true interstellar species and bring us into social equality with the eleven genuine empires stretching across the galaxy. Yandro, a planet that had been a complete and utter drain on Sol's resources ever since the first colonists had set out ten years ago with the kind of media whoop usually reserved for pop culture stars.

Yandro, the reason I'd been kicked out of Western Alliance Intelligence in the first place.

I looked at the dead face still pointed skyward. I have a pretty good memory for faces, but this one still wasn't ringing any bells. Shifting my attention back to the ticket, I skipped down to the passenger information section at the bottom.

And found myself looking at a digitized photo of myself.

I stared at it, the back of my neck starting to tingle. The photo was mine, the name and ID number printed below it were mine, and if the thumbprint wasn't mine it was a damn close copy.

Long experience had taught me that it wasn't a good idea to be caught in the vicinity of a dead body, especially one as freshly dead as this. I took a minute anyway to go through the kid's other pockets.

It was a waste of a perfectly good minute. He had no ID, no credit tags, no handkerchief, no pocketknife, no unpaid bills, no letters from home. Besides the ticket folder, all he had was a single cash stick with a hundred ninety dollars left on it.

From behind me came the sound of chattering voices, and I turned to see a party of four impeccably dressed young people emerging from the New Pallas for a night on the town. Casually, I stood up and stepped past the crumpled figure, heading down the street as quickly as I could without looking obvious about it. The movers and shakers who lived in this part of the city did occasionally have to deal with the distasteful business of death, but it was always done in the most genteel and civilized manner, which meant they had genteel and civilized thugs on the payroll to do it for them. I doubted that any of the theater-bound party tripping lightly down the steps had ever even seen a dead body before, and they were likely to make a serious commotion when they finally spotted him. I intended to be well on my way to elsewhere when that happened.

I'd made it to the end of the block, and had turned the corner, when something made me pause and look back.

There was a figure standing in front of the body. A slim, nondescript figure, his shoulders hunched and his head forward, clearly leaning over for a close look at the dearly departed. With the distance and the restless shadows thrown by the streetlights, I couldn't make out his face. But his body language wasn't that of someone horribly shocked or panicked. Apparently, dead bodies weren't anything new to him.

And as I watched, he straightened up and turned to look my direction.

With a supreme act of will, I forced my feet not to break into a full-fledged sprint, but to continue with my original brisk stroll. The man made no move toward me, but merely watched until I'd moved out of sight around the side of the corner building.

I walked two more blocks, just to be on the safe side. Then, as the wail of sirens began to burn through the night, I flagged down an autocab.

"Good evening," the computerized voice said as I climbed in. "Destination, please?"

I looked at the folder still gripped in my hand. Seven days until the train listed on the ticket. Slightly less than a seven-day flight from Earth to the Quadrail station sitting in the outer solar system near Jupiter's orbit. If I was going to catch that train, I was going to have to leave right now.

Awkward, and very spur-of-the-moment. But in some ways, it could actually work out to my advantage. I'd been planning on taking the Quadrail out into the galaxy sometime in the next couple of weeks anyway, buying my ticket with the brand-new credit tag in my pocket. This way, I could at least begin the trip on someone else's dollar.

Only I hadn't intended on heading out quite this soon. And I hadn't intended on beginning my journey at any of Earth's pitiful handful of frontierland colony worlds.

I certainly hadn't intended to leave with a dead body behind me.

But someone had gone to a great deal of trouble and expense to buy me a ticket to Yandro. Someone else had given his life to get that ticket into my hands.

And someone else had apparently been equally determined to prevent that ticket from reaching me.

"Destination, please?"

I dropped the folder into my pocket and pulled out my cash stick, wishing I'd taken the dead kid's stick when I'd had the chance. My credit tag contained an embarrassment of riches, but tag transactions were traceable. Cash stick ones weren't. "Grand and Mercer," I told the cab, plugging the stick into the payment jack. Fifteen minutes at my apartment to get packed, another autocab ride to Sutherlin Skyport, and I should be able to catch the next flight for Luna and the Quadrail station. If the torchliners were running on time this week, I should make it with a few hours to spare.

"Thank you," the cab said, and pulled smoothly away into the traffic flow.

The moonroof was open, and as we headed south along Seventh Avenue I found myself gazing at the few stars I could see through the glow of the city lights. I found the distinctive trio of Orion's belt and lowered my gaze to the star Rigel at the Hunter's knee, wondering if our own sun was even visible from Yandro.

I didn't know. But it looked like I was going to have the chance to find out.

ABOUT THE AUTHOR

Timothy Zahn is the author of more than twenty-five original science fiction novels, including the very popular *Cobra*, *Blackcollar*, and Dragonback series. His recent novels include *Night Train to Rigel*, *Survivor's Quest* of the Star Wars series, and *Dragon and Slave* of the Dragonback series. The first novel of the Dragonback series, *Dragon and Thief*, was nominated for Best Book For Young Adults. He has had many short works published in the major SF magazines, including "Cascade Point" which won the Hugo Award for best novella. He is also author of the bestselling *Star Wars* spinoff novel of all time, *Heir to the Empire*, among many other works. He currently resides in coastal Oregon.